# ERAFEEN

## BOOK 5

# The Sacrifice

David F. Farris

DAVID F. FARRIS



www.erafeen.com

Written by: David F. Farris
Cover illustrated by: Alessandro Brunelli

This book is a work of fiction.
All material was derived from the author's imagination. Any resemblances to persons, alive or deceased, are simply coincidental.



Thank you.

Sphaira Publishing, 2019

ISBN-13 978-1-7323585-2-2

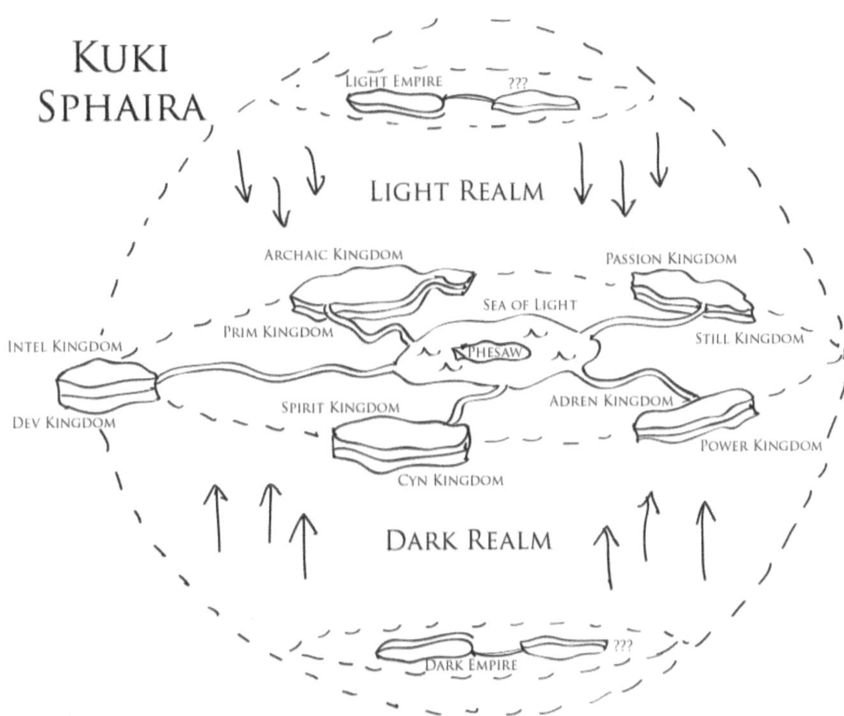


*This is a 3D diagram of Erafeen's world, Kuki Sphaira: a ball of air with floating islands and rivers. There are no landscapes or structures depicted within each kingdom because its purpose is a full-world view. Arrows represent flow of gravity. Dev, Cyn, Power, Still, and Prim Kingdoms (Dark Realm) hang on the underbellies of floating islands. Intel, Archaic, Spirit, Adren, and Passion Kingdoms (Light Realm) sit atop. More detailed maps of individual kingdoms ahead.

# INTEL KINGDOM
### (LIGHT KNOWLEDGE KINGDOM)

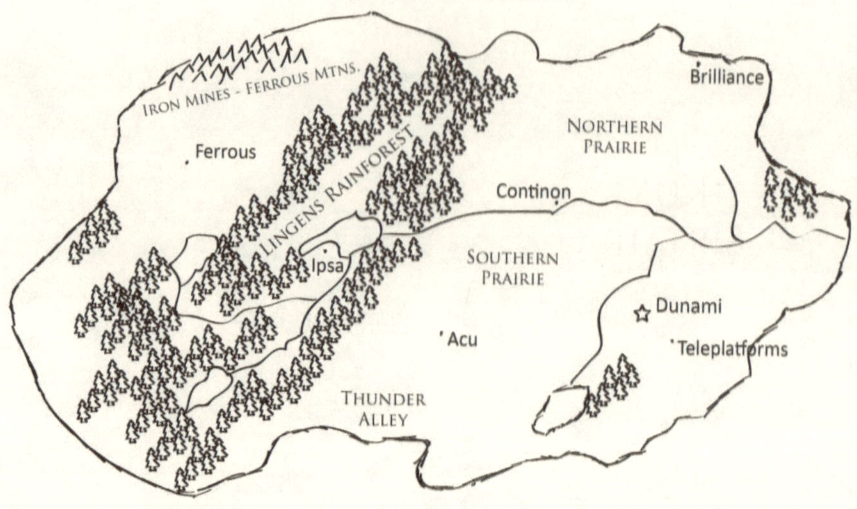


# ARCHAIC KINGDOM
### (LIGHT MORALITY KINGDOM)

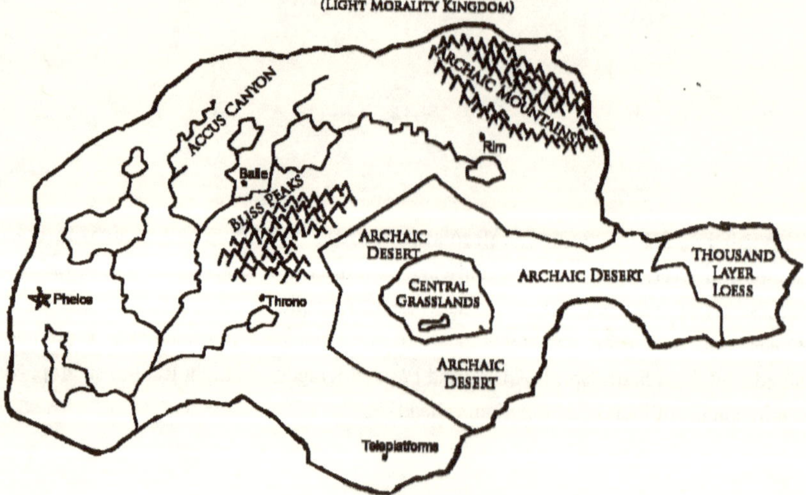

# DEV KINGDOM
### (DARK KNOWLEDGE KINGDOM)

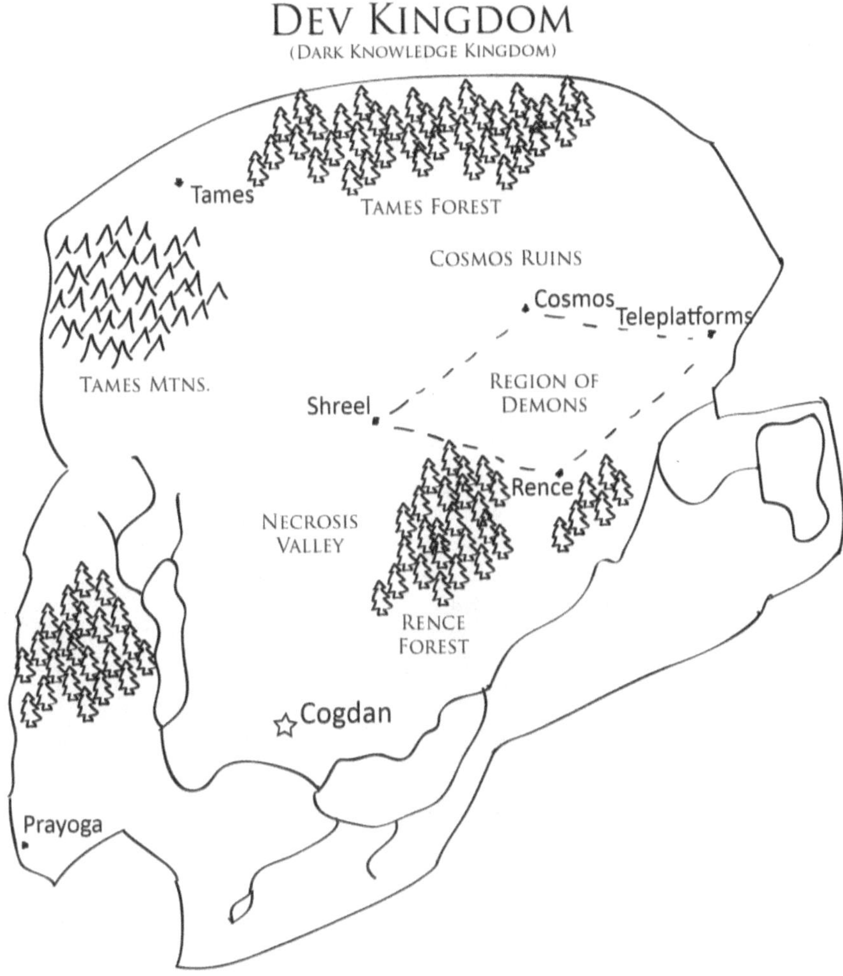

# POWER KINGDOM
### (DARK COURAGE KINGDOM)

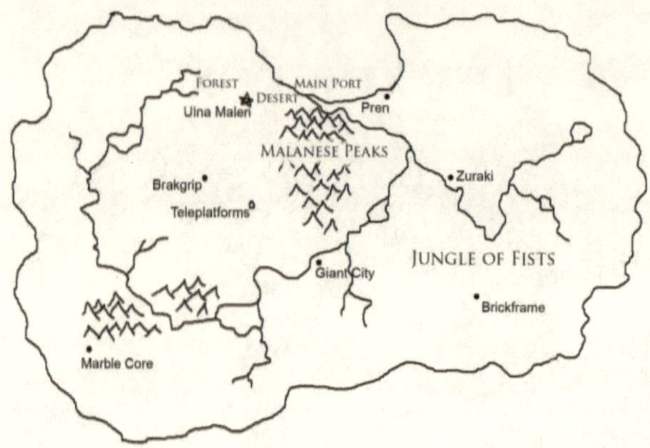


# ADREN KINGDOM
### (LIGHT COURAGE KINGDOM)

## <u>Light Realm</u>

### Intel Kingdom (mind, electricity):
Bryson, Lilu, Jugtah, Princess Shelly, King Vitio, Yvole, Frederick, Gracie, Limone, Wendel, Benedict, Tonitrua

### Passion Kingdom (heart, fire):
Olivia, Himitsu, Director Venustas, Fane, Horos, Barloe, Rayne

### Spirit Kingdom (soul, wind):
Jilly, Tashami, Director Neaneuma, Queen Apsa, Crole, Troy

### Adren Kingdom (body, speed):
Toshik, Yama, Director Buredo, Saikatto, Kolver, Soraku

### Archaic Kingdom (mind, ancients):
Agnos, Rhyparia, Itta, Prince Sigmund, Ophala, Musku, Captain Gray Whale, Kaylee, Prakriti, Creep, Poicus, Senex, Pluzina

## <u>Dark Realm</u>

### Dev Kingdom (mind, psychic):
Vistas, Flen, King Storshae, Illipsia, Tazama, Warden Gala, Mialo

### Still Kingdom (heart, ice):
Apoleia, Ropinia, Titus, Garlo, Moroza, Evelyn, Groto, Thyella

### Cyn Kingdom (soul, supernatural):

### Power Kingdom (body, strength):
Vuilni, Queen Gantski, Lana, Ernest, Rattius, Yesenia, Rose, Ruby, Prince Zorn, Stonebody

### Prim Kingdom (mind, ancients):
Iris, Queen Inedibus, General Pinillias, Quada, Catus, Dynamo, Atarax, Kakos, Therapif, Biaza, Moros, Dimiourgos

Not all characters are listed

# 1

# Neeko Lefolli

Spy Pilot Ophala Vevlu stood on the stage at the center of Archain Road with the lifeless body of Toth Brench lying in front of her. The sound of screams gradually subsided as civilians tried to calm themselves after observing the brutal scene. Ophala slowly scanned the surrounding multitude, catching the mortified gazes of children and adults alike. They had just witnessed their king—what felt like the third in as many years—fall to a gruesome death. He now lay facedown in a puddle of his own liquefied organs.

Her eyes dropped to the area between the edge of the stage and the crowd which surrounded it. On the ground lay three other bodies, a vulture perched on each of them: Vliyan NuForce and the two Dev Diatia—Jina and Halluci. Standing nearby, wielding bloody daggers, were their assailants: Elyol Brekton, Archaic Prince Sigmund, and Preevis NuForce.

Ophala's eyes roved toward the rooftops of the buildings lining the street and caught sight of five figures against the night sky. She recognized three of them as the assassins Himitsu, Horos, and Fane. The fourth one, whom she had yet to properly meet, stood next to Himitsu—a girl with silvery hair that glowed under the stars. The last figure belonged to a young man who, apart from Ophala, most would not know.

The abhorrent scene had all been part of the Spy Pilot's creation. Since the night she had aided in Rhyparia's escape two years ago, a new plan of deception had been conducted. One that required the acceptance of her own imprisonment and abandonment of her family the moment they had come to her rescue.

But it was over now. The Archaic Kingdom was back in its ruler's rightful hands, though they would not be her own. She wouldn't continue the trend that had plagued the kingdom for the past three years. She'd finally give this land to the young man to whom it justly belonged.

"King Sigmund," she said, regarding the man with the scarf standing next to one of the Diatia's bodies. "Come here."

He looked up at her, approached the stage, and climbed onto it. He looked scared, apprehensive about what was to come.

"Why do you look at me like that, Sigmund?" she asked with a sweet smile.

"You called me 'king.'"

"That's what you are now," she said, embracing him against her side.

"I'm not ready. Besides, won't you take over?"

"I will not," Ophala said. "This is your kingdom. You are the Archaic royal firstborn, which makes you the royal head since your father is no longer alive."

The crowd continued to watch in silence.

"But I cannot lead," Sigmund said. "You've seen how easily I am led astray."

"Your curse has been your impressionable mind, yes. However, I think these past few years have taught you plenty."

He shook his head. "I'm not—"

"I request your silence, milord." Ophala reached into her uniform and produced a crown of twigs. As she placed it on Sigmund's head, he cowered ever so slightly like a frightened puppy. She turned him around and gently nudged him toward the crowd. "Step forward," she said. "Present yourself to your people."

As he adjusted the crown of twigs on his head, Ophala looked down at Toth's body. A few years ago she would never have been capable of such an act, but a lot had changed since that time. If she wanted to defeat monsters such as these, she needed to become one herself.

*       *       *

Ophala sat in her office for the first time in nearly two years, a luxury she hadn't had since the Gravity Trials. She'd held a position in the Amendment Order at the time, leading the Archaic Kingdom alongside Toth Brench, Wert Lamay, Rosel Sania, and Grandarion Senten. They were to serve as a transitional piece, molding Prince Sigmund into a proper king unlike his father. Ultimately, the Amendment Order failed, plagued with corruption from the likes of Toth and Wert.

She gazed around the office, absorbing its stressful memories—the countless nights of trying to persuade Sigmund to stay on her side. He had lost faith in her during the trials. She looked at the chair on which Archaic Director Senex would always stand, giving his short stature a boost above the desk. He'd left Phesaw to help her defend Rhyparia in court.

Ophala grabbed the vase of artificial flowers from her desk, tipped its mouth toward her, and gazed into its depths. She cackled, then opened a bottom drawer and retrieved a mug. She poured the scarlet liquid from the vase into her cup, her eyes flaring with greed. She took a sip and leaned back, reflecting on the past several months.

It had been the most difficult mission of her life, which was saying a lot. As the Pilot of Spy and Sky, the only jobs she'd received throughout her life were ones her subordinates couldn't do themselves. She shook her head, thinking back to a decade ago. She'd been silly for believing her mission— being stationed in Rim and scouting the Archaic Mountains—had been meant to serve a purpose. It had been given to her by the now-deceased

Archaic King Itta and had turned out to be nothing but a ploy of misdirection in order to keep her far away from the capital.

She ran her fingers atop her chest, feeling the bumps of an ancient through her blouse. Living in Wert's skin had been painful for her. The patience she'd exercised impressed even her. There had been countless times when she had to stop herself from prematurely killing Toth and all of his underlings. That would have only accomplished the satisfaction of her own vengeful thirst. While she did indeed hate the man, she couldn't risk ruining everything she'd orchestrated. She often had to remind herself of the larger purpose. If she had attacked too early, Toth would have been her only sure victim.

Thus, she waited for all of her moving parts around her to fall into place. This included Himitsu and Elyol's theatrical battle; Intel General Lars's genuine sacrifice of his life by accepting a suicide mission through the teleplatforms; and the converging of all her allies in Phelos after Toth's regime let their guard down. Of course, the unexpected departure of Tazama—Toth's right-hand woman—didn't hurt.

Someone knocked, and Ophala's gaze slowly lifted toward the door. "Come in."

Archaic King Sigmund entered. She downed the rest of her mug and extended her hand toward the chair opposite the desk.

"Good morning, Ophala," he said, taking a seat.

She placed the mug on the desk. "Good morning, milord."

"Please, don't ..." he said, stirring uncomfortably.

"Get used to it," she said. "Last night was eventful. How'd you sleep?"

"I don't think I did."

"You don't *think*?"

He shrugged and leaned back with a posture very unbefitting of a king. "There were a few times when it felt like my eyes closed and my body dozed off, but my brain was still running at a thousand miles an hour."

"I'd be concerned if you *did* get a good night's sleep," she said. "Only an insane person would experience last night's fiasco, then fall asleep with ease."

"How'd you sleep?" he asked.

"Like a baby."

The king stared at her, likely fighting the urge to point out what she had just implied.

"I'm not insane," she said reassuringly. "I'm an exception to the rule. Last night's events presented a sense of closure for me. I had worked toward that moment for a long time, and I feel each of them deserved what they got."

"But ..." he trailed off, gazing emptily at the desk.

"But what?"

He frowned. "How is what we did any different than how Toth overtook the Amendment Order? He had me kill Rosel and Grandarion, forcing Vliyan upon me in case I backed out—which I did. He created chaos across the city."

"I'm glad you're thinking that way," she said. "But, did I take the lives of hundreds of soldiers and innocent civilians in the process?"

"No ... I suppose not."

"And did I do it to make myself queen?"

His posture diminished. "No, ma'am."

"I did this for our kingdom," she stated, leaning forward. "It now belongs to the proper family."

After a stretch of silence, he said, "I can't believe you were Wert the whole time."

"That was the point," she said with a wry grin. "It was the one piece of information I kept from everyone else, including those of you who decided to join me. Well, my husband knew."

"Was he the one responsible for wrapping Wert's wounds in the dungeons during the uprising?"

"Yes ... Even though those wounds were technically mine. I had already disposed of Wert and taken his place."

"Did it hurt?"

"The missing hand?"

He nodded.

"Of course!" she screamed, slapping her hand on the table with a laugh. "It was the most unimaginable pain."

The door opened abruptly. Himitsu and Horos sauntered in.

"Mom," Himitsu said, "it's our turn to catch up."

"My two favorite men," Ophala said, raising her empty mug. "Sigmund, I request your leave…"

The king sprung out of his chair like a plebeian who had been faced by his queen. She shook her head and chuckled as he left the room.

Horos plopped into the now-vacant chair while Himitsu rounded the desk and squeezed his mother tightly. He sniffed the air and his face knotted with disapproval. "Have you started drinking already? It's nine in the morning."

"Since when has a clock ever stopped me?" she asked.

"True," Hitmistu said.

Ophala studied her injured son as he backed away from her. His face and arms were badly scarred; bandages only covered the more vivid wounds. The young assassin had sacrificed a lot in order to sell his death on broadcast, even allowed himself to fall victim to magmatic attacks … he had put everything on the line for his kingdom. If she weren't his mother and he not her son, she would have snatched him up for her personal team in a heartbeat.

"Sit down somewhere," she said. When he decided to place his rump on the edge of the desk right next to her, she laughed. "How did you enjoy your living arrangements last night?"

"It was completely unnecessary," Himitsu said. "To have my mother force me to sleep in the barracks on what could have been our first night together in years … you are a monster."

"I needed someone to make sure none of the soldiers tried to kill each other." She grinned. "But you're here now … along with your father. How are you, Horos?"

"Displeased," he said with a rigid crease in his lips.

"You have to forgive me."

"No, I don't. You let me think our son had died."

"For only thirty minutes." After realizing the man's expression wouldn't change, she poured a cup of wine and offered it to him. "Here."

"I don't drink anymore," Horos said.

"That's right. I forgot," she said, raising an eyebrow at Himitsu. "You don't mind if I drink?"

Himitsu shook his head. "I wouldn't ask that of anyone. My problem isn't yours."

"That's good," she said, "because I wouldn't have been able to make any promises."

"I know."

As she took another sip, Himitsu asked, "Wasn't Poicus known for shape-shifting? I saw him do it once, back when a few of the Jestivan and I chased Dev King Storshae across his kingdom."

"He was," she said, setting down her mug. She reached for her blouse and undid the top two buttons.

"What are you—"

"Hush," she said. "This once belonged to Poicus." She exposed an iron-like emblem that had fused with her chest. It was the image of two identical rectangles standing vertically side by side.

"How'd you get that?" Himitsu asked.

"Remember when I visited your school to help deal with the Dev Assassins hiding in the Rolling Oaks?"

"Yeah."

"Well, that wasn't the only reason for my visit. I did a bit of bartering with Grand Director Poicus. Fearing for Phesaw's safety, he requested an ancient better suited for battle. Thus, I brought him a cane that could deal immense damage."

"*That's* where he got that from," Himitsu said. "When I flew over the campus on Gale, I saw him fighting Storshae. He was creating fissures in the land."

"Yes, it's very powerful," she said, pouring another cup of wine. "I believe it's in Toono's hands now. Regardless, that's neither here nor there. The point is that I didn't just give him such an ancient. I asked for something in return, knowing I'd require a new style of deception eventually. Since the whole world knows about Cheiraskinia and how I can communicate with and control winged animals, enemies were already wary of that. But, they never stopped to think that I had Poicus's shape-shifting ancient, Mutopellis."

"That was forever ago," Himitsu said, eyebrows halfway up his forehead. "You're amazing! Just how far ahead were you thinking?"

She chuckled. "I didn't know *what* I was planning for. I was only being preemptive." She paused and studied her husband. His stern glare had yet to soften. "Horos, we will talk about it later. Please … don't look at me like that."

Himitsu turned toward his father. "If you should be mad at anyone, it should be me," he said. "I'm the one who played dead in front of you."

"Under her orders," Horos said.

"You know the nature of my job, Horos," she whispered with narrowed eyes. "I divulge information in a methodical way. I needed a genuine reaction from you since there were a few Dev servants on that street. They definitely noticed you, and they would have realized the truth if your reaction hadn't been authentic."

Horos shrugged. "I could have *acted* traumatized."

"You're a terrible actor," she said flatly, "which is why you're an assassin, not a spy."

"Himitsu," Horos said, beckoning his son's attention. "Inform your mother of my own immaculate deception with Fane back at the orphanage."

When she looked toward Himitsu, his red cheeks said enough. She peered at Horos again. "You mean that ruse where you two pretend to be lovers?"

"You mean that wasn't the first time?" Himitsu gawked.

"Of course not," she said. "It's the only time he can play a role properly. He seems to be most comfortable when he and his boyfriend pretend to be cuddle-buddies."

Horos straightened up, folding his arms. "You're just jealous." He paused and smirked. "Fine … I'm over it."

"Good." She leaned forward and grabbed a folder from her desk. She opened it and shuffled through sheets of parchment. "So we have a few potential missions given to us by the royal heads. It's up to you two to decide which you want to take."

"I just got back from the longest mission of my life," Himitsu whined.

"You are no longer a child, nor do you attend school anymore," she said while spreading three sheets across the desk. "This is your career now,

Himitsu. You are a professional assassin. You've even garnered a nickname for yourself—or so I've heard."

"Shadow's Omen," he said, trying to sound cool.

"Yes, well … don't expect breaks … especially now, in the heart of a war."

Himitsu sighed, plopping his chin into his hand. "What are our options?"

"We have a job request from Passion Director Venustas, who as you know is currently running the Passion Kingdom. She wants a small team to travel to the Prim Kingdom and do reconnaissance work, hunting down answers as to what exactly happened the night of the Prim Prince's murder. It seems rather important, considering he was Toono's very first sacrifice."

"Did you not just call me an assassin?" Himitsu asked. "Shouldn't our missions be more focused on finding a dangerous target and eliminating it?"

"I don't have any of my talented spies left," Ophala said. "Wert Lamay had most of them killed off, so you will be taking their place, acting as a hybrid of spy and assassin."

"Fine. What are our other options?"

Ophala glanced at another sheet, ignoring Horos's chuckling. "A request from Intel King Vitio … he wants you to enter the Adren Kingdom and dispose of Yama and Kadlest, which reminds me …" She looked up from the parchment. "We've lost the Adren Kingdom."

"What?" Himitsu balked, standing immediately. He marched to the other side of the desk, putting distance between him and his mother. "Why am I just now hearing this?"

"A lot has happened, Himitsu."

He groaned, pressing his eyelids. "Yama has power over the Adren Kingdom? And what about King Supido?"

"Toono killed him. Supido served as his Adren sacrifice."

A few moments passed, during which Horos and Ophala watched their restless son squirm in place.

"You wanted a job that suits an assassin," she said. "This would be it."

"Two problems," Himitsu said, coming to a standstill. "One, that is Toshik's kill; he wants her more than anyone. And two, I can't defeat Yama."

"I agree." Ignoring his frown, she continued. "So that leaves this rather bland request from Spirit Director Neaneuma, who asks for assistance from a Jestivan at Phesaw not only to help guide the refugees, but to act as protection from potential outside threats."

This time, Horos spoke up. "As much as I loved Director Neaneuma when I was younger, I can't commit to something as boring as that."

Ophala shrugged. "Very well, then. It looks like you'll be taking on Felli's mission in the Prim Kingdom."

"No."

She leaned back in her chair and looked at Himitsu, who was now gazing out the window. "No?"

"I want to find Neeko," Himitsu said.

Her eyes narrowed. She hadn't heard the name in a very long time. "Neeko …? Neeko Lefolli?"

Himitsu turned away from the window. "I don't know his last name, and I don't know much about him. But I've learned enough in the past couple of months to make me curious."

"From whom?"

A flash of white split Horos's lips. "His girlfriend."

"Shut up, Dad!"

Ophala guffawed and reached for the flower vase. "I'll drink to that. I'm going to be a grandma!"

"Mom!"

Ophala continued cackling as she poured herself a glass and tossed it down her gullet. "Anyway," she said, smiling and smacking her lips. "I suppose the legend of Neeko Lefolli died out a few decades ago."

"What legend?" Himitsu said.

"I mean, it wasn't anything particularly epic—not like the Of Five, whose stories have stretched across all of the kingdoms. It was an innocent little legend contained within Phesaw's campus—a ghost story of sorts." She gazed at Horos. "Remember it, dear?"

"The Lost Boy," Horos said. "I knew the name had sounded familiar. Students wouldn't enter the Warpfinate by themselves because of that tale, nor would they venture too far into its depths, believing the deeper you traveled, the easier it was for the Lost Boy to find you."

"Never heard of such foolery," Himitsu said.

"Because the story weakened over the decades as students graduated and dispersed," she said. "In fact, it was likely on its dying legs by the time we had reached our late teens. It seemed nobody feared the building anymore. It was already an old tale by the time Horos and I were students."

"And you believe this Lost Boy was actually Neeko?" Himitsu asked.

Ophala crossed her arms and stared down at her empty lap. She paused as if reflecting on memories long past. "I was a star pupil of Archaic Director Senex," she finally said. "Because of this, he told me things. Over a cup of coffee one day, I inquired about his time as a student. After all, he and Poicus had been an iconic duo at the school when they were students. And while I wasn't particularly fond of the Grand Director, I admired the Archaic Director. I wanted to know everything about his life.

"He told me stories. During one of them, he accidentally let slip a piece of information. 'We were the stupidest three guys in the school,' he'd said. Being the astute listener that I was, I immediately pointed out that he'd said 'three' and not 'two.' He froze afterward, knowing he'd been caught. I asked him who the third person was."

"Neeko," Himitsu said.

She nodded. "Yes, a gentleman by the name of Neeko Lefolli. Apparently, they'd been a trio of misfits at a young age, wreaking havoc across the school and its campus. Poicus was the loud one, Senex the wise one, and Neeko the studious one. Neeko had a reputation of disappearing in the Warpfinate for hours. It was almost expected of him on a daily basis."

Himitsu hummed. "Lost Boy ... I see."

"Not quite yet," she said, shaking her head. "Eventually, Neeko began to disappear for longer chunks of time. He'd go days without showing up to classes. Senex and Poicus tried searching, but finding someone in the Warpfinate is not an easy task because of the way it expands according to one's scope of knowledge. With a genius like Neeko, he was impossible to find since nobody could reach his depths."

Ophala stood and approached a bookcase standing against the sidewall of her office. As she ran her fingers across a row of spines, she said, "Well, there came a day when Neeko never returned. Days turned to weeks, weeks turned to months, and months became a year. At some point during that span of time, the school had grown desperate enough that they sent Grand Director Modinus in, for he was the man who had taken a liking to the trio of Senex, Poicus, and Neeko. He'd mentored them."

Ophala pulled out a tome and returned to her desk. "Needless to say, Modinus wasn't successful. Over the years following, Neeko became known as the Lost Boy. Staff tried to sweep it under the rug, but it lingered for several decades. It actually became Modinus's undoing. He resigned as Grand Director and went to live in the grasslands of the Archaic Kingdom before dying of natural causes."

She held up the book. "This is one of dozens of class manuals Modinus had written while he was Grand Director, passed down to me from Archaic Director Senex. I used to read them when I was a student. Modinus had been a treasure trove of information, eventually superseded by the same pupils he had shaped. Neeko, however, developed an acumen that went beyond anyone's comprehension, including Senex and Poicus."

"He must have snuck out of the library when nobody was looking," Himitsu said. "It's the only probable explanation for how he wound up in an orphanage in the Archaic Kingdom."

"Eh … There were always eyes on that building," Ophala said. After a pause, she asked, "Humitsu, what is Kaylee's relationship with Neeko?"

"I guess he was a mentor and a guardian … until he vanished. She also said he chose three other students over his time spent at the orphanage to mentor, just like her. Agnos and Toono were two of them. She doesn't know who the other one was."

"So you want to do her a favor by finding him?"

"Not really," Himitsu said. "It's more than that. He has an interesting ancient that ties people to their dreams in life. He wrote them down in a book. I want to know what he wrote down for Toono. Maybe if we learn the guy's true dream, stopping him will become easier."

It was an impressive argument by her son—well thought-out. She gazed at Horos, who nodded in agreement. "I like where his head's at."

"Then you'll need my help," she said. "This won't be easy. Clearly, he doesn't wish to be found."

"Whatever it takes," Himitsu said.

"I need to arrange a meeting with this Kaylee girl," she said. "She'll prove useful in providing me with information about Neeko's appearance. Also, if Neeko deemed her worthy of his mentoring, then consider my interest piqued."

# 2

# Erafeen: The Queen's Introduction

Agnos drew a string down the centerfold and closed the chronicle. He'd spent the past few days slaving over translations, only to achieve a dozen pages or so. However, it was enough to confirm his opinion that this chronicle—documenting firsthand accounts of the Thunder Queen, a powerful ruler before the Known History timeline—was the most fascinating discovered treasure in Kuki Sphaira. He'd spent his life looking for answers to their world; he'd very nearly found them.

Agnos removed his glasses and placed them on the desk. He rubbed his eyes, strained from the countless hours of focus needed to decipher the Thunder Queen's unorthodox penmanship. Translating the already-complex language was only half the battle.

He stared emptily across his cabin. He may have been the captain of this ship—the Mythmaker—but he had neglected such duties since escaping the tumultuous sea that housed the cave on the seafloor. Tashami was running the ship with Barloe and Zorra providing support. The only people who'd been allowed in the captain's cabin during this time were Tashami, the doctor, and two cabin kids: Eet and Osh.

Only the doctor visited more than once a day to treat the wounds Agnos had received from his dive. When he'd searched the cave, he'd found a shield of light that he assumed to have been Tahara—a type of energy everyone possessed, but only beings of the empires could tap into. In order to retrieve the chronicle, he'd penetrated the light, shredding his arm in the process. Now it hung limply by his side. Constantly getting in his way seemed to be its only remaining purpose.

*Erafeen.* The word was etched into the chronicle's cover. At first, he didn't know what it meant. But after a little bit of reading and finding context clues, he came to the conclusion that it meant "Final Era." The Thunder Queen and her companion, the Mind King, had believed in such a concept, which was why the other leaders around the world had wanted to dispose of the two lovers at once. They were a threat of the greatest kind.

Agnos knew there was more reading for him to do, but for now he stood and headed for the cabin door. It was time he granted himself some fresh air.

He sluggishly made his way through the specialty quarters and out onto the main deck. He'd always been a weak person, but nothing could describe the fragility he now felt in his bones. Climbing the steps to the quarterdeck, he found Zorra, Barloe, and Tashami laughing amongst themselves. They all froze at his sudden presence.

He gave them a weak smile. "You guys see a ghost or something?"

"Feels that way," Barloe said.

As Agnos joined their group he noticed Barloe and Zorra's eyes fall upon his bandage-wrapped arm. "Where are Eet and Osh?" he asked, moving the discussion elsewhere.

"You didn't see them?" Zorra said. "They were in the specialty quarters, supposedly going to visit you. You should have run into them on the way out."

Agnos smirked. "Those kids ..."

"They're definitely snooping around your cabin," Tashami said. "You teased them with that story about the cave for a year. You didn't expect them to just forget about the book that was also supposed to be in said cave, did you?"

"Of course not," Agnos said, gazing at the sails. "I want them to read it. I've even been translating and rewriting it as I go. Let them snoop."

*   *   *

Eet and Osh cracked open the door to Agnos's cabin and took a precautionary peek inside. Once it was confirmed empty, they rushed in, shutting the door behind them. They ran straight for the desk where the chronicle rested. Osh climbed onto the chair and sat on her knees, scooping up the book and opening its cover.

"I can't read it!" she exclaimed.

"Where are his glasses?" Eet asked.

"Like we even know how to use them. We're not even Archain."

He shrugged. "Worth a try."

She began rummaging through the drawers. "I found them!" Just as she went to reach for the glasses, she noticed a stack of parchment beneath them. The first page read, *Erafeen Translated*. She brushed the ancient to the side and grabbed the parchment instead.

"Those don't look like glasses to me," Eet said, watching from the other side of the desk.

She narrowed her eyes as she brushed the cover page to the side. "Agnos has been translating it."

"Well, hurry up and read it!" Eet said.

She grinned and climbed onto the desk. She sat crossed-legged and began to read aloud: "My name is Tonitrua ..."

*   *   *

My name is Tonitrua, but I go by many names: the Bass of the Sky, the Blinding Strings between Clouds and Land, or simply the Queen of

Thunder. I wield lightning and possess an intellect far beyond most. The two exceptions lie with those known as Mialo, King of Minds, and Dimiourgos, King of Ethos. Their intelligence greatly surpasses anything I've ever seen. Alas, Dimiourgos is no longer with us, for he disappeared roughly a decade ago. Some say he was bested by Stonebody, King of Brutes.

I write this from the cabin of my ship. I fear my mission is hopeless. As the other eight Originators chase Mialo and me across the Sea of Light, I've been coming to grips with the fact that I won't be able to reach the location I truly seek. I'm not simply running from my pursuers; I'm chasing something. There is a large island that sits at the center of the sea, and it houses a structure without boundaries—an inexplicable phenomenon like no other.

I spoke with Tide Drifter, the Sea God, about my doubts. I told her about my desire to share Mialo's and my purpose with whichever brave soul tries to discover it in the future in case we fail. She then assured me that she could keep such information safe. All I'd have to do is reach a small island that sits outside of the grander one I seek. It is there where I'd surrender my ship and let it sink to the floor.

This is my way of sharing my knowledge. I hope whoever is reading this can finish what it was Mialo and I originally had set out to do. "Balance," a term heard so often in this world, has never truly been the objective. The scales must tip, and it must be done in a way that favors the Light.

A lot has led up to this point. I will share my story—from the moment I met Mialo to now.

# 3

# Father and Son

Ash rained from the sky, swirling in thick, black tendrils.

Rhyparia NuForce's shoes sank into the soot that swathed the ground as she cautiously descended the mountain. The ash spilled into the tops of her shoes, filling up any empty space within that her feet didn't already occupy. She cursed at herself for not packing boots all those months ago, but who could have predicted a scene such as this on the other side? Based off maps of the Archaic and Prim Kingdoms, she knew they'd resurface in a mountain range, but they assumed the final location of their egress would have been inside a cavern. Instead they had exited from the tunnel and ended up in an alcove. A small roof of land curved over the tunnel's mouth, protecting it from the falling ash.

As the group trudged along, Rhyparia, Prakriti, Rayne, and Saikatto used their hands to shield their faces from the ash. Atarax, the fox; Kakos, the wolf; Biaza, the honey badger; Therapif, the rabbit; and Moros, the weasel, all wore oversized cloaks, the hems already serving as barriers for their eyes.

They were dimiours, a species of humanistic animals—though labeling them as such was considered disrespectful. They were cousins to animals and humans, a bridge between the two species. The world didn't know of their existence—hence the cloaks—but they had thrived over a millennium and a half ago, before the Known History timeline. They've been living on the brink of extinction ever since.

Sunlight struggled to fight through the ash, so progress was difficult to track. Rhyparia felt like she'd been walking for hours, but with nature's ailments slowing them down, they'd be lucky to have made it a mile from the end of Realmular Tunnel. Hopefully the ash would disperse the farther down they traveled.

Prakriti stopped just ahead of Rhyparia and turned to wait. The group continued forward, splitting around him. Once she reached him, he continued, matching her strides.

"My father told me this mountain range was vast," he said, squinting and covering his mouth with his hand.

Prakriti's father, Musku Rao, was one of five original Jestivan from thirty years ago. Musku's death had occured just months ago. Rayne and Saikatto, who were currently at the front of the pack, were the only ones left.

In order to prepare Rhyparia for her trek through Realmular Tunnel, Musku had altered time, turning what had nearly been a year into eighteen years for Rhyparia and fifty-five years for himself. He eclipsed the century marker because of this maneuver and died of old age shortly afterwards ... all for her sake. She now had eighteen years of rigorous weaving training under her belt instead of the mere ten to eleven months the rest of the world had experienced. Of course, that meant instead of turning nineteen years old, she was now pushing forty.

"As long as we continue south, we should make it," Rhyparia said. She coughed up a cloud of ash. "We need to keep our words to a minimum until this clears."

Prakriti retrieved something from his pocket and brought it close to his face, using his other hand to shield the ash from obstructing his gaze. It was a special compass, designed specifically for the Dark Realm's altered gravitational force and poles. He tucked it into his pocket again. "We're still on the right path," he said.

She grunted as she ran into the back of a cloaked dimiour. Based off the height and stature, it was either Atarax or Kakos. Cursing under her breath, she searched for the reason for their abrupt halt.

All she could make out through the swirling ash ahead of them was a shadowed figure—definitely a person. What stood beyond looked to be a small building. Rhyparia reached for her waist and grabbed her ancient piece, an umbrella capable of altering gravity in the hands of a highly skilled weaver. It was what she had trained with during those eighteen years.

The figure stepped closer toward the group. His massive robes billowed wildly with the ash, reminding her of the Energy Directors at Phesaw. The man turned, waving for them to follow. She was the first to march after him. If the building meant reprieve from the elements, she'd accept the risk of entrapment or assault. Besides, she had more faith in her own abilities and those of her group than whoever waited inside.

*　　*　　*

The building was small and consisted of a single room. A fire raged in a pit at the very center with a large pot hanging above the flames. A single cot occupied one of the side walls, while a table with a lone chair sat against the opposite. Several wooden cabinets stood at the far end.

The robed stranger rifled through cabinets. Rhyparia's group stood in silence while the winds howled outside. There were four square windows, one at the center of each wall. The ashes smacked against the glass, only to be deflected, allowing the winds to errantly toss them elsewhere.

"We appreciate your refuge," Rayne said, "but we must ask who you are."

The man walked across the room, his arms full of green vegetation. After placing it on the table, he turned and regarded the group. He was squat, his beige robes dirtied by ash, his hair buzzed short. He sported the strangest mustache she'd ever seen, shaved in a way that mimicked whiskers. She made the connection immediately in her head. *Dimiourgos*— fabled deity that had lived before the Known History timeline, a lynx who had died seven times.

"I must ask you that first," the stranger said. "But before you tell me, take a seat on the floor. I'm sorry I have no other furniture; it's only me out here."

"Explorers," Rayne said as they all sat, "hailing from Concordia."

"I see …" he said, taking a handful of something stringy and green from the vegetative pile. He approached the fire and tossed the grass-like substance into the pot. "From Concordia …"

Sensing the distrust in his voice, Rhyparia tried a different approach. "Who do you *think* we are?"

As he scanned their faces, his gaze lingered on the dimiours still hidden inside their cloaks. Did he know? If he did, he didn't seem to want to address it directly. He looked at her, then her umbrella. "May I see your palm?" he asked from where he stood on the opposite side of the fire.

She stood and rounded the fire, extending both hands. He didn't lean in for a closer look, but inspected them from a distance. He gave her a nod, and she returned to her spot on the floor.

"You're not from Concordia … you aren't from this kingdom at all. You are foreigners walking upon sacred ground, defiling it."

Eyes widening, Prakriti said, "We are not here to disrespect—"

"Unless, that is," the man said, cutting off Prakriti, "you entered through a tunnel." The group hesitated, and the man smiled with apparent knowing. "It seems this situation is more complex than that of foreigners and natives," he said, stirring the contents of the pot with a stick. "Throughout the centuries, *Watchers* have lived and died while protecting Realmular Tunnel from desecration, but also waiting for a day to come when someone would emerge from its depths. It seems I've become the fortunate one to have witnessed that day."

"Who are you and what is a Watcher?" Rhyparia asked.

"There's always only one of us in existence at a time. When I die, the Monsignors will elect a replacement." He crouched and adjusted some logs in the fire. "My name is Iris. You'll have food and shelter for the night. Tomorrow, I'll lead you out of the Black Powder Mountains."

*   *   *

Bryson LeAnce was exhausted. After the journey from Kindoliya to the teleplatforms, then finishing with a carriage ride to Dunami, he could have passed out comfortably on the city's tar-paved roads. Two people kept him awake, and they were somewhere in the palace he was nearing.

Bryson, Olivia, Toshik, and Vuilni rode in a royal carriage through the innermost sectors of Dunami. Director Jugtah had already been escorted to his own carriage that would travel north to the city of Brilliance.

Vuilni continued to peer out the window since arriving to the Intel Kingdom. Citizens massed against the sides of the streets and cheered as their carriage rolled past. Children sat on the shoulders of their parents or reenacted the battles fought in the Blizzard of Blood.

"This is different," Vuilni said. "They despised you guys just a few months ago."

"Reminds me of when we first became Jestivan," Bryson said, glancing at Olivia. "Remember that? Signing autographs at Wealth's Crossroads or being honorary guards at the Generals' Battle?"

Olivia nodded, and Toshik said, "Seems like a decade ago."

Vuilni turned away from the window, facing the group. "So, what now?"

"I see my son," Bryson said.

She beamed. "Little Leon finally gets to meet his legendary father."

He gazed emptily at his feet. "Far from it."

*   *   *

Bryson showed little regard to anyone who tried to greet him upon entering the palace, including King Vitio. He sprinted down a sunlit corridor, windows on both sides stretching from floor to ceiling, as he headed for the nursery. He burst through the door and skidded to a halt on the marble floor.

Shelly whirled, the most incredulous of looks on her face. The baby she had been rocking gently in her arms began to wail. "Look at you what you did, idiot!" she screamed, fussing with a pacifier as she tried to stick it in the baby's mouth.

Flabbergasted, Bryson stood as if frozen. That was *his* son. He approached slowly, hesitant and unsure as to what he should do. How had he not planned this out already?

Shelly huffed, tilting her head up and glaring at the ceiling. "Why is the father of my child an imbecile?"

"Let me …" he said, extending his arms. After a long pause, she laughed and finally handed Leon over to him.

"Be careful," she said. "Support the back of his head …" She trailed off, for he had already positioned Leon perfectly in the crook of his arm. Leon grew quiet, staring up at his father with wide eyes and wet cheeks.

"How did you—?" Shelly began.

"My mom," Bryson said, leaning over to kiss her. "Before departing Kindoliya, she and my aunt taught me all I needed to know about holding a baby."

Her expression softened as she watched him study Leon's face. Before this moment, he'd never understood the infatuation adults had with babies. They always looked relatively the same to him—pudgy faces and big eyes. Now it made sense. He could see the subtle differences in his son. Leon's eyes were wide, developing a hint of their true color of blue. The little bit of hair he had was blond, and his cheeks seemed fatter than most. This brought Bryson's attention to the rest of Leon's body.

"Are babies typically this big?" he asked, gazing up at Shelly.

"Definitely not." She laughed then paused. "I make light of it now, but I've never been in such excruciating pain as I had been that night."

He nodded, looking down at Leon again. "Neither of us are big people," he said. "Lilu is practically my height, and she's taller than you."

"My mother is tall," she noted. "And your dad was a big man, so it's possible Leon got it from his grandparents."

Bryson clenched his jaw at the thought of Leon growing up knowing he was the grandson of such a monster. He wouldn't hide the truths of Mendac's actions to his child the way Debo had done to him.

"You can put him down now," Shelly said, stepping closer. "You've managed to ease him into slumber."

He smiled and transferred Leon to her, who then walked over to the crib to lay him down. She turned and sighed, leaning back against the crib's rail. "Have you been debriefed on happenings around the world?"

"I don't care right now," he said. "That can be saved for later. I've kept conversation of politics and war at bay since the battle. And I will continue to do so until I'm finished spending the rest of my day with you."

The princess flushed red and burst into a fit of laughter. Her green pixie cut had grown out slightly. Bryson swept toward her, enwrapping her in the mightiest of hugs. "I've missed you," he said.

"This is not the Bryson I remember."

He laughed. "Yeah … don't get used to it."

"My mother has prepared a celebratory ball to welcome back the group that traveled to the Still Kingdom," she said, stepping out of his embrace. "Expect friendly faces."

As they left the nursery, Shelly rang a bell that hung outside its door. A lanky middle-aged gentleman exited a room down the hallway to the right.

"Leon is sleeping," she said, "but do keep an eye on him for me, Yusif."

"Yes, milady."

They continued down a separate chamber while Yusif disappeared into the nursery behind them.

"When's this ball?" Bryson asked.

"Friday night." She gazed at him curiously, looking him up and down. "Have you ever had your measurements taken before?"

He shook his head.

"Well, you'll have that done tonight. My mother will not tolerate you showing up to such an event in a suit that either doesn't reach your wrists or is too baggy around your shoulders. I'll arrange for Layla to make a personal visit to our room."

"Layla?" he said, cocking his brow. "Since when do you allow those who aren't royals that deep into the royal quarters—especially in your room?"

"That would be a silly rule," she said as they descended a wide set of velvety steps. "Who do you think cleans our quarters? Definitely not the Intel family."

"Obviously the maids are an exception."

"There are a few others, too," she said.

"I think the real question is ..." he trailed off, pausing on the staircase as he began to flex his muscles in different poses ... "do they have a suit designed for such a physique?"

She took one glance at him before continuing down the stairs. "Never again."

*    *    *

Bryson stood as stiff as a washboard, his arms spread out on either side, while Layla, an older woman with short gray hair, measured his biceps. The entire process felt awkward, made even worse by the fact that she was measuring some fairly uncomfortable areas ... the diameter of his upper thigh, for example.

Thankfully, after much persistence, he had convinced Shelly into letting Vistas in her room while he went through the motions. She was elsewhere in the palace, doing something she deemed important for a friend.

"Friday night will be momentous," Vistas said, standing near the glass wall and gazing at the stars. "There is a lot to celebrate. Amongst all of the chaos surrounding the war, it's easy to forget nobody outside of the royal Intelian elites and some of the staff even know about the princess's pregnancy. And when they discover you're the father ..." He grew silent, shaking his head in wonder. "Well, a lot of things should arise from such an announcement."

"I think I catch your drift, but something tells me you're thinking far beyond my comprehension," Bryson said as Layla patted his inner thigh, causing him to spread his legs.

"The bonding of you and Lady Shelly is a first for many reasons," Vistas explained. "It makes one wonder about the new dynamics between two kingdoms. The princess is an Intelian royal firstborn; you, Bryson, are the Stillian royal firstborn. Not only are you destined to be the royal heads of separate kingdoms, but kingdoms that belong in two different realms. While it may not be an Untenable for two royal firstborns to lay with one another, it wouldn't be farfetched to question how other kingdoms would react to such an illustrious bond."

Vistas was right, and it got Bryson to thinking. Was he Stillian or Intelian? He considered himself both, but that meant he was a being of both realms. Did this mean he'd broken an Untenable by having a child with Shelly, a being of the Light Realm? Perhaps Thusia knew the answer. She'd said during their journey from Kindoliya to the Still Kingdom's teleplatforms that the presence of a Linsani at the battle meant higher beings had interfered. Maybe it was after him.

"Lift up."

He glanced down as Lyla patted the top of his foot. She was now on the ground with the tape measure. He raised his foot and stood on one leg with ease, showing off his years of balance and agility training.

"Did you ever stop to think about what kind of person Leon might grow up to be?" Vistas asked. "He's going to be deadly, powerful, and talented. He has the blood of two royal firstborns rushing through him. The world hasn't seen anything like it. Scientists will try to predict his traits. Will he have a Branian or Bewahr? Does he have Intel or Still Energy?"

Everything he said was terrifyingly true. "Why are we even making this public, then?" Bryson asked. "Did you not express these thoughts to Vitio or Delilah?"

"King Vitio already realizes all of this," Vistas said, turning away from the glass and walking toward the center of the room to take a seat on the sofa. "But it does not matter. Most of the Stillian elites already know about Shelly's pregnancy, and Queen Apoleia herself informed Vitio that she would inform her citizens. Thus, he must do the same."

"My son will be viewed as the biggest threat to the world ..." Bryson muttered.

"This isn't even taking into consideration which throne he'll be sitting on when he's older, Thunder or Glacial?" Vistas shrugged. "That should be interesting."

"So even those he should trust—while not fighting to kill *him*—would be fighting each other to bring him to their side." Bryson groaned. "Layla, give me a second please," he said, shaking her loose and walking away.

She stared at him grimly. "Five minutes. I must finish this swiftly or the queen will not be pleased."

As Layla sunk on the platform, Bryson pinched his eyebrows together in frustration. "And it's a fair deduction to say that some people in the Empires aren't thrilled with this whole situation." He gazed toward the stars through the glass ceiling. "Might the Bozani and Gefal be planning to hunt down my son?"

"It all sounds rather grim," Vistas said, slowly nodding. "But he's still only a baby. Those worries would come later down the line. For now, the immediate focus is the present war."

Bryson decided he wanted an answer straight from the source, so he called for his own Branian. A cluster of white lights formed next to him, taking the slender shape of Thusia. She began to say something, but Bryson didn't have time to waste.

"Am I the source of this tension you've been speaking of in the Empires?" he asked.

Thusia paused and frowned. "Hello to you, too," she said. "Why does it seem like whenever you summon me, it's to berate me with questions you shouldn't be asking?"

"Do the Gefal want me dead?" he asked, ignoring her question. "And my son?"

She crossed her arms. "You know I cannot answer any of these questions, for I am not at liberty to." She turned to the Dev servant. "Hey, Vistas."

"Good evening, Thusia."

The room fell silent while Bryson glared at her. "You're supposed to protect me from danger, are you not?"

"Don't even go there," she said with a fake chuckle. "You don't even summon me when you're in *actual* danger."

"If there are stirrings in the Empires that involve me and my family, you should inform me of them."

She sighed. "Stop sounding like a snob. Trust me … if the time comes, you'll know all you need to know."

The floor opened. It was likely Layla returning from her temporary relief.

"And who is that?" Thusia asked.

"Just go," he said, turning away from his Branian. "It's not someone who should see you."

She lingered for a moment longer with a pout before disappearing into a cluster of white lights.

"Well, that didn't help," Bryson said.

"I don't know," Vistas said. "If anything, the vague nature of her replies said it all."

Bryson looked up, spotting the shadowy underbelly of the bigger island that floated in the sky. "The Empires scare me more than anything down here."

Vistas's face grew austere. "That they should."

# 4

# The True Light Heroes

"You look dashing," Vitio said, brushing his hands down the front of Bryson's suit. "As a father myself, tonight means the world to me. I get to watch my daughter announce her child to the public. I might shed a tear or two."

Bryson grinned, knowing that he had a trick up his sleeve that could probably tear down Vitio's floodgates. "A lot to celebrate this evening," Bryson teased.

The king tugged at the young man's tie, tightening the knot. "You don't know the half of it."

"By the way, what's expected of me at the ball?" Bryson asked. "And who all will be there?"

Vitio placed his hand against Bryson's back and turned him toward a mirror. "As the True Light heroes? Well ... Olivia, Vuilni, Toshik, and Vistas of course. Then there will be Himitsu and Pilot Ophala."

Bryson's gaze darted from his own reflection to that of Vitio's. "What'd they do?"

"You've been back home for three days, and you haven't inquired about your best friend?"

"I guess I've been preoccupied with L.K."

Vitio's brows furrowed. "L.K. is going to take some getting used to. I do prefer just calling him Leon."

"What you call him is up to you," Bryson said. "But getting back to Himitsu and his mom. What happened?"

"They toppled Toth's regime in the Archaic Kingdom."

"What?" Bryson exclaimed, triumphantly balling up his fist. "How?"

"I'll leave that for one of them to explain; it's too complicated. However, all that really matters is the result. True Light has regained control of the Archaic Kingdom. Toth Brench, Vliyan NuForce, Jina, and Halluci are all dead—as well as Wert Lamay, I believe."

Bryson's glee vanished, and Vitio took notice. "What's wrong? I haven't gotten to the bad news yet."

"Nothing," Bryson murmured, lying through his teeth. He hadn't seen Toshik since returning to the Light Realm. The young man had already suffered enough, witnessing firsthand the deaths of his sister, mother, and girlfriend—all of whom, in his eyes, lost their lives because of him. Toshik may not have seen eye-to-eye with his father, a man who had clearly committed some heinous crimes, but that didn't mean he'd be okay with losing the only family he had left.

"What about this bad news?" Bryson said after a long pause.

Vitio shook his head. "Adren King Supido was murdered by the Rogue Demon, serving as his eighth sacrifice." This didn't surprise Bryson, but then the king said, "Yama and Kadlest are occupying the Adren capital. We believe they're filing SCAPD troops into the kingdom, stationing them across the land."

"Great, so we traded the Adren Kingdom for the Archaic Kingdom. I don't see how that helps us. Our enemies still have a kingdom in our realm."

"But now we have a kingdom in theirs," Vitio said. "All because of you. The Stillians will serve as great allies."

"Not only because of me. I had a lot of help."

"True," the king said. "My apologies, Bryson. You are such a force that I forget about those around you."

Bryson sighed and headed straight for the door. "I'll see you tonight, Vitio. We'll go over what's being done about this situation in the Adren Kingdom."

*　　*　　*

Bryson and Shelly flanked the vast entryway into a ballroom, shaking hands with extended royal family members, aristocrats, successful business owners, and other wealthy elites. Everyone was dressed to impress, locking elbows with their partners as they searched for their respective tables. Bryson had kept his attire simple despite Shelly's pleads. He hadn't bothered with cufflinks or tie clips, but now that he saw what a lot of these people were wearing, he couldn't help but feel naked. Not everyone could afford such luxuries. Even he balked at some of the accessories adorning the esteemed guests.

As he shook a gentleman's hand, he couldn't help but stare at his golden velvet jacket and the thin strings of sparkling silver hanging from its buttons. This man stuck out like a sore thumb, and not in a good way. His outfit was gaudy, reminiscent of Director Jugtah's thick golden glasses.

"Do you like my jacket?" the man asked.

Bryson closed his mouth, not realizing his jaw had been hanging slightly ajar. "Not really," he said, letting go of the man's hand. He rubbed his fingers together, slightly repelled by the clamminess. The man made a pointed frown before heading into the ballroom.

As the lobby's crowd thinned, Bryson snuck glances at Shelly. She looked beautiful in her silver and black dress, hugging her subtle curves before hanging loosely toward the floor. Several times she gave him the same icy smile in a way that sent chills up his spine. Honestly, he would have been enjoying himself more had it not been for the scene at the lobby's entrance.

While the two of them served as greeters for the connection between the waiting area and the ballroom, there were officers of the Intelian military manning the entrance to the lobby.

A while back, Lilu had made the suggestion of introducing a new classification system to the kingdom's people. Vitio had loved her insane idea so much he decided to implement it. Now citizens carried identification cards with them at all times, stating their energy and if they had control over it. It was a particularly unfair and unflattering system for Unables—people who weren't capable of weaving. Depending on which class you fell in, you were barred from entering certain establishments or areas of the kingdom.

Of course, these guests had already been checked and identified at the main gate of the palace grounds, but that was only the first checkpoint of several. Security was tight; Vitio was fearful of undesirables slipping through the cracks.

Bryson spotted two friendly faces enter the lobby: Ophala and Himitsu Vevlu. Himitsu's hair had grown considerably since Bryson had last seen him, though still nowhere near what it once had been. Ophala also looked different. There was a certain exuberance missing from her smile.

"Bryson!" Himitsu shouted, breaking into a sprint.

"Welcome back, stranger," Bryson said, catching his friend in an embrace.

"I heard about your miraculous lightning storm," Ophala said.

"And I heard about your puppet show."

"Good to see you again, Bryson," she said, placing her hand on his shoulder and walking through the doors. "Princess, you as well."

The remaining few people spilled into the room, leaving Bryson, Shelly, and Himitsu alone in the lobby.

After Himitsu and Shelly exchanged greetings, Himitsu asked, "Where's Toshik?"

"Haven't seen him for a few days," Bryson said.

"I need to make sure I meet up with him before I take off again. I told him that I'd keep in touch with him before splitting away from the group back in the Dev Kingdom, but that ended up being impossible with both of us on two separate missions requiring all of our attention."

"Understandable," Bryson said. "We'll talk later. I think Vitio is ready for the ceremony to begin. He's waiting for the superstars."

As the two young men chuckled and strolled inside, Shelly watched with lazy eyes. She stuck her finger in her mouth and pretended to gag before following them in.

*     *     *

At the table of heroes, sitting separately from the royal table, were Bryson, Olivia, Vuilni, Himitsu, Ophala, Vistas, and—to Bryson's surprise—Toshik. It seemed the swordsman had come out of hiding for an event of this scale, which was likely because of its mandated attendance. Intel King Vitio stood up from his table as he addressed the room:

"True Light has many reasons to celebrate, mostly because of the individuals seated over there." Vitio waved a hand in the direction of Bryson's group, causing heads to turn. "Zana Himitsu and Pilot Ophala, please stand." Both mother and son stood. "These two—along with several others who weren't able to make it here today—are responsible for the reacquisition of the Archaic Kingdom."

As the guests began to clap, Ophala and Himitsu nodded awkwardly before taking their seats.

"Then there are Zana Bryson, Lita Olivia, Zana Toshik, Vuilni, and Vistas." After realizing they weren't going to stand, he said, "Please stand. Don't be shy." They reluctantly did so. "This group defeated brigades from both the Dev and Power armies in battle. And with the expertise of Nyemas Jugtah, they added a new ally to the True Light alliance … the Still Kingdom."

More applause followed. Bryson waved, but then felt stupid seeing that nobody else did the same. As they took their seats, Himitsu elbowed him. "Real smooth."

Bryson grabbed his water glass and took a drink as Vitio continued speaking.

41

"But there was more to these accomplishments than the actions of those who are seated here," Vitio said. "I want to speak of a certain hero—a man who felt he had a lot to prove and was willing to pay the ultimate sacrifice to do so."

Bryson put down his glass and gazed at the king, his interest piqued.

"Intel General Lars is no longer with us; he died in Phelos, fighting one of the Dev Diatia known as Halluci. But the plan had never been for him to prove victorious. Both he and I understood the fate that awaited him. The same goes for every other soldier who took the teleplatforms into Phelos. It was designed to be a failed counterattack to Himitsu's false death, causing Toth's regime to relax, to feel as if they had achieved two massive victories."

Vitio paused, eyes falling toward the table. "I wasn't very kind to General Lars over the past several months. On more than one occasion I called him a coward based on his actions in a mission I had sent him on some time ago. He wanted to prove me wrong. He, as well as many of his soldiers, died valiantly in order to allow Pilot Ophala to strike with a finishing blow."

Applause thundered throughout the room, much louder than anything heard prior—and deservingly so. Bryson's eyes widened. Lars had really done that? Like the king, Bryson's treatment of Lars had been dismal because it had felt justified. But now, knowing this, a tinge of guilt stung at Bryson.

Vitio nodded in approval as he waited for the clapping to subside. "To give one's life is the ultimate act of courage. Tonight is about those men and women who crossed through the teleplatforms just as much as it is about those in this room. With that said, let us eat, dance, and appreciate all that we have because of those brave souls who protect our liberty."

Music began to play as several doorways opened simultaneously along the ballroom walls. Servers filed in, holding massive platters above their heads. They seemed to move in sync with the melody as they spun between the tables, time and time again making it appear they would collide, only to narrowly miss each other and continue spinning.

Bryson, catching the unmistakable sound of the piano, craned his neck, looking every which way for the source of the music. He eventually located it high above on a balcony that encircled the ballroom. He hadn't played since Jilly's funeral, and he'd keep it that way. It seemed that whenever he heard the instrument, unhappy memories surfaced.

Bryson stared at the meal a server had just placed in front of him. He scanned the faces seated around him. Olivia, Himitsu, and Vuilni wasted no time in chowing down; Vistas and Toshik took a more civilized approach, carving their steak with smooth cuts; and Ophala seemed more enamored with her wine than she was with the food. As the group conversed, Bryson gazed back at the royal table, spotting Shelly. Part of him wished he was seated only with her in a private dining room.

"Snap out of it, Bryson," Himitsu said.

Bryson turned back toward the others. "My bad."

"Why so glum?" Vuilni asked. "The biggest act of the night hasn't even happened yet."

"You're right," Bryson said, forcing a smile. He wasn't looking forward to revealing his child to the world, fearful of the enemies it'd create.

Ophala placed her glass of wine on the table and eyed him. "If you ever want to talk, Bryson, I'm available. We can have a one-on-one, parent to parent."

He nodded his thanks. His mood lifted after exchanging some light banter with Himitsu and his mother. Despite the jovial atmosphere, he couldn't help but notice Toshik's complacency. He appeared calm, unbothered by the news of Toth's death. Come to think of it, he was seated right next to the woman who had murdered him. Neither of them seemed perturbed by the other's company, but they were clearly avoiding eye contact.

Couples began to dance on the ballroom floor, although many remained at their tables to indulge in desserts. Bryson's group remained seated until a young woman with silvery hair and light brown skin approached the table. She wore a gray dress layered with deep blue frills and long matching gray gloves that reached her elbows. Freckles spotted her cheeks, and her eyes … one was hazel and the other silver like her hair.

Himitsu whirled in his chair and beamed. "Everyone," he said without averting his eyes, "this is Kaylee."

The others offered friendly gestures, but no real verbal exchange. After she gave them an awkward wave, she pulled Himitsu out of his chair and dragged him toward the dance floor.

They all watched as the couple joined the rest of the crowd. Toshik took a particular interest; his gaze seemed to linger longer than the others. "How in the world did he land someone like her?" he muttered.

"Who is she?" Bryson asked Ophala.

"Hopefully *the one*," she said. "Himitsu has always had a certain sense of humor that most females find undesirable—in a significant other, at least."

"He makes a great friend, though," Vuilni said, giggling after witnessing what had to have been the worst dance move in the history of time.

"That's my point," Ophala said with a sigh, turning back toward her meal. "Just like his father."

"It looks like Shelly's on the move," Vistas said.

Bryson looked toward the royal table and watched as Shelly slipped out a side door with her mother. He wiped his mouth with a napkin and stood. "I'll see you guys later."

As he exited the room, he could feel his heart pounding through his chest. For some reason, he was feeling shades of his induction into the Jestivan. Soon he'd be reentering this ballroom with all eyes trained on him. His mother, Still Queen Apoleia, had told him to do it with confidence if he was going to commit. Now was the time.

*     *     *

Himitsu danced nearly in step with Kaylee, her pace somewhat faster than he'd anticipated. He was surprised by her dancing ability. She didn't seem like the kind of person who'd feel comfortable with such an expressive act in public.

"Try and keep up," she said.

"I don't get it," he said through heavy breaths. "How do you know how to dance like this?"

"There were a few books on dancing in Neeko's library."

Himitsu managed a laugh. "You weren't kidding when you said his library covered anything and everything."

As they rocked side to side, she said, "Because of Neeko I am well-versed at many things."

"Can you cook a steak?"

"I don't eat meat, nor do I cook it."

"Hmm … There's still a lot to learn about you."

They fell quiet as they continued moving with the harmony. She glanced at the table Himitsu had been seated at. "It's quite sad that I could pinpoint Toshik so easily," she said.

"He has a very distinctive stature," he said.

"That's not what I mean."

He followed her gaze. "It was that obvious, huh?"

"I'm surprised he's able to sit so calmly in the presence of you and your mother. He hides the sorrow he feels from his face well enough, but his aura says all."

Himitsu stared at Toshik as they spun. He wasn't surprised by this, for his mother had killed Toshik's last living relative. Despite any ill will Toshik may have felt toward his old man, he probably didn't want him dead, which was why Himitsu had tried so hard to talk his mother out of it. Alas, there was no changing her mind.

"What does his aura tell you?" Himitsu asked. "Is he angry?"

"It tells me many things … so many things that I can't really read it. He's a mess." After a moment of silence, she asked, "What's next for a skilled assassin during war?"

"My father and I were presented with a few options, but I decided we should do something else."

"Such as?" she asked, placing her head lightly against his chest.

"Find Neeko."

A long pause followed. She lifted her head and looked up at him, brushing a few fallen strands of hair behind her ear. "That's impossible."

"I know he's a bit slippery, but with my mom's help I believe we can do it."

"Are you doing this for me?" she asked.

"I'm doing it for a couple of reasons, but yes, one of them is because of you." He grinned.

She nodded. "You not only want to find Neeko; you want to find his book in which he wrote our dreams."

After a stunned silence, he nodded. "You're an intuitive one."

"I can get behind this mission," she said. "Had this only been about finding Neeko to reunite me with him, I would have scolded you quite harshly."

"Is that so?" Himitsu said with raised eyebrows.

"I didn't come with you to distract you from your role in this war. If we are to be together, we must be useful to True Light."

"I see."

The ballroom's Intelights dimmed, and the music started to dwindle. Silence soon swallowed the room, and King Vitio rose to his feet at the head table. "If you would all clear the floor," he said. The guests did exactly that. "The Intel family has an announcement to make."

Vistas already had left the table of heroes and was now on the main floor in front of the head table, most likely recording what was about to unfold.

The ballroom's main doors creaked open. Vitio cleared his throat. "Let us welcome the new Intelian firstborn, Leon Kawi Still-Intel."

*    *    *

Bryson entered the ballroom and witnessed the change in the crowd. He saw the stunned looks on people's faces and heard their sudden gasps. He and Shelly flanked Queen Delilah, who walked in the middle carrying baby Leon in her arms. He glanced behind the queen's back at Shelly, who gazed back at him with the sweetest smile. Of course she'd handle this flawlessly—she was a princess, after all. Meanwhile, he had to adjust the underarms of his suit as discomfort spread across his body. For Bryson, this was the induction of the Jestivan all over again. He thought he had shaken loose his stage fright, but obviously not.

He made it a point to avoid the eyes of onlookers, though he couldn't get away from the swirling whispers. He spotted Himitsu off to the side standing next to Kaylee. Himitsu gave him a thumbs-up, but Bryson couldn't bring himself to respond.

As they continued along the empty section of floor space, a door opened near the royal table. Bryson caught sight of someone trying to sneak in, but since he was facing that direction he took notice immediately. He had to quicken his pace in order to return to Delilah's side; he had faltered slightly due to the unexpected appearance of Lilu Intel. As she took a seat next to her father, Bryson looked at the ground. Why did seeing her face again make him feel guilty? He shook his head and faced forward, this time allowing his eyes to wander. This was a big night. There was no room for hesitation.

As the trio stopped a few paces from Vistas, they turned and faced the ballroom. A few guests leaned over and whispered to each other. Bryson and Shelly leaned over Leon and kissed his forehead. He smiled back at them, saliva bubbles sprouting from between his lips.

Then Bryson stepped forward, separating himself from the two women. He turned and faced the princess, but quickly reached into his inner vest pocket and spontaneously genuflected right where he was standing. This brought forth more gasps from the onlookers, but he didn't care. He then produced a small case of crystal in the palm of his hand and opened it to reveal a ring topped with a crystal gem. He gazed up at Shelly, who did well in fighting back the tears … He, on the other hand, did not.

"Shelly, will you marry me?"

"Yes," she said without any hesitation. As she extended her hand, the room erupted. He slipped the ring onto her finger, a ring that—according to his mother—had a great history.

He stood while guests continued to applaud their union. The tip of his nose lingered in front of hers. They kissed, and Queen Delilah watched with a gentle grin.

In a life of tragedy, this would come to be remembered as Bryson's most picturesque moment.

# 5

# The Demon's Broadcast

Bryson sat next to Lilu as they watched Shelly make the rounds, brandishing her newest accessory in front of several female aristocrats.

"Looks like something you obtained while in the Still Kingdom," Lilu said.

"A parting gift from my mom," he said. "Apparently there's an amazing story behind it."

"Is there some ever-ice in it?"

"Ever-ice core, then a diamond shell to contain the freezing temperature. Without it, Shelly's fingers would be frostbitten by now."

Lilu sucked in air through her teeth. "The perfect illustrious gift for the princess of high-maintenance … good play, Bryson."

He laughed. "I appreciate that. By the way, your dad invite you?"

"I had to persuade him into letting me come, but I didn't come for this."

"How is the search for Mendac's lab notes going?" he asked. He leaned forward and grabbed a handful of almonds from a glass bowl.

"Not well," she said. "I've tried to follow your directions, but the sewers seem to have been renovated. The halls you spoke of do not exist."

He groaned. "Of course."

"Or …" she trailed off, giving him a pointed stare. "Perhaps your sense of direction is terrible."

"What do you want from me?" he said. "I can't go to Brilliance; it's too far away from everything."

Her gaze suddenly focused in another direction. He followed it and spotted Vistas, who was having a conversation at a distant table with his identical brother, Flen. "Vistas can't go to Brilliance, either," Bryson said.

"I want to witness the memory myself."

His mouth fell open. "I can't let you do that," he said, waving his hand dismissingly near his head as if to drop the subject.

"Don't you want to know why the Theory of Connectivity was in your dream?"

"That dream was years ago now, Lilu. While I'm still curious, it doesn't seem that important anymore. I told you about Mendac's lab research in the sewers in hopes that you'd be able to find it yourself. Otherwise, I can't do much besides that."

Her jaw grew rigid. "Mendac experimented on your body while reading from lab notes involving that theory, yet you don't think it holds any importance? You are not *that* dense, Bryson."

He shook the hand of a male elder who had come toward the front to congratulate him. After the man left, he snapped his head around at Lilu. "I'm already in enough trouble as it is for not only seeing the memory, but then telling Shelly about it. I'm not going to expand my mischief even further by involving you."

"You told me bits and pieces of it, so the damage is already done."

He groaned and leaned forward, letting his forehead smack the table.

"Oh, please," she said. "I'll admit to being very curious as to what Mendac was researching. You had mentioned a second theory in the memory."

"Fine," he said, straightening up.

Her eyes widened. "Really?"

"Yes. How long are you staying down here?"

"Very briefly. I had only planned to stay as long as it took to see this memory."

"Tonight, then," he said, standing up. "After the ball. That way you can head back in the morning."

"Thank you, Bryson."

He placed his hand on her shoulder before stepping away. "Take some time to enjoy the party. I don't know why you seek that man's evils with such eagerness."

*     *     *

Ophala staggered through a moonlit corridor somewhere in Dunami Palace, clueless as to what her destination was. She chuckled to herself as she felt the wine take control of her body. She reached down to remove her heels only to topple sideways, releasing a deranged noise in the process. Someone caught her just before she hit the floor.

"Easy there, Mrs. Vevlu."

She glanced up at her rescuer. "Toshik ..." She stood straight, trying to wipe the tipsiness from her face.

"Where were you headed?" he asked. "I can assist you there."

"My guest quarters," she said, holding her heels at her side. "I think."

He tilted his head toward the remainder of the hallway. "Let's walk."

She walked by his side, accidentally bumping his shoulder a few times. He gave a brittle smirk after each apology she uttered.

"How are you feeling?" she asked.

"I'm okay."

Even while inebriated, she had no trouble detecting such a blatant lie. "I'm sorry our conversation earlier today didn't turn out the way you envisioned it."

"Yes, about that …" Toshik said. They reached the foot of a marble staircase. He stepped aside to allow Ophala to ascend the steps first. "Are you sure there's no way of—"

"There is not," she said, turning halfway up the stairs. Her voice had now become surprisingly stern. "Gale has already done too much by helping me free Rhyparia from her execution. I cannot ask her to do what you desire. You simply want a method of transit into the Adren Kingdom. Gale wouldn't bother with something so minute."

She nearly toppled backward, but Toshik placed his hand gently against her back. "I understand," he said. "Even under the influence, you are unwavering … mentally, at least."

She spun around at the top of the stairs and held up a finger. "You tried to take advantage of me."

"I've become desperate, Mrs. Vevlu," he muttered, looking toward the floor. "And I can't just use the teleplatforms into the Adren Kingdom, for they're all so heavily manned."

"You want to chase Yama, is that it?"

"I want to visit my estate … and take a break."

Her expression softened. She pitied the swordsman, and she understood what it was he desired: tranquility and space for reflection. During her imprisonment, she had wished for those things also. While being locked in a dungeon cell had kept her at a distance from the world, it felt more like isolation than it did seclusion. She didn't reflect on life, but instead contemplated the next step in her calculated plan to overthrow Toth's regime. There had been no peace in that. She knew what Toshik wanted, but she couldn't give it to him.

"I can't get you to your estate," she said. "But I believe I know where you can find some semblance of what it is you're looking for."

"What do you mean?"

"You know of a man named Kuiku Fito?"

"He was my mentor when I was young. When I dropped out of the Adren Assistance Academy, my father managed to coerce him into leaving his position as the Adren Corporal."

"And in many ways, he helped mold you more than your father did, correct?" She shrugged. "One might even go as far as saying that he was a better father figure."

"How can you know any of this?" he asked, curious but understandably hesitant.

"I can bring you to Kuiku. He sought me out after he learned of your father's death. He is a good man it seems. I think spending time with him might grant you what it is you seek."

Toshik placed his hand against the banister as they reached the landing. He seemed to brood on it. Eventually, he spoke. "If that's the best you can do, I'll take it."

She turned the other way. "My room is just down the corridor. Thank you for the company, Toshik." She paused, remembering Horos's story about Toshik's companionship during Himitsu's drunkard spiral. "Thank you for what you did for my son. You are a good man plagued by bad luck."

*　　*　　*

The gardens of Dunami Palace were lively following the ball. Bryson had taken Himitsu and Kaylee into a secluded courtyard, one of the palace's more private sectors. It was here where he'd experienced countless training sessions with Shelly to improve his clout.

They took a seat on a wooden bench located at the edge of the courtyard, just beyond the marble walkways that bordered it. While Himitsu and Kaylee conversed, Bryson stared up at the firmament and became lost in thought. Just moments ago, he had seen two sisters off. Shelly had wanted to spend time with her mother and a few of her friends—something she'd been doing a lot of lately. As for Lilu, she was in the midst of a meeting with Vistas somewhere in the palace, likely experiencing Debo's memory. Bryson didn't want anything to do with it.

"You reek of fear."

He tore his gaze from the starless night sky to look at Kaylee. "Is that so?"

"She sees all," Himitsu said in a mysterious tone.

"Is it that eye?" Bryson asked.

Himitsu punched Bryson's shoulder. "Hey, man. Not cool."

"But he's right," she said.

"What's up with it?"

Instead of a response, she used her fingers to pry apart her top and bottom eyelid, then used the fingers on her other hand to dig into her eye socket. He cringed and leaned away in stupefied horror. Himitsu shook his head and smirked, looking into the distance as he bit into a roll of bread he had stolen from the ballroom.

She exhaled slowly, now holding her eye in her palm. Bryson stared at it, losing any concept of tact. Then again, was removing an eyeball and holding it like a handful of seeds tactful? He gazed into the pinkness of her empty eye socket.

"I can no longer see your aura, but it's unnecessary in this instance." She glanced at her detached eye. "Clearly, you feel disgust." She promptly popped it back in.

Bryson stuttered, wishing he could replay that moment. "Just stunned," he said, trying to pivot. "It's not something you see every day. Besides, it wasn't what I imagined. There wasn't anything attached to it—nothing gooey or stringy."

"That's because it isn't a body part," she said. "It's an ancient." She looked at Himitsu on her left, but only to avoid Bryson's eyes. "I thought you would be more like Himitsu. He described you as such."

Himitsu raised his brow. "I would have reacted the same way, had I not been trying so hard to court you."

"'Court you'?" she asked, placing her palm against her chest. "Is that what you were doing?"

Himitsu laughed. "Don't play dumb. You said it yourself over a dozen times. I am a pool of lust when I look your way."

"Aww, someone is smitten," Bryson said, reaching over Kaylee to pinch his friend's cheeks.

They continued laughing and conversing until the night's quiet swept over the courtyard. Bryson's mind, once again, began to drift. He thought about the war. After spending nearly a year being idle in the palace, barred from leaving by Intel King Vitio, Princess Shelly, and Branian Suadade, he had been given the chance to play a vital role. He, Olivia, Toshik, Vuilni, Vistas, and Jugtah crossed into the Still Kingdom to set a plan into motion: convert the Stillians from the SCAPD alliance to join True Light. They had done this by offering Director Jugtah's skills as a talented weaver, promising to heal the complete paralysis of Still Queen Apoleia's father.

They were successful, and Apoleia switched her allegiance just as two forces of the SCAPD alliance charged the Still Kingdom capital of Kindoliya. Her army fought alongside Bryson and his friends in a battle that had since been dubbed the Blizzard of Blood.

That had been Bryson's first taste of a live—and *fair*—battle. Unlike the massacre of innocents at the Generals' Battle or the Phesaw invasion, this hadn't been an ambush. It was a battle like those depicted in history books, taking place across a barren, ice-capped sea. Both sides knew what was coming, and everyone involved was there willingly.

Bryson shivered unexpectedly while images of a monster crept into the front of his mind. During the battle, a winged creature had appeared. It was a skeletal wyvern, cloaked by thick wisps of black smoke, equipped with a scream capable of piercing souls and driving men to kill themselves. Vistas had called it a Linsani, native to the Linsaniun Mounds of the Cyn Kingdom. Just the memory of the whole ordeal caused Bryson to doubt his reason to live.

He would have died that night had it not been for the support of Thusia and Apoleia. The Linsani, Tongku Feilong, had expelled all spirit from his body, driving him close to suicide.

"What are you doing?" he heard someone ask.

Bryson, clearly startled, turned to face Kaylee and Himitsu. They were both staring at him. He glanced back down at his hands. They were open, palms facing up. He'd been staring at them, impulsively trying to use his clout to emit electrical sparks, not even realizing it.

"Nothing," he said, letting his hands fall limp between his thighs.

"How much longer?" Himitsu said.

"What do you mean?" Bryson asked.

"Until your energy restores."

Bryson dropped his head and muttered, "Weeks, maybe months … maybe …" He trailed off, his face falling into his hands.

"Maybe never," Kaylee said.

Himitsu sighed, relaxing deeper on the bench and staring at the sky. "To weave a lightning storm, Bryson … of course there are repercussions."

Bryson grabbed a fistful of his bangs, fighting back tears of frustration. It was something he'd pushed to the back of his mind ever since the days following the battle. Director Jugtah had told him energy depletion was to be expected after such a display of clout and weaving, that it would last only a few days—a fortnight at the longest.

But now it had gone on for a month, the grim reality of the situation tightening its chokehold. He could feel his Intel Energy flowing through his canals—however weak it might be—but why couldn't he emit electricity? Why was his clout failing him?

His worries were interrupted by giggling in the distance. He looked up, catching sight of a rare face. Flen, once a Dev servant of the royal family, was strolling down an open walkway on the opposite side of the courtyard. A woman was attached to his hip, fawning over him and laughing entirely too hard at whatever weathered joke he had just told. Flen paid no mind to the trio in the courtyard, but this came as no surprise. He'd treated everyone with equal disinterest ever since being relieved of his duties—a luxury he'd earned by granting a favor for the Intel King.

As he disappeared through an archway, Kaylee asked, "Was that not the gentleman seated with you earlier at the ball? He seems a bit different."

"That was Vistas at the ball," Himitsu explained. "He's a refined gentleman. That person you just saw is his twin, but their similarities are only skin-deep."

"Flen is a surprising character," Bryson said with a frown. "I'm still baffled by the fact that he built teleplatforms."

"Didn't he have Joy's help?" Himitsu asked.

"Yes, but according to Vistas, Joy didn't contribute much. To see him now, strolling around the palace at his leisure, frivolously toying with young aristocratic women …" He trailed off, shaking his head at the thought.

"What is it?" Kaylee asked.

"It makes me wonder what it is he truly cares about in life."

Himitsu guffawed, toppling onto his side and clutching at his chest. Bryson joined the hysteria, expecting such a reaction.

"It's not that deep," Himitsu said, wiping tears from his eyes. "This is Flen we're speaking of."

"I know." Bryson then glanced at Kaylee. "What did you see when you looked at him?"

She shrugged. "A calm man …" She paused, eyes narrowing. "A hurt man."

The two Jestivan exchanged eerie looks, but that only ended in more laughter. "How could he possibly be hurt?" Himitsu asked. "Have you seen the kind of women he woos?"

She slapped Himitsu's chest, sending him into a coughing fit. She stood and exited the courtyard, her silvery hair glistening under the Intelamps that hung from nearby rafters.

Himitsu fell on all fours, clutching chunks of grass. Bryson chuckled. He'd always been the most naïve male of the Jestivan, but perhaps his time spent with Shelly had catapulted his young mind into something a bit more matured. He would have never said such a thing to her.

Himitsu had so much to learn.

*    *    *

Bryson stood patiently in the sitting area of Vistas's bedroom, waiting for the Dev servant to finish sharing Debo's memory with Lilu. He had arrived during the tail end, so he figured he'd hang out. While he waited, he watched the wondrous holopic atop the mantle of the fireplace. It was a bluish hologram repeatedly depicting the triplet brothers—Vistas, Flen, and Tristen—along with their best friend, Marcus, laughing jubilantly with their arms thrown over each other's shoulders. Bryson longed for such a memento, one depicting his own childhood with Debo by his side. He did have a painting of the two of them, but it was hanging in Debo's living room.

Bryson lowered his head and sighed with his hand grasping the mantle for support. His Intel Energy might have been temporarily defunct, but he still had his speed. If he was needed in battle, that skill alone would prove useful. He had Debo to thank for such an attribute. The man had drilled it into Bryson's training regimen as far back as he could remember.

He looked up again, pinpointing the faces of Vistas and Flen. This holopic was the one instance in which Bryson couldn't really tell the difference between the two. Their laughter was genuine, stemming from the same thing: friendship and brotherhood. But the Vistas and Flen who Bryson knew didn't share such similarities. Vistas rarely laughed; he was a mild man. Flen smiled constantly, but it always seemed playfully conniving. Despite this, he laughed even less than Vistas.

Shame washed over Bryson. *What did my father do to you guys?*

Sharp breaths pierced the silence. He whirled, catching sight of a winded Lilu as she placed her hand against her chest. Vistas stood, rising from the floor. He grabbed a glass of water from the coffee table and handed it to her before lowering himself into a cushioned armchair, crossing one leg over the other.

She downed the entire glass in a single swig. Bryson couldn't blame her, understanding the severity of what she had just experienced.

"That is not to be shared with anyone," he said, leaning back.

Lilu lowered the glass on her lap, staring blankly at it. "That goes without saying," she said.

"I mean it," he said sternly. "None of your new friends in Brilliance should know about this. If you are to look for this, you do it on your own. Or they can help, but must do so blindly. They cannot know about that memory."

"Clearly," she said, having regained control of her breathing. "I can't believe Director Debo shared that with Vistas."

"So did it help?" Bryson asked.

"Yes, I believe so. There's a passageway Director Debo traveled down that no longer exists. It must have been sealed off."

Bryson pushed away from the mantle, stretching his back in an arch. "Great. That's a wrap, then. Time for bed."

"Hold on," she said.

He made his way across the room, grabbing his cloak from the back of a chair. "What's up?"

"I had a conversation with Olivia earlier."

"And?"

"I told her she can be Leon's godmother."

He slowed as he placed his arm in the cloak's sleeve, frowning slightly to himself. What had made her come to that decision? "Okay ..." he said, putting on the rest of his cloak.

Lilu stared at him, an unreadable look in her eyes. She suddenly stood and made her way toward the door. It opened and slammed shut. He blinked a few times, then glanced at Vistas.

"That was a rather selfless act on her part," the servant said. "Your reaction wasn't ideal."

Bryson huffed. "She only told me because she wanted recognition. That's all she ever wants."

"Perhaps, perhaps not."

Maybe Bryson had overestimated his maturity process.

"Either way," Vistas said, "the two of you have always been a disaster to watch together."

"And whose fault is that?"

"Both of yours. Depends mostly on the situation—whoever is more combative and stubborn at any given moment." Vistas stood, grabbed the empty glass from the table, and took it to a cupboard. "With that said, it astounds me that her love for you has not died."

Bryson's heart sank.

"When I share memories—or do anything that involves the mind of someone else—I can sense a bit of what they're feeling as they watch. There was a melancholic subtlety to her anger. It was palpable, yet hidden. I can only imagine her discomfort when she's around you and Princess Shelly."

Bryson moved toward the door, not wanting any part in this conversation, but Vistas suddenly raced across the room with uncharacteristic haste. "We need to congregate in the war corridor right now."

Bryson gaped at the servant, who was now jogging through the corridor outside. "What in the world?" he asked, giving chase.

"I've been contacted by a Devish—a strangely powerful one," Vistas said. "She says she has a message from Toono."

*   *   *

Vistas stood at the front of the room with both eyes dilated, a holographic display hovering in the air. The Intelights were dimmed, giving more clarity to the display. Olivia, Himitsu, Toshik, Lilu, Vuilni, and Ophala all sat in foldable wooden chairs in the meeting area, while Bryson stood off to the side, growing impatient due to King Vitio's delayed arrival. Several others sat with the group, scattered around the main core of "heroes": elders, advisors, and Major Peter, who would soon be promoted to general, filling the void left behind by Lars.

The display pictured a room made of stone. Torches lined the far wall, a different portrait of someone in lavish royal attire between each one. Beneath the torches was an extravagant wooden coffin painted in swirling shades of burgundy, its edges seemingly stitched with gold string. It sat on a wheeled table. Apart from the flickering flames, the room was still. There appeared to be no one visible, but it was assumed someone was probably standing just outside of the periphery of the shot.

Bryson figured he knew who occupied the coffin … Dev King Rehn, or the man many called the Oracle. But why would Toono show this? He couldn't resurrect the man yet. With eight sacrifices obtained, he was still two short of Anathallo's threshold. He'd yet to gather the Intel and Dev sacrifices.

"What's taking him so long?" Toshik asked with an air of annoyance.

Ophala groaned, leaning forward and rubbing her eyes. Something told Bryson that her gripes stemmed not from Vitio's tardiness, but a massive hangover. It was now nearing three o'clock in the morning; she must have been woken from a drunken slumber.

"Once King Vitio arrives, the broadcast will officially begin," Vistas droned. "The other leaders of the True Light alliance have already assembled."

"Does that include my mom?" Bryson asked.

Vistas nodded. "Still Queen Apoleia, Lady Ropinia, and General Valp are also waiting, although with not as much patience as others."

The corridor's main door opened, and King Vitio rushed in, his hair a ruffled mess. It seemed even kings couldn't escape bed head.

"My apologies, Vistas," Vitio said, taking a seat at the front of the group. "Carry on."

Vistas nodded, then said, "The Intel King is here."

A cloaked figure stepped into the display from outside of the frame. He brushed back his hood, revealing the face of whom Bryson assumed to be Toono, based on the bandage circling his head. This was Bryson's first time actually seeing him. Dev King Storshae was always the face of the opposition's operations, for he was the one who'd show up in broadcasts. Even during Toono's participation in Phesaw's invasion a couple of years ago, Bryson had been too preoccupied with Olivia and Still Queen Apoleia to notice.

Toono looked nothing at all resembling the nickname the world had given him—the *Rogue Demon*. He was a rather unassuming man to have been labeled a demon, though it was difficult to tell beneath the cascading cloak of gray. His eyes weren't fierce, but soft with a lazy disinterest. He seemed to carry himself in similar fashion to Olivia during her emotionless years. His dirty-blond hair was untidy, striped with brown and gold.

While Toono had worked heavily with King Storshae, nobody seemed to understand his motives. Agnos once said he had come to a realization during his journey in the Void. Toono had always wanted answers to the purpose of life. At a young age, the two orphans had planned on finding some kind of book in an undersea cavern, but Agnos believed Toono gave up on that method. Instead the demon turned toward a darker route after meeting a strange woman, deeming it easier to gain answers about their world by asking Dev King Rehn. But that man was dead and had been for years. Toono then discovered a way to resurrect him, involving the sacrifice of ten powerful individuals, one from each kingdom who possessed a unique energy.

This was what made Toono the *Rogue* Demon. As an Archain, he had somehow involved himself with the Dev Kingdom, an inexplicable scenario in the eyes of the Light Realm's royal elites. How had this orphan gained favor with the likes of Dev King Storshae and Archaic King Itta? Had he been the reason why an alliance between the two kingdoms formed? Had he been the true catalyst to the Generals' Battle Massacre all those years ago? Many believe he was the silent force behind it all, a force that made powerful men believe their motives were the true reasons for this war, when the reality had always been in Toono's best interest.

He was a frightening individual. He'd sparked and successfully orchestrated a worldwide war, manipulating and killing royal heads in the process. He was a ghost, hidden by a layered, translucent shell of calculated deceit. Only a few others operated like him, those of high intelligence— Ophala, Agnos, and Tazama. Interesting that they all resided from one of two kingdoms: Archaic and Dev.

Toono came to a stop on the other side of the coffin, resting his hands against its edge. He stared at his recorder and said, "Welcome, True Light elites. This is a one-way transmission. I cannot see or hear you, so any attempts to communicate with me will be in vain.

"The past dozen-plus years have been an arduous journey for me. From wailing over the carcasses of rats I killed in abandoned alleyways to murdering royal heads as if they meant nothing more than a tin cup kicked on the side of a city street, I've devolved into something less human than I once was. This has been a strange expedition, conflicting and twisted, yet with a dream at the end that does not waver. I will stop at nothing to achieve it. My soul might be tethered to said dream, but even if it weren't, the course of action would not change."

Bryson frowned. *His soul is tethered to a dream? What does that mean?* He eyed Ophala, trying to read her reaction. She sat up with an alertness she previously did not have.

"Just behind me lies a legend to not only the Dev Kingdom, but the world," Toono said.

*But the coffin is in front of you*, Bryson thought.

"His name's reach is as extensive as the heroes of the *Of Five*. Dev King Rehn—the Oracle as the legends call him—spoke of universal truths that only he could obtain. But there was always one piece of information he kept to himself, or so I believe." He paused, gazing longingly down at the coffin. "The purpose of our world. I'm now as close as I've ever been to finding out this secret. Because of this, I am here in an undisclosed location of Cogdan, preparing myself for the climax of this journey." He paused again. "I want to show you something."

He reached across the top of the coffin, grasped its edge, and pulled it open. Only Toono's head remained visible behind the open lid. The Devish who was recording stepped closer, eventually reaching the coffin to peer inside.

Gasps erupted around the war corridor. Bryson's eyes widened. It wasn't Rehn, but his son Dev King Storshae. His eyes were a milky white, absent of iris or pupil.

Toono stepped back. "The ninth sacrifice." Four other figures came into view, all of them cloaked in plain black robes. They each took a position at one of the coffin's four corners, grasping onto the sides and wheeling it to the left. Toono followed. The broadcast's picture veered left, trailing the group as they proceeded through a wide arched doorway.

They entered a square room, modest in size but extravagant in décor. Gold decked the walls in several layers of paneling. Random treasures sat on mantles, some a matching gold and others dazzling silver. Torches sat in small mantles that were scattered throughout the room, their flames burning bright against the reflective sheen that swallowed them. Across the room was a small entryway with a narrow staircase that curved upward, disappearing into the shadows.

Despite all of this, the floor space was bare save a lone coffin that rested at its center. Unlike Storshae's resting place, this was more of a casket, but even that didn't feel generous enough a word. It looked to be molded of pure gold. The only other color came from the bed of flowers carved into its base, their petals painted black. A mosaic of eyes swathed the rest of the casket's side, acting as a backdrop to the flowers.

The cloaked figures wheeled Storshae's coffin to the casket's side. They lifted it off the table and set it on the floor, where it cowered next to the Oracle's bier. It served as an eyesore, unbefitting of such a room. What Bryson had first thought of as a rather beautiful coffin now resembled an oblong storage crate.

As the cloaked figures exited the frame, Toono reentered. "Storshae was an impetuous man. I had known the time would come when I would dispose of him, but I had to exercise patience, for he did have a role to play while alive. I figured I could do one good deed for him by allowing him to rest by his father's side … even if it is only for a short time."

He reached into his pocket and withdrew a handful of gems known as Anathallo, a relic he'd stolen from the Archaic Museum years ago around the time of the Jestivan's formation. It was the true beginning of the Rogue Demon's quest.

He spilled them across the top of Rehn's casket. Four of them gleamed, illuminating the space around them even more than the torchlight. The fifth one had a dull sheen. With only half of its sacrifice threshold met—that being the Devish half—it was not yet fully active.

Bryson's gaze became resolute, knowing what the other half was. Only one energy remained unclaimed by Toono.

"I know all of you have been keeping track of my progress," Toono said. "I have one sacrifice left, and it must be someone powerful who possesses Intel Energy. You may wonder why I've decided to announce this to you. Is it perhaps to cause you to overthink your next move? Either way, the fact remains that I know my next move, and your indecisiveness will likely render anything you do unsuccessful. Will you come to me or will you bunker up in your capitals? Now begins a game of cat and mouse in which neither side wants to assume either role."

He paused, and for the first time Bryson sensed emotion in his next words: "I will not fail."

# 6
# Cat or Mouse

Bryson stirred where he stood, clenching his fists with a slow pulse of his muscles. He wanted to move; he *needed* to move. He wasn't sure where to, but he knew what for. He needed to sever the head from the snake. Toono was the mastermind behind everything. And for the first time ever, he had stepped into the forefront. The end of this war was near.

The corridor was silent for a long moment following the conclusion of the broadcast. Vitio eventually stood, turning toward the group. Vistas joined those seated.

"What do you think he is playing at, milord?" an elder by the name of Unys asked.

"Some kind of deception," Vitio said.

"The Rogue Demon has a mind of many curtains," Ophala said sternly "not all of which hang with the purpose of concealment. If you were to peel most back, you'd find no window, just a wall. When you train to become a spy, you must learn such mind tricks. It's the only reason why I was able to counter Tazama over the past year."

"How should we go about this, then?" Major Peter asked, turning to her. "You are the Spy Pilot. As you said, you thrive in deception's haze."

Bryson wasn't a fan of mind games. He was a straightforward thinker. What would get him from Point A to Point B the quickest? "So we just rip back every curtain," he said, offering what he thought was the most obvious solution.

"Until you find the one that hides a trap," she said. "That headstrong mentality of yours might be helpful on a battlefield, but not in a situation such as this. Toono is a strategic mastermind. His plans are already in motion and have been for quite some time."

Bryson leaned back against the wall, waiting for Ophala to turn the other way before he frowned. Olivia shook her head. Despite his age, he was still a child.

Vitio sighed as he pulled out a watch from his pocket. He held the gold chain in his fingers, letting it dangle in front of him. "We'll reconvene tomorrow morning. For now, I must rest."

"Some of us have planned to leave in the morning," Ophala said. "I have business to attend to back in Phelos."

"Then you and I will speak briefly before you depart. As for everyone else—"

"And I'm taking Himitsu with me," she added.

"Can he not stay here?" Vitio asked, aghast. "We need all the Jestivan we have."

"You're not the only kingdom in True Light, King Vitio." Her tone was harsh. "Perhaps some of your allies could use the help. Why should you be able to hoard all of our most skilled men and women?"

"Probably because my kingdom is Toono's only remaining target."

Vitio had a point. How could she argue against that logic?

"Toono isn't going to ignore the rest of us," she said. "Tunnel vision is a dire flaw, and he knows this. If we put all of our focus into one kingdom, he will take advantage of our weaknesses elsewhere."

She stood and almost toppled over. Perhaps the alcohol was still in her system, somehow targeting her motor functions but leaving her acumen unhindered.

"Himitsu is returning to the Archaic Kingdom with me tomorrow. He has a mission that can prove useful to our efforts." She turned, stepping clumsily around those still seated. "Good night, friends." As she opened the door to leave, she glanced at Bryson with a smile. "And congratulations, groom-to-be."

*    *    *

Bryson didn't know what time Ophala was planning to leave the following morning, so he sat outside the palace's main entrance on the stone ledge of the grand fountain. He stared at the rising sun and could see the Intel Kingdom's familiar overcast sky already waiting to stifle its light.

He was surprised when he turned to find Ophala and Himitsu exiting the palace only thirty minutes after he had himself. He figured she would have desired a much longer night of sleep, considering the prior night's events. She was an impressive woman. Even Toshik couldn't hold alcohol like she could—not that the swordsman did much drinking anymore. He'd made it a point to rid himself of the habit following Jilly's death.

"Good morning, Bryson," Ophala said as she rounded the fountain.

"Hey, buddy," Himitsu said.

"Good morning. You're both up awfully early."

A horse-drawn carriage rode through the palace grounds, following the gently curving stone path through the grass.

"I could say the same to you," Ophala said.

"Couldn't sleep."

She nodded. "Had it not been for the copious amounts of alcohol in my system, I would have suffered the same fate."

"I wanted to talk to you," Bryson said. He then glanced back at the nearing carriage. " ... Before you leave, I guess. Surprise early morning departure?"

66

"I don't wish to speak with the Intel King—not in a face-to-face encounter, at least. I must leave before he rises."

"But the two of you need to discuss what happened last night," Bryson said. He was a bit caught off guard by the resentment in her tone.

As the carriage rolled to a stop several paces away, she said, "Never mind that. What is it *you* want to discuss?"

Bryson paused, staring at her curiously.

The coachman called out from behind: "Your bags are already aboard the carriage, milady. Whenever you're ready."

Smiling, she held up a finger, requesting his patience. Himitsu gave Bryson a hug. "I'm gonna get going. Good luck with whatever your role will be moving forward. Hopefully it involves staying far away from Toono."

"That's not a proper goodbye," Bryson said, frowning as his friend took a step back. "Actually, this wasn't even a proper visit."

Himitsu slapped his hand on Bryson's shoulder. "Kaylee is waiting for me."

As the assassin sprinted away, Bryson watched with furrowed brows. He spotted Kaylee on a bench just inside the carriage. "Why isn't she with you?" he asked, turning toward Ophala.

"King Vitio didn't want any Archains whom he wasn't personally familiar with sleeping in the palace," she said.

"*Really?*" he said in disgust.

"Unfortunately, yes. It seems the king has adopted a rather unflattering system of classifying his citizens, one that strictly limits what those from other kingdoms can do and where they can access. Himitsu, Toshik, and I are apparently exceptions ... because of our 'status.'" She formed air quotes with her fingers. "It was a miracle I even convinced the man to allow Kaylee access to the ball last night." She was speaking of the Socioenergenic System, an arbitrary system that only created greater division within the populace.

"I'm sorry," Bryson said. "I was against the idea when Vitio pitched it last year. To be fair, though, he didn't even come up with the concept. Lilu did."

She raised an eyebrow. "Oh? I figured it was one of his advisors." She sighed, looking blankly over his shoulder. "A bit shallow of the woman."

Her words made him flinch. They felt harsh—harsher than Lilu deserved in his eyes. Now he regretted telling her.

Bryson shifted uncomfortably, then asked, "Did you ever fear for Himitsu's well-being when he was under your care?"

Her thoughtful gaze refocused on him. "Wouldn't any sane parent answer that question with a yes?"

"I mean, of course you fear for your child's well-being," he said, "but have you—"

"Ever doubted my ability to provide that well-being?" she asked, finishing his question for him.

He nodded.

"Of course, and on more than one occasion," she said. "When Himitsu was a baby, I wasn't the Spy Pilot, but I was a spy. It still required long absences from home. Spy missions tend to be slow-developing."

*Oh really?* Bryson thought sarcastically. Ophala's recent overthrow of King Toth Brench had taken over a year of planning and execution.

"And Horos was still an assassin," she continued. "His missions also took time, involving a lot of travel. We were away from Himitsu a lot, and we probably shouldn't have been. Also, because of the danger and secrecy of our professions, Himitsu had to move frequently and was unable to stay in one location for more than a month at a time. He's never invited you home because he's never had one. Phesaw eventually became his home, but before that he had a unique life many children wouldn't understand."

She paused, then shook her head and laughed. "Talk about a tangent. What I mean to say is yes, you'll doubt yourself more times than not. And considering what's going on in the world now with your heavy involvement, you'll be in a similar situation to what I was in many years ago. Luckily for me, I had someone I could trust back then, someone who could stay by Himitsu's side while Horos and I were away." She smiled at Bryson. "I think you have that, too. Princess Shelly, who won't have the luxury of leaving the palace in the near future, is strong. She'll always be by Leon's side."

Bryson didn't know what to feel. She'd basically just called herself a terrible parent. She placed her hand on his shoulder with a thin smile and walked past. He stood there for a moment, confused. Nothing she had said made sense to him.

"Pilot Ophala," he said, turning around.

She slowed, then looked back.

"Isn't electing to spend time away from your child, especially for such long intervals, considered bad parenting?"

"Not if there is good reason," she replied. "You are a key to saving this world, Bryson."

"But L.K. is my *child*," he said. "Am I supposed to be so selfless that I risk my life for the world rather than stay alive to protect my son?"

"Which is more important?" she asked. "Your child or the world?"

He balked. "Obviously my child."

"The world." She turned back toward the carriage. "Without it, what would you give your son?"

*     *     *

The nursery was quiet. Bryson had relieved Yusif of his duties. Tears fell gently down his cheeks as he stared into the crib. The bluish eyes of L.K. gazed wondrously back at him. He hated Ophala for her wise words. The dilemma that faced him had seemed so complex in his mind—hide in the palace and keep his family safe or continue venturing into the world and risk leaving his loved ones behind—yet Ophala, when confronted with the same question, offered the most simplistic solution … and it made sense.

If he didn't stop Toono, what would come of Kuki Sphaira? The world could fall under the rule of the Rogue Demon and the Oracle, alongside the brutish Power Queen and ghastly Cyn King. This made the sudden appearance of a Linsani at the Blizzard of Blood even more unnerving. That, according to Thusia, had been the work of some otherworldly being from before the modern timeline. If this scenario were to unfold, L.K. would be one of the first to die … right after Bryson and Shelly.

*Or worse*, he thought, *they'd make me watch them die.*

He reached down and, placing his thumb against L.K.'s forehead, brushed away a few thin strands of hair. "I don't know what my next move is, bud, but I know it'll be in your best interest."

"I'd hope so."

He whirled to find the daunting presence of Intel Queen Delilah standing in the open doorway. She sauntered into the room with the grace of a royal woman. She approached the crib, reached inside, and lifted L.K. gently into her arms. "I figured I might find you here. My husband requests your presence in the war corridor. Afterward, Shelly would also like to see you."

He watched with a smile as she thrummed her finger lightly against the baby's lips. He left the room, comforted by the fact that there were a lot of people in this palace who would lay down their life for that child.

*      *      *

The war corridor was set up exactly as it had been the previous night. Bryson spotted several familiar faces—mostly advisors and elders. Toshik lounged in a chair at the rear of the seating area, far enough back that part of the wired module of Kuki Sphaira hung above him. Bryson crept toward the swordsman and took a seat. Vitio acknowledged his arrival with a small nod as he continued speaking to his audience. Bryson feigned a smile at Toshik. Shortly after, Olivia and Vuilni arrived.

"Milord, where is Pilot Ophala?" an elder asked.

"She departed early this morning without my knowledge," Vitio said. "But that's okay. I sent Radon with a message just a few hours ago."

Radon was one of Ophala's birds she'd given to important power players in the True Light alliance as another means of communication outside of Devish transmissions.

"Are the two of you on bad terms, milord?" the elder asked.

"I suppose I was a big factor as to why Rhyparia NuForce was captured and put on trial; I set the process in motion. Pilot Ophala was against the decision, but I didn't listen to her."

"And who ended up being right?" Bryson asked.

Vitio pressed his lips together. "She was … correct … just like Queen Apsa was correct about Toth Brench and Wert Lamay."

Why did he even bring up Rhyparia's name? While Jilly was fresh on Bryson's mind, Rhyparia had been pushed to the back. Nobody knew what had happened to her. Pilot Ophala and Archaic Director Senex had risked everything to help her flee her execution into the Archaic Mountains. Perhaps that was why her absence didn't feel as dire to him. He liked to believe that Rhyparia was alive, living comfortably in some kind of safe haven in the mountains. That'd be the only reason Ophala would have sent her there.

His brow furrowed. He hadn't seen Pilot Ophala in so long that he had forgotten to ask her about Rhyparia's escape. He dropped his face in his hands.

"She's alive, you know," Toshik said.

Bryson turned to look at him. "What?"

"Rhyparia … she's alive."

"How do you know?"

"I saw her."

Bryson's eyes widened, a chaotic mess of emotions suddenly swirling within him.

"I'd like *everyone's* attention!" Vitio called out.

Bryson gazed back at Vitio, who was eyeing him and Toshik with impatience. "Gossip *after* the meeting," the king said. "This is important."

Bryson begrudgingly shelved Toshik's revelation for later. He leaned back, allowing his muscles to relax.

"There are vacant missions that need to be filled," Vitio said.

"Which one involves hunting down Toono and ending his rampage?" Bryson asked.

"None of them. There are a few reconnaissance missions in the works, each manned by a spy chosen by Pilot Ophala. Those spies will work diligently, trying to extract information as to where Toono is exactly. It's likely he's in Cogdan Castle, but we can't assume that."

Bryson sunk in his chair. He had participated in the Blizzard of Blood a little over a month ago. That was all well and good, but the battle hadn't achieved the ultimate goal of this war: eliminating Toono.

"I think both alliances want to avoid large-scale acts of violence for the time being," Vitio said, turning toward the chalkboard. He listed missions at the top.

Bryson stifled a groan, realizing that almost everything listed involved the talents of a spy or scout. He wasn't going to have a repeat of his several months spent cooped in this palace back when Olivia had hunted Rhyparia in the Archaic Mountains. He needed an objective.

Vitio tapped the end of his chalk next to the first bullet point. "The Prim Kingdom. Because of their neutral status throughout all of this, True Light has disregarded them, deeming them unimportant. But Spirit Queen Apsa made a good point recently during one of our meetings. Where did Toono's first sacrifice take place?"

"The Prim Kingdom, milord," an advisor said.

"And who, according to one of Grand Director Poicus's rogue spies, was the sacrifice?"

"Prim Prince Gahn, royal first born," a woman said.

"Then that leaves us asking: why?"

"Because it was an easy target, milord. The Prim Kingdom holds no alliances and has no enemies. Security at their teleplatforms is laxed … even the capital is notoriously unguarded."

"But their royal headquarters is a fortress," another advisor said. "Though it may be ancient, it's also strong. Stone walls surround it as thick and tall as Kindoliya's ice wall."

"That is true," she said thoughtfully. "And Prince Gahn was supposedly killed in his own bedroom in the dead of night. It's such an impressive feat by Toono that one must question the legitimacy of Praetor Poicus's retelling of the story from his spy—especially considering that it was Toono's first sacrifice, so he was likely inexperienced."

Vitio shook his head. "I may not have seen eye-to-eye with Praetor throughout my life, but the man wouldn't have lied about this. Regardless, you're on the right train of thought, which leads us to the next question: How?

"Perhaps the Prim Kingdom was an easy target for Toono, but not because of the kingdom's political position in regards to the world. Director Venustas thinks there might be something deeper to Toono's first sacrifice. Since I think we'd all agree that his murder of the Prim Prince is more baffling than any of his others when considering the aforementioned circumstances, it's safe to say that it's worth investigating."

"Are we're sure we aren't grasping at straws here, milord?" Unys asked.

"I don't think so," Vitio said. He walked toward a table off to the side and retrieved a stack of parchment. He handed it to a lady at the front of the group, instructing her to take one sheet then pass the stack onward. As the parchment made its way toward the back of the group, he said, "These are copies of the penned letter written to Praetor from his spy years ago, informing him of the Prim Prince's death. Tell me, what other aspect of the murder stands out to you? Something that reeks of more than a simple sacrifice."

The papers had yet to make it to the back row, but Bryson already knew the answer. He couldn't forget the image Director Poicus had painted during that meeting years ago, when he informed the Jestivan of the Prim Prince's death.

"There was another strange murder that night," Bryson said, the remaining parchment just now making it back to Toshik's hands.

Vitio nodded. "Do tell."

Bryson's body shook at the thought, but he answered anyway. "The general ... he had the most inexplicable wounds, not the prince—though his missing iris and pupils were cause for alarm." Toshik handed the final parchment to Bryson, who merely placed it on his lap dismissively. "The general's chest and forehead had holes in them, apparently as the result of burns. King Damian feared it might have been a rogue assassin of his. After all, Passion Assassins use black flames that only prove most useful in dark places.

"But why would someone kill in that way?" he asked, as if carrying out a discussion with himself. "What's the point of burning holes into specific locations of someone's body only to leave everything inside intact? Director Poicus had said that the heart and brain went untouched."

"Venustas described it as a killing of passion," Vitio said. "She believes there was something deep-seated behind that murder, and it wasn't done by Toono, but by a companion of his."

"So this companion had ties with the general," an elder said.

"More important, since when can fire burn clean holes into someone's body?" a woman asked. "The way this is explained … fire doesn't seem possible."

"And if the heart and brain could be seen unobstructed, then more than just skin was penetrated."

"That means bones and muscle," said another. "Ribs and the skull."

Vitio sighed, scratching his scruffy golden beard. "An inexcusable oversight on all of our parts," he said. "Clearly, flame cannot burn through one's skull, especially in the manner described. It would take something a lot stronger." He regarded the group. "Any guesses?"

"Something corrosive," Unys said.

"Acid, perhaps?" Vitio said with a wispy air in his tone. Something told Bryson the king already knew the answer, but simply wanted to continue the discussion.

A general murmur of agreement crept through the corridor. Vitio turned to write on the chalkboard again. As he wrote, he read it aloud: "The Archaic Museum theft, Prim General's death, King Damian's death, Adren General's death, and the Adren Navy ship that returned to Sodai months back … they each have something in common. It took looking at them as a whole to see the trend."

He pointed at King Damian's name. "It took Director Venustas's inspection of King Damian's corpse to recognize his hand had been strangely burned. She noticed something odd about the bones of the finger. They had eroded slightly, hinting at an acidic substance.

"Even after discovering this, however, she didn't bring it to my attention or to that of the other royal heads. But when Yama recently infiltrated the Adren Kingdom and craftily killed Adren General Sinno through the use of a hole that seemed to have been carved out of the bottom of a carriage, it had confirmed to the Passion Director that someone was playing with acid.

That was the link she needed. She shared with us this information, and soon thereafter, other mysteries began to make sense.

"Spirit Queen Apsa had said the Adren Navy ship that returned to Sodai—the one that had carried Toono, Yama, and a mystery woman with brown hair according to sailors aboard—had a sizable hole in its hull. She had thought it to have been the work of someone's exceptional strength, but after hearing Venustas's revelation of acid, it clicked … another link."

Vitio pointed his chalk at the next bullet point. "Then, hearing all of this, Spy Pilot Ophala informed the royal heads of a discovery made by Himitsu, Horos, Fane, and a young woman by the name of Kaylee when they searched the Archaic Museum. A window at the very top of the towering wall of Relic Alley—one that should have been barred like the rest of them—was open. Its bars were no longer connected, somehow missing entire sections in the middle, creating a hole just big enough for someone to squeeze through. Kaylee, a practicing apothecary, believed it was acid because of the discoloring of the stone beneath the window."

Bryson sat slackjawed. It was like witnessing a thousand-piece puzzle being put together in seconds right before his eyes.

"Only recently, while the royal heads perused through information about Toono's history, trying to find more examples of acidic nature, was our attention drawn to his first sacrifice. It is, perhaps, the most glaring example of corrosion. Not only that, but it's the only sacrifice where there seems to be motivation beyond the simple act of getting it done. This means the answer to this question" —he slapped his hand against the board next to the word, *why*— "is likely personal. Crimes of passion are always personal. And as for the *how*, we believe there was a connection between Toono's companion and someone in that castle—if not multiple people."

"So our goal is to get someone into the castle to find out this information?" Bryson asked.

"Basically, yes."

"Why not send Fane, Horos, or Himitsu?"

"Horos and Himitsu are unavailable, for they have their own missions to attend to. As for Fane, he is an option, but I would want him accompanied by at least two elite fighters, such as the Jestivan."

Toshik shook his head. "Count me out. I will be on hiatus for the next couple of weeks."

Vitio's face flushed red. "A 'hiatus'? I trust you realize the scope and severity of this situation."

"I do," Toshik said. "And that's why I'm here right now. I could have left this morning with Pilot Ophala. Instead I wanted to remain in the loop. I promise when I return, I'll be right back in the thick of things."

Vitio paused for a moment; the struggle was evident on his face. "I understand," he finally said. "To have lost all that you have, it's a miracle you still sit here with a level head."

"I'll go," Olivia said.

"Me too," Vuilni said.

The king smiled, eyeing the two ladies. "Brilliant. How could Fane turn down such company?"

Fane was a Passion Assassin. He operated in the dark, using his black flames to cloak himself in the night. Meanwhile, Olivia and Vuilni's specialties were blunt force. They were physically stronger than most, capable of lifting boulders and punching through stone. They didn't rely on gimmicks.

But part of Bryson didn't enjoy this news. What was he to do while they were off exploring with purpose? He quickly scanned over the remaining missions on the board. Phesaw Patrol sounded like a snoozefest. The other—Rehn's Grave—piqued his interest.

"Let's move on to the next vacant mission," Vitio said. "Horos holds one spot, but he will be joined by one other. It is critical that we get to King Rehn's resting place. Luckily, Praetor Poicus left us with a little gift to aid our efforts. Praetor once decided to temporarily vacate his position as Grand Director in order to infiltrate the Dev army by impersonating a soldier. Doing so gained him access to places off-limits to outsiders, such as the Oracle's grave. When he returned to Phesaw, he made sure to map the casket's location, knowing that it might prove useful down the road. Of course, we don't know if destroying it prevents the resurrection process, so theft is more ideal."

Bryson's nose crumpled. "We'd be graverobbers."

"Yes."

At first Bryson was turned off by the idea of stealing someone's corpse, but then he realized the significance of a mission such as this. If he couldn't chase down Toono, then this was the next best method of stopping him: swipe his goal. While he was a frightening enough threat by himself, he still was only one person. The real disaster they needed to avoid was Toono's acquisition of a partner like Rehn, who possessed knowledge of this supposed weapon in the Dark Realm's sky known as Earth.

Bryson became giddy. If he were to successfully steal Rehn's body, then he could use it as bait to lure out Toono. If he took this mission, the war would give him a sense of meaning and plenty of avenues leading him to a face-to-face encounter with the world's most notorious villain.

"I'm going," he said.

"No, you're not."

Bryson turned toward his surprising opposition. A denial from Vitio would have made sense, but Olivia? Words failed him; he simply gave her a pitiful stare.

She remained firm, her expression unwavering as she looked him in the eyes. "Your arrogance renders you blind to the fact that your death would be the end of True Light. Toono has one sacrifice remaining, and it must be an Intelian—a strong one, at that. That leaves very few options for him: you, Shelly, Lilu, or King Vitio. As of right now, all four of you are in very secure locations, and that shouldn't change."

Vitio nodded in agreement. "I couldn't have said it better myself."

Even Toshik voiced his doubts. "Not to mention, your clout is weak right now. You have great speed, don't get me wrong, but without your electricity to complement it … well, Toono would be a daunting opponent."

Bryson's gaze veered toward Vuilni, his last hope. Her lack of eye contact said enough.

"I know how difficult this is to hear," Vitio said, placing his chalk on the ledge beneath the board, "but only an irrational mind would suggest letting you enter the Dev Kingdom. I don't know what Toono was thinking by killing off Storshae, but he has left himself weak and exposed. We have the upper hand, for he has to chase *us*. We simply need to hide a handful of elites while trying to figure out how to dispose of him."

"When is Horos beginning his mission?" Toshik asked.

"Would you like to accompany him?" Vitio asked.

"I would, after I visit someone in the Archaic Kingdom."

"You have two weeks, then," Vitio said. "Hopefully your travels don't take too much time." Vitio brushed off his hands and looked toward the board once more. "The last topic regards Phesaw security, and I will speak to Major Peter about that later."

Bryson drifted into a buzz of rage and wallow. What had been a brief moment of optimism had brought him crashing back down to reality. Did they really expect him to barricade himself in this palace? That wasn't going to happen. He was no mouse.

*　　*　　*

With a desperate need to clear his mind, Bryson took a walk into the northern barracks, which contained the Intelian archery units and training grounds. He'd yet to visit Simon since returning from the Still Kingdom, but he'd heard the gossip circulating the palace about a young red-headed boy who could strike the bull's-eye of a target from a mile away. They called him Torchtop.

Bryson nodded at passing archers as he strolled down the dirt path sandwiched between three-story flats. He was reminded of the envious students at Phesaw immediately following his induction into the Jestivan. But these were grown adults who were gazing at him with respect. They had heard the stories about his defeat of a Linsani.

He pressed on, doing his best to offer friendly glances to those with the confidence to acknowledge his presence. Little did they know, he was nothing but a dying Intelight only capable of producing mere sparks.

Bryson got lucky and found Simon in the first building he checked, a bow-and-arrow shop where the young boy worked for a small coin. He was a fletcher, a skill he'd apparently learned in Lingens Rainforest.

Bryson spotted the fiery ponytail in the backyard. Simon was seated on a stump, knifing at some kind of wood. He was bent over with eagle-eyed focus on his work, a pile of wood shavings at his feet.

"Hey there, Torchtop."

Simon looked up, sweat dripping from his brow. His face lit up. "The man who weaved a lightning storm!"

The two friends grasped hands and embraced in a powerful hug. Simon was only fifteen but had sprouted several inches in the past year, rising above even Bryson. The boy had to be at least six feet.

Bryson stepped back, grasping Simon's shoulders and holding him at an arm's length. "I can't believe it. Look at you."

Simon laughed. "I'm hoping to get as tall as Director Debo was."

"Even your voice is deepening!" Bryson said, now shaking the boy. He stopped and waved toward the stump. "Sit back down. Don't let me keep you from your work."

Simon took a seat, but didn't bother picking up his tools. "How's Olivia?"

"Fine, I guess. She'll be departing soon, though."

"She's got an assignment elsewhere?" Simon asked, finally picking up his knife and wooden chunk.

"Yep," Bryson said, gazing around the yard. "I can't really say much more."

"I figured." Following a pause, the boy shrugged. "One of these days I'll get to do something important."

"It will be something to see," Bryson said. "I've heard you can strike a target from a mile away."

A wry smirk wormed onto Simon's face. "The rumors never give me enough credit."

Bryson paused, then laughed hard enough to double over. "Okay, Torchtop. That ego of yours is something else."

Simon continued fletching as Bryson raised a brow at the deserted yard of tree stumps—not a single customer or employee in sight. "Where's Whistleblower or whatever her name is?" he asked.

"You mean Whistle?" Simon said. "She was discharged months ago."

"Why?" Bryson couldn't fathom it. Simon had spoken highly of her in the past.

"Well … when King Vitio implemented that new classification system, they discovered she wasn't Intelian."

"Because she couldn't weave electricity?" Bryson said in outrage. "Who cares if she's an Unable! That doesn't make her any less of an archer."

"That wasn't the problem, Bry," Simon said, setting his stock on the stump. He shook his head. "If she had been an Unable, she'd still be here. After all, I'm an Unable. No, she wove fire."

"A Passionian?"

Simon nodded slowly.

"Then what was she doing here?"

"Who knows?"

"Either way," Bryson said, "I'm fed up with these energy classes."

Simon pulled out a rolled-up piece of parchment from his trouser pocket. He untied the twine and unraveled the note, staring at it for a moment.

"Is that your ID paper?" Bryson asked.

"Yep."

Simon handed it to Bryson. The socioenergenic system had been such a large overhaul. Apart from the days he had spent watching Intelian officers raid the homes of Dunami citizens, he hadn't given much thought to what the documentation looked like.

"What does yours say?" Simon asked.

"I don't have one."

Simon frowned. Listed on the small sheet were several components: his full name, date of birth, occupation, energy, and socioenergenic class. Simon belonged to Tier 2, meaning he possessed Intel Energy but couldn't use it, marking him as an Unable.

Bryson handed it back. "The thing expires?"

"I have to get it renewed in four years."

A woman entered the backyard, approaching Simon and Bryson as she wended between tree stumps. "Torchtop, how's the job going?" she asked.

Simon nodded to the side, where a magnificent bow rested against a stump. "It's over there, Tisa."

She bolted for the bow, launching herself from one stump to the next. She was Shelly's age, somewhere in her mid-twenties. Her jet-black hair was tied in a ponytail that hung past her lower back. Light and loose, it danced with each bound like the hem of one of Shelly's silk robes.

Tisa picked up the ivory bow and examined it with lustful eyes. Shaped like a dragon's jaw, jagged teeth lined its inner edge. It had a sharp arch, giving it a fiercer look than a typical bow. It seemed less practical, too. Bryson wondered how such a bow would fare in battle.

Tisa drew an arrow from the quiver strapped to her back and nocked it. As she pulled back on the string, the bow's limbs bent inward, giving off the impression of a dragon's mouth closing around her. She didn't release her grip. Instead she gazed wondrously at the bow's teeth. Simon snorted.

Bryson looked down at him. "What?"

"She'd die if she tried to fight someone with that," Simon said, shaking his head in an amused state.

"That's what I thought."

"Oh well," Simon said. "It's more of a trophy bow, anyway."

"Ah …" Bryson nodded. "She's more of an image-before-practicality kind of person?"

"Definitely not, and don't let her hear you say that. She wouldn't try to fight with that thing in a real battle scenario." He looked up from his fletching. "She's very good."

"As good as you?"

"Ha! Not quite."

Tisa approached them. Her new bow hung at her side as she regarded Bryson. "You're not what I thought you'd be."

"And what were you expecting?" he asked.

She looked him up and down. "Someone taller."

Bryson found himself frowning, feeling she had a point. He'd always been jealous of Himitsu and Toshik, who tended to assert their dominance over others simply because of their height. In fact, she was so tall that Bryson couldn't think of any woman he knew who'd match her height. She would have given Himitsu and Toshik a run for their money.

"Yeah, well, my short stature helps me in battle," Bryson said, attempting to make his tone sound more prideful. "I'd imagine being as tall as you might make maneuvering difficult."

"Now you just sound bitter," Simon said.

She chuckled. "You're right. I'm not the most nimble of people, but my specific role as an archer doesn't require nifty feet—though I'm still more gifted than most. My talents come from these babies." She spread her arms.

"Your muscles?" He was skeptical since she lacked definition, but what else could she have implied?

"Her arms, Bry," Simon said, still shaving wood. He stopped and looked up. "More specifically, her wingspan."

"How does that help?"

She sucked her teeth. "Man, you don't know anything."

Bryson shrugged. He didn't care about archery.

"You see this, right?" she asked, holding up her dragon bow. "In the hands of most archers, it would serve no purpose. It's too big, the limbs and string too long. But for me, it's perfect. I have the wingspan to properly wield such a beast. Most others wouldn't be able to pull all the way back, causing a flimsy shot. I, however ..." she trailed off, gazing down at Simon. "Hand me an arrow real quick."

Simon absentmindedly grabbed an arrow from the ground and handed it over. Bryson's eyes veered toward her back. "Just use an arrow from your quiver."

She shook her head and laughed. "They're not long or strong enough for a bow like this."

"I have to fletch special arrows for that thing," Simon said. "Which is what I'm doing right now. Takes some time."

"Anyway, like I was saying," she continued, loading and raising her bow. She pulled back on the string, her lengthy reach on full display.

Bryson might have heard the snap before even realizing she'd released her grip. What followed wasn't a thud like he would have expected, but the sound of splintering wood.

"You're going to get me in trouble," Simon whined, spinning on his stump.

The target now had a hole at its center—no, more than a hole. It looked like someone had punched through it. And the wooden fence behind it had met the same fate.

Tisa relaxed, dropping her bow by her side with a satisfied nod. "Very good, Simon." She then gazed at Bryson, who had yet to pry his eyes away from the destruction. "You may be agile and fast, but that doesn't matter when you're a mile away from me and I obliterate your bones from a rooftop."

"So you fight with gimmicks?" Bryson said, finally looking at her.

She laughed and turned away, walking toward the shop. "So goes the life of an archer assassin."

# 7

# The Connection

Kaylee was beautiful.

It was all Himitsu could think about as he sat on the steps leading to the front door of Phelos Palace. She sat next to him, one leg crossed over the other, elbow atop her knee and chin in the palm of her hand. Not much of anything was taking place this morning. The courtyard was empty save a few servants tending to the lawns and gardens, yet Kaylee always had a look about her that made it seem like a groundbreaking discovery was inches in front of her face. Her slightly narrowed eyes, as if this discovery was too small for a normal gaze, embellished her already ferocious sense of focus. Or perhaps that astute glare was actually a squint, her unruly strands of silvery bangs flirting with her eyelashes.

"Your lust is showing again," she said without bothering to look at him.

He smirked and turned away to observe the main grounds. She didn't need to look directly at him to sense his aura. This, too, was reason for him to find her beautiful. She was unique and had a story—one with depth, one that molded her into who she was now. At least, that's what he assumed to be the case. How else would she have lost an eye and needed an ancient piece to replace it?

"That lust is evolving, however," she said.

"In what way?"

"Other emotional tendrils have begun to swirl."

He hesitated, then asked slowly, "You mean ... are you implying ... love?"

"Love is difficult to see, even for my eye," she said, brushing her stray bangs behind her ear for the fifth time in as many minutes. Her gaze remained astute, proving that it hadn't been her bothersome bangs. Sunlight, maybe?

He forced his gaze elsewhere. Why was he studying her with such obsession? What was so endearing about the nature of her stare? Surely, there were countless other things more alluring about a woman. Toshik thought so. Himitsu's attention turned toward the lanky swordsman, who was leaning against a tree trunk, enveloped in the canopy's shadows. No, he wouldn't have agreed—not anymore. Not after Jilly.

Himitsu sighed. *Stupid brain.* Why did every train of thought end with Jilly's corpse in a tavern room in Rim? He couldn't even imagine what it was like in the mind of Toshik. Not only did he have to live with her death, but his mother and sister, too. How that man still managed to wake himself every day was beyond comprehension.

An hour passed before a carriage finally arrived. Toshik lazily pushed himself off the tree and headed for the carriage's side door. The driver opened the door and allowed him inside.

Himitsu leaned back and groaned, tired of waiting on his mother. She'd said her meeting with King Sigmund would only require a few minutes.

"Patience is a quality you must develop," Kaylee said with her face buried in an open book on her lap. A bag of them sat on her other side. "Chasing a man like Neeko will require it."

"You're the one who told me we'd be able to find him. You seemed certain."

Turning a page, she nodded into her book. "Yes, because those who do not seek, shall not know. Thus, we will seek."

The twin doors behind them opened. Ophala stepped out, flanked by two guards. Her lips spread into a smile. "My apologies," she said to Kaylee and Himitsu as she descended a few steps. The guards remained near the door, keeping their distance. "Awfully difficult convincing King Sigmund he doesn't need his hand held anymore."

With his head tilted back and neck craned against the step's edge, Himitsu gazed up at his mother. "I hope you're going to at least proctor his decisions," he said. "I doubt this kingdom could handle another upheaval."

"Don't fret with politics, son. That's nothing you need to worry about—though if that ever does become the case ..." she drifted off, gazing ahead, eyes narrowed in dramatic fashion ... "we're all doomed."

Kaylee snorted, then covered her mouth and buried her face deeper into her book. Himitsu looked at her, and his lip curled on one end with annoyance. Ophala snickered and continued down the steps, pleased with herself as she motioned for the two of them to follow her. Kaylee closed her book and stood. Himitsu did the same, grabbing her bag before she could. He tossed it over his shoulder only to stumble sideways from the weight. She shook her head before continuing down to the stone pathway. He gave the bag an incredulous look. Had she mistaken bricks for books?

"I'll do whatever I can to help," Ophala said just as Himitsu caught up with the two women. "I'll have eyes peeled from above, but keep in mind he was once called the Lost Boy for a reason. We thought it hadn't been his choice all those years ago, that he'd merely been a victim of the Warpfinate's infinite depths, but clearly he never wanted to be found. And if that's the case" —she withdrew a drinking flask from her robes and took a swig— "well then, damn ... he must have been a godchild at hide-and-seek."

They reached the carriage and lingered outside it for a moment. The coachman returned to his seat at the front. "Good luck out there," Ophala said. "You'll have one other with you on the journey."

"You mean Toshik?" Himitsu asked.

Ophala tilted her head, gesturing toward the carriage's interior. Himitsu poked his head inside and spotted a man about his own age seated on a cushioned bench. It was the same person who had stood on the roof with him the night of Toth Brench's murder. He hadn't known the stranger back then.

"Who's that?" Himitsu asked, yanking his head back out of the carriage.

"He will tell you when he wants to," Ophala said. She embraced her son before he could argue. "Do have fun."

He nodded into her shoulder as he stood hunched over to meet her shorter stature. After saying her own goodbyes, Kaylee boarded the carriage. Ophala pulled Himitsu back as he tried to follow. With a devilish grin on her face she whispered in his ear, "Don't be scared, son. If the time arrives and both of you want it to happen, go for—"

"*MOM!*" Himitsu's cheeks flushed as he hopped into the carriage without looking back. He could hear his mother's maniacal laughter even after the door was shut.

Ophala banged on the carriage's exterior three times, signaling for departure. The two horses at the front neighed, and the vehicle began moving.

Himitsu took his seat, casually tossing his arm along the back of the bench. He made a point to not make eye contact with Kaylee, embarrassed by his mother even though no one else had heard her statement. Instead he took interest in the mysterious man with the buzz cut and worn, ragged shirt.

"Name's Himitsu Vevlu, and yours?"

The man gave a slight nod. "Sal." Apparently that was all he had to say.

Himitsu looked at Toshik, who lay across the length of the bench at the rear of the carriage with his eyes closed. He then risked a glance at Kaylee, but of course her nose was in an open book. He pursed his lips and decided to acknowledge Sal instead and challenge him to a conversation.

"Sal's a rather simple name. Is it short for anything?"

"Salvatore NuForce."

*　　*　　*

The Passion Kingdom was known for its grand lakes, and Lake Kaloge was the biggest of them all. Olivia and Vuilni stood on a bridge stretching over it from north to south. Sunlight sparkled on the water as they stared east across the widest section of the lake. Behind them, the Seph Mountains towered into the sky, bordering the lake's western edge.

As a pedestrian carriage passed behind them, Olivia hunched over the support rail to gaze below. The wooden rail was sturdy and a deep, healthy brown. It was a safety precaution that already should have been here but had only recently been built following the discovery of Passion King Damian's body on the lakebed—a mishap that likely could have been blamed on cheap financial backers when the bridge was built centuries ago.

"Could you even imagine what an underwater fight must have been like?" Vuilni asked.

Olivia stared emptily at a small fish that scooted by just under the surface. "No," she said. "Toono knew what he was doing. I guess at that point—since it was early on in his sacrifices—he wasn't fully confident in his ability to fight a royal head. Thus he chose an arena that would better suit the strengths of his bubble-making ancient while simultaneously negating King Damian's flames."

"Now he's committing reckless acts such as attacking entire royal transits and sparring Adrenian Kings," Vuilni said. "Much like Bryson, there is no such thing as subtlety to that young man."

"You can call him 'boy,'" Olivia said, lifting her head and gazing across the lake again.

Vuilni's expression soured. "I'm sorry, Olivia."

Olivia was disappointed in Bryson's handling of her departure. He'd been spiteful because of her mission. He couldn't have simply said good bye and wished her luck. No, he had to snatch L.K. from her arms and tell her to "go have fun." What did that even mean? She wasn't embarking on a frivolous adventure, but a meaningful quest that could provide answers to stopping Toono.

She nearly growled at herself. She'd once had a chance to stop the man. There was a short time when she had worked beside him, mapping layouts of Kindoliya Palace and studying the hierarchical structure of the royal elites. But her bond to her mother at that time had been too important. All she'd cared about was healing her, and if that meant joining forces with Toono to eradicate Queen Salia, then that was that.

Hooves clacked against wood, beckoning her attention back to the present. A rather mundane carriage approached. As it came to a stop, she was surprised to see Fane lean out and motion for them to join him.

They entered the carriage, taking a seat on a bench opposite Fane. Passion Director Venustas occupied the rear bench, looking quite comfortable among a pile of plush crimson pillows. She smiled, her teeth a brilliant white, her dirty-blonde hair tucked into the back of her robes. Her freckles, barely noticeable against her tanned cheeks, stretched up to her lower eyelashes. Her eyes … well, they were somewhat sunken, as if sleep was an elusive sea fairy.

"It's good to see you again, ladies," Venustas said. Despite the obvious lack of sleep, her tone was still as hearty as ever. She'd always talked and carried herself with a certain gusto befitting of a leader. Perhaps that was why she found herself in the position she was in now, serving as an interim head of the kingdom, allowing the queen to focus on her children following King Damian's death.

"How are you, Director?" Vuilni asked.

"Would you believe me if I said just dandy?"

"If you want me to."

Venustas gave her a gentle smile, then reached for a pitcher of water from a nearby stand. As she removed its lid and poured a couple of glasses, she said, "We'll keep this briefing … brief." She offered each of them a glass, then leaned back and set the pitcher back on its stand. "It's become obvious that acid is at play. And while it's still speculation, we believe the person using it is somehow linked to the Prim Kingdom based off the personal nature of the murders which took place there years ago. That and the fact the Primmish people use ancients just like Archains."

She rubbed her eyes, clearly stifling a yawn. "Your job is simple in objective, but difficult in execution. True Light needs you to discover what the link is between this acidic ancient user and the Prim Kingdom."

"Haven't we had spies in the Prim Kingdom for centuries?" Olivia asked.

Fane leaned forward. "We have, but since the Prim Prince's murder, the religious zealots and royal elites of the Prim Kingdom have tightened their chokehold on both their divine and political institutes. Information does not travel out of the upper circles. Also, the Light Realm kingdoms withdrew most of their spies following the incident, fearing potential discovery and retaliation."

Venustas nodded. "Besides, spies were never of much use in that kingdom anyway. The Primmish way has been to remain neutral for centuries. They do their best to avoid coexisting with other kingdoms from a desire not to play favorites. The most they do is simple trade. It is a culture with a religious foundation. Some believe their divine zealots hold more power than even the royal head."

"If trained spies were never able to discover anything meaningful, how are we going to?" Vuilni asked.

"That's what Fane is for," Venustas said. "Pulling information out of anyone is likely impossible. The alternative is to snoop and infiltrate places where powerful individuals mingle…" Her eyes followed a black speck that had been buzzing around the carriage for some time. As it landed on the floor next to her, she stomped on it. "Being a fly on the wall, so to speak."

"Sounds like a job meant for Ophala," Vuilni said as Venustas rubbed the sole of her shoe against the floorboards.

"The Spy Pilot wants to stay in her home kingdom, which is understandable when considering the constant hell it's been through this past century."

Olivia took a swig of water, then said, "So we'll use Fane's flames to sneak us into places at night."

"That's the idea," Fane said. "I may not be able to weave flames that can suck the light out of the sky like Horos and Himitsu can, but that isn't a desirable tactic for what we'll be doing anyway. Such techniques would only draw attention to ourselves. We simply want to pass by undetected."

"What happened to brief?" Venustas asked with a sigh. "Listen, when you arrive in the Prim Kingdom, they won't turn you away. In fact, expect to be welcomed. The Primmish aren't violent people. Seek out a Prowler— traveling deacons who are friendly and knowledgeable. They won't give you information on anything specific, but they like to preach of hope and peace. They'll also help guide you to wherever it is you want to go."

"Awfully welcoming for such a secretive culture," Vuilni said.

"They are," the director said, "until you begin digging too close to their core, which is their religion and politics. Anyway, that's all. The three of you can be on your way. I hope you've packed as little as possible. The journey from the Prim Kingdom's teleplatforms to Asalka is a long one."

Olivia and Vuilni exchanged glances, knowing that just outside the carriage lay both of their massive bags of belongings. Fane chuckled and rose to his feet, clapping his hands together. "These two ladies could pull this carriage to Asalka if they wanted to. Who needs horses when you have ox-like strength?"

Venustas and Vuilni joined in laughter. Moments later, Olivia, Vuilni, and Fane were headed north to the teleplatforms.

*     *     *

Toono stood at a window in the Cogdan Castle library, looking out at the great stone block of a building that sat just inside of the grounds wall. The prison, better known as the Confines of Consciousness, housed nearly a dozen Devish "convicts", its walls of Permanence entrapping their attempts at weaving Dev Chains. Supposedly, it had been a measure taken long ago to keep those inside from manipulating people outside—or at least that had been Storshae's explanation just a couple of hours before Toono killed him. Still, skepticism ate at the Rogue Demon. If the prisoners of the Confines were as talented and dangerous as implied, why not simply kill them?

He turned to find Tazama entering the library, her blue hair and eyelashes bright against the sunlight that streamed through the many windows that lined the far wall. Gala—once the Dev Warden of the Dark Realm's school, Ipsas—was already seated at a table off to the side of the main lobby with parchment strewn around her as she worked on improving the army's divisions. With an influx of soldiers from allied kingdoms, they were in desperate need of a new segmentation system. It was a lofty task, but he had faith in her ability.

He leaned back, placing his backside against the windowsill. "Any luck, Tazama?"

She came to a stop at the center of the lobby, the sleeves of her robe connected in front of her, grasped hands hidden within. "None."

He sighed. That was another thing that bothered him about the prisoners within the Confines. Who were they? Since first entering the building weeks ago with Storshae and meeting a woman named Homina, he'd tried to answer that very question, going as far as interrogating any of the elite officers of the military while having Tazama leaf through the castle's archives. And despite what should have been the most straightforward solution, he couldn't manage a single answer out of any of the prisoners.

They spoke in frustrating riddles that stemmed from their madness—through no fault of their own, he understood. Being locked away in a windowless, lightless box did things to people. Then to have that box filled with a sea of infinite Dev Chains carrying deranged thoughts and maniacal emotions, the result becomes an existence of mass paranoia. Even he would only last a few minutes inside.

"You search for the identities of these prisoners, yet you disregard the one person who could probably give you answers," Gala said, quickly scribbling something down without averting her eyes from the parchment.

Toono arched his neck and gazed at the cavernous ceiling with its rusted iron chandelier containing dozens of unlit candles, framed by countless eyes carved into the stone. "I cannot be too heavy-handed in my approach with her. She might break if my inquiries become too persistent, too aggressive."

"She is a unique case," Tazama said. "I sense she has an intellectual grasp of this world far beyond most, including myself, yet it all seems just out of her reach."

"Ah, well," Toono said, looking back down toward the lobby. "I suppose these worries aren't priority anyway. The Intel sacrifice is where our focus should be."

As Tazama nodded, another woman walked in, her black hair straight and full—a far cry from the greasy strings that had once curtained her face, spooling atop the cold floor of the Confines.

"Good morning, Homina," he said, a gentle smile spreading on his face.

"A very good morning indeed," she said, passing Tazama and stopping just between her and Toono.

Gala took a brief glance away from her work. "Heh, if that isn't a sign of the apocalypse, then I'm not sure what is."

He ignored the attempt at humor. While Homina didn't express much, that didn't mean it was as outlandish as Gala tried to imply. Then again, he'd once spent significant time with Olivia Still, a girl who could win a staring contest with a rock.

"And why is that?" Toono asked, immediately cringing at the softness of his tone. Why did he always feel the need to speak to Homina as if she were a child? Gala, still bowed over her work, shook her head, likely noticing the same thing.

"You wanted me to come to you once I made contact with my daughter," Homina said. "I think I have, though I sense her trying to push my connection attempts away. She doesn't recognize my weaving pattern."

He pushed away from the windowsill. "You need to tip her off before she successfully shuts you out."

"I'm trying," she said. Her eyes closed, and a thin line of focus formed between her lips.

"Despite the fact that Illipsia is in a separate realm, you'd think Tazama would have the skill to reach her for communication," Gala said, leaning back and fixing a stack of parchment in her lap.

"I'd risk connecting with the wrong person," Tazama said. Her hands were still connected in front of her, hidden within the large sleeves of her robes. She had yet to move from the spot she had arrived at earlier. "It's why I never had communication with Toono until he arrived in the Archaic Kingdom months back. Then I could easily speak with Illipsia. Prince Storshae had always been the only person in the Dark Realm I could speak with, and that had more to do with *his* weaving ability."

Gala raised an eyebrow, setting the stack of parchment on the table. "Hard to believe someone who can create teleplatforms can't create a cross-realm telepathic connection, yet Prince Storshae could."

Tazama finally turned, regarding Gala directly. "You were the Dev Warden of Ipsas. You should know that different abilities within one's energy depend on the woven patterns of their Dev Energy-Current Chains. Yes, I am proficient in certain areas of expertise, but Prince Storshae was dominant when it came to telepathy—just like you are dominant in regards to defensive holograms."

Gala nodded, smirking as she reached for her quill in its ink well. As she began to write, she said, "Toono, you've surrounded yourself with some of the most level-headed women I've ever known. Why does nobody fall victim to my bait around here?"

"I must request some semblance of silence," Homina said.

"See what I mean?" Gala said. "Get angry."

"Shush, Gala," he said.

The four of them waited in silence for several minutes. By the time Homina announced a successful connection, he had drifted over to a distant bookcase to rifle through a rather dry catalogue—even for his taste. When he returned to the lobby, Tazama was now seated opposite of Gala.

"If you wish," he said, "you can speak with Illipsia in private first. She is your daughter, after all."

"She's already requested your presence. I don't think she wants to speak to me alone."

A holographic display appeared in the center of the lobby, Homina's dilated eyes its source. The image framed Illipsia's face, her raven hair stopping just above her shoulders. Both of her eyes were burgundy as she recorded herself in a mirror, so that she could be seen.

"Toono!" Illipsia whispered.

He grinned, not realizing how much he'd missed her. He had a fondness for her; she felt like a younger sister. "Illipsia, is everything going okay?"

"I've made progress," she said.

"That's great, but I meant are *you* okay?"

She paused, then looked to the side, causing the broadcast's perspective to shift slightly. A toilet sat next to a white marble sink. *Good*, he thought. *At least she's in favorable living conditions.*

"I'm great ... made a friend."

"That's good," he said, despite knowing that, like the boy she had once befriended named Simon, it would be a fleeting relationship. The nature of her missions didn't allow for real bonds.

"I believe I've found the location of the levers to the stage platform," she said, "but to get to them I must unlock the latch that hides them."

"Well, that should be easy for someone of your skill," he said, stepping forward and grasping the top of a short wall bordering the lobby. She was gifted at picking locks.

Her face fell. "Not with these. There are five to be exact, and I have reason to believe they must be unlocked either in a specific order or simultaneously."

"No worries. We still need more time on our end, so don't feel rushed." He lifted a leg and sat on the wall. "Continue practicing your hallucinogenics. It must be refined before committing to the locks in the auditorium. If you're caught ..." He trailed off, stomach furling at the thought. "Just don't get caught."

"You can count on me."

He closed his eyes with a grin. "I know I can." He looked from the display to Homina. "And do make time to speak with your mother. She *is* your mother; I can attest to that."

The girl bit her lip in uncertainty. "Mendac killed my mother after my birth."

"Storshae lied to you," he said.

"I will give it thought."

"And action, hopefully."

Illipsia glanced to the side, and the hologram's perspective shifted toward a wooden door. "People are here," she said. "Bye."

The display disappeared and the library fell silent. The three women gazed at Toono; Gala with an eyebrow raised, Tazama with a smirk, and Homina with a more unreadable expression.

"What?" he asked Homina.

"How long has she been with you?" she asked.

"Four years, give or take," he said after some thought.

"And you've taken her on many of your quests, haven't you?" Tazama said.

"And all during her pre-teen years," Gala noted.

"Ah," he said, closing his eyes. "Yes, I guess I'm sort of like her brother."

Gala laughed with enough force for it to be more of a bark. Hand to her chest, she said, "More like her father."

His gaze fell to the floor. He sat halfway on the low wall in silence, reflecting on his fatherless childhood. A couple men had assumed that role for a short time, Neeko one of them.

Gala left, leaving behind her stacks of parchment on the table. Homina departed without word. Tazama remained for a moment.

"I'll be returning to my task," she said before heading for the door and shutting it behind her.

Toono exhaled and lifted his head, turning to gaze out the window he had been standing next to earlier. It was best to steer clear of fatherhood, for history had a habit of repeating itself.

# 8

# A Familiar Light

There was a kind of beauty in how terrible Lilu's team of weavineers was. Honestly, such an art could only be perfected by practice—or so she wanted to believe. Were they intentionally failing at every aspect of building her inventions, or were they actually that dense?

She sighed as she watched a smaller team of weavineers use a pulley system to drag a travolter from a kiln. The cave was entrenched into the edge of Steel Field, disappearing beneath the gigantic side wall of the Bastion of Intel, a cavern underneath Brilliance big enough to fit an entire town.

The travolter came to a stop after reaching level land. It was a massive vehicle, bigger than a royal carriage. The brainchild of a teenage Lilu, it could travel without the need of man or horsepower to pull it. Instead it used Intel Chains stored in Permanence vessels, and when those chains were released, it'd create rotational motion in the travolter's wheels.

But it was so much more than transportation. At the top of it sat a cannon, which was connected to its own Permanence vessel, capable of discharging electricity across vast distances, annihilating nearly anything in its sights—the perfect war machine.

Lilu, Frederick, Gracie, and Limone had created a successful prototype, but that had been months ago. Wendel LeAnce, the commissioner of the League of Weavineers and leader of Brilliance, had considered it proof that Lilu was ready to lead a bigger team of disciples here in the Bastion. Yet, as she watched a couple weavineers climb into the cockpit, she couldn't help but grimace, anticipating the result she had come to expect.

Sure enough, as a man gave a signal for the driver to initiate movement, part of the travolter's body blew as one of the vessels—if not a few— exploded.

*Great, another volatile vessel,* Lilu thought. For people who had been licensed weavineers for decades, they showed an awfully high level of incompetence. She refused to believe that she, Gracie, Frederick, and Limone—each of whom varied in age from twenty-one to twenty-four— were more capable of building these beasts than the seasoned veterans.

"Quite embarrassing."

Lilu turned toward the voice. Gracie Jugtah had slipped into a chair next to her to observe the entirety of Steel Field from the elevated platform. "Aren't you supposed to be proctoring your unit?" Lilu asked.

Gracie yawned, leaned back, and kicked her feet up onto the support rail in front of them. "I'm tired, so I took a break."

Lilu's gaze shifted from Frederick's squad to Limone's. They were inspecting one of the two travolters that had been successfully built during the past few weeks, taking notes as Limone pointed at random areas of interest. He had come a long way in two years since the first day he'd been put on Lilu's team.

Then there was Gracie's unit, tucked away in the far side of Steel Field, on the precipice of Lilu's vision. The field was enormous, and the sunlight that filtered through the hole in the cavern's roof didn't hit it the same way it did the town. But this was good, for she'd rather not see Gracie's team as they wandered aimlessly around their travolter. If the weavineers of Bastion were a diseased human, her team was the bleeding gash, open to infection, causing everything around them to rot. *Best to ignore it.*

"A team is a reflection of its leader," Lilu said, peeling her gaze away from the eyesore.

Gracie shrugged, eyes halfway closed, hands placed behind her head. "You gave me a bunch of people I can't connect with. They didn't even compliment my dress today."

Lilu rolled her eyes. "Who wears a sundress to this job without a lab coat to cover it up? They expect you to get your hands dirty just like them."

"Well, I'm offended," Gracie said, frowning. She reached for the bottom hem of her dress, a silky black one she'd definitely stolen from Lilu's wardrobe. "Look at this. Part of the fabric tore when one of those dingbats nearly nailed my leg to the provod."

"You're attracting the wrong kind of attention from Wendel," Lilu said, playing the one card that would work on her friend.

Gracie's eyes darted toward the cavern's farthest wall, past the town that sat between Steel Field and the provod storage caves. Balconies dotted the wall above those caves. One sat higher than the rest, belonging to Wendel LeAnce. Lilu couldn't tell if he was on the balcony at that moment, but she didn't care. The empty threat had served its purpose.

Gracie stood, huffing as she brushed off her dress. "Fine, I'll go continue my suffering."

"One more thing," Lilu said. "Tonight we enter the sewers."

"What for?" Gracie asked.

"To hunt for a couple of Mendac's secrets."

*      *      *

Lilu, Gracie, Frederick, and Limone were huddled outside of a gated manor, waiting for it to open. They were now above ground in one of Brilliance's illustrious sectors. Unlike the skyscraper-laden streets of the inner city, this area had more space, including yards, gardens, and buildings that spread to the sides rather than reaching for the night sky.

The gate opened on its own, undoubtedly due to some kind of Permanence device and a complex system of ropes and pulleys. They entered the grounds, walking briskly down the front stone path. The doors to the manor were already open, and the four of them slipped inside.

A butler with sleek white hair combed to one side motioned for them to follow. "The master does not wish to deal with you directly, milady, so he has directed me to lead you to the entrance. Dealings such as these are risky, and he could lose his seat because of it."

"I understand," she said, clasping her hand over Gracie's mouth before she could ask a stupid question.

They wound through opulent halls before descending a staircase that brought them to a basement corridor made of drywall, not a single mural or decoration in sight. At the end of the path a grate was set into the hardwood floor. The butler gestured toward it and said, "Do try to return before dawn. Otherwise the master will tack on five percent interest for each additional hour." He removed the grate and gave a nod. "Enjoy the view, milady."

"Thank you," Lilu said. She waited next to him while her friends descended the hidden narrow staircase. She then reached into her pocket and fished out payment.

The butler's eyebrows rose. "But you've already paid the master, milady."

"That's a tip … for you." She then flew down the steps herself, disappearing into the basement floor.

*　　*　　*

"Isn't anyone going to ask the obvious question?" Gracie said after a few minutes of travel through narrow halls made of uneven stone on either side.

"I paid someone who owns a balcony in the Bastion," Lilu explained. "It's a lower balcony, and he's definitely one of the lesser owners. He likes to rent it out to people who have the money to throw it away. But that doesn't matter. We just needed to get into the sewers."

"Why no stench?" Frederick asked.

"Because we're not near the sewers yet; we're deep inside a network of tunnels that branch off from them."

"Do you even know where we're going?" Limone asked in a voice tiny enough to have been smothered by the darkness.

"I just need to find the main pipe," she said, feeling her way down the hall. "The one under Mendac's statue."

"And do you know how to get there?" he asked again.

"Kind of. I'm following the tunnels in the general direction of where Mendac's statue is, relative to the manor." She paused, lifting her head and sniffing the air. "I'm also following the stench. The stronger it gets, the closer we are."

"Doesn't that sound romantic?" Gracie teased, causing Limone to blush.

The smell became rancid, and Lilu knew they were close. They soon emerged from the cramped halls and entered a larger tunnel with curved walls that formed an arched ceiling. Two platforms ran the length of both sides, bordering a stream of waste in the center.

Lilu glanced both ways, then recognized which tunnel she was in based off the color of paint on a stone block every few paces: blue, the fourth eastern appendage of the main sewer. She had Professor Jugtah to thank for her knowledge of the sewage system. While the only maps of the branched network of tunnels belonged to the board, the layout of the normal sewers was well-known. Access to them by the general public, however, was nearly impossible.

Their journey brought them to the spot where a latch loomed above, connecting with the base of Mendac's broken statue. Now all Lilu had to do was follow the path from Debo's memory. As she tried to concentrate, visualizing the sewers from Debo's perspective, Gracie bickered with Frederick out of boredom. She poked fun at his height; he was shorter than the average male, and gangly.

Lilu had to squelch a scream of frustration, realizing the sewers weren't quite the same as depicted in the memory. She came to a stop, staring at the wall where a branched tunnel should have been. She ran her hand down the stone while Frederick puked into the sludge behind her, marking his third time since entering the heart of the sewers. Gracie laughed, but doing so caused her to inhale more than normal. Her throat lurched, but didn't expel anything. She was just barely able to stop herself from suffering the same fate as Frederick.

"It's supposed to be here," Lilu said with a pout. She turned around and leaned back against the wall, arms crossed.

Frederick stood slowly, wiping his mouth with the back of his hand. "Maybe you're forgetting," he said weakly. "Let's keep looking."

Limone crossed a flimsy bridge extending over the waste to the opposite platform. As he inspected the wall, he called for them to join him. They crossed the bridge one at a time. He patted the wall as they arrived. "There's about a seven-by-ten foot section of stone here that looks newer than the rest of the wall."

Lilu stepped closer, narrowing her eyes. She soon realized it too. The difference was minor, but the stone was whiter than the rest. She ran a finger across a block, finding it rough instead of slick like the older stone. "It's Permanence," she said, eyes widening in shock. "There would only be one reason for using Permanence."

"Motion," Frederick said, holding his stomach and leaning lethargically against the wall.

She began slapping her hand against random spots of the wall. "Look for a—" She paused, the wall already lifting in front of her. Stone scraped against stone, as loud as a prison transit rolling over gravel. To her left, Gracie wore an evil grin, her foot pressed down on a secret switch in the ground. It was a slightly different shade than the rest of the floor.

"You sly demon, you," Lilu said, embracing her friend.

"My thirty-minute lunch break is now an hour," Gracie said.

Lilu was so ecstatic she didn't even argue.

The door neared the end of its ascent, following the sewer wall into the arched ceiling. Beyond was a tunnel, narrow and short. Chunks of cragged stone lay on the floor, most of it piled against the two side walls, both of which seemed to have been demolished by some powerful force. Even the ceiling appeared to have been a victim of the destruction. A makeshift path lay at the center of the debris, winding between rock and rubble.

Frederick stepped forward, careful to not twist his ankle; but Lilu grabbed a fistful of his shirt from behind, halting him. He glanced back at her. "What?"

She stared down the tunnel at something she had only seen once before in her entire life. It had shielded a closet door in the hallway of Bryson's home.

"What the hell is that?" Gracie asked.

"We must leave," Lilu said, having a hard time moving her feet. Light sat at the tunnel's end, contained within an orb by some inexplicable force … a shield created by Tahara, the energy of the Bozani.

She needed Bryson.

# 9

# A Knife of Hatred

As Himitsu's carriage neared Balle's western river, he couldn't help but think about how convenient a carriage such as this would have been months ago, when he, his father, and Fane were forced to travel on foot. Alas, that had been a journey of an inconspicuous nature, and nothing screamed "look at me" like a royal carriage, complete with plush benches and a laboratory compartment in the back.

Himitsu stuck his head out the front window, granting himself a view of the bridge as they approached. It was devoid of guards or horses, unlike his first visit to the city when it was still under Toth's regime. The coachman, who had begun to doze off, jumped at the intrusion and quickly grabbed hold of the reins. Face now red with guilt, he tipped his hat toward Himitsu.

"Good morning, Ilnu," Himitsu said.

"Good morning, Zana Himitsu. What is your destination in the city?"

"There should be a shoddy inn just across the river, in the rural reaches. That should do."

"Yes, mizana."

Himitsu cocked an eyebrow, having never heard such a title. It mimicked "milord", the latter half replaced by "zana". He retreated back into the carriage, finding himself perfectly okay with the title.

"Almost there?" Kaylee asked through a yawn as she rubbed her eyes. She was now sitting up, leaving Sal and Toshik as the last two to wake.

"Yes …" He paused, transfixed by Kaylee's body as she arched her back and stretched. Her dress was loose-fitting, but when it pressed against her chest … *Stop it*. His face suddenly felt burning hot, and he forced his gaze elsewhere.

"Wow, you need to learn to better mask your feelings," she said. "I don't even need to weave to see it."

He bowed his head, not offering a response.

Toshik and Sal awoke upon arriving at their destination. Ilnu rounded the carriage and opened the side door, acting as both the coachman and footman. Himitsu exited the carriage before the man could cup his hands beneath the step. He then brushed Ilnu away, turning to assist Kaylee. She placed her hand in his, then carefully stepped down into mud. It was a miserable evening. Dark gray clouds hung low overhead. He couldn't recall rain at any point in the day, so it must have mostly hit the city.

Toshik and Sal stepped out of the carriage by themselves; Himitsu was already guiding Kaylee to the inn's front door. He'd placed a cloak over her shoulders, lifting the hood over her head to protect it from the drizzle.

The innkeeper stood waiting just inside the entryway. His eyes grew wide at the sight of a royal carriage parked next to his inn. "Good morning … *milord?*" he said, uncertain of their status.

"Do you not remember me?" Himitsu asked while the innkeeper took Kaylee's cloak and hung it on a hook near the door. Toshik, Sal, and Ilnu entered behind them and promptly removed their shoes, placing them against a baseboard.

The innkeeper's eyes narrowed, studying the assassin's face. "Ah, yes, I do. I never knew you were so important, milord."

"I'm not a lord or aristocrat," Himitsu said. "I'm a Jestivan." The innkeeper froze as Toshik brushed past. "Do you think you can house us for the night?"

"Well ..." He looked the group over. "I don't have enough rooms, but I can make space for you in the barroom ... move tables to the side and lay down some blankets and pillows."

Himitsu beamed. "That'll do. I never got your name during my last visit."

"Grengil," the man said, stepping aside and gesturing toward the small barroom. "Please, make yourselves at home."

*     *     *

Himitsu sat on the floor of the bar, a mass of blankets twisted around him. A few tables and chairs had been pushed to the edges of the room in efforts to maximize space for the tenants. Toshik, Sal, and Ilnu were preparing their own sleeping areas in separate spots. They had decided to give Kaylee the lone guestroom upstairs. Toshik was closest to Himitsu. The swordsman dropped his pillow on the floor, an unreadable look on his face.

"Excited to see this Kuiku fella?" Himitsu asked as he crawled closer to his friend—if that was the proper term. He never knew how to label their relationship.

"I suppose it will be nice to see a friendly face," Toshik said.

"I'm sorry, Toshik."

Toshik took a seat next to his pillow. "If you're truly sorry, do something for me."

"What's that?"

"Don't repeat any of the mistakes I've made."

Himitsu frowned, wanting to tell Toshik he hadn't made mistakes, but that would have been a lie. He'd been responsible for taking his little sister into the woods to hunt spunka, leading to her death. That reckless act had lured his mother into giving chase, who then died trying to protect Toshik from the same fate as his sister. As for Jilly ... well, that wasn't his fault. That had been her decision—a selfless act to save her retainer.

"Don't let Kaylee die," Toshik said, lying on his side and tugging his blanket over his shoulders. His eyes began to glaze over.

Guilt washed over Himitsu. His mother had assassinated Toshik's father. A tear trickled down Toshik's face, falling onto the untreated wooden floor. "There is nothing more precious than the love of a fellow human. It doesn't wither away when that person dies; it gets stronger, and that only makes it hurt more."

Toshik's suffering was clearly intolerable. When Himitsu's parents had been captured and imprisoned, he had crumbled to pieces, relying on alcohol to drown his misery. Toshik had guided him to a better place. Now the swordsman was in a significantly worse position. His family was dead; the love of his life, dead. Yet here he was, breathing, still speaking words of wisdom to Himitsu.

Head limp on the pillow, Toshik wiped his nose. "I don't want anyone to hurt like I do."

*    *    *

Sleep was elusive. Himitsu would have had a better chance catching lightning in a bottle. He tossed and turned for hours, only to wind up stepping outside for a bit of fresh air. He walked a few steps toward the carriage still parked directly outside the inn. The horses were currently sleeping in a fenced-in pen behind the building. He climbed onto the carriage's roof, sighing as he lay on his back to do some stargazing.

Thankfully, the storm clouds had cleared. The Archaic Kingdom's night sky was quite the spectacle; the stars were plentiful. In places like Dunami, the clouds or the abundance of Intelights and Intelamps flooding the streets drowned out the stars.

Himitsu reflected on what Toshik had said earlier. He kept imagining himself in the swordsman's shoes, watching his mother die. His thoughts drifted to Kaylee. He might have not shared the same amount of time with her as Toshik had with Jilly, but he knew losing her would prove devastating. He looked over at the window of her room. A faint orange glow flickered against the beige curtains. Kaylee was probably reading by candlelight, unabashed by the late hour. Or maybe she was mixing some poisons … hopefully not. All they needed was Toshik to stumble upon them. Himitsu wouldn't blame him.

The inn's front door squeaked. He rolled his head to the side, catching the bulky frame of Sal in the moonlight. The man was a mystery. Since revealing his full name, he hadn't spoken much beyond that. He had to have known Himitsu's connection with Rhyparia. Ophala would have told him. Still, Himitsu allowed him to travel with them in silence, smothering the curiosities swelling within him. Was Sal Rhyparia's brother?

The carriage shook as the bigger man climbed to its roof. He sat near its edge, one leg bent along the surface, the other kicked up, knee toward the sky. He sat there like that for probably ten minutes, not speaking a word.

"What was my sister like?" Sal asked.

*That proves that theory.* Himitsu twisted his lips, trying to do her character justice. "Brave, but scared. Strong, but timid. There was a balance about her that I could respect. An inhumanely powerful girl with a genuinely humane heart."

"Adventurous?" Sal asked.

"Yes."

"Free spirited?"

Himitsu paused. "No, I wouldn't say that."

"Odd," Sal said.

Himitsu rolled over on his side, placing his elbow against the roof and resting his head against his hand. "How well did you know her?"

Sal shrugged. "As a child, she was a free spirit. She'd run through the streets, climb buildings, and cause innocent mayhem within the community … stealing a fruit or giving stray dogs to random families by sneaking them into homes."

"I guess people change," Himitsu said.

"When you go through something like she did, then yes." Sal's voice grew hollow. "You know, I genuinely thought it had been an earthquake that leveled our community when I was a child. And I thought my mom—a vile woman to the core—had been a hero for saving the family, or at least most of us. Then, when news spread that Rhyparia had been the culprit, I couldn't believe it. She was only seven years old at the time of those events, and it wasn't in her nature. But as the Gravity Trials progressed, I actually started to believe it."

Sal shook his head, evidently displeased with the memory. "I remember you taking the stand, and my mom doing the same. After that, I believed my evil mother over my younger sister. Now she's gone, alone, believing that the world despises her. She might believe it herself—that she's evil. My mother sucked that free spirit out of her."

"I believe Rhyparia's alive," Himitsu said, attempting to offer consolation.

"I know she is," Sal said. "Or that's what Pilot Ophala insists. However, she said she hasn't spoken with her in quite some time. It's no longer possible."

"You didn't have to approach me about this," Himitsu said after a protracted pause. "I would have respected your decision not to."

"I needed to get it off my chest. Our group feels like a pack of wounded dogs. I figured I'd expose my wounds, too."

Himitsu shook his head. "We're all wounded. The best we can do for those we've lost is try to heal. I know I've wallowed in grief enough."

*　　*　　*

Himitsu, Kaylee, and Sal entered the suburbs of Balle the following morning. Toshik had already departed with Ilnu, separating himself from the group to visit Kuiku in the aristocratic estate where Toth Brench had moved his bladesmithing business. This meant Himitsu's group no longer had the carriage for transportation.

"Despite living my entire life in this city, this is my first time really seeing it," Kaylee said. They waited for an officer on horseback to pass before crossing the dirt street.

"Not much different from anywhere else," Himitsu said.

109

"Are you kidding me? Dunami was breathtaking."

"Capitals tend to be exceptions. Fiamma is even more beautiful," Himitsu said. He grabbed Kaylee and pulled her to his side, saving her from stepping in a pile of horse dung. "Watch your step."

She made a disgusted noise. "Maybe I'll stick to the capitals."

Sal laughed. "Where I came from, it wasn't horse excrement you had to worry about stepping in, for nobody could afford such a majestic beast. Naw, it was the people who'd pop a squat in an alley."

"Yes, continue painting us such colorful imagery," she said.

"You make do with what you're given," Sal said. "Offered me perspective. Now I don't complain about much of anything."

They crossed into more congested streets where dirt kicked up by foot traffic floated through the air. "No, I understand," she said, glancing at Sal. "I would never try to compare my childhood to anyone else's."

"Speaking of which, how'd you lose your eye?" Sal asked.

"Dude!" Himitsu shouted, stopping abruptly and causing an older man to curse as he bumped into him.

"It's okay," she said, chuckling softly. "I was born missing an eye."

Himitsu stood still for a moment, then continued onward. "You never told me that."

"Well, you never asked," she said.

"I thought it'd be insensitive."

"And that's fine, but it wasn't something traumatic. I was simply born this way, and then Neeko gave me the gift of depth perception for surgical purposes."

"One of my little brothers was born without a finger," Sal said, unbothered by Kaylee's revelation. "He has an identical twin, but because of his nine fingers, we can immediately distinguish him from the other."

They made their way to Lost Wisdom, the orphanage that occupied an entire block of the city. A gated, perfectly manicured lawn bordered its perimeter. The front gate stood open, as it always did during daylight hours, allowing free entry onto the grounds. Access beyond the front lobby, however, was more difficult to obtain. Luckily for Himitsu, he had connections in high-up places.

Despite what must have been horrible memories for Kaylee, she strode to the orphanage's front doors faster than both Himitsu and Sal. This mission meant more to her than it did either of them. She'd had a personal relationship with Neeko Lefolli, so she wanted to find him more than anyone.

They entered the orphanage and approached the front desk, where the same secretary from Himitsu's last visit sat. He looked up from rifling through a filing cabinet. Spotting Kaylee, his eyes widened. "You're the girl who was stolen from her room in the middle of the night!"

"*Saved*," she said. "*Saved* from my room in the middle of the night."

The man's eyes veered toward Himitsu. "And you're the criminal who stole her!"

Himitsu gritted his teeth. "Shut it." He reached into his leather bag, retrieving a sheet of paper. "I have permission to—"

"*GUARDS!*" the man roared.

Himitsu's gaze grew lazy, fixated on the secretary. "Why are you an idiot?"

He heard scuffling feet and the scraping of metal to both sides. Six people, two swords drawn. As the secretary pushed himself away from the counter in his wheeled chair with terror etched into his face, Himitsu casually stepped back. A guard clutched at air and rammed into the counter. Himitsu grasped the back of his assailant's head and slammed his face into the wood.

The assassin sidestepped another fruitless attempt by a guard to apprehend him, then kneed him in the gut. A sword whooshed past Himitsu's chest, and he caught the woman's wrist, twisting it until the sword clattered against the floor.

He did all of this with his only free hand. The other held the paper, which he now placed on the desk. The secretary scuttled forward and read through it while Kaylee and Sal dealt with the remaining three guards.

"You guys aren't very good at your jobs," Sal said, locking a guard's arm behind her back.

The secretary slowly looked up with a hint of anger. "Welcome, honored guests of the royal court," he said, voice shaking. "How can we assist you?"

"By allowing us freedom to question whoever we want," Kaylee said, pressing a knife against her guard's neck. The captive grunted, chin tilted and eyes aghast. "And by never putting us in this situation again."

Himitsu raised an eyebrow at the aspiring apothecary. Her calm, inquisitive nature had been wiped clean; her face was coated in malice. Her blade was close to breaking skin, ready to coat the floor in red.

"Yes, of c-c-course," the secretary stammered. "You're free to roam!"

She removed her knife and shoved the man forward. As the guard pulled up again, a line of blood ran along his neck. He growled before marching toward the lobby's far corner, returning to his post as if nothing had happened.

"I want to speak with a boy named Raul Sanchia," Kaylee said. "Do you have his file?"

The secretary began digging through cabinets. He retrieved a manila folder and handed it to her. She poked through it. "He's on a field trip?"

"Yes, the ten-year-olds departed to Accus Canyon yesterday. They'll return in three days if you'd like to wait."

She handed the folder back. "We'll be back in that time. If he's not here, Himitsu will burn this place to the ground."

The secretary paused, mouth agape. "He'll be here, ma'am."

*Ma'am?* Himitsu thought. *That changed fast.*

Kaylee whirled and marched toward the exit. Himitsu and Sal ran to catch up. As they burst into the open air and trotted down the stone steps, Himitsu said, "That was an empty threat, right?"

"Obviously," she said. "But I will kill a few of the guards if I have to."

"And this Raul kid?" Himitsu said.

"He's the only one worth talking to." She waved flippantly over her shoulder, as if dismissing the topic. "For now, let's get a bite to eat."

The two young men came to a stop, watching as she continued out the front gate, her silvery hair refracting the sunlight. Himitsu turned to study the orphanage. What horrors lay within?

# 10

# Oppression

"Woah!" Kuiki yelled, narrowly dodging a barrage of slashes from Toshik's sword. "When did you get so good?"

Toshik wielded one sword, but the speed of his movements made it look like twenty. "Come on, old man!" he said. "I'm holding back here!"

Kuiku nearly toppled backward as the back of his heel hit a rock. Toshik's onslaught rescinded. He stood upright, back arched slightly, sword pointed down at his side. He bent over to pick up a piece of cloth. "It seems you've lost something that belongs to you."

Kuiku glanced down. The hem of his jacket had a chunk missing. He looked up, a smirk on his face. "You've gotten good, young man."

"Thank you," Toshik said, sheathing his sword.

The two of them walked over to a roofed patio, furnished with a few outdoor chairs and recliners. Toshik stood his scabbard against the small fence that circled the patio before taking a seat.

"Where have you been training?" Kuiku asked, pouring both of them a glass of water from a pitcher.

"Dunami Palace," Toshik said, taking a moment to study Kuiku's face. It had only been a couple of years since he had last seen the man, but he seemed to have aged ten.

Kuiku leaned back, placing his hands on his stomach. "You mean to tell me someone over there in the Intel Kingdom knows swordplay like what I just witnessed?"

"It'd be an insult to say my instructor uses a sword like I do," Toshik said. "I am half the fighter he is." The scars on his abdomen and chest began to burn as he spoke the words.

Kuiku gave Toshik a sideways glance. "And what was it that made you want to seek out such a dangerous individual?"

Toshik paused, three faces conjuring in his mind: Jun, Alina, and Jilly. "You know the answer to that question."

"And what about your father?" Kuiku asked. "How have you handled that?"

"You're not my therapist," Toshik said, nose wrinkled.

"I only ask because I don't want to be alone in my sensation of relief."

Toshik couldn't say the same. "I relieved myself of my father's burdens long before he died, back when I abandoned the estate with Jilly after the Phesaw invasion. After that, I ceased contact with my dad." He hesitated, that frustrating guilt creeping within him. "I think that broke him. I think he died unloved and unwanted."

"Befitting of such a man," Kuiku said.

Toshik sat forward with narrowed eyes, reflecting on the child he once was. "There was a time when I thought I deserved the same fate. Then my father gave me the gift of love in the form of Jilly, knowing he could no longer provide it to me following my mom and sister's deaths. And the world recognized I didn't deserve her, so she was taken from me."

Kuiku took a long sip of water, patting a wet towel against his forehead. "Is that why you haven't lost your mind?" he asked, lowering the cup. "Because you think this was karma coming your way? Because you deserved it? That's awfully shallow of you ... it's disrespectful of Jilly's sacrifice to keep you alive."

"That's the thing ..." Toshik said. "I was supposed to be the sacrifice, and she was to continue living, bestowing the world with her radiant soul. The world deserves *that*, not *me*."

"Well, you're still here, Toshik. Do something with that privilege. You can help eliminate the evil, and I'll come with you. Your dad, Wert Lamay, and King Storshae might be dead, but they were only pawns. Bigger game is out there." He paused, then asked, "And what was it your mother taught you about game?"

"You hunt it."

*     *     *

Vests, like anything that fell under the category of formal wear, had never been Bryson's thing. Yet here he was, strolling through the market streets of Dunami's most illustrious sector, Luminescence, like a stiff.

A black vest hugged his torso, the sleeves of his white collared button-up squeezing the life out of his biceps. He couldn't breathe and found himself gaining a newfound respect for the royal women who walked around in corsets as though they were as commonplace as a wristwatch. His black pants were straight-legged, a crease ironed perfectly down the front and back of each leg. They didn't even reach his ankles, which exposed his gray socks and left him feeling a bit insecure. He didn't like his ankles.

"Do try not to look miserable while in the public eye," drawled Benedict Ronal, a premier steward of the royal family. He and Shelly accompanied Bryson down the sidewalk. A band of guards set a perimeter around them to ward off swarming civilians.

"Why must we make a show of this?" Bryson whined with his hands defiantly tucked into his pants pockets. They were tiny and not very practical. He could barely fit half his hand inside.

"The people want to see the members of the most important couple in the realm as they prepare for their marriage," Benedict said. "Princess Shelly will be the Intel royal head one day, and you will be king. It's best they see you walking the streets like ..." he paused, pressing his lips together in thought ... "like common folk."

Bryson gazed at the guards. What kind of "common folk" had their own military escort?

"I like it," Shelly said with a smile, sauntering down the sidewalk like it was a runway, her silk golden dress molding to the shape of her legs with each step.

"Of course you do," Bryson said. There were a couple of reasons for this: one, she was a showman who thrived off attention, and two, this was a rare opportunity for her. Getting to leave the palace? Only twice had he heard of such an occasion. Once when she attended the Generals' Battle four years ago and once when the two of them ran away to the village of Yinyon in the Adren Kingdom.

"Ah, here we are," Benedict said, veering left. He pushed open a door, a tall rectangular sheet of glass—not a fingerprint or blemish to be seen— framed by newly polished wood. The sign above read: CASUAL SIN.

Bryson stepped aside, allowing Shelly to enter first. He then followed, but froze as he read a sign on the glass. Aside from the hours of operation, address, and name of the owner, a stomach-lurching message caught his eye: *Unables not permitted. Identification checked by the concierge.*

"Milord."

Bryson snapped to attention, his eyes darting toward Benedict. "I'm not going in there."

Shelly, who was already inside the shop pinching the sleeve of a suit jacket to inspect its material, looked toward the front.

"But we've come all this way, milord," the steward said. "Your fiancée specifically chose this store."

Bryson didn't move, his gaze fixated on the sign once again. A woman—likely the concierge—approached the main entrance from a podium just inside the shop. "It's an honor to host two royals," she said, taking a generous bow. "How may we be of assistance? Is something not to your liking, milord?"

"Unables are no different than you!" a small voice screamed from the crowd outside, casting silence over what had been a steady white noise of chatter.

Bryson turned and scanned the faces behind him. There were so many people blocking the street like a clogged artery. "Who said that?" he asked. "Step forward."

Nobody did.

"Prince Bryson!" someone yelled, but this voice was different. The rest of the crowd shouted for him, creating a frenzied mess.

He faced the shop again. Shelly gleamed while a shop assistant stood nearby holding four different suits on her behalf. Seeing that excitement, he couldn't let her down. He'd make sure that this special day outside of the palace's confines was one of the best of her life. Regarding the concierge, he said, "Take this sign down."

"The whole thing? People must know when we're open, milord."

"Just the idiotic bit about Unables," he said, sweeping past without glancing back. "I want it removed now."

If she said something, he didn't know. Benedict joined his side. "It would be wise to refrain from politics today, milord."

Bryson scoffed. "I don't stand for segregation or discrimination. That's not a political stand, but an ethical one."

"Very well, then, milord."

Bryson tried on all kinds of clothes over the next two hours, from modernized thigh-length dress shorts with suspenders over striped button-ups to the classical suit and tie with black trousers that crumpled ever so slightly upon reaching his shoes. As the assistant fitted him with an ebony tie, Shelly looked him up and down in the trifold body mirror. She nodded, but then frowned.

"Golden handkerchief?" she asked.

"I'd go with sky-blue, milady," the assistant said, now focused on folding back the cuffs of his sleeves. "It will complement the prince's eyes."

Shelly made eye contact with him in the mirror. She grinned. "I do love his eyes."

"I don't blame you, milady."

"You two are cute," Benedict said, standing several feet behind Bryson, but at an angle granting him view of the mirror. It helped that he was tall. "And you're making a great show for the public."

Bryson turned and looked toward the wall of glass that fronted the shop. Dozens of people crowded against it, smudging the glass. He could see the concierge cringe as she watched from her podium. He did the same, but for different reasons. He'd somehow forgotten about their audience.

"You shouldn't be ashamed, milord," Benedict said.

"That's not it," Bryson said, shaking his head. "All these eyes on me … it just makes me uncomfortable."

The assistant began running a lint roller down the front of his tuxedo and said, "You are a handsome young man, milord, marrying a young lady of divine grace and beauty; it's only natural they stare."

She stepped back, admiring her handiwork. Her eyes roved up his body, settling at the top of his head. "Although that" —she pointed at his hair— "needs a lot of work."

He frowned, running his hand through his thick golden locks, which stood in errant directions. It looked as if he'd just gotten out of bed. At least his bangs lay flat … for the most part. Surprisingly, it wasn't he who questioned the woman's observation.

"What's wrong with it?" Shelly asked, turning her head to face him rather than focus only on his reflection.

The assistant stammered, startled by the princess's question. "Well … Milady, he looks like a …" She trailed off. Bryson raised a brow.

"A child?" Shelly asked.

"Those were not my words, Princess," she said. It was clear by her expression, however, that the guess had been correct.

"I like that about him," Shelly said, putting her hand in his hair and ruffling it some more. He crinkled his nose. *Now* it was a mess. There was a controlled randomness—if that made any sense—to the directions in which his hair curled upward. But he stood by her act, appreciative of the support.

The assistant nodded. "Very well then, Princess."

Hours passed in the shop, spent trying on a plethora of different clothing combinations. Just when Bryson thought they'd settled on the classical tuxedo, it switched to a black vest with a blue cravat around the neck—a suffocating article of clothing. The only constant of his wardrobe was the color combination. Not wanting to dampen Shelly's spirits, he fought back a sigh as he observed his ensemble in the reflection.

They finally departed the shop around noon to excited murmurs from the crowd, which had somehow swollen to that of a mob. They strolled down the sidewalk, Shelly and Benedict discussing the dozens of outfits Bryson had tried on. Meanwhile, he studied the civilians, his elbow absentmindedly locked with his fiancée's—another stunt forced upon him by Benedict. Why couldn't Vitio have spared Vistas just for today? He preferred the Dev servant's company.

His gaze was drawn to a young girl with sandy brown hair like Meow Meow's fur. She peered around a guard's leg, her tiny hands grasping onto the man's pants. To the guard's credit, he didn't seem to mind. She was moving her lips, waving in his direction. Perhaps her voice was too tiny to rise above the din of the crowd.

He broke free of Shelly's hooked elbow and approached the girl. The crowd gasped, then quickly silenced. The girl's eyes widened.

"Milord, this is not wise," Benedict said from behind.

Bryson didn't care. Before the day had started, Queen Delilah warned him of the consequences if he partook in direct communication with a civilian, that he might not like what was said. But wasn't this whole act of shopping the streets supposed to display a connection between the royal elites and commoners? If that really was the goal, then shouldn't he actually *speak* to them? Besides, he didn't intend on addressing an entire crowd. This was a girl, barely eight years of age, with no interrogative prowess.

"Hey, young lady," he said, a beaming smile plastered on his face.

Her mouth fell agape and her hands squeezed the guard's pants even tighter.

"Are you enjoying your day?" he asked.

She seemed to want to speak, but her lips only trembled. The guard placed a hand against the back of her head and tried gently pushing her forward. She obliged.

Bryson tried another question: "What's your name?"

She shook her head. Did his presence really make her this nervous? She dug into her dress pocket, pulling out a small piece of parchment.

"What have you got there?" he asked.

A woman stepped forward from the crowd, grabbing the girl's shoulder. "I'm sorry, milord. I'll take her. She's my daughter." The mother appeared frazzled … scared.

He looked over the identification card similar to the one Simon had shown him. Her name was Sahala Jacayl, and nothing about what was written on the card seemed out of the ordinary—until he reached a section labeled: HANDICAPS.

His eyes froze; his heart began racing. Vitio had never told him about such a category. Anger and shame flooded through him. According to the Intel Kingdom, Sahala had two handicaps. One didn't come as too much of a shock. In fact, it made sense now. She was deaf, explaining why she hadn't replied to him. Either she couldn't read the lips of others or form words properly with her own. But the second handicap was wrong on multiple levels. And despite holding the same trait, he didn't recall Simon having it listed as such. She was an Unable.

He gazed up from the card, trying to subdue the tempest of rage within him. Sahala placed a finger in front of pursed lips. He understood why. She shouldn't have been here. There was another barrier of guards stationed at the crowd's perimeter, barring those considered unsafe or uncertain from joining the masses. If they had properly checked her documents, they wouldn't have let her pass. Her small frame must have allowed her to slip past.

He placed a hand on the girl's shoulder and offered a single nod, a stern flatness in his lips. He then stood from his crouched position and regarded the mother. "Can you hear me?" he asked.

"Yes, milord."

He leaned in, cupping his hand just behind her ear. "I will fix this," he whispered.

He stepped back and gazed down at Sahala. She didn't cry, nor did she appear hurt. She was strong, undoubtedly so. It was clear why the shop had such a sign on their door. The Intelian elites were sculpting something foul in this kingdom. Did they even realize it? Vitio thought this system would better protect the people, but all it did was protect those who didn't even need protection in the first place. And it was all at the expense of the civilians' freedom and pride. "Oppression" was a strong word, but it was becoming a reality.

He smiled at the mother before turning to join Shelly and Benedict. As he walked away from the crowd, he heard a kid's voice again, the one from earlier that morning. "Unables are people, too!"

He whirled, looking for the source. No luck. Judging by the crowd's jeers in response to the comment, they didn't agree. Of course they didn't. These were wealthy citizens, most of whom probably weren't Unables. The system didn't hinder them, so why would they care? Still, their exuberance from earlier had morphed into something sinister. Bryson listened carefully, pinpointing certain comments in the din.

"The prince *would* sympathize with Unables! He's just as bad as one! A half-Stillian!"

Many roared along with him—not all of them, but enough to make him feel sick. He liked to believe that those people who stayed silent, the ones who looked at those hurling insults in disgust, were considering what real deplorability was ... his father.

Had the public forgotten so easily? If there were any attacks at his bloodline, it should have been because of that man: Mendac LeAnce, the monster who raped, pillaged, and enslaved.

As Bryson watched the crowd, fights began to break out between citizens of various different political viewpoints: those who fought on behalf of their king and his socioenergenic classes, those who opposed it, and those who supported Bryson. There were likely many others with their own convoluted opinions, but at this point it had become chaos. Deciphering between those who fought and those who tried to flee was no longer possible.

Something hit Bryson in the face, hard and fast. His vision swirled, but he remained upright. Guards began rushing the crowd, apprehending people and disregarding all protocol. Civilians swung at the uniformed soldiers.

He reached up, touched the side of his temple, and lowered his fingers to find them coated with blood. A fist-size rock sat on the ground before him. Shelly tugged him away. A smaller unit of officers escorted them through a nearby restaurant and out its backdoor.

The angry cries of the mob carried even this far. The state of the Intel Kingdom was horrendous. Even if Toono didn't strike soon, they'd likely crumble from within first.

*    *    *

"I told you not to address the crowd!"

For the first time ever, Bryson was receiving a verbal tirade as vicious as the storms of Thunder Alley from Queen Delilah Intel, his future mother-in-law. He'd always feared her traditional stern nature, the disapproving stare or five-word sentence that could cast a tidal wave of shame upon one's soul. But this … this wasn't subtle at all.

As Vistas wrapped bandage around Bryson's head, Delilah continued her assault. For anyone else, it wouldn't have been considered yelling, but even a slightly raised voice sounded as such when coming from her.

"Yet you do the exact opposite of what I told you not to do!" she exclaimed. They were in one of the palace's many studies, rooms that had gone mostly untouched since Lilu's departure. Bryson sat on a stiff wooden chair. Shelly stood next to him with her hand on his shoulder. Delilah stood at the front of the room in a silk emerald dress, hands clasped behind her back. Vistas stepped back, removing his gloves and disposing of them in a nearby waste bin.

Bryson tried to speak up. "But the segregation problem—"

"Is now made even worse because of your actions today," Delilah said. "It's been an issue we'd been managing reasonably well."

"To be fair, Mother," Shelly said, "pretending there isn't a problem or that the problem isn't significant is a privilege of our status."

"Your father isn't 'pretending,'" the queen said. "He knows what he's doing."

Bryson shook his head; a bag of ice was pressed against it. "If he isn't pretending, then that means he's just woefully ignorant. If civilians have the gall to attack *me*—a royal who is to marry their future royal head—then what do you think they could do to a merchant, steward, or tradesman?"

122

Delilah's brows furrowed. "He is your king. You may have gotten away with speaking to him in such a manner because of his lenient nature and affection toward you, but I will not allow you to treat him with such disrespect."

"Imagine what they'd do to the lower class!" Bryson bellowed, ignoring her warning. "The factory workers! The homeless! The urchins!"

The door burst open and Vitio's burly stature marched in. He shut the door upon entering. As the years piled on for the king, so did the weight. No longer did he look like a man with fat atop muscle remnant from his youth, but a man who had let himself go, having grown comfortable in the confines of his frilly palace. Bryson vowed to never become such a man.

"Thirty-six arrests, fourteen injured, and four critically so," Vitio said, his face red, anger palpable.

Shelly's fist clenched. "Bryson didn't cause that," she said, defending him for the thousandth time today. "Some man in the crowd—"

Vitio waved his hand in dismissal, sucking the voice out of her lungs. "One casualty."

Bryson's stomach lurched. Someone *died?* Queen Delilah was right. His posture wilted, gaze fixed on the white carpet. What had he done?

"Today, a civilian died because of bad judgment," Vitio said.

Bryson didn't respond, mouth as dry as the Archaic Desert.

"A simple task was asked of you," the king said, remaining by his wife's side. "Despite what is heard or seen, don't make any noise. I specifically requested for you to bring any worries to me personally afterward. Then we could handle how they'd be addressed in a more professional setting." He fell silent for a protracted moment, as if for effect. "Nothing about a deadly brawl in the streets between civilians and officers is 'professional'; it's barbaric. For once, Bryson, you have failed me."

*And you have failed this kingdom*, Bryson wanted to say, but news of an innocent's death had dampened any will to argue. Shelly, too, had seemed to realize the same thing. Her silence spoke volumes.

"I will leave you to dwell on your decisions," Vitio said, turning to open the door. He allowed Delilah to exit first. "Come, Vistas."

The Dev servant hovered there for a moment, but eventually followed them out. The door slammed shut, leaving the engaged couple in deafening silence.

*　　*　　*

"I fear I'm no longer in touch with society," Bryson said. His voice sounded hollow as he lay in bed, gazing toward the star-strewn night sky above.

Shelly was curled up on her side, head atop his chest and one leg thrown over his. "It's what happens when your status and title becomes what it has. For someone who already had a reputation as the son of Mendac, your ascent up society's ladder has been unprecedented. It started when you became a Jestivan. Now you're the Still Prince, future Intel King, and possessor of a Branian. You're high up the food chain, which makes it difficult to notice the miniscule changes happening in society far below you … especially if you're not one to involve yourself in the political dealings where the tough decisions are made. Even my father leaves such matters to his council and the elders, for the most part."

"Are you defending him?" he asked.

"I'm offering perspective. It's difficult to govern everything that happens in a kingdom. And with the impending climax of the war and the threats on the lives of those he loves most, that task becomes impossible. He is to act as a general in these times, which forces him to delegate other duties to the council. While these identification cards have gotten out of hand, I do know that my father hasn't been an active part in their development since initiating the law. The last time he became so heavily involved was when Titus was found."

Bryson heaved a sigh. "If that's so, he needs to address it."

"You know he had a point," she said, running a finger across his exposed abdomen. "We should have gone to him directly."

"Someone died today, Shelly."

She nodded softly into his chest. "Yes. And it was avoidable."

124

"What if it was the girl?"

"It wasn't a child, according to Vistas. I already asked."

He squeezed his eyes shut, thanking the lucky stars. Still, that didn't mean the death didn't happen. "Was it an Unable?"

"We don't know the specifics," she said. "Get some rest."

He nodded. She reached up and kissed him, then rolled to her other side. He stayed awake for hours, reflecting on the day's events. He thought of the Still Kingdom, and how his mother had spoken about the discrimination toward men in their culture. She told him a story about Still Queen Francine and the eighth century Stillian Cleanse—or more properly known as the Stillian Massacre. The ruthless queen would enter labor wards and execute nearly every single newborn baby boy.

Bryson didn't want a culture where someone had to live with such fears, where they were chastised and abused because of a trait they'd naturally been born with.

No, not in his kingdom.

# 11

# Hallucinogenics

The grass beneath Yama was damp, but not from rain or dew. Blood soaked the sod, pumping itself out of a gouge in a man's abdomen beside her.

She sat with her legs crossed, sword lying horizontally in front of her. She glanced at the body for a moment, but then looked away, toward the flat skyline of the infinite prairies surrounding her. Why had he chased her into this kingdom? She may have been his pupil once, but that didn't mean she'd hesitate to kill him. Now, Adren Director Buredo was dead, just like his brother.

Yama had once been a tenacious individual, and for good reason. There was someone she chased—or something. She had never been entirely sure. Everyone had a dream, something they dedicated their life to pursue. Had she lost her way?

While her memory of her admittance into the Adren Assistance Academy wasn't concrete, it was there in some nebulous form, like the memory of a memory. Someone had dropped her off, saying that one day she'd return to a village where two oaks stood on a gentle hill, overlooking the farmlands. Under those oaks rested two legends.

Early in life she discovered such a place to be Yinyon, a small village near the Adren Kingdom's Edge, home of Ataway Kawi and Leon Suadade. Because of this, she had become distraught after discovering Intel Director Debo's real identity. Perhaps she could have asked him questions. Unfortunately, that opportunity was now gone.

She pushed herself to her feet, taking one last look at Director Buredo as she reached down to retrieve her sword. The time had come for her to separate herself from Toono … It was time she visited Yinyon.

*     *     *

Dozens of locks lay scattered around Illipsia. She sat on her dorm room floor, using her weaving skills to unlock them one by one. That, however, was the easy part. Even picking two at once had become a bore. It was when that number hit three that it became difficult. She strained herself, trying to weave three separate patterns of Dev Chains, manipulating their currents in a way that could fill each lock perfectly. It was like trying to read three books at once—an impossible task for any mind. Sure, she could switch her focus between locks, but that only caused her to fail against the other two. The goal was for all three locks to open at the same time. After that, four and five.

She had practiced like this for weeks, though opportune moments were few and far between. Sharing this room with three other girls didn't provide much privacy. Luckily, they were close friends, so when they left the dorm, they did so as a group.

She squealed in frustration as two of the locks dislodged, but the third remained locked. She could perform telekinesis while using clairvoyance— evidenced by her training sessions with Yama, levitating rocks from the ground while also tracking the swordswoman's movements—yet she

127

couldn't do a simple task like this. Were the intricacies of the lock's pins and springs that complex?

Something pulsed in her head, and her expression darkened. *Not tonight.* She didn't want to speak to her mother. That rare occasion she did was only because of Toono's request. She wove a dome of Dev Chains to shield her head, designing it specifically for her mother's telepathic pattern. The pulsing vanished.

A knock thrummed through the door. She scooped the locks into her arms and threw them under her bed, shoving them all the way against the wall. After another knock, she stood and strolled across the room, kicking two more locks beneath the bed.

She opened the door to find Beren holding a dandelion in his hand. He stood there awkwardly for a time before extending his arm, the plant bent at a pitiful angle. She accepted his gift and invited him inside. He was a year younger than her, yet a couple of inches taller. His hair was as black as hers and longer. Today he had it done up in pig tails. He liked to style it in ways very unbefitting of a boy, but perhaps society was wrong in how it categorized certain styles and hobbies to a specific gender.

He plopped onto a bed belonging to one of her roommates. "What are you up to?" he asked.

"I was on the verge of sleep," she said, taking a seat on her own bed and reaching over to place the dandelion on her nightstand.

His face fell. "I caught you at a bad time."

"I disagree." She turned to look at her window, where violet curtains blocked the sunlight. "Best not to nap at this time of day; it'd be a waste."

He hopped off the bed and approached the window, yanking back the curtains. Natural light swallowed the flickering glow of the candle on her nightstand. He stood in front of the window and gazed outside. Two pots of lilies sat on the exterior windowsill, soaking in the sun. He opened the window and leaned in to smell a few of them.

"This is a real flower," he said. "Puts my offering to shame."

He was right in a way. Technically, a dandelion bordered between flower and weed. However, the effort and thought made it even better than a flower. "I like dandelions."

He turned and smiled, then returned to the bed. "You are one of my few friends who are still here, Illipsia."

Ever since the Archaic Kingdom's reinstatement into True Light, refugee families had been returning to their homes in droves. "How many left this morning?" she asked.

"Thirty-six," he said, a frown forming on his face. "Two friends of mine."

"Well, I guess you'll be stuck with me for some time." This was partly true. Orphans were to remain at Phesaw for the foreseeable future, at least until Ms. Neaneuma worked out living arrangements with Archaic King Sigmund. Illipsia technically wasn't an orphan, but that was the role she played, so she'd remain here for now.

Beren straightened up. "As long as you're here, I won't lose hope!" She smirked. "Besides," he said, "I'm making a lot of new friends from the Adrenian refugees. It's unfortunate what happened to their kingdom."

Her gaze fell to the floor. The influx of Adren refugees meant Yama and Kadlest had been successful in taking hold of Katashi, the Adren capital. Based on the stories circulating around the campus, civilians survived the transition of power unscathed. Those who fled only did so because they feared the same fate as those who suffered during the Archaic Kingdom's uprising. Toono, however, had given Kadlest and Yama specific instructions not to hurt innocents.

She spoke with Beren for nearly an hour, even going across the street to grab some food before returning to her dorm. As they ate, she decided to practice a little high-level weaving without his knowledge. He'd be her secret test subject for the time being—not in a cruel way. She wouldn't prod him like a lab rat.

She weaved Dev Clusters that shrouded his eyes, unbeknownst to him. The special trait of Dev weaving was that the chains didn't form a visual ability, not unless the weaver wanted them to. With Passion weaving, fire was always the result; with Intel weaving, electricity. She shaped an image with her Dev Chains directly in front of his eyes while he absentmindedly chewed a potato wedge. Then he jumped.

She stopped weaving. Her eyes widened at his sudden movement. He stared at the window, half-eaten wedge now on his lap. "Did you see that?" he said.

She glanced at the window and shrugged. "It was just a cat."

"Yeah, but it landed on the windowsill out of nowhere," he said, getting up to approach the window. He stuck his head outside in search of the feline.

But she knew there would be nothing there, for the cat had been a hallucination cast on him. It may have been a simple version of a grander technique, but it meant she could do it. Dev weaving could achieve an abundance of results when mastered. The abilities were separated into tiers, and the top tier of difficulty, known as Grandeur's Three, were considered divine skills. Those who could achieve even one of them were hailed as icons in Devish history.

Illipsia had already achieved clairvoyance, the Tertiary of the three. Now she was on her way to perfecting the Secondary, hallucinogenics. Mastering two of them would put her in select company with only eight other people in history.

*But what about all three?*

The voice in her head made her jump. The question had come from her mother. How had she penetrated the barrier? Illipsia refocused, discovering a break in her shield that her mother must have caused. She quickly mended and reinforced it, interlocking Dev Chains so it was impenetrable.

*What a ludicrous question*, she thought. Only two people in history had mastered all of Grandeur's Three. Possibly three, if one were to count Dev Prince Storshae's Bewahr, Fenton Fonos. But even he'd never been documented using the Primary during his first lifetime, only clairvoyance and hallucinogenics. He'd likely learned the third one in the Dark Empire as a Gefal.

"Why'd you get so quiet?"

She regarded Beren, who stared at her with intrigue. "Nothing," she said.

*Focus on hallucinogenics*, she told herself. It meant nothing to distract herself with impossible fairy tales, and that's what Grandeur's Primary was. Teleportation was such a farfetched notion.

# 12

# The Search Begins

Despite her smaller stature, Kaylee's strides were that of an adult male as she marched toward Lost Wisdom's front doors, forcing Himitsu and Sal to jog in order to keep pace. Groundkeepers turned away from their work to watch the trio—or more likely, just Kaylee. She had gone from abused orphan to galvanized, vengeful woman in the blink of an eye to them.

As they burst through the doors, heads whirled in their direction at the sudden sound. Kaylee reached the front desk first. "Can someone take us to Raul Sanchia?"

The same secretary from their prior visit sat looking up at her. He cowered deeper into his seat. "Raul, nor the rest of the group, has yet returned from Accus Canyon."

"You said three days; I gave you three days."

"We don't know why they haven't returned," he said, eyes darting toward Himitsu, fearful that Kaylee's threat of arson would come to fruition.

After a prolonged pause, she turned toward Himitsu and Sal. "I'll go left," she said. "You two go right. Make sure you search every room."

She rushed down the left hall, whipping out a knife at a guard who tried stepping in her way. "But we don't know what this Raul kid looks like!" Himitsu yelled after her.

No response. He sighed, but followed her instructions anyway with Sal by his side. They searched every room they passed. Thankfully, none of them were locked. He had a feeling Kaylee would have expected him to kick the doors down if that were the case, which he had no desire to do.

"It feels like the deeper we go, the colder it gets," Sal said, gripping both arms with a shiver. "And this place just feels depressing."

Himitsu glanced at Sal's arms, bare and burnt brown by the sun. He always wore buttoned tanks with the sleeves torn off at the shoulders. "Maybe if you wore proper clothes, you wouldn't have that problem."

"I'm a big man. The meat on my bones insulates me well enough."

He did have stones for biceps and boulders for thighs. Even his height impressed, falling only a couple of inches shy of Himitsu, who had grown another inch or so in the past couple of years.

When they finally reached a locked door, Himitsu wiggled the handle in frustration. He pressed his shoulder against the sturdy wood. It didn't budge. He stepped back, observing it from a short distance. "Kick it down," he said.

Sal raised an eyebrow. "While I may not be the smartest, I don't think that's productive."

A pair of adults strolled past them from behind, their conversation dying as they watched the two young men with suspicious eyes. Himitsu waited for them to disappear around a distant corner. "Then what do you expect we do?" he asked. "Raul could be in there."

Sal reached into his pocket and pulled out a pin. He dropped to a knee in front of the handle and said, "Just give me a second."

"You can pick locks?"

"I grew up a thief," Sal said, tongue stuck to his upper lip with concentration. "While I mostly stuck to pickpocketing the middle class in busy market squares, there came a time when I grew too big for such a task. That's when Rhyparia took over that job, and I moved onto bigger game …

breaking into homes and stealing money from safes. Both required knowledge of a locking mechanism. Safes were a real pain, though."

"You're a thief," Himitsu said, frowning.

"As was Rhyparia," Sal said as a click sounded from the handle. He pushed the door open, then stood. "That's how you get by in a place like Olethros. We only took from those who could spare it."

"You don't know that," Himitsu whispered, poking his head through the door.

The room wasn't like the rest of the building—windowless and dingy, lit only by a candelabrum that stood in a far corner. A bed sat against a sidewall, and a plethora of stocky bookcases ran along two others. In a rocking chair at the room's center sat an elderly woman, her face wrinkled. She wore a tattered gray robe and matching shawl that hid most of her head.

Himitsu hovered in the doorway for a moment, but couldn't step inside. There was something off about this room, or maybe it was just the woman. She didn't acknowledge their presence. Her gaze remained empty above her hollow cheeks.

"She looks dead, mate," Sal said. After a pause, he added, "I feel dead, mate."

"You feel that, too?" Himitsu asked, a surreal sensation washing over him, like something bearing down on his chest and emptying his stomach.

Suddenly, the wooden floorboards beneath the woman began to rot, aging centuries in seconds. The effect spread across the floor, crawling toward the doorway. Himitsu gaped in shock, but then alertly slammed the door shut.

"What was that?!" Sal shouted.

"Trespassers!" a man bellowed from the far end of the hall. Four archers flanked him, two on each side, bows at the ready. What kind of place was this? They wouldn't try to shoot those things inside an orphanage, would they?

A snap cut through the air as the archers released their grips of the string. Himitsu wove a wall of black fire. The arrows instantly disintegrated within it. The two young men bolted down the hall, opening every door they passed. Guards began to spill out of intersecting corridors from in front and behind. Soon they were trapped. With arrows trained on them from both directions and only a locked door to one side, their options had run thin. A volley of arrows converged on them, and Himitsu wove two walls of fire on both sides. He was going to have to fight his way out.

*Bang!*

He whirled at the sound to find that Sal had kicked down a nearby door. Fortunately, there wasn't a creepy old lady in the room beyond, just an empty office that likely belonged to a staff member. As they ran through the room, Sal picked up a chair and hurled it at the window.

"We could have tried opening it!" Himitsu yelled as the window shattered.

Sal shrugged, then carefully made his way outside through the cragged glass. Himitsu approached it, found a latch, and unlocked it before climbing outside like a normal person. When his feet hit grass, he ducked as more arrows flew overhead.

The two of them scrambled across the lawn, tripping over daffodils in the gardens. Himitsu threw up walls of fire behind him, burning arrows and flowers alike.

They bolted for the front gate. He spotted Kaylee already sprinting out the front door. They converged near the gated entrance, dodging several guards, not even bothering to retaliate. Breaking free of the grounds, they stopped traffic as they crossed the dirt road. Horses neighed, lifting their front hooves, sending their coachmen into fits as they tried to regain control. Pedestrians pulled back either in surprise or anger, and wealthier gentlemen started wagging their sleek black canes at the hooligans.

The three of them careened around a corner into an alley. They bent over, clutching at their stomachs as they tried to catch their breath. Sal heaved the hardest, his bigger frame not suited for sprinting. Then they broke down and laughed in an adrenaline-induced hysteria.

Kaylee fell onto her rear with her back to the building's wall. She placed her blades back into their straps on her forearms and ankles.

Eventually they calmed down and regained their bearings. "Did you find Raul?" Himitsu asked.

"No, he wasn't anywhere," she said.

"Then what do we do?" Sal said, the only one of them still standing.

She wiped a tear from her eye, arching her neck and resting the back of her head against the wall. "Pack our things. We'll head to Accus Canyon."

*    *    *

Toshik and Kuiku rolled through the southern gate of Phelos Palace's grounds. Toshik yawned, stretching toward the carriage's roof. He'd rested well during the ride, and he planned to gather more during the approaching night. Tomorrow morning he'd be off to the Dev Kingdom, starting another long road of travel. He was okay with this … whatever kept his mind moving to distract his heart from the pain. It also meant he had an objective involving enemy territory and dangerous opposition, where he could put his training to the test and discover if he was actually ready to hunt Yama.

He stared at his spunka sword, its scabbard ribbed with glistening steel spines as it rested atop a plush bench. His father's bladesmithing business would continue, but not under the Brench name. Toshik had no desire to carry the torch passed onto him by force following his father's death. No, he'd decided to transition the company over to the Archaic Kingdom, making King Sigmund its owner.

The carriage stopped in front of the palace. Toshik and Kuiku approached the carriage's door as a pair of servants retrieved their bags. A steward trotted down the front steps, an open umbrella above him and two others at his side. He handed one to each of the Adrenian men. Toshik opened his and stepped outside first, hearing rain clatter against the nylon material. Holding it at a slight angle to fight the winds, he proceeded up the steps with Kuiku on his tail. He cursed as rain hit stone, splashing up his pant legs and onto his ankles before dripping into his socks. *Should have worn boots.*

They stepped inside the main entrance, a grand foyer with a vaulted arched ceiling, staircases running along the sidewalls to an overlook above. Toshik handed over his umbrella and gloves to the steward, then removed his dress shoes and kicked them off to the side. Looking down at the wet

136

streaks on the floor, the steward frowned, his arms full of the two men's extra clothing and accessories.

"Pilot Ophala and her husband await your presence in her office," the steward said, shuffling over to retrieve Toshik's shoes, being careful to not drop anything.

Toshik nodded and walked up the left staircase. Kuiku thanked the steward and followed. "You couldn't help the man out?" he asked.

"I'm tired," Toshik said. "I admit that the shoe thing was rude. I'll apologize to him later after I get some rest."

They reached the hall of Ophala's office. Her door was open, but Toshik slowed upon hearing the conversation from within. He hovered just outside the doorway, leaning casually against the wall.

"This is your call, King Sigmund," Ophala said. "It's an easy one. Don't come to me for help."

"But I botched Rhyparia NuForce's ruling," the king said. Toshik shook his head. Despite entering his mid-twenties, he still sounded like a child. That shakiness in his voice was nauseating. "What is to say that I won't do the same with Elyol Brekton?"

"Mr. Brekton has relinquished any desire to fight this trial," she said. "He made that clear a while ago, when he chose to join me in my efforts to take down Toth Brench and his regime. I had told him if he did so, he wouldn't escape punishment for past crimes committed during the uprising. He slaughtered hundreds of soldiers in a successful attempt to help steal the Archaic Kingdom from the Light Realm's alliance, milord."

"That means the jury will find him guilty," Sigmund said. "This I know. The severity of his sentence is up to me, though."

"Then make that decision and do it with conviction." The tone of Ophala's voice was stern and clipped, as if that was her final comment on the matter. After a prolonged pause, she said, "You are the king now. How many times must I tell you this? I am not here to make decisions for you, milord ... nobody is."

"I understand."

"Do you?" she asked. "If so, don't come back here with your tail between your legs, talking in circles in an attempt to get me to tell you what to do, King Sigmund."

Toshik made a noise of disapproval. Sigmund was king by law, but that didn't make him a good leader. If Ophala found it necessary to step in and take control, she would do so.

"Yes, Pilot Ophala. I will—"

Toshik began to whistle as he rounded the corner and strolled into the office with Kuiku right behind him. Sigmund spun away from the desk, his face turning red. "Zana Toshik …"

"Good afternoon, King Sigmund," Toshik said, taking a seat in a cushioned armchair in the sitting area. "Carry on. Don't mind me." Kuiku stood casually behind the sofa. To his surprise, Horos Vevlu also waited silently by a window.

Sigmund hesitated, his lips twisting with indecision. "I'll be taking my leave," he finally said, turning to regard Ophala. "Good day."

She nodded, and the king waddled across the room and out the door. *Pfft! What kind of king walks like that?*

"Hello, gentlemen," Ophala said, reaching into her bottom drawer.

Toshik stood and approached her desk with Kuiku. Horos Vevlu, husband of Ophala and father to Himitsu, remained standing by the window.

"I find myself drinking my liver into oblivion after every encounter with that young man," she said, pulling out a small glass cup from the drawer. She reached for her vase of fake flowers and poured herself a glass of red wine. "Hopefully this meeting goes more smoothly than that."

"Let's make this quick," Toshik said, sitting in one of the two chairs in front of the desk. Kuiku lowered himself into the other.

She took a long swig, then raised her glass as if to toast to such a notion. "Horos and I have 'business' to attend to, so I agree."

Toshik's nose crinkled, but Kuiku released a hearty chuckle and said, "I've only properly spoken with you once, but you are definitely one of a kind."

"Is that so?" she asked, a smile spreading on her face. "Perhaps Horos would like to invite you to our business meeting."

"Don't take her seriously," Horos said gratingly, running a finger down the aged scar on his cheek.

"I'm glad you've decided to tag along for this operation," she said, eyes on Kuiku. "Your skills will be of great use. Besides, three heads are better than one."

Horos walked over, placing his butt on the edge of the desk. His eyes narrowed as he inspected Kuiku. "You were quite a pain back when you were the Adren Corporal," he said. "I must thank you for retiring before being offered the promotion."

Kuiku grinned. "Of course."

Ophala reached for another drawer, and Toshik expected to find another glass in her hand. Instead, she brought out a roll of parchment and placed it on the desk. "Tomorrow morning, you will depart from one of Tazama's secret teleplatforms in the dungeons."

"How do we know they still work?" Toshik asked. "You'd think they would have destroyed their corresponding platforms in the Dev Kingdom already, restricting access to the kingdom to only the normal platforms. Less for them to defend that way."

"That is a possibility, but I doubt it. If anything, they'll keep both the normal and secret cluster secure while also keeping them in operation. They wouldn't want to destroy their only other means of slipping into Phelos, after all ... even if we have all of the platforms guarded."

"And what if it doesn't work?" Toshik asked.

"Then you travel to the normal platforms and teleport that way. But that's less than ideal since we're trying to avoid civilians. I don't want innocents sucked into a battle, which would definitely ensue upon arrival." She took another sip of her wine, then pursed her lips in thought. "I am worried about the strength of opposition that will likely be waiting for you. Last time you infiltrated the Dev Kingdom in search of the secret teleplatforms, you were met with over a dozen Dev Assassins."

"We can handle it," Toshik said with a nonchalant wave of his hand.

She raised a brow. "That's not what I heard. Himitsu and Horos told me it took the summoning of Bryson's Branian, Thusia, to dispose of such a large number."

"I'm better now," he said. "I can handle it. Horos could too if we were to arrive at night."

She shook her head. "You see, I'm not willing to take such a gamble. That's why I've already spoken with King Sigmund about it."

Toshik leaned forward, his face twisted with bewilderment. "What's he going to do? Soil himself and kill them with the stench?"

Horos turned away, but the grin was evident. Ophala didn't find it so humorous. "King Sigmund has a Branian," she said, leaning back in her chair and placing her hands on her lap. "That is an asset that cannot be topped. He will accompany you through the teleplatforms or nobody will be going anywhere."

"Doesn't he have business to attend to here, in the kingdom he rules?"

"Yes, and that's why he'll return the moment everything is clear for you three in the Dev Kingdom. He shouldn't be there for any longer than half an hour."

Toshik sat back. "Fine. As long as we don't have to drag him around. He'd only slow us down."

She studied the Jestivan, letting several moments pass without so much as a blink. "Once on Devish land," she finally said, "how the three of you decide to reach Cogdan is up to you. However, I wouldn't recommend travel through Cosmos or Rence, which would mean the two main roads are off-limits. My suggestion is to blaze your own trail, widely arching to the north or south."

She sat forward and untied the string around the parchment. It unraveled on its own, revealing a map not of a kingdom or any kind of land, but of Cogdan Castle. It definitely wasn't an official map; the lack of detail, measurements, and straight lines made that evident. Still, it was more than Toshik would have expected.

"How'd you get your hands on something like this?" Kuiku asked, now standing, hands on the desk as he gazed down at the blueprints.

"We owe thanks to Grand Director Poicus," she said. "Years ago he drew this during his stay in Cogdan, when he impersonated a Devish soldier to find proof of Dev King Rehn's grave. He figured it might come in handy in the future."

Horos snorted. "He could have saved us all the hassle by burning the body to ashes when he had the chance."

"Poicus also documented any secret passages to use and traps to avoid," she noted, pointing at certain areas where red ink had been used instead of black. "It is quite thorough, considering the limited resources and time he was working with."

"Do you think we'll run into Toono?" Toshik asked. His eyes landed on a square labeled *Throne Room*.

"I'd hope not, if Horos does his job right," she said. "Then again, this is Toono we're talking about. He isn't typically a victim of foolery."

Toshik's jaw tightened. Perhaps he could kill Toono on his path to Yama. After all, that man had been the one to land the finishing blow on Jilly. She served as his sacrifice, so he was equally at fault.

Yes, the idea of eliminating the Rogue Demon was euphoric—an extra layer of dead skin to scab over his wounds.

*    *    *

Toshik, Horos, Kuiku, and Sigmund stepped onto a teleplatform in a neglected chamber of the dungeons. Ophala stood off to the side, next to a podium that housed a lever.

Toshik set his jaw. His fist clenched the hilt of his sword, which was already drawn and at his side. Despite it being five o'clock in the morning, he'd achieved a full night of sleep. He longed for a battle; arriving to an empty field would prove disappointing.

"Are you not going to summon your Branian now?" Horos asked, glancing at Sigmund while tucking a few knives into the pockets of his leather belt.

"You aren't supposed to summon your Branian around commoners," Sigmund said. "Only if the situation is dire."

Horos frowned. "Bryson has no problem summoning his in front of his friends."

"From what I've seen and heard," Simon said, "Bryson has a reckless abandon of rules and regulations. In fact, my Branian says that boy has created quite a stir in the Empire. He's getting people in trouble."

"Heh, I guess that's why I've taken a liking to the boy," Horos said, smiling to himself.

Ophala approached the platform's edge and leaned in to give Horos a kiss. "Be safe, dear," she said.

"For once in your life, you can rest easy, love."

She took a moment to regard his company, surveying the group. "I suppose I can find comfort in the fact that Fane won't be around to steer you wrong."

He gave her a nod. "Get us out of here."

She pulled the lever, and the platform lurched into rotation. She waved, but her presence quickly became a blur that blended seamlessly with the gray of the chamber's stone walls. Toshik squatted low to the ground, ignoring the safety beams that stood around them. He had the balance to keep himself grounded, even within the torque's force. He had his recent training sessions to thank for this.

The platform slowed, and they could see the tall grass of the prairies swaying slightly under the starlight. Besides the subtle wind, there was no movement or sounds of alarm around them. But that didn't mean nobody was there. The last time they had visited the Dev Kingdom's secret telecluster, they had found the same stillness. Only minutes later had they been ambushed by cloaked assassins invisible to the naked eye.

"What are you sensing?" Kuiku asked.

"Nothing," Horos whispered. "But I can only sense an assassin if they're using their ability. If they're uncloaked, they could be simply hiding in the grass."

Toshik raised his sword to his hip, then flicked it effortlessly to the side. About a mile of grass ahead of him fell. He squatted lower and spun, swinging his sword throughout the motion. The grass surrounding them was shaved to that of a newly manicured lawn, revealing no signs of hidden bodies.

The others gaped at the clearing around them. Kuiku's incredulous gaze drifted toward the Jestivan. "You must tell me who's been training you."

Toshik stood, sheathing his sword. "You can head back, King Sigmund."

Sigmund closed his mouth with a nod. "I'll leave you to it. Good luck, gentlemen."

Everyone except Sigmund stepped off the platform. As the king initiated the platform's rotation, the three men began their journey northwest. They'd travel north of the Cosmos Ruins, following the southern edge of Tames Forest before arriving to the town of Tames. It may have been a longer, more unorthodox route to Cogdan, but it was safer and less predictable.

"Your pupils always turn out this crazy?" Horos asked Kuiku as they trailed several steps behind Toshik.

After a long pause, Kuiku said, "He's no longer *my* pupil."

*     *     *

The throne room of Cogdan Castle was noisy today, as a few carpenters worked on building a new throne—the last one being destroyed when Storshae had been tossed into it. Toono observed their work from the bottom of the stage's steps, Homina at his side. The doors to the room opened, and he turned to see Gala strolling down the burgundy carpet. Holographic symbols of various sorts slowly spun around her body.

"Warden Gala," he said. "How are you getting along with the soldiers?"

"Very well," she said. "But that's not what I'm here to discuss."

"I would expect not."

She stopped several paces away. "Our scout recorded activity at the secret telecluster. I watched the recording several times over, drawing from your notes about noteworthy enemies. I've concluded that Toshik Brench, Horos Vevlu, and a mysterious third man have entered the kingdom and begun traveling northwest from the cluster. Archaic King Sigmund was momentarily present, but he eventually returned to his kingdom."

He nodded and turned toward the throne again. "Not of much importance, but thank you for the update."

"But those are skilled fighters," she said. "Do they not pose a threat to us?"

His gaze remained locked on the workers, who had begun sawing a plank of wood that spanned two support rails. Usually, a commissioned project such as this would have been conducted out of a workshop, but he felt offering the workers the opportunity to work in a place as sacred as the throne room of their king would prove motivating—despite how impractical it might have been.

"It will take them quite some time to reach us here in Cogdan," he said emptily. "They're taking an indirect route that will likely see them circumvent the major cities and towns. With that said, do what you see fit, Gala. You are in charge of the military." He hadn't made such authority official with a title or rank yet, but she knew her role.

"I will send soldiers north from Cosmos in efforts to intercept the intruders if they plan on traveling to Tames," she said.

"Sounds good. Now, if you don't mind, I was speaking with Lady Homina."

A protracted pause followed, during which he could almost feel the warden's glare toward Homina. Gala hadn't taken a liking to his treatment of the woman. He did treat her differently, he supposed. This stemmed from a few things: he pitied her for all the time and sanity she had lost while trapped in the Confines, envied her for surviving, appreciated her for bringing Illipsia into this world, and—as strange as it sounded—*respected* her because he simply felt like he should.

As he heard the door shut in the distance behind him, signaling Gala's departure, he gazed at Homina in wonder. Her long raven hair wasn't tied up as it had been since being freed from the Confines. For the first time since seeing her on that day—adorned in a ragged shirt, hair spooling in greasy strings atop the cold, gray floor—her hair hung down her back, posterior, and legs, stopping just millimeters away from the floor. She turned to look at him, the swath of black curtains flicking effortlessly with the motion of her head.

"What is it, Demon?" she asked, smirking slightly.

She addressed him as such because of Gala, who had made a habit of teasing him with the alias given to him by True Light. Homina had decided to adopt said habit, finding humor in it each time.

He didn't mind being called 'Demon.' If it entertained Homina, then why would he stop her? He wanted her to be happy; he enjoyed that rare spectacle of emotion from her. Besides, was he not exactly that: a demon? Since the night of the museum theft, he had murdered and worked alongside men who had the audacity to slaughter children. While he'd had a reason, there were no excuses for such measures. Sacrifice was still murder in his eyes.

*I can't stop following this path even if I wanted to,* he thought. *Thanks for that, Neeko.*

His vision focused from the nothingness that lay just beyond Homina's head to her eyes, pulling himself back into the now. She had just said something. "What was that?" he asked.

"You were staring at me quite intently earlier," she said. "I asked you what was wrong, then you zoned out for a few seconds."

He chuckled. "My apologies. I was admiring your hair."

She frowned and tilted her head, raising a hand and running the back of it down a few strands. "Everyone has it," she said. "Or most do, at least."

"I noticed you've let it down today. Unless I've forgotten, the last time you allowed it to fall was—"

"The Confines," she said softly, nodding as she turned to regard the workers, gaze distant. "Forgive me, Demon. I am not perfect."

"What do you mean?" he asked, staving off a grin at the oddity of her statement.

"I possess insecurities," she explained flatly. "Wearing my hair down brings me back to the Confines, the uncleanliness of my quarters. The rancid depression in my heart." She turned away from the throne, her back facing him. "Thus, when I wear my hair down around others, I fear what they see ... a defeated *thing*, crumpled into a ball, held in place by atrophied limbs, a mask of black strings in place of a face."

His heart fell as the image filled his mind, and he hated that he understood her perception. Despite all logic, knowing that only Storshae and Toono had seen her in such conditions, in her mind the whole world had seen her, for that's how she saw herself.

She slowly lowered herself to the carpet that ran down the middle of the throne room. Confusion became sorrow as he watched what unfolded. She lay on her side, curled into a ball, and gently rocked back and forth, mumbling softly to herself.

He stepped toward her and knelt down, placing a hand on her shoulder. The workers had ceased their task, staring from a distance. "Lady Homina," he whispered shakily. "Can you hear me?"

She continued to sway and murmur, mentally gone from this world. He dropped his head and squeezed his eyes shut, refusing to let the tears seep through. He and men like him were the reason for this woman's suffering. He grabbed part of the bandage that covered his temple, regretting everything.

If he could take it all back, he would.

# 13

# Erafeen: To Crave Essence

Intel King Vitio lowered himself into an armchair in the war corridor, waiting as his top officers slowly made their way out of the room. The door eventually shut, and Vistas, the one person instructed to stay behind, stood in front of the giant wired module of Kuki Sphaira.

"This should be a quick meeting, Vistas," the king said, genuinely feeling a sense of guilt at how often he'd used the servant's specialties as of late.

There was a time, just a few years ago, when the royal heads would hold only one broadcast meeting per year, almost always being held a couple of months before the Generals' Battle. Looking back at them, they had been frivolous in nature. They'd discuss the location of the event, the money being put in by each kingdom, and casually banter about whose general would prove victorious. Never had a conversation stumbled into areas of war, for there was no need during a prolonged span of peace; commerce, for such matters were appointed to specialized individuals in their advisory teams and handled in writing; or politics, because each royal head dealt with their own kingdom's issues.

Then the final Generals' Battle happened.

Archaic General Inias was murdered, Dev soldiers slaughtered innocents in the stands, and Intel King Vitio and Archaic King Itta—two royal heads of rival kingdoms—finally unleashed their shackles of modesty in order to end the other's life. That caused the first summit between the royal heads in recent memory. Since that moment, broadcast meetings had become more and more regular. Now they were a daily necessity.

"One second, milord," Vistas said, standing with his hands clasped behind his back. "The others are lagging a bit."

Vitio leaned back, an elbow resting on the arm of his chair, fingers running through his scraggly beard. He regarded the servant with intrigue, then asked, "How has Flen been enjoying his freedom?"

"My brother's reputation of promiscuity has reached newfound heights," he said. "However, he has seemed different lately. I plan on speaking with him after we finish here. We have activities lined up for the night; it's been quite some time since we've had a ..." he trailed off, an inquisitive expression on his face as he gazed toward the ceiling. After a protracted pause, he glanced back at Vitio. "I think you would call it a 'guys' night.'"

The king chuckled, trying to imagine what two people as opposite as they tried to do for fun. "That makes sense. Well, now I feel even more pressure to end this quickly."

"I would appreciate that, milord." He paused, closing his eyes. "They're ready." His eyes snapped open. Burgundy flooded the iris of the recording eye. The other dilated, projecting three holographic displays that hung in the air. A benefit of Vistas's constant broadcasting was the practice it gave him. His abilities had become refined enough to simultaneously display multiple recordings.

Archaic King Sigmund occupied the display farthest to the right. He sat in his throne, though doing so made him seem smaller than he already was. While inheriting the spindly stature of his father and grandfather, he hadn't been blessed with their height. The back of the throne, shaped out of thick branches that wended between each other and stretched both to the sides and ceiling, dwarfed him. Instead of an intimidating aura, he looked like a squirrel at the mouth of a bear cave.

Passion Director Venustas occupied the display farthest to the left, seated in front of a glass window. Based on some of the equipment visible beyond the glass, it was a surgical room. Her hair was secured in a medical cap, and a disposable facemask had been pulled down around her neck. There was blood splattered across her cheek.

"That doesn't seem very sterile."

The comment brought Vitio's attention to the center display, housing what most would have rightfully considered the wisest of True Light's leaders: Spirit Queen Apsa. Had he and Archaic King Supido listened to her a couple of years ago—on a few different points—a lot of the recent turmoil could have been avoided. She knew better than all of them. Unlike Sigmund, she had an air of power, decisiveness, and confidence. The war had morphed her into something tough.

She, too, sat in her throne, one leg crossed over the other, silhouetted through a glittering blue dress that draped past her ankles. Two tidal waves of stone climbed up the sides of the throne's back, the barrels of the waves converging on each other at the center, framing her in a vertical ellipse and giving her the appearance of having wings. It was slimming, embellishing her height and straight-backed posture.

"What would make you say that?" Venustas asked.

Apsa raised a pointed finger toward her own cheek. Venustas glanced off screen to her right, then blushed. She used the back of a gloved hand to wipe it off, but that only added to the mess, for her gloves looked like they had been dipped into a canister of red paint. Apsa laughed quietly to herself as the director hurried off screen.

"Let's try our best to not drag this out today," Vitio said, though he was enjoying the lighthearted start to the meeting. If only it could continue that way. Alas, that pesky war.

"Let's begin with somber news," Sigmund said.

Venustas returned, settling back in her chair and patting a towel against her face. "Fantastic."

"Adren Director Buredo is dead," he said.

"No ..." Venustas muttered.

Vitio's gaze fell. "Pilot Ophala saw this, I assume?"

"One of her falcons that returned from the Adren Kingdom did."

"Who did it?" Apsa asked.

"The falcon found his body after the culprit had already fled, but Pilot Ophala says it's safe to assume Yama's the one responsible."

"Of course," Vitio muttered.

Venustas sunk deeper into her chair. "What of Toono?" she asked, voice hollow.

"He hasn't been spotted," Sigmund said.

"He could be anywhere," Vitio said, trying to rid the image of the corpse of another highly-esteemed member of True Light. Dwelling on it wouldn't do them any good. "We assume he's in Cogdan, but who's to say he isn't in the Power Kingdom or Void. And if he's in the Adren Kingdom, we really have a problem. He could travel by the Adren River to the Sea of Light."

"The Spy Pilot has birds all over the Adren Kingdom, and they all report back to her on a weekly basis," Sigmund said. "No word of Toono's presence yet."

"And I have the Adren Connector to the Sea of Light covered," Apsa said. "I've learned from my past mistakes and have adjusted the protocol of ships in the blockade. After letting Toono and his team slip through my last one at the Archaic Connector, I'll make sure such a blunder doesn't happen again. If someone makes it through, they'll have to do so by force—not stealth."

"The whirlpools," Venustas said. Her gaze was on the broadcast once more.

Vitio nodded. "You have a point, Felli. Whirlpools are difficult to predict. Navigators get their locations and times of arrival wrong all the time. Toono could travel through one and end up in the Sea of Light."

"Or worse," Sigmund said, lips twisting in discomfort. "He could be searching the Dev River for a whirlpool, which would bring him directly into the Intel River, past any of your blockades, Apsa."

She shook her head. "*That* is unlikely. Whirlpools in the Realm Rivers are rare and difficult to navigate. Their presence in the sea is more common." After a long pause, she added, "However, we must plan for anything. You make a valid point, Sigmund. I will deploy a dozen whirlpool scouting vessels into the Intel River. If one is spotted, the scouts will signal for a warship to approach and ready an attack … just in case something surfaces."

Sigmund's posture inflated somewhat at the praise.

"In any case," Vitio said, "I don't exactly feel secure about the people positioned at my teleplatforms."

"Do you not have roughly a thousand soldiers stationed around them?" Apsa asked. "I believe you've even begun building a military base and arsenal nearby."

"Yes, but who's to say Toono couldn't take care of a thousand soldiers on his own? And he'll have help with him if he were to travel that way."

"Well, I know you're not going to station Bryson there," she said.

"What about another Jestivan?" Vitio asked.

Apsa's eyebrows rose. "Such as? If I recall, they're all preoccupied with their own quests."

Vitio's eyes roved toward the Archaic King. "Sigmund, I need your help."

The young king's face turned red. "I cannot leave my kingdom," he said shakily. "Although, I am flattered."

"And he's not a Jestivan," Apsa said.

"That's not what I'm saying," Vitio said, leaning forward. "Speak with Pilot Ophala for me. Ask her to get a message to the Mythmaker. I believe a young man by the name of Tashami is its quartermaster."

Sigmund nodded, but Apsa replied, "I see … if it's Tashami's assistance you request, then I'll see what I can do." She waved her hand dismissively. "Leave Pilot Ophala be for now, for her skills are needed elsewhere. She's very useful to me with her seagull's eyes on the waters. The Mythmaker and Whale Lord will be arriving at DaiSo in a couple of weeks, and I think I have a better means of persuading Tashami to do what it is you ask. After all, face-to-face communication is always better than written."

*　　*　　*

151

Agnos set down his quill and reclined in his chair, heaving a sigh as he removed his circular-framed glasses. He pressed a hand into his face and squeezed his closed eyes, head pounding from the strain it took to translate *Erafeen*'s text. He gazed at the open archaic book, its tattered pages and sloppy penmanship within. The parchment wasn't like anything used today. It was unnaturally thick and sturdy, but even those qualities hadn't made it immune to a 1,500-year lifespan. Time had inflicted its toll upon the treasure, and he had to be careful while handling it.

Next to the book lay a disheveled pile of more modern, unbound parchment. They were the loose sheets on which Agnos scribed the Sphairian translations of *Erafeen*'s text. His progress had been sluggish. His patience ran thin after pouring hours into the text only to provide little yields. Still, each minor revelation of the text sparked a fire within his mind, driving him to persevere.

He swiveled in his chair, gazing out the grand window of his cabin. Sunlight cascaded in, the surface of the calm sea refracting its rays. He couldn't believe he was the captain of a ship with a successful voyage under his belt—a voyage many on his crew called the bravest, most foolhardy spectacle they'd ever witnessed. He had dived to the bottom of the sea, been carried in the mouth of a divine beast, retrieved an ancient text written by a god, and then resurfaced amongst dozens of waves, an unseemly tempest raging around him. And all that he had lost was a single arm.

Agnos had achieved the dream he had been tethered to by Neeko years ago. And like the name of his ship, he had shaped a story that sane people would call a myth thousands of years from now.

*Maker of Myths … Sixth of Six.*

The latter title wasn't a product of his own mind, but rather Spirit Queen Apsa's, according to Gray Whale. A lofty weight to put on one's shoulders, but he wasn't one to care much about it. What mattered most to him was the information contained within *Erafeen*. What would he learn from it?

Turning back toward his desk, he grabbed *Erafeen*, set a red string in the crevice of his page, closed, and placed it in the bottom drawer. A fine gold necklace lay on his desk, a tiny key attached. He grabbed that next, locked the drawer, and then bowed his head and placed the necklace around his neck—difficult for a one-armed man. Lastly, he neatly arranged the parchment of translated text into one pile, leaving it atop the desk as he headed for the cabin's exit.

It may have seemed odd, locking away the original text that nobody, outside of himself, could read, while leaving the legible version exposed for those who might trespass upon his quarters. But he did this for a reason. Curious children with wandering eyes were aboard this ship—two of them, to be exact. And seeing that Agnos loved the inquisitive nature of young minds—he had once been young, himself—he figured he could emulate what Neeko had once been to him: a cultivator of wisdom and knowledge.

*  *  *

The door to the captain's cabin creaked open. Two round faces peeked in: Eet and Osh. The cabin kids had seen Agnos enter the quarters of Firefighter Commander Barloe, but they still wanted to make sure the quartermaster wasn't lingering within, as Mr. Tashami would sometimes do.

Eet, the cabin boy, scampered across the room, as Osh, the cabin girl, slowly shut the door behind them. Eet had begun climbing Agnos's chair to get a better look at the translations when Osh swooshed in and pushed him off, climbing up in his place. She giggled quietly. "I'm the reader, remember? You're my audience."

Eet groaned from his defeated position on the floorboards, rolling his eyes in the process. She had always been stronger and smarter than he was, so it made sense, he supposed. Still, he wanted a turn to read.

She smiled and began flicking through the parchment, searching for where they had last left off. Meanwhile, he rounded the desk and sat in a chair, folding his arms with a pout. "Aha!" she exclaimed, eyes stretching wide at the ravaged stack. "Are you ready?"

He huffed. She may have been intelligent and mighty for a nine-year-old, but delicacy was not her forte. If she was to become a scholar, as they both were striving to be, she'd need to develop a proper respect for books. "Go ahead," he said.

She clapped giddily, and then began to read, "I want to begin with the Essence, a paradoxical entity …"

*     *     *

I want to begin with the Essence, a paradoxical entity that frustrates me so. The root cause of both my languor and vigor, it haunts me with dependence while taunting me with power. And I see no way of detaching myself from it, for the symptoms of withdrawal—frailty and mortality—are too a great price.

It feeds me; it loves me. Because of this, I owe it my loyalty. Those are the debts in which I pay. It is both human and metaphysical, taking its natural form of lightning in the Valley of Thunder while I'm away, but molding to that of a man when I come to harvest.

Considering this, do I refer to the Essence as "he" or "it?" Its preference is "he", but I may use them interchangeably in this text.

I've craved him my entire life, but I do not love him. Without his dedication to me, I am no longer the sole bearer of Intel Energy or lightning, but one of many. Civilians—homeless, farmers, and merchants alike—would suddenly have the potential to Weave, for Essence would burst without having me to harvest him, his form expanding around the world. He'd become scattered and lost, a billion tiny pieces of himself … "Currents," he called them.

This is why my loyalty is my greatest form of payment. While he doesn't possess a choice when it comes to feeding or loving me—for choosing not to would be suicide—I do have such choice. I could cease my visits to the Valley of Thunder and no longer harvest the sky, causing his metaphysical form to become too potent, too concentrated without someone to take it from him. His cognitive form would die.

But, for an extensive period, I could not do such a thing. Not because of love, but my lust for that power he gave me, just like the other Originators. Until I met another man, physical and tangible, I stuck by this notion.

154

Mialo, King of Minds, would be the one to help me break my chains. He, I can say, is someone I truly love.

# 14

# The Prim Kingdom

Olivia sat on horseback; Vuilni and Fane flanked her on their own mounts. She peered calmly at the back of the man who was leading them through the sprawling lands of the Prim Kingdom. He wore simple tan robes, a rope tied around his waist, and clogs on his feet. It was a style that reminded her of Agnos. The man's name was Journey, and out of the several dozen people who had been stationed at the Prim Kingdom's teleplatforms, he was the one who had elected to guide Olivia's group to their destination, the capital city Asalka. He called himself a Prowler, or one who traveled the land and shared life with nature. Its deeper meaning sat beyond her desire of inquiry, too abstract for her taste.

It was well past noon, and second-night was upon them. The stars and moon helped illuminate the road, which was more of a trail of grass naturally worn down by frequent travel. This section of road had taken them through the sparse woodlands of the Prim Kingdom's heart. Supposedly, they'd soon cross over Powder River, which Journey had said received its name from the thick coat of black powder blanketing its surface, its source being a mountain range to the northeast.

"I have yet to see a town or village," Fane said, breaking the silence. "This is the main road, correct?"

"Outside of Asalka, there is no road," Journey said. "There is only one trail—the one we currently travel on—connecting the teleplatforms in the west to the capital in the east. In order to reach the kingdom's remote villages, you must blaze your own trail." He paused. "Even then, you still might find that a village isn't anything like what you'd expect."

"Why is that?" Vuilni asked.

"Because our god believes in letting nature prosper unperturbed."

Olivia would have asked who their god was, but she knew better than that. She wouldn't receive an answer.

"Who's your god?" Fane asked for the hundredth time, trying to siphon concrete information out of the Prowler. He was resilient, foolishly so.

Journey turned in his saddle and smirked. "You are a funny one."

"Thanks," Fane said.

The first thing that the Prowlers at the teleplatforms had made clear before accepting the presence of foreigners was their most important law: *Discussion of religion and politics is forbidden.* Based on the severity of their tone, Olivia would have guessed the punishment for asking about it would have been equally so. However, Journey seemed not to mind, understanding the novelty in Fane's persistence. She hoped everyone in this kingdom was like him.

Despite the abstract nature of the Primmish, she found herself internally questioning the identity of their god. One thing was certain: he or she valued nature, maybe even more than civilization.

*     *     *

Black water ran down the mountainside like spilled ink on a gravel road, as rain and powder fell from the sky. Rhyparia took careful steps over rocks, shoes slipping against their slick surface, her umbrella doing little to keep her dry. She and Prakriti were the only two humans who could fit underneath it, while Moros the weasel sat on her shoulder. Therapif could have fit, but the sophisticated rabbit wasn't fond of the idea of being held.

Although it was somewhere between three and five o'clock in the afternoon, in the Dark Realm, that meant these were the hours of second-night. The sun wouldn't show itself again until roughly six o'clock, at which time second-day would begin. The combination of rain, powder, and night made for an impossible trek through the mountains. Iris, the Watcher in charge of protecting Realmular Tunnel, led them with a torch, but the fire died frequently. Rayne was in charge of weaving flame atop the torch, but combating the downpour proved exhausting for her energy, so they came to a stop.

While Iris might have been well-practiced in traversing the rocks in conditions such as this, everyone else wasn't. They situated themselves under a massive flat boulder that jutted out from the mountainside, rain spilling from its edge around them, a wall of black water splattering against stone. Dry stone beneath them offered comfortable footing.

They spread leafy blankets across the ground, the best they had in terms of comfort. After Realmular Tunnel and the early part of the Black Powder Mountains, they now had few belongings outside of what was already on their bodies.

Rhyparia lay next to Moros and Biaza, the weasel's tail absentmindedly brushing against her nose. She frowned and pushed it away.

Moros turned. "How rude," he said with a failed attempt at acting offended.

She stared at the wall of falling water, barely distinguishable through the darkness. Iris was right outside it, standing in the rain like a tree.

"Iris has a strange obsession with nature," she said.

"Is it really all that strange?" Biaza asked. She lay on her back on Rhyparia's other side, arms folded behind her head, gazing fixedly at the stone roof. "You should know by how nature is treated back in Epinio that it would be no different here in Dimiourgos's heartland. While Iris may not speak of it, I bet you he knows of the lynx." Moros writhed within his blanket, entertaining himself with childish shenanigans. "It probably also explains the vegetation he fed us earlier in his cabin."

"You think he's a vegetarian?" Rhyparia asked.

"Unquestionably."

She frowned. "I can't decide whether the Primmish are geniuses or fools."

Moros stopped wiggling about and poked his head out of a hole in the blanket. His beady black eyes locked onto her. "You know, I'm a dimiour. And since dimiours are Primmish, then that makes me Primmish. You better not think me a fool, girl." He said the last bit mockingly, an obnoxious air of primitive royalty in his voice.

"They've been neutral since before even our timeline," Rhyparia said, "during the days of the Originators. Perhaps that has brought them peace for thousands of years, but what wisdom has it gained them beyond what is contained within the Edge of this kingdom? They seal themselves off."

"And suffer less tragedy because of it," he said, his slender frame standing tall. "You know the story of Dimiourgos's downfall. The Dark Courage King slaughtered every animal and as many dimiours as he possibly could, enslaving the humans that followed Dimiourgos in the process. You would think that such a disaster would have a lasting effect."

Biaza, who had stayed relatively quiet, tipped her head to the side to gaze at Rhyparia. "This is her point, Moros," she muttered. He regarded her with a raised brow. "She questions the way of the Primmish not because of 'wisdom' like she says, but because of what was done to them. She questions their backbone."

Moros fell silent, but then looked at Rhyparia. "That's not it, right? This should be clear as day. The Primmish don't believe in retaliation. We don't harm others."

It was odd to hear him speak with such sternness, but his point was valid. However, the years spent training with Musku had not only molded her body at an accelerated pace, but her mind, too. And with it came perspective. All of that time didn't heal the scars her mother had given her, but caused them to fester.

Prakriti, who had been crouching over a medical purse near Therapif, turned toward them. "You know it better than most, Rhyparia," he said. "You spent more time with my father than anyone else."

She had to force herself to not shake her head. Prakriti had a habit of saying things that made her want to gag. His fear of conflict was insufferable. His ethos was very much like Musku's, but at least the old man had strength.

Noticing she wasn't going to respond, he recited that annoying quote that pierced her ears like nails on a chalkboard. "We embark on this quest not to take the lives of those in power, but to save the lives of those who aren't."

Her jaw clenched, masking her rigid gaze behind closed eyes, and she turned her face toward the stone above. The quote was stupid and sounded even more shameful from his mouth. Yes, she'd free the slaves, but she would kill the oppressors and beneficiaries while doing so.

For her dear friend, Vuilni, she'd slay the queen and, in the most literal sense, *crush* the city.

# 15

# Bryson Beckoned

It was just another day of disappointment for Lilu as she sat atop the stage at the head of Steel Field. Weavineers, supposedly the crème de la crème, handpicked by the League of Weavineers themselves, mulled about with a sickening nonchalance. There was no sense of urgency or excitement. And who could blame them? She would have felt the same way had she churned out one dud after another for weeks straight.

Limone's teams had been showing the most improvement, for he proved to be a better leader than Gracie and—to her surprise—Frederick. She'd thought that the licensed weavineer with tutoring experience under his belt would have shined in this position, but even he was having trouble.

She rose from her chair and approached the stairs next to the stage. She climbed down and headed for Frederick. During her walk, she wended between several other groups of weavineers as they huddled around prototypes constructed by Lilu herself. Their reactions to her presence said enough. They didn't scowl or look at her with contempt; they kept their gazes forward, locked onto their tasks, paying her no mind as she swept past. She would have preferred some kind of acknowledgement. Anything was better than pretending that she didn't exist.

*You came here not wanting to be acknowledged as a princess*, she thought. But that never meant she wanted to be treated like a leaf in the wind. In this new position that Wendel had given her—one that she had not earned by birthright—she had expected more respect. *Perhaps I should demand it.*

Part of the problem was the age gap. She browsed the faces of those she passed. Many sported wrinkles, graying beards, and balding heads; others, while not quite as weathered, still had a parental image about them. How did one demand such a thing from men and women more than twice her age? She knew how to command and motivate Limone, Frederick, and Gracie, but they were part of her gerneration.

When compared to other professions, weavineering was a toddler long past the stages of infancy. And while that made it relatively young, it had still been in practice for a couple of centuries. Only in the past few decades—after Mendac established an official trade deal with the Powish—had it begun to really take off. A lot of that progress was thanks to these older minds during their younger years.

She had to keep reminding herself this. Their years of innovation were behind them. They had made their groundbreaking discoveries, but since then had only focused on perfecting them. Now, she was the hatchling with an explorative taste, her trailblazers forced to wrap their minds around her innovations.

She slowed as she neared Frederick's team, standing at a safe distance to avoid distraction while listening from afar. He had a habit of faltering when she was near, not because he wanted to impress her, but because he wanted to look at her. She understood that desire, for she felt the same way about him.

He stood at the head of his group, a curved line of weavineers scattered in front of him. Between the weavineers and himself were five hardened chunks of provod, each the size of a small dresser, lying on the steel floor. At the center sat a lone regular Permanence vessel, a cube of gray stone like every vessel known to man since weavineering's inception. This was the supply source for the cannon, also known as a volter.

It was the circular vessels at each of the four corners that had given everyone the most trouble. They were the energy stores for the travolter's wheels as well as Lilu's patented invention, *rev discs*. These discs were to be placed just behind the wheels, hidden within the travolter's armored body. Their mouths were unique. Instead of a simple latch in the smooth side of a block, the disc had a funnel on one of its two circular sides, the other being perfectly flat. The travolter's wheels attached to the funnel connected to each respective rev disc.

"It's important that the weight distribution of each vessel is properly proportioned according to the percentages on Ms. Intel's blueprints," Frederick said. "A travolter, as you all know, holds five vessels: four rev discs and the volter supply. The rev discs should each represent twenty-two percent of the total vessel weight. That means the volter should only account for twelve. It should be light, creating little strain on the travolter's base, while the rev discs are heavier, serving a multifaceted function. Yes, they cause the wheels to rotate, but they're also the vehicle's anchors at the four corners. They will keep the vehicle from being blown over by a Spiritian's gale—not that we should ever have to worry about such a thing."

Everything he said was correct, although the sheer weight of the travolter itself should be enough to counter attempts at toppling it. Still, she didn't agree with what he was teaching them. What did the weight distribution matter if they couldn't even properly craft a rev disc in the first place? Without those, the vehicle couldn't move.

She approached the funneled side of a disc, gathering stares from Frederick's team. It stood as tall as her shoulders and had rubber wedges lodged between it and the ground to keep it from rolling on its own. She crouched, pressing her lab coat against her thighs with one hand while retrieving a tiny portalight from her pocket. It was a nifty invention, as small as her middle finger, that hadn't been seen beyond the walls of Brilliance yet. She had infused the tiny vessel at its base with EC chains the night before, so it probably had five minutes of soft light available. It wasn't the most practical device, but it did have it uses.

She clicked the button at the butt of its handle and pulled back the funnel's latch, exposing an opening in the shape of a ring that circled a sealed center. She shined the portalight into the funnel's ringed gap, angling it so she could get a proper look inside with one eye. The funnel should have appeared to have two walls, just a half-inch of space between them known as the membrane.

The weavineers struggled with such a concept. The crafting required a very delicate touch and meticulous detailing. Because not only did they have to simultaneously build two vessels—one within the other—but they had to attach the exterior of the smaller vessel to the interior of the larger one with rows of walls to maintain a constant width of the membrane throughout all sides of the funnel. She called these walls *spindles*, and there were hundreds of them that kept the membrane intact, skinny enough to not obstruct the flow of the EC chains within. It was such a time-consuming job, that she had dedicated a position on each team to tackle it.

Frederick tried to continue his lecture, but his stuttering implied she was distracting him. She studied the membrane, impressed by its consistent width. Alas, the mistakes were seen in some other aspect. She frowned as she eyed the ridges of the membrane's two walls, the roadways designed to guide the EC chains through the supply in a predetermined route. In a rev disc, they twisted with the funnel and were intended to guide the chains like the winds of a tornado.

"Who is responsible for crafting this disc?" she asked, standing up to see above the massive circular stone.

Frederick's mouth froze, as did the faces of those around him. Nobody fessed up, but someone volunteered the name of one of their counterparts: "Yila did, Ms. Intel."

Every face turned to a woman with olive skin like Gracie, though not as smooth. Her hair was tied back in a single tail, black streaked with silver. She was older, though not as old as most of the weavineers around her— mid-forties, perhaps. She gazed casually at the man who had ousted her for a moment, then turned toward Lilu. "What did I do wrong, Ms. Intel?"

Lilu's face relaxed. She had expected a harsher response, a tone laced with annoyance. "Take a look at this with me," she said, crouching low once again.

The hollow thuds of heels on the floor carried from around the disc. Yila joined her in a crouched position, white lab coat unbuttoned to reveal a black dress. After a quick peek, she said, "I botched the parallelism."

Lilu's eyes darted toward her, surprised by the quick acknowledgement. *Parallelism* was a method of grooving provod. It was inspired by Limone Lining, a grooving technique that Limone had suggested for the cannon of the volter over a year ago. The idea was to twist the grooves around the pipe to create torque in the Intel Chains, offering a straighter shot when the electricity was expelled into open air … similar to an archer who twisted the feathers of their arrows.

In the rev disc this concept was vital. And because of the two walls that ran parallel to each other, grooves needed to be etched into the minor funnel's exterior and major funnel's interior. Most importantly, the grooves on both walls must follow the same paths. This created a series of tunnels that ran through the membrane, forcing Intel Chains to remain in their lanes. If the grooves didn't align, chains would jump lanes and move erratically, which would ruin the rotational flow and create an errant shot.

"I will get it right," Yila said. "I promise. With each failure, I get better."

Lilu gave a nod and smiled. "I appreciate that drive. I will be keeping tabs on your progress."

Yila grinned and withdrew.

Lilu broke away from Frederick's group and browsed more of Steel Field, electing to hover near Gracie's team. Immediately regretting her decision, she turned away with a sigh.

On her way back to the stage, she felt the atmosphere had changed since she began browsing the field. Sluggish steps had become quick and decisive. Weavineers fidgeted with travolter parts and carved away at their workstations. Sweat even glistened on the brows of a few. She smiled, pleased with what her presence had accomplished. Then she reached the stage and paused; her fleeting satisfaction vanished.

Sitting in Lilu's chair was Wendel LeAnce, a newly pressed suit of blue hugging his lean torso. Today, his blonde hair was slicked to the side with product only the wealthy could afford, and of course his wrists and fingers were decorated with sparkling gold jewelry.

She hovered at the bottom of the steps to the stage. The weavineers hadn't been affected by her; they couldn't have cared less. No, it was the commissioner's presence looming over them. That's all it took for them to move?

She climbed the steps and strolled over to Wendel, coming to a stop at his side. She remained standing, refusing to drag over a seat. He looked up at her with a bemused smirk.

"Must you linger over me like that?" he asked. "It feels like you're one of my wards."

She took a step to her left, creating some distance between them.

He chuckled, resting his gaze on the weavineers. "Curious," he said, "I sit on my balcony oftentimes, but I've never seen them move with such vigor. Now I show my face down here and fear that some of these relics of human beings will throw out their backs with how they hustle." He paused, then asked, "How can we get you to have the same effect?"

Lilu could never achieve such a result with people like this. They were a different breed of Intelian. They'd spent their lives within Brilliance's walls, revering Wendel's last name. The LeAnce family made up the League of Weavineers' board of directors, and Mendac LeAnce was the most important icon of them all. She had destroyed his statue and slandered his name, and that had cast her in a negative light to people like this. However, she would never apologize for it. If that's why they hated her, then so be it.

"Perhaps they need to see you inducted as a LeAnce," Wendel said.

"No." The response slipped out of her mouth faster than she had thought possible, and she knew the man could hear the abhorrent shock in her tone. But if it had affected him in any way, he did a fine job of masking it.

He raised a hand to his face and gently placed closed lips against a ring on his middle finger. His eyebrows were flat, expressionless. He was brooding. "I understand," he muttered against the ring. "Besides, I couldn't undermine your father in such a way. You're an Intel, a royal, and the only family who I feel is my equal."

She was aghast. Had he really just implied that his family was equal to the most powerful, influential royal family in Kuki Sphaira? Centuries ago a man would have been jailed for such a statement. She held her tongue. After a prolonged period of silence, she came to a realization. For the past few weeks she had been trying to find a way to simply approach both Wendel and her father about allowing Bryson to visit Brilliance, never mind convincing them. But *this* … this could work.

"You would say the production of the weavineers has been pitiful, wouldn't you?" she asked.

"That's generous of you," he said.

"They only seem to move when a LeAnce is close by. Since your job mainly requires your presence in the capital above, none of your family can spare much time to visit the Bastion regularly."

He looked up at her. "What is your point?"

"Would you be opposed to welcoming another LeAnce to the city?"

A smile spread across his face. "Not at all."

*　　*　　*

Bryson stabbed at his mashed sweet potatoes, his fork hitting the plate with a clang. He poked and shoveled his food to the sides, toying with it absentmindedly. There was an unsettling familiarity to this scenario he found himself in—locked away in Dunami Palace, forced to sit on his hands. There had been a period of time just before the uprising in Phelos when he had spent nearly a year doing this exact same thing.

"You're doing it again."

He looked up from his meal of potatoes, asparagus, and an onion-smothered steak, locking eyes with Shelly. It was one of his favorite meals, and the princess had requested it for dinner to celebrate an evening with her fiancé. She deserved better. He straightened up and forced a smile, straining the muscles in his cheeks.

"I'm sorry, love," he said, finally scooping up some potatoes and bringing them to his mouth.

"So much sulking," Shelly said. "Yes, you're stuck here with me, but let's not forget what gift that gave us last time we found ourselves in this situation."

His smile softened to something more natural. She spoke of their son, L.K. And she was right.

She placed her fork down and gazed at him from across the table. They were the only two in the personal dining room. A grand window was open on his left, letting the humid, still air of summer seep in. He liked this room, for it lacked the decadence of the grander dining halls. The coziness reminded him of home, or what once had been home. He hadn't visited Debo's house in quite some time … doing so always broke him.

"I think what makes this time around feel worse is the fact that you get to attend meetings in the war corridor," she said. "Hearing about the finer details and strategies of the war while not being able to act on them personally is honestly just a giant tease … is it not? At least when you were stuck in this situation last time, my father didn't grant you access to any meetings, effectively keeping you out of the loop. You didn't know what you were missing."

"When you put it that way, perhaps I should be content with what I have now. I'd rather know what was going on, though."

"Suadade hasn't budged from his stance of silence," she said.

He shrugged. "Thusia must have gotten to him."

"Or maybe someone above him did."

"Maybe."

She had been berating her Branian about Debo's memory ever since learning about it from Bryson. There were several unknowns contained within it, raising more questions than answers. He'd once been adamant about discovering the answers, but Thusia's stance on the subject was firm. For the sake of Bryson and Shelly, she wouldn't divulge any information. Just the fact that they knew about the memory was enough to get them hunted by a Bozani. If that was the case, he wondered, why was he still alive? Months had passed since seeing the memory. But thinking about this only angered him, so he steered the topic elsewhere.

"How are you and your mother getting along with wedding preparations?"

"Just well," she said, lowering her glass of white wine. "Do you suddenly want to partake?"

"I was just curious."

"Listen, this conversation will go nowhere if you pretend to show interest in things you have no interest in. Let my mother and I focus on wedding stuff. I've found that I actually quite enjoy it. Besides, how else am I supposed to spend time in this place?"

"Of course I'm interested in the wedding, though," he said with a pout. "I can't wait for it."

"I know that. The preparations, however, are not your favorite part. And I know where your mind is at."

Silence wafted over the two of them as his thoughts drifted once again. This time he made sure to keep his head up. Two servers entered the room carrying dessert. One placed a plate of three macaroons—violet, green, and red—in front of Shelly. The other gave Bryson a bowl of hand-churned vanilla ice cream.

Halfway through dessert, Shelly dug into the bag at her feet. She held up some folded parchment.

"What's that?" Bryson asked.

"A letter from my sister requesting your presence in Brilliance," she said. "If you decide to accept it, you have my support."

He stood and reached across the small table to grab it. What could Lilu possibly want with him? He opened and read through it:

*Bry,*

*I can't say much. I know Ophala's falcons are notorious for their reliability. I've never heard of one being intercepted or traveling to the wrong location—as long as they know the person they're looking for. Still, the information I want to present to you is too sensitive. I will do my best to make sense while remaining subtle.*

*Before I left Dunami a couple of months ago, I was shown something. I told you I'd use that information to try to seek that something out. The good news is that I think I found it. The bad news is that I can't get to it without your aid. I don't possess what you and my sister do. It's protected by a force you could say you're familiar with. Those scars on your finger are a reminder.*

*That should be all you need to know. I know you're in the midst of certain ceremonious preparations, but I must request your presence. I've found a way to convince the person who leads my city; he is on board with this move. Alas, my father will prove more difficult. He knows of this request, for he has spoken with Brilliance's leader. He doesn't seem convinced.*

*Try to persuade him.*

*Your first friend.*

Bryson stared at the paper incredulously, holding it at a distance. "'Try to persuade him'?" he said. His last bit of ice cream was melting into a pool at the bottom of his bowl.

Shelly, having just finished her last macaroon, dabbed a napkin against her pursed lips. "I had the same reaction at first," she said. "But then I gave it some thought."

"There is no thought to give," he said, tossing the parchment to the middle of the table. "Your father will not agree to this. Besides, I'm not leaving you when we're this close to the wedding."

As he raised his bowl and tipped its contents into his mouth, she rolled her eyes. "The wedding is months away. There is plenty of time. And, once again, stop feigning interest. We both know you want to be doing something proactive in regards to the war. There might be something to Mendac's studies that could help."

"I doubt that," he said from behind the bowl.

"You need to get away from this palace." She sighed. "*I* need you to get away from this palace. You've grown antsy and irritable, and I know the only thing that will cure it is a quest of some sort."

He set the now-empty bowl on the table. Could he really get mad at her for pointing out the obvious? His temper had been quite short as of late. "This is hardly a quest. Besides, there is still the matter of your dad, who is going to say no. Then there's Thusia. Based off her reaction to me knowing about Debo's execution of my father, I doubt she'd be willing to then help me get into the very place where the memory took place. She's been all doom and gloom as of late, and I think she's in trouble in the Empire."

"Suadade has given me updates, however vague they might be. Both of them are going through their version of a trial, but neither of them is in any serious trouble."

"There is still—"

"Yes," she said, cutting him off. "There is still my father, and I know exactly how to handle him." She stood, clapping three times. A couple of servants swept in from a side doorway and began clearing the table. "We have a meeting with my father in ten minutes. Chop chop, love."

*     *     *

Their search for the king brought them to the western grounds, one of the most useless areas of the palace. Its purpose was aesthetics, a place to observe the scenery—massive fields of freshly cut grass separated by smaller gardens or hedge mazes. There were six fields to be exact, each as big as a city block. Bryson didn't envy the people who had to maintain the grass.

As Bryson and Shelly walked across an empty field, the crickets sung around them. The two moons hung overhead, their white light hazy behind the clouds. Barely audible over the chirping insects was boisterous shouting and chants in the distance, growing louder as they neared a hedge wall at the edge of the field.

They stepped through a gap in the hedge and made their way through a few twists and turns of the maze, its walls of thorny green leaves daring them to defy their boundaries. When they exited on the other side, they were welcomed with another expanse of grass. Unlike the previous two fields, this one was occupied.

Ten to fifteen people seemed to be running around like headless chickens. A few zigzagged, and the whole spectacle looked like a broken game of tag, but without the concept of someone being *it*. Everyone chased; everyone evaded. Occasionally, someone tackled. It was violent. This was not a game for children.

As Bryson stood there, motionless and dumbfounded, he slowly made out what was happening. There were sixteen people on the field, half in yellow and half in red to distinguish teams. One person on each team stood in front of a giant rectangular crate sided with rope and bound by plastic bars at the opposite ends of the field, not looking much involved unless the action of the other players migrated toward their end. He still couldn't make sense of the intricacies of the players' movements, but he could see something tiny and illuminated being flung between them. A lot of the action focused around that object.

"Shelly! Bryson!"

They glanced to their right and spotted King Vitio seated in a chair too ornate for outdoor use. He was a royal, however—and an Intelian one at that—so it wasn't that surprising. Bryson approached with Shelly, and a steward fetched two more chairs for them, stealing empty ones from a table of aristocrats nearby. Once the man returned, Bryson settled down and relaxed. He had told Shelly on the way here she'd do the talking since she insisted on not telling him what she had planned. She'd said it was best he stay quiet anyway.

"How was your dinner?" Vitio asked, attention drawn to the activity at the heart of the field.

"Splendid, Father," Shelly said, waving away a drink the steward was offering her. Bryson eagerly motioned for a glass of apple juice. "How has your new hobby been treating you?"

"It's exhilarating!" he said. "And it becomes more so with each night of practice. The players are learning, and because of it, the speed of the game is increasing, the strategies evolving."

Now that Bryson was closer, he saw what was being tossed around the field. It was a tiny glass orb, no bigger than one's fist. Inside was a light that sparked intensely—an Intelight—illuminating everything around it. Those dressed in simple yellow shirts and white pants passed it between each other, sometimes tossing it over great distances in order to cover ground and reach the other side of the field. However, if a pass was intercepted or someone fumbled it, and the orb exchanged hands to someone in red, it would discharge, a reddish flame filling it instead.

"Is this a game of Passionians versus Intelians?" Bryson asked, forgetting his plan to stay quiet.

"That it is, my boy," Vitio said.

The scattered aristocrats bordering the field gasped as a female Passionian threw her shoulder into an Intelian who had been running toward her teammate carrying the orb. He smacked the ground with enough force to leave him squirming for a few seconds, air knocked from his lungs. *So violent*, Bryson thought. *So fun*.

"It's still in its early stages of development, but the creator has been making big leaps in the process. Its evolution has been astounding to witness, and soon it will serve as the replacement for the Generals' Battle. I think the Light Realm has missed having that one annual event when everyone comes together."

Bryson watched as the orb switched hands from an Intelian to a Passionian, the electricity discharging outward as flame ignited within. "But how will other kingdoms get involved with a game such as this? What would an Adrenian or Archain fill the orb with?"

"That is something Rynoia is trying to figure out," the king said. "For now, it is Passionians against Intelians. It might not always be structured that way, however. We might compose teams so that they each have people native from different kingdoms, each serving their own role. We'll see."

Bryson nodded, in awe of the competition.

"Father, don't you think your focus should be on the Rogue Demon?" Shelly asked with little interest.

He groaned. "I spend the entirety of my days focusing on the war. This is my brief escape. And the realm could use a little escape once all of this is over." He smiled. "A sport such as this could provide exactly that."

They watched in silence for a protracted moment. Bryson had become entranced by a young man who had a habit of flipping over attempted tackles.

"Father, I assume you know why I've requested this little get-together," she said.

He clenched his teeth as he watched an Intelian just nearly miss a throw into the rectangular net. A group of Passionian elites cheered from a few tables over. Leaning back in his chair, Vitio looked at his daughter. "Lilu and the commissioner already tried convincing me, but I don't find their reasoning legitimate enough to risk Bryson traveling."

Bryson purposely looked away to hide his face, then stuck out his tongue in disgust.

"I don't know what they said to you, but I have a good reason of my own," she said.

"Is that so?" he asked, taking a sip of wine. "Let's hear it."

She sat up and puffed out her chest, as if to make herself seem more convincing. "As you know, Bryson still can't weave beyond mere sparks. He's practically reverted to a version of himself from four years ago." Bryson shot her a scornful glance, but she was too focused on Vitio and likely didn't care, anyway. "If the time comes when Toono decides to advance on us, having Bryson at full strength with his entire repertoire of skills would be vital. He is our best soldier, is he not?"

The king nodded as he reached for a glazed bread roll.

"He can't rely on his speed or sparring ability alone," she said. "He needs a way of striking over long distance."

"The boy can move in the blink of an eye," he said. "I think he has long distance covered."

"We have to assume that Toono can move just as fast; he did kill Adren King Supido."

Vitio rose from his seat, screaming as the Intelian man who had interested Bryson leapt and twirled over a would-be tackler. He broke away from the pack, his speed proving superior to everyone else on the field. The Passionian protecting the net spread his legs and bent his knees as a base, preparing to block the throw. The Intelian forcefully stepped to the right mid-stride, but then twitched to the left, sending the man in red toppling over his own feet. The Intelian threw the orb. It became a streak of white light streaming from his hand toward the back of the net.

"*GOAL!*" Vitio bellowed. "*Goal! Goal! Goal!*" He remained standing, celebrating his team's accomplishment with enthusiastic applause. He even cast a satisfied smirk toward some of the tables around him as he returned to his seat.

"Anyway," Shelly said, clearly annoyed by the outburst. "Nyemas Jugtah can restore Bryson's clout. He spoke about it when he came back from the Still Kingdom, before departing for Brilliance."

Bryson snapped his head around, eyes narrowed with suspicion. He had never heard Jugtah mention such a thing. But, if that was the case, then he definitely needed to go—regardless of Vitio's blessing.

It took several moments for the king to relax; his cheeks were still a hearty red from the celebrating. He chuckled and shook his head. "You know what … that's a valid point. If the man can bring people back to life, then the idea of him sparking a stronger current in Bryson's energy canals doesn't seem farfetched." A woman with braided black hair looked at him from the opposite end of the field, and he gave her a thumbs-up gesture. "Plus, you've caught me in a good mood."

That score had apparently won the Intelians the match, for the two teams were now shaking hands and mingling at the center of the field. A few players nursed certain body parts with gentle hands, the aggressive nature of the game having gotten the best of them.

Vitio turned, finally regarding Shelly and Bryson directly. "I must agree with you. Bryson's electricity is a crucial component to his arsenal. That was made clear in the Blizzard of Blood." He paused and pursed his lips. As he stared at Bryson, he scratched at his scruffy beard.

"I don't think I need to be fearful of anything or anyone on the road to Brilliance," Bryson said. "And even if I did, I have Thusia."

Vitio tapped his fingers against his beard, twisting his lips. "I suppose that city might even be safer than here." His gaze shifted to Shelly. "And what about you? You're okay with your fiancé disappearing with a wedding on the horizon?"

"I don't need him by my side all the time, Father. I am fully capable of handling things on my own. He has a job to do."

The king studied his daughter for a moment before nodding. "Wish granted. Let me know when you're ready to leave, and I'll make the arrangements."

*    *    *

"You are a frustrating child."

Bryson expected just such a comment from Queen Delilah. She was strolling through a ceremonial hall, wending between dozens of tables, each of them decorated with a different pattern or color scheme. As usual, L.K. was in her arms. He had a fondness for his grandmother. She passed a table with a sky-blue tablecloth, its ends hanging down the sides before stopping right above the carpet. The plates and bowls were a stark white, and the golden utensils dazzled underneath the Intelight chandeliers that hung from the ceiling. She took one glance at the table and shook her head. A gentleman by her side nodded and scribbled something onto parchment with a quill, a portable easel as a surface.

"I told Shelly I didn't have to go," Bryson said, trailing the queen and her assistant.

Delilah stopped at another table and picked up a goblet with her unoccupied hand, inspecting the gems circling the rim. "And all she heard was 'I don't have to, but I want to.'"

"She's the one who fought for me to go," he said.

"My daughter can be foolish sometimes, Bryson." She split away from the table and sauntered toward another. He had to jog to catch up. "I understood your reason for leaving to the Still Kingdom. That was important to the war and our kingdom's well-being. This, however, seems to hold no purpose."

"My Intel Energy," he said weakly.

She turned on a dime, standing stiff and straight. Her height not only matched his, but bested it—a trait that had been passed on to Lilu, but not Shelly. L.K. slept peacefully in her arms. "If you feel you must go, then who am I to argue? My one condition is that you return before your wedding date in three months."

"Of course."

She extended her arm and, rather unexpectedly, deposited L.K. into his. She waved him away and turned. "Leave."

Bryson stood there for a moment, his son now stirring in his arms. He couldn't help but feel guilty. He had missed the birth of his child, and now this. But he had to keep reminding himself of what Ophala had told him. Without the world, what did he have to give his son?

# 16

# Accus Canyon

The thick canopies above blocked the moonlight, casting ominous shadows across the forest floor. Without a torch for light, Yama minced through Spunka Forest, careful of the nocturnal snakes that liked to slither through the grass. But considering the jungle's name, snakes were the least of her worries. Spunka prowled in the shadows. Like most of the animals in this area, they were highly active at night, searching for rabbit holes or birds' nests to ambush. Their favorite prey was anything asleep, but if a human entered their territory, they wouldn't shy away from confrontation.

She traveled through the jungle's region unclaimed by the Brench Estate, simply trying to break free of its cusp and into the vast prairie that separated the sprawling jungle—the largest woodland outside of the Lingens Rainforest—and a tiny, remote village in the southwestern corner of the Adren Kingdom known as Yinyon, which sat about a thousand leagues away from the capital, Katashi. It was closer to the Edge than any other habitable community in the Light Realm.

Trying to remember her early childhood was like looking at a street Intelamp on a foggy morning just before dawn. She could see it was there, but deciphering any details was impossible. She remembered being taken to the Adren Assistance Academy at a very young age, but couldn't recall who had escorted her.

A woman with violet hair and a soft face with subtle angles to the jawline. She had given Yama a bag before leaving the little girl alone at AAA. Oblong and wonky, it was difficult to carry on her back, but she had managed. When she scoured the contents of the bag later that night, she had found a spandex bodysuit, sword, and note. The bodysuit was too large for her childlike frame, the sword too heavy.

The note had given her obscure directions, and she wound up following them for more than a decade. It all faltered after being inducted into the Jestivan. Jilly Lamay became her focus. Then, when that relationship disintegrated, she returned to Toono to aid his efforts towards accumulating sacrifices.

Only recently had it dawned on her, as she sat next to the corpse of Director Buredo, the man who mentored her at Phesaw. She didn't have the note given to her by that violet-haired woman anymore, but its message was engrained in her memory:

*When your speed percentage reaches eighty-two, return to Yinyon. You will fight the fastest person alive, and the outcome of said duel will determine if we teach you or not. Don't return prematurely. I beg you to heed this rule.*

*   *   *

"We'll call it a day here," Horos said.

He, Kuiku, and Toshik had finally made it to the outer edge of Tames Forest, where trees were sparse but just dense enough to enable one to hide from any wanderers—not that they should have had to worry about such things. There weren't any roads, villages, or farmlands nearby.

Horos wove a perimeter of regular black flames that would blend in with the forest's shadows. As the two older men worked on the tent,

Toshik collected sticks and a couple of fallen branches. He dragged the tinder to their campsite and dropped it in a pile. He drew his sword and hacked a couple of the bigger branches into smaller sections, adding a few of them to the pile as well. The rest he'd save for later. It took a few minutes to get a small fire going, its vivid orange light waning as it neared the wall of black flames surrounding them. He took a seat in the grass as Horos and Kuiku finished the tent.

An hour passed, and the two men talked and laughed, sharing stories about their lives to one another. Toshik simply stared at his sword on his lap, wishing he had the same kind of memories to share. But if he were to open his mouth, he'd only vomit words of self-pity. He did enough pouting as it was.

"Toono definitely knows we're here," Horos said after a short lull.

Kuiku nodded. "The fact that we weren't attacked at the telecluster was suspicious. A few scouts were probably nearby."

"Then why'd we take this long, arching path?" Toshik asked, forcing himself into the discussion. "If we were recorded going in this direction, then he knows about our plan to circle the kingdom and avoid the main roads. This whole idea was to move unpredictably."

"Not exactly," Horos said. "This route isn't about that as much as it is about being an inconvenience for Toono. Undoubtedly the man has forces spread across the entire kingdom, but the majority of them will be concentrated in the big cities or on the main roads as checkpoints. With the path we're taking now, he'll either have to rely on weaker forces in the distant towns or deploy scouting units to track us in the wilds. That's a hassle."

"That's if he's even worried," Kuiku said, pulling a gutted rabbit skewered on a stick from the fire. "There are definitely people searching for us, but he won't dedicate all of his resources to the task. As long as he's bunkered down in Cogdan—assuming he's there—he'll feel safe."

Toshik remained outside near the dying fire even after Kuiku had entered the tent to get some sleep. The fire was small enough to not require the wall of black flames anymore, so Horos relinquished it, standing with a groan. "My age is starting to show more and more as each day passes."

Toshik remained quiet, staring at his spunka blade. Just faintly, he could see the assassin's shadow lingering over him. "What is it?" Toshik asked.

Horos paused before answering. "Do you resent me because of my relationship with Ophala?"

The young swordsman bit his lip in frustration. Why did everyone think he held some sort of grudge toward that woman? She'd had every right to do what she'd done. Did they not think he understood this? Or did they simply pity him because Toth Brench was the last family member he had?

"I don't resent you or your wife," he finally muttered. Oddly enough, he thought of of the first time he'd met Olivia. She'd been such a strange girl, with that expressionless face of stone. Now he understood her. "I resent the human mind, its ability to create emotion, and the shackles of love and empathy, whose only purpose of existence is to bind us to an eventual heartbreak." He fought back tears, forcing a steadiness to his voice. "I resent living when all others die."

Horos's shadow remained still. "Foolish, but honorable. You have the heart of a warrior."

*　　*　　*

Himitsu stood at the edge of the western precipice of Accus Canyon, staring down at the boulder-strewn ground a thousand feet below. Nearly fifty leagues to the east stood the canyon's opposite wall, concave and even taller and more daunting than the one he currently stood upon. Having had experience with a natural formation such as the Dev Kingdom's Necrosis Valley, he hadn't expected much. But this canyon made such a place look like a shallow trough. It looked like the moon had crash-landed, carving out a winding chunk of the crust.

"For comparison," Kaylee said, squinting against the beaming sun, "if you were to place the tallest mountain in the Bliss Peaks on the floor of Accus Canyon, its summit wouldn't even reach this precipice, and this is considered one of the wall's shorter points."

He shook his head in awe. He'd seen the Bliss Peaks when traveling through them with Kaylee, Fane, and his dad. While they were by no means the grandest mountain range, they were still mountains.

"I've never liked the stories surrounding this place," Sal said from behind, keeping his distance from the edge.

"What stories?" Himitsu asked. "Those preposterous fables about monsters?"

"No, not that," Sal muttered.

"Archains grow up hearing tales about Accus Canyon," Kaylee explained, "how it's a place where people go to offer their life to the First of Five."

Himitsu balked. "They jump?" He inched backward in horror. "They kill themselves for the sake of some man?"

Kaylee shrugged. "I think it's just the kingdom's way of putting a not-so-depressing spin on it. In reality, it's where people who have given up on their life go to end it. Then they tell themselves that they're doing it for Gatal Accus, even though most people know the First of Five would never advocate such a thing."

He backed away farther, until he was standing shoulder to shoulder with Sal. Suddenly, his insides crawled with discomfort. Suicide was such a frightening idea. Even during his alcoholic rampage following the imprisonment of his parents, the thought of killing himself had seemed too drastic. He would rather have lived in misery.

She turned, brushing back a fallen strand of silvery hair behind her ear, and frowned slightly at the two young men. "Don't act so cold toward them. If anything, we should reflect on the flaws in our world that would drive someone to a point such as this. Take Lost Wisdom for example. That environment fosters depression or anger, or both." She turned toward the canyon again. "Do you know why the orphans are taken here as a 'vacation'?"

"This is not somewhere to bring children," Himitsu said, crinkling his nose.

"Exactly," Kaylee said, a gust of wind rippling her ankle-length skirt. "Fortunately, I was never brought here, but that was due to Neeko's sway. I never knew why they came here, and I still don't, but it's likely for an evil reason. Children never spoke of it whenever they returned. A lot of them spent days in the building's medical quarters after the experience."

Despite the heavy heat, Sal shivered. "Do they usually overstay when visiting?"

She paused, and her tone grew softer. "No. Something is wrong, and we'll find out what."

*     *     *

Himitsu looked into the eyes of Skyrise, the falcon assigned as a line of communication between his mother and himself. The winged predator was listening intently while perched on his gloved hand.

"Can you help us search the canyon? It's too vast for three people to comb. Let us know if you find anything out of the ordinary. We're looking for a group of children, possibly led by an adult."

The falcon took flight.

"So, were you speaking to your mom or the bird?" Sal asked.

"The bird," Himitsu said. He continued following the switchbacks of the canyon's wall. It was treacherous, just wide enough for two people to walk side by side. "My mom doesn't have direct interaction with a bird at this distance. She's all the way in the capital. That would take divine weaving ability. Still, Skyrise is familiar with me and will do as I ask."

"He can understand humans?" Sal asked.

"After decades of working with my mother, yes. He's learned the Sphairian language."

"Fascinating," Kaylee said. "Now if we could only get it to talk."

Sal frowned. "Please don't. That'd be weird."

Himitsu smirked at the thought of a talking animal. He wished they had met Meow Meow.

After an hour's descent, Sal had already emptied one of only a dozen waterskins they had brought with them.

"Slow down," Kaylee said. "I don't want to get stuck down here without water."

"I can't survive on the same kind of rations that you and Himitsu do."

"I may not have your bulk, but I'm tall," Himitsu said. "If I can get by on what Kaylee suggests, then you can, too."

"Hmm … where did you get your height from?" Sal asked. "Your dad is average for a male, and your mom, while taller than most women I've seen, is only about six feet."

"My grandfather on both sides," Himitsu said. "My mom's dad was six-three; my dad's dad was nearly seven feet. He actually suffered from unimaginable back pain, which made him hunch to about my current height."

Kaylee looked up at him. "Let's hope all of your growth spurts are behind you."

"Is my height stopping you from declaring your love?" he asked, playfully curling his lips.

She looked forward again, shaking her head. "This I do not like."

He pouted. "So it is my height?"

"No … not yet, at least. It's the shades of confidence that are beginning to swirl within your aura. Don't try anything foolish with me."

He laughed. "Is that what you take me for? A fool?"

Sal jabbed the back of his shoulder.

"More like a buffoon," she said.

*　　*　　*

The sun had set by the time they reached the canyon's floor. The cool wind nipped at Himitsu's ears. The terrain—rocky, dry, and uneven—was not suited for camping. Plant life was sparse, but weeds of some sort speckled the ground every hundred feet or so. Kaylee, of course, knew the names of all of them. What kind of sane adult would travel through this canyon for sport, let alone take a class of children along with them?

They relied on moonlight to guide them, sticking to the wider parts of the canyon so that the cliffsides wouldn't cast them into shadow. Eventually, they stopped near the western side and set up camp for the night. They didn't use a tent, for the ground was rock, and there was no way to hammer a stake into it. Perhaps Olivia or Vuilni could have made it work, but both of them were in a different realm, and he doubted Sal could match their strength.

Sal made himself comfortable on the stone ground. When Himitsu questioned his sanity, he explained his living situation as a child, and how he was used to hard surfaces for rest. Only his parents had been allotted a bed.

Now Himitsu found himself wandering, stepping across piles of rock that had long since crumbled due to erosion from the precipice above. If he was a religious zealot, the answer to what had caused all of this wouldn't have been something so mundane. He would have credited this canyon's formation to a Bozani, acting on behalf of a man named Gatal Accus, the *First of Five*. And not just any Bozani, like Bryson or Shelly's Branian.

He chuckled to himself. Out of the *Of Five* tales, the *First of Five* was the most unimaginable. Redirecting an incoming meteorite? Yeah, right. Sure, Gatal hadn't been the one to do it, but he had supposedly done the impossible task of summoning Magnifica, a female Bozani of some unknown rank, to act on his behalf. He wasn't a royal firstborn, so he shouldn't have been able to achieve this feat. The fairy tale credited the phenomenon to his religious past.

Of course, most scholars believed there never was a meteorite. Gatal Accus had simply escaped to this canyon to hide from the king of his time period. Back then, every royal family save the Primmish tried to eradicate anybody who practiced religion. It had been a major contributor to the loss of records about the time before Known History.

"What are you up to with that brooding face of yours?"

Himitsu glanced back over his shoulder to see Kaylee, hands grasped behind her back. He looked forward again, into the darkness. "Fairy tales and legends."

"Father Accus?" she asked.

His face twisted, but he kept it hidden from her gaze. "Father?"

"That was how you addressed a priest way back then." Stone jostled against stone, rubble tumbling down the pile as she approached. "Priests were the most powerful and insightful individuals during the first two centuries of Known History. They scared the royals. They did things that should have been impossible."

He looked at her out of the corner of his eye with suspicion in his furrowed brows. "Don't tell me you believe a giant rock from the sky actually crashed here."

"I don't know what I believe," she said. "But I've read a lot of books, a few cruelly-drawn almanacs from days past. Do you know the one constant about the maps depicting the Light Morality Kingdom during the first two centuries?"

"No."

"There was no canyon," she said. "This area had been farmlands and scattered villages, the main city being Balle."

"I didn't know that," he said with an air of intrigue.

"I don't think many do … except for Neeko and his few students. He'd obtained those almanacs from the deepest parts of the Warpfinate. I'd be willing to bet only a handful of people have reached far enough to find them." Silence followed. "Anyway, I don't know exactly how this canyon was formed, but I do know there was a time when this land was completely flat."

"Surely, there'd be a giant sky-rock sitting at the end of the canyon if the stories were true," he said. "No way could anybody have moved it."

"And that's a solid argument. But let's say the story didn't lie about Magnifica redirecting the meteorite … would it then be so farfetched to think she couldn't toss it back where it came from?"

He didn't respond. His stare roved toward the stars, finding the shadowed underbelly of the floating island believed to house the Light Empire. Could the Bozani see all of the kingdoms from up there? Did they watch certain individuals? To think Thusia and Suadade were part of only the bottom tier of the Bozani's hierarchy was mortifying.

He and Kaylee eventually turned to head back to camp—if one could even call it that. His foot caught on something long and narrow. He fell forward, arms extended in front of him. His hands received the brunt of the impact. Cursing under his breath, he pushed himself up. A cut ran across the palm of his right hand, causing blood to seep down to his wrist.

"What kind of rock ..." He paused as he glanced back, noticing the culprit. Kaylee was already crouched, inspecting the strange form. "Is that a bone?" he asked.

She gave a slow nod. "A tibia, to be exact."

# 17

# The Sixth of Six

DaiSo's harbor grew larger as the Mythmaker approached, signaling the end of Agnos and Tashami's second voyage as pirates. Working in tandem with Captain Gray Whale, Agnos had discovered a primordial text in a cave hidden within tumultuous waters. But nobody outside of Tashami and Gray Whale really knew the lengths he had gone to find it. From the mystical beast of the ocean's depths to the celestial light that protected the chronicle, the very oddity responsible for his now-inoperable arm, there were parts to the tale that would go unaccounted for.

It came as no surprise to Agnos's crew when they spotted a horde of pirates swarming DaiSo's beach, awaiting the arrival of Captain Agnos and Quartermaster Tashami. They were young, barely over the age of twenty, but their grandeur voyages dwarfed those of even the eldest captains.

Tashami smiled, leaning against the rail of the main deck, his ivory hair rustling in the gulf's breeze. Agnos also couldn't hide the bliss. He was returning home, and who would have thought it'd be a place such as this, where brawls were commonplace in the dirt streets and people practically bathed in alcohol.

Perhaps it was the appearance of the town—run-down wooden shanties, backwoods accents, dust-choked air, cramped roads, and horse refuse—but there had been a time when such a place terrified and disgusted him. Now he cherished it.

"Keep a careful eye on Erafeen while in DaiSo," Tashami said.

Agnos scoffed, as if he would forget such a thing. While he had grown accustomed to the way of living in the town, that didn't mean he was comfortable with every aspect. Thievery and pirates went hand in hand like Toshik and a flock of girls. He may have had a formidable crew and respected allies, but that didn't mean no one would try anything stupid.

Oftentimes, when a lesser crew returned from a voyage with riches, a rival crew would attempt to steal their treasures. This meant the assassination of a captain was also a common occurrence. These issues typically didn't apply to the upper strata of the piratical hierarchy, but Agnos thought it better to be safe than sorry. Though he took solace in the fact that his "treasure" wouldn't have meant much in the hands of anyone but him, why risk it?

Over the past few weeks it had seemed of little value to Agnos, too. The Technous language, according to Director Senex's discourse on the subject years ago, possessed over a hundred characters and symbols, each of which took a different meaning depending on the characters surrounding it. This meant there were hundreds of thousands of different patterns that needed to be deciphered before discovering the identity of one or two symbols. Translating Technous was challenging even for him, someone who had the aid of his relic and superior weaving skills.

The Thunder Queen's atrocious penmanship made the complexity of the Technous language only half the battle. Because of this, Agnos was forced to guess at certain symbols based off the context clues surrounding them.

As the Mythmaker entered the harbor, it headed for the Whale Lord. Gray Whale had gone ahead much earlier in the voyage, electing to reach DaiSo quicker than planned due to a lack of supplies on her ship. He had offered her some of his, but she was persistent on declining for some inexplicable reason. She had spoken of tending to matters in DaiSo, so clearly it had nothing to do with supplies.

"Drop the anchors!" Barloe shouted from the quarterdeck, where he stood next to Gunther on the helm. Zorra stood on Gunther's other side, wearing a long robe of midnight blue that draped over her shoulders and wrapped around her body. Her hair was woven into a single braid, long and thick. She grinned in Agnos's direction, offering a nod. He returned the gesture and turned back toward the beach.

"Do you hear that?" Tashami asked.

"I do!" Eet shouted, bouncing on his tiptoes, hands grasping onto the rail's wooden bars. He and Osh flanked Tashami and Agnos. The two children had spent the last few days of the journey moping, not wanting to return home. Now that they were this close, their attitude seemed to have changed.

"They're chanting something," Agnos said. The gentle sloshing of the gulf's waters and cries of the seagulls overhead made it impossible to make out any words.

They watched the pirates pump their fists in the air for a long moment until the longboats were ready to be lowered into the water. Agnos glanced over at the Whale Lord, half expecting to find Gray Whale standing on the deck, observing from a distance. She rarely left her ship, even when it was anchored in the harbor between voyages. Instead, he found it barren, sails rolled up and tied to their masts.

"Now what are they doing?" Tashami asked.

Agnos looked back at the crowd. It had begun to part near the right side, a path widening for two people. One hobbled and the other sat atop a great tan horse, an honor guard in sky-blue uniforms trailing her. They broke free from the masses, stopping upon a clear strip of beach between the pirates and the edge of low tide.

Gray Whale stood with her hands in her pockets, an unreadable line in her lips. The woman atop the horse, however, waved in the direction of the Mythmaker. She towered over everybody around her. From this distance and the angle at which Agnos was looking at her, she seemed grander than the downtrodden buildings serving as the beach's backdrop. That elegant blue dress hung down the horse's sides, sparkling like a kaleidoscope of ice under the sun.

The Mythmaker's safe return had been enough to beckon Spirit Queen Apsa into a town of pirates.

*     *     *

Agnos's longboat hit shore. He allowed Zorra, Eet, Osh, and Tashami to step out first. Tashami reached back to assist his captain. Agnos grabbed his hand and was pulled over the boat's edge, his feet becoming submerged in the cold waters. The chanting started again as he retrieved his clogs and tucked them under his arm. A few pirates rushed forward to grab the boat and drag it onto the beach. He looked up to see the queen smiling at him from her mount.

He stepped out of the water, his toes digging into the wet sand from an earlier high tide. The chanting was now thunderous.

*"SIXTH OF SIX! SIXTH OF SIX! SIXTH OF SIX!"*

He was both appreciative and amused. Did they even understand the significance of what he'd discovered? Never mind that. Did they even know *what* he'd discovered? It was unlikely. Only a select few knew of what he'd hunted.

The Spiritian honor guard thrust their hands into the air, palms open to the sky. Gusts of wind erupted from the ground, and the crowd fell silent. It was a Spiritian method of requesting silence.

Apsa gently tapped the side of her horse's neck, sending the stallion into a light trot toward the two former Jestivan. It was a beautiful animal with a spotless tan coat, its mane and tail a light cream. It snorted as it came to a stop just a few paces away.

Swinging her leg over effortlessly, the queen stepped down from the mount without the need of assistance, proving true the rumors about her height. The fact that she was wearing a dress made it even more impressive—even if it was one suited for riding.

"To be in the graces of the Sixth of Six and his great companion," she said, pearly whites exposed. "What an honor."

"No, the honor is ours, milady," Agnos said as both he and Tashami bowed.

She raised her chin just a bit and might have given a prideful nod—and deservingly so. She was a royal head, the most powerful rank outside of the Empires. And she'd been the main reason why Toth Brench never received his shipment of funds to aid his upheaval of the Amendment Order. She'd persuaded Gray Whale to chase the galleon and do whatever it took in regards to the Adren naval fleet serving as escort. If any of that hadn't happened, who knew how powerful Toth's clutches would have been on the Archaic Kingdom. Most would have called her the integral piece of causing the man's plans to flounder.

"I hope the thing you've been chasing was worth the effort," she said.

"It was. And now that I have it, it seems the effort I put into chasing it was only the first hurdle."

"Well, I don't doubt your capabilities to figure it out."

"While your presence here is flattering, Queen Apsa," Tashami said, "I'm assuming there is an ulterior motive outside of welcoming us home."

"Of course, but we must retire to somewhere private."

Agnos looked toward Zorra, who was standing off to the side, watching with wide eyes. "I believe my navigator can accommodate us, milady."

*    *    *

Agnos, Tashami, and Apsa walked up the stairs to Flailing Fin's second floor. Eet and Osh trailed them, struggling to drag a case of Agnos's belongings up the steps. Osh pulled with two hands from the top, keeping both feet planted and squealing as she yanked. Eet stood at the bottom end, using his shoulder and entire right side of his head to push it upward.

"Are you sure you don't need help?" Tashami asked, turning around and walking backward.

"We've got this!" Osh screamed.

Once they entered the room, they waited for the two cabin kids to drag the trunk in. A minute later, Eet dropped the raised end of the trunk on the wooden floorboards, sweat lathering his face. Agnos thanked and dismissed them with a wink.

The door closed. Agnos took a seat on his bed, Tashami sat on the floor, and Apsa remained standing. There weren't any chairs in the room. Maybe he should have offered her the bed?

"You must have a lot of stuff in that trunk," she said.

Agnos almost admitted to not having many belongings, but then that would have raised unwanted questions. Inside the trunk was *Erafeen*, but it was the other item that worried him: Orbaculum. The ancient piece would have been immediately recognizable to a woman like Apsa. The royal heads had been briefed many times about Toono's old ancient, the staff that could create elastic orbs of steel. If she discovered Agnos had it, the tone of this meeting would take a terrible shift. He had no intention of telling her he knew Toono had been in the Spirit Kingdom.

"I like to keep my property under personal surveillance," he said.

"That makes sense," she said. Her gaze grew austere. "How much information have you been privy to about happenings on land?"

"None," Tashami said. "Unless Agnos has been withholding information from me, Pilot Ophala hasn't been keeping in touch with us."

"She hasn't," Agnos said. "What news do you have, milady? I'm sure a lot has happened."

"We'll start with the good news," she said. "Thanks to Pilot Ophala, Toth's regime wound up being short-lived. She executed a clever, manipulative scheme that resulted in his death by her hands."

The two Jestivan exchanged looks. "Do you know how Toshik is doing?" Agnos asked.

"Considerably well, to the surprise of many. He's currently on a mission in the Dev Kingdom. We don't know if we should be impressed or concerned with the composure he's shown."

Agnos dropped his head. "Concerned."

"It's created a resolve in the young man that I have no intentions of extinguishing."

He frowned, taken aback by the lack of empathy in her statement. He remained silent, however.

"Toono has achieved his eighth and ninth sacrifices," she said, "taking the lives of both Adren King Supido and Dev King Storshae."

Agnos chose not to meet eyes with Tashami, knowing the judgmental gaze he'd receive. If there was one thing Tashami had always been vocal about, it was Agnos's refusal to outright acknowledge the evil that was Toono.

"As one can assume," Apsa continued, "True Light is now preparing for the climax of the Rogue Demon's plan. He has one sacrifice left to obtain … an Intelian."

"That should narrow down his targets considerably," Agnos said. "Bryson, King Vitio, Princess Shelly, or Lilu. Each of them is bunkered within a highly secure area, correct?"

"They are, but they don't have much protection outside of high-ranking military officials. And it's not like royal heads of other kingdoms can spend their time playing guard at the teleplatforms."

"No offense, but if the past is any proof, even royal heads won't be able to stop Toono," Tashami said. "Unless they possess a Branian."

She nodded. "I know this. Archaic King Sigmund and Intel Princess Shelly are the only two Light Realm royals with a Branian. Bryson counts as a third even though he is, by definition, a Dark Realm royal." She glanced at the floor, pressing her lips together and furrowing her brows. "I still don't understand how that young man has a Branian and not a Bewahr."

"What about other Jestivan?" Agnos asked. "Can't they act as guards to Dunami and Brilliance? You said Toshik is away on a mission, but there are a few others who'd be willing to play the part."

"They're all occupied with their own missions," she said, shaking her head.

Tashami raised a brow. "Why? Shouldn't their focus be on the direst threat?"

"We believe we can make a better decision on how to handle Toono if we know more about his past and the people he works alongside. Himitsu, Olivia, and Vuilni are chasing those answers."

Agnos scratched at his chin. "And Rhyparia's whereabouts—if she's not already dead—are unknown, Lilu's in Brilliance, Yama's a traitor, and Jilly's dead." He paused, sharing a glance with Tashami and coming to an unspoken understanding. He regarded the queen. "So you've come to us, the only two remaining Jestivan."

"That I have," she said, face grave. "The two of you are best friends. You've been by each other's side since the Jestivan formed, have you not? Agnos, you helped Tashami find his father in the depths of the Void, and Tashami, you helped Agnos find his dream on the bottom of the ocean."

"I suppose," Agnos said. "What do you need from us?"

She fell silent, her gaze flicking between the two pirates. "I need the two of you to split up."

Agnos was up from his bed in a heartbeat, face incredulous. After prefacing her request with praise of their uniformity, he had expected something along the lines of a team mission. But to split away from the one man who had stayed by his side through thick and thin? Well, that was absurd!

"Whatever it is you want us to do, Queen Apsa, I assure you we'd be better together!" Agnos exclaimed.

"It would be physically impossible."

"Can we not both stand guard at the teleplatforms?" Agnos pleaded. "Or do you plan on splitting us between Dunami and Brilliance? Please don't fault me for pointing out the obvious flaw in such a tactic, but I cannot fight—especially not alone and missing an arm."

She waited, perhaps for him to slow his breaths and regain his composure. "I want to station Tashami at the teleplatforms."

"Then let me—"

"As for you, Agnos," she said softly, somehow overpowering his desperate rebuttal, "I require your presence to remain on your ship, the Mythmaker. It needs its captain for what lies on the horizon. The crew, an exceptional one at that, will lose motivation if you're not leading it. That would be a death sentence when embarking on a journey through a whirlpool."

"Whirlpool? I've never used one in my life. What would make you think I could guide a ship through one?" After a pause, he asked, "And why would I want to?"

"To infiltrate the Dark Sea and attack the Dev Kingdom from water rather than land. And you'd have the help of the Whale Lord. Captain Gray has agreed to travel alongside you, just like she did on your previous voyage. She can guide you through the whirlpool."

"You don't need me for that," Agnos said.

Apsa tilted her head, peering at him with intrigue. "I'll admit. People who know you have only raved about your temperament to me, yet I am not witnessing it. Tashami matters very much to you." She gave an understanding nod. "I see. Well, I want both of you to talk this over."

She pulled up the sleeve of her dress, exposing a silver watch that wrapped around the widest part of her forearm. "I do ask that you come to a decision quickly. I must return to Saido by nightfall. I hope you come to the right decision, for I've already brought over some of the most talented members of my navy and a special guest. I would hate to have wasted their time." And with that, she turned and exited the room.

Tashami spun to face Agnos. "The time has come."

Agnos balked, lowering himself onto the bed. "Are you kidding me?"

"Not in the slightest. This plan makes sense, and at this point we need to do what's best for the world. I know we've identified as pirates as of late, but what are we really?" He sighed, gazing at the floor. "I'm a Zana of the Jestivan, as are you. We were given this position to fight bad people. Right now, there is an immediate threat to the Light Realm's safety, and that's Toono. We need to make sure he doesn't succeed at bringing Dev King Rehn back to life, and we do that by defending one front while attacking the other."

Agnos stared at Tashami, words struggling to escape his trembling lips. Why was committing to this so difficult? Was it because he didn't want to experience losing a best friend again, like with Toono?

Agnos had let Toono go, and that boy he had known died and been replaced with something evil. If he were to allow Tashami to escape his clutches, it was possible that death would come for him. But was this not selfish thinking? Just a month ago, he'd gone into the depths of the Sea of

Light, risking life and limb to find a book, knowing that death was far more likely than escape. He had been willing to leave Tashami stranded.

"This can be your retribution, Agnos."

Agnos's gaze refocused on Tashami, knowing what those words implied. He had sat idly by for too long while Toono wreaked havoc around the world. It did eat at his heart, becoming an ethical conundrum. While Toono committed evil acts, Agnos refused to scorn him for it. He'd ignore the evil in favor of the memories he had shared with that innocent boy in the orphanage. He couldn't defeat evil by pretending it didn't exist, all because he had that privilege. He needed to stop playing the ignorance card and take action. He could storm the Dev Kingdom and end Toono's reign.

*No, I can't*, he thought. *That's not who I am.* Realizing this, he muttered, "I'm not a fighter, Tashami."

"You'll have fighters around you. You just need to lead them."

Agnos gazed at the trunk resting askew against the far wall. No matter what Tashami said, it didn't change his mind. But if Tashami wanted this, then who was he to say no? He lay back onto the bed, placing his hand over his wet eyes. "Tell Queen Apsa we accept her request."

After a long pause, Tashami asked, "Can we not bring her back in here?"

"Leave me for now. I need a reprieve."

# 18

# Asalka

Rhyparia's group had escaped the Black Powder Mountains a day ago. According to Watcher Iris, they'd reach the outer reaches of the capital just before first-nightfall, putting their arrival time between eleven o'clock and midnight.

They used the eastern bank of Headless Lake as guidance south to Asalka. The lake, however, was difficult to see when consumed by grasslands as untamed as this one. The grass was as tall as Rhyparia, permitting distant vision to only the tallest of the group: Atarax, Saikatto, and Kakos. Benefitting from his smaller stature, Moros had hitched a ride on Atarax's shoulder, careful to keep his body and face cloaked.

Rhyparia shook her head as she watched from behind. This really had been a terribly thought-out plan. While the dimiours had tied their tails to one of their legs with rope, keeping them from absentmindedly lashing about beneath the cloak, one couldn't look past the smaller statures of Moros, Biaza, and Therapif. Perhaps Biaza could be mistaken for a child, but not a weasel or rabbit. They were too short, their frames too odd. And Therapif could barely walk without accidentally hopping every several steps.

"Why have you not questioned us further, Iris?" Rhyparia asked. "Why were you so eager to lead us here? Did you actually see us escape the tunnel?"

"Quite a barrage of questions," he said. "I suppose I'll answer the last one first. I didn't see you escape the tunnel with my own eyes, but I believe you when you say you did. Certain individuals in your group intrigue me, which should come as no surprise."

"Are you making fun of my height?" Moros asked from his perch atop Atarax's shoulder.

Iris gazed back at the veiled pair, smiling. "Even your tone is strikingly unique."

"This is why I ask," Rhyparia said. "What are your plans with us?"

"Let me first assure you of your safety," he said, turning forward again. She cocked a brow. "There is no ill intent behind my guidance. However, I am bringing you to the capital for judgment. The Monsignors won't be happy I abandoned my post, but when I present them with your group, they will understand—or so I hope."

Her eyes narrowed. Judgment? Were they to be put on trial for nothing? Her disdain for Iris's vagueness had grown exponentially over the past two weeks. It was beginning to boil over. "If anyone tries to harm us …"

"Then you will retaliate," the Watcher said, nodding. "But do not fret about such an implausible outcome. The Primmish may be stern—and on the rare occasion, violent—but in regards to foreigners, their desire not to create international friction casts a lenient nature upon their judgments. With that said, the kind of trial you will be faced with is unordinary, to the point of never-before-seen. The Monsignors are never summoned, for they are religious recluses. Priests normally act as jurors."

Kakos growled, and she glared at him. Nothing about it sounded human. The wolf didn't seem to care. "You all sound like lunatics."

"Perhaps it works in our favor," Iris said. "It might explain why other kingdoms do not bother with us. Besides, to us, the rest of the world is ludicrous—blasphemous, even. The abolishment of religion in Known

History's first two centuries was a curse to their cultures. Heretics, they are."

Nobody disturbed Iris for the next few hours. The group split into smaller ones, conversing amongst one another as they walked. Rhyparia found herself next to Rayne and Saikatto, the only two living members of the original Jestivan.

"What do you think?" Rayne asked, eyeing a handful of the mysterious vegetables Iris had been feeding them since the night they had exited Realmular Tunnel.

"I think we prepare ourselves for an unfavorable outcome," Rhyparia said. "But we'll play along until that outcome presents itself."

Rayne nodded, and Saikatto said, "We don't need anything from them. We're only here because it's the only route to get to the Power Kingdom. If we must, we'll flee and find our way to the teleplatforms."

"That could be difficult," Rayne said. "Musku's map has proven to be inaccurate thus far. Sure, there are general accuracies, but the specifics have been far from reliable. We would have never escaped those mountains had it not been for Iris's assistance. Who's to say we'll be able to find the teleplatforms by following the map?"

Rhyparia hated to admit it, but the woman had a point. They'd need the aid of a Primmish native in order to make their way across the kingdom, which could prove difficult if these Monsignor people declared them enemies of the kingdom.

Saikatto's gaze veered toward the lake on their right. He hummed quietly to himself, then said, "The lake's name must pay respects to Dimiourgos. 'Headless Lake' is too peculiar to be anything else."

"Do you think it's where Dimiourgos and the Dark Courage King fought for the last time?" Rhyparia asked.

"Either that or it's simply a monument of sorts," Rayne said.

"Stonebody." They each glanced forward, where Iris continued leading the pack alone. "That was the name of this Dark Courage King you speak of. His proper title was Stonebody, King of Brutes." He turned to regard them, eyes narrowed. "Yes, as I thought, you are a peculiar group. To possess such knowledge ..." He trailed off, turning forward and shaking his head. "I think the Monsignors will be pleased ... or scared."

Rhyparia, Rayne, and Saikatto exchanged uneasy looks. After a few more hours of wandering, Rhyparia began to question their guide. Where was Asalka? Surely its skyline would have ascended above the horizon by now. All she saw ahead of her was a wall of trees against the orange backdrop of second-dusk.

"Is the city behind the forest?" she asked.

Iris let out a hearty chuckle. "Ah, such blasphemous things, you are. The forest *is* the city."

"They're giant willows," Prakriti whispered, leaning toward her. "Like the ones in Epinio that we humans aren't allowed access into."

"What are those things called in your kingdoms?" Iris asked. "Buildings?"

"A building is a foreign concept here?" Rayne asked, a bit bemused.

"Yes ... Or, not exactly," he said. "There is one building in Asalka ... the *castle*, where the *royals* live." He practically spat two of the words with contempt. "We, zealots, tend to pretend it does not exist."

"It seems like there's quite a rift between the religious sect and the royals here," Biaza said. "It's hard to believe this kingdom has gotten by without war for so long."

"Our god does not condone violence," Iris said. "This rift you speak of is nothing but a stubborn and silent dispute ... though recently it's grown worrisome."

"What does your god condone?" Biaza asked.

He shook his head. "I have said too much already." He paused. "The peculiarities of your arrival have caused me to let down my guard. I will speak no further until our arrival to the Glades."

The group fell silent, and it stayed that way until meeting Asalka's edge. It was decided shortly before entering the wooded city that the Craftmasters—Atarax, Kakos, Moros, Biaza, and Therapif—would remain in the sparse woodlands of the city's exterior. They needed to remain behind in case they roused suspicion from civilians, risking the revelation of their identities. Who knew how people would have responded in such a case?

It was also better the group split, offering the opportunity of one helping the other in case of imprisonment … or worse. Iris was staunchly against this plan, but he eventually ceased his rebuttals.

As the smaller group crossed into the forest capital, their eyes feasted upon the scenery. Roads were nothing but winding strips of grassy clearings, bordered by streaming green branches that hung to the forest floor. The willows here were somehow grander than those back in Epinio. An occasional birch tree stood amongst the willows.

Young adults sat in the grass below the birch tree canopies, socializing and laughing, while adults enjoyed their nights in more reserved fashion. The black sky of first-night settled upon the land, yet light was plentiful. Thousands of fireflies fluttered through the forest, their lights seemingly everlasting. It had the atmosphere of a modern city, but with trees in place of buildings and grass in place of tar or stone.

A few seasoned men broke free of a willow's branches just ahead, laughing as they turned to head down the clearing. One of them stumbled drunkenly, saved from a fall by his companions.

"You allow humans to enter the willows?" Saikatto asked.

Iris stopped and turned around, a curious expression on his face. "As opposed to what, exactly?"

"Animals," Rayne said.

The Watcher tilted his head slightly, studying the cloaked human. Was he trying to see beneath the hood? "Once again, peculiar," he said.

Shrouded by weeping branches, the purpose of the willows was unknown. The abnormally thick birch trees seemed to act as all kinds of establishments. She spotted a tavern, restaurant, general shop, and several other unmarked trees. Each birch had an open doorway at the trunk, and most had ovular windows scattered around the base. Fireflies seemed to flutter in and out of the trees without any complaints from the people.

She stopped, catching her breath as something small skittered past her. It sprinted toward the base of a nearby birch, climbing its trunk before leaping for a branch and hanging there. She couldn't believe her eyes. "Is that a monkey?"

"Yes," Iris said. "Native to the Prim Kingdom. Actually, the same can be said for a lot of the animals here. We share the land with them, but something tells me you already knew this."

As they moved deeper into the forest, paths became less crowded. It seemed the opposite of a normal city, but what else would one expect from a place as odd as this. Every hundred paces or so, they'd pass a man or woman in plain white robes. Civilians would surround them, listening to the robed lecturers with interest.

"Who are they?" Prakriti asked.

"Priests," Iris said. "They watch over the city, occasionally giving sermons to the civilians. Nothing too detailed … usually vague remarks about wisdom or ethics."

Rhyparia recognized a trend with these priests. Each time they passed one, usually standing just outside of a willow's branches, the priest's eyes would follow Iris. Some bore expressions of shock while others narrowed their eyes with skepticism, their gazes lingering on the cloaked group following the Watcher.

"They don't seem fond of your presence," Rayne said.

"Of course not. Leaving my post is an unforgivable sin." He paused. "Unless for good reason, which I believe this to be the case. Regardless, I outrank them, so they will keep their distance."

"Why is the city becoming emptier the deeper we get?" Rhyparia asked.

"The heart of the capital is sparsely populated while the outer reaches are rich with markets, housing, businesses, and other recreational establishments. The heart is where the zealots live. And the Glades are the heart's center, where the Monsignors reside."

Rhyparia surveyed her surroundings, searching for a castle. Iris had mentioned the royals living in the only man-made structure in the kingdom, but she had yet to see any signs of one.

Iris came to a stop and turned. Behind him was the largest willow tree she had ever seen in her life. The cascading wall of branches stretched to the sides for what seemed like forever, creating what had to have been a perimeter wider than Wealth's Crossroads. Its height was nothing to gloss over, either, as it dwarfed every other tree in the forest.

"I really do wish you would have brought everyone," the Watcher said.

He turned toward the willow, splitting the branches with two hands and stepping inside. They followed and were met with a grassy glade that glowed beneath a canopy of thousands of fireflies, like a golden throne room straight out of a fairy tale.

Rhyparia had underestimated the size of the willow. Now that she was within its confines, it seemed twice the size of Wealth's Crossroads, big enough to contain five humble birches just within its branches, an open doorway carved into the base of each one. The willow's trunk at the center of the Glades was thicker than a naval galleon's main mast.

Iris stepped deeper into the Glades, and Rhyparia reluctantly followed. Something about this place unnerved her. He approached the willow at the center, but maintained a healthy distance. He dropped to all fours and bowed his head—less of a bow and more of a child impersonating a dog. She watched with uncertainty, eyes skittering around the glade, freezing momentarily on each black void of a doorway.

"Watcher Iris." She jumped at the booming voice, curious of its source. "Your presence here is deplorable. Who are these civilians?"

"Now, now, Brother Catus," a woman said. "If Watcher Iris has come to visit us, I assume it's for good reason."

"That still doesn't explain the civilians, Sister Quada."

"This is true," she said, their voices unnaturally loud. "Watcher Iris, why are they cloaked?"

"They aren't civilians," Iris said, still on all fours. "They're foreigners."

Gasps followed, enough to make Rhyparia question the amount of people around them. *"You've brought foreigners into the Glades?!"*

The voice of Catus rolled like thunder around them. This time, nobody refuted his anger.

"Study them!" Iris said, his voice desperate. "I believe they are something we've given up seeking a long time ago."

"What are you implying, Watcher?"

"I believe you know, Brother Catus," Quada said. They seemed to be the only two who spoke. "But it's a rather ridiculous claim. Have you seen these foreigners, Iris? Why are they cloaked?"

"I have not seen them, but they came from the tunnel." More whispers. "That's why I'm here."

After a long pause, a figure emerged from each of the five birch trees. Rhyparia's hand slipped into her cloak, grasping the handle of her umbrella. But she faltered as humans exited the birches, their faces veiled by strange masks.

"Animal heads?" Prakriti said. "That is the most morbid thing I've ever seen."

Perhaps because of her familiarity with Meow Meow, the image didn't bother Rhyparia as much. She recognized a gorilla, ram, ox, and panther. The last one was a mystery to her … some kind of bear?

"Get up Iris." The deep voice came from the man in the gorilla mask, who had to have been Catus. The Watcher slowly rose to a stand. "Bring them to the willow."

Iris turned and waved the group over. Rhyparia allowed the others to move first, deciding to stick to the rear and watch their backsides. She remained wary of the Monsignors, watching their hands to make sure they weren't wielding anything. Perhaps she was being too cautious, but she couldn't shake the habit. Ever since learning of her mother's manipulation of her clout as a child, she made sure to always be observant. As they neared the massive trunk, the Monsignors stepped away from their birches and converged at the center. Rhyparia's grasp of her ancient's handle was enough to make her fingers numb.

"We should have brought one of the Craftmasters," Prakriti whispered.

He was right, but she felt better knowing they weren't here. What would have become of them had they been exposed to fanatics such as this? The Craftmasters probably would have been worshiped, but that wasn't what they were here for. They didn't come to the Dark Realm to linger in the Prim Kingdom. The Power Kingdom was their goal.

Catus stepped forward from the group, his gorilla head too large for his human frame. He stopped a couple of paces away from Prakriti, staring into the hood of his cloak. Prakriti bowed his head slightly, as if intimidated by the man's gaze.

She watched with curiosity as Catus made his way down the line. She then studied the other Monsignors who remained at a distance. She felt safe knowing these people worshipped Dimiourgos, the lynx that once led the Dark Morality Kingdom before Known History. All signs pointed to it:

their refusal to eat meat, a symbiotic lifestyle with animals in the city, and the name of the lake just outside of the capital. But how was wearing the heads of dead animals a sign of respect? Surely, Dimiourgos would have condemned such a practice. Did these Monsignors think they were dimiours by impersonating their image? That would have only made it worse.

Finally, Catus reached her. She grimaced, noticing the torn edges around the gorilla's neck. Had they ripped this directly off the animal, then cleaned and gutted it? Now she was questioning her acceptance of Meow Meow years ago.

She remembered her first encounter with Olivia, underneath the school after being inducted as Jestivan. She had taken a particular interest in the kitten hat because of the feeling it had given her, similar to that of an ancient. Because of that, she had always thought of it as such: a device or relic that somehow did things that logic couldn't explain, like her umbrella or Agnos's glasses. But to think she had been staring at a girl wearing the head of a dead god … that should have been mortifying.

Catus grunted and stepped back. He turned and gave a simple wave to his comrades, heading back in the direction of his birch. "Watcher Iris," he said. "Take them away; you have wasted our time."

Rhyparia's eyes widened. "We need your help!"

He paused, but didn't turn around. "You will receive no such thing from us. What you do in Asalka is up to you. You may leave or stay, but I advise the former. We cannot promise your safety here, now that you've seen us. Foreigners are strictly forbidden access to information about our religion. The moment you entered the Glades, you broke the most important law of our society."

"Then why aren't you taking action against us right now?" Rayne asked.

Catus turned only slightly, the side of his gorilla mask barely visible. "Because I can see in that woman's eyes that she is not to be crossed. We are not fools. If we were to cast the judgment you deserve, you'd fight back, and that might end poorly for us." He started walking again. "Please leave. Perhaps we can arrange for a Prowler to escort you to our kingdom's teleplatforms, so you can safely return home."

Rhyparia cocked an eyebrow as the Monsignors disappeared into their birches. From the sounds of it, foreigners had never entered the Glades. They likely had never seen the Monsignors or the animal masks. Spies who had infiltrated the city for over a millennium had never mentioned this place. Considering this successful track record of secrecy, why would they be willing to allow Rhyparia and her friends to walk free? Because of fear?

Rayne, Saikatto, and Prakriti walked toward the willow's wall of branches, but Rhyparia's feet remained planted as she stared at Watcher Iris. He stood with slumped shoulders, facing the willow's trunk, the cavernous void of a doorway swallowing him.

"Let's go, Iris," she said.

"I cannot."

"What are you talking about?" she asked. "It's over. They don't want anything to do with us."

"Watcher Iris is to remain here," Quada said, exposing her as the panther.

Rhyparia set her jaw. "And what is to become of him?" she said softly, trying to quell her anger.

"That is none of your concern."

Rhyparia's grip on her ancient's handle stiffened, but Iris turned to regard her. He smiled. "I will be fine," he said. A rogue firefly fluttered past his face. "As I've stated before, we are not a violent culture. Please go and enjoy the city for the night. When the Prowler comes to aid your journey to the teleplatforms, accept it." He turned away. "Good night."

She hesitated. The others had already exited the Glades. Why did she find it so difficult? She said she wasn't going to get distracted by anything that may arise here, that she'd find a way to the teleplatforms the moment the chance presented itself. This was her chance. She had no ties to this man, so why worry?

She bit her lip, but forced herself to exit. Iris would be all right. It was time to find an inn and get some sleep—if she could even manage it. Hopefully by morning, this Prowler person would be ready to lead them to the teleplatforms. They were within reach of the Power Kingdom.

*　　　*　　　*

Olivia stood at the bow of the longboat, violet hair flowing behind her in the gentle winds of Headless Lake. Vuilni and Fane sat behind her, rowing in unison to keep their path straight. Journey was seated on the boat's last bench, smiling as he leaned over the vessel's edge, letting the water run through his fingers.

Olivia had been standing like this ever since boarding the boat. For some odd reason, this lake meant something to her. It offered her a sense of comfort she hadn't experienced since having Meow Meow atop her head. Despite the mysteries of her feline friend, she missed him dearly.

There had been holes in his memory—gaping and black like a bottomless pit. But she had come to accept that at a young age, learning not to question those missing pieces. What was he exactly and how did he come to exist? Toono had called him an ancient, like Rhyparia's umbrella or Ophala's Cheiraskinia. But if that were the case, how could Olivia use him all those years? She wasn't an Archain, but a mix of Intelian and Stillian.

Maybe logic wasn't the route to take. She herself seemed to defy it, somehow using the ability of water a few years ago. She possessed just as many mysteries as Meow Meow, but one thing was certain: this lake meant something.

"You're on your own once we reach the shore," Journey said. "I'll have to return to the teleplatforms."

"But all I see are trees," Vuilni said through heavy breaths.

"Asalka is a city of trees," he said.

Olivia opened her eyes. The lake's curling mists obscured the shore ever so slightly. The tress glowed faintly, shrouding the distant mists in a yellow hue.

She closed her eyes again, allowing the cool wetness of the mist to wash over her face. It was a marvelous sensation, and she found herself smiling. She felt at home, but not exactly her own. There was peace in that.

She had found a missing piece of Meow Meow's shattered memories.

# 19

# The Demon's Plans

The road between Dunami and Brilliance was long and bumpy. Bryson had gotten used to the tar-paved roads of the capital, a luxury he hadn't fully realized until now. He winced as one of the wheels hit a bump.

A small portion of King Vitio's honor guard traveled alongside the carriage on horseback. Inside was Bryson's only company: Benedict Ronal. Why they had been forced to travel in such a shoddy vehicle was beyond Bryson. Vitio wanted them to appear unassuming, but what was inconspicuous about an escort of guards on mighty steeds? Might as well have painted "I'm important!" on the carriage's exterior.

"Prince, for someone who I've been told is not fond of unappreciative or snobby people, you seem to possess such traits in strong dosages," Benedict said lazily.

Bryson curled his lip downward, displaying the very quality the steward spoke of. "And who did you hear this from?" he asked.

"Reliable sources."

"You've been speaking with the queen far too much."

Benedict smiled. "Well, she is whom I spend the most time with. You would have known this had it not been for your constant avoidance of her presence throughout the past few years."

"She scared me."

The steward nodded. "Rightfully so. She can intimidate without the need of weaving talents, the raising of her voice, or flaunting of her money. She is soft-spoken, but stern; expressionless, but expressive."

Bryson held his tongue. He would have only pointed out the obvious flaw in this statement, and he felt that's what the man desired. He wasn't going to get roped into another philosophical discourse. It would have been the fifth one since embarking on this journey.

"Do you love Princess Shelly?"

Bryson groaned. "Do you love pissing people off?"

"Do you always counter deep conversation with shallow remarks?"

Twisting in his seat, Bryson threw an arm across the back of the bench. He peered out the open window, watching the horses trot through the tall prairie grass. "I counter stupid questions with shallow remarks. Of course I love her."

"Then why, for the hundredth time, are you leaving her during one of her most important times of need?"

Bryson raised an eyebrow and looked at the steward. "Because she always tells me to—even if I fight it."

"Fight it harder."

Bryson paused, a lethargic flatness to his eyes. "If it was that simple, do you think I'd be in this carriage right now?"

"I know this," Benedict said, "but it frustrates me. This is where the queen and I see things differently."

"Even Queen Delilah hasn't minded my journeys," Bryson said.

"And she is a ..." he trailed off, looking toward the carriage's floorboards. "And she should have fought you."

"Oh, so you don't back the queen on all of her thoughts and decisions?" Bryson asked, surprised by this revelation.

"I do not, which is why she has kept me by her side for so many years. She desires someone as resilient as she. I stand firm by my beliefs and will refute her claims when necessary. I am probably the only person, outside of Lilu, who she allows to do so." He shook his head and chuckled. "Needless to say, when I discovered she was letting you commit to this frivolous vacation to Brilliance, I was aghast. I argued with her for hours. There is a great wedding being planned, and her daughter's groom-to-be should be present during all of the preparations."

"It's not a vacation," Bryson said. "There are matters of importance I must attend to in Brilliance, and Shelly understands this. Just because you aren't privy to the reasons why Shelly and I have decided I should come up here doesn't mean they don't exist. There is purpose in this trip."

Benedict crossed his legs, one knee over the other, as he narrowed his eyes. "I see. But that—"

"And don't question my feelings toward Shelly ever again," Bryson snapped. "I love that woman from the bottom of my heart."

The steward's expression remained skeptical, but he soon nodded and clasped his hands together above his knees. He closed his eyes and leaned his head back, facing the roof. "Very good … very good."

*　　*　　*

Phesaw's curved main lobby, which circled the auditorium, was dotted with lingering students on break. Illipsia and Beren occupied a bench against the outer wall. They sat directly beneath a tall, skinny window that stretched upwards toward the ceiling dozens of feet above. Sunlight splashed over them as it fell across the floor of the lobby in a rhombus-shaped patch.

Illipsia observed a tall man, his frame bent to the side as he leaned on his cane. His name was Yvole, a new addition to Ms. Neaneuma's security team. He had become of particular interest to Illipsia because of his seemingly equal particular interest in her. Considering this, she had decided to make him a subject of her experiments. She had already practiced her hallucinogenics on Beren plenty, but that had become easier with time. Not to mention, his mind was not that difficult to fool. Someone like Yvole would pose a challenge.

"Imagine being dubbed *the Oracle*. Did they call him that during his life or did he have to die first?"

She peeled her eyes away from Yvole and glanced down at the textbook Beren was reading. Based off the first passage she spotted, it was a text regarding Devish history. This particular chapter focused on Dev King Rehn.

He'd been struggling in his Interrealmular History class. She found it fascinating Phesaw included studies of kingdoms from the other realm. That didn't happen in Ipsas, a school crippled by segregation just like the realm it belonged to.

"He had been given that alias long before death," she said. "And while the Light Realm enjoys painting him as some sort of villain, he was nothing of the sort. He was, in many ways, a symbol of prosperity to the Devish."

Beren gave her a quizzical look. "How would you know that? You're only fifteen."

"I used to have a tutor who knew a lot about Dark Realm history," she lied with a shrug.

"And your tutor told you the Oracle was a hero; not a villain?"

"Basically."

He inhaled through closed teeth and shook his head, turning toward the open book again. "I don't know about that. From the sounds of things, he was a bad, bad man."

"Textbooks tend to construe details in order to reflect the author's desired perspective. It's called 'pushing an agenda.'"

"Look right here," he said, flipping back a few pages and pointing at a sentence. "'During the annual Cosmos Festival, King Rehn would expose one truth of the world to his people. But in order to do so, he would sacrifice an innocent child to the Dark Empire's Gefal, slaughtering him on stage.'" He read the last part with a shiver.

"Let me see that," she snapped, snatching the book from his hands. She'd never bothered reading anything about King Rehn while in the Light Realm, knowing that most of it would have been propaganda, but this was just absurd. She scanned over the page, face twisting with disgust after each sentence. These weren't just construed facts, but perverse lies, something straight out of a dark theatre act of the Void. This author was depicting King Rehn as an evil almost congruent to that of Still Queen Francine, a woman who slaughtered newborns. Did they really teach such nonsense in school?

"Don't just believe everything you read in a book," she said, passing it back to him. "King Rehn didn't sacrifice children."

"Why is that so unbelievable?" he asked, pouting as he read the words again. "The Rogue Demon is currently doing the same, and he's doing it to royal heads, too. People from the Dark Realm are scary."

The Rogue Demon. She bit her lip in an effort to stifle any comments on Toono. If she started down that road, her mouth wouldn't stop. She'd likely say something she'd regret, putting her entire mission here at jeopardy. Still, she couldn't help herself.

"But do you think he's really from the Dark Realm?" she asked. "Don't they say he once belonged to an orphanage in the Archaic Kingdom? He even worked at the Archaic Museum."

Beren closed the book and leaned back. "Yes, but he aligned himself with the Dev Kingdom and worked alongside King Storshae. Now he allies with the Power and Cyn Kingdoms. That makes him a Darken."

She scowled. Thankfully, a bypassing group of girls caught his attention and distracted him from her reaction. In Phesaw, "Darken" had slowly become the slanderous name of anyone from the Dark Realm. Kids flung the word around like it was nothing. It was foul and it scarred her heart each time she heard it. "Bryson LeAnce and others recently befriended the Still Kingdom," she said, trying to expose the flaw in his logic.

He shrugged, eyes still following the girls. "The Stillians made the right decision. That makes them a little better than Darkens."

"Stop calling them that."

He frowned, finally regarding her during a stretch of silence. He then closed his book and slung his open bag to his chest, stashing the book inside. He zipped it closed and flung it onto his back. "I don't know why you sympathize with them," he said, tightening the straps. "But it's weird."

Illipsia watched him as he walked away. She had grown fond of the boy, even going as far as calling him a best friend, but that was the first time she had heard anything like that come out of his mouth. If he thought of her people with such disgust, how would he react if he knew she was a Devish?

A man approached Illipsia and stood next to where Beren had been seated. He groaned and lowered himself onto the bench next to her. She turned and nearly leapt upward, thankful she didn't—that would have cried guilt. The man sat back, kicking out his limp leg. As always, a pipe hung loosely between his lips. He didn't smoke it, however, for that was strictly forbidden while indoors. She recalled a scene where Grand Director Neaneuma scolded the man for it in front of all the refugees. Ever since that moment, he chewed on it instead.

"Mister Yvole," she said, sliding off the bench and dropping to her knees as she began packing up her things.

"You know of me, young lady?"

"Of course, sir." She screwed on the top of her inkwell and tossed it sloppily into her bag. "Everyone knows who you are."

"I disagree. Most people pay me no mind, perceiving me as something inconsequential … like the school janitor or the assembly line assistants at the lunch buffet." He removed the pipe from his mouth, its tip cragged from his constant chewing. "If anyone does recognize me, it's usually due to my limp or my pipe."

"That's what I mean, sir," she said, tying the string on her bag's flap. She slung it over her shoulder. "You're not difficult to miss."

"Do not lie to me," he said. Though her face remained impassive, it was clear he could see more than she'd intended. "You see, while my foot may not be what it once was, my eyesight is still pristine. You don't move around this school in a manner befitting of a normal student; you tend to creep."

"I keep to myself, sir."

"That you do. Are you Archain or Adrenian?"

"Archain."

"Do you not want to return home, now that your kingdom is safe again?"

"I have no home."

He nodded, grabbing his cane and pushing himself to stand. "No need to flee with such haste," he said, eyeing her bag. "You seemed comfortable here. I only wanted to talk. I'm sure I shall see you around."

She remained on both knees as he limped his way through a throng of students who had the proper sense to move aside. Her mannerisms needed reassessing. Yvole knew something was off about her. The good news was that if he knew exactly what her plans were, he would have surely acted by now. At this point, he could only continue to observe and wait for her to do something rash.

This meant anything she did in the future would require hallucinogenics. But she wasn't ready for that yet. She needed more practice. It was time she focused less on the locks and upped her attention on deception techniques. Until she could manipulate the minds of those like Yvole and Neaneuma, this mission would prove impossible.

*　　　*　　　*

Toono stood atop the steps leading to Cogdan Castle's main entrance, flanked by Gala, Homina, and Tazama. At the bottom of the steps stood a bevy of Devish intelligence officers, their burgundy eyes turned toward him, feeding their recordings to dozens of their comrades scattered throughout the city as they broadcast to the civilians.

Holographic displays hovered above the streets, illuminating the darkness of second-night. Just beyond the recording officers, swathed across the castle grounds, were rows upon rows of neatly organized soldiers all donning the same shade of burgundy. Gala had made great progress with disciplinary protocol. Toono addressed the soldiers directly, relying on the broadcasters to do the work of amplifying his voice for the rest of the city.

"For those of you who do not know me, my name is Toono. During what should be a brief period, I will act as your interim king. Dev King Storshae is dead, slain by my hand, serving as the ninth sacrifice."

He paused, offering the city a moment to soak in his words. He could tell by the reactions of the soldiers in front of him—as subdued as they

214

tried to appear—that this would be difficult to come to grips with. The soldiers may have had suspicions reserved deep within about the sudden disappearance of their king, but without proof, they had relied on faith that he was still alive. This was the confirmation they feared.

"I understand the confusion surfacing from this. Why would I kill the son of the very man I'm trying to bring back to life? To put it simply, he would have struck first had I not. He believed there were others out there who could achieve this goal outside of me. He would have been in for a rude awakening. Only I can wield the ancients necessary for such a task.

"Storshae had refused to make this public, but now that he's gone I will do it for him. He had a child a couple of years ago. The boy's mother is a mystery to me, but I promise you I've committed no harm to the baby. He is the distant future of your kingdom and will take control of the throne after Dev King Rehn. I don't intend to be in this position forever. The sooner I can bring the Oracle back to life, the better."

He turned slightly, eyeing Dev Warden Gala. He tilted his head, gesturing for her to step forward. As she did so, he turned forward again, regarding the intelligence officers and soldiers.

"The military is already familiar with this lady, but I want to introduce some of the key players to the masses. Once the Dev Warden of Ipsas, Gala Prasidia will become the Dev General, leading the military as Ossen once did several years ago."

Gala brought two fingers to her nose. The soldiers yelled, mimicking her gesture as a sort of salute. After dismissing her, he called for Homina. She stepped forward, her hair tied up in a bun.

"Homina will become the Intelligence Ambassador, acting as the head of the intelligence unit. She will orchestrate war tactics on a more deceptive level, using the special skills of her officers."

She stepped back, allowing the third lady to take her place by his side. "Then there is Tazama, once a renowned scientist in the city of Prayoga before being captured and enslaved by Mendac LeAnce. She will serve as my proxy, my most trusted advisor."

Tazama nodded before retreating to her spot next to Gala and Homina. While Toono had never cared much for Toth Brench and Wert Lamay, he had taken a liking to the title of proxy, stealing it for his own.

"With these three ladies, the Dev Kingdom is in good hands. Including Kadlest, who is acting as an additional general in the Adren Kingdom, we find ourselves in a powerful position. In addition to our Cynnish and Powish allies, I have spies hidden within enemy kingdoms. Our presence can be felt all around Kuki Sphaira."

He surveyed the field of soldiers, jaw rigid. "*I will bring back the Oracle!*"

And with that, the city roared.

# 20

# Kolver's Refusal

The broadcast hovered in the sky, illuminating one of Tames's busier market squares. Toshik, Horos, and Kuiku lingered just outside of an alleyway to avoid the square's congestion. While the moon and stars might have been out in full force, that didn't mean the daytime activities had come to a close. It was the heart of afternoon. Most people had just gotten off work, which meant these were peak traffic hours in the markets.

Today the routine wasn't quite the same. All eyes were on the broadcast, Toono and three women pictured within. Kuiku stood straight-backed with his hands in his trouser pockets, Toshik stood casually to the side, and Horos leaned against a wooden building, tossing back handfuls of sunflower seeds. The broadcast ended with a rally cry about the Oracle's rebirth, but the citizens of Tames didn't respond with the same vigor. As the hologram disappeared, the torches became the main source of light once again.

Kuiku frowned, watching as people slowly returned to their shopping and mingling. Toshik narrowed his eyes, listening for anything of interest among the conversation. "It seems that speech didn't have the same effect out here than it did in the capital," Toshik said, recalling the cheers that erupted from the broadcast following the speech's conclusion.

"I don't think the identity of the person sitting on the throne matters too much out here," Kuiku said. "Tames is labeled on the Dev Kingdom's map as a town of note, but not much attention is given to it—not like Cosmos, Shreel, or Prayoga. Even Rence gets more love, acting as a checkpoint on the main road between the teleplatforms and Cogdan. It's a shame, really, considering much of the kingdom's raw supplies come from Tames's farmlands, forests, and mountains."

Horos nodded. "These sunflower seeds are pristine."

Toshik continued to scan the market street. "I guess that works in our favor. If they don't bother themselves with royal issues out here, then nobody should be looking for us."

"That doesn't mean there aren't spies," Horos said, spitting out an empty shell. "But I suppose it is my job to recognize them, so don't you fret. If there is one thing I know like the back of my hand, it's a spy. I married a pretty good one."

Kuiku turned toward Toshik and Horos, hands still in his pockets, sword at his hip. "What scares me is the calmness of Toono's delivery. He talks such a big game because he knows nobody doubts him, allies and enemies alike. He backs all his talk with results. He has an unprecedented résumé to prove it."

"It is a bit unnerving," Horos said.

Toshik didn't care about any of that. He was more focused on the women who had accompanied Toono. Where was Yama? He had spoken of everyone else, even mentioning some woman named Kadlest in the Adren Kingdom, where Yama was supposed to be. It would have made more sense had he named her the general. Surely, this Kadlest woman wasn't a more talented fighter.

He supposed it didn't matter. Yama's path would end the same way no matter what … skewered by his blade.

*     *     *

Toono blew through the castle. Marble pillars that stretched up the corridor's side walls blurred as he past. He wrestled off his ornamental coat he had worn for the broadcast, handing it to a nearby aide. Tazama waited for him at the end of the hall.

"Kadlest is waiting patiently," she said, turning and matching his strides through the eastern rotunda. "But we must be quick, for she had to leave the Adren Kingdom in order for her Devish officer to connect a telepathic link."

"She's at our teleplatforms?" he asked, unbuttoning the cuffs of his dress shirt and folding them up to his elbows.

"The Cynnish. She thought it best to enter an ally kingdom, where True Light forces likely aren't trying to attack."

That was good. He could always count on Kadlest's savvy when it came to war. It was a specialty of hers—or had been long ago. It only took one glance at the woman's broad shoulders and rugged features to realize she had once been hardened by battle.

They eventually entered the throne room where Homina stood by the throne and Gala sat on a step leading up to the stage.

"She can't be away from Adren for too long, so let's make this quick," he said. Homina nodded, one eye burning burgundy, the other dilating to display a hologram of Kadlest.

"Dearest Toono. How are things?"

"Better than expected," he said. "What do you have for me?"

"Troops are prepared for deployment through the teleplatforms whenever Illipsia finishes her job in Phesaw. I have over a thousand stationed at the Adren teleplatforms. I've been keeping busy in the capital, making sure nobody tries to maneuver their way into a position of power. But when the time comes, I'll be ready."

"Have you been keeping in touch with Illipsia?" he asked. "She's making steady progress."

She nodded. "So I've heard. I speak with her from time to time, but I don't have quite the relationship with her as you do. I'm proud of her, though. The feats she is accomplishing are quite rare."

"And you questioned my mindset when I pitched her just such a role in the mission," he said, smirking slyly.

"I still do."

"I assume the Adren Director was taken care of," he said.

"Yama handled him."

He hesitated, fearing the answer to his next question. "And where is she?"

"Well, the director's body was found where Yama had said she would fight him. As for her, she's vanished without a trace." She shook her head. "You knew this would happen eventually."

His gaze fell. He may have foreseen it, but that didn't make it hurt any less.

*     *     *

Yama broke free from Spunka Forest and into meadows that rolled as far as the eye could see, a deceptive vastness caused by the near-distant Edge of the kingdom.

It had been a long trek southwest, a week at the least. In no rush, she had stopped on several occasions to either rest or try her hand at hunting for food. Her full stomach was a testament to her success. She'd had a couple of chances to bathe at two crossing rivers, and even paused a couple of times to lie on her back and stare at the stars. Leisure was a foreign concept to her, but it was a welcome change. She deserved some time to herself, and more importantly, she needed it to reflect on her crimes.

She had killed Jilly, the one person who accepted the bold swordswoman for everything she was worth without feeling obligated to. Toono may have always accepted her, and she appreciated him for that, but the truth remained that she held a utilitarian purpose with him.

She'd spent most of this journey reminiscing on her relationship with Jilly. She saw the Spiritian everywhere, hanging from branches by the back of her knees in the forest, golden hair streaming toward the ground, or thrashing about in the shallow waters of the riverbanks, giggling uncontrollably. She was always close enough for Yama to make out the faint freckles on her cheeks, but too far to reach out and touch. Even now, as Yama kicked her way through the thick grass of the meadow, she heard Jilly's infectious laughter as she tumbled down a nearby hill.

It was some cruel form of torture. There had been a time when she could picture a future with the girl. The weekends spent perusing Tabby's Gift Shop, watching her jump into barrels of stuffed animals; the early evenings spent walking around Phesaw Park; and the many times Yama had to yank back her sword from her too-curious hands.

What made these manifestations torturous wasn't the realization of what she had lost, but the way in which they always ended. She sighed and closed her eyes. Jilly had just rolled down a hill ahead of her, disappearing within the grass. Yama neared the spot and froze, opening her eyes as tears already streamed down her face. In the grass lay a motionless young woman, eyes halfway open, exposing a dullness that didn't belong. Her lips hung slightly apart, and blood running from a diagonal gash between her left shoulder and right hip soaked the sod beneath her.

Perhaps the most haunting aspect of it all was the silence—no gags, shallow breaths, or final dying words. Yama had become such a skilled wielder of the blade—such a skilled *killer*—she had cut deep enough to eviscerate Jilly's ribs, muscle, and heart in one swing.

"Damnit," she muttered, squeezing her eyes shut.

It should have been Toshik. Why had Jilly sacrificed herself in his stead? Only yesterday Yama had realized that was the question that made her truly upset. Did Jilly love the idiot that much? Yama found it insulting. And she recognized how self-centered that was, but she couldn't help it.

She *despised* Toshik. He'd been a womanizer for most of his life … she'd been a victim of it on several occasions. But somehow he wound up with a woman as pure as Jilly, discovering yet another method to scorn Yama.

She wished there could have been some other way. Witnessing Jilly's death and Toshik's suffering should have struck a chord of deep regret within her, but it only fueled her flame. She may have killed Jilly, but he was equally responsible.

For that, she'd kill him.

*　　*　　*

Yama approached the village of Yinyon. Its main road stretched across the front like a moat of dirt. A tiny inn sat against the road, sprawling pastures and farmland behind it. A lone hill rose above the village somewhere in the middle, two massive oaks standing at the top.

She crossed the road and entered the inn. Like the exterior, the décor was rustic and one giant shade of brown. Dust caked the floor and cobwebs hung in the corners of the humble lobby.

She strolled toward the vacant innkeeper's desk, floorboards groaning with each step. She leaned over, as if to find a mythical dwarf, but all she found was a ream of parchment. She almost mistook it as a ledger since it would have made the most sense. However, the top sheet showed an upside-down detailed sketch, complete with crosshatchings for shadowing and lines of various widths to signify distance. She narrowed her eyes and craned her neck, trying to make out the image. There was definitely a swordsman, but the composition was befuddling—at least from this angle.

She reached down for it, but suddenly a hand smacked hers away. She stepped back and drew her sword in one swift heartbeat, her general response to a worthy adversary. Anyone who could sneak up on her was someone to be reckoned with. That meant they had moved with not only impeccable stealth, but deadly speed. She narrowed her eyes at the red-headed young man who now stood behind the desk. His hair was buzzed short, making his already-large ears appear more like wings for his head. He had to be only a few years younger than her.

"Don't wanna start your visit to Yinyon by committing a crime, do ya?" he asked.

She paused, sword still drawn in front of her, one foot back. "And what crime is that?"

"Invasion of privacy, ordinance number one hundred and six."

"More of an ethical dilemma than a legal one," she said, not relaxing her stance.

"Not in this town," he said. "Regardless, you've already broken a more severe law."

"Breathing?" she asked sarcasticly.

He smirked, relaxing his posture. "Not quite. Drawing one's sword without proper reason, ordinance number two."

She straightened up and lowered her sword. "You snuck up on me," she said. "To me, that poses a threat. To me, that is proper reason."

"Don't put me at fault for your lack of awareness," he said. "Either way, it's in the past now. Consider your excuse valid. I won't bring it to the attention of higher authorities."

She cocked an eyebrow. Higher authorities in a place like this? And why had his voice changed from uneducated countryman to that of a scholar?

He picked up the ream of parchment and shoved it in a compartment somewhere behind the desk. She heard the jingle of keys and the click of a lock. He stood and stared at her. "What are you doing here, Yama Fuuna?"

She balked, sword now hanging limp in her hand. Not only did he know her first name, but he had given her a last name. "I don't have a last name," she said hoarsely.

"Maybe not out there, but here you do." He chuckled, scratching at the unkempt patches of hair along his jaw. "My mistake. How rude can I be? My name is Kolver."

She stepped forward slowly. "Why was I supposed to return? Why was I taken away in the first place?"

"I don't know much. I've only heard bits and pieces of your story during lessons."

"Who do I need to find to tell me more?" she asked.

The glee slipped from his face, and his stature stiffened once more. "No, what am I doing? Yama Fuuna, you are no longer desired in this village. Those you seek will not tolerate your presence. While Yinyon doesn't force anyone to leave, my advice would be for you to evacuate our village."

She stammered. "But there were written instructions for me to return here."

"And now they realize it had been a mistake."

"But I've been working—"

"No!" he bellowed, cutting her off. His gaze was fierce. "Yama Fuuna, you are a disgrace to our people. We don't want your representation."

# 21

# The Hero of Brilliance

Lilu had never seen such a crowd, shutting down all traffic throughout Brilliance's main street and its adjacencies. Onlookers poked their heads out the windows of the surrounding tenements. On the flattop roofs, some sixty to a hundred feet in the air, people sat on the edges, their legs hanging down the sides of buildings—an obvious safety hazard and violation of city law. But nobody cared, for all eyes were on the city's southern gate.

Lilu, Gracie, Frederick, and Limone stood well ahead of the masses and just behind the LeAnce family. They were donned in their finest attire: neatly pressed suits for the men and nearly similar attire for the women, with skirts taking the place of pants. This line of golden-haired board members would be the first to welcome their guest, while Lilu's team would come next.

She turned to regard the crowds. Officers barked orders at the civilians, many of whom were trying to push their way through the barricade. It was a pathetic scene. To think the last name of a man like Mendac beckoned such reverence from the public … she became queasy just at the thought.

An officer fell victim to a left jab, sending him stumbling backward. A higher ranked official, who stood behind the barricade overseeing his subordinates, quickly ordered a dozen others to rush the gap. The civilians who penetrated the barricade were apprehended and shoved back into the crowds. The man who had punched the officer was cuffed and separated from the others.

"This is utter madness," Gracie said, watching the chaos with Lilu.

"Vile," Lilu said.

"I thought this city hated Bryson LeAnce," Gracie said. "When he broadcast the crimes of his father's rape."

"I think there are a lot of emotions happening right now. A lot of these people choose to ignore Bryson's comments because of his status. He is the son of Mendac. They can't see past that."

Lilu paused, carefully surveying the faces of the civilians. Not everyone stirred with excitement. Many stood perfectly still, faces coated with malice. These were likely the people who believed Bryson had betrayed his father.

Lilu whirled as the gate opened. Gracie would have noticed that. She watched with anticipation as the massive door lifted into the wall, operated by some complex system of levers, pulleys, and weavineering technology.

A mundane carriage rolled through. The city erupted, causing Lilu to flinch and clasp her hands over her ears. Gracie shook her head with arms crossed, an uncharacteristic sternness in her expression. "I find myself annoyed," she said.

"You should."

*　　*　　*

Bryson poked his head out of the carriage's window, watching the gate lift to reveal the most astounding city street he'd ever seen in his life. While the tar-paved roads weren't anything special, nothing could have prepared him for the monstrous edifices that soared into the sky. He looked straight up in awe. He hadn't explored much of the world, but he couldn't help but think there was nothing else like this. Faces looked down at him from countless windows. Most waved and smiled.

He retreated back into the carriage, shaking his head as he took a seat. Benedict stared at him with intrigue, but he wasn't the only other person in the carriage anymore. Two guards sat next to the steward, making sure he didn't try to look outside.

"How is it?" Benedict asked. "You appear … dumbfounded."

Bryson sunk into his bench, brows furrowed. After a moment of thought, he asked the guard, "What am I to this city?"

"A symbol, milord."

"Of what?"

"The highest acumen."

Benedict chuckled. "I would say this city is in for a rude awakening."

"He's right," Bryson said. "I'm not smart."

The guard shrugged. "Don't tell the people that, milord."

"Are they that judgmental?"

"It would be wise to feign an air of intelligence," the guard said.

The steward wore a smirk. "Do you think you can manage that, Prince?"

Sighing, Bryson relaxed his shoulders, his head falling back atop the bench. "I'm not going to fake it."

"Milord, if I recall my conversations with Lilu years ago correctly, she spoke of your obsession with talking a big game. After a childhood of being belittled and berated for not being your father, you felt the need to prove it whenever the opportunity presented itself." Benedict paused. "In a way, you feigned confidence."

Bryson's gaze remained glued to the carriage's roof even as it came to a stop. Part of him wanted to retaliate; he was not fond of being analyzed. It was truth, however, and he had the Jestivan to thank for ridding him of those habits.

He looked down, regarding Benedict. "I am no longer that boy."

"I can see that, milord."

The door opened, and an armored escort stepped inside. "Prince Bryson," the woman said. "Brilliance is ready for you."

He stood and flattened the creased front of his navy blue coat. It was an extravagant thing, white buttons running up the left and right side of his torso, its long, pleated hem stretching to his knees, causing a pair of sleek black slacks to be barely visible underneath. It was an outfit Shelly had told him to wear on the day of his arrival, believing it'd impress the weavineers rather than his typical unzipped hoodie exposing his scarred chest.

"You look ravishing, milord," Benedict said, rising to a stand. "Have fun and be the idol you want to be; not the one they desire."

Bryson extended a hand. Benedict froze, staring at the gesture. "Shake my hand, Benedict. You annoy me, but that doesn't mean you aren't worthy of my respect."

"Forgive me, milord, but one does not shake hands with a prince as though he's a business partner."

"But we *are* partners; that is the proper relationship between royals and civilians. We exist to serve each other. No longer will people bow."

Benedict hesitated, eyebrows raised. Bryson almost thought the steward would refuse, but eventually the man grabbed his hand, firm and resolute.

"Thank you," Bryson said.

He turned and headed for the exit, the mouths of the two guards hanging open. Was it really that odd to see a royal shake hands with someone who was considered "below" him? That was a problem Bryson would fix as soon as possible. Once this war blew over, a tectonic shift in political etiquette was in store.

As he stepped down from the carriage, a slew of officers bowed to him. He closed his eyes and sighed. As much as he wanted to grab them all by their shoulders and straighten their backs, he couldn't do that yet. Baby steps.

Cheers rang from the blockaded section of street. He couldn't tell how far the crowd stretched while on level land, but he had a feeling that it went on for miles in several directions. He faltered as he noticed the men and women who fronted the crowd, confounded by their unified appearance: all blond-haired, donning suits with dazzling pocket chains and cuff links. He inched his way toward them, legs inexplicably weak. The man at the front wore a toothy grin.

Flowers and confetti began to rain on Bryson, littering the streets and catching in his unkempt hair. Intelights swarmed the sky, fluttering and zipping about like the Passion Kingdom's spring honey bees. They sunk lower and lower until finally flooding the street. There had to be thousands of them, offering a celestial glow to the otherwise murky weather. The hairs on his arms and neck stood tall, as if drawn to the Intel Chains. Many Intelights stretched their shapes, mirroring a string of rocks across a brook. He even spotted the faint tendrils of some, extending from whoever wove them in the distance.

He managed to pry himself from his spot again. As he reached the line of suits, he spotted Lilu's green hair just beyond them. She wore a white lab coat over a simple yellow sundress. He waved, and she offered a nod.

The lead man from earlier stepped into his vision. The celestial currents of Intelights reflected in his blue eyes, and what he went on to say eliminated all sense of wonder from Bryson.

"Welcome to Brilliance. I'm this city's commissioner, Wendel LeAnce."

*    *    *

After a painfully long horse ride throughout the wealthier blocks of Brilliance, during which the same events that had occurred on the main road continued to play out, Bryson eventually wound up in the dining hall of Wendel LeAnce's villa.

He sat at a grand table with the rest of the Board of Weavineers. He had been putting in his best effort during conversation, but it was clear to others he didn't want to be there. Even Lilu, who they had purposely sat him next to, seemed scared to look at him. And he knew why.

She'd lived in this city for a couple of years now, yet she'd somehow forgotten to mention the last name of those who ruled it. That wasn't something that just slipped someone's mind.

Anger boiled over inside of him, but he continued to smile his way through dinner. It took Olivia's voice in his head calling him a child for him to finally stop sulking and get to the point.

"Are all of you my biological family?"

The buzz of conversation died. All eyes finally regarded the mostly silent Bryson. It was astonishing how they all sported the same shade of blue in their irises. The only exception in the hall was Lilu, whose green hair and eyes stuck out like a sore thumb.

"Yonoka LeAnce, who is my mother, adopted Mendac when he was a child," Wendel said, setting his knife and fork beside his plate.

"So we're not related by blood," Bryson said.

"What else would his words have implied?" a woman said. She'd introduced herself earlier as Periphan. "Mendac was a step-sibling of ours long ago. Our mother took him in because of his unnatural charm and intelligence, even at the tender age of seven. His physical attributes were an added bonus."

Bryson scanned his companions, then asked, "You're all siblings?"

"Correct," Periphan said, looking up from her plate. "Our parents had ten children. Our mother had eight siblings of her own. In the LeAnce family lineage, one child is assigned the task of procreation. The rest cannot."

Shaking his head, Bryson reached for his glass of water. "That's dumb."

She scowled. "We have our reasons."

After a quick sip of water, he looked at Wendel again. "So you have a lot of kids?"

He chuckled softly. "I was chosen as the commissioner, not the parent."

Bryson raised a brow. "I see." He leaned into Lilu and whispered, "Did you know they were this weird?"

"I didn't know about any of this."

He straightened up again and shrugged. "Well, I suppose this makes my request a little easier to make ... if we're not blood related."

"Anything for you," Wendel said.

"I don't want to be addressed as LeAnce."

Periphan's knife clattered atop her plate. "Don't you think—"

"Periphan," Wendel said, raising a hand for silence. "If that's what the young man wants, then so be it. However, we can't guarantee the civilians or weavineers will give you the same respect."

"I understand," Bryson said. "That will take more time. When do I get to meet these weavineers, anyway?"

Wendel smiled. "Tonight."

*     *     *

Bryson walked down an incline as wide as the open fields of Dunami Palace's eastern grounds. It was perfectly smooth and made of stone, a giant canvas of gray. The two walls and ceiling were both a lighter shade of gray. Sheets of glass in the ceiling housed unusually bright Intelights within, giving the space a sterile atmosphere like that of Dunami Hospital.

It was a cavernous tunnel that slowly descended below the city, big enough for him to question the reasoning behind it. Even as they reached the bottom, a massive gray wall blocked them from proceeding.

The commissioner pressed a button in the wall, and it jerked into motion as it crept its way upward. Stone grated against stone as some kind of weavineering contraption went to work, revealing an enormous field of steel where hundreds of weavineers were at work. Just beyond them was a low-rising town. Intelights fluttered throughout the top of the cavern.

"Welcome to the Bastion of Intel," Wendel said. "This particular area is known as Steel Field. While the town of Bastion houses thousands of weavineers, only the elite are allowed access here. This is where we work on the most important inventions. As of late, Steel Field's focus has been on Lilu Intel's greatest invention: the travolter."

Weavineers stopped to stare at Bryson as he passed. Most piled materials into crates; some were aboard the travolters, wiping then down with wet rags; while others combined their efforts to manually push the wheeled machines off to the sides. It must have been the end of the workday.

To his felicity, nobody bowed. They simply exchanged whispers here and there. Some made it a point to look the other way, focusing on their tasks instead.

"There are a lot of these travolter things," Bryson said, eyes drawn to the strange vehicles. "Looks like a success."

Lilu forced a laugh. "Ninety percent of these don't work, and the ten percent that can be considered operational are only halfway so. Only my prototype functions the way it's intended."

"So why don't you just make them all?" he asked.

"Because making a single travolter takes an entire month."

He scoffed, then spotted a travolter raised on a stage at the front of the field. That must have been the prototype. The exterior's sheen suggested a daily polishing, and the size of the monstrosity dwarfed everything else on the field. He couldn't find a single flaw in its appearance, and its functionality was likely flawless, too.

Bryson, Lilu, and Wendel climbed onto the stage and observed the weavineers ending their day. Dozens of people rolled mop buckets onto the field, slapping soapy water onto the steel floor. He cringed, imagining the amount of time it took to mop a floor of this size.

"I thought only weavineers are allowed down here," Bryson said.

"Yes," Wendel said.

"Then why do you have a custodial crew?"

"They are weavineers, too," Wendel said. "But a much lower rank. Everyone has done it at least once before."

"I don't recall mopping any floors," Lilu said.

"That is true," Wendel said, stroking his smooth chin. "You and your team have been an exception." He looked at her teasingly. "Perhaps we should change that?"

"No, thank you."

"I was under the impression you didn't want handouts because of your royal status," Wendel said.

With her trademark eye-roll, she groaned. "Using my words against me. But yes, you're right. I don't want handouts because of my title of princess. However, I'm willing to accept privileges that stem from my merit as a successful weavineer."

After the field had been cleared, three people approached the stage. He remembered seeing them upon his arrival to the city earlier in the day, standing next to Lilu. Despite what must have been a long, arduous day, they didn't seem exhausted or annoyed. They guffawed and moved with a bounce, lab coats tossed over their shoulders. They weren't just colleagues, but good friends. And as they neared, he noticed their youth. *They* were leading groups of elite weavineers?

Wendel stood. "I think I'll turn in for the night. It's quite a trek back to my villa. Do enjoy your stay, Bryson."

Bryson shook Wendel's hand. Lilu had already headed for the front of the stage and was now jumping down to the floor, hands pressed against the front and back of her dress. He followed.

She looked at him, gesturing toward the three strangers. "Bryson, these are my friends: Gracie, Frederick, and Limone." She then turned toward them and performed the gesture in reverse. "Guys, this is Bryson Still, my future brother-in-law."

Bryson shook Gracie's hand, who looked at him with narrowed eyes. Limone's grip was clammier and unsteady, the line of sweat trickling down his forehead suggesting anxiety. Then he regarded Frederick, a dark-skinned young man who matched his own height. They were both short in stature when compared to the average male, but Bryson had the muscle to make up for it. Frederick was scrawny like Agnos.

When he started to bow, Bryson grabbed his shoulder. "Please don't."

Frederick nearly fought Bryson's guiding hand. "But it's a sign of respect."

"If Lilu deemed you worthy enough to consider you a friend and colleague, then that speaks volumes enough. If anyone needs to show respect, it's me. I'm the stranger who has appeared on your doorstep, not the other way around." He extended his hand. "Shake it."

Frederick did exactly that. Bryson looked at Lilu. "What do we do now?"

"We find our place of residence here in Bastion. It seems now that you're here Wendel wants us to spend more time in Bastion rather than in Brilliance."

Gracie dropped her shoulder and tilted her head, a profound frown on her face. "It's dark and dreary down here."

Lilu whirled, heading in the direction of the town. "I'm sure you'll have a change of heart once you see our townhouse."

*　　*　　*

Lilu entered the bedroom she had apparently claimed days ago when Wendel showed her the place. An irate Bryson followed her inside, closing the door behind him. The others were busy admiring the kitchen downstairs.

"I'm sorry, Bryson," she said, sinking into the frilly sheets of a four-poster bed. "I really am."

"We're supposed to be friends, Lilu," he said, marching away from the door to stand at the foot of the bed. "I can't believe you never told me about the people who govern this city!"

"Keep your voice down. I don't want their first impression of us to be that we fight all the time."

Bringing his hand to his face, he seethed quietly into his palm. "We're not fighting," he muttered. "I just … I can't …" He bent over and placed his hands on his knees. "They are the people responsible for raising my father to be the man that he became."

"Oh, dear," she said, a pitiful frown on her face. "If you think that's unnerving, just wait until you discover how this city treats Mendac's legacy."

"Your story of how the city responded to you breaking his statue said enough," he said. "I will do my best to avoid public places." He began to peruse the room, fidgeting with Intelights contained within small glass spheres. They sat atop stone holders on nightstands, desks, and other surfaces. He picked up one from its stone base. The buzzing white light suddenly dwindled to a dull yellow. He had no idea how these things worked.

"You took it off its permanence vessel," Lilu said, noticing his confusion. "Thus, it no longer has a renewing supply of Intel chains. Its glow will continue to fade until the final chains die out."

He eyed her curiously, then returned it to its home. "Whatever that means," he said, looking elsewhere.

"I can't believe my dad actually let you come up here," she said, removing her heels. "Was it hard convincing him?"

"It would have been a stern no had Shelly not thought up something evilly genius," he said, now fidgeting with a needle and compass, spinning it in his hand. This room was full of useless junk.

"And what was that?"

He turned toward her. "Well, you're aware of my inability to weave ever since the Blizzard of Blood." She nodded. He raised his hands and emitted sparks from his fingertips. "It seems I'm still suffering from dysfunctional clout. And how effective would I be in a war without my electricity?"

"Very," she said matter-of-factly. "You still have your speed."

"It's not enough," he said. "Perhaps, if I had a sword to pair it with, but Debo never taught me how to wield one." He grunted. "Anyway, if Toono is to be my opponent down the line, then I need every asset."

"And what does coming up here have to do with your electricity?" she asked.

"It's a long shot, but Shelly thought maybe Director Jugtah could be able to do it. Didn't he revive Vistas after his heart stopped beating? Something about restoring a pulse to the nervous system. Perhaps he can do the same to my energy system."

"Bryson ... I don't think it works that way."

"It doesn't hurt to ask or try," he muttered.

"Maybe we'll go visit him in the coming weeks."

Someone screamed Lilu's name from downstairs. "I guess we should get back to your friends before they think something's up," he said, looking back at the door.

"Yes, please," she said, getting out of bed. "For Gracie's sake, at least. The extremes she jumps to sometimes."

"What about the sewers?" he asked, setting down the needle and compass.

"That might take some time," she said. "Wendel hasn't let me or anyone else enter them recently. And nobody is allowing me to use their private entrances into the tunnels after my last visit. It seems the man I paid didn't enjoy finding out I hadn't used his balcony, but instead snooped beneath the city."

Bryson opened the door, allowing Lilu to pass through first. "All right, then. I suppose we'll find a way."

# 22

# Leecher

Days had passed since Himitsu, Kaylee, and Sal had discovered the mangled skeleton contorted within a pile of rocks. Himitsu and Kaylee had continued to be on edge, while Sal possessed an eerie sense of composure. When questioned about it, he'd mentioned his brush with death as a child in Olethros. He had returned to the sector following its collapse, met with the remains of an entire neighborhood strewn within the wreckage. The worst of it? He had found his newborn sister, Atychi, crushed and lifeless.

Himitsu had seen plenty of death in his lifetime, much of it by his own hand, but the idea of killing a child was terrifying. And while he had been saddened by the tiny skeleton he'd seen, it was the anger that kept him up at night.

What bothered him most was Kaylee's analysis of the bones. A skeleton should have meant complete decomposition, implying the person had been dead for quite some time. But she found chunks of body matter, fresh enough to have been only days old. What were they dealing with here?

This brought to light stories of Gatal Accus, First of Five. The fairy tale had mentioned the arrival of strange beasts following the meteorite crash, but that had always been an outlandish idea. In fact, most modern versions of the tale omitted it altogether. Even Kaylee had dismissed it as a possibility the moment he mentioned it.

With resources running low, they'd need to find a way out of the canyon soon. Unfortunately, they didn't know where they were. They had traveled countless miles without bothering to lay a trail down behind them, believing they could rely on Ophala's birds. But, like the group of orphans, they seemed to not exist.

"Either of you can contribute whenever possible," Kaylee said as they followed the canyon's southern wall.

"Not all of us were taught everything in this world," Sal said, grunting from exhaustion. "Just because you can navigate doesn't mean we can."

"It's one of my weakest skills," she said. "We're getting nowhere."

"I hope this Raul kid is still alive," Himitsu said.

"Hopefully they've already returned to the orphanage," she said. "I'd rather us be out here for no reason rather than find the kids, only to discover they're dead."

Himitsu stopped. "I guess we'll find out exactly what's happening in a second," he said, pointing to a bird flying toward them.

Skyrise landed on the ground, and then took flight, zipping past the trio in the direction of which they had come. They turned, eyebrows raised. Then they bolted after the falcon, failing miserably at keeping pace.

"Doesn't it realize we aren't damn birds of prey?!" Sal shouted, falling behind considerably.

Himitsu didn't respond. He was too focused on breathing properly. Skyrise was still in sight, for he wasn't flying at his maximum speed. Kaylee was behind him by a good margin. Still, Skyrise was moving too fast. The falcon understood the difference between his speed and theirs, yet he continued to pull farther away. This must have been something dire.

They had already gone this way, but had turned back before traveling too far because of the lack of supplies. It seemed they had only needed to venture a little deeper to reach what they had been looking for.

The canyon's walls tightened as they ran, swallowing them in a shadowy fissure. Skyrise was no longer visible. To make up for this, he released a screech that echoed violently down the narrow passage. They were on the right track.

Himitsu came to a stop, spotting Skyrise perched on a spire of rock that jutted from the fissure's wall. His eyes raked his surroundings, Kaylee and Sal arriving several minutes later. Both of them leaned against a wall, gasping for air.

"Wood," Himitsu said, reaching back toward Sal.

Sal tossed the rod of wood toward Himitsu, who caught it and swiftly sparked a fire with flint. He narrowed his eyes as he crept down the rift, torch in hand. Kaylee and Sal remained behind for now as they tried to recollect themselves. The fissure narrowed to that of a crevice, forcing Himitsu to turn sideways and shuffle his way through. He held his torch awkwardly in front of him, pain shooting through his shoulder from the awkward angle.

This was stupid. He could get stuck down here. His chest pressed against the wall with each breath, which only heightened his anxiety. He couldn't do this. He had to turn back.

As he began to shuffle his way back the way he had come, a feeble cry from behind made him stop. Slowly, he turned his head, gazing into the waning orange light. There was a child down here, somewhere.

He pressed forward again, doing his best to overcome the claustrophobia. Rock dug into his back, forcing him to readjust. But that made him twist his knee to the wrong side. He fought back a noise, not wanting to draw attention to himself from anything or anyone that might have been dangerous.

"Did you hear that?" said someone behind him.

Himitsu couldn't turn his head anymore, but he recognized the voice. "Kaylee, how did you catch up so quickly?"

"I'm smaller than you," she whispered. "Sal's staying behind. He can't fit."

Himitsu's eyes widened at a strange sound that rumbled through the crevice. It was low and grating, almost like that of a demonic entity in theatrical plays—something that would have damaged the voice box of most humans. Another child's scream followed, this time a girl.

He picked up his pace, shuffling with little regard for his body, nearly dislocating his knee a time or two. Kaylee was pressed against his shoulder, moving with much more grace. He wished she had gone first; she would have already reached the children.

The crevice widened, and he faced forward again. He ran down the narrow corridor, unaware that there was no longer sky above him. He stopped on a dime, Kaylee colliding with his back.

In front of him rose a ten-foot creature, skin pink like a hairless cat, back hunched slightly, and claws roughly a foot long. A group of dirty children were huddled against the wall behind the beast. Many of them wore torn clothes.

A lone girl sat in the middle of the rift, shaking uncontrollably as she tried not to look at the thing. It leaned over her with heavy breaths, releasing that low grating noise. She screamed in short bursts, her rapid breaths getting in the way. She was petrified, fully aware of death's proximity.

Himitsu darted forward, weaving black flames that sucked the rift of its little light, including the torch he had passed to Kaylee. The children's screams were swallowed by the beast's roar, its unique sound raising the hairs on his body. He used that sound as a guide, moving at a speed that would have made Bryson proud.

He reached for his waist and unsheathed his spunka sword. He dispersed his flames, letting light return to the rift. The creature turned, but its response was too late. Himitsu couldn't read its face; its eyes were framed by loose skin that drooped in bags. There was no nose, just more loose skin. And its mouth ... he almost faltered in his attack at the sight.

It was white and bony, skin stripped away. Its jaw was exposed from ear to ear, but there were no teeth. Tiny holes ran along it, like the grates of a vent.

Himitsu hacked downward. It dodged, stepping back with its left foot and straightening its posture. It had been an effortless motion, reading the assassin's speed with ease. He landed and stepped forward, thrusting his sword toward the creature's abdomen. But it only smacked his blade away.

Now that it stood without its hunch, it towered even higher than before. It wore no clothes and sported no hair, but it didn't possess a human's anatomy. There were no genitalia, only loose pinkish skin that drooped around its frame. Despite all of this, his eyes were drawn to the grated jawbone. It seemed every detail of *The First of Five* had been correct …

Leechers were real.

As children scattered, Himitsu adjusted his strategy, realizing he couldn't get too close. If he wanted to kill this thing, he needed to do so from a distance with weaving techniques—if he were to go by the legends.

Leechers fed off pure energy. The holes in their jaw were capable of sucking a human's body dry of it. However, energy woven into EC chains was useless to them, the belief being that the presence of nature's currents made the energy inedible.

A knife whizzed past Himitsu's ear and nearly struck the leecher in its chest, but a timely dodge rendered the attack useless. He whirled to find Kaylee with a bouquet of knives protruding from between every knuckle of her closed fist, her right foot kicked back in a fighting stance.

She glared at him. "Well, get on with it!" she screamed, a horde of orphans crowding behind her, some grabbing hold of her back leg.

He turned and studied the beast. Scientists and explorers had come to study this canyon over the centuries since Gatal Accus's heroics, but nobody had ever mentioned proof of the leechers or a meteorite—or at least they'd never made it public knowledge. Had they always known?

He shivered. Why were children being fed to these monsters?

The leecher roared. It tilted its head toward the cavern's ceiling above as it arched its back, its stretched arms falling to the ground. Himitsu relaxed. Since he knew what it was, killing it should prove easy. According to the tales, this was likely a smaller one anyway.

Himitsu swung his sword. Black flames emitted from the metal and sweept across the rift. They ran through the leecher, causing it to writhe in pain. Taking advantage of its distraction, he lurched forward and sliced off its head.

*　　*　　*

Himitsu nursed his knee while seated on the hard ground, leg extended in front of him. Sal was several paces in front of him, doing his best to help Kaylee escort the orphans into the open expanse of the canyon. She was focused on guiding them through the fissure since she was most suited. Sal had tried entering the gap, but that only led to her shoving him back out from the other side. Despite all the children had been through, the scene had brought a smile to a few of their faces, motivating him to continue the charade at the expense of her patience.

Himitsu wished he could share their enthusiasm, but he was bothered by too many things. According to one orphan, four children had died already. Their proctor—the only adult who had partaken on this adventure with them—had been the first to fall victim to the leecher. Following her demise, the children were stranded until they were eventually dragged through the rift and into the strange hollow on the other side. Perhaps he could find solace in the fact that they claimed to have only seen one leecher—the one he'd killed.

But there had been attacks in the open area of the canyon. Was it the same leecher or were there two of them, raising the question of the other's location.

Night had fallen by the time Kaylee exited the crevice with the final orphan. Sal held the torch, a smile on his face as he provided light for the children surrounding him. She retrieved two waterskins from her bag, giving one to a child on each end of the group with instructions to share and pass them around. Though she forced a smile, the exhaustion and heartbreak on her face was clear to adult eyes.

They were all weak and in desperate need of a wash. Himitsu could no longer distinguish their collective stench. He finally managed a smile, spotting a young girl who pointed with intrigue at Kaylee's silver eye. She took it in stride, popping it out by smacking the back of her head, collecting a smattering of disgusted or amused expressions in return. He would have never been able to describe his perfect woman, but after knowing Kaylee for some time, he knew it was her.

She spent close to an hour looking into each child's eyes and pressing her fingers against their wrists, checking for a safe pulse. It seemed nothing was out of the ordinary, as she eventually made her way over to him. He tried to stop grimacing from the discomfort of his joints. Of course, she saw through his attempted pride, likely not even needing the use of her ancient to do so.

"I wish I had brought some medical supplies," she said. "Stupid of me."

He looked at her, his gaze flat. "You don't need to always think of everything."

"Yes, I do."

He looked forward again. There was no use arguing with her about it. Sal was busy lodging himself into the crevice, pretending to get his butt stuck to the glee of the children. To hear them laugh with such strength … it was strange, yet promising. Perhaps they weren't as broken as he would have expected.

"Sal is showing his worth," she said. "The man is a real softy."

"He grew up with six younger siblings in the poorest of households," Himitsu said. "I'd guess it was always his job to provide a positive outlook in bleak circumstances. Rhyparia had herself a great older brother."

He noticed Kaylee glance at him out of the corner of her eye, likely trying to read his aura. She didn't comment on it, however. Thinking of Rhyparia made him depressed; she didn't need to point it out.

They sat in silence for a long moment before Himitsu finally remembered the reason why they'd ventured into the canyon in the first place. "Is that Raul kid here?"

"He is, and he's in the worst condition out of everyone."

He scanned the children, eyes landing on a young boy who didn't laugh along with the others. He sat near the rear, head drooping slightly, his black hair a matted mess. He was scraggly and tiny, but that could have been the wear and tear of days spent away from civilization.

"I guess we wait before we start interrogating the poor thing," he said.

"That'd be wise. Our focus should be getting them back to Balle." She sighed. "And not to Lost Wisdom. We need to get word to your mom about that place."

"And about what we've discovered here," he added. "Leechers …"

"I doubt it could be considered a discovery," she said. "People have known about this, I'm sure of it. They've just kept it hidden … like most other dangerous things in this world. In fact, I read a book once about someone who had claimed to find one."

"I guess so," he said, cringing as he rubbed his knee. "Gale Thrasher turned out to be real, and nobody had believed that."

"If monsters like the Linsani exist, then I won't rule anything out." She looked up, where the shadowy underbelly of two islands floated high in the night sky. "There are so many mysteries to this world. Those two islands … what are they, exactly?"

He followed her gaze, but then glanced back at the children. "The only mystery I'm worried about is how we're supposed to get these kids back to Balle alive. We don't have any food, and that's the last of the water."

"Fair point," she said, rising to her feet. "I think we should depart now, not even bothering to wait for morning. I'm scared if they fall asleep, some of them won't wake back up."

Himitsu stood gingerly, letting slip a small groan. She grabbed his arm and tossed it around her neck. He had to lean over considerably to reach her smaller stature, but he appreciated her gesture.

She smiled at him, trying to blow her fallen bangs out of her face with no success. They stared at each other for a moment. Her silver eye dazzled in the moonlight, and his smile slowly slipped from his face as she moved her head toward his. Their lips were inches away from each other when Sal interrupted them.

"Have any of you children learned about the birds and the bees?" Himitsu yanked his head back and glanced at the man, who was pointing in their direction with a sly smile. "For such a lesson, I present to you: Exhibit A."

Some of the children cackled, while others—likely not understanding the joke—stared at the pair incredulously.

Himitsu pulled away from Kaylee, wobbling on his one good leg. He didn't know how she had responded to Sal's interruption because of how quick he looked away. He glanced at her. She was gazing at the ground with disappointment, eyes lazy. *Damnit.*

"We need to get going. We're not far from the city," he lied, gazing back at the kids. "Come on."

He turned and began to walk. The canyon's walls appeared to split farther apart in the distance. Kaylee walked with him, but she didn't speak. At least she stayed by his side. After a while, he said, "About what just—"

"It's okay," she said softly. "I see your regret. It was a missed opportunity, but I'm sure the chance will come again."

Butterflies filled his stomach. She was something special. He nodded, his posture straightening despite the limp.

A falcon swooped down from the sky, landing on a small stone with one talon. It dropped something from the other—a dead snake, the biggest one he'd ever seen ... *food.*

He hobbled toward the bird of prey. "Thank you, Skyrise!" he said, slowly dropping to his good knee. Then he laughed as he noticed what was in its beak—a branch of ripened berries. He turned back to Kaylee. "See how smart he is! He even got something for you!"

As she approached, Skyrise hopped to the ground and walked toward her. Stopping in front of her, he dropped the berries on the ground. He looked up at her, spreading his massive wings and twitching his head.

She ran a finger down his beak. "Thank you."

"Wow," Himitsu said. "That's how my mother's falcons show their respect. I've only seen them do that to her."

She picked up the branch and plucked off a berry, eating it with a smile. She leaned in, her face dangerously close to the falcon's beak. "Can you inform Pilot Ophala of what we've found here?"

Skyrise took off in an instant, but Himitsu didn't watch the bird as it flew into the sky. Instead he gazed at Kaylee, like he had done so often since meeting her. She was the most interesting person he had ever met in his life.

# 23

# Erafeen: The Man who Crossed Realms

Recently the Cracked Pearl had become a landmark of sorts in the pirate town of DaiSo. What once had been a mostly deserted bar, home to the washed-up or downtrodden of pirates, was now a thriving social hub with more customers than product. The barman, simply known as Twig, was forced to begin taking out dirty loans from some of the shadier pirate crews in order to pay for more booze and food to stock his bar. Alas, the demand was growing exponentially while the incline of supplies was steady at best. One would think an increase in business would have been a welcome change for a poor barman, but his baggy eyes and shakiness suggested a lack of sleep from unimaginable stress.

Agnos had been coming to this bar with Tashami on a daily basis since discovering it years back. He had grown fond of its atmosphere, granting seclusion from the crowded streets or rowdy Whale House. Now, as his eyes raked the barroom and its dozens of customers, he questioned his reason for continuing to visit. It was as loud as the crew house, vulgarity and a strong stench commonplace.

Perhaps it was guilt. The reason the Cracked Pearl had become such a sought-out destination was because of his frequent visits. Pirates came to see the captain of the Mythmaker and his mighty quartermaster. Even if they weren't here, customers stayed just for the chance of their arrival. Some wanted the ability to say they had dined in the same establishment as the Sixth of Six, according to Twig.

Agnos saw opportunity in this information, but not because of what most might have thought. A lot of pirates came to the bar in hopes of getting luckily recruited by Captain Agnos, but he had no interest in them—no matter how skilled they were.

He wanted Twig. Every crew of pirates—or every elite crew—had a member who filled one of the most important roles: the informant. Many would argue the informant was more important than even the navigator or utility commanders. Agnos saw them all to be on the same level, though the informant was a very special case.

Informants didn't partake on voyages. In fact, they almost never stepped foot on the ship at all. Their job required their permanent presence in DaiSo, discreetly collecting information to then pass it on to their captain. If a crew had a good informant, then the captain knew how to maneuver within both the political field of pirate crews and the battle field of the open sea. They knew who to avoid and who to follow, which allied crew plotted to backstab you, and which rival crew was preparing to chase a hefty treasure. These were just a few of many questions a good informant could provide answers to.

Considering Agnos's sudden propulsion into pirate lore, he needed someone to fill the position. Gray Whale had one, though she had yet to give Agnos or Tashami the person's identity, bringing to light the most desirable trait in an informant: their secretive nature. Only the captain could know their identity, and in some special cases, the quartermaster, too.

Agnos had to pick someone who nobody would predict. Gray had told him to not pick an enemy or anyone who had wronged him. Those relationships were always the first to be questioned by a rival captain or informant.

This was why, today, Agnos and Tashami entered the Cracked Pearl through its backdoor rather than the front, directly into its storage room. Twig was already waiting for them, making himself busy by dragging sacks of flour into a vacant corner of the room.

Agnos and Tashami removed the hoods of their cloaks, pinned at the lapel. Twig turned, dusting off his hands against his trousers. "Hello, boys."

He was an older gentleman well into his early fifties, so hearing him address them as such was understood. They may have been approaching their mid-twenties, but they were still children in his eyes. It seemed a full beard didn't do much to hide it for Agnos.

"Good evening, Twig," Agnos said, stepping forward to shake the man's hand. Tashami followed suit, then found a sturdy crate to sit on. Twig remained standing.

"How are Eet and Osh doing?" Agnos asked, deciding to ease into the conversation with something light.

The barman nodded. "Good, good. They're excellent busboys."

Agnos smiled. "I'm glad. They do enjoy having something to do when not at sea, and this grants them a small coin. They're also getting older now, so this is a good learning experience."

Tashami lifted the lid of a nearby crate. "Can I have one of these?" he asked, pulling out a green apple.

"Of course," Twig said. "Apples are a bit more expendable than other goods, considering Tsubasa Forest grows them in generous amounts."

Agnos regarded Twig with pursed lips. "Obviously, we requested you in a setting such as this for an important reason."

"I figured."

"Have you ever thought of joining a crew?"

Twig paused, an unreadable expression on his face. "No," he said. "I'm not fond of the sea, despite my mother's constant nagging to follow her out there."

"Well, that's perfect," Agnos said with a smile. "This role wouldn't require your presence during voyages. You could remain right here in your thriving bar."

Twig raised an eyebrow. "Is that so?"

"Yes, and nobody needs to know you're a member of the Mythmaker, including my own crew. Only Tashami and I will be privy to this information."

Nodding, Twig closed his eyes as he leaned against a shelf of spices with folded arms. "You want me to be an informant."

"Precisely."

"That's a dangerous job."

"If it's done poorly, yes," Agnos said.

Tashami, who had been crunching on a chunk of apple, wiped the corner of his mouth with the back of his hand and said, "You have the perfect cover, Twig. It's the captain's job to make sure their informant is someone in a pristine position to observe both the masses and individuals." He extended his hand toward the bar beyond the closed door. "You have one of the busiest establishments in DaiSo on what has become one of the most trafficked streets. Pirates from every crew gather here. You hear all kinds of stories every day while you stand behind the counter."

"This is true," Twig said, gazing distantly at the door to the bar. "And I have the two of you to thank for that."

"Unnecessary," Agnos said with a wave of his hand. "If you accept this offer, you can expect to be paid handsomely, like any elite member of my crew. Another added perk is that I will pay you consistently and uniformly. Unlike other crews that pay their informants on a commission basis—the more useful the information they provide, the better their pay—I will always pay you the same amount. And it will be quite generous."

Twig grinned, displaying a few missing teeth. "I've always liked you, Captain."

*Captain?* "Does that mean what I think it does?" Agnos asked.

"I'll be your informant."

Tashami stood and tossed his apple core into a waste crate. He walked over to Twig and shook his hand. "Welcome to the Mythmaker, Twig. You start today."

*　　*　　*

Agnos sat on DaiSo's beach later that afternoon, letting the sand scorch the bottoms of his bare feet. Since living in the pirate town, he'd grown accustom to the sand. His soles had calloused to a point of near-numbness. Because of this, even his clogs had become less an accessory and more a decoration on the floor of his room back at the Flailing Fin.

Tashami and Barloe flanked him, also seated in the sand. They were in the midst of a conversation about what this "gift" was that Spirit Queen Apsa was supposedly sending today. Agnos, meanwhile, dwelled on the chronicle hidden beneath the floorboards of his room.

*Erafeen* was the most rewarding yet most frustrating book he'd ever read. Translating it didn't get any easier as he progressed through its pages. He was lucky to have his relic. Without it, the chronicle would have served no purpose, for he wouldn't have been able to read it.

The way Tonitrua told her story perturbed him to no end. While he had learned a lot of intriguing information about certain Originators and their essences, she had yet to mention the mystery of Earth once. Also, she didn't speak much on this thing she was chasing. The closest she had gotten to this topic was her mentioning of a structure with no boundaries on an island at the center of the sea, but that had felt like a teaser for a bigger revelation. Perhaps she'd speak more on it later.

The obvious possibility for what she had described was the Warpfinate. And if that was the case, he would have been livid with himself. He'd spent years at Phesaw, several days a week in that very building, but his own fears had stopped him from venturing too far into its depths. His scope of knowledge was vast enough to have let him explore more, but he'd been scared he might not escape one day. At certain depths, there were *things* in that place.

People around him began to stir with excitement. He looked up toward the gulf's horizon, where blue sails stood faintly against the sky. A small warship was making its way toward DaiSo.

"Do you think she's giving you the ship?" Tashami asked.

"Who knows?" Agnos said, not ruling out anything at this point. If Queen Apsa had once gone to the extent of having a galleon as big as the

Mythmaker made for him, there was no telling how much further she'd go to help him.

"I don't know who would captain it."

Agnos turned at the familiar voice. Crole, a squallblaster of the Whale Lord, stood behind them, staring toward the horizon with narrowed eyes. His mullet was dripping wet, as was his tunic.

"You just get done going for a swim?" Tashami asked.

"Nah, I had to run all the way here from the Whale House. Nobody woke me up."

Agnos shook his head and laughed. "It's three o'clock in the afternoon, Crole. Your body should have woken itself up hours ago."

"Oh well," Crole said. "The question remains … Who would captain it?"

Agnos and Tashami exchanged looks, both knowing the answer had it still been a possibility. Tashami's time as a pirate was nearing an end. They were simply waiting for instructions for him to depart. Hopefully they'd never come.

"Probably Barloe," Agnos said, regarding the sea again.

"I don't know if I have the patience," Barloe said, voice gruff.

Agnos raised an eyebrow at him. "You were once a quartermaster, which requires the most patience on the ship, you buffoon."

The ship reached the harbor an hour later. Agnos remained seated, waiting as a longboat was lowered from the side of the ship. From this distance, he couldn't get a headcount of those onboard. As the boat reached the shoreline, he made note of the woman at the front first.

She was fair-skinned with hair the color of the sky, made even bluer by a crystalline substance entwined within. It sparkled in a dazzling display of lights underneath the blazing sun, making the sea's surface seem dull. She stepped out of the boat, her bare feet submerging in the shallow water. Those who followed were all men, most of whom were shorter than her. Despite the elegant look of her hair, the rest of her was typical of a sailor. Her tunic's sleeves had been torn off, exposing the lean muscle of her arms. And her breeches were baggy around the legs, rolled up at her knees.

"Have fun with that," Crole said, a hint of fear in his voice.

Agnos shrugged. "She's like a younger Gray."

"How's her hair doing that?" Tashami asked.

"Diamonds?" Crole said.

Barloe guffawed, clutching at his stomach as he rolled forward. "Entering a haven for pirates with diamonds in your hair? Is she asking to get robbed?"

The woman stepped onto the beach, a group of nine men trailing her. She stopped near a man who was busy dragging his own boat onto the beach and said something to him. He replied by turning and pointing at Agnos's group. She nodded her thanks before approaching them.

"Captain Agnos," she said, extending a hand as she came to a stop in front of him. "We're your reinforcements for you voyage to the Dark Sea. My name is Evelyn Tesai."

He stared at her for a protracted moment, observing the crystals in her hair—no, that was *frost*. His eyes widened, noticing the drop in temperature as she stood there. It wasn't unbearable, but it was definitely noticeable.

"It's bloody cold," Crole said.

Agnos stood and shook her hand. Her palm felt like ice. "Are you … Stillian?"

"That I am. Still Queen Apoleia has been sending some of her troops to the True Light kingdoms since the new alliance months ago. She sent me to Spirit Queen Apsa, who, in turn, has now sent me to you."

"So you're a soldier?" Tashami asked, rising to his feet.

She glanced at him and smirked. "Not quite. I'm a Diatia."

The two Jestivan stared at her in shock, and Crole asked, "What's that?"

"A group of elite students at Ipsas formed to counter the Jestivan," she said.

Crole's eyes skated between Agnos and Evelyn. "So you're rivals."

"Not anymore," she said, scanning the beach as if no longer interested in the conversation. "I'm looking forward to the voyage. Anywhere to find a bite to eat?"

"I know just the place," Agnos said.

*     *     *

Eet and Osh barged into the Flailing Fin long after early evening hours. The sudden intrusion caused Zorra to drop a tray of drinks onto a customer. She grabbed a rag from her shoulder and began to wipe the customer's vest. "My apologies, sir."

The two children laughed as they darted for the stairs to the side of the bar. Zorra glanced back at them with fiery eyes. "You brats! I'm coming for you later!"

Skipping steps two at a time, they reached the top and ran into the first room on the right. Eet giggled maniacally as he slammed the door shut, leaning back against it and sliding down to the floor. Osh was already on the far end of the room, pushing a nightstand away from a section of floor that wasn't coated in dust. She knelt down and lifted a loose plank, wasting no time in snagging a stack of parchment from within.

"Hurry up!" Eet said. "Before Zorra comes and rips us a new one."

Osh ran to a desk and climbed onto it. She found the sheet she had last finished reading, then cleared her throat. "Mialo, King of Minds, was my epiphany …"

*      *      *

Mialo, King of Minds, was my epiphany. But long before he visited me, he had visited others. He was a special case when it came to the Originators. He could teleport, much like Dimiourgos, King of Ethos. While the rest of us refused to travel between realms because of the risk involved, Mialo didn't have to worry.

Rumors circulated over the years. Apparently, the King of Minds was making appearances in the Light Realm kingdoms. This was odd, considering the Originators didn't step foot between neighboring kingdoms, let alone an entire other realm. We kept to ourselves, refusing to stir conflict with our adversaries. And yes, simply trespassing was enough to spark a major war in such times. Our world was and still is a volatile one, especially after centuries of countless wars.

As time passed, I communicated with a few of my fellow Originators to discover what Mialo wanted. They didn't say much—perhaps, because he didn't say much to them. Or maybe they simply didn't want me to find out, fearful of what my response would be.

Mialo was pitching a proposition, one that was frightening enough to put the Originators on edge. Speculation consumed me following this news. What could the man have been suggesting that would give immortal beings such as myself a reason to cower? Was it the promise of a powerful alliance or the threat of war? He was crossing into the Light Realm after all, and while there have been hundreds of wars fought within the realm, there had never been one that spanned across both.

After news spread that the other four kingdoms had received visits—all ending in refusals—I feared I was next. How would Mialo respond when I became the fifth and final "no"? The question I should have asked myself was: how would the world respond when I became the first and only "yes"?

# 24

# Priestly Constables

Illipsia sat in bed while Trish, one of her three roommates, packed her bags. Trish sniffled quietly as tears stained her cheeks. She'd been crying for close to thirty minutes, and Illipsia could do nothing but pretend to read a book on the classification of ancient pieces. Many pitied her whenever she did this, for everyone knew her as an Unable.

Trish finished packing by stuffing a raincoat into the top of her last bag. She pulled the drawstrings, pinching the mouth closed. Then she grabbed four of her bags and tossed them over her shoulders, allowing them to hang down her back. The other two she lifted with her other hand. She stood as straight as her strength would allow her to under such weight, and then turned toward Illipsia.

Illipsia looked up, noticing the sound of ruffling had come to a stop. Trish was leaving Phesaw, a foster family in the Archaic Kingdom awaiting her arrival. She had been adamantly against returning to her home kingdom, favoring the freedom and social life garnered here at what was essentially a refugee camp. But this was never supposed to be a permanent solution. That reality had become apparent as Phesaw's population dwindled over the past couple of months.

Her tears were leftover from her heartfelt goodbyes with their other two roommates. The three of them had built a relationship akin to sisterhood, while Illipsia had become the recluse. This goodbye would go a little differently.

"Well, Illipsia, it was nice knowing you."

"Likewise," Illipsia said, understainding they really didn't know each other.

"I hope you break free of those shackles one day," Trish said.

This gave Illipsia pause. She stared at Trish with calm eyes. "I'm not bound to anything."

Trish smiled, wiping a tear from the corner of her eye. "I think leaving you is the saddest part." She paused. "Perhaps it's regret ... regret that I never tried harder to connect with you."

Illipsia gazed down at the open book in her lap. "It's better you didn't."

After tilting her head, Trish said, "I believe that." She sighed, taking one last look around their room before heading for the door. "See ya, Illipsia."

The door closed, and Illipsia stared at it, the sun beating down on her neck from the open window. If she could, she'd make no friends. Alas, it wasn't as easy as that. Humans were drawn to company; she understood this. Nobody wanted to be alone. She just wished she could defy this law of human nature. It'd save herself and others from the heartbreak of her eventual treason of their trust.

She got up and shut the window, then closed the black curtains. Darkness swallowed the room, accompanying what felt like a pit in her heart. The nature of her missions definitely took a toll on her, but she had to keep reminding herself there was a reason for all of it. The Intel Kingdom had struck first, going after Dev King Rehn and enslaving hundreds of her people. Even if it had been before her time, that fact still hurt her. Toono was working toward revenge. As long as she kept telling herself this, she could soldier on.

Her other two roommates would be gone for the rest of the day. They had studying to do in the Warpfinate, and based off the books she'd heard them discussing, they'd need to travel quite a ways into its depths—if they could even make it far enough to find them. Still, it granted her time to work on the lock situation.

Ever since her encounter with Yvole in Phesaw's main lobby weeks back, she had become hesitant in her movements around the campus—almost to a point of standstill. Did he know exactly what she was planning, or had he simply noticed a pattern to her suspicious behavior? Either way, laying low was her best option for now.

This gave her time to focus on simultaneous weaving, once taking a backseat while her focus turned toward hallucinogenics. A big part of this mission would rely on her ability to perform multiple weaving techniques at the same time. While she was working on picking the locks, she'd need to also track movement outside the auditorium using her clairvoyance.

She retrieved a box from beneath the bed and lifted the lid. Dozens of bolt locks stared up at her, ranging in levels of intricacy. She had been able to unlock all of them individually, but there were a few that were more stubborn when she tried to pick them as part of a group. Those were the ones she reached for.

She began to work on four at once, only managing to unlock two. As she droned through the process, her mind drifted to the moment she'd finally take action in the auditorium. She had a plan in the works, but it would require Beren's assistance.

*　　*　　*

"This is the strangest city I've ever seen in my life," Vuilni whispered.

Olivia walked between her and Fane, eyes slowly raking over what was more of a forest than a city. A mix of birch and willow trees surrounded them, and there might have been just as many wild animals stalking about as there were humans. She felt something here … something homely and familiar, derived from memories not her own.

"How are we even supposed to know where we're going?" Vuilni asked.

"We don't," Fane said.

"Aren't you an accomplished assassin?" she asked. "How is this shocking to you? You've worked closely with spies over the years. Aren't there some here?"

"The spies who operate in the Prim Kingdom don't need assassins, for their objective isn't assassination. In a kingdom such as this, what you seek is information … that's it." He paused. "But even that is impossible to come by in a culture of self-guarded secrets."

"Then how did Grand Director Poicus find out about the first sacrifice?" Olivia asked.

"Long ago, before becoming the Grand Director, Praetor had a chance of becoming the Spy Pilot. He was an expert at the art. He knew a lot of the most skilled spies, and I think he might have had one in Asalka." He frowned. "Who knows? That person might still be here."

They continued through the city, grass reaching higher as they went. Birch canopies shrouded the sky, thousands of fireflies lighting the forest. The willows were humongous, seemingly acting as a place of gathering, people entering and exiting the curtains of branches that streamed toward the ground. As curious as she was about what was inside, she stuck to the clearings.

As the paths grew more untamed, the crowds dispersed. She began noticing a few men and women who would walk the streets in white robes, absent of design or accessories. They weren't like normal citizens, who dressed like any common person would from another kingdom. They also wore thick, silvery headbands that fell to a triangular point between the eyebrows.

"Do you think those headbands are purely decorative or do they serve a purpose?" Olivia asked.

Fane followed her gaze toward a dark-skinned priest with long black hair. "They might tell themselves they're religiously symbolic in some way, but they look ornamental, like something to distinguish themselves from the commoners."

Olivia shook her head. "I don't think so, not in a place like this. These people take their beliefs very seriously."

"It's strange," Vuilni said. "They don't look like constables or officers, but the way they strut around the city seems to imply it."

As Fane and Vuilni began discussing the purpose of the mysterious robed persons, Olivia remained fixated on the headband. It was abnormally wide, as if to hide something on the forehead. She thought of Toono, who had become notorious for the medical bandage wrapped around the top of his head.

She'd never asked him about it, but perhaps what he was hiding pertained to these robed people. It could explain why he had targeted this kingdom first. Maybe he had a personal vendetta against them. Had they betrayed him?

She raised an eyebrow as a robed woman came to a stop just outside of a willow's reach, facing away from it. A group of twelve to fifteen civilians congregated around her, listening intently as she began to speak. Olivia, Vuilni, and Fane stepped closer to better hear her, but they hadn't realized they were the only people still standing in the path. This brought the woman's eyes from her audience to them.

"Come here," she said after surveying them with narrowed eyes.

Olivia approached first, with her two comrades closely behind.

"Show me your palms," the woman said as they stepped through the audience.

As they held out their hands, it took no more than a glimpse for her gaze to become suspicious. "You aren't Primmish. What is it that you desire here?"

Olivia glanced back at a few of the civilians, all of whom wore fingerless gloves. They were hiding something just like the robed people. Many of the civilians hid their hands, grasping them behind their backs.

"We are Stillian Unables," Olivia said.

The woman nodded. "I should have known based off that violet hair. Are you related to the queen?"

"I am," Olivia said, trying to walk a tightrope between lies and truths. "A cousin of Olivia Still."

"I never knew Princess Ropinia had a child," the woman said.

It was a good thing Olivia instinctively showed no emotion. Otherwise, the surprise of the amount of information this woman knew would have shown on her face. "It's been a well-kept secret," Olivia said. "But now that we've aligned with True Light, the city of Kindoliya has decided to break out of its shell."

"I see," the woman said. "And who are these two?"

"Revered advisor of Still Queen Apoleia, ma'am," Fane said. "Newly appointed to the position ever since the queen's subtle shift in stance about male inferiority."

"Ah, yes. I've heard about that woman's philosophical differences to her predecessors," the woman said, posture stiff, neck elongated. She hadn't moved a muscle since confronting Olivia. Her gaze roved toward Vuilni.

"I'm simply a warrior, tagging along to protect Lady Olivia," Vuilni said. Both she and Fane impressed Olivia, falling in line perfectly with her ruse. They hadn't discussed this at all beforehand.

The woman studied Vuilni's body, eyes tracking up the bulging muscles in her calves and forearms. She nodded, then looked at Olivia. "I see they've put you in good hands, but I must ask again: What is your purpose?"

"To try and discover why Toono and his accomplice targeted your kingdom first," Olivia said flatly.

The woman faltered, her lips opening slightly. She addressed her audience and waved them off. "We'll reconvene later, at the break of second-night," she said. "I hope to see you all here."

The civilians slowly dispersed, many of them glancing back over their shoulders. One young girl lingered for a moment. "Thank you, Priest."

The woman gently pushed her away with a genuine smile. "Enjoy your morning, little one."

The girl ran away and disappeared within a willow's branches.

"A priest?" Fane said.

She ignored Fane and regarded Olivia instead. "You're very direct," she said. "Clearly, you aren't a spy."

"My intentions are not to be deceptive," Olivia said. "I'm here to gather information that can prove useful in the war against the Rogue Demon."

"Though you may have lied about your identities," the priest said, "I can tell you speak truth of your purpose."

"We haven't lied about anything," Vuilni said.

The priest smiled at the self-proclaimed warrior. "This Olivia woman might be a question mark, but the two of you are definitely not Stillian. While a common Stillian can't be so easily distinguished, a warrior mighty enough to protect a royal would be. I'd feel your freezing body temperature cut through the atmosphere around us." She looked toward Fane. "As for you, I'd go out on a limb and assume you don't have the distinctive scars across your back that every male in the Still Kingdom possesses, reminding them of their inferiority."

"If you know so much about my culture, then you know how shameful it is to expose such scars to the public eye," Fane countered.

"I don't really care," the priest said. "I'm not worried about your identities. Do you think this is the first time we've had liars visit our capital? Most of the time, however, it's because of our religious practices. But it seems what you seek involves the political branch."

"Does that mean you'll help us?" Vuilni asked.

"I cannot," she said, closing her eyes and shaking her head slowly. "The religious zealots and royal elites are separate entities in the Prim Kingdom. We keep our distance and, for the most part, don't interfere with each other. The matters of the Rogue Demon and his assassination of the Prim Prince are strictly theirs."

"Very well," Olivia said, turning away from the priest. "We'll be on our way and out of your hair."

"Strangers," the priest called out as Olivia walked away. They didn't turn back. "I advise you adapt the same philosophy … if you favor your lives."

*     *     *

"We need to get to the Power Kingdom now. I don't care how it happens," Rhyparia said.

As Saikatto raised a spoonful of noodles to his scarred face, Rayne leaned back and crossed her arms. "That requires us knowing how to get to the teleplatforms first," she said. "Do you suggest we simply wander westward and hope we get lucky and stumble upon them?"

"That's better than sitting here," Rhyparia said. She poked at her soup, scooping up broth only to dump it back into the bowl. Despite promises of a Prowler, they hadn't received one.

Saikatto cleared his throat and stared at the two ladies. He was an observational man, speaking mostly when spoken to. He was the complete opposite of a woman like Thusia, who made her voice heard whenever the opportunity presented itself. She wondered how the two got along back during their days as Jestivan.

"Why didn't we just bring the Craftmasters?" Rhyparia asked. "The Monsignors were wearing damned animal heads. If we had shown them a dimiour, they would have done anything for us."

"Is that so?" Rayne asked. "But what if, instead, they decided to go out of their way to make sure we couldn't leave? Do you really think religious fanatics such as the Monsignors would allow the very beings they worship to walk away, especially after a millennium and a half of never seeing one?"

"And what would they have done to try to trap us?" Rhyparia asked. "There is nobody here who could overpower any of us."

Rayne laughed. "We know nothing about this kingdom. If they can keep the details of something as big as their religion a secret to the rest of the world, how easy do you think it'd be for them to potentially hide powerful and talented fighters?"

"If you doubt yourself, that's fine," Rhyparia said. She glanced down at her umbrella that leaned against the table. "But I know what I'm capable of. There is no one who can stop me from achieving this mission."

"You're doing this to save the slaves, correct?" Rayne asked.

Rhyparia's gaze snapped toward the original Passion Jestivan. "Why even ask that? Of course I am." Rayne and Saikatto exchanged glances, and Rhyparia narrowed her eyes. "What?" Neither of them replied, so she confronted Saikatto. "You will give it to me bluntly. What is it?"

He placed his spoon in his bowl and straightened up. "Ever since your training with Musku, you've" —he looked off to the side, struggling to find the right words— "lacked patience."

Rhyparia stared at him during a long silence. Then her jaw relaxed and eyes softened. "Those twenty years did something to me," she said. "I think they messed me up."

"And we're trying to understand that," Rayne said in an empathetic tone. "We can't fathom the toll it took on you. After all, it was only ten months for us."

"It was torture," Rhyparia said, her voice weak. "Absolute torture." She looked down, knowing her expression had gone from convicted lunatic to wounded pup. "You've lived long lives. Imagine twenty years of it, but constantly training and only spending time with one other person."

"I'm afraid nobody can imagine it unless they experience it firsthand," Rayne muttered.

"And that's the problem," Rhyparia said. "Everyone expects patience from me. I can see the frightened looks in their eyes when I exert aggression I didn't have as a teenager. While that training only took close to a year from your perspective, you have to remember that I'm approaching my forties now."

"Despite all physical evidence," Rayne said, glancing down at Rhyparia's chest without shame, "I still see that young girl who showed up at our cabin's front step."

"That needs to change," Rhyparia said. "That was two decades ago—two decades of doing nothing directly fruitful toward saving the slaves, followed up by several months traversing a never-ending tunnel in the ground. I don't have time to spend more weeks here."

"We just want to make sure you aren't committing to anything rash," Saikatto said after finishing his bowl of soup.

Rhyparia's face scrunched at the center, as if offended by his words. "Of course not. I just want to save those who can't save themselves."

They studied her for a long moment before nodding. Had she really caused this much doubt in their minds? If it was this bad with them only noticing her shift in attitude, she was glad they didn't know her full intentions. Saving the slaves was only half of it.

A knock came from the door. She glanced toward it and noticed a folded parchment slip through the bottom crevice. She got up and approached it slowly, as if it was some sort of weapon. She picked it up and unfolded it. The message was short and simple:

*Your presence is requested this Sunday for the execution of Watcher Iris.*

# 25

# Moroza's Reinforcement

Intel King Vitio had become a fixture of the war corridor, almost as commonplace as the three-dimensional module of Kuki Sphaira that hung in the center of the room, hovering only inches above the floor. Every day he spent hours in the room, either with elders and advisors or officers and spies. Another common presence had become Vistas, since an hour of the day's schedule was dedicated to a broadcast meeting with his fellow True Light leaders.

Today was no different. Vitio sat in a plush ruby armchair near the center of the room, the wiring of Kuki Sphaira's module serving as his backdrop. Vistas sat across from him in a more prosaic chair. Three holographic displays hovered between them, the servant's dilated eye the source. His other eye, a deep burgundy, recorded Vitio.

Vitio had remained silent for longer than usual during the broadcast, allowing Spirit Queen Apsa, Passion Director Venustas, and Archaic King

Sigmund to carry the discussion. He put on an interested face and pretended to listen closely, though he was actually annoyed.

Every time Sigmund spoke, Vitio would glance at the young king's handsome face, making his annoyance more difficult to hide. He was trying mightily to not look at him the same way he had seen Apsa in the past—like a child. That perceptional flaw had been what led to the uprising in the Archaic Kingdom and allowed Toth Brench to establish control. He never heeded her warnings because he hadn't taken her seriously.

It didn't completely have to do with Sigmund's presence, but more so the absence of Pilot Ophala. That woman had meant everything to the swift upheaval of Toth's regime in the Archaic Kingdom. Without her working her skills as a spy, conducting grand schemes from veiled positions, Toth Brench would still be king. And that, coupled with Yama's control of the Adren Kingdom, would have been a disaster. SCAPD would have had two kingdoms in the Light Realm, and True Light would have only been three kingdoms strong.

Over the years the relationship between Vitio and Ophala had been a rocky one, and that hadn't changed. He saw her as the reason why the Amendment Order failed, and she was responsible for Rhyparia NuForce's escape from the noose. She had gone against most of the plans he had made for the Archaic Kingdom following King Itta's demise—and she was right in doing so. Vliyan NuForce had possessed the Cloutitionist's Necklace, and Toth Brench covered up this fact by replacing it with a decoy. Ophala had tried informing the royal heads of traitors and liars, but none of them listened.

And Vitio realized all of this when it was too late. During Pilot Ophala's recent visit to Dunami, during the ceremony where Shelly and Bryson introduced their child to the world, she had turned a cold shoulder toward him countless times. When she did speak to him, it was clipped and scornful. Even when he tried to apologize for everything, she wouldn't accept it. She claimed he hadn't changed, that his new socioenergenic classification system was a discriminatory travesty. Perhaps he shouldn't have ousted Himitsu's lady friend from the palace that night, claiming he couldn't trust her to sleep so close to his family.

Over the last few months, something unsettling had dawned upon him. While he may have not been an evil quite like Mendac LeAnce, one could argue he was no different than the likes of Archaic King Itta or Dev King Storshae. That was a catastrophic revelation, and he possessed nothing but respect for a woman with character like Ophala.

"Pilot Ophala has been bringing me a slow but steady influx of information about happenings in the Adren Kingdom."

The name ripped Vitio from his trance. Sigmund was in the middle of briefing the leaders about Ophala's findings from Adrenian lands. Since she was stationed in Phelos, she couldn't use her ancient to directly control the birds in a separate kingdom. But she'd established such a good relationship with the creatures of the sky over the decades that they were willing to act as scouts for her.

"SCAPD forces have swarmed Adrenian lands," Sigmund said. "She believes there are more Cynnish, Powish, and Devish troops stationed there than there had been in my kingdom when Toth ruled."

"Seems like they're bunkering down," Venustas said. "Preparing for the long haul."

Apsa nodded. "A strange siege of sorts, perhaps."

"Yama has been conducting suspicious behavior as of late," Sigmund said.

"Hopefully she's not preparing for another target," Vitio said.

"Not really ... she seems to be withdrawing from the main SCAPD forces."

An eyebrow shot up Apsa's forehead. "Oh? What kind of crafty maneuver are they planning now?"

"She's been traveling through the distant reaches of Spunka Forest," Sigmund said. "Pilot Ophala thinks she's headed for Yinyon."

"The home of Ataway Kawi?" Venustas asked. "Besides that distinction, it's the most irrelevant village in our realm. What in the world does she want out there?"

Vitio leaned forward and scratched at his beard. "Shelly and Bryson went out there once," he said, reflecting on his fury after waking to a rather unapologetic note from his daughter. She had taken Bryson to visit her Branian's grave—or so he had assumed.

"Well, Pilot Ophala is in the process of scavenging for any information on the village, including tales about the Third of Five," Sigmund said. "She wants to know why Yama deems it a worthwhile destination."

"Watch it be something personal and insignificant to us," Venustas said. "She might want to visit the graves of legends, possible iconic beacons of a skillset she wishes to achieve."

"Or maybe that's her home," Apsa said.

Venustas frowned, raising her eyebrows. "Maybe. None of the Energy Directors knew about her home life. Grand Director Poicus had recruited her from the Adren Assistance Academy."

"If she's that far removed from the main forces and the teleplatforms, we should take it as a temporary win," Vitio said. "I don't think Toono would try striking while his most skilled fighter is on the opposite end of the Adren Kingdom."

"Pilot Ophala had originally been worried that Yama was trying to lull us into thinking that," Sigmund said. "Apparently, everyone in the Adren Kingdom has become extremely cautious when outside or near any windows, fearful of the birds, so she must take what her birds hear and see with a grain of salt. She doesn't want to be lured. They might be doing something tactically similar to that seen in Phelos during the uprising— constructing secret teleplatforms. However, nobody was traveling with Yama, and she doesn't have reason to believe such a remote village would possess provod or own a Devish, let alone one that could be capable of such weavineering feats."

"We'll let Pilot Ophala continue to research the village," Apsa said. "For now, that's all we can do. We should move on to news regarding the seas and rivers. I have gone out of my way to personally seek out two Jestivan, Agnos and Tashami."

"Please give me good news," Vitio said, sitting forward with anticipation.

"Tashami has agreed to leave his life in DaiSo to act as the premier guard at the Intel Kingdom's teleplatforms," Apsa said, causing Vitio to sigh with relief. "He will be stationed there for the foreseeable future, until we feel the threat Toono imposes to be abolished."

"And how did Agnos take that?" Venustas asked, following a sip of water. "If I remember their relationship at Phesaw correctly, they were inseparable."

"They decided to put their realm ahead of their friendship, which is admirable," Apsa said. "As for Agnos, I decided to offer him the chance to partake in the war."

Vitio laughed. "He was on the ship when Gray Whale attacked the Brench Hilt and its Adrenian naval fleet, so some would say he was part of *starting* the war."

Apsa nodded gravely. That fiasco was a touchy one for her, seeing that she had quietly orchestrated it behind the backs of her allies, albeit for the greater good of the alliance. "I told him that he and Gray Whale should infiltrate the Dark Sea and prepare to head for the Dev River, with their ultimate goal being Cogdan's main port."

"I understand the main port is right next to the capital and at the heart of the kingdom," Vitio said, "but they'd have to sail through the kingdom, passing many lines of defense. Not to mention that word would reach the capital before the ship would—or *could*—even arrive."

"There are ways around that," Apsa said. "If they must disembark before reaching the port, they can do so wherever they want. I've also lent them several people who can prove useful ..." She paused, her gaze growing sincere. "Just trust me."

Vitio, Sigmund, and Venustas nodded without hesitation.

Apsa smiled, then reached for something located on her desk offscreen. It sounded like she was shuffling parchment, until she eyed the page she was looking for. "I've finally received word from the ships that partook in my ambush tactic in the Stalagmite Sea."

"About time," Vitio said.

"I'll admit, I'm surprised," Venustas said. "It's been so long that I just assumed the maneuver had been a failure, complete annihilation being the reason why no communication had been received."

"The exact opposite, actually," Apsa said. "Of course, the enemy ships had been prepared for anything, knowing we were onto Toth Brench and Wert Lamay's roles as moles in our alliance. The battle didn't go anywhere near as planned, but our side ended up victorious. The reason for the delay in communication was because the lone Devish I had in the fleet had suffered a shock-induced coma."

"Does that mean we still have our ships stationed in the Dark Sea?" Sigmund asked.

Apsa sucked her teeth, tightening one eye. "Not quite the numbers we once had ... we're down to three ships, and they're docked in the Still Kingdom for now."

Vitio sighed. "It's better than none, I suppose."

"As for the potentially unflattering news ..." Apsa trailed off, turning in her chair to look at a map of the sea and Realm Rivers swathed across the wall. "Our ships in the Dark Sea have noticed a frightening pattern in SCAPD vessels."

"And what is that?" Venustas asked.

"There are countless ships gathering near possible whirlpool locations," Apsa said. She turned to face the broadcast again. "We need as many ships as possible doing the same here. But whirlpools can be erratic at times. We can't predict them all, so there will be avenues into our realm that will likely go unprotected."

"I don't understand," Vitio said. "Does Toono plan to attack or defend? His tactics are all over the place."

Apsa closed her eyes. "He is exceptionally deceptive and has proven that anything Storshae, Itta, or Toth has done has been mere child's play. We speak so much about his physical talents because of his victories against some of the most elite individuals in Kuki Sphaira, but we fail to appreciate the unprecedented intelligence he possesses." She gazed straight into the broadcast, eyes as fierce as the Great Flame of Jarfait Meadow. "We prepare for an invasion by sea."

*　　*　　*

Ophala leaned against an armchair in the study of her office, both hands grasping its back. She stared at the small coffee table, where she'd accumulated as many books as possible regarding the village of Yinyon.

Unlike most of her scavenging sessions in the libraries throughout her life, this time she hadn't finished with a mountain of books to scour. Instead, she stared at the pitiful three books, each stacked atop one another to make it look like she had achieved something grander.

Was she looking too hard into this? Was she being led astray, like when King Itta had stationed her in Rim to scout the Archaic Mountains? She had never wanted to fall victim to such a misdirection ploy again, but she also knew to not let that fear stop her from chasing a lead—a frustrating conundrum, indeed.

She groaned, bowing her head and staring at her recently manicured nails. It was times like these that made her miss the Warpfinate. If one was dedicated and smart enough, they could find anything in that place. She rounded the armchair and took a seat, reaching for the top book in the stack. She stared at the cover for a moment: *The Third of Five*. Not favoring the idea of reading a fairy tale for the sake of studying, she tossed it onto the nearby sofa for later research. Perhaps she could read it before bed.

The second book, while having more promise than the fairy tale, still didn't spark a fire in her. It was a biography about Ataway Kawi, the man who became the legend of said tale. She slid that to the side of the table, revealing the final book. She stared at its cover for a moment: *Yinyon, the Village of Mundanity*. The title didn't sound promising, but it was the most logical place for her to start. She had read the other two texts countless times in her life, so she would have remembered anything unordinary mentioned about Yinyon. Thus, her best bet would have been something she had yet to read.

She picked up the book and leaned back in her chair, kicking one leg over the other, and opened to the first page. She reached for her wine glass on the end table and raised it to the level of her head as she began to read, lightly swirling its contents. The first few pages were dry, so the rich wine was welcome company. As she tipped the glass against her lips, in her peripheral vison she spotted a figure in her open window. She glanced over to see Skyrise, her favorite falcon.

Excited for a reason to escape her tedious task, she rose from her seat and approached her desk, waving at the falcon with a smile. Skyrise's eyes were as fierce as always, but that was typical of any falcon. Ophala grabbed her ancient, Cheiraskinia, from its spot leaning against her desk. It was a long staff with a single loop at the top, a rod stretching horizontally through it to serve as a perch. Skyrise swept into the room and landed on it.

Ophala smiled. "What is it that you have to show me, Skyrise? Good news, I—" She froze, having instinctively began the weaving process already, jumping into the bird's mind. She saw everything: the remains of a child, Himitsu and Kaylee's struggle through a narrow crevice, and a creature that wasn't supposed to exist, its mouth a grated strip of bone.

A leecher … It couldn't have been. She stopped weaving, then stared at Skyrise with wide eyes. Why were orphans being brought to such a place?

"Thank you, Sky. We'll speak more later."

The falcon took off, bolting across the room and out the window. Ophala placed her backside against the desk, body furling limply. She needed to send skilled scouts into Accus Canyon. And perhaps it was time she investigated Lost Wisdom.

*       *       *

It had been a long time since Toshik had gone to a theatre to attend a play. As a child, his father had taken him to many, since it was an expectation of a man of his status. While his mother was out hunting exotic beasts, his dad's idea of fun involved sitting on his rear and watching people pretend to be heroes. Instead of living it himself, like Mom, Toshik watched it from a safe distance.

This explained the sick sensation within Toshik's stomach as he followed Horos and Kuiku to their seats. Several rows of wooden bleachers stretched away from the main stage. They lacked cushions and armrests, leaving him even less thrilled to be here. At least when attending plays with his father, he could distract himself with the food of their luxury suites, not to mention they had been indoor venues. This place was exposed to the elements, granting the gnats free reign over any bare skin.

He sat down next to his comrades, a low buzz of conversation surrounding them. Torches ran along the pathways that split the rows of benches, aiding the stars and moons to illuminate the festivities. Vendors walked the paths with baskets hanging in front of them by rope around the back of their necks. They sold sweets and meats that had been cooked in the concessions behind the crowd, spreading a mouthwatering aroma in the air. Toshik called over a vendor and bought a food item he'd never seen before: several cuts of meat and peppers on a stick.

He sat in silence and enjoyed his food while Horos and Kuiku talked. The two men had grown fond of each other, which he was appreciative of. The more they interacted, the less he felt he had to. He preferred the company of his thoughts, though even they seemed to betray him lately.

While he'd been in Dunami, the distractions of his training had kept him from dwelling on his shortcomings that had led to the deaths of the women he loved. Now he felt he was at a standstill, and all the time he spent hovering in Tames allowed those painful memories to seep through again. He wanted to get out of this town, finally make the move toward Cogdan. Alas, Kuiku and Horos both agreed to exercise patience. They couldn't rush to the capital. It was best to throw Toono's timing off.

His eyes wandered as he bit into a green pepper, his taste buds receiving an instant kick from the spice. Families filled the benches … boys who were lucky enough to still have their mothers; boys who teased their sisters, unknowingly from a place of love. Then there were the couples, and his heart wrenched. Youthful love was abundant at such an event, and he found himself questioning how many times he had done something like this with Jilly. The instances were too few and far between.

The stage, which had been enveloped in darkness since his arrival, finally became visible as staff set flame to the torches running along its perimeter. A man stood in front of the stage, facing the audience with hands behind his back. He wore clothing from the earlier ages of Known History: velvety material with a ruffled collar. Toshik knew it to be stiff and uncomfortable, but the gentleman pulled it off quite nicely.

The chatter died down, and the man nodded in thanks. "We here at Tames Theatre are blown away by the turnout tonight. We always know to expect good attendance whenever we debut an act, but this was unforeseen." The man's eyes raked the crowd. "My apologies to those of you who must watch from the grass."

Toshik leaned forward and gazed down the length of his row, spotting a lot of spectators sitting on the ground. They seemed to have come prepared, however, as many of them had blankets lain beneath them. Some even had picnic baskets, distributing their farmed goods to their companions. Tames could thrive because of its self-sustainment.

"We all know the significance of tonight's act," the man said. "The three starring roles, as well as a fourth character, depict boys who once lived in this very town as best of friends at a young age. It was just after the death of Dev King Rehn and before the arrival of Mendac LeAnce to our small town. Tonight, you will witness a story of betrayal unlike any other. We ask that following its conclusion, the crowd remains calm. We understand a tale such as this can rile up certain emotions … especially for those of us who once knew these boys."

Toshik heard someone sniffling and glanced to his left. An elderly woman touched a napkin to her cheek. An older man sat on her other side, his arm draped across her back. Despite the stoic expression on his face, a tear also ran down his face, hanging for dear life on a loose fold beneath his chin.

"Well," the man said, glancing off to the side of the stage hidden behind a massive wooden wall. "It seems our talent is ready to get started. Without further ado, I present to you a play about the Inson brothers, *The Traitorous Triplets.*"

*      *      *

Perhaps because Toshik knew two of the men being portrayed, he found the play to be haunting. He'd never met Tristen, but knew of him. Bryson had told him the story once, how Tristen had acted as a double agent for Intel King Vitio over the span of several years, gathering information from the Dev Kingdom and King Storshae. He had even gone as far as to sacrifice his own life to show King Vitio and Lilu where Olivia was after she had been kidnapped. It had been a noble act, a cause worth dying for. Tristen had achieved something Toshik could not.

The actors who played the roles of the triplets each had a letter stitched into the front of their tunics—a *V*, *F*, and *T*—making it easier for the audience to distinguish between them. The story had a strong focus on the boys' backstory. He watched with intrigue, enamored by the skill of the young actors. He almost expected to glance to his right and see his father and little sister. The sight of two battle-tested men in Kuiku and Horos, however, brought him back to reality.

The triplets had been something special to Tames since they were the first of their kind in the village. The fact they each became highly talented in a certain skillset by a young age only heightened society's expectations. Vistas became known as the future scholar; Tristen, the future warrior; and Flen, the future Prayoga scientist. And despite the vast differences in their specialties, they were inseparable. Eventually they added the talented weaver, Marcus, to their circle of companions.

Each of them suffered mightily during Mendac's invasion of their town. Marcus was taken away from his family, and the triplets lost their parents to a massive fire said to have been sparked by Mendac himself. But one boy's story affected Toshik more than the rest.

At the age of fifteen, Flen was poised to become the youngest admitted student to a prestigious university in Prayoga. He'd been in the midst of packing for his departure on the very day Mendac arrived, with Brintlen, his girlfriend of two years, at his side.

"I'm so excited for you," she said. She sat on the floor. Apparently, the Inson family was too poor to afford anything outside of the necessities. Chairs didn't make that list.

"Should I be worried that you don't seem shaken up by my early exit?" Flen asked.

"And why should I seem that way?"

He stopped packing to gaze at her, dumbfounded. Eventually he shook his head and laughed, focusing on stuffing books into a travel sack again. "For someone who loves me, you regularly display the opposite."

"If we're to go by the adults in town, we don't even know what love is," she said.

"My brother may not, but we definitely do." He winked.

She guffawed, rolling backward as she covered her face. "It was one kiss!" she managed to say.

"And our first," he said, rising to his knees. He gazed around him, where a poor man's luggage lay in tattered sacks. Frowning, he asked, "Do I not get a keepsake to remember you by?"

She dug into a pocket of her holey pants. From how the actress played her part, she might have been a tomboy. She pulled out a flower: a Chocolate Cosmos, its petals as black as the sea on a cloudy night. The crowd gasped. Toshik took a look around, struck odd by the reaction.

"Where'd you get one of those?" Flen asked, taking it from her in awe.

She smiled. "There's a festival held in the Cosmos Meadows, silly."

"But you've never gone to it."

"Remember when I told you I was visiting family in Shreel a couple of months ago?"

He paused. "Uh, yeah."

"I actually went to the festival," she whispered playfully.

He lowered the hand holding the flower, expressionless. "And you didn't invite me?"

She crossed her arms and rolled her eyes. "Because you would have tried to drag your brothers."

"And rightfully so!"

She sighed. "Can't we ever do anything without them around?"

"We are the same person."

"Well, if that isn't a stretch …"

They both fell silent. Flen's gaze dropped to the flower in his hand. After a protracted pause, he smiled. "What was he like?"

"Who?"

"The Oracle."

"I've never met a greater man." Her response was immediate, as if knowing the answer before being given the question.

He rose to his feet, placing the flower behind his ear. "I hope the rumors my parents have been speaking about aren't true," he said. "I've heard Mendac has returned, seeking a shot at redemption."

"And King Rehn will simply lay waste to him like he did to that other Jestivan," she said. "I don't know why the Light Realm thinks they can just push us around. If they continue to trespass, especially with harmful intent, our king will do what it takes to punish them."

Flen nodded and looked toward a window, which was simply a rectangular wooden frame that hung nearby. His eyes narrowed.

"What is it?" she asked.

He approached the frame. "There's an orange hue in the sky … and … is that smoke?"

She ran toward him, mouth agape. "The mayor's estate is on fire," she said.

What followed was a tragedy, and Toshik found himself happy about the production's low budget. If this had been a show at a theatre back home, they would have showed every miserable detail. Flen and his brothers found their parents dead downstairs, slain by two men in golden military uniforms. The triplets were captured and bound by chains. As for Brintlen, she was killed the moment the Intelian soldiers had seen her, Flen watching hopelessly as he and his brothers were overpowered.

Toshik began to wonder what the point of this play was. Was its sole purpose to upset the audience? It was twisted and depressing, and there were no heroes. But his question was answered as the play progressed through its acts. In the second act, the triplets were painted as traitors, their helpful deeds to the Intel Kingdom put on display. Onlookers shook their heads in disappointment, and the elderly couple that had been sitting next to Toshik rose from their seats and exited the theatre.

The third act was different than the first two, depicting events that had yet to happen. The Dev Kingdom wound up victorious in the war. Flen and Vistas were brought back to Tames, where their eyes were gouged out with spoons before being stoned to death. They even went as far as having the ghost of Brintlen return during Flen's moment of death.

It was all very dramatic, but understandable. Who could blame Tames citizens for thinking the way they did? Mendac had been a ruthless monster, yet a lot of the Devish who had been enslaved by him continued to serve the Intelians in peace. It seemed the true blight on this town belonged to the Inson triplets.

The crowd cheered as the performance came to an end. The cast formed a line, linked hands, and simultaneously bowed. Toshik, Horos, and

Kuiku stood and clapped along with the rest of the audience, if only to keep up appearances. Remaining seated and unmoved would have only beckoned unwanted attention.

Horos leaned into Toshik and muttered, "The hatred these people have for the Intel Kingdom is unprecedented. If King Rehn is brought back to life, it would spell doom for True Light."

The three men were thinking the same thing; it was clear as day. If the kingdoms of True Light wanted to win this war, they'd need to find the Oracle's body.

*     *     *

Flen sat up in bed; another nameless woman stirred next to him in her sleep. He stared at her, studying the length of her fake eyelashes, the vivid red of her lipstick, a dark shade in the shadows cast by moonlight. She hadn't bothered dressing down her face before drifting into a deep slumber. He gazed at the empty bottles of bourbon on the nightstand next to her. Perhaps that was to blame.

Had anyone noticed the trend in the women he courted? Hair of honey, just long enough to brush the seat whenever they sat down; a face of makeup that only highlighted their natural beauty; and a body of delicate curves. He could never hide his guilt.

He was chasing someone who no longer existed, foolishly believing he could find it in someone else. He was a coward; this he knew. Even after the death of Brintlen, during which he stood chained to his brothers, wailing for the Intelian officers to lower their swords, he could never find the will to grow stronger. Instead, he tried to compensate for his lack of physical strength by forcing a witty tongue and an air of nonchalance. The fleeting bursts of bliss these random women provided him healed nothing.

He slipped out of bed and slinked over to a bolted door. He pressed a finger against the lock and weaved a pattern of Dev Chains until it clicked. He opened the door, stepping into a corridor as big as the main room.

277

Easels stood scattered across the floor, each of them depicting the same girl: Brintlen Edrania.

He couldn't sleep, and his depression had begun to mount. So he approached a half-completed easel, grabbing his palette and cup of brushes from a table on the way. He unscrewed the lids of his paint jars resting on the bottom of the easel, and then dipped his fine-tipped brush into the red paint. He smudged some onto the palette, mixing a bit of yellow with it.

The disasters of that night ran through his mind as he gazed at the painting, absentmindedly preparing his mixed colors. The cuffs on his wrists and ankles as he'd been dragged behind burgundy carriages stolen from the capital, watching the flames swallow the mayor's estate, smoke furling into the sky.

He placed brush against canvas and continued filling in the fire. That took only a few minutes before he moved onto the smoke. As he painted the shades of gray into the abstract shape of Brintlen's face, he began to cry. Tears slipped from his chin and diluted his colors. What would she think of him now, living illustriously under the roof of his captors, her murderers?

She'd never speak to him again.

His gaze flicked over to a painting he had completed years ago—an image depicted within he was sure never happened, but it was one he liked to imagine. A laughing Dev King Rehn with a hand to his gut and his other arm thrown around the back of Brintlen's neck, a forest of black flowers hiding their feet.

She had never mentioned personally meeting the Oracle, but Flen liked to think she did. If she had gotten to meet the hero of their kingdom, maybe Flen could hurt a little less … sleep a bit easier. Or maybe, he could do something more useful than play pretend …

He could help bring their hero back.

*    *    *

"Have you ever heard of the Warpfinate?" Toono asked, scanning through a book.

"Yes, I have," Homina said. Stacks of books in the middle of the table separated the two of them. "It's a shame such a phenomenon exists in the Light Realm, where I don't have access."

He paused at the end of a paragraph, looking up to scan Cogdan Castle's main library around him. While this was a grand room, complete with multiple levels and dozens of sections, it was nothing compared to what he'd been told about the library at Phesaw—the place of no boundaries. He'd never set foot in it, which was his biggest regret. Neeko had spoken of the wonder he felt … and the fear; he always made sure to mention that.

"Why?" Homina asked after a long pause.

"No reason," he said, continuing to read through his book about Kuki Sphaira's grandest landmarks.

Minutes ticked by in an awful silence, allowing Toono's thoughts to run amuck. He straightened his posture and exhaled slowly. He'd been avoiding a certain topic he'd planned to discuss ever since retrieving Homina from the Confines of Consciousness. He couldn't smother the urge to inquire any longer.

"Homina … when I saw you for the first time in the Confines, you muttered something about you and I being alike. You called yourself a primordial remnant, but said I was a more direct line. What did you mean?"

A hand slipped through the space between two stacks of books, pushing one to the side. Homina stared at him, her raven hair disappearing behind her back. "Let's put it this way," she said. "If Dev King Rehn had known about you like he had with me, he wouldn't have even bothered locking you up. He would have killed you on the spot. Your ancestors and his were not kind to each other, nor did they see eye to eye."

"And who were our ancestors?"

She shook her head and closed her eyes. "Of this we do not speak. Most do not know this, but discussion of events before the Known History timeline is considered an Untenable. And I don't have much of those memories anymore anyway—not since leaving the Confines. The only reason why I made such comments the first time you saw me was because of my state of mind."

He stared at her for a few seconds, but then simply nodded. He wouldn't pester her about it if that was her wish. The library doors opened.

Homina twisted in her seat, looking over her shoulder. General Gala sauntered in, followed by her former colleague: Still Warden Moroza. A young man nipped at her heels, tall and dark, frost radiating from his skin.

Toono placed a golden reed in the crevice of his pages and closed the book, standing tall and rounding the table to approach the group. Gala stepped to the side, introducing the Still Warden first.

"It's a pleasure to finally meet you, Moroza," he said. "I've heard about your dedication to the Dark Realm's cause even after the Still Queen shifted her allegiance."

"And it's an honor to finally meet you," she said, shaking his hand. Her fingers were clammy and cold, a feeling he had experienced when infiltrating Kindoliya Palace with Apoleia, Olivia, and Titus years back.

"How is Ipsas?" he asked, releasing his grip.

"Crumbling to pieces," she said with little emotion. "Nobody has seen Power Warden Feissam in years, and now Cyn Warden Pinako is dead. The Head Warden has retired because of this, not fond of mine and Gala's preoccupancy with your efforts in the war. He'd rather us stay out of it. And thus, the Prim Warden has stepped in to fill those shoes."

Toono raised an eyebrow. "Did he not form the Diatia specifically to combat the Jestivan in case of war?"

She belched a laugh, throwing her hands into the air. "Right? He didn't make any effort to use the Diatia properly, so that's why I figured I'd take matters into my own hands."

She stepped aside and allowed the taller gentleman to approach. He had an unsheathed sword strapped to his back, and Toono noticed that's where most of the frigid steam was radiating from, rising toward the library's cavernous ceiling. It wasn't a typical blade. It was huge, crafted of ever-ice, and likely heavy enough to only be wielded by someone with mighty strength.

"I know Gala told you I promised reinforcements," Moroza said, smiling at the young man. "While I couldn't gather the Prim Diatia for obvious reasons, this is one of my Still Diatia, Groto Yuln."

Toono studied him a moment longer before extending his hand. Groto grasped it firmly and looked him in the eye. "My queen may have forgiven them," he said. "But I won't. The wicked man raped my queen, and I will do anything to help your cause as long as it's in spite of the Intel Kingdom."

Crossing his arms, Toono gave a nod. "Welcome."

# 26

# The Duo Splits

Bryson stretched toward the overcast sky, inhaling deep with satisfaction. He placed both hands against the back of his head as he walked down the sidewalk of a congested street. It was nice to have a day outside of the Bastion. He thought this day would never come, based off the strict guidelines laid down by Wendel. Fortunately, the man had folded after a couple of weeks of berating him on the subject.

He and Lilu were on their way to the Intel Weaving Academy, the school she'd attended following Phesaw's closing. She told him stories about the curriculum and the difficulties she had faced during her first year. He was surprised to learn she had failed her first couple of classes; her weavineering skills not up to par at the time. He had grown so used to her excelling at everything academic when he had known her at Phesaw.

"I'm interested in seeing the remnants of Mendac's statue," he said.

"We need to stay away from that intersection—at least in the daylight," she said. "I don't know what kind of surveillance it's under now that you're here."

"Does Wendel know what you've been trying to do?" he asked, lowering his voice so the surrounding crowd overpowered him.

She glanced around, eyes stopping briefly on a passing constable carriage, distinguished by horses draped in yellow cloth. Three armored officers sat in the backseat, the coachman in the front.

"Let's not discuss this in the public," she said.

He agreed and dropped the subject. Truthfully, he felt anxious. The reason for their visit to the surface was to meet Director Jugtah, hoping the talented weavineer could find a way to spark a current in Bryson's Intel Energy. Months had passed since the Blizzard of Blood, yet his ability to expel energy from his body was minimal. And with Toono's imminent completion of sacrifices, this was the most important time for Bryson to have his full arsenal of weaponry. What good would his speed serve without something to pair with it? Even Adrenians had their swords.

They walked alongside a small black fence with a perfectly manicured yard on the other side, gardens dividing it from a four-story building. It seemed squat and swallowed up when compared to the edifices surrounding it, but its architecture was more intricate and primordial than the sleekness reflected in the rest of the city. This struck Bryson as odd, considering the fact that IWA served as a hub of innovation. He'd expected it to look more like Weavineer Tower, a place he'd only caught a glimpse of when first entering the city.

If he thought he had received too many stares while outside walking the streets, nothing could have prepared him for IWA. He and Lilu stuck to areas designated for staff and faculty only, all of whom gave them blatantly curious looks. They asked a female secretary if Jugtah was in his office, and she told them they had caught him just before lunch.

They found his door open as they approached his office. He, as well as most professors, had an open-door policy during work hours. They poked their heads inside to find him already withdrawing the contents of a packed lunch and organizing them on his desk.

Lilu knocked on the frame, drawing Jugtah's gaze and exposing his golden spectacles. Bryson hadn't missed those obnoxious things.

"Lilu, hello," Jugtah said. "And Bryson … ah, what a delight."

Bryson strolled inside. "Miss me, Director?"

"I'm not a director anymore," he said.

"Well, that's what you are to me."

He paused, slowly placing his sandwich on the desk and releasing a slow breath. "Ah, yes. How I have not missed your insolent nature."

Bryson took a seat across from Jugtah, kicking his feet up onto his desk in a manner of which Himitsu would have been proud. "We need a favor, Director."

Jugtah lowered himself into his chair. He glanced at Lilu, who frowned and shrugged as an apology. He extended an arm toward the empty chair next to Bryson, offering her a seat. She accepted.

"What makes you think I'd want to help you after the experience you had with me at Phesaw?" Jugtah asked, picking up a knife and cutting his sandwich into two triangles.

"Because Gracie said you would," Lilu said, clearly struggling to fight back a crafty grin.

Jugtah nodded. "Of course, the trump card." He leaned forward and took a gigantic bite out of his sandwich. After chewing for a few moments, he asked, "What can I do for you, Bryson?"

"I haven't forgotten about what you did in the Still Kingdom," Bryson said.

"Nearly soil myself every time that Apoleia woman looked at me?"

"Not quite," Bryson said. "Though I'm impressed by your stab at humor."

Jugtah smirked. "My niece rubs off on me."

"I mean what I witnessed outside Kindoliya, when you revived Vistas," Bryson said. "Or what you apparently did with my grandfather, curing his paralysis."

"Of course," Jugtah said, pausing to take another bite from his sandwich. "Do you have a paralyzed friend in need of assistance? Because I'm beginning to think I should charge for my services."

Bryson hesitated, mouth open in shock. Jugtah laughed, leaning back and placing a hand on his pudgy midsection. "Another joke, Bryson. Don't worry. Seriously, what is it you need?"

Bryson lifted his hands. "Ever since unleashing that lightning storm over the Diamond Sea, I've had a problem." He tried to emit electricity from his hand, only to leak sparks. "I still can't weave."

Jugtah gave a pronounced frown and leaned forward, causing the front of his shirt to hover an inch above his food. "I think you misunderstood me when I spoke to you about this the first time. This has nothing to do with weaving. I believe your clout isn't operating properly, like a bodybuilder who suddenly loses the ability to flex."

"You can fix it, right?" Bryson asked, nearly cringing at the frailty of his tone.

"I'm afraid not."

"But you've brought someone back to life!" Bryson exclaimed, scooting forward in his seat, looking as if he was about to drop to his knees. "You said you weaved your Intel Energy with the electrical currents of nervous systems. Can you not do the same with my energy system?"

"No," Jugtah said. He looked at Lilu. "What's the most basic rule of weaving, Lilu?"

"Energy cannot be woven with energy, for it will yield no results," she recited.

Jugtah nodded, glancing back at Bryson. "You see, if I were to try to use my Intel Chains to spark a current in your energy system, nothing would happen." He paused and his expression softened "Besides, I'm not familiar with the anatomical structure of a human's energy system. Nobody is, really. It's impossible to see with the naked eye. I wouldn't be able to locate the canals and guarantee a safe procedure. Most of the studies regarding the energy system speak of theories, but nobody can prove them."

"So I'm to be without electricity for the rest of my life now," Bryson muttered.

Setting the other half of his sandwich on the desk, Jugtah gave Bryson a consoling gaze. "I wish I could inject you with false hope, but you know that isn't me." He sighed. "To go for this long without any signs of progress is a bad omen. I don't think you'll ever wield electricity again."

*     *     *

"The man is blunt, but at least he's consistent … I'll give him that," Bryson said later that night while seated at the dining table of their townhouse with Lilu and Frederick. Gracie and Limone were busy on the sofa in the living room. A mug of coffee sat in front of Bryson, a drink he didn't typically consume. He had no idea why he chose now to drink it. Perhaps he was looking for a jolt of positive energy. It wasn't working.

Frederick and Lilu both had glasses of white wine in front of them, trying their best not to stare at the sulking Bryson. No amount of effort could wipe the sorrow from his face—not that he was putting in that much. His elbows were both on the table, his forehead resting in his palms.

The reality of his situation had finally sunk in. He'd no longer weave electricity. Since he could emit sparks, he wasn't an Unable by definition, but he considered himself one. The fact that this devastated him was frustrating. Did he really think so little of Unables? Had he not just got done scolding Vitio for how he treated them? Was he a damned hypocrite?

"I think it'll return," Lilu said after a swig from her glass. "I've never heard of someone losing their clout. Sure, people have entered comas or died because of energy depletion, but you've done neither. You're alive and well. In fact, those who've had energy-induced comas always come back with the ability to weave again—if they wake up at all."

Bryson continued to stare at the lacquered surface of the wooden table, not bothering to give her false hope a response. If there was one thing he'd learned from Debo, it was that there was a first for everything. That man had been the first Bozani to leave the Light Empire in order to permanently reside in the mainland amongst commoners. Who was to say Bryson wasn't unlucky enough to be the first person to simply lose his powers? He'd woven a storm of lightning, after all. Had that been a first?

"I can't believe something like this would happen to a man of your caliber. You deserve better."

Bryson looked up at Frederick, befuddled by the compliment. Even Lilu gave the weavineer an incredulous look.

"Why do I deserve better?" Bryson asked.

"The way you exposed your father to the world," Frederick said. "Not many would have done that, knowing their father was the reason why they were perceived in such a positive light. You risked bringing a lot of negativity upon yourself in order to expose him."

Bryson held Frederick's gaze, setting his jaw and shaking his head. "I regret telling that story the way I did."

Gracie whirled from her spot on the sofa, face peaking over the back. "Why would you regret that?"

"It wasn't my story to tell," he said, gaze falling to the table again. "I never asked the person it actually happened to if I could share such a vulnerable tale. My mother went years and years without telling anyone, so what made me think I could break her silence?"

Lilu nodded, placing her glass of wine on the table. "You've matured, Bryson. I hadn't thought of it that way."

"Most people hadn't," he said, voice distant. "When I spoke with my mother following the Blizzard of Blood, she brought it up to me. She admitted to being angry after finding out what I had done. But, I was lucky. Apparently, she had told her kingdom the story around the same time I did in the Intel Kingdom."

"We all make mistakes," Frederick said.

"None as grave as mine," Bryson said. "That had been a selfish act— being so angry at my father that I wanted the world to feel it, too. And considering the actions of my father in the past, there comes a degree where a mistake is no longer a mistake, but a deed done with intent. I don't want my selfishness to cause me to make choices out of ill intent."

Lilu reached over and grabbed Bryson's hand. He was instantly reminded of his first year as a Jestivan, when the connection between both of them had grown like an untamed wildfire. He looked up to see her eyes glazing over. "You're twisting your fears into your reality. Don't do that. You are nothing like Mendac LeAnce."

All eyes were on the two of them, Frederick's gaze fixated on their interlocked hands at the center of the table.

Lilu smiled. "You are Bryson Still, a prince in a long line of dominant women. You may weave electricity, but ice runs through your veins, as strong as the ever-ice from the tips of the Still Mountains."

He continued to stare at her, stuck in a hypnotic trance.

"It may seem like fate is working against you in your mind, but you can be as unyielding as both your mom and sister." She gave a firm nod. "I believe that."

Gracie pursed her lips. "She's a damn poet, too."

*     *     *

Tashami and Agnos walked up the stoop of a short, narrow house crammed between two near clones. The entire street was lined with architecturally similar homes, the only difference being their color. This one was a pastel green, complimenting the pink house to its right and yellow to the left surprisingly well.

Agnos was a bit nervous, considering this was only his second visit here. The last time he'd come here, Phesaw had just shut down for good, fresh off his second year as a Jestivan. He had come to hunt down Cheiraskinia, an ancient that allowed communication with sea life. Little did he know he'd been taking his first steps to becoming a pirate.

Tashami unlocked the door and walked inside. He had made sure to come and visit as often as he could over the past couple of years. Seeing that they had been at sea for most of that time, the opportunities were few and far between.

Agnos recognized the scents wafting down the narrow hallway from the kitchen in the back. Mimi was an excellent cook, and Tashami made sure to bring leftovers back to Agnos after every visit. However, today he was looking forward to tasting her food hot out of the pot.

As they reached the kitchen, Mimi scampered over, moving quite nimbly for a woman of her age. She wasn't Tashami's grandmother by blood, but she might as well have been; she'd taken care of him since he was a child.

"Good to see you, Mimi," Agnos said, getting the words out before she could squeeze the air out of his lungs.

She twisted her hips, shaking him to and fro. "I'm supposed to be angry with you, but I can't hold grudges!" She still had that infectious spirit he remembered from his last visit, reminding him of Jilly. Considering what had happened in the past two years, such a reminder was now bittersweet.

"I don't get a hug first?" Tashami asked, chuckling to himself as he approached the fire pit and gazed into the pot. "Ooo, asparagus and" —he looked into a nearby pan— "steak?" He frowned. "Why don't you ever bring out this stuff when I visit alone?"

She finally released Agnos and turned toward Tashami. "This is different, Shama-Lama." Agnos broke into a fit of laughter, and Tashami smacked his own face in embarrassment. She went on, not seeming to care about their reactions. "This is to celebrate yours and Agnos's friendship. This is a special occasion."

One side of Tashami's mouth curled upward. "Sounds more like a funeral," he said. "Like we're never going to see each other again."

"Who knows?" she said, rushing toward the fire to toss some seasoning into the asparagus pot. "From what you told me, it'll be quite some time before your paths cross again. Agnos will be venturing all the way into the Dark Sea, and that is a lofty voyage indeed." She shrugged. "But at least it sounds fun." She turned to glance at Tashami. "You, on the other hand, will play border control. That sounds boring."

Tashami waited for Mimi to return to cooking before rolling his eyes. Agnos couldn't help but think she had a point, for their tasks were completely different. His voyage was more of a life-endangering mission, while Tashami's stationing at the teleplatforms was more of a routine assignment. How likely was it that Agnos would die? He'd escaped death twice already while at sea; once when in the battle with the Adrenian Navy and again when he chose to dive into the depths of the Sea of Light in search of the Thunder Queen's chronicle. The reality of this night began to sink in. This was the last time he'd see Tashami for a while—maybe ever.

Mimi looked up from the asparagus, turning to glance between the two friends. A long silence had followed her words. She sighed. "Nothing can get between your friendship. Not even death. I'm telling you … I've never seen a bond quite like it."

Tashami groaned. "Can you not be so depressing, Mimi?"

"It's not depressing, sweetie," she said, frowning at him. "The opposite, in fact. It's absolutely beautiful. I don't know what kind of influence that Grand Director Poicus had on you Jestivan during your time at Phesaw, but it was something special, something that cannot be manufactured. He planted a seed, and the lot of you nurtured it into a family." The steak began to sizzle. She turned, using a pair of tongs to grab the meat and press its sides against the bottom of the pan, giving it a good sear. "Are all of you like this?"

"Most of us," Tashami said, answering before Agnos could mention Yama. "But we have our flaws."

"As to be expected," she said, flipping the steak again. "Beauty requires scars."

After her words of wisdom, the two men took a seat at the small table next to the window. Mimi happily placed some asparagus and a generous cut of steak on each of their plates before taking a seat herself and chowing down.

Conversation over dinner was lighter and full of laughs, complete with stories of the two Jestivan's adventures. Mimi's personal favorite was hearing how Agnos discovered the rats aboard the Whale Lord, and how taking them down led to the eventual finding of the Brench Hilt.

Dinner ended, and Mimi headed upstairs to prepare for bed. Tashami and Agnos remained downstairs to clean the kitchen and dining area. They did so in silence for a long stretch of time, but Tashami finally broke it.

"You'll kill it out there, buddy."

Agnos paused, grasping a wet rag as he wiped down the table. "It'll be different without my other half."

Tashami smiled. "It is true you've had a partner in crime throughout all of your voyages, just like your fellow *Of Six* legends. But, I believe you can do anything you put your mind to. For goodness sake, you had a dream at the age of seven and set a goal to achieve it. Fifteen years later, you did exactly that."

"A pep talk, eh?" Agnos said. "That's what you're going with?"

"Not that you really need one," Tashami said, brushing asparagus tips off the counter and into a waste bin. "I don't think you ever needed one. Even in the Void, when we went to find my father, you displayed more mental fortitude than anyone else by conquering your fears. When everyone ran at the sight of spirits, you remained in that house, walked into that room, and confronted the gruesome shell of my father."

Agnos began wiping the table again. "I appreciate that."

"And it's great that you appreciate it," Tashami said. "But I need you to know it." He shook his head, dropping the waste bin to the floor and approaching the table. "Do you know it?"

"Know what?"

"That you're a badass," Tashami said, leaning in and intently eyeing Agnos.

"That would be Bryson," Agnos said, head down as he wiped the table. "Or Himitsu, Rhyparia, Olivia, Toshik, or you."

"None of them have your willpower!" Tashami snapped, raising his voice. This was becoming more than just a pep talk. "It's not all about physicality! How many times must I tell you this? It's about mental fortitude and perseverance." He paused, squeezing his eyes shut. He opened them, revealing a softer gaze. "Tell me you know this."

Agnos paused with his mouth ajar. Finally, he regained control of his jaw and said, "I know this."

Tashami tightly grabbed Agnos, pressing his face into Agnos's shoulder. "We are more than friends, Agnos."

Agnos lifted his arms and wrapped them around Tashami's back. "We'll see each other again."

# 27

# Paths Cross

"Do we find it wise to target the holy trees rather than the palace?" Vuilni asked.

Olivia, Vuilni, and Fane were seated in a secluded area of a restaurant. Of course, like every establishment in Asalka, they were inside of a hollowed-out birch tree. Their table sat next to a wall of bark that curved around the building, forming a vast circular shape to the interior. They occupied one of the higher floors. It followed the curve of the wall, forming a ring. A wooden guardrail allowed people to lean over and gaze down at the lower walkways. The main lobby sat several floors beneath them, in the base of the birch's trunk.

The restaurant didn't have a name, but it was one of the busiest in the city from what they had seen. Thankfully, the multileveled structure of the floor plan allowed for secrecy. It was also easy for Fane to spot any possible spies.

"I think we should focus on the palace," Vuilni said.

Olivia shoved a leaf of lettuce into her mouth, grimacing at the crunch. After taking some time to chew, she said, "I agree with her."

Fane sighed and leaned back. "I see my plan is outnumbered."

"What would be the point of focusing on the holy trees?" Olivia asked. "Our goals here involve the royals, not the priests. Let's stay far away from them."

"Either way," he said, "the longer we stay here, the more impatient this city will become with our presence."

"Oh well," Olivia said mid crunch. "We have a job to do, and it is vital to the war. We aren't going to let anyone scare us away."

He nodded. "I understand this better than anyone. I'm simply stating that the longer we drag this out, the more difficult the task becomes."

"Then why waste our time with the holy trees when the castle should be our target?" Vuilni asked.

"I wouldn't waste our time. The holy trees are important because they'll serve as diversions. We need to bring the city's focus away from the castle," he said.

"I see," Olivia said, taking a sip of a drink too bitter for her liking. She spit it back into the cup, sticking out her tongue in disgust.

"We need to split up over the next few days or so," he said, leaning in and lowering his voice. "Vuilni and I will roam the city and discover which willows are the most important to this place's culture. We'll move only during the nightime, under the cover of my flame. While we're doing that, Olivia, you will need to scout the castle's defenses. You said you used to live in a forest, so I expect that background to aide you immensely when maneuvering through the trees. They will serve as your cover."

"And when do we act?" Vuilni asked.

"Slow down," he said, resting his hand on the table. "The prep work is the most important phase of the mission. If we get it wrong, everything after crumbles—if we even make it to the 'after' part." He lowered his voice to a whisper. "Once Vuilni and I find the two most important holy trees, we'll prepare for the following night to cause a diversion at the two locations."

"Do I get a warning?" Olivia asked.

He shook his head. "No, when night falls, you must be ready to strike at any time. You'll know when the diversions are in play. I expect those around the castle should respond accordingly. I have faith that by the time we make our moves, you'll know how to infiltrate the castle."

"Very risky," Vuilni said.

"A necessary risk," he said. "This is the Prim Kingdom; there is no other way. They don't simply grant requests to foreigners, especially if it involves scouting."

Olivia straightened her back, pulling away from the conspicuous huddled image they had created. She nodded silently, closing her eyes. "We'll begin scouting tomorrow second-day. It's a solid plan, Fane."

He laughed. "You sound like the assassin with decades of experience under your belt."

"But I'm not," Olivia said, opening an eye to look at him, "which is why we'll listen to you."

"I appreciate that."

They finished their dinner composed of vegetables and bread—a typical meal in Asalka—then made their way down a staircase that wound with the birch tree's bark wall, passing several ringed floors on the way. They each remained wary of their surroundings. According to Fane, Prim Assassins did exist, making them one of only a few races to not have gone extinct.

The second-day air was cool, but warming quickly. The Prim Kingdom suffered from bipolar temperatures. At night, it was cold to the point of chattering teeth for Fane and Vuilni, while the daytime would make Olivia sweat profusely.

If there was a glaring positive about Asalka's unique layout as a forest city, it was the crisp, clean air. A deep breath was oftentimes the highlight of Olivia's day. Looking up to the canopies of green, with sunlight streaming through thousands of tiny gaps in the leaves, only reminded her of her home in Lallopy Forest—though there the trees were yews. Some days she couldn't see the canopies because of the fireflies, but today the insects had decided to remain hidden.

They turned down a grassy street and headed for their place of residence, pointing out each new species of animal they spotted on the ground or in the trees. The mixture of humans and wild animals was still fascinating to them. The only animals seen in the cultivated areas of the Light Realm were domesticated pets and livestock or wild birds.

But no animal caught Olivia's eye more than the woman who briefly made eye contact with her as they crossed paths. Her face seemed familiar, and she looked to be in her forties, only slightly younger than Pilot Ophala. Everything about her was matured, yet two things stood out above the rest: the layered brown hair and a burgundy bandana tied around her neck like a collar. She knew this woman, but as a girl. And that bandana should have been on her head.

Olivia whirled, coming to a stop as the woman continued in the other direction. Was that Rhyparia's mother? The resemblance was uncanny. What was even more peculiar was the way their gazes lingered on each other, as if the woman knew Olivia.

Vuilni stepped closer and whispered, "I see you noticed the same thing."

*      *      *

"Iris doesn't deserve this," Rhyparia said in a clipped tone.

She took long strides through Asalka, a benefit of her growth spurt during her decades training with Musku. She was far taller than most women. While Saikatto strode by her side, Rayne and Prakriti struggled to match her pace, remaining on her heels with some effort.

"Who are we to interfere with Primmish customs?" Rayne asked, nearly tripping over a massive tangle of roots.

"I'm not letting the poor man die," Rhyparia said.

"And what is telling the Craftmasters going to accomplish?" Rayne said.

"It'll resolve everything. Besides, they deserve to know, anyway. The fact that Iris is being executed for our own error won't sit well with Atarax. We should have brought them with us originally, like Iris wanted. He had faith in us, and we let him down."

Prakriti stammered, but eventually found words. "This is impulsive. I thought we had a discussion about this."

Rhyparia spun, forcing the three of them to stop on a dime. "Impulsive would have been my original reaction. Would you rather have had me hunt down Iris and snatch him from the grasps of his captors, stopping at nothing to escape with both of us alive—including slaying those who would stand before me?"

With eyes wide, Prakriti stared at her in a stunned silence. "Was that actually your first reaction?"

She turned around and began walking again, this time with less fervor. "Yes, it was. But I stopped and allowed myself a moment to think, to breathe. Ultimately I came up with something better. And that involves getting—" She paused, but continued to walk, trying her hardest to remain stoic.

"You okay?" Rayne asked.

Two young women strolled past Rhyparia, one with violet hair and a missing kitten hat, the other with dark skin and thick braids. She couldn't believe her eyes, but there was no denying it. She thought she'd never see any of them again. Two dear friends from her youth at Phesaw were within inches from her. Not intangible manifestations in her dreams, but the real thing.

Quickly, she looked forward. As they passed, she closed her eyes to trap the inevitable tears.

*     *     *

Rhyparia descended a slope that led to the muddy bank of Headless Lake. She then followed the water's edge, the slope evolving into a short bluff the farther they traveled, hiding them from Asalka. Once she found an outcropping of rocks, she climbed her way through to find an empty alcove. Rayne, Saikatto, and Prakriti stopped behind her.

"You're good to come out," Rhyparia said, her gaze raking over every shadowy corner.

296

Five dimiours stooped out of separate shadows, their postures suggesting exhaustion and food deprivation. Her shoulders sunk. "I'm sorry. It's been a tough few days, but that's honestly no excuse."

Atarax stepped forward, his rancid breath reaching her even from a distance of several paces. He growled, showing a side of himself that she hadn't witnessed before. "What news do you bring?"

Kakos, his body still rugged despite the lack of nutrition, leaned against the wall of the bluff. His pointed teeth were exposed, and his eyes fierce. "It better be good news. You can't cage us away like circus animals and expect us not to regress … at least not Atarax and me. We don't have the same control as the others."

Rhyparia scanned the faces of the smaller dimiours: Therapif, Moros, and Biaza. They seemed more composed. "It's not good news," she said after a long pause. "They've announced an execution of Watcher Iris and requested our presence, whether as spectators or criminals, I do not know."

Atarax's eyes narrowed. "They can't do that. They wouldn't do that. I refuse to believe it—not from the kingdom that used to belong to a leader such as Dimiourgos."

"I don't think they practice what they preach," Rhyparia said. "There is something corrupt about the people Iris brought us to meet … the Monsignors. They wore animal masks, but didn't carry themselves like the beings they worship."

"And when you say they requested 'our' presence," Biaza said, "did they mean us, too?"

"No, they don't even know about you, but I think it's time they do." Rhyparia's face became grave. "Are you ready to show yourselves to the world?"

Atarax walked forward, placing his paw on her shoulder as he passed. "Let's go."

# 28

# Like Father, Unlike Son

Although there were plenty of chairs, Bryson chose to sit on the floor of the townhouse's balcony. He leaned back on his hands and craned his neck to stare up at the hundreds of thousands of Intelights floating just below the Bastion's cavernous ceiling. How were there so many? He tried to imagine the amount of manpower it must have taken. He sulked, remembering he could no longer do something as simple as weaving an Intelight.

His gaze drifted down the gigantic wall of the cavern with its balconies jutting out at random spots. He couldn't see the occupants of the higher ones, but the lower balconies were easier to spot. As usual, most of them were vacant. The wealthy spectators seemed to come during the late afternoon, just after the end of their workday, granting them a couple of hours to watch the weavineers work on Lilu's travolters. At this time of night, however, Steel Field was empty and nearly impossible to be seen from such a distance—not without the sunlight streaming through the hole in the ceiling.

He had a plan for these strange balconies, but was losing faith because it required the participation of a very important piece: Thusia. This shouldn't have been a problem, but it had been weeks since he'd last summoned her—and not from a lack of trying. She wasn't answering his calls, and he was beginning to lose that sense of comfort. It unnerved him. What was happening in the Light Empire?

Frederick served as Bryson's only companion for the night. Gracie and Lilu were having a girls' night out, while Limone had committed his team of weavineers to extra practice in one of the Bastion's dozens of labs.

"How do you like it here?" Frederick asked, leaning forward with his forearms resting atop the guardrail.

Bryson shrugged, twisting his lips in thought. "It's definitely fascinating, but the longer I'm cooped up down here, the quicker the novelty of it wears off."

"Yes, the Bastion feels like a cage at times, that's for sure," Frederick said.

"Brilliance, however, is magnificent," Bryson said. "A real marvel."

"I've been here my entire life, so it's quite mundane in my eyes."

"You're telling me you've never left this city?"

Frederick turned and laughed. "Of course not. Have you not seen how this city operates? Weren't you just saying how you never knew how this city was constructed? That level of secrecy wouldn't exist if the city's citizens were able to simply leave. It's only allowed on rare occasions to elite individuals in society."

"True," Bryson said, recalling the maxim engraved on the city's wall: *What is seen does not leave.* "I suppose it's just difficult for me to fathom living your entire life without visiting a location away from home."

Frederick smirked, shaking his head. "How were you raised, Bryson?"

"What do you mean?"

"Forgive me if this is too personal or forward, but would you consider your childhood privileged?" Frederick asked.

Bryson wrinkled his nose, as if the word "privilege" had the foulest stench. "I grew up being ridiculed and harassed by my peers for not living up to the image of my dead, rapist father. I never knew my mother, and I had no siblings. I wouldn't call any of those circumstances a privilege."

Frederick closed his eyes and nodded. "Let me reword my question; I can see that it upset you."

"Obviously."

"I shouldn't have used that word," Frederick said. "I meant, what was the financial situation of whoever raised you?"

Bryson paused. "Very good, I suppose. I was raised by an Energy Director, of which there are only five in the world, so they make a lot of money. I lived in a very nice house in a suburban neighborhood right outside of Dunami."

"Well, ninety-nine percent of the world doesn't live like that," Frederick said. "Most people live their lives in one town or village, only leaving it to hunt and gather in nearby woodlands. Maybe they go out fishing, if they're lucky enough to live by a lake. However, they don't have the luxury to explore distant towns or experience one of the Light Realm's magnificent capitals."

"They can't travel?" Bryson asked.

"No ..." Frederick said, gaze solemn. "Horses are extremely rare outside of the major cities because of how expensive they are. And the mass populace isn't going to decide to just walk hundreds of leagues for a vacation, not when they have families to feed. Families that rely on their plantations and ranches to produce their food and milk, which doesn't always yield desirable results because of faulty weather patterns ... not to mention the government taking most of their crops, underpaying them in the process."

Bryson's gaze grew distant, imagining the strife of such a life.

"Therefore, like the wall around Brilliance that literally entraps its citizens, money can do the same. Only a handful of people possess the luxury of the freedom you've had throughout your life. So, for you to be shocked about me never leaving Brilliance seems backwards; such a life is common. You, on the other hand, have traveled all over Kuki Sphaira, including venturing into the Dark Realm."

Bryson didn't respond. He stared at the guardrail in front of him. He had grown up wealthy because of Debo, and over the past five years, he had surrounded himself with people who shared his status: Jestivan and royalty. It had narrowed the scope of his perception. He glanced at Frederick, looking him up and down. He always looked dapper.

"You have lots of money," Bryson said.

Frederick glanced down at his suit, then clutched his stomach and guffawed. "I have a lot of debt. In order to sell yourself in a city like this— in a profession such as mine—you better play the part, and that means presenting a wealthy image ... even if it's phony, like mine. Thankfully, I landed this position under Lilu, so I can pay it back faster than I had feared it would take."

Bryson nodded, returning his gaze toward the banister.

"I'm sorry," Frederick said. "Who am I to lecture a prince?"

"Don't be sorry," Bryson mumbled. "I actually appreciate the perspective. You've helped me with a problem that's been bothering me for a while now."

"And what's that?"

"The stupid idea of socioenergenic classes and those identification cards that go along with it," Bryson spat.

"Ah, yes. I have mine in my vest pocket at all times," Frederick said, lightly patting his chest.

"You know..." Bryson paused, debating whether or not to reveal who had come up with the idea in the first place. Did he need to throw Lilu under the carriage like that? It was clear to him that Frederick fancied her.

Frederick raised an eyebrow. "Huh?"

"Nothing."

Then, as if Frederick had read Bryson's thoughts, he asked, "What's Lilu like when she's out there ... in her royal settings?"

"A stubborn, unyielding headache," Bryson said, smirking. "But she is humble, generous, and professional. I don't know many royals who leave the comforts of their palaces and castles to attend school at a public establishment like Phesaw." He paused, looking off to the side in thought. "In fact, I've *never* heard of such a thing."

Frederick's face lit up, motivating Bryson to continue talking a big game for Lilu—which wasn't difficult to do, surprisingly. The compliments sort of rolled off his tongue. "I know she wants to lead a normal life, achieving things by her own merit, and not the merit of her social status and political identity. I respect that. Alas, the two of us are very similar and bump heads because of it. Our relationship doesn't have a steady track record, per se." He paused. "I suppose we're 'steadily unsteady.'"

Frederick laughed. After a long pause, his face fell. "Do the two of you still share feelings?"

"Absolutely not," Bryson said. "Not in the way you're thinking. We share feelings of admiration. She admires my physical skills; I admire her mind. I am very much in love with Princess Shelly, my fiancée and the mother of my son."

"Do you think I have a chance with a woman of Lilu's caliber?" Frederick asked, cutting straight to the point.

Bryson smiled, nodding as he pictured Lilu's expression every time Frederick entered a room. "You have more than a chance, man."

*　　　*　　　*

The oak's canopy spread above Yama, casting a shadow below with its healthy green leaves and thick, sturdy branches. She sat in the cool shade next to the headstone of Ataway Debonicus Kawi, reflecting on her time spent speed-training with Bryson, Lilu, Toshik, and Directors Debo and Buredo. That whole situation still frustrated her. She couldn't believe she had been so close to an Adrenian legend for that long.

She moped, an aura very unbefitting of her personality. She knew this, but with where she found herself now, what else could she do? She had lived her life believing one day she'd return to this village and discover what she was supposed to be doing with her skills. She had been told to train relentlessly and discover the true nature of her abilities on her own, then, when the time came, to return and challenge the "fastest man in the world." The goal of such a difficult task had been daunting and alluring, pushing her to excel past her classmates and comrades. Now she was near the completion of this lifelong objective, yet she had been denied access.

She sighed, turning her head slightly to look upon the pastures and plantations that stretched until they reached the sudden canvas of blue—the Edge. She had visited this hill several times over the past week, observing the Edge, debating her next move. With Kolver shunning her from any inside information or participation in the village's activities, her existence now felt hollow. His superiors—whoever they were—didn't want anything to do with her, deeming the path she had taken in her life to have been toxic.

Yama no longer had a purpose to continue living. Perhaps, the Edge could serve as her departure from this world.

*    *    *

Shelly strolled through the gardens of Dunami Palace along with her mother while Benedict followed closely behind. A florist guided them through, frequently stopping to gesture toward a crop of flowers, lecturing the two royal ladies about them. Flowers were an important aspect of any wedding theme.

Shelly's gaze was distant. Her eyes seemed to gloss over as her mind vacated the present. She was trying to place herself in Brilliance, next to Bryson and Lilu, trying to imagine how much fun they were having up there. She'd heard the stories about the city while growing up—buildings as tall as the highest towers in Dunami Palace, stretching like fingers toward the sky—but it was still hard to picture in her head, for she had never seen anything like it.

"Can you give us a moment?" Queen Delilah asked of the florist.

The woman, who was presently on her knees pointing out the details of a blue rose's petals, nodded and rose to her feet. "Of course, milady," she said, offering a generous curtsy. She then wended her way between flower patches and went to talk to a few assistants near a distant gazebo.

Shelly groaned as her mother turned toward her. "Mother, stop it."

"Give us some space, please, Benedict," Delilah said, eyes still glued on her daughter.

Once Benedict retreated, Shelly said, "I don't desire a discourse."

"And I don't desire depressed daughters … or alliterations." Delilah smirked—an odd expression for such a formal woman.

"Comical, Mother. You can bring the florist back. I've been paying attention."

Delilah raised her eyebrows. "Oh, really? Why is it, then, that flowers can prosper in a kingdom like ours, where the sun never shines?"

"Because flowers don't actually prosper in our kingdom; they only survive in artificial locations where there is weavineering technology to provide light, such as the dozen or so Intelamps surrounding the gardens currently." Shelly lazily pointed toward a few of them. "They turn on at night, and that's when the flowers see the most growth." She stuck her tongue out at her mother, knowing the only reason she could answer such a question was because of Lilu.

"As impressive as that was," Delilah said, "the florist never discussed any of that. You simply recited that from memory." She paused, looking deep into Shelly's soul. "What's wrong?"

"This is the third time I've allowed Bryson to venture off, either on a dangerous mission or a distant one, during a pivotal moment in our collective life," Shelly said, words spilling out of her like vomit. "Am I doing this spouse thing wrong?"

Delilah gave a gentle smirk. "You are not. You both are learning as you go, and it's difficult to acquire a balance while in the midst of war. Honestly, I wish I could offer more than that, but your scenario with Bryson is very much different than mine was with your father. I never advocated for Vitio to put himself in harm's way, but it helped that he never intended to do so himself. He was never a fighter, but more of a traditional royal head. He had his soldiers do the work for him."

Shelly's face fell toward the ground. "But Bryson is a soldier."

"And I don't know if you'll ever shake that out of him," Delilah said, placing her hand on her daughter's shoulder. "He isn't your typical royal; politics aren't his thing. And as much as that young man despises his father—and rightfully so—that is the one thing about him that makes me see his father when I look at him …" She paused, her gaze growing distant.

"They both possess a penchant for confrontation and thirst for victory, no matter the differences in their reasoning behind it."

Shelly's expression morphed into something of disdain throughout her mother's explanation. "But Bryson isn't Mendac at all."

Delilah's gaze refocused. She raised her hand and gently slid her thumb down her daughter's cheek. "Of course not. I'm letting you marry him, am I not?"

After a long pause, Shelly nodded. "Let's hurry this up. I want to spend time with L.K."

Delilah smiled. "Who am I to separate a mother and her child?"

# 29

# Erafeen: Solar Glare

Agnos stood next to the helm on the quarterdeck of the Mythmaker. His posture was casual, hands grasped behind his back as he surveyed his ten new crewmates lent to him by Spirit Queen Apsa. For the most part, they were a muscular bunch, and he still had a lot to learn about them. The only person he'd taken a severe interest in since their arrival a week ago was Evelyn Tesai, the Still Diatia. Even then, he knew less about her than he desired.

Evelyn leaned against the mainmast while the other nine—all elite sailors from the Spirit Navy—sat strewn across the main deck. Her ice-blue hair blew gently in the harbor's winds, frost occasionally trailing from its lengths and glittering through the air before disappearing in the distance. Her arms were crossed, one hand grasped onto each of her exposed biceps, making Agnos's arms look like noodles. That was the only part of her that seemed guarded; everything else was relaxed, from her tranquil facial expression to her left foot casually kicked back against the mast.

With the date of the voyage quickly approaching, Agnos had decided today was the perfect opportunity to brief the newest members of his crew about the ship and their roles on it—while it was empty, save the couple of boatswains who were fixing weather damage.

He had gone through three of the men, inquiring about their past positions on Spirit naval vessels and learning their strengths and weaknesses before assigning them new roles as pirates. It only took several minutes before the tables had turned and he was the one being interrogated.

"Captain Agnos, is it true you were in the captain's cabin when Gray Whale led the Whale Lord into the battle with the Adrenian navy?" one man asked, his hair buzzed short like the rest of them.

"Yes," Agnos said hurriedly, not wanting to remember such a day. "Moving on to—"

"And Tashami Patter was the sole reason why the Whale Lord did the impossible by clearing a record-shattering wave in the midst of a torrential sea storm?" the same man asked.

"Not solely, but largely," Agnos said. "Now if we can move—"

"And you caught the rats in Gray Whale's crew, didn't you?"

"Yes, but—"

"How exactly did you lose your arm?"

That question gave Agnos pause. Suddenly he no longer felt like a captain. His main crew—the one who had joined him on his voyage to retrieve the chronicle—would never have questioned him in such a way, interrupting and berating him. And to ask something like that—something so blunt and rude! What would make them think he'd want to discuss the absence of a limb? Sure, here in DaiSo, people knew him based off his reputation at sea. But if he were to walk through a random city, people would see him as a cripple—not only frail and small, but inoperable. It was a sensitive matter for him.

His eyes drifted toward Evelyn, who remained standing behind the former sailors. She continued to study him with a passive gaze. She had probably expected more from a Jestivan, having heard of their reputation— the likes of Bryson LeAnce, Rhyparia NuForce, Olivia Lavender, and Lilu Intel. Yet here she was, standing beneath this ragged *thing*. He could see it in her eyes, the gears ticking in her head. She was an observant one.

"My apologies, Captain," the man said. "I was too forward."

Agnos regarded the man again. He had lost track of time. How long had he been silent?

"That you were," Agnos said, trying to force a sense of authority in his tone. "What was your name again?"

"Troy Sulia, formerly the second-in-command to Admiral Ren Tonlo."

"I see," Agnos muttered, internally losing his mind at the revelation. He was in over his head. Had Queen Apsa really placed such a high-ranking man beneath him? No wonder they felt they could interrupt him on a whim. He cleared his throat. "Anyway, barring any other intrusions, I'll make this quick."

He spent the next half hour discussing roles and responsibilities. He quizzed them on emergency protocols in case of sudden attack or storm, and tactical maneuvers depending on the type of battle being fought. To his pleasure, they passed with flying colors, which was expected of men of this caliber. Everything Gray Whale had taught him seemed to have been already drilled into their heads. Throughout it all, Evelyn didn't speak, electing to stare at him with those tranquil eyes instead.

Hours later, after a tour of the ship, the former sailors boarded a longboat and returned to the shore. Evelyn remained on board, at his request. It was a couple of hours into the evening, the sun having long since set. Oil lanterns hung around the crew's quarters, orange light flickering across a bevy of hammocks, shadows stretching in multiple directions. Agnos sat awkwardly in one, his feet planted firmly on the floor. Evelyn remained standing, her back against a pillar. A lantern hung just above her, eerily pooling her face in shadows.

"What do you think?" Agnos asked.

"I think you worry too much about how you're perceived," she said.

"Well, I am in a position that relies on the respect of my authority."

"Demand it, then."

Agnos's lips curled upward. "Is that attitude how you've wound up with a horde of experienced sailors following you around like you're their captain?"

"I was supposed to be a sailor, myself," she said, gazing down at her forearms, which were, once again, crossed in front of her. "But then I was picked to be a Diatia, putting a hold on any of my personal dreams."

Agnos frowned, leaning forward with an elbow resting across his knee. "How did Queen Apsa come to trust you, and why should I? I've had experience with a couple of the Diatia before. One of them wasn't that pleasant."

"You speak of Bruut, I assume," she said. "He's not a good person, I know. Vuilni, on the other hand, was one of my dearest friends, which are hard to acquire in a group like the Diatia. But you don't have to worry about me. I follow my queen, and if she has forgiven the Intelians, then I can do the same. I'm here to do right by her, which means doing right by my prince and princess."

"Bryson and Olivia," Agnos said.

She nodded.

"And where is your fellow Still Diatia?" he asked. "Doesn't each kingdom have a pair?"

"Yes, structurally, we are composed just like the Jestivan. However, politically, it's been a disaster from the start. There is no cohesion within the Diatia. I'm sure you've wondered why we've been separated and in small numbers the few times we've been seen on a global scale."

"I just thought the school might have operated differently than the kingdoms," he said. "But I guess not. I recall Vuilni mentioning it once."

"Ipsas mirrors its realm perfectly," she explained. "Corrupt wardens, toxic ideologies, and constant strife festers throughout the campus, where impressionable children, unfortunately, soak it up like sponges."

"I'm sorry," he said, reflecting on his childhood in Lost Wisdom. "I'm familiar with such an environment. Luckily, I escaped early."

She stared at him for a protracted moment, observing him like he was nothing more than a piece of wood. "If that is true, I'm impressed with the composure you hold yourself with now. Not many can escape with their minds intact."

"You seem very composed," he said.

She finally allowed herself to smile. "That is the nature of a Stillian woman. We hide our emotions; taking the reins of our vulnerability … though, Queen Apoleia has been working on evolving our maxims."

He nodded. "I know Olivia very well, and she was raised by Queen Apoleia. The girl was expressionless."

"Yes, well, to answer your original question, my fellow Still Diatia has decided to follow our dear Still Warden to work with SCAPD," she said, closing her eyes. "Unlike me, they don't accept our queen's decision. They've joined the Rogue Demon, believing he's the man who will take down the Intel Kingdom alongside the Oracle."

Noticing the dissent in her face and tone, Agnos sucked his teeth. "I get it. The Jestivan also possessed a traitor in Yama. We've had our fair share of dysfunction and turmoil."

Her eyes opened, and she pushed herself away from the pillar, arms remaining crossed. "To them, I'm the traitor. I don't think you understand how disastrous the Diatia have been. We started off poorly and it only grew worse. The reason why we were vacant during worldwide catastrophes was because we were too busy fighting evils in our own school—some of that evil being ourselves. Then Chelekah was killed by the Rogue Demon, serving as his second sacrifice. Then Vuilni, Bruut, and Power Warden Feissam left for your school, never to return. Then it was Gina, Halluci, and Dev Warden Gala who abandoned us to join Dev King Storshae. Then Cyn Warden Pinako and Still Warden Moroza left to fight in the Blizzard of Blood."

She raised her hand, pressing her fingers into her temple. "Most of them are now dead. Don't get me wrong; I'm not bitter, necessarily. However, we were supposed to achieve more." She looked up at him, eyebrows furrowed. "Do you know why I've been studying you all day long, staying silent? Or why I even agreed to come here in the first place?"

Slowly, Agnos shook his head.

"To learn," she said. "To learn from the man they call the Sixth of Six. To learn from a former Jestivan, a rank of students that achieved meaningful results for their side in this complex war. To recognize what it takes to be a team." She paused, lowering her gaze toward the floor. "To be part of something bigger than me. Because in a school like Ipsas, there was nothing bigger than the individual."

Agnos pushed himself out of the hammock with his one arm and stood in front of her, smiling. She looked down at him, as if wanting to step back and recreate the distance.

"You want yourself a team," he said.

She didn't respond, but her silence answered everything.

He reached out his hand, and she grasped it firmly. "Well, you've got yourself one."

*     *     *

Eet and Osh burst through the door of their captain's room in Flailing Fin. Eet, a boy who had grown three inches in the past six months, ran across the room, but his best friend and archrival tripped him before he could reach his goal. She pressed her boot onto his back and raised a fist to declare victory.

"I, Oshila Gray, am the victor!" she declared.

Eet flailed without luck. Even with his growth spurt, he was no match for the girl. She finally relieved the pressure of her boot and tromped the rest of the way toward the nightstand, retrieving the translated documents from beneath the floor. She then ran toward him and slid across the floor before coming to a stop in front of him, likely ripping a few more holes into her trousers and multiplying the tally of scrapes across her knees.

She took a seat in front of him and found the proper page, then brought her fist to her mouth and cleared her throat. "Alas, the dreaded day came when the Mind King arrived outside my castle grounds ..."

*     *     *

Alas, the dreaded day came when the Mind King arrived outside my castle grounds. How can I forget the disarray of my officers when they

311

came to inform me? They shouted of a man who appeared out of thin air, his hair blonde and eyes as yellow as the sun. To this day, I have never heard of such a trait … golden eyes. He did give me an explanation, but that will come later.

Naturally, I told my men to calm down, knowing damned well that even I was anxious. They offered to escort the man to my energy chamber but were visibly relieved when I told them not to bother; that I would journey down to the gate and speak with him briefly. Something told me they understood the status of such a man, even if they didn't know his exact identity.

I ambled across the grounds of my castle, my gaze trained on the distant gate. Soldiers watched from a respectable distance, knowing that they held no purpose in a meeting of this magnitude. If things went south, which often was the case in this world, any aid from them would serve as nothing more than a gentle breeze against a bolted iron gate. We were Originators, after all. We could have obliterated an entire city in one fell swoop if we wanted to.

His golden eyes struck me before anything else. Even his massive stature was indistinguishable until I grew nearer. Those eyes weren't natural. And I'll admit, without shame, they scared me.

Mialo waited patiently, hands partly tucked into the front pockets of his long kingly coat. His skin was the color and texture of milk chocolate and smooth despite his age. I remember how peculiar his aura was because as I approached him, my guard lowered. It wasn't an unnatural effect, but simply the way he carried himself. He oozed a sense of security.

"The drifting rumors are true, it seems," I said, standing on the other side of the iron bars. "Mialo, the King of Minds, is paying visits to every kingdom of the Light Realm."

He smiled. "May I have a moment of your time, Tonitrua?" His voice was deep.

"Why should I grant you that privilege? I have been forewarned of your dastardly requests."

"You know the specifics?" he asked, an eyebrow rising slightly. "I recall the other Originators I've visited shooting me down the moment I opened my mouth. They didn't get to hear much beyond my initial statements."

"With good reason, probably," I said.

"I am not here to be an endangerment to you or your people. If that were the case, I would have teleported directly into your castle."

The man had a point. Of course, that could have been his tactic—baiting me into trusting him. Either way, if he had visited the other kingdoms without bringing harm, why would that change with me? The thought occurred to me that he could have possibly worked out a deal with one of the other kingdoms and was now executing a plan to take me out, but that seemed farfetched. Plus, I had enough faith in my ability to defend myself if that were the case.

I granted him access, standing my ground as the gate squealed open. He could have easily teleported across, but he refrained from doing so. My eyes skittered about me, observing the soldiers and staff, the tension so thick I could feel it squeezing me like a girdle. What kept the soldiers from running wasn't the fear of what I'd do to them for such cowardice, but the confidence and respect they had in me. I was not a typical Originator. I ruled with compassion, and the rumors said the same about Mialo. Perhaps this was why I opened my door to him.

We shook hands as he neared. I then turned and headed for the castle with him by my side. Even in my peripheral vision his eyes glowed, and I wanted to interrogate him about them right then and there. But I quashed that urge.

"Do you have a preference for the setting of our discussion?" I asked.

"So the rumors are true," he said, raising an eyebrow. "You are a different beast than the others."

"I pride myself on that fact," I said.

"The rest of them took me straight to their energy corridors as a display of dominance," he said.

"A pitiful gesture of self-righteousness is more like it."

He paused for a moment, turning his head to look at me. "So I've learned. They are very different than the Dark Originators. They flaunt their energy corridors and superior power, but when they speak ..."

I finished his sentence for him. "Their voices sound frail."

He nodded. "And that is a problem that must be addressed."

I didn't respond, but I noted the statement's peculiarity. Why would that matter to him? After walking in silence for a few minutes, he inhaled and closed his eyes.

"I have a good feeling about this," he said. "We should meet over dinner and mead. I've seen enough energy chambers over the past few months."

A pair of guards pushed open the front doors of the castle, and we stepped through. "Consider your request granted."

# 30

# Olivia's Infiltration

Rhyparia sat in the same restaurant she believed Olivia and Vuilni had been leaving when she had crossed paths with them a few days ago. This was the fourth straight day of doing this, and she was beginning to believe her intentions were hopeless. Her brief chance to speak with her friends from a life she thought to have been dead was now gone. It caused her gut to wrench as she sat at the table alone.

Her table was on the inner path of the ring, next to the banister where she could gaze down to the ringed balconies and main floor. She only took her eyes away when the waitress came to ask if she wanted anything else besides the drink she'd ordered an hour ago. Bittersap wasn't the best tasting thing she'd ever had in her life, but it seemed to be the drink of choice amongst customers. Perhaps their palettes had grown accustomed to the bitterness and sticky consistency. She desired something a little sweeter.

She turned, feeling the presence of someone else and expecting it to be the waitress again. Instead she found a young lady with violet hair and a stone expression, Olivia Lavender. Next to her stood another woman who Rhyparia had only known over the course of several months as a teenager, but had grown closer to than anyone else in her life, Vuilni Gesluimant. They both bore muscles akin to a power lifter, arms and legs ripped even more than Rhyparia could recall.

A tear escaped her right eye, tickling her cheek as it raced for her chin. Olivia and Vuilni were here, right in front of her, in the flesh. She got up and embraced them both, forgetting Olivia's disdain for such physical contact. However, she didn't push Rhyparia away or try to slip out of it. Her arms remained limp at her sides, but she accepted it. Vuilni returned the hug, wrapping an arm around both women.

For a long moment—extensive enough to draw the attention of others at their tables—they remained in that position. None of them wanted to let go, and Rhyparia could have allowed her head to rest atop of theirs for hours. She was considerably taller than both of them.

Finally, she released her hold and backed away, wiping tears from her cheeks while trying to stifle the euphoria fixing to blow a hole in her chest. She gestured for them to sit as she lowered herself into her own chair. They followed suit, regarding her as if she were a mythical creature. She expected this.

"I don't even know what to say," Vuilni said.

"I do," Rhyparia said. "I've missed you so much."

"Likewise," Vuilni said, shaking her head in disbelief. "I just can't believe my eyes."

"Have you been in Asalka this whole time?" Olivia asked.

Vuilni leaned forward, pointedly gazing at Rhyparia's chest as she whispered, "What do they put in the food here?"

Rhyparia paused, allowing the question to sink in. She then broke into hysterics, setting her elbow on the table and placing her face in her hand. More eyes darted toward their table, and she quickly tried covering her mouth, but without much sucess. Vuilni laughed along with her as Rhyparia tried fanning herself with her hand, trying to regain her breath. As she looked at Olivia, her laughing stopped.

"Are you smiling?" Rhyparia asked, tilting her head at the oddity.

"She does that now," Vuilni said. "Though, it's still hard to pry it out of her."

"I've missed a lot!" Rhyparia exclaimed.

"So have we, apparently," Olivia said.

Rhyparia closed her eyes and exhaled, leaning back with a slouch. She could still feel the overwhelming heat in her face from the laughter. She hadn't felt such jubilance since years ago, during her time as a Jestivan … before being put on trial as a suspect in the Olethros collapse.

"I've only been in Asalka for a few weeks," she said after a pause. "Before this, I spent a few months traversing a tunnel that connects the Archaic Kingdom to the Prim Kingdom."

"Uh, what?" Vuilni asked.

"Long story," Rhyparia said. "Longer than you could imagine, quite frankly."

"What happened on the night of your execution?" Olivia asked, frowning as the waitress returned with two mugs of hot bittersap for the new dinner guests.

Rhyparia waited for her to leave, then said, "Pilot Ophala and Director Senex saved me, along with a few others. She had a gigantic bird fly me into the Archaic Mountains, where I then met a man who led me to the other side."

"I thought those mountains weren't traversable," Vuilni said, taking a sip of her bittersap. She didn't seem to grimace at the taste. "Especially after my little adventure through them."

"They're not as bad as some might think. Don't get me wrong, they're deadly, and most who enter do die. However, the reason for a sizable number of the disappearances within the mountains is because of the existence of a village on the other side of the mountain range, crammed between it and the Edge."

"You're kidding," Vuilni said, now sipping her bittersap with reckless abandonment.

"Yes," Rhyparia said. "And I tell you this in good faith. The people who live there don't want to be discovered for good reason. When the time comes, they'll reunite with the world on their terms."

"You don't look your age," Olivia said. She had always been one to cut straight to the point. "You should be—what—nineteen years old?"

"By the logic of your timeline, yes," Rhyparia said. "But I'm no longer the youngest of the Jestivan; I'm the eldest." She chuckled at Vuilni's confused knot in her lips. "In order to pass through Realmular Tunnel— the tunnel I spoke of earlier—I needed to partake in a special kind of training, led by a man I met in the village. That training resulted in nearly twenty years passing in ten months—at least for me. The rest of the world experienced the typical passage of time."

"How?" Olivia asked.

Rhyparia sighed, dragging her finger around the rim of her mug. "I won't discuss the specifics. The important part was that it was necessary to achieve the goals—those of my new friends as well as my own… goals that I have yet to accomplish and do not plan to discuss." She paused, then looked toward Olivia and Vuilni. "I'm thirty-nine, by the way."

She watched as they both studied her. At least there wasn't much to Olivia's gaze, even if there was a lot going on in her head. The next closest Jestivan to Rhyparia's age would have been Yama, who was twenty-five by now.

"Have you had any children?" Vuilni asked.

Rhyparia nearly laughed again. "No, there hasn't been the time or opportunity for any of that." She paused, realizing what this meant. She was rapidly approaching forty, yet still a virgin.

"Do you not want any?" Vuilni said.

"A child isn't on my radar. I have more pressing matters in front of me." She feigned an air of confidence, but in her head a weight had been dropped on her.

"What about you two?" Rhyparia asked. "What are you doing here?"

"Digging for information about Toono's first sacrifice," Olivia said. "We're not getting anywhere, though. The Primmish are protective of both their religious and political practices."

"You think that sacrifice was significant?"

"We do," Olivia said, lowering her voice. "We believe it can answer certain questions about his relationship with a woman he's been working alongside."

Rhyparia nodded, lifting her mug to her lips and taking a slow sip of its contents. The bittersap was beginning to grow on her as it cooled and thickened … either that or it was getting sweeter. "I, too, am struggling with some of the elites in this city. But I believe I have a solution." She set her mug on the table. "And I think I can help you, too."

Vuilni had fallen silent for a good portion of the conversation. "What is it?" Rhyparia asked.

"Did you escape those twenty years of training unscathed?"

Rhyparia frowned. "I didn't fight anyone, but I'll admit to suffering from energy exhaustion several hundred times."

"I think she means mentally," Olivia said.

Rhyparia's gaze slowly transitioned between both of them. Was it that obvious? She pressed her lips together. "I'm not the same girl you remember from Phesaw," she said. "I may have similar goals, but the extent I'll go to reach them is now far beyond anything a naïve child could imagine. That stems not only from the twenty years of training, but my experience during the Gravity Trials. I have little patience."

Vuilni looked up from the table, regarding Rhyparia with fearful eyes. "Don't do anything you'll regret."

"I've done plenty of that in my life already."

"Don't try to overcompensate for the mistakes you feel you've made in the past," Vuilni said.

Rhyparia remained silent.

"I trust whatever it is you're doing," Olivia said, causing Rhyparia's stomach to lurch. She would betray that trust.

*     *     *

Olivia sat on a branch high up in a birch, gazing at the stone wall that wrapped around the grounds of Prim Castle, barely visible behind hundreds of other branches. Guards stood at the foot of the wall, allowing not a single gap in their line as it followed the perimeter. Torches jutted from the wall every dozen feet or so, only hanging a few arm lengths above the heads of the guards. She wasn't worried about their numbers because she had faith in her ability to defeat all of them if she had to. But that would then defeat the purpose of a covert mission.

The wall was too high to be cleared in a single leap, even with the strength of her legs. And it was too distant from the nearest birch trees for her to reach it from the canopies. Her only option was to wait for Fane and Vuilni to begin their diversions. Vuilni had hinted that tonight might be it, so Olivia was trying to remain more attentive than she had the past few nights. The conversation she'd had with Rhyparia earlier, however, made this difficult.

Rhyparia's pointed looks toward Olivia's hair hadn't gone unnoticed. She may not have mentioned the absence of Meow Meow, but those looks had been enough to spark Olivia's insecurities. And for some reason being in this city didn't help, making her feel more naked than she ever had in her life. And jumping through trees only made it worse, reminding her of being back home in Lallopy Forest with Meow Meow on her head.

There was a lot for her to process about the meeting earlier that day. Unfortunately, she couldn't dwell on it. They had important, time-sensitive missions to carry out. All she could do was hope Rhyparia was headed down the right path.

Olivia leapt to her feet from a crouched position, noticing movement amongst the guards at the bottom of the wall. She pushed forward, leaping carefully between branches in search of a better vantage point. Based off patterns from her previous scouting trips, it wasn't time for shifts to rotate.

She stopped near the outer layer of trees, spotting the uniforms of officers as they directed guards in separate directions. Olivia's eyes raked the sky, looking for the "obvious" diversion that Fane had mentioned. Then she spotted it, an unnatural mass of black framing a few of the castle's eastern spires. They were the flames of a Passion Assassin, but these were not meant to blend in with their surroundings. They stuck out like a horse in a pack of dogs.

Some guards ran toward the inferno while others split the opposite way, likely heading for whatever distraction Vuilni was creating. Olivia only hoped the two of them weren't causing any actual harm to people, as they had agreed. She regarded the wall again to find the guards' numbers split in half, the gaps between them having doubled in length. Even the caved-in section didn't have the same protection as before, four guards at most.

This would be the only opportunity she would have. The Prim Castle's defenses were tighter than anything she'd ever seen, and while she could have powered her way through without problem, that wasn't the goal. She dropped from the tree and landed in the shadows of the thicket. This maneuver would rely on speed—speed she had acquired from countless days running in Rhyparia's increased gravity at Phesaw. If she could move faster than their eyes could track her, this should work.

She dug the ball of her back foot into the sod, preparing for the push off. According to Bryson, that was the most critical part to get right. Just as she pushed, her calve bulging through her skin, something heavy and hard slammed into the back of her head.

She collapsed, and blackness pooled her vision.

# 31

# The Execution

Olivia opened her eyes to a fuzzy splotch of gold. She blinked a few times, slowly distinguishing a pool of fireflies above. Was she still in the birches outside of the castle? She rolled her head groggily to the side, spotting branches that stretched into the distance before wispily drooping toward the ground. She was within a massive willow's canopy.

She groaned and squeezed her eyes shut, rolling her head so that she was facing the firefly-shrouded treetop once again. It was easier this way, requiring the least amount of physical effort. Her memory was hazy, but it slowly returned as the ringing in her head softened.

She moaned again, this time from embarrassment. She hadn't even taken a step toward the castle's walls before being spotted. How long had they been watching her? Not only had she been spotted, but someone had snuck up on her and knocked her out. Who possessed that kind of skill? She may not have been the stealthiest Jestivan, but she was still a Jestivan. In order for someone to do that to her ... she groaned again.

Someone grasped her bicep and yanked her up to her knees. She lurched, nearly puking at the sudden motion. But there was no time to calm her stomach, as she was yanked up even farther onto her feet. Her knees shook beneath her, and a sharp pain shot up her back.

She looked up in search of her handler's face to find a man with a silver headband. He wore white robes with a rope tied around his waist—a priest. He spun her around, bringing her face-to-face with a ghastly sight.

"No!" she screamed. The terror in her own voice scared her just as much as the scene before her.

Vuilni and Fane were on their knees, their bodies slumped awkwardly, necks resting across a short, knee-high wooden rail. Judging by their closed eyes and motionless faces, they were unconscious. Another man she didn't know was in the same position, but awake. The priest led Olivia to the only remaining vacant beam.

"You awoke earlier than planned," the priest said. He pressed her toward the ground by the neck. "We do not take kindly to spies—especially heretics."

Olivia tried to fight back, but her muscles were too weak, her mind too groggy. Had they drugged her, too? This wasn't how she had ever envisioned dying—not like this. She had underestimated this kingdom and its people, even after learning about its dangers at Phesaw. The Primmish people could afford the luxury of neutrality for a reason. Nobody knew anything about the kingdom for a reason … Yet she thought she could simply walk into the capital and sneak into its castle? What made it scarier was the fact that, somehow, Toono had punctured their defenses and slain their prince.

She tried to scream, but all that escaped was a raspy croak. "Vuilni, Fane! Wake up, please!"

She gasped for air as the priest slammed her neck against the wood, causing something inside to pop. Nothing broke, but the pain was now immeasurable. Her vision multiplied. Her hands were bound behind her back by rope. She saw priests in the distance, just inside of the willow's streaming branches. She couldn't tell if her mind was playing tricks on her, but she even saw a birch with a hollow at its base, large enough for a human to walk through.

A pair of boots stepped into her field of vision, and she craned her neck to see the person's face. A brutish woman stood above her, an axe in her hand. She didn't wear robes or any kind of ceremonial gear, just simple trousers and a tunic. Olivia began to panic, the realization of decapitation sinking in.

"The Primmish people try to stray away from drastic acts such as execution," the priest said. "But there comes a time when our hands are forced, whether it's because of a man who's betrayed his duties, such as Watcher Iris abandoning his post at Dimiourgos's tunnel or because of foreign spies committing heretical felonies in our lands. We do, however, make sure that even evil receives some sort of respect. Primmish executions are done by beheading for a reason. That was how our god was killed."

The priest paused and gaze down at his captives. "We're offering you the same departure from this world as our god."

Olivia's eyes began to tear up, a sensation she'd only experienced once before, when her mother had attacked Bryson and Thusia to a pulp. She was partly thankful for this occurrence. The last time this had happened, she had created a twister of water—the only time in her life she'd shown an elemental ability.

She blinked several times, trying to force out the tears and spark something within her, but nothing happened. She clenched her fists and tried to pull her wrists apart, but she didn't have the strength to tear the rope. How much longer were they going to drag this out?

The priest turned toward the distant willow branches. "Bring in our guests."

*　　*　　*

Rhyparia, Prakriti, Saikatto, and Rayne headed a group of hooded figures. This group varied in size, from a two-foot stature to someone who was nearly seven feet tall. Rhyparia marched ahead. A priest who had been assigned as their escort to the execution lengthened his strides to match her pace.

"The only people invited were you and those three," he said, looking back at the trio without hoods. "I cannot allow you to bring the others."

"Stop us, then," Rhyparia said, tightening her grip around the handle of her umbrella.

The priest glanced toward it, knowing it posed a threat somehow. She had never explained what it was to any of the Primmish people, but he seemed to have a clue. As they reached the wide-sweeping curtain of the willow, several priests stepped in front of her group. She came to a halt and glared at them. "Move."

They stood their ground, but only for a moment. She used her clout to expel her Archaic Energy from her hand into her ancient, weaving with the currents that flowed within it. She then forced the Archaic Chains from the ancient and into the open air. The priests were pushed by a sudden force to either side, their bodies traveling quite a distance, like rocks slung from a slingshot. Behind where they had stood, the willow's branches blew apart, like someone yanking open the curtains of a window at the dawn of a new day.

She dithered, catching a glimpse of the scene before her in the Glades. She'd expected to see Watcher Iris in some kind of unfavorable position, but not three others. She raced inside just as the willow's branches closed, the rest following her in. A priest at the center of the Glades was already looking back at her.

"We were just calling for you," he said. His face sunk, noticing the cloaked figures behind her. "Where are the Fangs that were standing watch?"

"Temporarily disposed of," Rhyparia said as she rushed forward, assuming the Fangs had been the priests standing guard outside. She ran straight for Olivia and Vuilni, but a brutish woman wielding an axe caught her by the throat with one hand.

Olivia's face was turned toward Rhyparia. Olivia seemed absent of any bodily harm, but the expression on her face was a different story: defeated and weak. Rhyparia had never seen such emotions from the unwavering Passion Jestivan—not even when they had rescued her from Dev King Storshae's captivity.

Rhyparia flipped her umbrella, reversing the grip of its handle so the tip pointed upward. She rammed it through the executioner's forearm. The tip protruded from the other side, dripping in blood. It had happened in an instant, and she doubted anyone had seen the motion.

The woman dropped her axe and screamed, releasing her grip of Rhyparia's neck in the process. Rhyparia ripped the umbrella back out of the woman's arm, turning to face the only priest at the center. The rest circled the Glades, near the willow's leafy wall. He had backed away a considerable distance.

"I want this to stop," Rhyparia said, speaking over the executioner's muffled screams.

The priest studied her, but Olivia was the one to speak. "Be careful. They have someone formidable. I know it. It's why I'm here."

"I don't want to use force," Rhyparia said, disregarding Olivia's comments. "Unless you push me to do so."

"What is it that you suggest?" the priest asked, eyes narrowed. "I understand your desperation to save Watcher Iris; you feel he's done nothing wrong. However, the other three were caught trying to vandalize our holy trees while simultaneously attempting to infiltrate the castle. We cannot have a repeat of the events that unfolded on the night of the Prim Prince's assassination."

"I suggest you take a look behind me," Rhyparia said.

The priest's head tilted, his eyes narrowing further. After a pause, he slowly looked that way, as if wary of a trap. The cloaked figures removed their hoods, and a chorus of gasps followed. Whispers emanated from the priests circling the Glades. It only took seconds before every single one of them dropped to their hands and knees, bowing their heads in reverence.

Rhyparia's face softened as she watched the spectacle. Her hunch had been correct; they wouldn't defy proof. She headed for Olivia and untied the rope around her wrists. She then did the same for Vuilni and the other man, who were slowly gaining consciousness. Watcher Iris was last.

"Oh, get up," Kakos growled, his fierce wolf eyes looking down at the priest with disgust.

Therapif hopped over to the trunk of the willow at the center of the Glades, opening up his purse and retrieving gauze and ointment from within. As he began tending to the executioner's forearm wound, the unnamed man slowly pushed himself up to his feet. She recalled seeing him with Olivia and Vuilni the day she had crossed paths with them for the first time. He was older than Rhyparia by a few years, judging by the tight wrinkles of his face and the brown spots on his balding head.

"I recognize your face," he said weakly. "But I'm not sure from where."

"If you had ever paid attention to the Gravity Trials—"

"Ah," the man said. "I recall you being much younger, however." He coughed. "Name's Fane."

Rhyparia nodded, but then moved away from him to approach the priest. He had risen to his feet, but the bowed stature of his body implied he didn't feel comfortable standing in front of the dimiours. She stood at his side to observe the dimiours with him, but his wide-eyed gaze was aimed toward the roots, his mouth agape.

What were the dimiours to him? Did she honestly care? She scanned the five birches that formed a ring around the willow's trunk, eyes trained on the hollows.

"Where are the Monsignors?" she asked. "I'd like a word with them."

A person stepped out of each hollow, each one wearing an animal mask.

"That's disturbing," Moros said. He climbed up Biaza's back and onto her shoulder for a better look. "I hope those aren't actual animal heads."

"Priests, you may leave," Catus, the gorilla-masked man, said.

The priests slipped through the willow's branches, giving the dimiours a second glance before doing so. The executioner, with her forearm freshly bandaged, got up and retrieved her axe before following them out.

"That includes you, Gregariant," Catus added, regarding the priest standing next to Rhyparia.

Gregariant hovered for a moment, eyes glued to the fox that stood at the forefront of the dimiours, before finally hurrying across the Glades and disappearing through the branches.

Once they were all gone, the Monsignors dropped to all fours. They growled, low and heavy, like a lion on the prowl.

"I'm fairly certain a gorilla doesn't make that noise," Moros said, smirking at his own joke.

"A lynx does," Catus said, unfazed by the weasel's tease.

Atarax stepped forward. "What kind of monsters claim to worship Dimiourgos, but wear the heads of animals and decapitate people?"

Silence. Even Catus couldn't muster up words.

Rhyparia took interest in Vuilni, Olivia, and Fane, all of whom were fixated on the dimiours. Olivia's expression was the most interesting of them all. She leaned forward, as if some sort of force drew her toward them. Did she recognize the connection between the dimiours and Meow Meow? Did she even realize the mention of Dimiourgos just seconds ago referred to the very beast that had sat on her head for years?

Quada, the woman in the panther mask, was the first to finally respond. "Holy laws have evolved over the centuries, Lord Dimiour."

"You represent nothing of what Dimiourgos did," Biaza said. "His ideologies don't align with yours."

More silence.

"May I ask, Lord Dimiour—"

"Stop calling us that," Biaza said, cutting Quada off. "And get up, please."

"Very well," Quada said, her voice trembling as she rose to her feet. The rest of the Monsignors followed. "May I ask where you've been?"

"Where Dimiourgos wanted us to be, millennia ago, when he sent our ancestors through Realmular Tunnel," Biaza said, arms crossed, a pronounced frown on her face. She was clearly disgusted by what she was witnessing from this city.

"How many of you are still alive?" a different Monsignor asked.

Rhyparia whirled, for the voice had come from one of the birches behind her. She was shocked by the soft, childlike tone. Her eyes narrowed. She hadn't noticed it during her last visit here, but the figure topped with the head of an ox was no taller than five feet. How old was this person?

"There are several others outside of ourselves, but they've remained in our haven," Therapif said, hopping back to join his fellow dimiours, having just finished repacking his purse of medical supplies.

"Do you know Meow Meow?"

Everyone turned to regard Olivia, who was on her knees, hands flat atop each thigh. She had made the same mistake Rhyparia had made when first speaking about the kitten hat to the dimiours: referring to it as "Meow Meow."

Moros began to laugh, breaking down in tears as he held onto Biaza's shoulders for dear life. Biaza rolled her eyes, and Atarax shook his head disapprovingly.

"Rhyparia has told us about the blasphemous name you've given our god," Atarax said. "The being you refer to as Meow Meow isn't simply a silly hat or ancient piece, it's the decapitated head of the Primmish Originator—and his name is Dimiourgos."

Olivia's eyes widened, but she didn't say any more.

Rhyparia held up her hand. "That's enough. We've been trying to get out of this kingdom for over a month now, and this is our opportunity to do so."

"Whatever you need," Quada said.

"Take off those masks, first of all," Kakos said, sneering as he stepped forward. "It's foul."

"These animals died of natural causes," Catus said.

"I still don't like it," Kakos spat, fangs bared.

The Monsignors lifted the masks, exposing their faces and bald heads. Their skin was as pale as chalk, likely from not having seen direct sunlight in years. Most of them bore wrinkles in the edges of their eyes and lips, but the person who had worn the ox mask turned out to be a young boy— possibly fifteen years old. Their foreheads all sported the same tattoo: a five-pointed star.

Olivia gasped, and Rhyparia turned to look at her old friend. "What is it?"

"That's the same symbol engraved into Meow Meow's fur," Olivia said.

Rhyparia studied Quada's forehead, the panther mask now at her side. Was that what the priests were trying to hide with their headbands? She shook her head, ridding her thoughts of irrelevant material.

"We need your help getting into the Power Kingdom," Rhyparia said.

"Why are you going there?" Vuilni asked.

"To rescue the slaves. It seems slavery has been going on there before even the dawn of Known History. Except the Primmish humans were the slaves back then."

"You're going to get yourself—"

Rhyparia's head snapped toward Vuilni. "Don't you worry about me; I'm decades older than you and my abilities are far beyond what anyone can comprehend." The fierceness in her gaze subsided as she realized who she was speaking to. "What was it that I told you almost every night when we shared a dorm in the Lilac Suites?"

"You said you would free my people."

Rhyparia paused, then nodded and regarded the Monsignors once again. "How about it?"

"We can get you there," Quada said. "Anything for our holy lords."

"I could get used to this," Moros said, cackling softly to himself.

"We can smuggle you into the Power Kingdom through trade ships," Quada said. "And we'll provide you with our most skilled stealth force."

"And one more thing," Rhyparia said. She pointed toward Olivia, Vuilni, and Fane. "You will assist my friends here with anything they request. I assure you, they're not here to harm anyone ..." She trailed off, raising an eyebrow at the trio. "Thought I must admit their actions seem odd." She turned back toward Quada. "But all they seek is information from the royals. Can you help them with this?"

Quada hesitated, and Catus answered instead. "The royals will not simply do as we say."

"But we can persuade them," Quada quickly added, likely noticing the anger on Rhyparia's face. "We will help them."

"Good," Rhyparia said. "When will we depart for these trade ships you speak of?"

"Tonight, if you're prepared," Quada said.

Rhyparia spun, facing the dimiours. "That sound good?" They nodded in unison. A few of them wore relieved smiles. "Tonight it is, then."

# 32

# The Toxic Pair

Moonlight splashed through the window, blanketing Illipsia in twilight blue. She sat in her bed, legs crossed, hands clasped on her lap, and eyes closed. She was allowing herself a moment of meditation while also tracking nearby movements via clairvoyance, expecting the arrival of company.

She felt the movement of a presence outside, likely several rooms down. As always, when she had requested something of Beren, he came through. The presence inched its way closer to the window. She exhaled slowly, preparing herself for the complex weaving she'd have to execute. She opened her eyes and glanced to her left, where her two roommates were sleeping.

Beren's presence approached, and she began to weave a wall of Dev Chains against the window. These chains were composed of millions of tiny fragments of a whole image she had conjured in her mind. To her and anyone in the room, they'd see nothing different if they were to look out the window. However, to someone outside trying to look in, they'd see whatever she was imagining in her head.

To take something from one's imagination and weave it into a perceived reality—something with solidity, an image with objects that didn't waver around their edges—was art far beyond the realm of painting, sketching, or sculpting. It was the ancient art of projecting, but now more commonly known as hallucinogenics. It took more than elite creativity and artistry; it required rigid focus, a keen eye for detail, and a photographic memory like no other. And that was just the crafting of the image. The weaving patterns were a whole different story.

Beren appeared in the frame of the window. He looked inside, then squinted and leaned forward, pressing his cupped hands against the glass. Illipsia watched him attentively, but remained concentrated on the image she was weaving in the window. If all went according to plan, he'd walk away soon.

He pressed his cheek against the glass and tried to look at a downward angle toward her bed. She could see the sorrow flood his face. He knocked, nearly causing her to let slip a gasp. Across the room, her roommates stirred, forcing her to spontaneously shift certain patterns in her Dev Cluster to adjust the image in her mind.

Beren backed away, arms falling limp at his sides. He didn't frown, but the sadness in his eyes was unmistakable. As he left, she instantly hated herself. He liked her; she knew this. She, however, couldn't reciprocate those feelings. She had sworn to refuse her heart that pleasure the moment she'd entered Telejunction. She knew she'd have to use someone, and Beren had gained that responsibility. If a bond developed with him, it'd be devastating when the time came to disappear …

Just like what had happened with Simon.

*　　*　　*

The next day, Illipsia walked with Beren by the lake in Phesaw Park. With the steady departure of Archain refugees, the campus had grown peaceful. She playfully kicked the fallen pink petals of the cherry blossoms as they walked. The ground was a carpet of pink. Even the lake was hidden beneath the petals.

"I can't believe you stood me up last night," Beren said with a notable pout.

Illipsia bit into her chunk of chocolate and shrugged. "*You* stood *me* up," she lied. "I was in my room waiting the entire night. Didn't fall asleep until four o'clock in the morning."

"What were you doing? Hiding under your bed?" he asked, pulling a petal out of his collar.

"I was sitting on my bed."

He snorted, gaze growing lazy. "I don't know what you get out of messing with me."

*Practice*, she thought. "I'm honestly confused," she said. "Are we going to spend all morning on this?"

He sighed. "I guess not."

She turned her face away from him, trying to hide her shame by feigning fascination with a group of starlings fluttering between trees. Last night had been a huge leap forward. Beren hadn't seen her. He had looked into the room only to find it empty, even though she and her roommates had been in plain sight.

*     *     *

Bryson sat in one of the chairs occupying the stage at the far end of Steel Field. He slouched, an elbow resting on one arm and his cheek plopped into his open hand. The days had begun to drag, and he didn't care that his presence was improving the performance of the weavineers. If anything, that only pissed him off. To think these people envied him because of a last name he didn't even claim anymore. He wasn't a LeAnce; he was Bryson Still, soon to be Bryson Intel. Honestly, he still wasn't sure how that would work.

Why did this city revere a man like Mendac? Did his accomplishments in weavineering outweigh the evils he'd committed? No, they simply didn't believe their icon did such things, which explained a lot of the looks of disdain Bryson received on a daily basis. They saw him as a liar and traitor. The disgust was visibly painted on some of the weavineers' faces every time they looked toward the stage. He preferred that. At least it meant they couldn't believe his supposed lies because of their atrocious nature ... At least they knew the acts were atrocious.

He sighed, lazily tipping his head to get a better look at Lilu, who was enthusiastically inspecting a newly finished travolter. It had been completed by Limone and his team of weavineers, proving the extra work they were putting in outside of Steel Field was worth it. A couple of weavineers snuck glances at Bryson to see if he was watching them.

Sucking his teeth, he redirected his attention to the right, where the distant cavern wall stretched high above. The sunlight streamed through the sky hole, illuminating the town of Bastion and the balconies scattered around the curving wall.

He wanted nothing more than to get into the sewers. The sooner he accomplished this, the sooner he was out of this city and on his way back to Dunami. Alas, he could do nothing without Thusia, and he still he couldn't summon her. Something was blocking his ability to do so. He thought it might have been an occurrence on Thusia's end, fearing the Light Empire was punishing her for something she did. After all, she had apparently broken a lot of rules that made little sense to him.

But then something else occurred to him. He could no longer use his clout, so maybe he could no longer summon a Branian either. Maybe Bryson hadn't only lost his Intel Energy, but his Tahara, too. He bowed his head, a sunken demeanor to his posture. He needed to contact Shelly and ask her to interrogate Suadade on the subject. Maybe he had answers.

*     *     *

"Bryson, is Thusia in trouble?"

Bryson shrugged at Lilu's question, but didn't respond. They walked down a Bastion street, Intelamps illuminating it in splotches. As they stepped in and out of shadowy gaps, squat townhouses bordering both sides, he rocked his head side to side, popping his neck to release tension. All the ramifications of not having Thusia at his disposal were beginning to pile up in his head. Not only did it make getting into Mendac's lab impossible, but it meant he had another missing tool in combat. How would he fair against Toono without both his electricity and Branian?

"We're running out of time," Lilu said. "You're due back at the capital within the month. This isn't a mission we can request an extension for."

"You're berating me with this useless information as if I don't know this already … or as if I can do anything about it. I don't have any control over my Branian if she chooses not to answer me. She is a being of divinity, Lilu. I'm a mortal."

Following a pause, she said, "Understood. I suppose we'll simply wait for Radon's return with my sister's response."

"That's all we can do," he said, pleased to be dropping the subject as they turned down another street.

Mostly silence bathed the block, save a couple of young weavineers who seemed to be holding a friendly conversation on the stoop of their townhouse. Feeling uncomfortable in the quiet, Bryson tried to search for another topic. Luckily, the couple kissed, bringing to light the perfect conversational piece.

"I like Frederick," he said.

Lilu gazed at him, eyes narrowing. "He's a good guy, I suppose. And Limone and Gracie?"

"They're cool, too. But Frederick's a great guy."

She expelled a single, forced laugh. "Don't circle your point; cut straight to it."

He smirked. "Do you like him?"

"I love our friendship," she said after a pause.

"It's okay to admit it. I see how you look at him."

"You mean my gazes of admiration? I admire his mind and generosity, Bryson."

"Don't you have a date with him tonight?"

"I have a meeting!" she exclaimed.

He turned to look at her, his gaze flicking up to the flower in her hair. "Your cherished begonia all for a meeting?"

"I'm not in love with him!"

Bryson stopped walking. She had shrieked with such ferocity that the couple retreated into the house. He stared at her, his eyebrows pinched with a mixture of shock and anger. Why had something so minor set her off? She had also come to a stop, but didn't look at him. She looked down and away, her breathing heavy. The redness of her ear, exposed between two wavy locks of green, told him she was likely just as angry as he was. Then he heard sniffling.

"The guy likes you, and I know you like him," Bryson said softly, unaware of the idiocy in his words. "Why can't you let your guard down?"

She slowly turned her head, allowing only the right side of her face to be seen while her shoulders remained squared. "Thanks to your father, I know what a man can do to a woman."

Bryson balked, unable to find words. What came next, however, might have been just as bad.

"And thanks to you, I'm scared to love."

*     *     *

Bryson didn't know how long he spent standing in that exact spot. Ten minutes? An hour? He didn't care if he was in the middle of the street, and he wasn't bothered by the few people who walked past with dragging stares. Honestly, the street didn't exist in his mind. Neither did Bastion. All he could see was red.

Had she really just taken a jab at his father to hurt him? This shouldn't have bothered him, but it did. Mendac deserved all the hatred he received, but the way she had worded it implied Bryson should have felt personally responsible for it … as if she was saying, "Yeah, Mendac did it, but you're to blame."

Then to follow it up by saying he was the reason for her guarded heart. Such a notion was ludicrous and enraging. His relationship with Lilu had been toxic for a long time. There wasn't one side on which to pin the blame. They both made mistakes, causing their relationship to flounder quickly. It didn't help they were both extremely stubborn, so most of their quarrels resulted in week or month-long vows of distant silence rather than apologies.

He arched his neck and looked toward the cavernous ceiling of dimmed Intelights. Clenching his fists as his sides, he yelled for the entire neighborhood to hear, forgetting he was supposed to be some sort of icon. How many people were now watching from their windows as this man screamed to the Empire, the echoes becoming as heavy as his misery?

He finally ceased his cry and dropped his gaze toward the street ahead, heaving as he tried to rein in his flooding rage. How could she have clumped him in with his father?

# 33

# An Orphan's Clue

Olivia awoke in a daze, vision swimming and mind heavy. She hadn't been knocked out again, so why was she like this? Had they sedated her?

As she began to make sense of her surroundings, she realized she was in a cage—or something close to it. Instead of steel bars, sturdy rods of wood encircled her, arching near the top until they converged at the center. She was leaning against a skinny tree trunk that stretched from the ground to the top of the cage.

She crawled forward, arms shaking as she put weight on her hands. She reached out for a wooden rod and tried to snap it. Despite its size and feeble appearance, the rod remained firm. What kind of wood was this?

"Olivia."

She turned to see Vuilni sitting calmly in a nearly identical cage just a few paces away. Fane was in the same predicament just to the right of her.

"It seems your Jestivan friend's rescue didn't result in the most flattering of accommodations," he said, eyeing the bars with a frown.

Olivia rubbed her thumb and index finger against her temple in an attempt to massage her headache away. "Why did they stick us in here?" she asked, too weak to reach a volume above a mumble. "I thought those masked people would comply with Rhyparia's requests."

"Apparently not," Vuilni said. "We've been in here for well over a day."

"Really?" Olivia asked.

Vuilni nodded. "They seemed to sedate you much heavier than they did Fane or me."

Olivia tried shaking the cage again, but with no luck.

"Brute strength doesn't affect them," Vuilni said. "Not even my Powish strength."

Olivia looked at Fane. "Have you tried your flames?"

"No," he said. "They won't work. I know from recent experiences."

"Try it anyway …" Olivia said.

He shook his head. "Best to practice patience. They might be contemplating their decision elsewhere." He looked around, but all that surrounded them were the weeping branches of a larger willow. "This could simply be a safety precaution, which I honestly understand. While I didn't set fire to anything important, they still think that was my intention."

Olivia plopped onto her stomach, now sprawled atop the grass.

"Is that okay with you, Princess Olivia?" Fane asked. She could hear the attempted humor in his tone.

She simply let out a muffled groan into the ground. Her thoughts drifted to what had unfolded the day before. She had witnessed the revelation of a new species—or an ancient, forgotten species, considering what had been said. Bipedal animals that spoke the Sphairian language and possessed intellect on par with humans. She had never learned of such a thing in school, not even from her scholarly mother.

While there were still many questions she had about the dimiours, she knew one thing. Meow Meow was once one of them, and he'd been a sort of god to them. A shiver raced up her spine. She'd shared a mind with a deity for most of her life, yet she had never seen a single shred of evidence regarding this supposed past.

Minutes later, a priest stepped through the greater willow's wall. He strolled toward their cages in silence, then somehow lifted one of the wooden rods from the sod with only his hand, freeing Vuilni first. He moved toward Fane, saving Olivia for last. As the three of them stepped out of their cages and rose to their feet, he turned and headed for the branches he had just entered through.

"Follow me."

*     *     *

Half an hour later, they were led through the branches of another willow tree, the grass surrounding it strewn with its gnarled roots. She stepped carefully, fearful of snagging her foot in a pit. Three priests, clasping their hands behind their backs, stood in front of the willow's trunk.

They finally reached a place where their escort instructed them to stop. He then bowed to the priests and retreated from the willow.

"What were the intentions of your actions two nights ago?" a woman asked.

"To gain access to the royal castle," Olivia said.

"That makes sense. We had come to the conclusion that your purpose wasn't to target the holy trees, but to pretend as if you were. You set fire to the area surrounding it. While some of the birches were destroyed because of this, none of them were establishments or places of residence."

"Yes, I thoroughly scouted the areas beforehand," Fane said. "I don't murder innocent people."

The second of the two female priests nodded. She had short ivory hair. "Since you weren't attempting assassination, what were you seeking in the castle?"

"We're trying to find information about an acidic ancient," Olivia said. "We believe someone in the castle knew about one. And this is relevant to the assassination of the prince years ago … or so we think."

"Priests don't use ancients," the lone man said. "We would know nothing about this thing you chase."

"I need an audience with the queen," Olivia said flatly.

340

"That request would require weeks of negotiations," he said, a hint of disdain in his tone. "The royal and religious sectors of Asalka have separated themselves from one another. The priests don't have the respect of the royals. Only a specific Monsignor could execute such negotiations." His lips pressed together, creating a thin line. "And as of this morning, they have departed to the Black Powder Mountains for a spiritual mission, where they will try to determine where their philosophical ideologies went wrong."

"Those dimiours shook them a bit, eh?" Fane asked.

The man's eyes dragged toward the Passion Assassin, his face dull. "They have some soul-searching to do." He paused. "All of us do."

Olivia glanced at the roots just ahead of her, contemplating the offer. They had spent a lot of time here already, and she had no clue what was happening anywhere else in the world. Asalka felt even more isolated than Kindoliya.

"How long before they return?" she asked.

"Anywhere between one week and three."

Olivia closed her eyes, releasing a slow breath. "We'll wait."

＊　　　＊　　　＊

Kaylee sat at Raul's bedside on the second floor of Balle's premier medical ward. Premier was quite a stretch, however, considering the state of the building's infrastructure, furniture, and supplies. It was a miracle they hadn't killed any of the orphans she had rescued from Accus Canyon by now. After the first couple of days of noticing the amount of filth coating the surgical instruments of the nursing staff, Kaylee had taken it upon herself to hand-wash every single object she could.

The second floor was one giant room, lined with twin beds on both sides. Wheeled curtain rods separated the beds, most of which were drawn closed to offer some form of privacy. Orphans occupied a majority of the beds.

Lost Wisdom had a medical sector in their building, but Kaylee had made the decision to keep the children away from such an evil place. And they soon discovered anyway that the building had been locked down and occupied by Archaic officers—and not just local officers of Balle, but high-ranking officials and soldiers from the capital. It seemed Pilot Ophala had taken the issue seriously, and Kaylee loved her for it. She even sent scouts into the canyon to further investigate Kaylee and Himitsu's bone-chilling discovery.

Kaylee would have loved to take part in the investigations, but her mission required her presence by Raul's side at all times. The young boy wasn't suffering from anything critical, such as a coma or shock. But, like his fellow foster brothers and sisters, he was malnourished, and she didn't have the heart to interrogate him about Neeko this soon after such a traumatizing experience. She simply stayed by his side, cracking jokes and telling him stories. She even created her own chemical concoctions at the inn she was staying at and brought them to the ward to help heal him faster. She did this every day over the span of two weeks for hours on end.

Himitsu and Sal contributed to the investigation into Lost Wisdom during the downtime, trying desperately to be of use. Their presence wasn't ideal here in the medical ward. Raul didn't respond well to them, and he usually bottled up. He felt more comfortable with her after learning she had also been an orphan, which was the only time he mentioned the name of their mentor. Since then, he had steered clear from the subject. Today, Kaylee's luck would change.

"You're super skilled at this," Raul said, placing a mug of her most recent elixir on the bedside table.

She smiled. "I would hope so. I do aim to be an apothecary, after all."

"You could find a job today," he said, resting his head back onto his pillow. "I'm recovering faster than anyone else because of you." He tilted his head to the side, glancing toward the other beds. "You should help them, too."

"I only have enough supplies for one person ... maybe two."

"What made you decide on apothecary? I know you've read thousands of books from Neeko's library."

She paused, thankful to hear the man's name again. This was her chance, but she would have to ease it into the conversation. "I suppose it relates to my ultimate dream in life. There is something specific I wish to achieve down the line, and such a profession will provide the greatest avenue to achieving it—that combined with some surgical skills, too."

"I see," Raul said. "Do you mind me asking what the dream is?"

"I can't tell you that. I know your studies with Neeko didn't reach the extent they did for me or his three other students that came before me, but there's more to it than what you can imagine."

"Very ominous and obscure," he whispered, almost as if mocking her. She cracked a smile. He gazed at the ceiling. "Neeko had told me to pay attention to which subjects caught my interest while reading a second time through. He wanted me to narrow it down to three."

"Then he would have had you choose one from those three," she said, nodding. "I remember it quite well."

"Honestly," he said, "I knew what I wanted to study after the first read-through. Every single book on the matter fascinated me."

"And what was that?"

"Botany."

"Ooo!" she exclaimed, nearly forgetting her objective in this conversation. "An apothecary's best friend is a botanist."

"We can be partners once I grow a bit older," he said.

"That we can," she said.

Raul's face softened. He reached for his glass of water from the bedside table and took a sip.

"What's wrong?" she asked.

"I only wish I had the opportunity to reach the stages of Neeko's education that you did. He never got to hear my newfound aspiration."

Was this what it felt like when adults used to speak to a ten-year-old Kaylee? She couldn't believe this little boy's vocabulary and maturity. He was well beyond his years.

"What happened to Neeko, Raul?"

His shoulders sunk, gaze falling slightly. "I don't know. He changed."

"How so?" she asked, weaving through her silver eye to catch every shift in the boy's aura.

"He became ... depressed. And it wasn't a gradual shift toward degradation. It was sudden—almost jarring, really." He shook his head, gaze distant. "I remember going to his office one day, more excited than I ever had been in my life."

"Why?"

"He was going to give me an exam, one tailored for only his most special students … like the four who had come before me, you being one of them."

She nodded, knowing exactly what he was talking about.

"But when I arrived at his office, he was sunken into his chair, eyes open but unresponsive." Raul regarded Kaylee with scared eyes. "I didn't know what to do. I called his name several times, but he just sat there, staring at a silver medallion resting on his desk."

She leaned forward, eyes narrowed. "A medallion?" she asked. She had seen most of Neeko's belongings, but she couldn't recall anything of that nature. "Did you notice any details? Was anything engraved into it?"

The boy shook his head. "Of course not. It belonged to him, and I'm not one to snoop—especially on someone of his stature. I had nothing but respect for that man. Anyway, he eventually responded when I shook his knee." He paused, trying to find words. "His gaze was haunting, Kaylee. The way it dragged onto my face, the hollowness that seemed to fill his pupils. He was a very old man, but it seemed as if his wrinkles had multiplied exponentially in just a week's time."

Kaylee released a slow breath, hating every detail of the imagery. She loved the man. He had been a father figure to her.

"He was like that for weeks," Raul continued. "He bathed in wallow. While I continued to read the books for a third time, my lessons came to a halt. He had no desire to teach me."

"And he never explained why he was sad?" she asked.

"While he had never stated it explicitly, I believe he lost his passion for reading and learning," he said. "He told me, 'Raul, stay away from books and connect with people. You commit your entire life to the past and future of the world like I did, then realize at the end of it you never made time for yourself and your friends.'"

As Raul fell silent, Kaylee tried to decipher the message. There was an obvious lesson in the quote, but something had to have caused Neeko to realize this. Where did the lesson stem from? What occurrence acted as the catalyst to such a mindset?

Raul's eyes narrowed. "The day before he disappeared, he made a very cryptic statement to me. Seeing that you knew him a lot better than I did, perhaps you can make greater use of it."

"What was it?"

"He claimed all the evil currently plaguing the world was indirectly his fault, as if he was taking the blame for the massive war between True Light and SCAPD. He said he had to make sure nobody ever discovers the tool that started it all."

Kaylee closed her eyes and sighed. "I see," she said. That may have been cryptic to Raul, who had never reached the final stage of Neeko's teachings. But to her, there was no mistaking his words.

Neeko felt responsible for guiding Toono toward the path he eventually took in life. And the tool he had used was his ancient quill.

*　　　*　　　*

"Raul just gave us the biggest clue we could have asked for," Kaylee said, as she, Himitsu, and Sal watched several Lost Wisdom employees be loaded onto a convoy of prisoner wagons.

"So we know Neeko regretted teaching Toono, or he regretted writing down his dream at least," Himitsu said. "He also feels guilty for the war. But where does that put us in terms of knowing where to find his book?"

"He mentioned valuing people over books," she said. "Something happened that triggered this mindset. Raul described Neeko as being in a nightmarish daze. Perhaps a significant death?"

"Based on what you've described, that'd make sense," Sal said through a mouthful of grits he had purchased at a pop-up diner. "My father had that look for years after what happened in Olethros."

"If we consider all the major deaths that have occurred since Toono's first sacrifice, whose would have affected him the most?" Kaylee asked.

"That's easy," Himitsu said. "Grand Director Poicus or Archaic Director Senex."

She raised an eyebrow. "Why?"

"My mother said Neeko Lefolli was once a student at Phesaw. He was best friends with Praetor Poicus and Mynute Senex. Long story short, he spent a lot of his time in the Warpfinate until, one day, he never came back out. That's how he became known as the Lost Boy, a ghost story that was told to students at Phesaw over the next few decades."

A long silence passed. "Why did you never tell me this?" Kaylee asked.

"Slipped my mind, honestly," Himitsu said.

Sal laughed. "What an idiot."

Himitsu's brows furrowed, turning toward Sal. "What are you talking—"

"He's right," Kaylee said. "You're an idiot."

Himitsu frowned. "Fine then."

She sighed and shook her head, gazing back at the road where the prisoner wagons sat. "So we should find places of importance regarding Senex and Poicus," she said. "Where did they die?"

"Senex died in the midst of a rescue attempt of Rhyparia in Olethros," Himitsu said. "I was there. I don't know what they did with his body, or if they even found it. I believe he was swallowed by lava."

"And Poicus?" she asked.

"Nobody knows where he actually died," Himitsu said. "But reports indicate his body was found at the Archaic Kingdom's teleplatforms."

"Okay …" She scoffed. "Two complete opposite ends of the kingdom."

"Visiting both spots would be a waste of time," Himitsu said. "I think we've done enough of that up to this point."

She nodded in agreement. "We need to speak with your mom again. Raul mentioned a silver medallion, which was likely an ancient piece. That would mean Poicus or Senex would make sense."

"Well, luckily my mom will be arriving here within the next couple of days."

"Really?"

Himitsu looked at her with eyebrows raised. "You like her that much, eh?"

She beamed, eyes twinkling. "I absolutely adore that woman."

# 34

# The Forgotten Hybrid

The crew's quarters of the Whale Lord was dark, with only a small section illuminated by an oil lantern resting on the floorboards. Gray Whale lay in a hammock; Agnos was trying his best to do the same. Ever since losing his arm, he was scared to lay in the death traps. All it took was one wrong movement and he'd topple out like dead weight. He'd underestimated the amount of security that second arm had given him.

It had been a while since the last time he was aboard the Whale Lord. The storm currently pummeling the harbor was fitting, reminding him of the nights he'd spent in the ship's cargo hold as a swab. Those nights ended up being what propelled him to relevance, as he caught two rats aboard the ship. Once they were apprehended, Gray Whale hunted down the Brench Hilt with ease.

"I know you think you know everything, son, but that's simply not the case when it comes to whirlpools," Gray said, gazing at the ceiling as she rocked her hammock side to side with a planted foot. "They are one of the most fascinating beasts of Kuki Sphaira, but also the deadliest. No amount of book reading can prepare you for it."

"And you're letting Eet and Osh come along for the voyage?" Agnos asked.

"Of course I am. They understand the dangers. Just because they're kids doesn't mean they're not pirates. When they commit to something, they don't turn around with their tails tucked between their legs."

"I don't want them on my ship," he said.

"Well, they want to be on your ship."

"I don't care."

She chuckled softly to herself. "They'd find a way on regardless." He didn't entertain her with a response. "Anyway, a whirlpool requires mighty squallblasters—ones who can both weave creatively and with a lot of clout."

He rolled his eyes. "So now it makes a ton of sense why they'd take Tashami away from me."

"Calm down," she said. "Queen Apsa gave you a very formidable group of sailors. I can vouch for them. While Tashami is a considerable loss, you've been given a considerable gain to make up for it. Those are some of the best squallblasters in the world, and who knows what that Diatia could provide."

"I just don't want to die doing something completely avoidable before even finishing my translation of the Thunder Queen's chronicle," he said.

"Now, now, Anus, you're beginning to sound a lot like that boy I met in the Chasm."

"Ha, ha. Don't start calling me that again."

She coughed several times before hacking up a wad of spit. "If it makes you feel any better," she said, "I'll be entering the whirlpool first. All you have to do is follow my lead."

"Way easier said than done."

She cackled. "Damn right it is!"

*　　*　　*

Once again, Yama sat against the oak's trunk that neighbored Ataway's grave. From the depth of her slouch she could have been mistaken for a corpse. Part of her wished she was one. Her chin sat atop her chest while her violet hair draped her face. She didn't care that it had been weeks since she had last bathed and wasn't fazed by the absence of her sword, something that had been at her hip throughout her entire life. Now it lay forgotten in a nearby gnarl of roots.

She finally looked up, spotting a bowl of gruel and a jug of water a few paces ahead of her. She had neglected them since morning, partly wishing thirst or hunger would claim her. But who was she kidding? Such deaths were too painful. Even now, as her stomach gurgled only slightly, she wanted to nourish it immediately.

She crawled forward and scooped out the cold, slimy substance with her hand, lifting it to her mouth and letting it coat her tongue. Despite the terrible texture, it had a lucid taste of strawberries. She took another scoop and tipped her head back, pouring the sludge from her hand into her mouth, causing excess clumps to roll down her chin. She wiped them off with the back of her hand, reached for the jug, and then chugged the warm water it contained.

Lowering the canister onto the grass, her gaze drifted toward the Edge in the distance. When was she going to commit to her leap? Today? No, she didn't feel like walking. And yesterday it was raining. The day before that it had been too hot … She was running out of excuses.

A glimpse of red crested the hill in her peripheral vision. She glanced that way to find Kolver, the young man in charge of the village's only inn. Sometimes Yama thought he was the only person in the entire village. He stood roughly fifty paces away, keeping his distance between the two of them.

"What do you want?" she asked.

"You should go, Yama. There is nothing for you here. It's hopeless."

She looked off to the side, eyebrows furrowed. "You don't have to keep telling me this. I'll be leaving soon."

*     *     *

While Rayne, Saikatto, and Prakriti loaded their belongings onto their carriage, Rhyparia helped the dimiours load theirs. Most of the items they brought were only meant for the journey to Prim Bay. After that, they couldn't take much of anything since they'd be smuggled into the Power Kingdom via cargo holds of ships. That would only allow for some food, water, and the clothes on their backs.

Moros had transferred from his typical spot on Biaza's back to Rhyparia's shoulder. He didn't offer much to the loading process, electing to lounge against her head and giggle at any mishaps from his friends.

Most of what went into the carriage's storage unit underneath the floorboards was food. They were chiefly leafy products, most of which were either green or yellow in nature. The Primmish were vegans, which shouldn't have bothered Rhyparia. During her time training with Musku, he had weaned her off meat. However, at least in Epinio, the vegetation was cooked and prepared. The Primmish preferred to eat their plants raw, and if they did cook them, it was only to rid them of deadly bacteria.

She hopped out of the carriage and bid the dimiours farewell for the time being. Moros climbed down her back and leapt for the steps, skittering across the floor and hopping onto a seat. She approached the second carriage, gazing to her left where a wall of birches acted as Asalka's border. As unique an experience the forest city had been, she was happy to depart.

Outside of Rhyparia and her companions from Epinio, the only other person with them was an unnamed man who the priests had referred to as a Prowler. He sat atop a horse ahead of the two carriages. He apparently knew the geography of the kingdom like the back of his hand.

As reassuring as that was, she still hadn't forgotten the promise of reinforcements, which were nowhere to be seen. Were they waiting at the bay? And did she even want reinforcements? They could sabotage everything in the Power Kingdom.

Realizing she was the last person still outside in the beaming first-day sun, she lightly jogged to her carriage. As she went to board, it shook, and she caught a glimpse of something just above. She stepped back and looked toward the roof, shielding her eyes against the sun. A man stood there. He wore a long black trench coat, broad at the shoulders and buttoned all the way down.

"What was that?" Rayne asked from inside the carriage.

"Nothing," Rhyparia said, tilting her head at the man. He had clearly landed hard enough to disrupt those within, but the collision hadn't made a sound. "Who are you?" she asked. Her umbrella was in the carriage and, therefore, of no use.

"Your reinforcement," he said with a bit of an accent.

He dropped to the ground effortlessly, landing in the grass in the same stance he had taken atop the roof. Once again, he made no noise. His hands were tucked inside his trench coat pockets, and he stood with a slight arch to his back. He was older than her by a couple decades, but his build was that of a man in his twenties. His beard was long, full, and black, with splotches of gray throughout. He donned hard black eyes in the crevices of his wrinkled face. They were shifty, skittering just around her face, unable to focus on one thing.

"Where are the others?" she asked.

"I'm all the reinforcements you'll need, Lita," he said.

She froze, leaning forward and narrowing her eyes, as if a closer look would help her remember him. "How do you know who I am?"

He smiled. "I can see you scouring your memory banks, but you won't find anything up there. For now, let's just say I know things." He tilted his chin up and inhaled. "Let's get this mission going, shall we?"

"What's your specialty?" she asked.

"I am a hybrid."

She paused, then finally said, "Of what?"

"Spy and assassin."

She looked him up and down. His appearance wasn't exactly inconspicuous, nor was his accent. She snorted, walking past him. "Just carry your weight and don't get in the way."

"Like I got in the way of your friend, Lita Olivia?" he asked, not bothering to follow.

She whirled only to be facing his back. "You were the one who captured my friends?"

He turned his head only slightly, exposing one eye. "I did, and rather effortlessly I might add."

# 35

# The Dahlia Effect

A week passed, and despite having to be seen together on multiple occasions, Bryson and Lilu had yet to speak to each other. They had fallen into the same cycle as usual. He wasn't surprised by it. In fact, he was more caught off guard by how long it took for it to happen. Usually, they couldn't stand the sight of each other after just a few days.

Living up to his stubborn ways, Bryson was already returning to the townhouse earlier than he was supposed to. Weavineers bustled with activity on Steel Field, for there were a few hours remaining in the workday. He should have been on the viewing stage, but he couldn't take it anymore—at least not today. While Lilu spent most of her time on the field, proctoring her weavineers, that didn't mean there weren't long moments when she had to sit on the stage next to him … as if they were a royal couple on their thrones.

Perhaps that was what bothered him most. He wasn't only being lauded as the son of Mendac LeAnce, but the city was flaunting him as if he was the partner of their weapon's specialist. He couldn't stand the thought, especially not after what Lilu had said to him a week ago.

"Bryson!"

He turned, surprised someone had the gall to address him—not that he would have minded it. He had simply gotten used to the civilians watching him from a distance, speaking with their friends in a hushed silence.

A young woman with sleek black hair, olive skin, and a white lab coat was sprinting toward him. "Gracie?" he muttered.

She stopped as she reached him, leaning forward with her hands on her knees, heaving for air.

"You should stand up straight," he said. "Place your hands on the back of your head, elbows pointed out. Then breathe in through your nose and out your mouth."

She followed his instructions without question, straightening up in a heartbeat. As she inhaled, she nodded her head. "Yes, that's much better."

He smirked. "Tips from Debo."

"Who's that?"

His smile disappeared. "Nobody."

She shrugged. Then, after a few seconds, she dropped her arms and continued past him. "Take a walk with me, Bryson."

He frowned and crinkled his nose. Out of Lilu's friends here in Brilliance, he had spoken with Gracie the least. Because of this, the tone she had just given him was kind of comical. Still, he did as she asked, if not simply because it was the most direct route to the townhouse.

"I notice things," she said, gazing forward.

He guessed at what she was referring to. "It's not like we're trying to make it unnoticeable."

"You definitely are. At least, for the weavineers and the public. But a good eye, one that knows Lilu very well, can see it clear as day."

"Okay ..."

"What did you do to her?" she asked. "I just want to hear it from your mouth."

"Are you seriously assuming it's my fault because she's your friend?"

She turned toward him and smiled. "Not at all. I know she said something stupid, too. I've already had this discussion with her the night she came back to the townhouse in enraged tears. I could talk to her in that moment because, like I previously stated, I know her. However, I didn't feel comfortable approaching you because we barely know each other. But after a week, I can't sit idly by any longer."

"I suppose I can understand that," he said.

She nodded, looking forward. "I made her realize the stupidity of her words, but she also told me the way everything unfolded. You're also to blame, and I'm here to make you realize this."

"Are you now?"

"Some people need a little prodding, but personalities like yours and Lilu's need more of a shove."

"Good luck," he said.

"You're both prudes with alpha personalities," she said. "Let's get that straight." His head snapped toward her, but she continued her rant. "It's no wonder things never worked out. And despite the fact that there's been so much tension released between the two of you, there's still an unimaginable amount pent up."

She paused and sighed. "From what I've gathered, you and Lilu started out with a bang. I don't know the extent of your relationship when it was on good terms, but I can assume there was promise."

"Yes, but that's in the past," he said. "*Way* in the past."

"And I get that. Most importantly, she understands that. But understanding doesn't imply acceptance. She's had to watch you grow close to her sister, make a baby with her, and now you're going to marry the woman. Don't get me wrong … jealousy has played a factor in her moods regarding you, but there have been times when she's come to grips with the reality of your relationship with Princess Shelly. And that's when I see her at her best."

"Then why don't I ever see that?" he asked.

"Because you always, *somehow*, do or say something stupid that triggers her old habits."

He groaned and threw up his hands. "And that's why I stopped speaking to her! Even when I'm simply trying to help, it's not wanted."

"Bingo!" she yelled. "She doesn't want it! So stop trying to tell her what you think is best for her."

"I didn't know being a good friend was a bad thing."

Gracie slapped her face, clearly frustrated. "Role reversal time. How would you feel if Lilu was the one with a child and on the verge of marriage with some guy, and you were the one separated from all of your friends in a faraway city?"

He twisted his lips. "Like crap, I suppose."

"And if Lilu then came to visit you, only to push you onto another woman?"

"I get it," he said.

"Do you?"

"Who and when she chooses to love again is up to her," he said, understanding dawning upon him. "It's not my choice, and I should show respect to that fact."

Gracie gave an impressed frown, but then smiled. "Wow, you caught on to that quicker than I thought you would. You're right. She's a strong, highly independent person. The last thing she wants is someone she used to have feelings for trying to dictate her direction in life, even if that isn't your intention."

He came to a stop at the foot of their townhouse's stoop. He regarded her sullenly. "I messed up and didn't know it," he said. "I'll apologize."

She clapped giddily. "Do you mind hugs?"

As he stared at her, he saw Jilly for a split second. Despite the differences in skin tone and hair color, the similarities were uncanny. "Of course I don't mind them."

They embraced, and she whispered, "I also have a way for you to get into the sewers without being noticed. Let me know when your Branian is ready."

His hug tightened. "Thank you so much."

*     *     *

Bryson entered an empty house; Gracie sprinting back to Steel Field. He walked through the breakfast nook and living room before heading up the

356

stairs and finding his room near the end of the hallway. He entered to find a sealed parcel on his bed. Dashing over, he leapt onto the bed and snatched it up, breaking the seal and untying some string to reveal two narrow boxes with a note attached.

*I wish I could help with your question, love. However, I can't receive an answer, for I face the same predicament. Sorry.*

*P.S. Pick a flower for the wedding theme. I love you and hope to see you soon.*

Bryson dropped the note on the floor and flopped back onto his bed, groaning in frustration. It was worse than he had imagined. While Shelly had tried to keep her wording as cryptic as possible, the message was clear. She couldn't summon Suadade. Now he knew it wasn't only a problem on his end.

Thusia and Suadade had led somewhat reckless existences as Branian—at least while bound to Bryson and Shelly. They had spilled information that was strictly confidential, and Thusia had shown herself on several occasions to non-royals, which was an offense in the eyes of the Empire. The royal firstborn had to be in life-threatening danger in order for it to be permissible.

A wave of guilt crashed over him. What kind of punishments were the two Branian suffering because of him? He had never been coy when it came to pressing them for information regarding the Light Empire. Or did it pertain to the fact that he was a product of kingdoms of separate realms? He slammed his fist down onto the mattress. Would he ever see Thusia again?

He lay there for nearly an hour, toxicity swirling in his mind, until eventually he fell asleep.

*　　　*　　　*

A knock thrummed through the door, penetrating Bryson's dreams. He awoke drearily, rising slowly from his bed. "Come in."

The door creaked open, and Lilu poked her head in. "Gracie said you wanted to talk to me."

He rubbed his eyes and nearly laughed. That girl was not one for wasting time, apparently. "Yeah, come in."

She entered tentatively, closing the door with too much care before inching her way toward a neglected desk and taking a seat.

"I'm sorry," he said, not wanting to make a show out of this.

She remained quiet, but her shoulders relaxed.

"At the time, I didn't realize what I was doing," he said. "But I'm beginning to learn that in some instances, it's better to just shut up rather than to give advice—especially if it's not my business. You don't need my advice; you're capable of making your own decisions whenever you feel like it."

She continued to stare at him. Heat rose into his face, discomfort clamping its jaws around his head.

Finally, she gave a nod. "And I'm sorry for what I said. I retaliated in a very unflattering way because of jealousy and anger." He tried to respond, but she held up her hand and closed her eyes. "I'm over it, Bryson. It's just that, there are times when you spark remnants of my disdain for how our friendship took a wrong turn. That's it. Let's move on."

He paused, mouth slightly ajar, wanting to respond. Instead he laughed. "To think it only took a week to break the silence."

Her lips curled upward. "That's a new record for us."

"Gracie's pretty awesome," he said.

"I've made great friends up here." She looked toward the two boxes that lay forgotten next to him. "What are those?"

He eyed the note. "Bad news from Shelly. She's having the same problem with Suadade that I'm having with Thusia."

"That's not ideal when we're in the midst of a war," Lilu said, frowning. "Especially if Toono is hunting down Intelians."

"I know," he muttered. "This isn't good."

"We'll figure it out."

"Maybe," he said with a shrug, eyes roving toward the two boxes. "Want to do me a favor?"

She paused. "Depends."

He reached for the parcels and lifted the lids. He wasn't much of a flower guy, but their beauty still managed to strike him speechless. "Wow …" he said.

She stood and walked over to see what it was. She gasped. "My goodness."

"They're gorgeous," he said.

"That one is a golden dahlia, found only in a few places of the Light Realm" she said, pointing at a flower with dozens of yellow petals layered on top of each other, their ridges stained maroon. She glanced at the other one, which didn't look like a traditional flower. Instead of sitting on a stiff stem, the flowers sprouted from a vine-like plant. "And those are yellow orchids."

"I've never seen either of them," he said.

"That's because you've never explored Lingen's Rainforest, Oros Jungle, or Tsubasa Forest. The golden dahlia is home to the first two, while those orchids can be found in the latter—as well as a few other remote areas."

As she took a seat on the bed, picking up the parcels to inspect them closer, he eyed her. "I want you to pick one," he said. She glanced at him, confused. "Shelly told me to choose one for the wedding theme. You're an expert on flowers, so I figured I'd ask for your input … if you want to give it, that is."

She gazed back at the two flowers, basking in her thoughts. "You really don't have to answer," he said, feeling it had been a terrible idea to ask.

"The orchids," she said, handing him the box. "Because of how they grow in groups, oftentimes from the same stem, I believe they're better suited for something like a wedding. That one, specifically, has grown as a pair, representing a partnership that should last until they wilt."

He stared at the two flowers, much smaller than the dahlia by comparison. She was right. The only thing missing was a third flower to represent his and Shelly's son, L.K. He'd make that a request in his return letter.

Lilu lifted the dahlia from its box and held its stem delicately between her fingers. She studied its infinite, concave petals. "The golden dahlia," she whispered, "is a flower of solitude—more stubborn, less inclined to share the land surrounding it. But, every now and then, it will sprout next to another, a phenomenon known as the Dahlia Effect."

She looked up, just past the flower as if staring at something only her eyes could see. "I'd like to keep this," she said emptily.

"Go ahead."

She removed the sunflower from her bangs and replaced it with the dahlia. It was big enough to hide some of her face, so she tilted it more to the side of her head, pinning her bangs farther back. "Perhaps, it's time I manifest that phenomenon," she said.

As she got up and left the room, he grinned. He felt happy for both her and Frederick, and he was grateful to Gracie.

# 36

# A Ruthless, Deadly Duo

Toshik entered the northern funnel of Necrosis Valley following a two-day recess spent in Shreel. When Horos and Kuiku had been planning their next route toward Cosmos a week ago, he had suggested cutting southeast to Shreel instead of continuing the arching path they had been entirely too committed to this entire journey. While he had made arguments about the practicality of such a method, explaining that Shreel would have been an ideal resting point on the long road to Cosmos, those were not his true reasons.

Horos and Kuiku had wanted to arch around the main cities, possibly crossing through the foothills of the Tames Mountains. That raised several red flags for Toshik. He never wanted to see another mountain in his life. In Tames, the sight of their peaks on the horizon had been torture enough, so he didn't even want to think about the trauma entering them would impose. Thus, he argued until he was blue in the face—until he won. Now they were committing to something likely even more foolish in the eyes of Horos and Kuiku: traveling the length of Necrosis Valley.

Like the mountains, the valley would also resurface old memories, but at least they weren't bad ones. When he had come here years ago with Bryson, Jilly, and Himitsu, they were met with success. It took the unexpected assistance of a few others, but they had been able to rescue Olivia in the end … and he had kept Jilly alive. He supposed the death of Debo had been heartbreaking, but it was nothing like other deaths he'd experienced in life.

They survived the valley by relying on the food, water, and supplies they had stocked up on while in Shreel. Two days in, they approached the section of valley where Bryson had killed Dev General Ossen before nearly dying at the hands of King Storshae and his Bewahr. It had taken a timely arrival from Debo and, later, Thusia to keep him alive. For Toshik, Jilly, and Himitsu, who had been fighting on the eastern ridge in the distance, they had also received a bit of help from the most unexpected person.

"What in the hell happened over there?"

Toshik followed Horos's eyes to find that exact ridge. Only it was no longer the clean-cut precipice. It had crumpled in on itself. An entire chunk of land appeared to have been blasted from the cliffside, piling debris and rocks as large as shanties atop the valley's floor.

"Rhyparia happened," he said.

"The Jestivan who was on trial?" Horos asked incredulously.

Toshik nodded.

"What was she doing here?"

"This was where the clash between the Jestivan and Dev King Storshae happened."

Horos's eyes widened. Even Kuiku scanned their surroundings, likely taking note of the countless signs of battle.

"I had been imprisoned by Passion King Damian during all of that. It's kind of an honor to be standing here, witnessing historic grounds," Horos said, still gazing fixatedly on the valley's crater. "How old was Rhyparia when she did that?"

"A month before her sixteenth birthday, I believe," Toshik said.

"Well, I'll be damned," Kuiku mumbled. "Imagine if we still had her on our side. I think we'd be unstoppable."

"Itta had been the only one who knew what the girl could offer," Horos said. "It makes a twisted sort of sense that he referred to her as a weapon of mass destruction."

Toshik's gaze grew distant, recalling the image of an adult Rhyparia standing over him and Jilly's corpse. She had instilled fear the likes of which he'd never seen into the eyes of forces such as Yama and Toono. He never would have thought it on the day the Jestivan formed, but she was the most terrifying person he'd ever met in his life.

*     *     *

"Of course we're meeting in a bar," Sal said, as Himitsu, Kaylee, and he entered a tavern door.

"She owns every bit of who she is without shame," Kaylee said, as if she were a proud mother speaking about her child.

While Himitsu scanned the crowded barroom, Sal retorted, "It's a miracle nobody noticed her lust for wine when she was undercover as Wert Lamay." He snorted. "That was too risky."

Himitsu looked up, but there wasn't a second floor despite its impressive height from the outside, just a vaulted, triangular ceiling. Finally, he saw someone waving a hand at him to the right of the barroom. He sauntered across the bar, wending between tables seating rowdy patrons. He climbed a few steps onto an elevated section of floor, where there were fewer tables and more windows to bathe the space in sunlight. His mother sat at a booth directly beneath the grandest of windows.

"Good afternoon, boys and girls," Ophala said as the three of them slid into the booth. She leaned in and gave Himitsu a kiss on the cheek. "What are we discussing today?"

"We have questions about Directors Poicus and Senex," Kaylee said, her pitch much higher than usual.

Himitsu regarded her with a ridiculous gaze. She was seated with an unimaginable arch in her back, her hands clasped on the table. She looked like a child waiting for cake.

Ophala beamed at Kaylee. "You are too cute."

Kaylee leaned into Himitsu, shielding her mouth from his mother with her hand. "She's smitten by me," she whispered.

Rolling his eyes, he decided to lead the discussion. "Mom, we believe Neeko was suffering from grief just before his disappearance. You said he was best friends with Directors Senex and Poicus, correct?"

Ophala lowered her glass of wine, smacking her lips as she nodded. "Inseparable, those three … except for when books were involved. According to Director Senex, Neeko always chose books over everyone and everything else."

"Do you know anything about a silver medallion?" Himitsu asked.

She paused in the midst of twirling noodles around her fork. Her gaze slowly drifted up from her plate. "Unless they're fakes, silver medallions are usually ancients that involve mutating one's body. Instead of being worn or wielded, however, they're absorbed as if being stitched into a person's skin. And, as most of the world knows, Senex and Poicus were notorious mutants. Poicus could transform into other people, while Senex could grow or shrink the size of his body."

Kaylee shivered. "I've never loved the idea of being a mutant Archain."

Ophala's face was grave. "They're not for the faint of heart. Most steer clear from such ancients, for they can hurt those who possess smaller energy stores than others. They're also valuable and can attract the attention of *ancient thieves*, who will sell them for unimaginable amounts of coin." She fell silent for a moment. "When I had to use Poicus's ancient over the past year, it wasn't easy. It takes a toll on you." She shook her head and laughed. "Anyway, a 'silver medallion'—not that they're technically *silver*—is fairly vague since there are several of them. What do you want to know about them?"

"Do you still have Poicus's ancient?" Kaylee asked.

"Yes, it's in a safe and secure location in order to protect it from falling in the wrong hands," Ophala said.

"What about Senex's? Was his ever discovered?"

"No. That, I'm afraid, could be in the hands of anyone. Nobody really knows what happened to Senex's body after falling victim to Elyol's lava. Since I was captured in the middle of the fiasco that was Rhyparia's escape, I wasn't privy to any of the search and rescue information that followed."

"But I'm sure you've searched records of the kingdom's efforts," Kaylee said. "They did document their findings, right?"

Ophala smirked. "What kind of spy would I be, had I not gone searching?" Kaylee flushed red. "According to documentation, Senex's body had never been found, which means his ancient could be anywhere."

"Like in the hands of Neeko?"

Ophala tilted her head at Kaylee. "Possibly, but I think the world forgot such a fabled boy even existed ... though I guess he's far from a boy now."

Kaylee explained her conversation with Raul, describing what the boy described as massive grief over someone Neeko might have lost and how he regretted his decision to value books and knowledge over friendship. Once she mentioned the shape of the medallion, Ophala's eyes widened.

"You're on to something, young lady," Ophala said. "Senex's ancient was exactly that. And while there may be many mutant ancients with such a shape, and nobody could know for sure unless they saw what was engraved into it, I'd say your guess is an educated one."

"The only problem is that Neeko has disappeared," Kaylee said, lowering her voice to a whisper. "Where would his grief have taken him?"

Ophala gazed out the window in thought, humming quietly to herself. Feeling they would only serve as a distraction, Himitsu and Sal had taken a backseat during the conversation, allowing the two women to arrive at a conclusion themselves.

"One of two places," Ophala finally said. "He either traveled to Senex's childhood home in one of Phelos's poorer sectors, Thriskia, or he ventured into the Central Grasslands at the heart of the Archaic Desert, which is where Senex's widow lives ... It's also the resting place of his mentor, former Grand Director, Modinus."

"Somewhere of sentimental value to Senex," Kaylee said, nodding in agreement. She pulled out a jar of ink, a quill, and piece of parchment from her purse. She began to write down locations. "Anywhere else you can think of, Pilot?"

"I'd be going out on a limb by suggesting this, but Olethros. Senex had grown an attachment to Rhyparia and, because of it, had succumbed mightily to guilt during her trials. Neeko might have wanted to visit such a landmark just to see what kind of disasters had struck the city and his friend."

Kaylee stabbed a period at the end of her sentence and leaned back with satisfaction. "Got it."

Himitsu cleared his throat, leaning forward to join the conversation. "Mom, can you help by searching Thriskia when you return to the capital? Phelos is kind of out of our way."

"I'll do what I can," she said. "I'm beginning to feel like your personal assistant. Don't forget that I still must counsel Archaic King Sigmund. The young man has not a clue how to function without me holding his hand, and I'm afraid he might try to commit to something reckless in this war."

"If anyone can knock some sense into him, it's you, Pilot Ophala," Kaylee said after blowing the ink dry on her parchment.

"You, dear, don't have to address me as that," Ophala said with a smile.

Kaylee froze, her face burning red again. "Understood, Mrs. Vevlu."

Ophala stared at Kaylee with a look of amusement. She then looked toward Himitsu and shook her head, chuckling. "Hold on and don't let go, son," she said, wiping her lips with a napkin. After a final swig of wine, she rose from the table and left.

*     *     *

Those in the two carriages didn't stay separated for long. Rhyparia eventually found herself with Prakriti and a few of the dimiours in one carriage while everyone else occupied the other. They'd shuffle around quite a bit. She appreciated the company of Atarax, Biaza, and Moros, but Prakriti had become a nuisance. Ever since Realmular Tunnel, she had grown a strong dislike for the man. He was mentally weak.

He reminded her of her past self, when she couldn't face the truths of her actions during the Gravity Trials, how she had broken down in tears

366

following Archaic Prince Sigmund's final vote in favor of her execution, how Director Senex had sacrificed his life and Pilot Ophala her freedom to save her. But that was no longer who she was, and she would never become that frail little girl ever again.

Honestly, she would have preferred Kakos's presence in place of Prakriti, for the wolf had a bite to which she could relate. This would have scared her younger self to the bone. Alas, she was nearing forty now, and the passing of decades had sculpted her into something cynical.

She listened to Biaza and Atarax attentively while they discussed plans for the Power Kingdom, keeping herself from shooting disdainful glares at Prakriti each time he tried to remind the group of their ultimate mission of peace. The two dimiours would always agree with him, but that never raised the same level of anger in her. Perhaps that should have alarmed her. If everyone in the group agreed that a peaceful rescue was the only acceptable goal, then why did she single out Prakriti?

She smothered the likely answer: he was fragile, useless, and pathetic. Ever since his hiccup in Realmular Tunnel—nearly leading to everyone's deaths—she now entered every conversation with him under the preconceived notion that his opinion didn't matter.

"Everyone seems to have a role but Kakos," Biaza said. She was sprawled across a bench, her furry tail flipping awkwardly to and fro in the air. It was doing a good job at keeping Moros occupied. Despite him being the oldest of the dimiours, he was mostly a child.

"Kakos just needs to just stay out of the way," Atarax said. "If he refuses to dig with the three of us, then he'll do nothing."

Prakriti nodded. "I'm afraid he'll draw attention to himself if he tries to do anything else."

Moros caught Biaza's tail with two hands and gave Prakriti a strange look. "Any of us would draw attention to ourselves just by simply walking into a public place. We're furry."

Rhyparia smirked.

"That's not what I meant," Prakriti said. "I meant if he's not watched, he'll do something stupid that will reveal everything we're trying to accomplish. It's best that he stays idle—if he doesn't want to dig, that is."

Rhyparia wasn't fond of the plan they had contrived. It may have been the most practical in terms of rescuing slaves, but it did nothing beyond that. Atarax, Biaza, and Moros were to spend most of their time digging. The proximity of the Power Kingdom's main shipyard to Ulna Malen made a tunnel system plausible, especially with natural diggers such as a fox, honey badger, and weasel at their disposal.

It'd take several weeks to create. Therapif would enter the capital during the first half of the mission's timeframe, seeking out possible locations for tunnel entrances. He'd then return to the tunnels and help heal slaves as they were freed.

Rhyparia was to also infiltrate the city, which shouldn't be too difficult. Ulna Malen may have been separated into ringed sections of land encompassing a mountainside, but only the highest three stratums had walls of defense between them. The rest were protected via manned checkpoints on roadways.

Her job was to weed out servants, which were slaves that lived outside of Stratum Zero. They may have had a slightly more glamorous lifestyle, but for them that only meant getting to live in a manor's cupboard instead of a shack swimming in mud. She needed to free as many servants as possible. The dimiours had advised staying away from the higher stratums, adding emphasis when speaking of Stratum Nine, which housed the royal palace. But Rhyparia would do what she felt necessary. If that meant attacking the palace, then so be it. Freeing servants wasn't her only objective.

"How are you going to pass between stratums without getting caught, Rhyparia? It's going to be quite a hassle."

Rhyparia looked at Prakriti. Sunlight from the carriage window reflected against his clean-shaven scalp. It was a fair question. She had never prided herself on stealth, oftentimes relying on Himitsu to provide such a skill in the past.

"I'll figure it out," she said.

"Infiltration is my specialty, so allow me to provide aid in that regard."

All eyes went to the back of the carriage, spotting a bearded man in a trench coat seated on the floor against the rear door, a man who had not been there just seconds ago. He was leaning to one side, one knee in the air, his forearm resting atop it. Rhyparia caught a glint of silver just beneath the cuff of his sleeve.

"How do you do that?" Atarax asked, raising an eyebrow.

"I'm sneaky," he whispered unnecessarily. "Hence the name: Creep."

"Short for 'creepy'?" Moros said, drawing a laugh out of Biaza and Prakriti.

"My mentor used to call me that," Creep said with a smirk. "Anyway, I'm here as reinforcements, so put me to use."

Rhyparia saw the promise in this man. He was special. "I'll take you with me."

*     *     *

Days later, Rhyparia and Creep sat in a longboat as they rowed toward a trade ship in the harbor. The others were separated into other longboats, but far enough away to give her privacy.

"I don't much like the idea of being trapped for days in a supply crate," Creep said.

"A bit claustrophobic?" she asked.

"I guess you could say that," he said, gazing toward the ship apprehensively. "Reminds me of my teenage years. Training to become an assassin requires learning to cope in small spaces." He shook his head. "I always failed those lessons."

Their oars sloshed almost silently in the gentle waters with each stroke. "When we enter Ulna Malen, I don't want you to think of it as a rescue mission," she said.

"I knew I saw something different in your eyes every time your group discussed it, like you were trying not to roll them."

She tilted her head, brows furrowed. "You were never present during those discussions."

"It's good that you think that. Means I'm not rusty."

"I'm in desperate need of a skillset like yours," she said.

"What do you want from me?"

"I want someone ruthless."

He held her gaze for a long moment while they continued to row. "That weak-minded man and the others wouldn't be fond of this conversation."

"I don't care. I'm done watching the less fortunate be stepped on."

"I can be ruthless," he said. "We'll work well as a pair."

She looked toward the sky, where both moons hovered high above. "I'll pulverize every elitist scumbag in the city."

# 37

# Erafeen: The Five Gods

Agnos lounged in the Mythmaker's crow's nest, elbow up and a hand resting behind his head. He gazed at the morning sky, lucid white clouds drifting by. Far below him, his crew was readying the ship for departure. It seemed like every voyage was tougher than the last, even if that should have been impossible. From obliterating entire naval fleets, to finding lost treasures at the bottom of the sea, to funneling through a whirlpool into a different realm ... he was some sort of crazy.

He'd gained more confidence after experiencing such successes, but also because of the people around him. He had a crew composed of dozens of squallblasters, firefighters, and seashockers, and a navigator in Zorra who knew the sea and stars like the back of her hand. Queen Apsa had given him the second-in-command to Admiral Ren, the leader of the Spirit Navy. He had an ally in the Whale Lord's crew, led by one of the greatest pirate captains to ever live, Gray Whale. Then there was Evelyn, a Still Diatia who might have held talent near the level of his former Jestivan peers.

On paper, he looked unstoppable, yet something didn't feel right. How had he arrived in such a position? He wished all of his focus could have gone into translating *Erafeen*. The quicker he did that, the quicker he'd receive answers to his lifelong questions.

But this war felt pressing. He had a personal obligation to stop Toono. He hated himself for continuing to mistake the villain as that young orphan who had taken him under his wing. Toono wasn't a good guy. There was nothing morally just about his actions. Did remembering that really have to be such a struggle?

Thus, Agnos felt he needed to accept this mission. He'd break that annoying attachment to Toono by playing a critical role in eliminating him from this world.

Barloe bellowed a command from below, his booming voice carrying all the way up to the crow's nest:

"Set sail!"

*　　*　　*

Agnos sat at his desk in the captain's cabin. DaiSo's harbor was now out of sight. He had just finished a round of one-on-one meetings with important members of his crew, such as Barloe, Zorra, Evelyn, and Troy. Now he could kick off his clogs and bask in the silence of his cabin, staring at the bookcases that lined the walls—his own personal library.

He leaned forward and retrieved a stack of parchment from his bottom drawer. He left his glasses, not needing them since these were the translated documents. He wanted to reread the last chunk of translations, for it had caught his attention more than anything else up to this point. It spoke of the "Essence" once again, and he had become enamored by the concept of such an entity.

His eyes scanned the first sentence ...

*　　*　　*

I never expected my dinner with Mialo to be as enlightening as it was.

I want to return to the Essence, the entity I spoke of earlier in this chronicle. As I said, each kingdom had one. Mine resided in Thunder Alley, and Mialo's—Dev Essence—could be found in the Cosmos Meadows. They were both nature and person. They exuded love, but only for their respective Originator. It was our job to accept that love. Otherwise, the Essence would disperse and become currents, feeding the masses. For most of our existence, we followed that universal law.

So, imagine my face when Mialo told me he was beginning to wean himself off of the Essence's addictive grasp. This was unheard of and, quite frankly, frowned upon. It was a frightening notion, and when he had revealed this during dinner I suddenly understood why the other Originators had turned him away with such haste.

"Do you ever grow tired of relying on your Essence?" he asked before even receiving our first course of what would become an abnormally long meal.

"There are times I wish I could function on my own, yes," I said. "The frailty that descends upon me if I go too long without returning to Thunder Alley to harvest is terrifying."

He leaned back as a steward placed a plate of salad in front of him. He nodded his thanks, then said to me, "I'd select a different choice of words. Instead of frailty, I'd say humanity." He stabbed at a cherry tomato and raised it in front of his mouth. "Instead of terrifying, I'd say humbling."

I watched as he popped the tomato into his mouth and began to chew. The more he said, the more I understood the hesitation of my peers. His words were blasphemous. For me, however, he was saying all the right things. Only, it was difficult for me to admit it.

"I went three years without harvesting Dev Essence," he said.

"That's a lie," I said in utter disbelief.

"It's true. I'm not the man I once was because of it. I'm weaker than the other Originators, weaker than you."

Between mouthfuls of green leaves, I searched his golden eyes. Did that explain their color?

"Tonitrua, I saw something the last time I harvested. Usually, when an Originator visits their Essence, they simply absorb part of it. Doing so keeps the Essence contained in its geographical location. When we do this, somehow that part of the Essence interacts with the energy in our body, which allows us to use our abilities."

"Yes, I know all of this," I said.

"I tried a different approach," he said, placing his fork on the table. "A few months ago, when I returned to my Essence after years of neglect, she was not pleased and had already begun the process of dispersing across my kingdom. Still, she desired my harvest. I acted as if I would do exactly that, but just as I was about to absorb part of her, I rejected it by expelling my own energy from my body and into her." He paused, jaw becoming rigid. "What followed was nothing I could have prepared myself for."

My half-eaten plate of salad was swiped from in front of me, replaced by a plate of grilled green-scale fish. "So you released your psychic, telekinetic, or telepathic abilities into the Essence?" I asked.

"Not at all. Remember, it had been years since my last harvest. My store of Essence inside my body had depleted by that time, so all that I had expelled from my body was energy. There were no abilities ... or, at least, there shouldn't have been." He looked down at the table with narrowed eyes. "I felt the collisions between my energy and Essence, even though it was happening outside of my body. It was as if my sense of touch had expanded to include my now-external energy. The sensation overwhelmed me ... until I went numb and had a vision."

Mialo gave me pause by this point in his story. His revelations were becoming increasingly more absurd, and had I not possessed the amount of patience I did, I would have stopped him at that point and requested his leave. Instead, I fought back that urge, seeing something unnatural in his golden eyes that reeked of a story equally as unbelievable.

"And what did you see?" I asked while I carved into my fish.

"I saw our purpose," he said. "We are nothing but a means to an end, Tonitrua. In that brief flash of a vision, I saw our gods."

I raised an eyebrow. "Tide Drifter ... Land Molder ... Gale Thrasher ..." I named all three of them slowly; mighty beasts who were credited for sculpting Kuki Sphaira during prehistoric times. If he couldn't hear the disbelief in my tone, he saw it in my face. He didn't seem to mind.

"And two of our forgotten gods."

"'Forgotten gods?'" I repeated as if I was some Sphairian-speaking commoner trying to learn the language of the Originators.

He nodded and asked, "What are the Essences?"

"Intel, Passion, Spirit, Adren, Archaic, Dev, Still, Cyn, Power, and Prim," I recited.

"You only named ten."

I looked at him, but didn't respond. Was he implying there were more?

"There is an eleventh and twelfth Essence, both of which are considered the sources of the other ten. They are also the fourth and fifth gods."

I finished chewing a delicate cut of fish and washed it down with a swig of white wine. I decided to finish off the glass, searching for a buzz that could help me come to grips with his story. I let out a sigh of satisfaction, placing the glass back on the table. I smacked my lips and looked across the table. "And who are these 'forgotten gods'?"

"Tahara, the Essence of Light, and Mulawith, the Essence of Darkness."

"And why has nobody ever found their locations?" I asked.

"Because they're shrouded in the depths of a structure with no bounds, on an uninhabited island at the center of the Sea of Light."

I knew exactly what he was talking about. Everybody knew of the island, but because of its central location, nobody was allowed to lay claim to its land. Not only that, but it was practically impossible to traverse the tumultuous waters surrounding it.

"The Region of Raging Tides," I said.

# 38

# A Close Encounter

Groto Yuln was an impressive fighter. Toono watched from an atrium balcony as the Still Diatia sparred with Warden Moroza below. It was the same atrium where Yama and Illipsia had once trained a couple of years ago, before their trek into the Archaic Mountains. While Groto didn't possess the same level of talent as Yama, he looked good enough to put up a fight against most of the Jestivan.

Toono wasn't completely certain how many Jestivan were in the Intel Kingdom, preparing to defend their elites, but he wanted to make sure he had plenty of reinforcements to counter any number. He thought about Bryson and Shelly, and the Branian they possessed. That was the major hurdle he'd yet to overcome. While he had confidence in himself, trying to defeat Bryson, Shelly, and both of their Branian would have been a suicide mission. Nobody on his side could summon divinity—or nobody willing to leave their home kingdom. The Power Queen had made it clear she wouldn't send her son into the war.

Groto swung his massive sword of ice down at Moroza, who threw up both her hands, using frozen talons as a shield. Ice clashed against ice, sounding even sharper than the swords of two dueling Adrenians. While Groto rarely landed any blows, he was able to keep Moroza on her heels. She was fighting defensively, only committing to calculated strikes, relying on the icicles that stretched out of her fingers like talons.

His techniques were exaggerated, but fast and powerful. He fought like a wild boar, while Yama had always resembled a butterfly with the grace of her swordsmanship. She packed a lot more speed and effectiveness in a swing with less effort.

Of course, Groto was currently fighting without his trump card. He liked to coat the ground in ice, causing his opponents to lose traction while he could maneuver flawlessly. Against someone like Moroza, however, such a strategy was ineffective. *Nobody* could traverse ice like a Stillian woman.

Toono heard footsteps behind him. He turned to find Tazama standing in the corridor just outside the archway. She had finally returned from her trip across the kingdom. He left the balcony and entered the softer orange torchlight of the hallway.

"Welcome back, Tazama."

"Thank you."

"How was it?" he asked. A few weeks ago, he had sent her to inspect the Dev Kingdom's teleplatforms. The fact she had returned without once telepathically contacting Homina or Gala told him it was likely bad news.

"Everything is taken care of," she said. "It was probably the most difficult project I've ever been assigned, but that only made it more rewarding."

"And you can trust this man?" he asked. "Hasn't he been serving the Intelians for well over a decade?

"It is a risk," she said, "but I feel it is one we must take. His weavineering skills are on par with mine, and nobody else can make such a claim."

"I hope you're right, Tazama."

"He's been serving the Intelians because he's had no other choice—and the ridiculous amount of money they pay him. But I've showed him there are people fighting for him now. I think that has given him the confidence to betray those who enslaved him." She set her jaw and her gaze became rigid. "Toono, I mean it when I say few revered Dev King Rehn and hated Mendac more than Flen Inson."

*　　*　　*

Toono strolled through the dungeons of Cogdan Castle, passing vacant jail cells that had gone unused since Storshae's death. Most of the prisoners who had been down here had been guilty of speaking their minds, which shouldn't have been a crime in the first place.

He paused at a cell that looked nearly identical to the rest, but despite this, it would remain vivid in his memories forever. Praetor Poicus, a man who Toono used to read about, had sat in this very cell. The man had been a hardened youth, but took a path of enlightenment as he grew older. He became an educator … only for Toono to ultimately imprison, starve, and kill the man.

He pressed his face between two cold bars. He wanted to speak with Kadlest, and not through a broadcast. He missed her, for she was the only one with whom he could have a candid conversation. The longer he was away from her, the more he doubted he could do this.

"An update from Illipsia, Demon."

Toono turned, once again caught off guard by a woman of high rank. Her sleek black hair disappeared behind her back. "Homina, what is it?"

"My daughter has completed a rather unimaginable step in her process, fooling a skilled set of eyes in Phesaw."

*　　*　　*

Illipsia stood behind a tall potted ficus in Phesaw's main lobby. It was afterschool hours. Dusk's warm glow was streaking through the narrow windows. She watched through the leaves as the final students trickled out of the school for the weekend. Yvole was likely just outside the door, ushering them out while keeping his eyes peeled for Illipsia. However, she didn't plan on leaving—at least, not yet.

Every other school exit was locked down or guarded, forcing all refugees to funnel through the main entrance. Her absence would make him suspicious. He'd first check in with the authorities posted at the smaller exits, asking them if they'd seen her. Then he'd search every inch of the school.

The twin doors shut, casting a good portion of the lobby in shadows. Yvole stood just inside the doors, peering curiously to his left and right, as if she would suddenly show herself. She gathered her breath and wove a cylindrical wall of Dev Chains around her, trapping her in an invisible tube. Anyone who looked in her direction should see nothing.

Purposefully, she rustled the ficus. Yvole's gaze snapped toward it, eyes steady as he searched for something that wasn't there. He approached with long strides, as if to catch the culprit before it ran away. As she stepped from behind the ficus and into the open, his eyes didn't follow her, but remained on the plant. *This is working!*

But it wasn't time for celebrations because the closer he got, the more difficult the weaving became. From a distance, minor discrepancies in the imagery she was projecting wouldn't be decipherable, but when up close to her tube of Dev Chains, a skilled eye could spot any mistakes. The only thing working in her favor was that nobody was looking for a hallucinogenic trick, for that was a skill so uncommon, several generations would pass without a single Devish accomplishing it.

As Yvole neared, she feared he'd hear her heart thrumming through her chest. His eyes were narrowed as he limped toward the plant. He stood a safe distance away, recognizing something was awry. A door opened to the right, and Illipsia panicked.

An elderly woman exited the auditorium and stepped into the lobby. Her gray hair was pulled back into a tightly coiled bun, and she walked with a hunch. Despite the feeble appearance, this woman was not someone to take lightly. She was well into her nineties, yet she was the most skilled weaver on this campus: Shea-Ley Neaneuma.

Yvole regarded her with a look in his eyes that cause Neaneuma to raise a skeptical eyebrow. "What's wrong?"

"We must talk elsewhere," he said. "I have a theory."

She scanned the lobby, and her eyes paused in the vicinity of Illipsia. Illipsia's heart caught in her throat, as the woman's soft gaze bore right through her. She made sure to continue focusing on the image in her mind.

Eventually, Neaneuma nodded and guided Yvole through the lobby. As she passed, her stare lingered in the spot Illipsia occupied, yet she didn't seem to react.

Illipsia watched as the two of them diappeared around the lobby's bend. She should have been excited that she had fooled people of Yvole and Neaneuma's caliber, yet all she could think about was this "theory" he had mentioned. Were they on to her?

# 39

# One Last Try

Olivia stepped through the weeping branches of the Glades, where she had once been on the brink of being beheaded. One of the Monsignors had summoned her, for they had finally returned from their journey in the Black Powder Mountains after three weeks. Her patience was running thin, and she felt she had already spent more time here than she should have. She couldn't help but wonder if Himitsu and Toshik were having the same issues on their missions.

Observing the five birches that encircled the Glades, she waited for whichever Monsignor requested her presence to show up. Finally, a woman exited the hollow of the closest tree. She didn't wear an animal mask like last time. Her scalp was perfectly shaven, her nose flat on her face.

"Good morning, Olivia," she said. "My name is Partus Quada, and I will be spearheading the task of coercing the royals into granting an audience with you."

"Haven't you been back for a few days now?" Olivia asked. "Have you not started working on it already?"

"The Monsignors needed time to recover. Our time in the mountains wasn't one of leisure."

"I'm running out of time," Olivia said. "I need to find out any information I can now, that way I can return to the Light Realm and try to help with the war. They have Dimiourgos, after all. He's in the wrong hands."

Partus studied Olivia for a long moment, as if wanting to believe the claim that the Primmish deity was still alive. It would have been difficult to deny, considering the shocking appearance of the dimiours.

"If it is true this Toono character is trying to use the ability of resurrection, it means Dimiourgos will die for good."

"What do you mean?" Olivia asked.

"Resurrection can only be used nine times. A long time ago, he used it seven times after dying several times in battle. On his seventh life, he was decapitated, and his head was taken as a trophy. He brought himself back to life an eighth time, but without his body. If he's still alive today, as you claim, that would mean he's yet to die since then. However, if Toono uses him to resurrect Dev King Rehn, that will be the ninth and final life."

Olivia froze, incapable of responding. She had never thought of Meow Meow's life being in danger.

"As powerful as Dimiourgos once was, he's not immortal—nobody is."

"Please," Olivia said, "move quickly."

Partus gave a genuine smile. "I'll do my best."

*　　*　　*

Kadlest appreciated the modesty of the Adren Kingdom. If she hadn't hated the Light Realm as much as she did, she could have seen herself residing here permanently. Homes were one-story tall, constructed of basic wood, plaster, and drywall. Every house had at least one garden, complete with bamboo or eucalyptus trees and a manmade pond. They were easy to maintain because of the kingdom's frequent rainfall. Even the royal headquarters was more of an estate than the typical palace or castle seen in the other kingdoms.

She stood in the doorway of the estate's front entrance, watching as her mixed forces trained across the sprawling green hills. This had become the daily routine with there not being much else to do. She was playing a waiting game, hoping Illipsia and Toono were completing their ends of the objective.

She became fixated with the soldiers in silver, who were busy marching in the distance. At least, they were supposed to be marching. Some strolled, others stood defiantly. Adrenian soldiers were notorious for their work ethic and sense of duty. If they were given a job to do, they did it without question—as long as it was just. But they were loyal people, so taking orders from an invading force didn't sit well with them, especially one that had slain their king and his brother.

Kadlest frowned. Did any kingdom really need a king? They still had their queen, which was more important in her eyes. Even the newborn prince had gone unharmed. Neither Yama nor Kadlest had intentions of hurting anyone who didn't pose a threat.

Yama's absence had been a large part of the problems Kadlest found herself facing. The daunting, tenacious swordswoman had kept the Adrenians in line at first. With her barking orders, they'd listened to everything without question. Because they knew if they defied her, she'd cut them down without mercy, and there would have been nothing they could do about it.

An aide approached Kadlest's side. "Milady, a letter from the Dev Kingdom."

She snatched the parchment from his hand and broke the seal. It had been more than a month since her last contact with Toono. As she read through the letter, her excitement died. It was a routine update on his and Illipsia's progress. Apparently, the girl still needed more time.

Kadlest groaned and ripped the note into pieces, letting it flutter onto the stone steps. A fight broke out between an Adrenian and Powish. Of course, dozens more joined to create a brawl. She stepped down and took a seat on the stone, sighing as she placed her head into her hand.

*        *        *

For the first time since arriving to Yinyon months ago, Yama had decided to take action. Before making a final decision such as suicide, she wanted to make sure they weren't testing her determination. Maybe they wanted to see how easily she'd give up.

Since her first visit to Ataway and Leon's graves atop the hill, the mayor's building had caught her eye. It was the largest structure in Yinyon, which still didn't amount to much. She figured she needed to speak to someone who wasn't Kolver. If she could just get to someone whose status in society was more important, she could finally argue her case. Kolver was nothing but an innkeeper.

The entry foyer to the mayor's building was rustic, with untreated wood floors, unwashed windows, and nothing but a few candles to try to make up for the lack of sunlight. To her surprise, there seemed to be no semblance of security. The only presence in the room was an older woman who sat at a receptionist's desk. She looked up from her half-moon spectacles without lifting her head. After spotting her guest, she glanced off to the side at nothing of note.

Yama sauntered over. "I'd like to speak with the mayor."

"That's not going to happen, Ms. Fuuna."

Yama snorted. She was getting tired of everyone knowing her identity, but her not knowing any of these people. "I'm not leaving until I do."

The lady shook her head while writing a letter. "I'd advise you leave, Ms. Fuuna."

"I'll force my way upstairs."

The woman slowly looked up from her parchment, spectacles low on her nose. "And we'll force you outside."

Yama couldn't believe the audacity of the people in this village, a village barely worth being marked on maps with a population that didn't eclipse one hundred. Why did they think they could turn her away so easily? She

384

needed to assert herself and show them why the world had come to fear her. She would not lose her purpose in life.

She rounded the desk and headed for a narrow staircase that disappeared above. Two blurs of color streaked across the room and stopped at the foot of the stairs, halting Yama in her tracks. They had moved with freakish speed, nearly rivaling her own. They both wore spandex bodysuits that stretched up their necks and around their heads, hiding their identities. There were knitted sections where their eyes, nostrils, ears, and mouth were, allowing for air, sight, and sound. Both were men, judging by their rugged physiques and lack of curves in certain places.

Yama squeezed her eyes shut and opened them in disbelief. She hadn't even drawn her sword. Had she become that rusty since her arrival, or were these guys that good? They also hadn't drawn their weapons, which were strapped to their backs.

As she studied their bodysuits, she said, "Those are like mine. Only mine doesn't have the ribbons that drape from the back of the neck."

"Yours also doesn't have the mask, shoes, or gloves," the receptionist said, apparently unfazed. She hadn't moved from her seat and had returned to writing. "Those are items you could have acquired, but you've ruined that."

"I can fix it," Yama said, eyes remaining on the two silent guards. "Let me show you my remorse for my actions."

"We don't care about your remorse, Yama Fuuna. You should have thought about that remorse before committing all the evil you did in your young life. You will never win back the trust of your family and friends here in Yinyon." She sighed. "And that's a shame."

The two guards grabbed her biceps and began to drag her across the foyer. "I want to see my family!" she screamed. "You did this to me! You turned me into this! This is your fault!"

The receptionist looked up just before Yama was escorted from the building. "Your resolve is weak, Ms. Fuuna."

Yama was slung outside. She skidded across the dirt path before rolling to a stop. As she lay there, Jilly stared down at her with a smile that stretched into her eyes. Yama shook her head, ridding the hallucination from her vision.

The receptionist's statement had been wrong. Yama's resolve wasn't weak; it was nonexistent.

The end was near.

# 40

# The Lab

Bryson stood on the balcony of his townhouse, leaning against the banister and gazing down at the tiny backyard. Lilu, Frederick, Gracie, and Limone were on a double date, celebrating the completion of three more operational travolters during the past week. It seemed Bryson's presence in Bastion was achieving something—or at least it was in the minds of the LeAnce family. He didn't feel like it had anything to do with him, rather the relentless leadership of Lilu finally paying dividends.

He missed Shelly and L.K. He missed his bedroom in the palace's tallest tower, floating above the Intel Kingdom's low-hanging clouds. In there, he could always look up through the glass ceiling and gaze at the stars. It was so much more than the view here. The horde of Intelights that fluttered just below the cavern's ceiling had grown stale.

He pouted as he looked down at his feet, longing to feel Shelly's lips against his. And as much as he enjoyed seeing Lilu open up with Frederick, he hadn't realized how much more that'd make him desire companionship.

Even Gracie and Limone, while eccentric and unorthodox, had become a close-knit pair.

Desperate measures would need to be taken to remedy Bryson's sudden bout of loneliness. It had been an entire week since the last time he tried summoning Thusia. He had honestly given up. But his current situation had him prepared to try anything, so he closed his eyes and called for her once more. He even tried envisioning her, as if that would make a difference.

"Hello, Bry."

Bryson spun around so fast he almost toppled over the banister. "Thusia!" He leapt toward her to give her a hug, but he stopped almost immediately. She was seated on a wooden patio chair, her posture slumped and head drooped. She wore a dirtied white gown, like what patients wore in hospitals, and nothing else. Even her signature diamond-encrusted collar he'd always seen her wear around her neck was missing. Scars wrapped around her calves and forearms.

"Thusia … what happened to you?"

She looked up and grinned, exposing more scars around her neck. "Nothing that I can't handle."

"Who did that to you?" he asked.

"I can't tell you that, or more of the same will definitely come my way."

"This is my fault," he said shakily. He had a feeling her absence had to do with him. He and Shelly should have never pushed their Branian for information. Thusia said they'd get in trouble.

"No, it's not." She stood and approached him, embracing him in a hug. "You deserve to know the things you're hunting. Part of me has always known this. While there are certain topics a Bozani isn't supposed to discuss with mortals, those lines become blurred when the bond between a Branian and their charge is a personal one. I knew your father, Bryson. For me to become your Branian is astronomically rare. I will do what it takes to help you find answers."

"How are you here right now?" he asked, holding on to her and not letting go.

"There is a war brewing between the Empires, Bryson. In order to sustain their numbers, the Light Empire's elites needed to free me from my cell and prepare me to fight. This was under the explicit rule that I refrain from returning to the main kingdoms."

He left her embrace. "Then why are you here?!"

"Because you need me. I've felt you trying to summon me."

He stared at her, dumbfounded. "A war between Empires?"

She nodded gravely. "It's the scariest thing I've ever heard of. When someone becomes a Bozani after death, they learn about the history of the empires—or most of it, at least. Apparently, such a war has never happened before."

"Will we feel the effects down here?" he asked.

"Most certainly, but not in the way you'd think."

"You need to go back," he said. "I can't have you getting in more trouble for my sake."

She gave that annoying smile she showed so often whenever pessimism began to rear its ugly head. Jilly always used to do that. "I'm here, and that's that. Besides, I'm only a Branian, so it's not like they have a method of tracking me. It will take them some time before they can find me."

He looked over her shoulder, hearing commotion stirring downstairs. The others must have returned from their date. Thusia turned with an inquisitive look, observing the sliding glass door that sat open. "Where are we?" She looked up at the Intelight ceiling. "Bizarre ..."

"Long story, but we're underneath the same city that Mendac grew up in."

"Brilliance ..." she said softly.

He nodded, then spotted Lilu in the hallway just outside his bedroom's open door. She froze at the sight of him and Thusia. She wore a long black dress that hugged her body, the top of it forming a single strap at one shoulder that dipped underneath the opposite arm. The golden dahlia she'd taken an interest in was pinned to her hair.

She burst into his room and reached the balcony in only a few seconds despite wearing heels, putting her skills of balance that she had learned from Debo on display. "Thusia! It's so great to—" She paused, eyes dropping to Thusia's neck, then falling to her forearms and legs.

"Don't ask," Thusia said, waving dismissively. "Nothing for you to concern yourself with." She stepped back and admired Lilu's outfit. "You look beautiful."

Lilu hesitated, still fixated on the Branian's scars. However, she forced her gaze upward. "Thank you," she said, turning her body and displaying a model's pose. "Do you think I'd give my big sister a run for her money?"

"You and Shelly are equally gorgeous," Thusia said, reaching over to give Lilu a hug.

Frederick, Gracie, and Limone were now huddled at the entrance to Bryson's room, looking toward the balcony in awe. He knew what it was they were feeling—that unnatural feathery light consciousness as if they could sprout wings and take flight. He recalled having that exact sensation many years ago. First, when meeting Shelly's Branian, then when he had summoned Thusia for the first time while fighting Dev King Storshae and Bewahr Fonos.

Bryson waved them over. They were timid at first, stepping across the room as if he was an abusive father with a belt in his hands. Thusia, being the kind of person she was, eased their uncertainties by offering them a friendly face. After quick introductions, they talked, laughed, and shared stories. Thusia graciously answered their innocent questions, while respectively declining those that crossed the line.

Gracie was the most eager, berating Thusia with a barrage of questions. Lilu had told him about Gracie's habit of sensationalizing men based solely off their gender. He was happy she got to see a woman like Thusia—even if Lilu should have been a good enough example herself.

Either way, he wished he could show Gracie all of the influential women he'd met in his life. Brilliance was only a small corner of the world, and it showed in its culture. The city did its best to establish male intellectual dominance at an early age, forcing most women to not even bother trying to become weavineers. It was engrained into their minds at the very beginning, so the potential for women like Ophala Vevlu, Apsa Spirit, Felli Venustas, Shea-Ley Neaneuma, Apoleia Still, Lilu Intel, Thusia, and countless others was slim to none.

He looked at Lilu, observing the way she stood straighter than the others, much like Thusia did. There was confidence in her that couldn't be broken.

He made the decision. After getting into Mendac's lab and retrieving the theories, he would remind this city of who really was the force behind the travolters. It wasn't him; it was Lilu Intel.

*　　　*　　　*

The following day was a Sunday, allotting plenty of time for Bryson and the others to take care of business outside of the Bastion. Wendel LeAnce had given them Sundays to roam Brilliance since the weavineers had time off. Limone had stayed underground today, electing to proctor a few weavineers at Steel Field.

Gracie led Bryson, Lilu, Frederick, and a cloaked Thusia through a wealthy neighborhood. He hadn't visited this sector of Brilliance, so he was shocked to see sprawling yards of green, oak trees, and gated manors that were constructed more like the traditional buildings across the world. They were only three to four stories high, stretching to the sides rather than reaching into the sky.

"Because of Uncle Nyemas's critical role in convincing Lilu to study in Brilliance a couple of years ago, the LeAnce family gave him a home here," Gracie said as they walked down a chalk-white sidewalk. Unlike in the heart of the city, it was clear this pavement was washed regularly. "But they only recently gave it to him, as more travolters were built."

"No offense, Gracie, but aren't you supposed to be helping us get into the sewers?" Bryson asked.

"Yes, and doing so requires visiting my uncle's house first."

They passed several gated properties before finally reaching a villa constructed of some kind of smooth, sandy brown stone. It sat at the center of a flat yard, with a lone pathway cutting between two nearly identical pebble ponds before reaching the building's twin front doors.

A pair of guards greeted Gracie, Lilu, and Bryson by name before opening the front gate, eyeing Frederick and the cloaked figure as they passed. The sky was dark for midday, signaling a chance of storms. Bryson picked up the pace, feeling droplets hit his face.

Gracie retrieved a key from her pocket and unlocked the door, welcoming her friends to a vaulted foyer with archways to the right, left, and straight ahead. Two flights of stairs stretched up the sidewalls to an overlook above, where a brilliant chandelier of Intelights bathed the space in a white light.

Frederick closed the door behind the group, and Bryson gaped at the beauty. It was different than what he was accustomed to. He may have spent his past few years in the gaudy palace of one of the wealthiest families in the world, but he found himself preferring the muted luxury seen here.

A pudgy man in a bathrobe appeared from a hallway that branched away from the foyer, waddling onto the overlook. He paused at the center and surveyed his guests, adjusting his golden spectacles. "Has my niece briefed all of you on the rules?" he asked.

"We don't even know what we're doing here," Bryson said.

"Bryson hasn't done this before," Lilu said.

Jugtah gazed at Gracie. "Why must you be so difficult?"

"Because I like to mess with you."

Turning on his heels, he headed for the staircase to the left. "Very well, then," he said while descending to the main floor. He paused at the bottom, eyeing the woman in the hooded cloak. "Follow me."

Their destination was only a couple of rooms over and one floor down. During their walk, Jugtah explained everything Gracie hadn't.

"Besides the residences of the LeAnce family, this is the most exclusive neighborhood in Brilliance. The people who live here didn't purchase these properties, but contributed something of great importance to the Board of Weavineers, which doesn't necessarily mean something of monetary value. The man behind those blinding white Intelights, for example, lives next door to me."

"Like the ones in your foyer's chandelier?" Lilu asked.

"Yes, he invented the weaving pattern and holds its patent. In fact, the Board likely already has a property lined up for you, Lilu. You've brought more to this city than anyone."

She snorted. "I'm not sure I want to live here beyond a few years."

"I don't blame you," he said. "Just make sure you bring Gracie with you when the time comes. Anyway, the most cherished perk of being a home owner in this neighborhood is that it grants you access to the Bastion's balconies."

"You own a balcony?" Bryson asked.

"As of two weeks ago, yes. And now, here I am, already breaking the rules."

"I figured," Lilu said. "We used an entrance like this months ago, in the neighborhood right next door. The man who allowed me to do so wouldn't do it again, however."

They came to a stop in an empty basement, floored with plush white carpet.

"If that's the case," Jugtah said, coming to a stop, "then you know it won't put you directly into the sewers, but a couple of miles away from them. You'll have to travel through a series of passages to get there." He scanned their faces and lifted an eyebrow. "Limone not joining you on your journey?"

"He wanted to work with his team at Steel Field," Lilu said.

"That young man will work himself to death," Jugtah said. "Well, I do ask that all of you make this as quick as possible. The longer you're down there, the more suspicious Wendel will become when he notices he hasn't seen any of you all day."

He grabbed a fire iron from the wall, stabbed it into the floor, and yanked it back to reveal a carpeted trap door. He stood back and waved them over. "Just follow the flames, and you should be on the right path. I lit the torches earlier today. When you get to the main pipelines, just grab a torch from the wall."

As they filed down the ladder and into a tunnel, he whispered down to them, "Good luck."

The door above them shut, and they were on their way.

*     *     *

The group formed a line as they squeezed through the narrow passages, Frederick acting as the caboose. Bryson had to turn his head to the side as they shuffled through a crevice.

"Thusia, why is there such little information on you about your time before Phesaw?" Frederick asked.

"I suppose because my family wasn't important to the world," she said. "Windwynder is a small, distant town, after all."

"That's it?" Frederick said. "I always wondered why we only brushed over you in my history classes. You did help kill a demon. I thought that alone should have been reason enough to meticulously study you."

"Everyone always thinks that a 'hero'" —she did her best to raise an arm and symbolize air quotes with her fingers— "needs an enthralling backstory. Like if you weren't born an orphan or traumatized youth, then what kind of conflict could propel you to achieve great feats? But, it doesn't take suffering to realize changes need to be made in the world. And, as you should know, trauma oftentimes leads to evil. For every Bryson, there is a Toono."

They broke free from the crevice and wound up in a warped corridor that sloped downward. Bryson nearly tripped on the rugged rock beneath them, too focused on Thusia's story. He'd never asked her about her childhood before Phesaw.

"Like most remote towns, Windwynder's specialty has always been agriculture. It was also a pristine fishing town, for it sat next to Wynding Lake. That was my family's expertise. My father and mother would take the family boats onto the lake every day and return with a pile of fish that I could have jumped into and hid myself in had I wanted to. They were the best fishermen in the town, and because of that, we lived lavishly." She chuckled to herself. "Which didn't mean much in that town. Our house only had two bedrooms and a few other rooms."

"The mundaneness of your past makes it unique," Frederick said. "It's a fresh take when compared to the other icons in Kuki Sphaira's history."

Bryson took an awkward step down the slope and lurched forward, letting out a squeal for help. Gracie and Lilu both grabbed the back of his shirt and dug their heels into the jagged edges of stone.

Thusia turned and laughed. "Haven't you spent your life on a peg course being trained by one of the greatest Adrenians of all time?"

Bryson stuck his tongue out at her as he straightened up. As Thusia turned forward again, he whispered his thanks to the two ladies. They reached level ground again, and the corridors began to widen. Thusia grabbed a torch from the wall, its flickering light no longer reaching the sewers' boundaries, instead waning into the shadows.

"When I was eight years old, my parents sent me to Phesaw for my first year of schooling. That was where I met some of the most interesting people of my life. But, I guess my story truly didn't begin until joining the Jestivan."

"How big was the demon?" Gracie asked.

"Sixteen feet, roughly."

"Wow ..."

They finally stepped into a smaller sewer, and Lilu took a moment to study the map. She had already found the lab before, but it had been from a different location. She looked to the right. "Just a couple of miles that way, then a left, and another right before hitting the main sewer."

Bryson pulled the collar of his hoodie over his mouth and nose. "Let's get this over with."

It took a little over an hour before Lilu brought them to a halt at a random spot in the main sewage line. Bryson frowned at the path of sludge cutting between two platforms.

They crossed a flimsy bridge. As the group gathered on the other side, Lilu pressed her foot into a secret switch in the floor. A section of wall began to lift, stone grinding against stone. Bryson eyed it peculiarly; this hadn't been in Debo's memory.

"I believe Wendel—or one of the LeAnce's—tried sealing off this passageway with a fake wall," Lilu said, watching as the wall lifted, curving with the sewer's arched roof. "It may appear to be typical stone like everything else down here, but Limone had noticed a slight difference in its color when we last visited. It's actually Permanence."

"If Wendel's known about this, then why do we expect to find anything in here?" Bryson asked. "He's likely already scooped up anything of importance."

"Because of that," Lilu said, pointing down the passageway. "Use your brain, Bryson. Did you already forget why we needed Thusia?"

He nearly retaliated, but Gracie placed a hand on his shoulder, likely noticing the anger in his face. He took a deep breath and stared at the shield of light just beyond a divided pile of rubble.

"We can't simply rule out the possibility that Wendel also put up that light," he said.

"I highly doubt that," Lilu said. "How many people outside of the Bozani have you known or heard of who can produce something like that?"

Thusia nodded, stepping ahead of the group and splitting the piles of rock. "Just one …" she said. "And I know it's not Wendel."

Lilu turned to Frederick and Gracie. "I need both of you to stay here and keep watch."

Frederick, who had been fighting back vomit ever since entering the heart of the sewers, gave a thumbs-up.

"I got you covered, boss," Gracie said.

Bryson and Lilu ran to catch up with Thusia, who was already standing near the light. "This is definitely the work of someone who's had centuries of practice with weaving Tahara Chains," she muttered, inspecting the orb of light in awe. "It's been here for well over a decade, too."

"You think it was Naipa?" Bryson asked.

Thusia's gaze snapped toward him. It was the name of the woman from Debo's memory, a woman who ranked higher than both him and Thusia. He probably shouldn't have mentioned her name, seeing how the ordeal with the memory was probably a huge reason as to why Thusia had found herself in trouble with the Empire.

"I would say that's a fair deduction," Thusia whispered. "Breaking this will be very difficult."

Lilu frowned. "Suadade was able to break Debo's."

"Yes, well, Debonicus was only a Pogu. Naipa is much more than that." Thusia leaned in for a closer look. "Back away. Give me some time to study the weaving patterns. Luckily, this has been here long enough for the bonding of her Tahara Chains to weaken significantly. I should be able to crack it."

Bryson and Lilu exchanged looks before doing as they were told, realizing they'd only serve as a distraction in this scenario. Neither of them could use Tahara, nor did they know much about it in the first place. As they retreated to the secret entryway, they could only cross their fingers in hopes that Thusia would find success.

*    *    *

"Bryson ..."

Bryson awoke to the sound of his name and felt someone shaking his shoulder. He looked up from where he was seated on the cold stone floor of the sewer platform, spotting Thusia's face above him. Her golden blonde hair dangled down the sides of her face.

He pushed himself out of his slouch, wiping a trail of drool from his chin. Had enough time passed for him to have fallen asleep? "What time is it?"

"Late. Now get up."

He twisted his neck to see Lilu standing in the secret entrance, impatiently tapping her right sandal against the floor. He rose to a stand and rubbed his eyes before joining her in the doorway. The light at the end of the passage was gone, revealing a plain wooden door. He had expected something a lot more secure from something that was supposed to seal off the most important laboratory in Mendac's possession.

He and Lilu began walking toward it, but Thusia remained behind with Gracie and Frederick.

"What are you doing?" Bryson asked.

Thusia's face was hollow, her eyes wide with a forlorn expression. "I don't think I could stomach going in there," she said. "I'm more comfortable out here."

He stared at her for a moment before nodding. She didn't want to face the truth; she didn't want to see the hard evidence of Mendac's heinous downward spiral. After all, this was supposedly the room in which he had carved open a young Bryson for experimental purposes. Even *his* stomach quivered in an unsettling way as they pressed forward.

Lilu reached the door first. It was perfectly intact, without a blemish to be seen. Bryson would have thought it had been recently built had Thusia not just said the light had been protecting it for over a decade. As Lilu reached toward the handle, she looked back at Bryson. He closed his eyes and gave a nod.

She pushed open the door, revealing the very same laboratory that he'd seen in Debo's memory. It was surreal and chilling, the destruction from the fight between Ataway Debonicus Kawi and Mendac LeAnce still evident. Lab tables were toppled over, some lying in pieces against a wall; craters had been blasted into the walls; areas of stone were still black from Mendac's electrical attacks; and ink-strewn parchment lay scattered across the floor.

Lilu tiptoed her way across the wreckage while Bryson remained frozen in the doorway. His gaze had fallen on an operating table at the far end of the room—the eye of the storm. It seemed as if the battle had touched every corner of the room except the area where a five-year-old Bryson had laid, innards exposed.

Lilu was already next to the operation table, staring incredulously at a lectern nearby. Excitement lit up her face as she grabbed some papers resting on it. As she ruffled through them, he wondered if she even realized the weight of what they had walked into. Part of him hated her at that moment.

Finally looking up from the papers, her smile faded. Shame took its place, and she dropped her treasure with haste. "I'm sorry, Bryson."

Somehow, he managed words. "That table has haunted my nightmares since I was a child. At five years old, I lay there with my organs and rib cage exposed ... and I was awake, and I felt it all. I was in such fear that I couldn't even force my eyes open."

She didn't respond, her gaze falling to the table in front of her. "I am sorry, Bryson. I don't know what else to say."

He stared at the rusted steel. There was nothing she could say.

*     *     *

Back in the Bastion townhouse, Bryson paced in the breakfast area, leaving the dissection of Mendac's lab notes to Lilu and Frederick. The two weavineers poured over them, one focused on each theory. Gracie and Limone had already retired for the night upstairs.

Bryson occasionally came to a stop, only to look toward Lilu and Frederick in the hopes that they would offer something worthwhile. Instead, they sat mostly in silence, save the frequent whispered exclamation of how amazing of a find this had been. They flipped over countless pages of essays and lab notes, unfolding canvases that displayed complex equations, detailed graphs, and diagrams drawn by someone who clearly hadn't been an artist. It looked like one massive headache to him.

"Bryson, can you stop moving so much?" Lilu asked.

He stopped and turned toward her. Her expression wasn't hard or annoyed, just pleading. He sighed and sat on a stool at the breakfast bar, spinning it so he faced the living room. Gazing down at his hands, he tried to create an Intelight, only to emit mere sparks—like he was a novice Jestivan again. He groaned.

Hours past, during which Limone had shuffled down the stairs and into the kitchen to grab a boxed carton of milk from the ever-ice fridge. The buttons at the front of his pajamas were askew, a few of them undone. His hair was a matted mess atop his pudgy face. The look was enough to draw smirks out of Frederick and Lilu. It explained why Limone had rushed up the stairs earlier in the night.

Bryson began to swivel on his stool repeatedly, stopping himself after several rotations. The sofa leaned sideways inside his swirled vision, making it appear as if Lilu and Frederick were defying gravity. He closed his eyes for a moment, regaining his bearings before spinning again, using the counter of the bar as his push-off.

"It's a shame Mendac was as despicable as he was," Lilu said. "He was an absolute genius."

He froze, grateful for a disruption to the silence.

Frederick nodded, eyes still glued on the theory he was focused on. "If that Theory of Connectivity is anything like this Energy Gate Theory, I can't wait to read it."

She sighed and leaned back, plopping onto the sofa's soft cushions. She rubbed her eyes and shook her head. "Everything about it is groundbreaking and intuitive, but the methods taken to prove his hypotheses correct were despicable."

Frederick leaned over and squinted at her stack of lab notes. "The Energy Gate lab notes don't have an experimentation or conclusion section … just the hypothesis, theories, and diagrams."

"Same for mine," she said. "But I've connected the dots between what's written in these notes and certain actions Mendac took in his life …" She trailed off and glanced at Bryson, pity blanketing her face. "And I can make an educated assumption as to what his experimentation was."

Frederick glanced back at his own papers. "Do you think we need to go back and search for the rest of the information? Maybe he recorded his results separate from the essay."

"No need," she said softly, gaze still locked on Bryson. "The conclusion, the result, the *law* … he's sitting in this room right now."

# 41

# Mendac's Laws of Energy

As all eyes fell on Bryson, he remained quiet and thin-lipped, eyes empty. He'd already assumed a very long time ago, even before entering Debo's memory, that his father had conducted experiments on him. It only made sense after all the horrible things he'd learned about the man. However, Lilu seemed to be implying there was more to it than that.

"What are you getting at?" Bryson finally asked.

"Are you sure you want to talk about it right now?" she said. "I think it might do you well to get some sleep."

"Even if I tried, I wouldn't be able to."

They held each other's gaze for a protracted moment, until she leaned forward and shuffled through the papers scattered across the coffee table. "All right, where should I start?" She paused and shook her head. "Actually, let's preface this by speaking on the kind of mind and aspirations Mendac possessed."

"Let's not," Bryson said, rolling his eyes.

"It's necessary," she said. "Mendac grew up in Brilliance. Because of this, he was raised as a mind that bases all of his beliefs on logic. If it couldn't be proven through experimentation, it wasn't fact. The same applied to proving if something was false or incorrect. First and foremost, he was a theorist—not in a philosophical sense, but a rational one."

"A savant," Frederick said, listening intently while seated next to her. "A sage of logic."

"Skip the praise and jump to the point," Bryson said, trying to mask the venom in his voice.

Lilu nodded, glancing back at the lab notes. "Mendac dedicated his life to the scientific process: hypothesizing, experimentation, theorizing, and proving said theories as law. That's all he cared about. He was known for it as a Jestivan, but it had taken a backseat after meeting Thusia—or so that's what was believed. It took her death to send him over the edge, until he gradually lost any care in the world for the repercussions of his experimentation.

"He has a lengthy research essay at the beginning of these lab notes." She lifted a few of the pages off the table. "In the introductory chapters, he speaks briefly on laws he'd already discovered: The Laws of the Eleventh and Twelfth Energy, Law of Energy Gates, and Law of Polarity. Two of these laws—the eleventh and twelfth energy—are already known to a certain degree by primary bloodline royals, but not to the depth at which he describes them. However, the other two laws—energy gates and polarity— are groundbreaking."

"Based off the dates recorded in these notes, it makes sense that he refers to the energy gates as a law," Frederick said. "So this theory I'm reading came before yours, Lilu."

"Correct."

Becoming annoyed, Bryson tried to hurry them along. "Can we just get to—"

"Sit down over here, Bryson," Lilu said, standing tall and pointing at a vacant armchair. "Based off what I've read, this will be of interest to you not only because of the negatives, but because of what it can provide you." She approached the massive charcoal board on the sidewall and grabbed a piece of chalk from its baseboard.

He did as instructed, leaving his barstool and entering the living room to sink into the plush chair. She was seriously about to give him tutorage like they were in the Warpfinate again, holding lessons on weaving. She took some of her hair that fell down the front of her right shoulder and brushed it behind her, allowing it to flow down her back in waves of green. She reached up and wrote on the board: *The Law of Polarity*.

"This was what probably started it all. I don't know how Mendac came up with this theory, but it ended up being right." She drew an outline of the human body and then sketched symbols inside of it: a heart in the chest, brain in the skull, a wispy ball in the stomach, and a few random shapes in the arms and legs, which she explained immediately. "These are muscles, by the way. I'm not going to bother drawing all of them; we'd be here all night."

"And what's that ball of magic dust at the center?" he asked, earning a laugh from Frederick.

"According to Mendac's diagrams, the soul," she said.

Bryson raised an eyebrow. "That's an *actual* thing?"

"Apparently so," she said. "And it makes sense, for what else would create Spirit Energy?"

"Wait a second." He paused and stared at the diagram, thinking back on his studies at Phesaw. Not once had he ever learned about a specific location creating energy.

"I know what you're thinking," she said, looking back at the board. "We've been taught all our lives that our bodies just sort of create the energy of whichever trait we're born with. If you're an Intelian, your body just *creates* Intel Energy by some kind of chemical reaction. If you're half Archain and half Passionian, like Himitsu, your body will simply produce the energy of whichever cultural trait ends up dominant. In his case, that means Passion Energy. Turns out, however, it's nowhere near that simple. You have a brain, don't you, Bryson?"

"Obviously."

"What about a heart?" she asked, pointing toward the symbol in the diagram. "Muscles and a soul?"

He nodded, though he was still trying to wrap his mind around the "soul" thing.

"And what if I told you each of those organs was responsible for creating one or multiple types of energy?"

"I'd tell you you're crazy," he said.

"And that's an understandable reaction," she said, twirling the chalk between her fingers like it was her weapon of choice. "In theory, that would mean everyone is capable of possessing all of the energies—which we know is not the case. Even Mendac states this in his notes." She looked toward the diagram and twisted her lips with uncertainty. "Look, I'm not going to delve into the finer details of the man's research. We'd be here for days, then months, just for you to comprehend it. I still need to read through it properly several more times, so let's put this in layman's terms."

She wrote another word on the board. "The hereditary trait that determines your energy is called the D.E. trait—also known as one's dominant energy. That trait doesn't trigger your body to start producing a certain energy; it triggers a compartment in a select organ to begin producing its energy."

She pointed at her sketch of the heart. "According to Mendac, there's a container within the heart located between the left and right ventricle that he calls the *Cavity of Emotion*. It's tiny, nearly invisible to the human eye. This cavity's function is to produce one of two energies. Can you guess what those are?"

Bryson gave it some thought. "Well, the Passion Kingdom is known for being kind-hearted, but that's more symbolic than literal. They're passionate individuals, oftentimes emotional ... the cavity of emotion." He shrugged. "Passion Energy?"

She smiled. "Despite the strange logic, that's partially correct. The more direct route your line of thinking should have taken, however, is one based on history lessons. Mendac's use of vernacular for the naming system of these cavities is old. What happened in 842 K.H.?"

"Don't ask me that, Lilu. I have no idea."

"The Sphairian Summit," she said with a sigh. "The first time all ten royal heads came together in one location for a meeting. It was to discuss the naming of the kingdoms and how the world perceived their peoples. Before the year 842, kingdoms weren't named by their energies, but by a combination of what realm they resided in and what trait they specialized in. For example, the Passion Kingdom was the Light Emotion Kingdom. On the flipside, the Still Kingdom was the Dark Emotion Kingdom. They were natural rivals that occupied the same floating island, only on opposing surfaces like a reflection of each other. Together, they were the *Mirror of Emotion.*"

He slapped the arm of the chair. "So the Emotion Cavity in the heart doesn't only have the capability of producing Passion Energy, but Still Energy, too."

Frederick, who was now sprawled across the sofa, chuckled softly.

"For someone who despises learning, you sure do show a lot of exuberance when you've had epiphanies," she said.

Bryson crossed his arms with a smug gleam. "I'm smarter than Shelly, that's for sure."

"You're both equally dumb," she muttered, turning toward the charcoal board.

He sat up. "What was that?"

"Nothing!" she exclaimed, turning with a guilty shrug. "Anyway, back on topic … If two Passionians make a baby, that baby will have Passion Energy, obviously. This means the Emotion Cavity won't produce Still Energy. As for the Law of Energy Gates, Mendac says every cavity in the body—emotion, knowledge, soul, courage, and morality—has a gateway that controls the output of energy spilling into the body's energy canals."

By this point, she had drawn dozens of lines that flowed through her human diagram, representing someone's energy canals. And there were gateways connecting the canals to the cavities. She looked back over her shoulder. "You following me still?"

He nodded. "Is this the Theory of Connectivity?"

"Not at all, but we're getting there. This is simply a summarized version of the Law of Energy Gates and an explanation on cavities." She faced the board again.

"Now, what if we had a Spiritian mother and Adrenian father?" she asked, pointing her chalk toward the wispy soul then to the biceps. "As far as Mendac is concerned, the chances of the baby inheriting one over the other are random. Based off historical data, he can't decipher a trend to validate any theories, and he didn't have enough time or subjects to dedicate to such studies, himself.

"One thing is certain though: the offspring will always favor one over the other, for both cannot exist in the human body at once. In the case of parents with different energies—let's say Spiritian and Adrenian—when the child starts producing energy, both the Soul and Courage cavities will activate inside the body. This means, for a split second, both Spirit and Adrenergy will flood their canals."

Bryson was now leaning forward with focus. "Then why can't they possess both abilities of wind and speed?"

"Because one will reject the other," she said. "And once that happens, the losing energy's cavity will stop functioning, sealing off its gateway permanently."

"Because of the Dominant Energy trait?" he asked.

She grinned. "Because of *polarity*, Mendac's other theory that he eventually determined to be law. Dominant Energy is a myth—at least, now that I've read this. What's the difference between Intel and Dev Energy, Bryson?"

"Is that a trick question?"

"Geographically, what's the difference?"

He paused, not wanting to give what he thought was the obvious answer. He finally succumbed. "Intel Energy is of the Light Realm; Dev Energy is of the Dark Realm."

"Spot on," she said. "Intel, Passion, Spirit, Adren, and Archaic Energy belong to the Light Realm. Dev, Still, Cyn, Power, and Prim Energy belong to the Dark. And this doesn't only apply to geography, but remains true throughout all of nature, your body included."

She walked over to a dresser against the wall. As she pulled open its drawers, rummaging through its contents, the two men exchanged looks. Frederick appeared enamored.

Bryson leaned over and whispered, "I take it you like it when she gets in this mode?"

"There is no teacher like Lilu," Frederick said. "You know our relationship started with me as her tutor?" He stared at her in wonder. "How quickly the tables turned."

Bryson retreated back into his seat as Lilu returned with two metal rods in her hand. "What do you know about magnets?" she asked.

"They're awesome because they stick to stuff like magic," he said.

She laughed. "Okay, Jilly. What about the law of magnetic forces?"

"Opposites attract, likes repel."

"A very simplistic answer," she said, frowning at the metal rods, "but I guess it's all I need for what I'm about to explain. I suppose we're not here for a physics lesson."

She dropped to her knees and placed a metal rod on the coffee table, pushing scattered parchment out of the way. She pointed a finger at one end, where a plus sign was engraved. "That's the positive side." She pointed at a minus sign at the other end. "And that's the negative side." She picked up the second rod. "This magnet has the same engravings. When I try to approach the positive end of one rod with the positive end of the other …"

She trailed off, doing exactly as she said. The rod that lay on the table moved on its own, trying to avoid the touch from its counterpart. "Essentially, they're repelling each other just like you said. Now, what if we applied the same logic to energy? What if energetic forces acted like magnetic ones?"

"I get it," Bryson muttered. "So that's why one energy overpowers the other when two parents hail from different kingdoms. The two energies repel each other, one eventually rejecting the other."

She nodded. "Triggering the losing energy's cavity to shut down. For Himitsu, there was a split second, sometime during his childhood, when both his Emotion and Morality Cavity booted up. His Passion Energy won the battle, causing the Morality Cavity, which is located in the left half of the brain, to shut down."

Her face became grave. "This is where the Theory of Connectivity comes into play … this is where you come into play, Bryson." She flipped the rod in her hand, the negative end pointed outward. His eyes widened, watching as she pushed it toward the positive end of the other rod.

"While likes repel, opposites attract," she said, the two rods snapping together. She looked up at him, her jaw rigid. "The procreation between humans possessing energies of separate realms is considered an Untenable. Apparently, there's a reason for this beyond cultural taboo. If our energies are like magnetic forces and two energies from the same realm repel each other, then that would imply two energies from opposite realms would …" Her sentence tapered off.

"Attract to each other," he said.

A long silence followed, pierced by Frederick releasing a low whistle. "Your dad's Intelian and your mom's Stillian," Lilu said. "This means during that split second when you gained the ability to produce energy long ago, both your Knowledge and Emotion Cavities kicked into gear, sending Intel and Still Energy coursing through your canals. But instead of repelling each other, they were drawn together, meaning there was never a catalyst telling your body to shut down one of the cavities."

"Are you saying I have two energies inside of me?" he asked.

"According to Mendac's Theory of Connectivity, yes." Her eyes narrowed. "For as long as I've known you, you've complained about suffering from chills—even when it was dead hot outside. It was why hoodies became your clothing of choice. And you've told me that had always been the case … ever since you could remember."

"I chalked that up to me being part-Stillian once I found out about my mother," he said.

"And that's right, but you weren't digging deep enough … into the nitty gritty, scientific details. It's more than a simple birth trait affecting your body temperature. What's causing that chill is your Still Energy."

"Then why can't I weave ice?"

"That's a good question, and one to which I don't have the answer," she said. "Alas, I've only done a few hours of digging into Mendac's research, which isn't proper enough time to gain a real understanding of it all. It hurts that there isn't any section in his research about specific experiments he performed, even though we can guess at what a few of them were. I'll try to figure it out, though."

He fell silent, staring at the diagram while she stood aside. She had labeled each of the cavities and which energy they produced: the Emotion Cavity in the heart, Spirit Cavity in the soul, Adrenaline Cavities in several muscles, Morality Cavity in the brain's left half, and Knowledge Cavity in the brain's right half. She had also made it a point to draw the eyes.

"Any reason you drew the eyes?" he asked.

"Speaking of eyes, that's quite a good set you have," she said, writing two more words on the board: *Light* and *Dark*. "I'm not going to dive into the depths of the eleventh and twelfth energies, but Mendac believed the eyes held the cavity that produces them. He also calls them parent energies. Basically, what the ten lesser energies are derived from. He didn't know the proper terms for these energies, but I know that what he refers to as Light Energy is actually Tahara." She paused. "And I'm sure the royal families of the Dark Realm know the name for Dark Energy. They've kept that a well-guarded secret, though."

"But it seems only the Bozani or Gefal can tap into those," Bryson said. "I guess the trigger happens after death, when one is chosen to be reborn in an empire."

"That's complete speculation," she said. "The royals who are aware of the parent energies believe everyone has a little bit of both inside of them. Mendac believed this, and he took it a step further by offering a deeper explanation, a luxury granted to him from all of his research. Besides an Unable's inability to produce energy, what is unique about them, Bryson?"

"No idea," he said.

She huffed. "It's sad how little you remember from your studies. Have you never met an Unable before?"

"I have. Some have been great friends in the past, but I never ask them about that kind of stuff."

"Unables can't see the Empires," she said.

"What?"

"When they look into the sky, they don't see the underbellies of two floating islands like you or I do."

His chin disappeared, head recoiling back into his neck. "Really?"

"You've spent your entire life around talented weavers and cloutitionists, so I guess this would come as a shock. But no, they can't see them." She turned and pointed toward the board. "And Mendac theorizes it has to do with the fact that their body doesn't produce any energy, which means there is no energy in the parent cavity of their eyes. Because of this, they cannot see things such as the empires."

"Interesting," he said, eyes narrowing. "Do you remember my pal, Simon?"

After a pause, she said, "Yes, the foolish boy who idolizes you? I believe the archers in my father's military are now referring to him as Torchtop, the sharpshooter of the millennium."

"He's an Unable, yet he's specifically pointed out the Light Empire to me on a few occasions. He can see them."

Her eyebrows climbed her forehead. "Then he's lying to you, Bryson."

"About what? Seeing the Empire or being an Unable?"

"That's an answer only he'd know. Either he's keeping an innocent secret, trying to make you believe he can see the same things that his idol can …" She trailed off … "Or there's something about him that he really doesn't want you to know."

He frowned and looked off to the side at Frederick, whose eyes had grown heavy. It was late, and while Bryson was long overdue for sleep, he doubted he could grab hold of it tonight.

Lilu returned the chalk to the base and approached the coffee table, taking a seat on the floor and rummaging through the parchment again. "I suggest you two get some sleep," she said.

"And what about you?" Frederick asked.

"I'm good. This won't be my first rodeo pulling an all-nighter. Besides, I have a hunch, but it requires a little more digging. With all of this coming to light, I may know how to fix your issues with your energy, Bryson. The hard part will be convincing a certain someone to partake in the solution."

Bryson sat up, suddenly alert. "Are you serious?"

She looked up at him with cautious eyes. "Hold off on the optimism. This might take a few days to figure out, then a few more of persuasion. Give me some time." She smiled. "I got you, Bry."

# 42

# The Power Kingdom

*Tha-dunk.*

Rhyparia's body lurched forward, jarring her awake. She was still in the darkness of her crate, the slits between its planks granting dim light. The way it swayed told her she was being transported. A few people carried her, grunting with each step, and she wondered if they knew she was inside. How many people on the ship were aware of their presence?

A door squeaked on its hinges, and sunlight spilled through the crate's slits. She nearly sat up and tried to peek through a crevice, but that would only raise suspicion. If the people carrying her weren't privy to the presence of stowaways, they'd surely find it odd if the cargo moved on its own.

Sometime later, the men lowered her to the ground and walked away. She was thankful to not hear their conversation any longer. It seemed even the Primmish had some bad seeds despite their obsession with morality. She wanted to bathe, and not only because of the grime coating her skin.

Hours passed, and she was teetering between starving to death in this death trap or blasting her way out and risking the chance of being caught by any wanderers. The silence around her suggested nobody was close. She could hear distant shouts, likely those of sailors or harbor workers—if she was even near the harbor. She didn't know where she was. She wanted to scream out for any of her friends, but what if someone else heard her?

She felt the crate shake, but heard nothing. A side of the crate fell open, thrusting freedom right in front of her. As eager as she was to escape, she wasn't certain if doing so was the right move. Nobody lingered outside—not within eyesight, at least. Perhaps they had laid a trap. Considering this, she remained hunched forward, eyes narrowed as she stared outside, vision slowly adjusting to the darkness. She had no clue if it was first or second-night.

The crate silently shook again, and she tightened her grip on the handle of her umbrella. An upside-down face slipped into view from the top of the crate.

"Creep ..." she muttered, releasing a long breath.

His full beard remained rigid despite gravity, but his graying hair dangled toward the ground. "Shall we begin tonight?" he asked, his hard black eyes skittering in a hundred directions, as always.

She stepped outside, releasing a groan as she arched her back and stretched. They were in a shipyard, illuminated a deep blue by the sparkling night sky. Barrels, crates, and massive metal containers were stacked around them, trapping them in a maze. She could see a port in the distance just over one of the container stacks, shrouded in a faint flickering orange from hundreds of torches. How far had she been carried earlier?

"Where is everyone else?" she asked.

"I've only seen the weasel, rabbit, and that man with the terribly scarred face," he said. "They're currently seeking out the others."

She approached some barrels stacked in the shape of a pyramid nearby. "Well, let's help."

"I was really looking forward to reaching Ulna Malen right away," he said, heading for a crate a few paces away.

"I'm not leaving my friends stranded," she said, inspecting each barrel for a tiny black *x*. The Prowlers had marked each of the containers holding a person with the same symbol using tar. "But rest assured we'll be in the capital by …" she trailed off, glancing at the moons … "dawn."

She leapt off the pile and approached a shaking barrel, its lid clearly marked. She unlocked a couple of latches and lifted the lid. A clean-shaven man rose from within, his lanky frame lending similar imagery to that of a snake winding out of its vase. Creep grunted and turned away, obviously displeased by the luck of their draw.

"Good evening, Prakriti," she said, immediately walking away to look elsewhere.

He struggled to lift his leg out of the barrel. It was a tight fit, and only one of the smaller dimiours or a skinny, feeble man like him would have been able to survive in such a space. Suddenly, she was thankful for her crate, a mansion in comparison.

While she and Creep continued to search through cargo, Prakriti became enamored by the gigantic metal containers. They were rectangular, as long as a fallen yew. She hadn't given them much thought.

"This is steel," Prakriti said in shock. She turned to watch him, annoyed he wasn't providing any help. He crouched and gazed at something near the bottom of the container.

"Are you going to help or not?" she asked.

"There are handles at the bottom," he said, his gaze following the container's length. "Three of them. One at the front, one in the middle, one near the rear." He tried grabbing a handle, positioning himself into a squat. He pulled upward with no success.

She shook her head and refocused on a stack of crates. "You're going to throw your back out," she said.

Creep leapt to the top of a container. "I'll keep a lookout around us. Someone needs to keep watch with that idiot prancing around."

During the search, Prakriti finally joined Rhyparia. She found herself cursing Creep for abandoning her.

"You and Creep will handle yourselves well in the city, correct?" he asked.

She fought back a sigh. Did he realize how different they were? He must have. Why else would he have constantly brought up her mission in the city? His sermons about peace and morality had become redundant and exhausting. If anything, they made her want to rebel against him more, like a teenager told not to stay out past curfew.

"Stop worrying about me," she said, doing her best to keep her tone level.

He stepped around a crate, looking for a mark. "It's not you I'm worried about, but the Powish civilians."

"And why is that?"

"Because of you."

"What's that supposed to mean?" she snapped. So much for civil.

"Before my father left to train you, he told me about you. He said you were the most frightening individual he'd ever met in his life." He paused. "He said training you would prove to be a massive gamble."

"Musku said that?" she asked, dumbfounded.

He nodded. "Your story goes one of two ways according to my father. You either become a martyr, or you become a tragedy the likes of which could annihilate thousands of families." He looked at her with soft eyes. "I'd rather not have it be the latter."

"I would never do such a thing," she said. "And I can't believe Musku would say that."

"All it takes is one bad influence, Rhyparia. Don't allow Creep to serve as that. Our objective here is to free the slaves … that's it."

"I know that. We've gone over this dozens of times."

They fell silent, but Prakriti continued to stare at her while she searched through cargo. "Rhyparia, my father trained you as tenaciously as he did only to give you the tools to get us through Realmular Tunnel. Don't forget that. It wasn't for the purpose of combat or destruction."

"Shut up." That's all she could say.

*　　*　　*

The light of the setting sun was not yet gone. With everyone found, they had gathered in a compact square of land surrounded on all four sides by

414

container stacks, some three stories high. A narrow pathway ran through one corner of the wall, between two neighboring containers.

As Atarax and Rayne went over the long-term plan, Rhyparia zoned out, mind focused on her mission in the capital. Anxiously, she fidgeted with the cloth of her black cloak. She couldn't hide the tic. This had been a long time coming. Nearly two decades of work—most of it spent training—to get to this point. For all those who were suffering and had suffered in the past, slaving away beneath the whips of their taskmasters, she would seek their revenge … for Vuilni Gesluimant, whose family had been abused and torn apart.

Atarax was in the midst of his briefing. "Therapif is already on his way to Ulna Malen to seek out escape routes for inner-city slaves. The rest of us, save Kakos, who will stand guard and watch for intruders, will begin work on digging the tunnel here."

"And what will the almighty and all-knowing Prakriti be doing to enrich our mission?" Creep asked sarcastically from the back of the group.

"He'll act as a guide to the slaves we free from Stratum Zero," Atarax said.

Kakos cackled, exposing his canines. "In other words, he's a waste of space."

"*Shut up*," Saikatto spat. "Do you forget, Kakos, that Prakriti is the son of Musku? How dare you disrespect him?"

The wolf's laughter turned into a gentle thrum. "I don't care."

"Rhyparia and Creep will spend the next few weeks in Ulna Malen," Atarax continued, ignoring the squabble. "I don't have to speak much more on that subject; they know what to do."

Prakriti turned and looked at her.

"And that's that," Atarax said. "After years of preparation, the time has finally come. The mission starts now."

*    *    *

Rhyparia and Creep waited a few hours for second-night to fall. Once the sun disappeared behind the blue ball in the sky, they made their way across the tops of containers. Creep ran with a lot of speed, but he made no noise despite this. Rhyparia lightened gravity around her significantly to help ease her footfalls, strides unnaturally long like a gazelle. She stopped atop one of the shipyard's exterior containers. They both lay on their stomachs so their silhouettes blended in with the containers.

Just outside the shipyard, men and women were hard at work unloading and loading ships docked at the port. They carried crates, barrels, and sacks of items, some of which looked too big for a normal person to carry. Torches ran across the sides of the port's maze of pathways, giving light to second-night's air. People in uniform were stationed at checkpoints along the port, whips in hand, ready to lash anyone who faltered.

Since the Powish were some of the strongest people in the world, their Power Energy somehow being able to feed their muscles, they should have been able to withstand such weights easily. Yet the malnourishment was evident in a lot of them. Shoulders slouched and backs hunched. Some slunk along the port even if they weren't carrying anything. Food and rest were likely difficult to come by in an environment like this. The only necessity provided was water. Each time a slave returned to a ship to grab more product, they'd pass someone who stood by an open barrel. That person would dip a ladle into the barrel and then spill its contents down a slave's gullet.

"Well," Creep said, "that answer's Prakriti's question about the handles."

Rhyparia followed his gaze to the right, toward the other side of the port. A monstrous ship, unlike anything she'd seen in her life, towered above the entire bay in a shadowy black mass. Its deck was too high for her to see it at all from this vantage point, but she did see what they were unloading from it.

Her eyes widened and her jaw dropped. A massive doorway sat open in the ship's hull, a gangplank connecting an upper deck to the port. This gangplank, however, was more like a roadway, wide enough to stand thirty grown men shoulder to shoulder—and for good reason. A steel container, five wagons long, was being carried up it, a man or woman stationed at each handle. It only took six people to carry that monstrous thing?

"And look at that," Creep said, pointing away from the port.

She followed his finger toward the edge of the shipyard, where a figure as tall as the containers themselves stomped toward one.

"A giant ..." she muttered. He was bigger than Power Warden Feissam, though it was hard to distinguish an accurate size from this distance.

The giant squatted at the end of a container and reached forward, grasping onto two handles set into the container's door. He roared and pulled. His thighs, calves, triceps, and forearms threatened to rip out of his skin. After the difficulty of the first tug, he began to drag it across the dirt with relative ease. He pulled it toward a separate port ramp, wider than the rest to accommodate for the container's unique size, before approaching the gangplank to the galleon.

"I think it's time I should warn you, Rhyparia ... do not fall victim to a physical blow from a Powish giant," Creep said.

As intimidating of a display it had been, she wasn't worried. She had ways of countering such strength. Her gravity-altering ancient was the perfect tool for such a purpose. "So these are all slaves?" she asked.

"For the most part," he said. "The giant isn't. He likely gets paid a lot of money. They're very important people in Powish culture. It's believed that they're descendants of some sort of powerful ancestor from before Known History."

She knew exactly who that ancestor was, recalling the story Musku had read to her upon meeting the original Jestivan for the first time. The Dark Courage King, the man responsible for killing Dimiourgos seven times and beheading him on the seventh attempt. Watcher Iris had referred to him as *Stonebody*. While the story had never mentioned the man's size, it wasn't out of the realm of possibility he'd been a giant.

"It's a miracle the port doesn't collapse under all of that weight," she said.

"One of the Prim Kingdom's greatest commodities is their holy trees," he said.

"You mean the willows?"

"Yes, but they're more than the typical willow found in the rest of the world. Holy trees are unfathomably sturdy. It takes extraordinary force to break them. Because of this, their wood is highly sought after across the world, and the Power Kingdom is the Primmish's most important trade partner in regards to it. That port is made of holy wood. There could be twenty giants carrying containers across that thing and it still wouldn't break. That ship is called a leviathan, and it's constructed of the same thing."

She hummed in thought. "I'm surprised the Prim Kingdom trades something that means so much to their religion."

"That was the decision of the royal family centuries ago," he said. "And it's the main factor as to why the royals and holy men don't get along."

"I see."

He turned to look at her. "Up for a fun fact?"

She cocked an eyebrow. "Sure."

"Most of the structures in Ulna Malen's upper stratums are constructed of holy wood. After the 1200s, the capital laid in ruin from nearly a century's worth of rioting and arson. That was when King Unop made the decision to rebuild the important parts of the city with an architectural strength that could match that of the people living in it. While the riots continued into the 1300s, they found no success in the upper four stratums because of the holy wood buildings."

She turned back toward the port. "Interesting. One thing still bothers me, though."

"Shoot."

"With holy trees being such religious landmarks of the Prim Kingdom, what did the Powish have to offer in return?"

He nudged his head in the direction of the galleon. "Exactly what's in those steel containers."

"And what's that?"

He sighed. "The most desired commodity in the world ... provod."

"What's that?"

"What?" he said, forehead crumpling. She shrugged. "I guess provod is still new in the Light Realm. It's unlikely you learned about it in school. The Dark Realm did well in keeping it a secret for centuries."

"So what is it?" she asked again.

"Basically, a material that repels EC chains when crafted and hardened properly, becoming a substance called Permanence." He paused. "Of course, that's a very simplistic explanation. In other words, fire, electricity, wind, ice, or anything created by woven chains cannot affect it. In fact, such attacks would be repelled … if the Permanence is made correctly."

"Not even my gravity alterations?" she asked.

He nodded slowly. "Ancients use woven Archaic Chains, so no." He rolled onto his side, gazing in the direction of Ulna Malen, the capital of the Power Kingdom. Built on a small mountain, it wrapped around the hillsides in stratums like a layered wedding cake. It was bright, illuminated by white lights that made no sense.

He continued to explain: "That's why the wealthiest two stratums—Stratums Nine and Eight—have buildings that aren't just constructed with holy wood, but then reinforced with an added layer of Permanence. There is no destroying those buildings. Nothing short of an act of the goddess could achieve such a thing. A holy tree's weakness is lightning, but how can electricity reach the wood if it can't get past the exterior shell of Permanence?"

"Basically what you're saying is, it would take someone with extraordinary brute strength to topple those buildings," she said.

He shook his head and laughed. "No, *impossible* brute strength." He shrugged. "Or a combination attack of unimaginable strength to break the Permanence and electrical clout to then shatter the holy wood. I don't know who could provide such a combo, though."

She placed her face against the container and sighed. "Well, I suppose if my objectives had been easy, they would have been done already by someone else."

He grinned. "Yes, but there's a first for everything."

*　　*　　*

Rhyparia leapt across the Power Desert, flying over several sand dunes at once. She soared through the night sky toward the empires before increasing gravity around her and plummeting back toward land. She pounced in an explosion of sand with both feet, then hurled herself back into the sky. She moved with grace, arcing gently as she appeared to glide across the stars.

Then there was Creep. As smooth and stealthy of a man as he was, he couldn't achieve the same effect as her when airborne. He was out of his element, and for once, she could spot discomfort in his motions.

He'd land awkwardly, making contact with one foot at a speed that required two, sending his body lurching forward. By that time, it was too late to plant the second foot, his body already parallel to the ground. Instead, he'd throw out his hands to protect his face from the inevitable impact, sometimes with success.

His palms skidded through the sand until he rolled his body and allowed his shoulder to hit next, completed by a rapid and nauseating tumble down a sand dune. She broke into a fit of laughter as she watched from the sky, waiting for him to regain his footing, which he finally did halfway down the slope. He sprinted uncontrollably down the dune, unable to stop his momentum.

She tightened the grip of her umbrella and did a bit of simple weaving to lighten the gravity around him. His strides grew longer, and after the third step he leapt into the air again. He flailed his arms and legs, like a baby tree bent over in a hurricane, flapping its twig-like branches in the gales.

She shook her head and smiled, looking forward again. They were closing in on Ulna Malen. The hill had grown into something more daunting, something that had to have been on the cusp of a mountain. After a quick count of the stratums, she realized she was eye-level with Stratum Seven, a modest wall of white stone separating it from Stratum Eight.

It took only a short while to reach the desired distance from the edge of Stratum Zero. This time she landed with care, not allowing the gravity around her to return to normal until she hit the side of the dune that faced away from the capital. Creep soared a ways behind her, but he was moving quickly. His trajectory had him headed clear across the desert's final dune, a landing spot likely in the middle of Stratum Zero.

In need of an immediate adjustment, she turned and pointed the tip of her umbrella just ahead of Creep. She wove an invisible wall of Archaic Chains with enough gravity to stop him in his tracks. He hit her cluster of woven chains and plunged toward the ground as if something had smacked him from above.

She broke the chains of the wall, allowing normal gravity to take over. She pointed her umbrella at the ground below him and wove a multi-layered floor of clusters, some forty feet thick. Each layer contained a different gravity alteration, growing successively lighter from top to bottom. His plunge went from a free fall to a gentle sinking until he was hovering inches above the sand.

She broke the chains and allowed her umbrella to rest beside her. Creep dropped onto the sand and lay there for a long moment, recovering from the jarring gravitational shifts. His slight movements meant he was alive, at least.

She peeked above the crest as he rose to his feet and climbed up toward her. "Aren't you an assassin-spy hybrid?" she asked. "You should be able to handle heights a little better than that." She couldn't hear his breaths, but his flaring nostrils and heaving chest were clear indicators.

"I can scale buildings and climb trees like any talented being of stealth," he said, breathing now audible. "That, however, doesn't mean I can fly."

A few miles away, Stratum Zero lay in waste. Unlike the rest of the city, where lights blazed a brilliant white, it was encased in a dull orange. It was impossible to see people, which meant she couldn't get a good feel for the security at the stratum's edge. She didn't want to risk moving closer, though.

"Very few guards and a simple wooden fence a stallion could clear," Creep said.

"How do you—" She paused, turning to find a looking glass against his eye. "Ah …"

He lowered the instrument, pressing the skinny end to shorten it. As he returned it to his trench coat pocket, he said, "I may not be able to fly, but I know how to prepare for a mission such as this." He looked at her with a pronounced frown. "And what tools did you bring besides your umbrella?"

She didn't respond.

He shrugged, looking toward the city again. "I suppose that bandana can serve as more than just a pretty necktie. Perhaps, you can hide your face like a ninja and become invisible because, you know …" he cracked a smile … "that's totally how that works."

"How do you suppose we get in?" she asked, ignoring his sarcasm.

"We fly."

"Because two people in the sky doesn't scream 'look at me!' to everyone below," she said.

"Do you know what light pollution is?" he asked.

"Of course I—" She paused, considering the white lights that littered the capital. The sun may have not been out, but it was still three o'clock in the afternoon at the latest. This meant the city was abuzz with activity.

"This was why I wanted to commit to this during second-night and not first," he explained. "The city sleeps during first-night. Ninety percent of its Intelamps are off. But now, thousands of them are on. To the citizens, they can't see the stars because of it. Have you noticed how the stars have appeared to grow weaker the closer we've gotten to the city?"

She looked up. He was right.

"Besides," he said. "It's not as if we'll be flying above the entire city—only Stratum Zero, which isn't even on the hillside by the looks of things. It's spread across the flat deadlands circling the hill's base."

"All right," she said.

"Now, here's the weird part," he said, sighing. "This maneuver will require holding hands."

"What?" she exclaimed, sinking below the crest and regarding him with stern eyes. "Are you an idiot?"

"I wouldn't suggest it if it weren't necessary," he said, lowering himself. "It'll make sure we don't become disconnected during flight, but it will also allow you to guide both of us as one person instead of trying to split your weaving into two."

"Then I'll make sure we stay next to each other if that's what you're worried about," she said. "I'm not holding your hand."

"There's more to it than your gravity," he said. "When we land, we need to do so quickly and in silence. Normally, you'd suggest lessening the gravity so we land softer, but doing so would make us sink unnaturally slow, causing us to hang in the air and increasing the likelihood of being caught."

She bit her tongue, suppressing the urge to counter his logic.

"We need to plunge to the ground, and doing so will require my ancient of silence upon landing. I'll land first, making contact with whichever surface we choose. Then you'll land a split second after, but without noise since I'll have already silenced the surface. Also, the landing will inevitably expel some kind of grunt or gasp from you. But if you're in contact with me, nobody will hear it ... hence, the hand-holding."

Her eyes narrowed. "So let our bones break by allowing normal gravity to splatter us against the ground?"

"You can still manipulate the gravity somewhat, but not to the extent of what is necessary to stifle the noise of our impact. I've heard Stratum Zero is covered in mud, so our impact should be soft even if we don't greatly lessen the gravity."

She groaned and lay on her back. "Fine."

"Are you ready to do this?"

She set her jaw. "I've been ready.

# 43

# A Stratum Strewn in Sewage

If it wasn't for Creep's silent ancient, this mission would have failed the moment they landed in Stratum Zero.

Rhyparia's hair fluttered above her as she dropped them out of the sky. Creep's mouth hung open, a look of horror on his face. She was certain he was yelling bloody murder. Her hand was numb, his grip tightening the closer they got to the ground.

She wove a layered cluster of Archaic Chains below them, but not with the same drastic alterations in gravity as she had earlier with Creep in the desert. While these would slow their fall, it wouldn't do enough to silence their impact. Hopefully they wouldn't break any bones.

She aimed for a dark crevice between two shacks. She didn't want to land on any buildings—not in this stratum. There was no holy wood or Permanence holding up these structures, so they'd definitely blow a hole through a roof. No suffocation of sound could get them out of that mess.

She altered the gravity around them, rerouting their path toward the shadowy alley at an angle. If they were to stick to this trajectory, they'd split the gap, but immediately hit the side of the shack. This called for a drastic and risky maneuver.

Creep gawked at her just as they were about to enter the gap and hit the wall. She wove a powerful blast of gravity just above them. A force pushed the top of their heads, smacking them down through the gap at an alarming speed. They should have hit the ground immediately after, but her reflexes and weaving prowess were fast enough to accommodate that unforgiving time constraint.

She wove two gentle forces of gravity that moved inward from the walls of both shacks, catching them in the center. This slowed them, but she wove another gravitational buffer below to prevent injury.

Instead of crashing into the hard crust of land, she splashed into a puddle of slime. The impact was noiseless, Creep somehow managing to keep grasp of her hand. Even as she forced herself to stand, fighting against the gooey substance trying to keep her pinned, his hand remained entwined with hers. She wanted to yank it away, but she knew he was only trying to silence her breathing. The succession of weaving techniques had taken a lot out of her.

She clasped her hand over her mouth and nose. A rancid stench the likes of which she'd never experienced wafted over her. Creep's nose wrinkled, his mouth twisted, and his eyes narrowed in disgust. She looked down at the brown sludge dripping from her forearm.

Her entire body convulsed, not even needing to take a closer sniff to realize what this was. A sensation sprung up within her, a tingly prickling that climbed up her throat and into her mouth. Her body lurched, turning her mouth into a faucet of vomit.

Creep turned away, leaning against the shack while keeping a hold of her hand. His shoulders slunk, his back ebbing and flowing with heavy breaths. He was likely feeling the same thing, but doing a lot better at holding it in. She went to wipe her mouth, but then remembered what coated the back of her hand.

It took close to a minute for them to recover, nausea overtaking any worries of bodily damage from the impact. They hadn't prepared for this. She needed to move elsewhere.

Creep finally turned away from the wall. Sweat lathered his paled face, and webs of red ran across his irises. His graying beard dripped with what must have been excrement—and a lot of it. The entire alleyway was blanketed with a thick layer of it.

"You good?" he asked, his breathing becoming more audible as he spoke.

She nodded wearily, but her twisting insides told a different story. She wanted a bucket and a bath, but she wasn't sure if any amount of water could cleanse the filth off her.

He lifted a foot and glanced down at the bottom of his boot. There were strings of brown stretching between it and the ground. "Seems like we're going to have to hold hands for a little longer," he whispered. "This footing is not ideal for stealth."

She nodded again. She didn't care if she'd have to hop on his back. She might have preferred that.

They crept down the short alley. Torches lit the street just ahead. To her dismay, the condition of the roads was no different. She gazed around the corner of the shack, spotting a line of slaves walking in their direction at the far end of the road. They were barefoot and bare-chested—men and women alike—their necks strung together by rope. Holes peppered their trousers, the only article of clothing they did wear.

Behind the line of slaves was a taskmaster, a giant of a man mounted on top of a giant of a beast she had learned about in Phesaw. Because horses couldn't support the weight of Powish riders, the job fell onto barrelers.

Native to the Jungle of Fists, it was believed they had been imported all the way to Ulna Malen and trained for the purpose of war even before the Known History timeline. Their skin was reptilian, scaly and dry, though their facial features were quite human-like. Their frame was similar to that of a gorilla, but entirely more massive in size. Their chests and shoulders were as wide as a royal carriage when exposed. They even walked on all fours, using their front knuckles as feet. Their name, 'barreler,' was derived from two things: their unrelenting barrage of fists and kicks when enraged and the barrel-like girth of their forearms and thighs, lending them the strength to clear chasms in a single leap.

Mighty beasts indeed, they relied on raw power, a stout frame, straight-line speed, and cast-iron skin. Their weaknesses lay in their agility and lack of claws and teeth. Since they were herbivores, they didn't sport impressive canines. Pivoting and changing direction didn't come easy for them, making a skilled Adrenian the perfect counter. They killed humans not for food but for sport, making them even more terrifying.

A taskmaster sat atop the animal. He was a smaller giant when compared to Power Warden Feissam or the woman Rhyparia had seen at the shipyard, but anyone could look intimidating when perched on top of a barreler with a whip in hand—a whip that got way more use than it should have. All it took was a slight misstep from a slave for the thing to come lashing down on one of them.

The image was enough to flood her vision with red fury. While Vuilni had told her some stories about life in Stratum Zero—or Cascade's Closure as she'd called it—she'd always avoided the finer details. Vocalizing them in such a way only caused her to relive them. Rhyparia never blamed Vuilni for this because she, too, understood that problem. Even during the Gravity Trials, she would have rather been hanged by the court than forced to defend herself by recounting the events of the Olethros Collapse.

However, now she wished Vuilni would have told her. She would have worked even harder in order to reach this kingdom and make sure every single citizen who ignored or benefitted from these slaves got what they deserved. And shame on the Light Realm for allying with these scumbags and turning a blind eye to their abhorrent practices. Why wasn't Powish slavery in Phesaw's curriculum? This was sickening.

"I'm trying to figure out where all of this crap came from," Creep said, indicating the filth coating the road. "Certainly not the barrelers."

"Notice how it seems to be moving at a snail's pace, too?" she asked.

He frowned. "You're right."

She pulled back into the shadows of the alleyway, cringing at the sight of another lashing. That didn't stop her from hearing it, though. The lack of a reaction from the slaves bothered her more than anything. Had they been conditioned to the pain? Or did they stifle their screams in fear of being whipped again?

Her breathing grew heavy as heat rose to her face.

"I know what you're feeling," Creep said. "But, we can't lose focus on the greater goal here."

"I know that."

"If we were to make a scene here and now, everything would be ruined."

She glared at him, and that put a stop to his words. They retreated deeper into the alley as the line of slaves crossed just outside, barefoot in the sludge. Now that she could see them up close, the scars coating their shoulders and backs glowed against the surrounding torches. Their skin was a lattice of fresh wounds and aged scabs, making them appear less human. On closer inspection of the patches and ragged clumps of hair entangled around scars on their scalps, it was clear that several of them could no longer sport a full head of hair.

As the barreler-mounted taskmaster rode by, she engrained the image of his face in her mind. He was an unnaturally big man, bordering the threshold between human and giant. She didn't care. He would die, and she'd make sure it was by her hands.

"We need to find a residential district," Creep said. "Someplace where there's a crowd."

"Do they even have such a place?" she asked. "I'm getting the impression that every area of Stratum Zero is monitored by a taskmaster, and it's likely they have a strong tally on their slaves. If they spot someone unfamiliar in the crowd, they'll know it."

He crept toward the alley's end again, peeking to the left where the slaves were now hidden in front of the barreler. "I don't know about that," he muttered. "You saw them, Lita. Nothing about them stands out individually. I mean, their condition is quite striking to the eye, but when clumped together as one, it's a giant glob of defeated things masked in wounds."

"So we need to blend in," she said, ignoring his description of the slaves.

"That's the safe and smart play. Infiltration is complete, now it's time for spy work."

She looked down. "So we should roll around in the filth?"

He nodded apprehensively.

"And what about our backs?" she said. "We don't have their scars. And it's not as if we can hide it; they walk around topless."

"A few of them wore shirts, but you're right, I suppose. Even the shirts had rips in the back and shoulders, exposing their wounds." He hummed in thought. "That's a tricky one, requiring certain sacrifices on our part."

She turned and lifted her shirt, feeling air hit her back. "I'm sure you have something on you that could mimic a lash wound." She bit down on her rolled up shirt, eyes squeezed shut as she braced for impact. It never came. "Well, come on, then."

"I have several blades on me, no whips," he said.

"Use what you think is best. Just hurry up."

A pause. He grabbed her hand, obviously with the goal of silencing her. "Are you sure?"

"Just do—"

Her sentence was cut short, and so was her breath. A blade tore across her back. She screamed into the cloth of her tunic, but there wasn't any sound. It was like the nightmares she used to have as a child, being back home in Olethros, standing in the middle of the street as buildings collapsed around her … as her neighbors crumpled under the weight of her gravity, dying slowly and painfully. Her cries were always muted. Instead, she'd hear the screams of those she loved amongst the destruction.

A blade slashed her back again, then thrice more. Each time she clawed deeper into the shack's rotting wood. It continued well past the point of losing count, until she finally dropped. Creep's grip of her hand kept her from being fully submerged in the sludge. He forced her back to her feet. She wanted to fall over again, but he took her arm and slung it over his shoulders, acting as a crutch.

"You cannot allow your wounds to soak in that filth, otherwise you'll have about ten different infections within minutes." He shook his head. "I doubt you have the same kind of immunities as these slaves, who have been conditioned to such an environment."

She couldn't speak. All she felt was the searing pain in her back.

"Give it a few minutes, and you'll do the same to me." He fell silent, likely weaving to silence their breaths. He gazed distantly at the other shack, as if staring through it. "You are something else, Lita Rhyparia." He paused, his expression unreadable. "You remind me of that old geezer before he became a softy."

*     *     *

They found a residential street during second-day. While the same rancid stench of sewage emanated from the land, the atmosphere was different. Instead of slaves strung together by chain, they roamed freely in tangled crowds. Taskmasters didn't ride barrelers through the streets; they remained posted at interesections.

Roads were more like random pathways that branched out in several different directions, cutting between shacks. It was all one giant canvas of brown, from the ground to the buildings to the grime darkening the skin of the slaves. Most slaves wore shirts if they weren't on some kind of job. They may have still been peppered with holes, but at least they had something. This allowed her to scratch her original plan of walking the streets bare-chested, which was something Creep had been highly against, stating it would only draw more attention to herself. In a place dominated by male taskmasters, it wouldn't have taken much to catch their eye.

She'd never seen Creep without his trench coat, but for this mission, he had no choice. As morbid as it might have been, they both had to scavenge trousers off the bodies of a couple of dead slaves they had found earlier. Their original clothing would have stood out because of the quality of material, even while tattered and covered in waste. A slave's attire was entirely monochromatic, a giant shade of beige or tan.

She'd strapped her umbrella to the outer portion of her leg using a few of Creep's spare knife bands. It made her walk with a limp, but that only added to the image of the poor, injured woman she was trying to depict. Within her closed umbrella were Creep's boots and gloves, making for a rather wonky concealment job. Luckily, the boots were light and easily foldable, forming only a subtle bulge around her knee. The looseness of her trousers made up for that.

They did their best to remain glued to the denser sections of the crowds. Despite the deplorable conditions, she saw a few children running around and playing, oblivious to the fact that this life was neither normal nor just. It struck a chord within her, for she had once been that naïve little girl in Olethros, racing her big brother through the streets and gaining a thrill by stealing produce from unsuspecting merchants. She hadn't been able to see life beyond that.

They drifted through the crowds of slaves with relative ease, receiving no suspicious stares. As she proceeded down what they believed to be the main street, she tried to get a grasp of what the slaves were doing. They didn't seem to be working or following any kinds of orders. And although the street resembled a market, there weren't any shops or stalls for commerce. It seemed they were simply mingling, many of them taking a stroll through the sludge.

It was strange. Here was a large population of people treated less than human, whipped on a daily basis and forced to trek through feces, yet in this moment their mannerisms displayed a façade of tranquility. Why didn't they look miserable? They didn't look happy, but they seemed … content. It wasn't just the children, but also the adults who had accepted this reality.

Stratum Zero circled the hill of Ulna Malen. It was the only stratum that didn't touch the actual hillside. Because of this, a towering wall—perfectly smooth and in no way climbable—ran along the stratum's inner wall. Seeing that no structure reached higher than two stories here, it was visible from anywhere in the stratum of slaves.

The wall grew larger the farther Rhyparia and Creep followed the main road. Despite their proximity, the amount of taskmasters didn't increase like she would have predicted. Maybe they were confident none of the slaves would find a way into Stratum One. The closer she got to the manmade wall, the more this made sense. It may have not been the High Sever, but it was still a behemoth of a barrier.

She'd been refraining from using her ancient in order to infiltrate the higher stratums, but that was starting to look impossible. The best bet would have been to wait until first-night when most of the city slept, and then simply throw herself to the top of the wall with altered gravity.

They walked a considerable distance, and the crowds thinned. It didn't take long to realize why, as she tugged her foot out of the sludge that was now up to her ankles. She looked down in disgust before scanning the street around her. She followed Creep's gaze through a throng of people. Her eyes widened, spotting the source of the stratum's sewage problem. The wide mouth of a pipe—probably as big as a shack itself—jutted from the bottom of the stone wall at a dead-end, spilling into the road. The sludge was likely deep enough to drown in if one stood directly next to the pipe.

"It seems the capital's sewers are built in the hill, this being their exit point," Creep whispered. "There are probably dozens of them scattered across the inner wall."

She couldn't believe it. These slaves lived in a sewage dump. Hundreds of thousands of people used Stratum Zero as a toilet, giving new meaning to the name: Cascade's Closure. It was worse than she could have ever imagined.

Creep sighed. "As vile as it might be, I think I found our way out."

*　　*　　*

First-night came without incident, but it required unbearable patience. Once the sun had set and darkness swept across the stratum a bit past midnight, Rhyparia and Creep snuck their way over to the proximity of the pipe they had seen earlier. It was deep enough to reach their chests, placing the stench directly beneath their noses.

She trudged her way through, her spine stiff from thick bandages circling her upper torso. They had been a special kind Creep carried with him, the exterior made of water-resistant material. The idea was to keep the sewage from seeping into their cuts.

"This is the most disgusting thing I've ever done in my life," she said.

432

While they were outside in the unobstructed view of the residential sector's main road, they were far enough away to look indistinguishable from such a distance. Several taskmasters patrolled the roadways at night, but none of them seemed to get close to the far end of the road, where the sludge was at its deepest. And why would they? There were no buildings or torches down here, and who in their right mind would venture to this point? It was a quarter-mile of waist-deep sewage.

"Do you feel yourself stepping on lumps?" she asked.

He nodded. "There's more stuff in this pool than just excrement."

She shivered at the thought, but tried not to dwell on it. They neared the pipe's mouth, which was tall enough for Toshik or Himitsu to stand comfortably in, and gazed inside. Without light, sight was limited. After a few feet it was pitch-black.

"Constructed with steel," Creep noted.

"I'm guessing they got the iron from the Intel Kingdom," she said. "In exchange for provod."

"That's the deal in this day and age. But no, this pipe has been here for a long time—longer than the iron-provod exchange has existed. I'm guessing this has been here since the mid-500s, when iron was traded for marble."

She frowned, disappointed in the Intel Kingdom for doing business with the Powish for so long. But should she have been all that shocked? The Intelians never had a flattering history in regards to ethics. Mendac was the most recent example of that. She closed her eyes and exhaled slowly. She no longer had a right to judge the actions taken by those who believed them to be just … Not when considering what she had in store for this city.

Creep, now equipped with his gloves and boots, grasped the bottom rim of the pipe and pulled himself upward. He turned and reached down, gesturing for her hand. She grabbed hold and jumped as he pulled, freeing herself from the pool of sewage. The pipe vibrated beneath her, but emanated no sound.

She tried to stand, but the surface was slick with waste. Instead she crawled on hands and knees, trying not to vomit like she had earlier. The stench had intensified in the pipe's confined space. After some distance, she reached out a hand and felt an incline just ahead. It was steep and definitely not scalable.

"Now we know why the taskmasters don't stand watch over the sewer," he said. "Nobody can climb this, not even someone with strength like a Powish."

"Well," she said, finally managing to stand. "Luckily, I'm more than a mere nobody." She looked to her right, where he must have stood based off the sound of his voice. "Have you ever swum through air?"

"No, but I've swum in water like a normal person."

She smirked. "Nearly the same thing, I suppose. I'm going to lighten gravity for the time being. We'll float, then we'll follow the pipe until we find the first grate."

She gripped her umbrella and began to weave. Their feet lifted from the ground.

"You're a piece of work," he said.

She kicked her legs, propelling her upward. "No time to waste."

# 44

# Scattered Missions

Agnos stood at the bow of the Mythmaker, gazing across the marvelous blanket of blue before him. The Sea of Light was calm today, allowing his crew to appreciate a brief period of rest despite the mid-afternoon hours. The Whale Lord had slowed ahead of them, contributing to the leisure. Despite nonexistent winds, Gray Whale didn't seem to be making use of her squallblasters to fill the sails. Thus, he followed her lead, assuming his squallblasters were likely resting in the fighting tops of the three masts.

In this dual-ship voyage, Gray Whale acted as the lead, the complete opposite set-up from their last voyage. Agnos had led that, Gray only acting as an emergency line of defense just in case he needed it—something he hadn't asked for at the time.

"We must get it done before arriving at the whirlpool, Agnos," said Barloe, the newly engaged man who stood next to Agnos, leaning forward against the bow's rail. He proposed to Zorra last night on the main deck for the whole crew to see. She said yes.

"How much longer before we find one?" Agnos asked, ignoring his quartermaster's haste about the wedding. Such a formal event on a pirate ship seemed absurd.

"It can take anywhere from days to weeks to years," Evelyn said. She stood on Agnos's left side, arms folded in front of her, back straight as a washboard. "But with a woman like Captain Gray doing the hunting, it should be on the shorter end of that spectrum. Right, Barloe?"

He nodded. "Her whales are extraordinary whirlpool hunters."

Agnos glanced at Evelyn. "Gray Whale's reputation stretches even into the Dark Realm, eh?"

"Only amongst the sailing community. As I've said previously, I was an aspiring sailor before the Diatia formed."

He looked forward again. "Nobody on my crew has ever gone through a whirlpool."

"That goes for pretty much all of the world," she said.

"Not even me," Barloe admitted. "Gray stayed away from them. I didn't join until after her legendary first voyage. Apparently, it had been a frightening enough experience to have made her avoid them for several decades."

He paused, and they all fell silent. Chatter from the crew buzzed through the air as the sun beamed down on them.

"Large loss of life if not perfectly prepared for," Barloe said. "All it takes is one hiccup from a squallblaster, and the ship will be in danger of capsizing in the whirlpool's current. But I suppose that's why Queen Apsa gave you Troy Sulia. He's traversed four whirlpools in his life, directing the complex maneuvers and weaving combinations of a talented team of squallblasters each time."

"Four?" Evelyn asked, impressed. "That's on the high end—so much so that it's actually an anomaly."

"The Spirit Navy is the king of the seas for a reason," Barloe said. "Still, I would love to get this wedding out of the way before we risk our lives. Eet and Osh are more excited than anyone."

Agnos closed his eyes and stifled a sigh. Gray had been right. The two cabin kids had somehow snuck their way onto the ship before departure from DaiSo. Now they were in a potentially life-threatening situation, likely trying to sneak into his cabin at this very moment to read more of *Erafeen*.

The sea was a terrifying place, and he couldn't even imagine what that voyage had been like for the Thunder Queen and Mind King millennia ago, when their fellow Originators chased them across the Sea of Light. That threat made whirlpools sound tame.

*     *     *

Ophala wore a thick leather glove that reached her elbow. Skyrise, one of her most reliable falcons, was perched on her guarded forearm, pecking away at a dead mouse grasped tightly in her other hand. She held her ancient, Cheiraskinia, in the hand of the arm that supported the falcon.

Her eyes were closed, focused on her weaving as she jumped into the falcon's mind. She saw everything in its recent memories, including the approaching arrival of Himitsu, Kaylee, and Sal to the Central Grasslands. After informing them of Neeko's possible desire to visit the home of Director Senex's widow, they'd chosen that route over the other possibility of Olethros.

She opened her eyes and smiled at the falcon. "Thank you, Sky, for all that you do for me. My son may not be a royal firstborn, but you are his Branian in my eyes. Continue to keep watch over him." She lifted her arm. The bird took flight, gliding toward one of several open windows.

The bird tower of Phelos Palace was active almost every day since Ophala's return to prominence. She had dozens of messenger, scout, and spy birds coming in and out of the tower on an hourly basis. It was her favorite means of communication with powerful members of the True Light alliance. She left the responsibility of broadcast meetings to Archaic King Sigmund like she was supposed to. She didn't care how annoyed this made King Vitio.

As for her scout birds, they were the most useful. Alas, their presence was rare since their objectives usually involved a higher degree of difficulty. Updates were few and far between. It had been some time since she had

437

received a visit from Abyss, the raven seeking evidence of leechers in Accus Canyon. This worried her, for Abyss was her best nocturnal scout. She didn't believe that Himitsu and Kaylee would lie to her about their sighting of such mythical creatures, but surely the raven would have found one by now.

"You okay there, Pilot Ophala?"

She refocused her attention, turning to regard Preevis. Father of Rhyparia NuForce, he was a thin, feeble man. He leaned back against a thin strip of wall that stood between the bird tower's gaping windows.

She smiled. "A lot on my mind, as you already know."

"How is my boy doing?"

"Sal is fine—a good companion for Himitsu and Kaylee."

He grinned and lowered his head, resting his chin atop his neck. His arms were crossed in front of him. "He waited a long time to be of use. I hope he's happy … or as happy as one can be when considering his past."

"I hope you know I'm happy, Preevis," she said. "And that's because of people like you and your son. Without your help over this past year, taking back this kingdom would have been impossible."

His nose curled up, as if he had smelled something foul. "I know you placed that spawn of Itta as this kingdom's ruler, but you are its rightful queen."

"I'm no such thing," she said, shaking her head as she looked toward the light of dawn. "I'm the Pilot of Spy and Sky … which sounds a lot cooler, don't you think?"

He chuckled and pushed himself off the wall. "The Inebriated Pilot of Spy and Sky is more like it."

She batted her eyelashes, turning away and purposefully acting coy. "You flatter me, Mr. NuForce."

He pressed his lips together and shook his head. "I would do no such thing. Horos would kill me with one fell swoop of a knife." He paused and sighed, turning to search the sky.

She knew why he was here. He came up here every time she made a visit. She waited for the question.

"No sight of Boltshot?" he asked.

She held his gaze, but didn't respond. She respected his resiliency, but seeing the disappointment in his face every time she gave him the answer had begun to wear on her. She, too, wanted nothing more than to see Boltshot flying toward the tower, but the reality was sinking in: Rhyparia couldn't be found.

Ophala *did* know that Rhyparia had made it to Epinio, which had been the pilot's main objective. Based off information from Boltshot, the powerful Jestivan had also entered Realmular Tunnel. But, since that time, the eagle hadn't returned with any news. Rhyparia could be dead. In fact, it was the most likely scenario. The chances of survival in Realmular Tunnel were miniscule. Ophala only wished Musku had provided her with more information about the tunnel back during the days when King Itta had her scouting the Archaic Mountains.

"Very well, then," Preevis said, heading for the top of the spiraling staircase.

"Like I said, I'm sure she's okay," she said, succumbing to guilt and injecting him with false hope. "I had Director Senex send her that way for a reason."

He stopped at the top of the stairs and beamed back at her. "I believe in you, Pilot Ophala. Good day."

As he began to descend the stairs, he stopped and moved to the side. She narrowed her eyes, curious as to who else could have been visiting her.

"Good morning, milord," Preevis said.

She had to fight back the urge to roll her eyes. Instead, she reached into the inner pocket of her vest and pulled out a drinking flask. Quickly, she unscrewed the top and tossed the stinging liquid down her gullet.

"Good morning, Pilot."

She lowered the flask, placing it back into her pocket. "King Sigmund, how are you?"

There was a way to Sigmund's movements that irked her. His hesitant step was one thing, but the unbridled anxiety in his tone when he opened his mouth to speak was absolutely nauseating. She had expected to care for this young man like another son, advising him the few moments he really needed it, but he had become a nuisance. Why could he not understand the fact that he was king now? She had even appointed him a worthy set of advisors to speak to when decisions became tough.

"King Vitio would love it if you could attend the broadcast meeting today," he said, following a long, drawn-out *uhhh*.

"I've been maintaining a healthy conversation with him through Radon," she said, turning to tend to one of her crows.

"He says writing is a restricting medium."

"What of the teleplatforms?" she asked, swiftly changing the subject.

After a pause, he said, "Destroyed. All the secret teleplatforms that had been constructed by Tazama are no longer operational."

"Good. And what of the indictment against Elyol Brekton?" She already knew the answers to these questions, but she wanted to hear them from the king's mouth. She also wanted him to think he was giving her information she didn't already know. Perhaps, it'd make him perceive her as reliant on him.

"The jurors seem to be sympathetic toward the man because of his major part in taking out Toth and Wert." He paused. "However, they don't seem to forgive all of his past deeds. He did kill over a hundred soldiers during the uprising, acting as a key player in Toth Brench's forces."

"Have you spoken with Elyol?" she asked.

"I have. He expects to be executed, but is hopeful for a life of imprisonment."

She nodded. "The jury might believe execution is the ultimate form of punishment. However, keeping him alive and locked up in solitude for a lifetime is infinitely more brutal. He knows this; he wants that kind of torture because he feels he deserves it."

The sun had fully risen above the horizon and was now beaming against her face. A long pause carried between the two of them. The sound of fluttering wings and bird cries overpowered the silence.

"I've sent more reinforcements to the Intel Kingdom in case of invasion by the Devish," he said.

"As long as you're still here, I don't care."

"Right …" he muttered. He'd spoken of temporarily vacating his throne in order to travel to the Intel Kingdom and provide aid, but she'd shot down the idea every time. This kingdom needed its king, especially one who had a proper Branian. If something catastrophic were to happen to the Archaic Kingdom, the Branian would be the key to stopping it.

"Any progress on the interrogations of the Lost Wisdom staff, Pilot?"

She extended her hand, allowing the crow to hop onto a perch. She turned and regarded Sigmund. "Very little, but I'm looking forward to getting my hands on their paperwork. I want to learn about their operations. We're still trying to figure out what the item was that we discovered in certain rooms of the orphanage. It's something unnaturally ominous and depressing and, from what we've gathered, needs a Cynnish wielder in order to make it work."

He sighed. "To think the kingdom has housed Dark Realm natives, and *Cynnish* of all ethnicities. Makes you wonder how they got here."

"Come now, milord," she said, walking across the room and stepping past her king. "We both know it had to have been either Itta or Dolomarpos." She swept down the stairs. "We'll talk later, Sigmund."

*      *      *

"Fun fact about the Central Grasslands," Kaylee said, as the trio spotted the tall prairie grass just beyond the desert sand.

"More meaningless words from the human encyclopedia," Sal said, sweat running down his face.

The multiday trek through the desert had been hard on the man built like a furnace. Himitsu had traversed through part of the desert a couple of years ago after retrieving Bryson, Olivia, and others from Rim. That journey hadn't lasted nearly as long, for they had moved with a greater sense of urgency. They also didn't have Sal slowing them down.

"People often question how there is a prairie smack-dab in the middle of a desert," she said, ignoring Sal's jab. "The belief is aquifers. Some believe an underground river flows from the west, underneath Throno, the Bliss Peaks, and the western half of the Archaic Desert. Then, at a certain point underneath the desert, the river disperses into layers of rock traveling up toward the surface of the land, acting as an aquifer and nourishing the soil. That's why grass grows here. It also explains the random lake in the center of the grasslands."

"Riveting," Sal said, lifting the bottom of his shirt to wipe his face.

"Underground rivers …" Himitsu said. "Nature is wild."

Kaylee grinned and nodded. She looked up, watching as Skyrise turned and flew in the direction from which they had come. The falcon had been guiding them since departing from Balle. Now that they were approaching the grasslands, he was likely going to inform Himitsu's mother.

"Do any of us know exactly where this woman's house is?" Sal asked.

As they crossed through scattered patches of grass, Himitsu shook his head. The grasslands were vast enough to require days to search properly. Homes were few and far between save for a very tiny market that, according to his mother, only popped up once a week … on a Tuesday. Since today was Thursday, their best bet at asking around for directions wouldn't come for nearly a week. Either they'd have to wait for Skyrise to return or get lucky by accidentally stumbling upon the home of Senex's widow.

"Imagine living in a place like this," Kaylee said, scanning the stretch of green before them.

"My mom would have never allowed it," Sal said. "She thrived on relevance, and there is nothing relevant about this place. While the same could have been said about Olethros, at least it was close to stuff."

"Was it hard growing up under your mother?" Himitsu asked. "Forgive me for my brashness, but she was an evil woman and I'm glad she's dead."

Kaylee's head snapped toward him, her silvery hair whipping around to her other shoulder. There was a fierce slant to her eyebrows, but they relaxed as she looked at Sal, likely noticing something in his aura.

"My mom was confusing," he said, looking toward the sky. "She was the most unassuming lady, round and physically unfit, yet she had an indescribable power over our family. I guess I didn't really learn why my father feared her as much as he did until discovering her prowess with weaving and ancients. She was a lady who revered King Itta when he was alive, and I remember her speaking highly of King Dolomarpos, too. She'd always wanted Itta to match his father's intensity."

"Not the best idols to have …" Kaylee muttered.

"Not at all."

Himitsu's nose wrinkled as he squinted into the distance. "I wonder why she was so skilled with ancients."

"I don't know," Sal said. "I never met any of my distant relatives, and my mom didn't speak much about her past at all. However, she did mention being raised in the Thousand-Layer Loess."

"Don't they have a lot of healers?" Himitsu asked.

Sal shrugged.

"They do," Kaylee said. "The Thousand-Layer Loess is comprised of hundreds of villages, all of which specialize in a category of healing. And they're all connected via a network of underground tunnels and caverns for easy travel between layers of the loess. It's like an ant farm, but on a massive scale for humans."

"You should go there and learn some things for apothecary," Himitsu said, smiling at her.

"That was once an option, for they have fantastic apprenticeship programs." She paused. "But I want to focus on this for now. I want to know what happened to Neeko, and if it helps True Light in the war against the Rogue Demon, even better."

Himitsu came to a stop, Kaylee and Sal following suit. Ahead of them, gentle hills rolled in green waves. "That's a lot of land to comb. This should be fun."

Sal pressed forward, muttering under his breath. He wasn't thrilled with all of the lulls in this mission, and Himitsu couldn't blame him. Reconnaissance work was boring. He supposed there was a reason why he was an assassin and not a spy.

*　　　*　　　*

Rocks and boulders dotted the lands between Necrosis Valley and Cogdan. Toshik, Horos, and Kuiku were exhausted after a long journey through the barren valley. They had brought just enough water and dried meat to last them until their arrival at the capital, but it had required consuming only meager portions.

Toshik had underestimated the valley's length. When he visited it years ago to rescue Olivia, he hadn't seen much of it. They had approached from the eastern side and remained in that one section. Now he understood the measures Dev King Storshae had taken to avoid encountering any threats. To forgo the comfortable route through Rence in favor of the sweltering heat wave of the valley said a lot. It felt like it was hot enough for Toshik's sweat to evaporate the moment it leaked from his pores, and there wasn't a single source of water anywhere nearby.

Now that he was at the cusp of civilization, he counted his blessings. His time in Tames had softened him. The distant town had been a relaxing place without any real threats, which worried the three of them. Horos had mentioned it a while ago. Where were the spies or scouts? Why hadn't they been confronted by any soldiers? With Toono aware of their presence, wouldn't he have sent men to handle the intruders?

Toono peeked out from behind the right side of a rock; Horos and Kuiku did the same on the left. The capital's main gate, which stood at the northeastern corner, was open. The wall was made of blanched white stone that glowed blue beneath the starlight of second-night. Instead of carrying torches, guards stood with them floating by their heads—likely a result of their telekinesis.

He recalled the first time in his life he'd seen the Devish's signature ability. Was it four or five years ago now? When Devish soldiers had somehow infiltrated the Generals' Battle, assassinated Archaic General Inias, then laid waste to hundreds of innocent spectators largely because of telekinetic attacks. That had been the start of all the chaos—a mere two months after the Jestivan had formed. They hadn't been prepared, placing Kuki Sphaira in a world war that still raged to this day.

"How do we go about this?" Kuiku asked. Toshik watched as a convoy of carriages filtered through the main gate. While it was dark outside, second-night meant it was the heart of afternoon—busy trade and travel hours.

"I'd say it's time we finally put my flames to use," Horos said.

Toshik sucked his teeth. "I'll just run."

"And how is that going to help us?" Horos asked, untwisting his body and returning to a seated position behind the rock.

"Keep up," Toshik said.

Kuiku chuckled. "I can't keep up with you anymore, Toshik. And I doubt I can move fast enough for my movement to be untraceable by their eyes."

"Well, I can, so I'll run."

Horos scowled. "Why must you be a pain in the ass? My specialty is stealth, so let's put it to use."

Toshik turned to regard the man's scarred face and bearded chin, none of them had been able to groom in over a week. "Let's make this a competition, old man," Toshik said. "I'll run and you can use your black fire. Whoever gets into the capital first wins."

"As if I'd do something so reckless during a mission this impor—"

Toshik dashed toward a rock closer to Cogdan's wall, not hearing the rest of Horos's sentence, though it was clear what the man was trying to get across. He darted behind another rock, then another, moving like a rain droplet through the crevices of a brick wall. Back and forth, following the only path given to him.

It didn't take long before the sky became black. He looked up to see white dots speckling the sky, but not emitting light. He then looked down and extended his arm, trying to find his hand with no luck. Horos was on the move, and he wasn't trying to be inconspicuous about it. Toshik had figured the assassin would have woven his normal black flames, disguising them as a distant backdrop of the night sky. He didn't think Horos would commit to something like this, something so obvious.

Toshik turned and felt along the boulder's cold, smooth surface. He peered around the side in search of the main gate. While everything directly surrounding him was pitch-black, he could see dim light in the distance. It still wasn't enough to illuminate details of the gate's surroundings, but he could spot the flame of the torches. That was the direction he needed to run, and he needed to do so quickly.

The Devish were prepared for such a scenario. As Toshik sprinted at his highest speed percentage toward the gate, the flames of the torches disappeared, likely doused by the savvier officers. He also assumed they were trying to close the gate as quickly as possible. If he hadn't been running at such a high speed, wind whipping against his ears, he would have probably heard the squeal of the gate.

He could only keep running straight. Otherwise, he would splatter into the wall. The images of torchlight were engrained in his memory, so he was sure he was on the right path. The cacophony from the panicking crowds somewhere beyond the gate also helped.

Suddenly, the darkness disappeared and the starlight returned. His eyes skittered around. He was in the center of a busy road. A lot of people had scattered, cowering at the sides of the street and hugging against buildings. Many adults had simply dropped where they were standing, shielding their children with their bodies just in case of attack.

Toshik adopted a role, like the actors in the play he had watched in Tames. He looked around in confusion, acting as if he had just risen out of a crouch. As his eyes adjusted to the return of starlight, he spotted other civilians doing the same. The screaming had stopped, but whispers quickly commenced. Most of them—if not all—had no idea what could have created such a phenomenon. Even Passion Assassins hadn't been known to achieve something like that.

Toshik turned, and his jaw nearly dropped to the floor from what he saw. The gate was quite a ways behind him. He had underestimated his speed percentage and the distance he could travel in a small window. Seeing this did more than reassure him. All of his training was coming to fruition. Soon, he'd be ready to go after Yama.

Torches sprung to life around him, slowly spreading warmth throughout the street. Civilians began to stir, but they wouldn't get far, for constables had begun to sweep the street. They apprehended everyone—men, women, and children alike. The screaming commenced once again, and children wailed desperately as they were separated from their parents.

Toshik's eyes raked the area of street around him, watching as the ordeal unfolded. He glanced right, then left, catching sight of a darkened alley. His eyes narrowed as he sniffed at the air. He frowned, sensing a foul odor. Were Horos and Kuiku in that alleyway? No, they couldn't have made it this far already.

He glanced up, toward the roofs of the surrounding buildings. Knowing Himitsu for as long as he had, he'd become familiar with an assassin's preferred maneuvers. Sure enough, he saw a slight alteration in the blackness of the night sky. There was a wall of black flames surging down the rooftops, invisible to all of the untrained eyes in the streets. Horos and Kuiku were likely sprinting just behind it.

Toshik scanned the street one last time. Two constables had taken an interest in him and were now headed his way. He stepped to the left and found himself in the alleyway almost instantly, covering more than a dozen yards with ease. He glanced back out the alley, spotting the two stunned constables. To their eyes, he had vanished into thin air as if teleporting.

Something grabbed his shoulder. He whirled, grabbing the hilt of his sheathed sword at his waist. He straightened, spotting a grin from Horos Vevlu. Kuiku stood just behind him.

Toshik released his grip of his sword. "I win, old man."

Horos chuckled and nodded slowly. Before he could respond, a dazzling light lit the street. They looked up to find the source. A holographic display hovered high above. Inside was a dark-skinned woman with deep blue hair and eyebrows—a woman both Toshik and Kuiku were very familiar with: Tazama Bandia.

"We have intruders in the capital," she said, her voice echoing across many holograms throughout the city. "True Light has sent what they believe to be elite warriors into our lands. It is time they learn the difficult truth of Devish might. To those intruders, I ask you this, are your lives worth it?"

Toshik's brows furrowed and his jaw clenched. Kuiku placed his hand on Toshik's shoulder. Horos grumbled and muttered, "Death is likely, but that must not come until we find the Oracle's grave and dispose of his body for good."

"Easier said than done," Kuiku said.

Toshik balled up his fists. "I'm not dying before Yama."

# 45

# A Surgeon's Shock

Toono watched from a balcony as the peaceful star-speckled sky of the Dark Realm's afternoon turned into a smattering of luminescent holographic displays that hung above several sectors of the city. Tazama's face occupied every single one of them, and he raised an eyebrow at the spectacle. What had happened?

Following her warning, the displays vanished into thin air. He straightened up, replacing his resting elbows on the banister with his hands. He had told Tazama a while ago to raise the alarm bells if something significant ever occurred, but for some reason, he had doubted her ability to do such a thing. She wasn't one for overreactions after all.

"There's an issue at the city's main gate, Demon."

He turned to see Homina stepping onto the balcony from the parlor. He tried to choose rooms where people would least likely find him, but she always had a knack for sniffing him out. He was beginning to believe she had the ability of clairvoyance; it'd explain her daughter's prowess.

"What kind of issue?" The balcony he'd chosen for his personal reflection tonight faced the south side of the city, so the main gate was nowhere in sight.

"Still Warden Moroza had spotted a large shadowy mass consume the main entrance, like a dome of black had swallowed the streets and sky. It absorbed all light, including the stars. Soon after, we received confirmation from our intelligence personnel stationed at the gate that someone had likely entered the city. They don't have an explanation for the blackout, however."

He turned away, returning to his relaxed position against the banister. He knew it was a Passion Assassin—a very skilled one at that. "Thank you for the update," he said. "You may leave. This is my lone moment of solitude for the day."

"Why are you so calm?" she asked. "Should I remind you there are also True Light vessels sailing down the river at this very moment? They'll approach Cogdan Lake in two weeks' time."

Toono glanced toward the port of the lake, a massive stretch of black to the south of Cogdan.

"Let them come," he said.

*     *     *

A detailed map of the Dark Sea was sprawled across a massive, unpolished table. Spirit Queen Apsa leaned over one side of it, making mental notes of the most recent positional updates of every True Light vessel. They were making great time, descending upon the Dev Kingdom's mainland river a week faster than predicted. Her forces were running through SCAPD ships with relative ease.

"Milady," someone behind her murmured.

She turned to find Joy, her most valuable Dev servant, standing in the open doorway. "Hello, Joy."

"I have news from Captain Yiro, milady."

"Shut the door," Apsa said, waving her inside.

Joy entered the room and did as instructed.

"What is it?" Apsa asked, preparing herself for bad news. Captain Yiro wasn't stationed in the Dark Realm, but was on one of the smaller warships in charge of patrolling the Sea of Light.

"Enemy forces have finally been spotted spilling through multiple whirlpools," Joy said. "Some have crashed, but many have successfully gotten through. Captain Yiro wasn't trying to downplay this warning, milady. He said Cynnish and Devish galleons have been seen. Ships from the Adren Kingdom have also begun confronting our blockade at the Adren Connector."

"Did he give any exact numbers?" Apsa asked.

"He's personally seen ten through whirlpools. Other captains are also starting to report similar sightings. He's estimating north of sixty ships, milady ... not counting the galleons from the Adren Kingdom."

"Sixty?" Apsa echoed, gawking at the map of the Dark Sea. It was no wonder why her forces in the Dark Realm's waters were making such progress. The opposition impeding them was thin—and purposefully so. Was Toono planning an assault? Was he on one of the ships? Or was this all a ruse, and the ships simply sacrificial pawns to a greater strategic maneuver?

Sixty warships were enough to put up a fight against the blockade she had formed at the connector between the Intel River and Sea of Light. But who was to say there weren't more on their way?

She looked up and stared out the window of the cartographer chamber, gazing emptily at the blue sky. What would the Intelian, Archain, and Passionian ships do when confronted by a Dark Realm foe? She had confidence in the Spirit Navy to counter such unique circumstances; her sailors prepared for it at a young age. However, her allied kingdoms wouldn't understand how to battle Powish, Cynnish, or Devish ships, save a few of the specialist crews who were sent into the Dark Sea.

Like the Spiritian squallblasters, Passionian firefighters, and Intelian seashockers, the Dark Realm kingdoms had utility specialists, too. How would an inexperienced True Light vessel react to the tidal waves of a Devish waveweilder, the hurtling projectiles of a Powish stoneslinger, or the inexplicable sensation of a Cynnish woodrotter?

She closed her eyes and exhaled slowly, trying to calm herself. She had planned for this, assigning one of her top Spirit sailors to every True Light ship. Now she needed to get word to all of them as fast as possible about a potential attack, that way they could hammer down on teaching the crews about Dark Realm battle tactics at sea. And she knew exactly how to alert them.

"Are you still there, Joy?"

"Yes, milady."

"I'll be speaking with the royal heads later today, but I need you to get in touch with Spy Pilot Ophala immediately. I need the assistance of as many of her messenger birds as possible. They must be sent to every single one of our ships, alerting Spirit sailors as to what is happening. They must be prepared for what is to come."

"Of course, milady."

The chamber door shut, and Apsa studied the Dark Sea's map. Her prior elation now felt foolish. She had been naïve. Toono wanted her ships to penetrate the Dev Kingdom's rivers. The deeper they traveled, the less possible it was for them to turn back and search for a whirlpool in a timely manner.

She thought of Gray Whale and Agnos. Had they already found a whirlpool and crossed into the Dark Realm? If so, she had made a grave mistake.

*　　*　　*

Bryson lay shirtless in bed early Sunday morning with the covers flung across the floor as he stared at the ceiling of his room. One hand was resting beneath the back of his head while the other sat atop his chest, his fingers occasionally dragging across the scars that read "T2". Ever since finding Mendac's lab and learning about his theories, Bryson had tried to piece together the connection between the significance of his scars and the information in the theories. So far, he had found nothing that correlated, nor had Lilu.

451

He rolled over on his side and stared at the wardrobe standing against the far wall. One thing was certain about Mendac's theories, and it had bothered Bryson for the entire week since discovering them: he'd been nothing but the subject of an experiment. He now had an even greater understanding of his mother's blind hatred toward the man. Mendac's objective in the Still Kingdom all those years ago was to bed Apoleia with the ultimate goal of producing an offspring who could prove his theories correct. After failing to seduce her, he forced himself on her. Bryson became the result. Thus, she had viewed him as the reason for Mendac's crimes. In a way, Bryson felt responsible.

He had struggled with this revelation, spilling tears of rage on a nightly basis. His father had raped a woman all for the purpose of an experiment, viewing her as a means to an end. Bryson couldn't even comprehend the kind of evil that had to stir within someone for them to commit something so heartless. Mendac was a snake—no, worse than that. He was a demonic thing that twisted and writhed like a snake, but too massive and vile to be considered something so simple. A basilisk would have been too kind a word.

Bryson rolled further, placing his face in his pillow. How much had his mother known about Mendac's objectives? It was unlikely she had known beforehand, but had she learned after the incident? Bryson had never known much about Olivia and Apoleia's involvement following Mendac's crime. He didn't know if Olivia had been operated on like he had or if she had even been around following their birth. In Debo's memory, there was no sign of her in the lab. Had they been separated in their early years?

A knock thrummed through the door. He tilted his head and looked toward it. "Who is it?"

"Lilu."

He dropped an arm off the side of the bed and retrieved his shirt. He sat up, pulled it over his head, and stuck his arms through the sleeves. He wiped his eyes and cheeks on the collar. "Come in," he said, forcing depth into his tone.

The door opened, revealing the royal Jestivan in simple trousers and a pretty blouse of blue, a daisy pinned to her bangs.

"It took some convincing, but I think it's time we try to fix your clout problem," she said.

"How?"

"How do you feel about surgery?" she asked. After a long pause of silence from him, she nodded. "I understand what I'm asking of you. Putting you under a scalpel isn't ideal. It can resurface awful memories, and the pain might be extreme." She sighed. "But I don't know what else to do. This is the best solution I can think of."

He looked off to the side, his eyes growing distant. How would he react to lying on an operation table? The image of Mendac's lab was still vivid in his mind, with their discovery of it happening just a week ago. As his hands hung limp between his knees, he tried to emit a surge of energy from them. All he got were sparks.

He stood and grabbed his hoodie from the bedpost. He put it on, zipped up the front, and threw the hood over his head, shrouding his face in shadows. He reached for his hair and pulled several thick locks down in front of his face, then walked toward Lilu and the door. He stepped past her, gazing at the floor. It was a pitiful sight; he knew it. He had reverted to his younger self, before becoming a Jestivan. Sulking. Depressed. He didn't care.

"Let's go," he muttered, not a single ounce of conviction in his voice.

After a moment, he heard the door of his room close behind him and Lilu's footsteps against the wooden floorboards as she followed him down the hall.

*     *     *

Bryson didn't mutter a single word throughout their walk. They covered a lot of ground, traveling across the Bastion of Intel, crossing into Brilliance above, and then turning down many streets in the city. He didn't question her about anything she had planned. This was mainly because he didn't want to know, but also because he trusted her judgment and had faith in her ability. He was sure whoever she had picked as his surgeon was well-suited for the job. This meant even if it was a LeAnce, he wouldn't put up a fight. The war was too important, and his electricity was vital to it.

They wound up walking along the gated front entrance to IWA's grounds, a rare acreage or two of grass just beyond, crammed between towering buildings at its sides. As they entered the academy's grounds and approached the front steps, he had a feeling he knew who they were going to see. Sure enough, after scaling a few staircases and winding down hallways, they came to a stop just outside of a classroom's open door.

They peeked inside and saw a class of seventeen- to eighteen-year-old students. Bryson remembered those years. Even though he was only twenty-one, it felt like ages ago. Just over five years had passed since his induction into the Jestivan.

Professor Jugtah stood at the front of the room. Surprisingly, his thick-rimmed golden glasses weren't crowding his face, but resting peacefully on his desk. Bryson had never seen the professor without them on. As students began to spot their guests at the doorway, whispers were exchanged, some leaning across desks to tap their friend's shoulders.

Jugtah turned with squinted eyes, making his face look pudgier than it already was. Apparently, his spectacles were necessary. His eyes relaxed, distinguishing who had disrupted his lesson. "Ah, Lilu and Bryson." He picked up his glasses and put them on, then looked down at his wristwatch. "You're a few minutes earlier than expected, but ..." he trailed off and sighed, turning away to regard his students. "I suppose I can end class now."

His class wasted no time jumping at the opportunity. Chairs skidded against the floor as students nearly jumped from their seats, retrieving their bags and belongings before making a mad dash toward the exit. Lilu and Bryson stepped out of the way to clear a passage. Some students purposefully looked away as they passed, others stared without shame.

One girl stopped and asked to hug Lilu, who accepted the embrace without question. After letting go, the girl looked at Bryson and bowed her head slightly. "It's an honor, Prince Bryson."

"You don't have to bow," he said, frowning. "Why can't I get a hug, too?"

She leapt forward and squeezed him tightly, pinning his arms at his side. It was the kind of hug Jilly would have given; a hug you'd expect from a child. Lilu smiled at him.

"Thank you," he said after being freed. "I don't want people bowing to me."

"You and Princess Lilu are just alike!" she said. "Wait until I tell my little brother I spoke to both of you!" With that, she whirled and sprinted down the hall.

He pressed his hand against his ribs in efforts to massage them. Lilu laughed. "Come now, Bryson. Anyone who knew Jilly should be used to that."

One more student filed out, each footstep accompanied by a jingle. Bryson looked for the source of the sound, and then hated himself for doing so. The young man wore a belt around his waist, metal rods dangling from hooks. Heat climbed Bryson's neck. It had been years since he last saw such an accessory, an image that paid homage to Mendac LeAnce.

Bryson tried to pursue the student, but Lilu's hand grasped a chunk of his hoodie. He looked back at her, and she shook her head. "Not worth it," she whispered. "Believe me, I know. You must pick and choose your battles here. We'll make a change, but it must be done on a grander scale. Confronting him will do nothing."

"As per usual, Lilu's right, Bryson."

Jugtah had appeared in the doorway of his classroom, leaning against the frame. "You let him wear that thing in your class?" Bryson asked.

Jugtah's lips thinned, his gaze following his student as he disappeared around a corner down the hall. "The students can wear what they want. I can't push my political or moral agenda on them. It's unfortunate and frustrating, but that's the rules of IWA. The young man isn't harming anyone, so I can't do anything."

Bryson pulled his hood over his head again, eyes growing fierce.

"Anyway," Jugtah said, "it's time we head elsewhere. We can't do this here. I'm sure you understand the risks involved in what will be unfolding."

Bryson nodded, staring at the floor.

"Very well, then. Lilu, you know where to go."

*       *       *

Hours later, Bryson found himself in Jugtah's new home, the same home they had used a week ago to sneak into Brilliance's sewers. He stood in a room small enough to be considered a walk-in closet. A large viewing window stretched across one wall next to a side door. The other wall housed racks for the hanging of lab coats, protective goggles, gloves, and other medical and safety equipment. A sink and some kind of shower crowded the small far wall.

He and Lilu watched Jugtah through the window. He was in the much grander operation room, preparing his workspace. Bright neon Intelights gave the room a bluish hue. A narrow bed with white sheets stood menacingly at the center, carts of surgical tools surrounding it, a foldable Intelamp to the side.

Bryson had begun to sweat, forcing him to remove his hoodie. Surprisingly, this didn't help. Now he felt a chill, causing his limbs to shake and skin to crawl. He wiped a bead of sweat from his eyebrow. What was happening? He felt two conflicting temperatures at once.

"Are you okay?"

He nodded but didn't look Lilu's way. As he watched Jugtah fidget with objects that made no sense to him, all he could see on that empty bed was his five-year-old self, chest sliced open and ribs exposed.

His hands trembled as illness grabbed ahold of him, causing him to lurch forward. His chest tightened and his mind fogged. And suddenly he felt himself lying down, his bare back pressed against the cold steel of the operating table, tears flooding his eyes as he stared at the dirty ceiling of a dingy room. His father leaned over him, a surgeon's mask covering his mouth and nose, eyes a fierce blue. Then he lowered the scalpel to Bryson's chest and began to carve.

"He's going into shock!"

He didn't know who screamed it, but it was loud enough to penetrate his visions. It sounded like Lilu. He felt the blade cutting into his chest, but at the same time felt someone trying to grab onto his arm and squeeze him tight.

"Snap out of it, Bryson," she whispered gently, her voice shaking with desperation. "This was a bad idea."

"He's sweating profusely," Jugtah said, sounding as if he was submerged in water. "Let me …" His voice trailed off, and Bryson wanted to reach out and try to grab hold of it. Seconds later, he felt a wet rag pressed against his face. Cold water jolted him from his episode, and he was back in the prep room outside the surgical area.

He was seated on the floor, back against the wall. Lilu sat next to him, holding on for dear life, as if she was his only anchor to reality. He wanted to puke. His chest was constricted, and it felt like ants were crawling up his throat.

"We need to take him to a bedroom far away from here," Jugtah said. "He needs rest, and we'll have to sedate him before even bringing him back."

Weakly, Bryson slumped against Lilu, her shoulder serving as a head rest. He shivered as another chilly blast rushed up his spine. She didn't let go of him, and he trusted that she wouldn't any time soon.

# 46

# Lord Rattius

It took a couple of weeks for Illipsia to muster up the courage to commit to her next test of hallucinogenics. She walked through the empty halls of Phesaw's school building, using clairvoyance to make sure nobody occupied any surrounding classrooms or adjacent hallways. She slowed as she approached an intersection, poking her head around a corner where a lavish, ornate door sat at the end of the hall. It was the door to Ms. Neaneuma's office, once belonging to the Grand Director.

Illipsia crept down the hall, the thick silence proving bothersome to her psyche. Her clairvoyance told her there was a presence in the office. Based off the signal's intensity, it was clearly Ms. Neaneuma.

She slid to the side of the door, pressing her back against the stone wall. Dusk's amber light splashed across sections of the hall. Refugees were far away from the main building, either playing in Phesaw Park or enjoying the activities elsewhere. The school should have been empty at this time save Ms. Neaneuma and Yvole.

Illipsia waited patiently and remained quiet. The last thing she wanted to do was make the woman think someone was outside her room. That would have been too suspicious.

After waiting roughly an hour, the door finally opened. Illipsia wove a cylindrical wall of Dev Chains around her, replacing reality with an image from her mind, an image that only showed the floor and wall, not her.

Ms. Neaneuma stepped out of the room with a fan in her hand, waving it at her face in efforts to cool herself off. The elderly lady stopped and glanced to her left, staring at the exact spot where Illipsia stood. Her eyes narrowed, a hand reaching out to grasp at the air. Illipsia jumped back, but her focus remained on the weaving. She had to alertly adjust thousands of Dev Chains to keep the projected image consistent. She steadied her breath as Ms. Neaneuma pulled her hand back, gaze locked on the spot. After a protracted pause, she returned to fanning herself as she limped down the hallway.

Illipsia watched intently until the woman disappeared. She ran down a separate corridor until she felt safe enough to fall to the floor and crumple against the wall. Her bold test had been worth it. She had come a long way, to the point where she could fool a pair of eyes like Ms. Neaneuma's. Now that she knew this, she could focus entirely on the locks. Her mission was nearing completion.

*　　　*　　　*

A couple of weeks had passed since Rhyparia and Creep had decided to split ways upon their arrival to Stratum One after maneuvering through the sewers. Since then, Creep had spent his time gathering information by observing the civilians and snooping in on conversations. Doing so had led him up the hierarchical ladder of Powish society with little to no effort at all. Of course, he was a master spy who had spent his entire life doing such work, so this was second nature to him.

He stood in the side yard of the lofty estate of House Gromel, pressed against the building. It was half past five o'clock in the afternoon, which meant the sun was slowly slipping from behind Earth, signaling second-day's dawn. Soon the property would be blanketed in a dim gray, as if a sheet of black tint hung above them.

This served Creep well. It lent him a darkness he could work with. And with the carriages and guests gathering at the front of the estate, that's where most of the security's focus was. He'd infiltrated House Gromel's grounds a few hours ago, during the darkest moments of second-night. Rhyparia had stopped by to provide her gravitational assistance, for the walls of the estate's property were too high for him to climb in a timely manner. After assisting him, she'd left to focus on her own objectives elsewhere in the city.

House Gromel was throwing a grand ball today, and Creep had to get in the house before sunlight splashed across the grounds. For now, it was just dim enough to scale the wall without being spotted from afar. The hedges that hugged the bottom of the estate also served as sufficient cover, though their leaves stabbed him in the face with prickles.

Typically, his trench coat could protect him from something so minor, but that was long gone and now replaced by a blue suit, something more suitable for a ball. He was happy to have been lent money from Rhyparia. His Primmish coin would have held no value in a Powish tailor shop. He was also thrilled he got to keep his beard, a fashionable trend for Powish males.

He turned and looked up, already positioned between two columns of stone that jutted out from the wall. There was just enough space between them to press a hand and foot against the side of each one.

He began to climb, pushing himself up with his boots, and then reaching up farther with his gloved hands. It was a common maneuver of a stealth specialist, so he did it without much thought. The key was to always keep either one's feet or hands pressed against the stone. If a hand and foot lifted at the same time … Well, have a fun plunge.

He reached the third story and pressed his feet against a ledge that extended from the pillar. Just above him, on the estate's top floor, was the underside of a balcony. He walked outward, until his back was no longer against the wall, and then came to a stop at the end of the pillars and looked up. Did he trust himself enough to jump at such an awkward angle and grasp onto the floor of the balcony? He had studied it earlier in the night from below and determined it was doable, but now that he was directly beneath it, he began second-guessing himself. He wasn't a young lad anymore.

He shook his head and smirked; Praetor would have had his head for such a mindset. That man would have been able to achieve this at the age of ninety. Creep couldn't be shown up. Besides, the sun had slipped from behind Earth, the tint across the land brightening. If he didn't commit to this now, he'd be exposed.

He craned his neck, preparing for the awkward jump. He leapt and twisted his body so that he was facing the building. Thrusting both arms upward, he clung to the wooden balcony. One hand slapped the floor while the other grasped onto the base of a support beam. If this wasn't holy wood, the beam would have likely snapped. He'd be plummeting toward the shrubbery four floors below.

He pulled himself up, allowing only the top of his head to peek above the floor. He checked for any guests or tenants before yanking himself up the rest of the way, grasping onto the banister and placing his feet between the beams. Then he kicked both legs over, leaping onto the deck.

He inched toward the sliding glass door and looked inside at what appeared to be an office. A large desk sat to the right side, bookshelves lining the wall behind it. The room was paneled with sleek dark brown wood, and the floor was a matching hardwood. An armchair, sofa, and coffee table occupied the space just in front of the desk, an opulent red carpet with golden etchings sprawled below it all. It was a warming space, but more importantly, it was vacant.

He tried to slide open the door, but it wouldn't budge. Obviously, entry wouldn't come easy. With the sun showing itself and the crowds growing louder near the front of the estate, he needed to get inside now and take advantage of the chaos in the public areas of the building. With the importance of this ball, getting lost in the shuffle shouldn't prove too difficult.

He pressed a button at his wrist. A blade slipped down his forearm and into his gloved hand. It was his most precious knife, crafted of spunka steel by one of the most skilled craftsmen in the Light Realm—and no, not a member of the Brench family. This was the product of Soraku, a woman who called Yinyon her home. Nobody compared. Her stern glare as she operated her grindstone flashed through his mind, and he smiled, yearning for something he hadn't had in decades … a companion.

In his twenties, he had been assigned the mission of gathering intelligence from the village of Yinyon. Soraku quickly stood out as an important member. He spied on her, grew close to her, and then ultimately received information that could have demolished everything the woman loved and represented. He was supposed to relay this information to his superior, Praetor Poicus—this had been before his shocking transition to the role of Grand Director of Phesaw. However, Creep had chosen to avoid Praetor after returning to Phelos in favor of reaching out to Mynute Senex, another elite spy and the leader of a separate unit.

Such an act had been taboo. One didn't go around the back of their direct superior in favor of their colleague. Still, Creep didn't regret it, and Mynute didn't scold him for it. Instead, the man known as the Critter assigned Creep a mission of his own: travel to Asalka in the Prim Kingdom and act as a spy, but most importantly, never speak of what was learned about Yinyon to anyone. Doing so would only destroy the village.

Creep continued to stare at the knife, remembering the day Soraku had offered it to him as a gift. She had done so with a rare smile, and it had followed her revelation of Yinyon's greatest secret. She had entrusted him with everything, going as far as breaking the first ordinance of her people: *Never reveal our true nature.*

That night, he'd left the village and abandoned her, vowing to never work under the likes of Praetor Poicus again. He'd keep Yinyon's secrets safe, but he couldn't stay any longer. If so, Praetor himself would have hunted him down—the last thing that village needed. Creep had abandoned Soraku just when she laid it all on the line for him. He should have left the knife; he didn't deserve such a gift. But a selfish part of him wanted to keep a piece of her with him.

His gaze roved up to the door. He pressed the tip of his knife into the glass, piercing it like butter. Spunka steel was a cherished commodity, which was why the Brench family became filthy rich. However, even they never understood its real potential.

Soraku did. The strongest spines didn't come from an adult female; they came from an elderly female—a spunka well into its fifties. They could live for sixty years, but because the Brench family slayed most of them in their twenties, they'd never reach that age. Soraku, on the other hand, knew the proper targets.

Creep ran the knife through the glass, carving a circular section out of the door, angling the blade so the glass would fall outward. If it fell inside the room, he wouldn't be able to stop it from shattering against the hardwood. He caught the sheet of glass and placed it on the balcony. He then stepped through the hole, bending over considerably to squeeze through. He straightened up on the other side, returning Soraku's knife to his forearm brace hidden beneath the sleeve of his suit. He closed the curtains to hide the glass; then, buttoning up his cuff, he swept across the office.

The door opened before reaching halfway across the room. He dashed to the right and slid across the top of the desk, constantly weaving in the process to make sure he didn't make any noise. He landed in a rolling leather chair, but quickly slipped off and crawled beneath the desk, its grand size allowing plenty of shadows in which to disappear.

He heard footsteps approach the desk and walk around it. His breathing was heavy, but noiseless. A young man came to a stop in front of the bookcase directly behind the desk. He seemed to skim through the spines of the books, searching for a specific one. He crouched for a better look at the bottom shelves, and Creep prayed the man wouldn't turn around.

The man was a slave, and not one of the well-treated ones. The sleeves of his dirty tunic were rolled up at his elbows, exposing bandage and bruises around his forearms. His trousers were also raised to his knees, brandishing even more punishment to his calves.

Creep had come to House Gromel for a reason, learning it was the worst house in terms of its treatment of slaves. Most of the wealthier families treated slaves poorly, but none compared to Gromel's wrath. Their torture methods were primitive, dating back to the first few centuries of the Power Kingdom. It was one thing to have your muscles and bones slowly contorted and broken down by a Powish grip, but for it to be done by the mighty hands of a giant ... there was no mercy.

How many times had this young man's limbs been mangled? It would explain his ginger movements, the gasps of pain when he tried pushing himself up to a stand, and the limp in his step. He must have been close to the final punishment, the pinnacle of judgment: the slow destruction of his spine. Creep almost wanted to reveal himself, grab the slave, and run. There was a greater goal here, however.

Once the slave found the proper book and departed the room, Creep crawled from beneath the desk and stood. He returned to the door and opened it slightly, peeking through the crack. This was likely a private sector of the manor. The hallway was empty and homey, the complete opposite of how he envisioned the main floor, likely bathed in gold and marble.

He found his way through the manor mostly without obstruction. Twice he had to dip into a room after hearing what he thought was footsteps or conversation. On the second floor, a slave met his eye, but eventually moved on with his duties without question. Creep's lavish suit spoke volumes to a slave's eyes. They wouldn't confront someone who was clearly above them.

Creep walked onto an overlook that hung over a blindingly bright rotunda. There was no chandelier that hung above, but the Intelights circling the walls could light the deepest abyss. The Powish had made great use of the Intel weavineers lent to them years ago.

The rotunda buzzed with conversation, as aristocratic guests mingled before departing in groups into the grand hall. Unlike most balls Creep had been familiar with from his younger years in the Light Realm, there weren't any gowns or dresses. Men and women both wore suits that squeezed their bodies, exaggerating the shapes of their muscular frames. The only difference lied in the color palette. Men wore powder blue or charcoal black, while women wore eggshell or gray. He found it all to be quite ugly.

A few guests were scattered across the overlook, lending him a perfect entry into the festivities. He descended a wide set of steps at the center, joining the fiasco below. As he walked through the crowd and scanned the faces, he thought of his history as a hybrid.

He'd been more of a spy than an assassin in his life, but that didn't mean he was flawless in the art. There were different kinds of spies. His specialty was observing from the shadows; his ancient dictated this. Operating in the thick of things, however, was more suited for talents such as Praetor or Mynute. Their abilities to either shape-shift into another person or shrink to the size of an ant allowed them to gather information while looking someone straight in the face.

Creep remained wary, but moved with a sense of direction. He needed to seem like he belonged here. He entered the ball room, avoiding the private parlors some of the more experienced aristocrats ventured into. A band played stringed instruments on a balcony at the far end of the hall. Below them was the head table, where Lord Rattius Gromel guffawed heartily at something his wife had whispered into his ear. Tables dotted the elongated floor space. Those closest to the head table were assigned to specific families. Creep would have to pick a table near the back, where people were free to choose where they sat.

He took a seat at a table draped in cinnamon brown, eyes trained on the slaves wending between tables. Surprisingly, their attire was no different than what he had seen in the office four floors above. Despite the presence of the Powish upper class, the slaves were dressed in rags, their bruises, scars, and bandages brandished as if they were to be gawked at like jewelry. Yet they continued to serve food and take orders with smiles, as if this was the norm.

He fought back a sigh as he watched a woman at another table toss the contents of her wine glass at a young slave boy, staining his ragged tunic a bloody red. Nobody laughed at him, but perhaps their glares were even worse. They found no humor in his status as dirt; they simply despised it.

"Typically, it's bad manners to sit down at an occupied table and not introduce yourself."

Creep turned, forgetting where he was. A man with beady black eyes gave him a hard stare. In any other kingdom, it would have been rude to glare at someone in such a way, but the Powish believed there was only one way to regard an equal, and that was to set one's jaw and focus the eyes.

"My name is Hansen, of House Troy," Creep said, returning the austere expression.

"House Troy?" the man asked, frowning with a nod. "A minor house like my own. I suppose that's why we're here in the outskirts of the hall."

"And your family?" Creep asked.

"House Itria," a woman to the man's side replied. She was big—seven feet or so. Powish like her were the reason why these tables were so abnormally tall. "Where is the rest of your house?" she asked.

"They retreated to a parlor room. I prefer not to partake in the business and politics of such meetings, so I came directly here."

She nodded gravely. "Yes, but finding yourself in any meeting at all is a good omen, is it not? That means you're working your way up the stratum ladder."

"Or it means someone wants us to think that, when they're really just prepping us for slaughter," Creep said, reaching for a glass of water.

She paused and turned toward the man who first addressed Creep. "This is my husband, Ernest Itria. My name is Lord Lana Itria." She gestured to her right, where a little girl with a violet bow in her hair sat facing the other way. "This is Yesenia, heir to House Itria."

The girl turned with eyes too big for her face. He was immediately struck silent by her resemblance to another girl he'd known, another person he'd abandoned. Her eyes flirted between green and amber, and her dark brown hair was tied up in a too-tall bun. It was a wonder how she kept her head from tipping sideways. She wore a simple vest over a white dress shirt, and her hands were gloved like the rest of the guests. It was a rather convenient style for Creep, a man whose ancient involved gloves.

"Hello, mister," she said.

"Nice to meet you, Yesenia," he said with a smile.

After offering a grin of her own, she turned and observed the grand hall again.

"Forgive her," Lana said, flicking Yesenia's ear and causing the girl to frown at her mother. "She doesn't have much of an attention span."

Creep nodded, but continued to regard the girl. He found her to be quite attentive. Only her attention was elsewhere.

"I must ask how Lord Holland Troy has acquired a meeting in the parlors," Lana said, leaning back to wave over a slave. "Stratum Five families are only invited to these balls because of tax benefits. To think one of us have been selected for a meeting … well, that's promising news for the rest of Stratum Five. Perhaps, the upper stratums have discovered our worth."

Lord Holland was the leader of House Troy, and he was actually not in attendance due to illness. Creep knew this, but the Itria family wouldn't, for their estates were on opposite sides of Ulna Malen's hill.

The slave Lana waved over finally reached their table after being stopped by a couple of others on the way over. She was a battered thing, like every other Gromel slave, but she smiled despite this. "Yes, Lady Lana?"

Lana regarded her with disdainful eyes. "Why haven't I received my risotto yet?"

"Hmm …" The slave looked down at a clipboard she had pressed against her chest. "My apologies, Lady Lana. Was it lobster or scallop?"

Creep raised an eyebrow at this. While they were aristocratic families, ordering such a dish was far too expensive for a family of Stratum Five.

"You can't even remember my order?" Lana asked, bewildered.

"I'm terribly sorry, Lady Lana. Please forgive me, there is a lot happening—"

Lana smacked the clipboard out of the woman's hand, silencing her explanation in an instant. The metal clip careened into her face. As it fell from her grasp and clattered against the floor, the slave reached up to press a finger against her bloodied lip, another wound to complement the many others that already spotted her face. Creep's gaze hardened, but he couldn't interfere.

The slave crouched to retrieve her clipboard, but Lana's massive palm came plunging down on the back of her neck. She crumpled atop the floor, quivering for a moment. Creep forced himself to remain seated.

"Mommy!" Yesenia screamed.

Lana whirled in her seat, staring daggers at her daughter. "What did I tell you about pitying them?"

The girl shrunk down into her chair, silenced by her mother's wrath. It seemed this despicable behavior toward slaves wasn't a natural trait, but a learned one. Children watched their parents, who had in turn watched their parents when they were children—a toxic cycle not easily broken.

"I believe it was the lobster risotto, Lady Lana," the slave said, already having recovered. She continued to smile, and Creep almost hated her for it. The woman had every right to show her anger toward her abuser. "My apologies."

Lana grabbed the young woman by the back of her neck and yanked her closer, so that they were face-to-face. "How close are you to having your spine snapped in half, slave?"

This got the reaction Lana was looking for. The slave's smile slipped from her face, replaced with a horrified gape, eyes hollow. "Lady Lana, I'm seventy percent there."

"Make it eighty," Lana hissed. "After I report your mistake to the closest taskmaster, you'll have to step on eggshells from here on out."

A slave had ten mistakes to make throughout their life. After Lana's threat, this woman had two more left. Each error brought physical punishment upon them. Creep hadn't nailed the system yet, but he knew the wounds on their arms, legs, neck, and face served as a tallying system. Lana had likely already deciphered this before calling the slave over, and was looking for a reason to add to it.

Lana thrust the slave away, disposing of her as if she had swatted away a fly. "Bring me my risotto and don't give me a reason to give you your ninth mark."

As the slave limped away from the table, Creep stared down at his lap, finding it difficult to mask his rage.

"The Gromel slaves really are something else," Ernest said, poking through a bowl of rolls. He found one suited to his desires and began to butter it. "Their reputation precedes them."

Yesenia had resorted to sobbing into her hands, while the guests at the table surrounding them seemed not to have noticed—or maybe they just didn't care. Lana's scene was likely a common occurrence, so much so that it was expected.

"He executes his estate flawlessly," Lana said. "Lord Rattius yields very little wiggle room when it comes to the productivity of his slaves. We've gone to how many balls over the past two months and seen countless slaves with only minor marks on their arms."

Ernest nodded as he chewed on a chunk of warm bread. He swallowed and said, "Too many."

Creep's eyes raked the grand hall once again. The couple was right. He had never seen so many slaves severely wounded like this.

"And that's why Lord Rattius doesn't have to worry about runaways or rebels. His slaves are kept in strict order."

"But they die young because of it," Creep said, realizing he had become silent for too long. "I believe the average lifespan of a Gromel slave is somewhere in their early twenties, correct? That's even worse than the slaves of Cascade's Closure."

"But that's the beauty of it!" Lana said, smiling and leaning forward. This was a sick lady. "Nobody wants the elderly as slaves. Most houses end up killing them off in their fifties anyway because of Powish law. With Lord Rattius, he doesn't have to worry about that."

Ernest, who had shoved another roll in his mouth, swallowed and raised a finger. "And that's because nearly all of his slaves receive their tenth mark while in their twenties. Then it's" —he squeezed his hands together and made a crunching noise with his mouth— "off to a giant to have your spine crushed."

Creep glanced at Yesenia. She sobbed uncontrollably, and it only worsened as her parents continued to speak. Lana noticed this, her gaze shifting from him to her daughter. She smacked the back of Yesenia's head. "You're embarrassing us!"

This only made the girl cry harder.

"You don't have to do that," Creep whispered. "Really, it's quite all right. I've had the same issues with my own son. That's why he's not here tonight. I made him stay home and reflect on his disgusting affection toward our slaves."

Lana's eyes narrowed. Yesenia looked up, regarding him with bloodshot eyes. Even Ernest slowly stopped chewing his third roll, tilting his head with curiosity.

"That's rather un-Powish of you," Lana said slowly. "A peculiar approach to handling a foolishly affectionate child. Queen Gantski enforces a strict policy that children must be thrust into the thick of things. The only way to rid them of their pity for slaves is to expose them to the brutal truth as much as possible. Continue to wound their youthful heart until it permanently scabs."

"Of course," Creep stammered, unaware of such a cultural practice. His weeks of recon work leading up to this hadn't prepared him for everything, apparently. "That's why I'm making him witness the tenth mark of one of his favorite slaves," he said, conjuring lies from midair.

Lana's eyes remained narrowed, but she eventually sunk into her chair. Ernest's chewing sped up again, and Creep felt the heat drain from his face.

"Mother, may I be excused to the lavatory?"

Lana waved her daughter off. "Be quick about it. Lord Rattius will address the hall soon."

Yesenia scooted off her chair and sprinted toward the hall's exit in search of the restroom. She wore shorts with suspenders, and his eyes widened at her calves, the size of a teenage male in any other kingdom.

"How old is she?" he asked, turning back to Lana and Ernest.

"Eight," Lana said with disinterest, too busy straining her neck as she tried to see over some of the taller guests at the tables. What was she looking for? Ernest, meanwhile, had his eyes locked on Creep.

The hybrid's stomach dropped to his feet, instantly recognizing what was happening. He had been too suspicious, and these two idiots weren't fooled. He glanced right and saw a massive man stomping through the grand hall. Pushing twelve feet, he was definitely tall enough to be considered a giant, his beard dangling in braids down to his chest. He was headed straight for their table.

Creep shot out of his chair and swept through the hall toward the exit. A clamor rose behind him, the giant picking up speed.

"Stop that man!" he heard Lana yell from behind.

He burst into the rotunda just as two guards tried to apprehend him. One man was able to grab his arm, but Creep slipped through his grasp and sprinted through the rotunda. With most guests either in the parlors or hall, the crowd had thinned tremendously. This made it difficult for him to blend in, but made it easier to flee and maneuver. He glanced at the estate's twin front doors to find them secured by a giant and a bevy of guards.

His only other option was the staircase, so he dashed up the steps two at a time and crossed the overlook, the giant on his heels. The chambers and hallways were cavernous, constructed purposefully for the use of giants, but that would mean nothing if the giant's speed couldn't keep pace with Creep's.

Creep darted past bewildered slaves and stewards. If anyone noticed the absence of sound when he moved, they'd know to look for it in the future. Thus, he made sure each footstep clunked and every collision with a wall or slamming of a door could be heard through the floor.

He sprinted down a hall on the third floor in search of the flight of stairs that would take him a level higher. His goal was to escape through the sliding glass door he had entered.

He turned a corner and saw Yesenia standing at the dead end of the corridor. He paused, and she waved him over. He turned back, apprehensive of the decision. The giant's shadow could be seen against the wall, signaling his approach from an adjacent corridor. Creep set his jaw and ran toward the girl. As he reached her at what he thought to have been a dead end, he noticed a hallway split to both sides.

"Go that way," she said, pointing right. "I'll tell the giant you went left. Go up the stairs and into the second room on your right."

He followed the directions, for he had no time to question them. He raced up the stairs and reached the fourth floor, heading straight for the door she'd indicated. He burst through, now making use of his ancient once again.

He stopped. A burley red-headed man with a matching beard stood on the opposite side of the room, just in front of a glass door that led to the balcony. He was built like a pile of rocks, his noble suit squeezing every angle of his rugged chest and abs. While he didn't possess the height of a giant, he seemed to have a presence about him that imposed such an image. The child had let him into a trap.

"You are not Hansen of House Troy," the man rumbled. "Tell me who you are, and I'll offer you a proper introduction."

Creep turned to flee, but two men and three women sat on the floor in front of the doorway. Their legs were crossed and bodies slouched, elbows resting on their knees, daring him to test them. A massive war hammer stood upside down next to each of them, their wooden handles pointing toward the ceiling.

"Make no mistake, stranger," the man across the room said. "I don't believe I want to harm you, but don't give me reason to change my mind. Tell me the truth."

Creep closed his eyes, slowly turning to regard the man. "I'm a spy of House Troy—"

The man shook his head, silencing Creep. "I want the truth," he said. "I know House Troy very well. I despise their reverence of my house, idolizing my wife's treatment of our slaves. Tell me, stranger, do you pity the slaves?"

After a prolonged pause, Creep nodded. "I do."

The man's eyes regarded the five armed Powish behind Creep. Each of them stood, and Creep suddenly felt vulnerable and ashamed. Had his skills perished while in Asalka? He had established himself there so many years ago that his skills as a spy had become unnecessary. He obtained information because of the trust he had built with the Primmish elites. That kind of deep embedding took years to build. He shouldn't have charged into this kind of mission so carelessly.

"You probably already know my name," the man said. "But I'll properly introduce myself to someone of your nature. I respect what you represent."

Creep looked up, eyebrows furrowed in disbelief.

"My name is Lord Rattius Gromel, and I want you ..." he trailed off, uncertain of what to call the intruder.

"The name's Creep."

He nodded. "I want you, Creep, to help me flip this city on its head. I've been slowly freeing slaves by integrating them into society over the past ten years, and you can join my efforts. What do you say?"

Creep's body relaxed as he turned toward the five people behind him, war hammers slung atop their shoulders as if they were as light as swords. Each of them smiled. "We can use someone with your skill," a woman said, her hair black and skin dark. "Breaking into a ball of this stature unnoticed? That's impressive."

He faced Lord Rattius. "If you think my skill is something, wait until you meet my partner."

"It would be a pleasure," Rattius said. "Should I consider that your acceptance?"

Creep nodded. "I came here to free the slaves. With our combined forces, this just might be doable."

Rattius lifted an eyebrow and scratched at his beard. "There are more than two of you? Tell me more."

# 47

# The End of an Era

"An awfully lonesome looking place, isn't it?" Himitsu said as he and his two companions stepped out of a thicket of grass.

A clearing sat in front of them, a humble two-story cottage at its center. It was the first sight of tamed grass since departing from the pop-up farmer's market a day prior. After five days of mostly aimless wandering, the directions they received at the market had rejuvenated their search. Himitsu was a bit annoyed with his mother over Skyrise's disappearance. The scouting falcon had been a fourth partner during their entire journey, and its absence hadn't gone unnoticed.

They approached the cottage, walking down a path of smooth scattered stones, as if someone had planted them in the ground, flat-side up. They followed it through what looked to be a massive patch of weeds on both sides.

"That's rather unflattering," Himitsu said. "Where are the flowers?"

Kaylee stopped and crouched, inspecting the mesh of green vines blanketing the ground. "You're too used to the frivolous palace gardens, where their sole purpose is to look pretty. This is a garden of practicality. These are pea plants."

Sal bent over and joined her. He cupped a green pod in his oversized hands. "They're delicate things," he said.

"They are," she said, offering a smile.

Himitsu curled his lip, observing the rest of the patch from a distance. "Still looks like weeds."

They continued toward the roofed porch, where potted flowers hung from wooden rafters. Himitsu knocked on the front door.

After a stretch of silence, Sal asked, "Do you think it's too early? Dawn was just a couple of hours ago."

Himitsu frowned, walking across the porch and stopping at a window next to a rocking chair. He brought his face close to the glass and cupped his hands against the window. Lacey curtains granted little sight. He stepped back, hearing the door open.

"Hello?" came a shaky voice.

He returned to the door, hoping she hadn't noticed his snooping. She was taller than he would have expected. For a woman who was supposedly in her nineties, her posture was stiff.

"Good morning. Are you Mrs. Senex?" Kaylee asked.

"Yes," she said following a pause, "but I'd rather go by Pluzina." Her eyes skated over Sal and Himitsu. "And who are all of you?"

"My name is Kaylee, and these dingbats are Himitsu Vevlu and Salvatore NuForce."

Pluzina tilted her head. "Vevlu and NuForce … intriguing." She turned and walked away, leaving the door open. "Come in for tea?"

They removed their shoes at her request upon entering. They settled down in the living room while she prepared their drinks in the kitchen. Seating was limited, so Himitsu made himself comfortable on a rug at the center of the room while Kaylee and Sal shared a loveseat. They left the only other chair, a ragged armchair, vacant for Pluzina. The three of them exchanged glances as the scent of honey wafted through the room. The topic they wanted to discuss wasn't exactly a gentle one.

Pluzina stepped out of the kitchen with a tray of wooden teacups and a kettle. It seemed almost everything in this place was made of wood, making Himitsu question where the lumber came from. The grasslands didn't have many trees.

As she rounded the room, holding out the tray and allowing them to grab a cup, Kaylee said, "This is a lovely place, Pluzina."

The woman smiled while pouring tea. "Built it myself."

"*You* built this cottage?" Sal asked, twisting in his seat to inspect the building's bones.

"Well, I did all the carpentry and architecture. I drew the blueprints, built the foundation, and carved the wood. Mynute, of course, helped with constructing it. His ancient was quite handy when it came to areas of the structure that were out-of-reach."

"You're a carpenter?" Sal asked.

Pluzina gingerly lowered herself into the armchair, offering Himitsu an appreciative smile. "My skillset is well-versed," she said, placing her own teacup on the end table next to her chair. "I'm a chef, carpenter, architect, herbalist, farmer, teacher, welder, and the list goes on from there." She chuckled, looking down at her hands. "Where do you think I got these calloused hands from? Or these shoulders?"

Sal chuckled. "You're not the typical grandma."

"Oh, honey. In order to be a grandma, I'd have to be a mom—which I'm not."

Sal's lips flattened. "I'm sorry."

She shook her head with a smile. "No worries. I never wanted to be one."

"What made you take on all of those hobbies?" Kaylee asked.

"I'm an Unable," Pluzina said after taking a sip of her tea. "One must busy themselves somehow. Especially when your husband is one of the most celebrated weavers of the century."

"I'm an Unable, too," Sal said.

She regarded him with an unreadable expression. "And don't you ever forget it," she said. "Own it, and prove to the world you can survive on your own without energy. Look at me thriving in life, living off the land and my own two hands." Her gaze grew distant. "I think the privileged and elites forget the Unables represent seventy-eight percent of the population."

Kaylee nodded. "And factor in the people who have energy but don't know how to use it, and that percentage jumps up to ninety-one."

Himitsu raised his eyebrows. "Seriously?"

"Leave it to a Vevlu to think otherwise," Pluzina said. "The people you've surrounded yourself with throughout your life have warped your perception of reality. It's a different world away from the royals and aristocrats. Imagine being a child raised in the slums without a lick of energy to rely on. The world is against you."

"I know it all too well," Sal said. "I was that child once."

"Mynute was born and raised in the ghettos of Phelos, but he was lucky," Pluzina explained. "Out of his dozen or so siblings, he became the only one to harbor energy. That trait opened up hundreds of opportunities an Unable child would never get to sniff at."

"Like a free ride to Phesaw?" Kaylee asked.

"Like a free ride to Phesaw," Pluzina echoed with a slow nod. "Ever wonder why you don't find many Unables in attendance at that school?"

"I thought it was because there wasn't much to gain from it," Himitsu said.

Pluzina laughed, shaking her head. "No, it's because they have to pay tuition—an astronomical amount. It was something Mynute tried to change during his few decades there as the Archaic Director." She scoffed, a look of disgust flashing across her face. "Praetor didn't agree, proving he hadn't completely changed from the man he once was when the two of them had been military elites back in the day."

"I would have loved to meet Mr. Senex," Kaylee said.

"He was kind of boring," Himitsu said.

Kaylee whirled, staring daggers at him. But, Pluzina smiled. "That he was," she said. "He was a mild-mannered man, but morally just."

"A hero in my eyes," Himitsu said.

"At least you realize that," she said. She sighed, gaze drifting to a mantle above the fireplace. "When they found Mynute after the lava cleared in Rim, he had been badly burned. It's a miracle I was able to obtain his body."

They all stared at the lone item on the mantle: a wooden urn with the initials M.S.S. carved into the side.

"How'd you get the body?" Kaylee asked. "I would have assumed the corrupt powers in the Amendment Order would have confiscated it in efforts to scavenge Mr. Senex's ancient."

Pluzina's gaze roved toward Kaylee. "You're a clever girl with a mind much like Mynute's. You would have fit in well with his group of friends at Phesaw." She looked toward the urn again. "But, to answer your question, I have my ways."

"Do you know a man by the name of Neeko LeFolli?" Himitsu asked, considering that his cue.

Pluzina's eyes closed, exhaling softly. "It's been a long time since I've heard someone mention that fool."

"So you do know him." Himitsu said.

Her lips thinned. "Neeko was, in all honesty, the most intelligent being I've ever met in my life. Everyone likes to speak of Mynute and Praetor, but I was around when they were students at Phesaw. Their acumen paled in comparison to Neeko's. The reason why *they* received the recognition in later years was because they didn't disappear off the face of Kuki Sphaira like he had."

"So, you haven't seen him since the day he entered the Warpfinate and never returned?" Kaylee asked, leaning forward with intrigue.

"No one has."

"But I have," Kaylee said.

A long pause followed, the two women exchanging inquisitive stares, as if they were trying to read each other's soul. "I don't believe that," Pluzina said.

"He mentored me for a few years," Kaylee said. "But he vanished again. I'm trying to find him, for I believe he holds information that can help win True Light the war."

"I don't know why you've come to me," Pluzina muttered, looking away. "I haven't seen Neeko in eight decades."

Kaylee continued to lean forward, elbows resting on her knees, hands grasped in front of her. After a moment, she sighed. "I guess we've hit a dead end."

Pluzina stood, grabbing her cup and placing it on the tray lying on the coffee table. "I'm sorry I can't be of more help. This war has been quite an ugly one from what I've heard." She gathered the rest of the cups, pausing after realizing Himitsu had barely touched his tea. She frowned.

"It's okay," Kaylee said. "You were of more help than you think."

"I have to tend to my plants," Pluzina said, lifting the cluttered tray and holding it in front of her. "I'll be outside for a couple of hours, but you're welcome to stay if you like. I could never dream of shooing away a member of the Vevlu family. There are two spare bedrooms upstairs."

As the widow took the tray into the kitchen, Himitsu attempted to read Kaylee's eyes. The backdoor in the kitchen opened and shut.

Himitsu collapsed backward, sprawling across the floor on his back. "We came here for nothing."

"Off to Olethros?" Sal asked.

"She's not telling the full truth," Kaylee said. "I saw it in her aura, though she's very good at obscuring it. We've come to the right place."

*　　*　　*

Bryson woke to a pounding head and tightened chest. His eyes peeled open, a gentle orange glow flickering in his hazy vision. He was in an unfamiliar bedroom, furnished like any other. A breeze entered the room from the open window, the night sky just outside. A set of candles stood on the nightstand to the right of his king-size bed. He had grown so used to Intelights that the light of the tiny flames seemed insufficient. To his left sat a sleeping Lilu, skin oily and bags beneath her eyes. He looked down at her lap, where her hands were crossed over a pink begonia, the flower she had worn the first day they met.

He tried to sit up and prop his back against the headboard, but he quickly fell back into the mattress, his chest feeling as if it would tear open from any movement. He drew back the covers a bit, but he was bandaged too heavily to see the surgery's aftermath. He was thankful for this.

He reached up for his head, feeling bandage that squeezed the entirety of his cranium. *Wait a second ...* Why was his chest wrapped? Hadn't Jugtah operated on his knowledge cavity? That was in his brain according to Lilu. He glanced down at his chest again. What had Jugtah done in there? He shivered, feeling a chill rush through his body. He yanked the covers back up to his neck.

"Bryson?"

He turned his head to find Lilu now awake. She rubbed her eyes, clearly dreary.

"Good morning, sleepy head," he said.

She stood and approached his bedside, placing her hand on his forearm through the blankets. Now that her eyes were open, their sunken state was even more evident. "How are you feeling?" she asked.

"I feel like I just fought Thusia and Suadade at the same time. How about you? Have you been sleeping?"

"Not really," she muttered. She reached back for her chair, pulled it next to the bed, and took a seat again. "I've been here since your surgery."

"And how long has that been?"

"Three days."

He looked up at the ceiling. "You've sat here for three whole days?"

"I'm not that pathetic," she said, rolling her eyes. "I explored different rooms."

"You know the bathroom doesn't count, right?"

Her lips quirked upward. "I suppose cracking jokes is a good sign." She leaned back, crossing one leg over the other. "I don't know why I worried."

"Because we're friends," he said, turning his head to regard her again.

She nodded and threw the begonia at him. It landed on his stomach before sliding down his side. "That's why I got you this," she said.

They both laughed, though his was much weaker.

"What about the travolters?" he asked. "Have you seriously missed three days at Steel Field?"

"Yes, but that's no big deal," she said. "Frederick is running the show, and he's visited every day to keep me updated. Besides, there is this thing called vacation days, Bryson. I may have never imagined using them, but hey, there's a first for every—"

She paused, likely noticing his shivering. It was constant now, and clouds of frost expelled from his mouth with each rattled breath. "I'm going to get Professor Jugtah," she said, rising from her chair.

As she ran out of the room, he tried to clamp his teeth together to keep them from chattering. The shivers became convulsions, entire sections of his body shaking violently as he felt the room's temperature plummet. He'd never experienced this before. Had something gone wrong during surgery?

*      *      *

The gales were violent, tossing snow and ice through the air in all directions—sideways, downward, and up. Bryson pushed his way through the blizzard, each step taking the mightiest of efforts, as he planted and dug his boots into the snow. The storm tugged at him, trying to rip him from the land and send him flying into the sky, but there was something ungodly about his strength. He could tell just from his movements that this wasn't his perspective, but that of someone else—someone far stronger than he could have imagined.

He climbed a slope slick with snow so compact it might as well have been ice. As he looked up in search of the top of whatever it was he was climbing, he had to press his hand to the side of his face to keep the hail from cutting him. The blizzard's wrath limited sight to only a few feet. And he didn't know why he knew this, but he understood the source of the storm's rage. He hadn't harvested in years, sending the Still Essence into an uncontrollable rage.

The ability to power through this storm was befuddling, for no normal person—no, *nobody*—should have been able to withstand this incredible force. Even Thusia or Suadade would have been blown away like a leaf in the wind.

He came to a stop at what seemed to be a random area and then screamed, "Stillinia!" Though he knew it in his bones, the octave of the shriek told him he was experiencing a woman's perspective.

The blizzard stopped, practically falling out of the sky. The air grew calm, and the stars loomed large and bright directly above. He turned and his heart jumped into his throat. He was at the peak of a gigantic mountain, surrounded by a vast range of other snow-blanketed monsters. These were the Still Mountains, and he stood atop Mount Stillinia, the mother of them all.

He turned forward again. A woman walked toward him, fair-skinned in the face with crystallized hair of blue and white. Her eyes looked like the surface of a manicured diamond, her lips were a faint blue, and her eyebrows were as white as Grand Director Poicus's. She was unclothed, but her skin looked as if it was scaled in crystal. Her silvery skin crumbled as she walked, creating a trail of glittering dust behind her, reflecting the light of the moons and stars in a million directions. Despite all of these inhuman peculiarities, she was one of the most beautiful women he'd ever seen.

"Have you come to your senses, Thyella?" Stillinia asked. "The other Originators have gone mad. I feared you had joined them."

Bryson had never heard of an Originator or anyone by the name of Thyella or Stillinia, yet he knew every detail about them. For example, he understood this crystallized woman was a complex entity. She wasn't just a human, nor was she only the blizzard he had just fought through. She was the Essence of Still Energy.

"I've required time for reflection, Stillinia," Thyella said.

Stillinia's eyes narrowed, her hair shedding crystal fragments behind her. She dazzled beneath the night sky, and the snow blanketing the ground only intensified her sheen. "Three years is an awfully long time for reflection," Stillinia said.

"Well, I'll admit there was more to it than that. Ever since Tonitrua and Mialo died in the Region of Raging Tides five years ago, the remaining Originators have been questioning their supposed ideas. Had the two of them been on to something?"

"Tonitrua and Mialo weren't the issue," Stillinia said. "That imbecile, Stonebody, ruined everything a couple of years before those two even began chasing their delusional dreams of grandeur. He killed Dimiourgos, and because of that, Archaius lost the only person who could harvest him."

As Stillinia spoke, Bryson made sense of every obscure name instantly. Tonitrua was the Queen of Thunder; Mialo, King of Minds; Stonebody, King of Brutes; Dimiourgos, King of Ethos; Stillinia, the Still Essence; and Archaius, the Archaic Essence.

"Yes, and around that same time, the Intel and Dev Essence had begun to disperse," Thyella said. The two women stood several paces away from each other. "Depending on their roots, commoners began to show electric or telekinetic abilities. It offered a whole new perspective to the world. Those three kingdoms began to build armies, which threatened us Originators."

"And the rest of the Originators followed suit," Stillinia said, her face grave. "You are the only one who still has their Essence, since you've harvested most recently—though I hardly call three years 'recent.'"

"And now I'm the only one with a kingdom absent of weavists," Thyella countered. "I am only one person."

"You are an Originator!" Stillinia yelled. An echo swallowed the sky, turning into a howling wind across the mountains.

The two women studied each other. Stillinia's skin began to leak steam. She looked down at herself, breaths heavy from anger. "No amount of plebeians can take you down," she explained.

"If multiple kingdoms banned together, I believe they could," Thyella said. "Originators have been considered immortal because of our sluggish aging process, immunity to disease, and inability to be affected by blades or arrows. The only thing that could kill an Originator was the attack of another. Now, anyone can possess such abilities. And it doesn't matter if their powers don't compare to mine, for even fractions eventually equal a whole number when enough of them unite."

"You are far beyond their—"

"*I AM NOT A GOD!*" Thyella screamed, interrupting Stillinia without any regard. "Nor are you! Your mother and father, Tahara and Mulawith, are the forgotten gods! Tide Drifter, Land Molder, and Gale Thrasher are gods! That's it!"

Stillinia's face twisted into something foul, crystal scales crawling up her neck and around her chin. "Now you're speaking of Mialo's blasphemous claims of some forgotten gods, as if there are Essences greater than me?"

"Tahara is your mother, Essence of Light," Thyella said in a steady voice, trying to pull more rage from the twisted being. "And Mulawith is your father, Essence of Darkness. Do you refute this?"

"*SHUT UP!*" Stillinia fell to her knees, squeezing her forearms against her ears. "Do you understand the repercussions, Thyella? You are the last Originator! If you don't harvest me, I will be the last Essence to burst into the atmosphere. You, like your fellows, will age rapidly and die within months."

"I'd rather I die than my kingdom be lost. I want my people to flourish, Stillinia." Bryson felt Thyella's smile spread across her face. "And your death will grant them that opportunity. Tomorrow will be the first day of a new era in Kuki Sphaira."

Stillinia howled as the gales returned, the blizzard swallowing the mountain once more. The woman disappeared in the blur of white, and Thyella kept her feet grounded. The storm raged for only seconds before bursting. A shockwave thundered across the mountain range and into the distance, triggering hundreds of roaring avalanches. The storm vanished, but the destruction was just beginning.

The tenth Essence had dispersed into the atmosphere. Originators were no more, and a void between timelines was set to begin.

# 48

# SLO

Bryson gasped and bolted upright in bed, his chest nearly tearing at the sudden movement. He groaned as hands grasped his shoulders and pushed him onto his back again. His entire body was freezing cold, and for a moment, he thought he was still on that dreadful mountain.

"Are you okay?"

He looked up, refocusing his vison. Jugtah stood above him with a concerned look, his gold glasses now replaced by something more normal. Bryson still breathed clouds of frost, but they diluted more and more with each breath. He tried to rack his brain and hold on to the images of whatever dream he had just been in, but it was gone already.

The room was ablaze with candles. He had never seen so many in such a confined space. Surely, this was a fire hazard. Lilu stood just behind Jugtah, a horrified expression on her face. He looked to the right in search of the other person who had pinned him to the bed. His eyes widened when he saw Wendel LeAnce.

"Why am I so cold?" Bryson asked, pulling the covers up to his mouth. "What did you do to me?"

"During surgery, after fixing the problem in your knowledge cavity, I decided to do some exploration in your chest," Jugtah said.

"I'm fixed?" Bryson asked.

"I believe you are, but we won't know until you try to use your clout," Jugtah said. As Bryson pulled down his covers to free his hand, Jugtah grabbed his wrist to stop him. "Now is not the time. Your body is still recuperating. You've awoken sooner than I'd foreseen."

"Isn't that a good sign?" Bryson asked.

Lilu had begun placing several more candles on the nightstand next to the bed. It was providing some heat, but not enough to lessen the chill.

"I suppose," Jugtah muttered, looking down at Bryson's chest. "But I wanted you to sleep longer while your body became acclimated to the new energy flowing through you."

Bryson's brows furrowed. "What did you guys do?"

"I was curious as to what Mendac had been searching for in your chest, so I tinkered around in there myself." Jugtah frowned. "I found some things, but ultimately discovered something abnormal with your heart. And according to Mendac's theory notes, the damage seemed to have been right where he believed the Emotion Cavity to be. I don't know what the man did to it, but he somehow broke the energy gate."

"And how did you fix it?" Bryson said, fighting back a shiver.

"A delicate touch."

Bryson regarded Jugtah's hands. "But you have fingers like tiny sausages."

"Surgical instruments are quite delicate, Bryson," Jugtah said, closing his eyes and staving off a smile.

Wendel laughed, beckoning Bryson's attention. "What are you doing here?"

"Nyemas informed me of the procedure beforehand," Wendel said. "And I notified the royal family in Dunami." His eyes narrowed. "How did you know about the secret passage in the sewers? How did you get through the strange light? And how did you know what was beyond it?"

Lilu stepped forward. "Okay, we can save the interrogation for later, or you can simply ask *me* at a better time, Commissioner." She glared at him. "He is not in any condition to be berated with questions."

Bryson appreciated her for this. Wendel wasn't exactly the man he wanted to talk to. Besides, he was too busy trying to remember his dream, knowing it had something to do with the Still Kingdom.

Lilu eventually convinced Wendel and Jugtah to leave. Bryson tried sliding across the bed to get closer to the candle-strewn nightstand. The chill was still unbearable. She returned to her wooden chair at his bedside, anguish plastering her face. Sweat trickled down her forehead, making him think the room's heat would likely suffocate any normal person.

"You don't have to stay here, Lilu."

She shook her head and smiled. "I know your brain has never worked too well, but do you remember my visit to the hospital after the restaurant collapse on Generals' Battle weekend?"

"That was so long ago," he said.

She looked down at the floor, gaze distant. "Many years," she muttered. "I had a few broken ribs and was bedridden for days."

He nodded, recalling the disastrous weekend. He thought about the anxiety he had felt the first night of her stay in the hospital, being ushered out of her room as she screamed in pain, doctors and nurses rushing in to tend to the princess behind closed blinds.

"You stayed there with me," she said softly, grinning at the memory. "The least I can do is return the favor."

*     *     *

Prakriti waited in the mouth of a burrow that hugged the side of a steel container. The entrance might have been small, but the tunnel itself was big enough for several people to stand comfortably shoulder to shoulder. The entrance sat in a rectangular patch of dirt surrounded by containers. They had chosen this location because of the lack of activity surrounding it. It seemed they were too deep in the cargo yard to warrant being touched anytime soon.

As comforting as this was, a lookout was still necessary. This was usually the job of Rayne or Saikatto. Today, Prakriti served more as a host than a watch guard, waiting for the arrival of Therapif, the dimiour who had been responsible for scouting Stratum Zero for suitable tunnel entrances for escape.

Prakriti felt isolated here. He didn't connect well with Atarax, Moros, Biaza, Kakos, Rayne, or Saikatto, most of them far stronger than him. Even Moros, the tiny weasel, was too crass for Prakriti's taste. Therapif's personality would be a welcome change, however fleeting it might prove to be.

A pair of long white ears jutted from the corner of a container. The fuzzy face of Therapif followed, the rabbit being extra cautious in his approach. He sniffed around, and then finally turned the corner and hopped toward the barrels Prakriti hid behind. Therapif squeezed between the barrels and slipped into the burrow, sliding right past Prakriti until landing in the tunnel.

"It's good to see you again," Prakriti said, brushing off the knees of his trousers.

"Likewise," Therapif said, turning to inspect the tunnel. "Nice and spacious, but that burrow entrance won't cut it when we're trying to escape."

"We'll fix that when the time comes," Prakriti said. "For now, it can't be too obvious."

"How far have they gotten?" Therapif asked.

Prakriti sighed, raising his hand to his chin. "It's difficult to say. I've been doing my best at calculating the distance relative to the map of the kingdom's surface. My best guess is that we're halfway to Stratum Zero's edge."

Therapif nodded and turned toward Prakriti. "Well, a few updates from my end. I've been making great progress on the escape tunnels, though it started out rough. They have a sewage problem in their streets, so I've had to find places that aren't swathed in waste, which are few and far between."

"Have you managed to speak to any slaves?"

"I'm still hesitant about that," Therapif said, ears folding forward with a droop. "I'm not sure how they'll react to—in their eyes—a talking rabbit. I'm waiting for the right moment. If I'm not careful about it, I might cause an uproar and tip off the taskmasters."

"Nobody has found it strange that a 'rabbit' is hopping around such an environment?" Prakriti asked.

"It depends on which side of Ulna Malen I'm in. If I'm in a sector facing the desert, then yes. But in the other sectors that neighbor the woodlands I can move a bit more freely. When I'm spotted, they simply think I'm a wild animal that's unknowingly wandered out of my natural habitat." Therapif smiled. "Even so, what else would someone think when seeing me? None of them have any idea what a dimiour is, so they only see me as one of two possibilities: an animal or food … definitely not a threat."

Prakriti's eyes narrowed lazily. "Don't you get yourself eaten."

"Of course not."

After a brief pause, Prakriti eyed the dimiour. "Speaking of food, you appear absent of supplies."

"And how would you like me to carry these things, Prakriti?"

"I don't know …"

"I'm supposed to be a wild animal. What kind of rabbit hops around with a satchel over his shoulder?"

Prakriti laughed. "None, I suppose."

"Isn't Saikatto supposed to be going out every couple of days to gather material?" Therapif asked, looking back toward the shadows.

"He does," Prakiti said. "It'd just be nice to have someone else, too. Stockpiling enough material for a horde of slaves is daunting."

"If we can make it through Realmular Tunnel, we can achieve anything," Therapif said. "Don't fret."

"Speaking of tall tasks, how are Rhyparia and Creep making out?" Prakriti asked.

"They're doing fine so far. Both have had a couple of close calls, but it's been worth it. They've made great strides in finding ways to free the upper stratum slaves. I don't know too much because I've only gotten to rendezvous with Rhyparia once. Trekking into any stratum above Zero is very risky for me."

Prakriti exhaled and closed his eyes. "Rhyparia isn't doing anything reckless, is she?"

"I don't think so, but how am I supposed to know this? It's not like she would tell me."

"That's what scares me …" Prakriti murmured, gaze growing solemn. "I don't like that Creep guy."

"He's efficient," Therapif said. "That's all I know."

"Personally, I find the guy to be the perfect complement to Rhyparia," a new voice growled.

They glanced into the shadows, recognizing the menacing wolf strolling toward them. Kakos's arms were crossed, his neck framed by broad, lazy shoulders. "I had noticed something different about that woman when she returned from Musku's training—something I liked. It was why I had joined her in the mountains to find her little friends."

"What are you talking about?" Prakriti asked.

Kakos stopped and leaned back against the tunnel's wall. "You didn't know her before Musku's training. She was physically strong, but mentally soft. That changed, though. And now Creep has fueled it even more. She has an edge." He smiled, exposing his jagged teeth. "She has something to prove."

Therapif frowned at his comrade. "And what's that, Kakos?"

"That her power didn't come from her abusive mother, but herself. She can kill on her own watch, and she'll dispose of all the evil in the world on her own." Kakos cracked open an eye and glanced at them. "And I'm sure you realize why that is so frightening."

Prakriti stood in silence, a horrified expression on his face.

The wolf nodded, closing his eyes and facing forward again. "Because in the mind of Rhyparia, 'evil' encompasses a very broad spectrum of people. Not just those who commit the crimes, but those who benefit from them … and those who simply spectate without remorse." He leaned his head back against the wall, gazing up at the ceiling. "All of you believe she's some sort of martyr of peace. I'm not so foolish. Ulna Malen is in for a surprise. Death will swathe their streets."

*　　　*　　　*

Creep stood casually to the side of a cabinet room with his gloved hands inside his trench coat pockets. It was like any other chamber designated for small gatherings—furnished with bookcases, end tables, plush seating, and boring artwork—but grander in height for the sake of the giants. His eyes were presently drawn to such a being, an oversized gentleman pushing eleven feet, who sat on the floor yet remained at eye level with many of the other guests.

Creep had met him days prior. His name was Hupert. He wasn't like most giants, who were as bulky as they were tall. He was lean and, surprisingly, equipped with a sword at his hip. And since he was young— mid-twenties, perhaps—he still had some growing to do. Giants didn't stop growing until their late thirties. Because of his frame, Creep feared the poor lad would blow over in the wind. He also couldn't see Hupert in a swordfight, struggling to keep his balance.

Creep's eyes roved over the others in the room. It had been five idle days since his infiltration of the House Gromel ball. Lord Rattius Gromel had asked Creep to stay in his estate during that time. A few of the people in this room he'd already met while twiddling his thumbs in Gromel's luxurious premises.

He only knew code names, Hupert included. There was Rose, a red-haired beauty maybe a decade younger than Creep seated in an armchair. Her daughter, Ruby, stood behind her, hands entwined on the back of the chair. They both were lean, the muscles in their arms cut cleanly, as if their skin were the muscles themselves. He'd seen Rose's temper flare on one occasion, when Ruby had defied her and left the estate past curfew. The woman's arms had inflated to thrice their normal size, and he wanted no part of it.

There were others—too many to take note of—scattered throughout the room. The most important, however, was Lord Rattius, who had just arrived and placed his suit jacket on a coat rack. He smiled at his guests as he passed them, shaking hands with some and slapping the backs of others.

They were obviously a close-knit group. Despite Creep's distance, Rattius still managed to spot him and offer a nod.

As Rattius took his place at the front of the room, just beneath a painting of a group of armored giants, Rose smiled and said, "Have a little trouble with your wife, Rattius?"

Creep raised an eyebrow. Were they so close they didn't even bother addressing him as 'Lord'?

The man chuckled. "Not as much as she'll have when we succeed in freeing the slaves in the coming weeks."

People shared apprehensive looks, but Rose was the one to speak up. "Coming weeks? What happened to our five-year forecast?"

"You sound foolishly optimistic, Rattius," a man said from the back of the room. This was Creep's first time seeing him. "I wouldn't expect such illogical predictions from a man like you."

"It is no longer illogical, Biccini," Rattius said.

"And what, may I ask, has created such a drastic jump in our time table?" Rose asked.

All it took was Rattius's brief glimpse in Creep's direction for every pair of eyes in the room to turn toward him. His lips thinned as he gave a half-wave. "Hello, my name is Creep." It sounded like an introduction from a recovering drunk at a rehabilitation meeting. Perhaps, it had been just awkward enough to siphon a smile out of Rose.

As a few others laughed, Rattius nodded and said, "Creep is an asset who comes with a team behind him—a team in places we have no way of breaching."

"I've never even seen this guy before," another man said. He was somewhere in his late fifties, gray hair streaked with strands of ivory. His jaw was chiseled, like most Powish.

"If Lord Yosetti doesn't recognize the man," Biccini said, now walking across the room toward Creep, "then that doesn't bode well in my eyes."

Creep's gaze narrowed at the older man. Lord Yosetti, of House Equious? If that was so, then he understood Biccini's doubts. Yosetti Equious was the leader of a Stratum Eight aristocratic family, above even House Gromel. He was important enough to make them regard him as Lord, despite the cordial atmosphere of the group.

"Lord Yosetti," Rattius said, "Creep is a specialist who has lived his life in the shadows."

"Do you even know where he's from?" Yosetti asked, an air of boredom in his expession.

Rattius hesitated, and Creep knew exactly what the man was thinking. If Creep was ousted as a foreigner, he'd likely be kicked out of the room immediately. While he could see this dilemma stirring in Rattius's eyes, he didn't want the man to lie.

"I'm from the Prim Kingdom," Creep said. He watched as their reactions soured.

"A Primmish?" said another new face, this one a woman with jet-black hair in a ponytail. She scowled. "Besides the few sailors on their trade ships, since when does a Primmish flee his land? Have you finally chosen a side after centuries of cowering in your haven?"

Creep smirked. "We've chosen no sides in interrealmular affairs. We have no interest in the present war. We do, however, know an unethical practice when we see one. And this capital suffers from one … on a catastrophic scale, no less."

"I'm assuming he knows the details of our group if he's here?" Biccini asked, turning toward Rattius.

"He knows our purpose," Rattius said calmly, connecting his hands behind his back. "He strives for the same goal."

Biccini stepped closer to Creep, brows furrowed. Creep remained calm in what had become his signature pose since his teenage years: an arch to his back, hands in pockets, and laziness in his expression. His height had always allowed him to tower over most, but it seemed he was on the shorter side in the Power Kingdom.

"Let the man be," Rose said calmly, closing her eyes as she lifted a glass of water to her mouth.

Biccini growled at Creep, but ultimately backed away. Creep looked Rose's way and offered a nod. She avoided his eye, but there was the slightest evidence of a smirk that flashed across her face.

"How do you expect us to trust him?" Lord Yosetti asked.

"That question could be flipped on its head, in all honesty," Creep said.

As Yosetti and Creep held each other's gazes, Rattius approached the wall and slid back a panel, revealing a weathered map of Ulna Malen's hill. "Creep has a point," he said, briefly turning away from the map. "He has more to lose than us. It'd be easy for us to quell his propaganda if he chose to approach anyone of significant importance. Besides, Lord Yosetti, the only people more influential than you are those in Stratum Nine … Queen Gantski and the rest of the royals."

Yosetti, whose eyes were still trained on Creep, finally looked away. "Then inform us of what he can contribute to our efforts. Convince me."

"Of course, milord," Rattius said. "Since the forging of SLO and Creep's team will be a symbiotic relationship, let's start with what we'll provide his unit."

"SLO?" Creep repeated.

"Yes, like you're a little *slow* in the head," Rose said, deadpan. Ruby giggled behind her mother, and a few others placed their hands in front of their mouths.

Creep liked this woman, so he grabbed the handle of his special knife in his pocket. There was only one lady for him.

"SLO, or S.L.O., is an acronym that stands for Slave Liberation Operation," Rattius said. "It's the name of our group."

Creep scratched at his beard. "Perhaps I should give my group an awkward name, too." He hummed and then flicked his fingers. "Slippery Sewage Slide of Sovereignty."

Rattius chuckled. "I like it."

Rose, however, crinkled her nose. "Okay, I don't like what that title suggests."

"We free the slaves via the sewage grates in the basements of our estates," Rattius said.

Several groans escaped from those in the room, obviously disgusted by the proposal. Ruby spoke for the first time. "Even cracking open the lid of that grate causes a wretched stench to take over most of our house."

"What's more important, Ruby?" Rattius asked, frowning at the young lady. "The potential freedom of the slaves or the condition of your villa?"

She sighed. "You make a fair point."

"Who's to say they'll survive the plummet through the sewers?" Gerald asked. He was one of the first people Creep had met after Rattius had instructed him to stay in the manor. "Nobody knows their path. What if they narrow at a certain point? Wouldn't people get stuck? And what if they plunge directly down? Then we'd be sending the slaves to their deaths."

"Logical worries," Creep said. "However, my partner has been scouting the city's sewage line for a couple of weeks now. She has found no such dangers."

"And how has she—"

"She's special," Creep said, cutting off Biccini. "And she's not someone we must doubt. In all honesty, she's the leader of my group."

Biccini scowled from afar, but Rattius cleared his throat. "The sewers' exits, as we all know, are at the bottom of the hill, where they spill out into Stratum Zero. When the time comes to start freeing the slaves, Creep's team will be waiting at the bottom, ready to escort them far away from Ulna Malen."

"Have you met any of these people, Rattius?" Biccini asked.

"You do have a bad habit of trusting too easily," Rose said. "I meant to ask this a few days ago, but how did you find this man?"

"He infiltrated my house's most recent ball and showed signs of remorse for the slaves, yet didn't know how to hide it. He was a complete amateur and clearly knew nothing about our culture—besides the fact that we practice slavery."

"Or he's just a very clever spy," Rose said, eyeing Creep once again.

He wished that was the case. His purpose at the ball had been spy work, but his efforts were shoddy from a lack of practice. He was discovered quickly, but luckily ran into likeminded individuals.

"Listen," Creep said, "I can't stop my partner from committing to whatever bold, reckless, and likely catastrophic plan she has brewing. Either you put your trust in me or not, because when the time comes to escape through the sewers, there will be no opportunity to question it. She told me the signal will be obvious … and big. And those who remain in the city will regret it."

"What's to stop us from killing you right now?" Lord Yosetti asked with an apathetic stare. "I'm sure my good man, Hupert, would hold no reservations in doing so."

Creep glanced at the narrow giant seated on the floor, his long legs folded, yet still taking up too much space. The swordsman didn't strike fear in Creep, but he couldn't admit to that. "Because I'm the only way you can go from five years to two weeks," he said coldly. "How many slaves would such a shortening of the timeframe save?"

"Hundreds," Ruby said.

Rattius frowned at the floor, lost in thought. "Pfft! Hundreds would be if you were only considering my wife's wrath. I swear that woman kills one slave per day. I can't walk around this place much longer and have to stomach seeing which poor souls are brandishing new wounds."

"And don't forget I don't need you guys," Creep said, turning fully to face Yosetti. "I hadn't planned on coming here and running into a group like this. Sure, you'll make my job easier, but either way it's getting done regardless. Running into Lord Rattius was simply a convenient perk."

"Don't give chance so much credit," Rose said. "If it hadn't been for your miserable attempt at blending in, you wouldn't have caught his eye."

"He actually caught the eye of someone else, but that's neither here nor there," Rattius said. "Now that Creep has found us, we can provide him with dozens of likeminded power players who own property all throughout Ulna Malen. Over the next two days, we'll designate certain estates as gathering spots for slaves. Then, when the time comes for everyone to escape, we'll use each estate's sewage grate to flee." Rattius looked them over. "We must do our best to free every single unfortunate soul who has had to play a subservient role in this rancid city."

"And what will Creep be doing during all of this?" Biccini asked. "Sitting back and watching us do all the work?"

"Obviously not," Rattius said. "My plan is to give Creep an alias and fake title in my house. He will then attend balls of the lower stratums—three and four, let's say—where he won't be recognizable since nobody from those stratums attended my ball. There he will meet some of SLO's lower ranking lordlings and the slaves we've freed up to this point."

The room fell quiet, and many eyes were still on Creep.

"What do you say?" Rattius asked. "How many of you accept his contributions?"

Hands slowly rose into the air. Only a few people remained rigid in their stance against Creep. Biccini, of course, was one of them.

"That's the majority," Rattius said. He looked toward the back of the room, where Lord Yosetti stood. "But I'd feel better if you were also in favor."

"Do what you must," Yosetti stated. "I hold no objections. If he turns out to be a spy of Power Queen Gantski—"

Creep punched the window he was standing next to, shattering it into pieces. Those who had seen it in their peripheral vison looked at him, aghast. Those who weren't looking at him didn't even notice.

Biccini gawked at the window. "What in the world?"

Others turned, their eyes widening. "When did you do that?" a woman asked.

Creep shrugged. "Just now."

"But I didn't hear anything."

"My ancient allows me to move in silence," Creep said. "Only Archains and Primmish can use ancients, so now you should know that I'm definitely not a spy of the Power Queen."

The silence that followed was interrupted by the pattering of drizzle against the windowsill. Yosetti finally showed some emotion, displaying a grin across his face. "Well, I'll be damned." He raised his hand, showing his approval of Creep's participation.

Biccini scoffed, but then dropped his head and raised his hand, too. Rose leaned against the arm of her chair, gazing at Creep with interest.

Rattius clapped his hands together. "Welcome to SLO, Creep."

# 49

# The Leviathan

The Mythmaker and Whale Lord floated next to the each other somewhere in the Sea of Light with anchors nestled on the seafloor. Agnos and Evelyn found themselves in Captain Gray's cabin aboard the Whale Lord while she prepared them for the morning ahead. During Agnos's absence from his own ship, his quartermaster, Barloe, temporarily held command.

Both ships sat just outside of a brewing whirlpool, not yet mature enough for passage. Even if it was mature, the fact that the sun had long since set wouldn't have allowed them to pass through, anyway. Traversing a whirlpool without sunlight was a suicide mission. Luckily, the whirlpool's development would complete by morning.

"This will be the most complex maneuver you've ever faced as a pirate, Agnos," Gray said, standing over her desk and shaking her head while studying the blueprints of the Mythmaker. She had marked a dozen X's across the ship, each one representing a location that should be manned by a squallblaster when entering the whirlpool.

Agnos and Evelyn stood on the opposite side of the desk. He leaned over the blueprints with his one hand on the desk's edge while she stood erect, arms crossed. "This is impossible," he croaked.

"You've achieved the impossible before," Gray said.

"Yeah … by luck," he said, looking up at her. "What are the chances a sea monster comes to save the day for a second time?" He said sea monster, but something told him that beast had been something far grander.

She looked down and took a slow breath. "Fair point."

"We'll be fine," Evelyn said. "Troy's been working with all of the squallblasters throughout the voyage. They are prepared. And I must admit that I've been quite impressed with the guy. He's living up to his reputation as the Spirit Admiral's second-in-command."

"I'd feel a lot better with Tashami," Agnos said.

"Tashami's gone, Agnos. You cannot dwell on the man," Gray said.

Agnos turned away from the desk, sat on its edge, and stared emptily into the distance. "What are we doing?"

"Excuse me?" Gray said.

He whirled, eyes wide. "Why are we doing this? This doesn't make any sense. We're so far away from everything. There's a war happening, and the climax is approaching … if it hasn't already arrived!"

She held his gaze as silence swept through the room. Activity from the deck above thrummed lightly through the ceiling. "I get it," she said. "You're scared. It's been a long time since you've operated without your best friend."

"It's more than that," he said.

"Is it?"

Agnos bit his lip and gazed out the window behind her. "Maybe I haven't changed," he finally said.

Gray looked at Evelyn. "Can you give us a second?"

The Still Diatia swept out of the room. The door shut, and Agnos continued to gaze outside. He didn't want to look at his former captain. The floodgates would open if he did.

"Look at me, Agnos."

He continued to bite his lip, and he felt it quivering. He feared death. He had found the chronicle he'd spent his childhood and teenage years hunting, but after translating nearly half of it, he realized how empty his achievement had been. It had been a bridge to something bigger, and the blasted thing didn't even offer instructions. It only gave him another location to chase—something that had been right under his nose for years.

Gray stepped into his field of vison. She was old—too old to still be captaining a crew of pirates—yet here she was, stoic and proud. Despite the wrinkles, her face was chiseled. Despite the age of her bones, she still stood tall. Despite the horrors she had experienced in her life, she still persevered.

He broke down the moment he saw that face, reminded of the first time he'd met her in the Chasm. Tashami had taken the lead during that adventure, beating the snot out of a thug and gaining the respect of Gray Whale with little effort—though they had known her as Silvia at the time.

"Stop crying," she snapped. He buried his face into the collar of his shirt. "If your crew saw you like this, you'd have a mutiny on your hands."

He couldn't stop the tears spilling out of him like rainwater from a gutter. He was a coward. He was selfish. The man he'd become with Tashami by his side had been a farce. At least when he was younger, he had had two arms to rely on.

"It's useless," he said through gasps of air.

"You sicken me sometimes," she said. "You need to develop a backbone and stop relying on someone else to be it for you. Why must you always lean on someone?"

He knew the answer, but managing words through his hysterics was impossible.

"Will you look at me?" she begged.

He looked up from his collar, and he winced at his candlelit reflection in the window. His cheeks were red, overgrown bangs stuck to his face. It was a shameful image. And all he could do was use his one hand to peel off a few strands of hair.

Gray's lips thinned as she observed the young captain. "Positive reinforcement isn't my strong suit," she said. "I am not your mother; I am not one to coddle."

"I don't want to be coddled!" His words came out as a jumbled shriek, and he wasn't sure she could even understand them.

"You want a crutch."

"I want faith!" he yelled. He heaved as she fell silent. His voice grew weak. "Something only a family can give me. Tashami was that. He was a brother." He refrained from mentioning Toono.

Gray's head fell. And for the first time in three years of knowing her, he spotted a glimpse of vulnerability. Her expression softened. She reached back for her chair and lowered herself into it. She slouched and stared at nothing, the silence that followed stretching into eternity. Perhaps she was waiting for him to calm down.

"Let me apologize," she said. "I have a very archaic approach to captainship. I make it a point to ignore the pasts of my crewmates. I don't want to know anything about them, and I try to avoid bonds. I'm sure you've noticed this. When we're at DaiSo Harbor, I spend my time on the ship. When we're at sea, I stick to my cabin." She shook her head. "And I wonder why we had a couple of rats aboard our ship for decades."

Agnos sat across from her. "You can do that," he said. "You're the most feared captain in the world."

"Perhaps, but it only works if I maintain the rule. With you, I haven't done that. And because of that, a bond has formed. But how helpful is that bond if I'm forgetful of whom you are at your core?"

"I don't understand," he said.

"I forgot you're an orphan," she said. "You have every right to be nervous. I think what bothers me is I don't want that fact to hamper your confidence. I want you to commit, and I want you to do it on your own. You're strong, Agnos. You own a ship as big as mine and lead a crew of elite pirates."

"What does any of that matter?"

"How important are the lives of your crew?" she asked.

"Very."

She nodded. "Well, their lives depend on your belief. If you don't believe in yourself, they'll notice it. That attitude will become infectious and spread throughout your ship. And there is nothing more daunting than entering a whirlpool with a crew who thinks they're destined for death."

"Do you believe in your crew?" he asked, wiping his face.

"Without question," she said. "And I believe in you."

Another tear trickled from his eye, his gaze dropping to his knees.

"My childhood wasn't ideal," she said. "My parents weren't good people. I strived so hard throughout my life to not become my mother that I refrained from finding love and bearing children—though Eet and Osh make me think otherwise at times. And that's great, I'm not a mom, but that doesn't mean I haven't become my mom. As I've aged, my crew has become less a family and more an establishment of employees. You can still salvage a proper relationship with yours."

Surprisingly, Agnos smiled. He thought of Barloe, Zorra, Eet, and Osh. He had fostered a beautiful atmosphere on his ship, one which he should have been proud of.

"I've learned from observing your captainship from afar," she said. "You're a superb leader, and I wish I could have met the people who instilled that quality in you."

Images of his crew shifted to those he had known at Phesaw: the Energy Directors, Bryson, and Olivia.

"I want you to keep reminding yourself this, Agnos." She leaned forward against the desk. "Family doesn't require blood ties."

*　　*　　*

Agnos felt like an insect approaching a groundhog hole. The whirlpool was massive, dwarfing the Adrenian naval fleet that had served as escort for the Brench Hilt over two years ago. It could have swallowed the capital city of Dunami whole.

The crew was frantic, racing every which way to get into position. Barloe, Evelyn, and Troy stood at power positions across the deck, barking orders at crew-elected leaders who then relayed instructions to their units.

Agnos looked up, thankful for a clear sky. Storm clouds would have caused the whirlpool's edges to become sporadic. One minute a ship could

502

be thousands of yards away from the monstrosity, the next moment it could be clearing a wave on its way into the belly of the beast.

The Whale Lord led the charge, and he pictured Gray Whale operating the helm. She'd said she would, but the thought was still mindboggling. He turned and surveyed the controlled chaos of his crew, nobody looking his way for guidance. He had done his part already. At the crack of dawn, after a night of no sleep, he'd given his oath of faith in his men and women via an improvised speech. All he could do now was stand at the bow of the ship and watch. No matter what dangers came his way, he wouldn't move. He was the leader of this ship, which made him the man on the frontlines in his mind.

He looked down at his shoulder, where an arm should have been. He may have lost a limb; he may have lost his brother. But, as Jilly would have pointed out, he still had his spirit. His lips curled upward. *Jilly, give me strength.*

His smile faded, however, noticing a disruption in the movements of his crew. People began shifting directions as leaders shouted with more urgency. He turned toward the sea, and his mouth fell agape.

A ship cleared the whirlpool's edge, dwarfing both the Whale Lord and Mythmaker. It sported sails of gray and black, a logo of a fist painted at their center. He'd never seen a Dark Realm ship, and nothing could have prepared him for one like this. What kind of ship could make a galleon seem like a foothill at the base of a mountain?

Apparently, one from the Power Kingdom.

# 50

# Sea of Gray

Evelyn came rushing toward the bow. "Agnos, we have to turn this around."

He could do nothing but balk at the behemoth of a ship. It was essentially the size of four galleons combined, making the Whale Lord—the largest ship in the Light Realm—look like a child. He'd read about Powish ships once, while studying under Neeko. They had a specialist branch of their navy that flaunted six mega ships called leviathans, but they shouldn't have been a threat to the Light Realm.

He shook his head. "No, we can take it on. Between us and Gray's contingent of blue whales, this is doable." He honestly felt like this was true. He'd seen what Gray's whales were capable of.

"Listen," she said, glancing back at the scattering crew, "I admire this newfound confidence, but you don't take on a leviathan with two galleons. We need at least five ships to put up a fight!"

"It may be huge, but it's beatable," he said. "The whales will weaken the hull, and the combined utility specialists from both crews will handle the Powish sailors."

"That ship is constructed of holy wood!" she bellowed. "Unless you have any world class seashockers on board, you're not sinking that thing!"

Holy wood changed things. He'd forgotten about that detail. It made sense when considering the amount of weight a leviathan had to hold. A Powish crew weighed tons, especially with several giants also onboard.

"What do we do?" he asked.

"We turn around and haul ass out of here," she said. "Take advantage of one of a leviathan's weaknesses, which is its lack of speed."

"But Gray is too close to retreat," he said, grabbing his looking glass from his coat pocket. "She'll need our help." He bit down on the instrument and extended it with his lone hand. As he brought it to his eye, the view rocked back and forth until he spotted the Whale Lord.

"Damn it," he said, watching as his ally's sails began to shift. The two sails that extended like wings from its sides had rotated drastically, and there were likely squallblasters unleashing gales into them in efforts to get the ship to turn. "They're directly below it! They'll be crushed!"

Evelyn pulled out her own looking glass. "Gray is at the helm. She should be able to maneuver her way out of this mess. Her proximity to the hull might put her at an advantage."

"How?"

"The leviathan's other weakness is, surprisingly, its size. If a smaller ship gets close enough to its base, it can't be seen from any decks or windows. That means the stoneslingers won't be able to attack it. Also, because of its sluggish steering, it can't maneuver fast enough to try to crush the bugs sailing beneath it."

He dropped the looking glass and swallowed spit. He'd never imagined the Whale Lord as a bug, but that's exactly what it was when faced with *that*. He turned toward Evelyn. "We may not commit to a fight, but we must, at the very least, serve as a distraction to allow Gray a chance of escaping."

"And how do we do that?" she asked.

"We sail a bit closer, within range to draw interest from the leviathan. Once we've hooked them, we turn and flee, luring them away from the Whale Lord."

Her gaze hardened. He knew his plan was suicidal in her mind; even he had doubts. But, their previous goal to traverse a whirlpool was dumb, so this strategy seemed like child's play in comparison.

"You said we have some of the most talented squallblasters on this ship," he said. "We even have *the* Troy Sulia. With them in our family, wouldn't you say we could easily outrun that leviathan?"

She looked up and squinted at the massive ship, giving it thought.

"Months ago, you told me you wanted to learn under me. You wanted to find out what it was like to put everything on the line for the sake of a team." He pointed in the direction of the Whale Lord, his gaze still focused on her. "Well, the pirates on that ship were once fellow crewmates of mine. They are my extended relatives. It's time you put up or shut up, Evelyn!"

"Very well, then, Captain," she said with a smile. "Go ahead and give your orders."

He beamed from ear to ear and ran for the banister that ran along the forecastle. He caught it with one hand, came to a stop, and then bellowed across the decks: "*CHARGE!*"

*     *     *

Gray Whale's breaths were rapid and unsteady, her age more evident than it had ever been in her life. The wheel's handles nearly slipped from her grasp as she spun it with all her might. As the leviathan's keel reached for the sky above her, looming over the Whale Lord and swallowing it in a massive shadow like a low-hanging storm cloud, she knew how much rode on this first turn. If she didn't get the ship out of the way, that was it.

Her crew was in disarray. Her entire utility personnel were above deck. The other pirates occupied the lower decks, boarding up windows and keeping an eye on the hull for damage. When this close to a leviathan, the sea was unpredictable.

A wave crashed onto the main deck just below Gray as she continued to steer on the quarterdeck. Squallblasters were posted in the fighting tops and crow's nests. Her four best were on the stern deck at the tail of the ship, weaving gales into the winged sails. They might have been even more important to this maneuver than she was.

Seashockers dotted the perimeter of the decks, concentrated on the starboard side since that was the side that'd face the leviathan if their turn was successful. They unleashed electrical attacks onto the leviathan's holy wood-constructed hull. Unsurprisingly, this didn't achieve much. It took an extraordinary talent to simply scorch holy wood, let alone fully damage it.

Gray leaned to her left, putting all of her body weight into the helm as it hit its stopping point. Now, all she could do was hope her squallblasters did the rest of the work necessary to get the Whale Lord to safety.

She glanced left, where Marigium lay on the deck. She had carelessly dropped the ancient upon noticing the leviathan earlier. It served no purpose in this scenario, for her whales would have been useless against holy wood.

She closed her eyes, the effort necessary to keep the wheel from snapping back overwhelming her. As she'd aged, she hadn't realized just how much she relied on her skills as a weaver in battle. She'd stand in her cabin or on the decks, orchestrating battles via Marigium, controlling her whales through weaving. Physical strength, on the other hand, had fallen by the wayside. It was something she hadn't resorted to since her forties.

A deafening snap jarred her back to her senses. Surely, that wasn't a noise she wanted to hear. She looked to her right, which was difficult to do, considering the current position of her body. She had to lower her shoulder and arm to see above them.

Her eyes widened. The mast jutting from the right side of the Whale Lord, serving as the skeleton to the winged sails, had snapped upon colliding with the leviathan's hull. The far end scraped against the holy wood before ultimately falling limp, swooping downward in a violent arch and disappearing beneath the railing. She braced herself, hoping they'd get lucky. But if the direction of the mast's pendulum-like arch stayed true, it spelled doom for the Whale Lord.

The ship shook violently beneath her, a resounding crash thundering through her eardrums. Her body jerked and was nearly pulled from the wheel, but she managed to keep her boots planted. Gritting her teeth, she growled at the unfavorable twist of fate.

A woman climbed up from the lower decks, a firefighter whose name Gray didn't know. The woman raced across the main deck and climbed the steps to the quarter deck. She paused at the sight of Marigium on the floor, but quickly recovered and continued forward. "A mast just shattered the walls of the crew's quarters and the orlop, Captain!"

Gray squeezed her eyes shut at the news, continuing to lean against the wheel. It had destroyed a big enough section to encompass two separate floors? *Oh, seas.* This was it.

"What do we do, Captain?"

Gray looked up at her. "You do what you can."

The firefighter froze, and Gray saw the fear in her eyes as the magnitude of the situation hit her like a ton of bricks. The tears streaking down Gray's scarred cheeks likely only made it worse.

"Are we going to die, Captain?"

The hardened captain looked down at the deck, still wincing from the effort to keep the wheel pinned. "Pirates and sailors who go down at sea never die," she said. "We become part of it, and we live on in its spirit."

Gray felt the ship beginning to tilt to the right as water flooded the lower decks. Even over the crashing sounds of the leviathan's destructive waves, she heard the screams of her crew below the decks. So much death.

The ship's starboard side careened into the leviathan. The holy wood didn't budge, and the Whale Lord was crushed against it. Crole, one of her best squallblasters and a rambunctious man with an awkward mullet, was tossed off the deck.

Gray lurched, losing grip of the wheel's handle. She caught hold of a beam in the deck's banister. The wheel recoiled, causing the galleon to straighten out and continue to ram into the leviathan. The unnamed firefighter tumbled uncontrollably down the deck before crashing into the side rail with her back. Her breath was knocked out of her lungs, and any sign of life disappeared from her eyes.

Squallblasters fell from their positions high up in the masts. Those higher up were lucky enough to miss the ship, plunging straight into the sea, while others splattered against the decks. It sounded like boulders were raining down on the ship. Gray screamed as the Whale Lord rolled onto its side, positioned awkwardly against the leviathan.

This was the end of her journey. She had led her crew to slaughter—a crew she barely even knew.

*     *     *

Dread washed over Agnos as the Whale Lord, the grandest pirate ship in all the Light Realm, was flattened by the leviathan. It wasn't an explosion of shattered wood, like when Gray's blue whales had assaulted the Adrenian naval fleet, but more like meat churned through a grinder—excruciatingly slow.

"We have to turn now," Evelyn shouted. His eyes were wide, shock overwhelming him. "There's nothing we can do for them."

He remained mum. She stared at him for a few moments, waiting for a command. She looked toward the disaster. "If you don't say something, I will."

*Good*, he thought. He didn't want to speak it into existence. Let her do it.

She whirled toward the decks and screamed, "Turn her around!" The crew roared in earnest, Evelyn's message being relayed across the length of the ship.

Agnos continued to watch the vessel of his nautical mentor perish. He had many friends on that ship. His mind drifted to Crole, a good friend of Tashami's and one of the first crewmates to show Agnos any respect. The Whale Lord had served as his home for nearly a year. He could rely on it always being there if his ship failed. A woman who communicated with whales. A woman who he'd spent countless nights with in the harbor of DaiSo, conversing in the hammocks of the crew's quarters. A woman who had seemed invincible.

As his ship turned, he gripped the banister and squeezed his eyes shut, bowing his head. He wouldn't cry. Just last night, that very woman had told him not to for the sake of his family. But what would she say now, when half his family was dying right before his very eyes?

He bit his lip, fighting back tears. She would have told him it was okay to cry, but not in front of his crew. Right now they needed to see fortitude in his guidance. He needed to get those who were still alive out of this mess. Once that was accomplished, he could retire to his cabin and wail into his hammock, possibly burrow his face in *Erafeen*'s pages until the end of eternity.

He looked up, eyes wide, remembering who else was on his ship. Last night, he'd instructed them to stay put in his cabin until the whirlpool was cleared. Had they listened?

He spun, eyes skating over the crowded decks. He bolted across the forecastle, pirates doing their best to get out of his way amongst the chaos. Despite the immediate danger in front of them, they had the awareness to acknowledge the presence of their captain.

He stomped down the stairs to the main deck, stormed across it, and then burst through the door leading to the specialty quarters. He ran down the narrow hall, lit by the natural light spilling in from the open doors of vacated rooms. His cabin door was closed at the end of the hall. Reaching into his coat pocket, he pulled out a key and unlocked it. The door opened, revealing two youths in his grand cabin.

Eet sat in the middle of the floor, Osh sitting cross-legged on Agnos's desk. A stack of parchment—his translated documentation of *Erafeen*—sat in her lap. She panicked, thrusting the stack of papers behind her back.

He heaved a sigh of relief. "I'm glad you listened."

Twisting his body with a lazy gaze, Eet said, "You kind of didn't give us a choice. Locking us in here was a bit overdramatic."

"Put those translations back," Agnos said. "I need both of you to head down to the hold and remain near the front of the ship."

Osh's face turned beet red, but she did as she was told, rounding the desk and returning the parchment to its proper drawer. "What's happening?" she asked. "Have we entered the whirlpool?"

He smiled, even though it hurt him to do so. He had to lie to them. The woman who'd acted as their grandmother throughout their life was dead, but he couldn't break that news yet. "We have," he said. "And considering some unforeseen conditions, you need to get as low in the ship as possible."

They ran past him, and he followed. Not wanting to bring them to the main deck, where they'd clearly see the leviathan looming in the distance, he instructed them to turn into a cupboard. An emergency trapdoor sat in its floor. He pulled out his ring of keys and unlocked the padlock.

The door fell open. Eet and Osh jumped down first. Agnos was more careful with his one arm, slowly climbing down the unraveled rope ladder. They landed in the crew's quarters, where hammocks and lanterns swayed maniacally with the movement of the ship. He wended between hammocks, guiding the kids to the nearest latch in the floor.

As he crouched and swung it open, he looked up at them. "Keep going all the way down to the hold. They need me above."

They regarded him with bug eyes. Despite the roundness of their faces, he saw the beginning of their maturation processes. Eet's shoulders had become broader and Osh's head had grown into her ears, allowing them to hide behind her raven hair.

Both of them began to cry, catching him by surprise. They may have been young, but he had always seen Gray's resolve in them. They were even brave enough to continue embarking on voyages with the two most dangerous crews of pirates of the modern day. In their guts, they knew something was wrong.

Osh leaned into the embrace of his one arm, while Eet leaned into his other side. Agnos rested his cheek against the boy's mop of unwashed hair. "You know all those men and women on the decks above have your back, right?"

They nodded, sniffling quietly into his ears.

"They're hard at work, making sure we get through this unscathed," he whispered. "It's frightening, I know. But I believe in my crew. Your family will take care of both of you." He paused, allowing the shakiness in his voice to disperse. He bit his lip—a recent habit to stop his lips from quivering. With Gray now gone, he'd need to step up for them. "And when all is said and done—when this voyage comes to an end—I want to adopt both of you. And I promise to be the best father the world has ever seen."

He gently palmed the back of Osh's head and kissed her forehead. He turned and did the same to Eet. They each kissed one of his cheeks, sandwiching his face between them. He didn't know whether to cry or laugh.

"Hurry up now," he said, guiding them down the hole. "I'll come down to get you later."

After watching them disappear into the shadows, he closed the latch and stood tall. Gray was right. He didn't have his brothers, Toono or Tashami, by his side, but he was surrounded by family. And the two most important members depended mightily on his courage right now. He was only a decade older than both of them, but they felt like his children.

He looked up, hearing dozens of footsteps thundering above. His face became stern, and he raced toward the ladder leading up to the main deck.

# 51

# Stoneslingers

The main deck was a mess, and following a quick assessment of their surroundings, Agnos noticed the Mythmaker was only a quarter of the way through its turn. He stopped at the top of the ladder to make sense of the chaos, but that was impossible. Did his crew possess any strategy or were they simply running around aimlessly?

Barloe barked orders from the quarterdeck, but it was pointless when considering the noise and disarray of the crew. Most couldn't hear him.

Agnos raced toward the steps that led to the quarterdeck. If they wanted to evacuate unscathed, they'd need to intelligently delegate commands and ration information.

Barloe spun, relief washing over him as he spotted Agnos. "Captain, this is maddening!" he shouted above the din. Gunther stood behind him, manning the helm.

"I need every utility commander, except the squallblaster commander, gathered here right now," Agnos said. "Get on it! Get others to help find them if needed. We don't have much time!"

"Yes, sir!" the quartermaster said, immediately heading for the stern deck.

Zorra stepped around Gunther and approached Agnos. "You have a plan?"

"Hopefully he hurries up," Agnos said, glancing to the left where the leviathan was pressing forward. "Once we're halfway through this turn, we'll be exposing the entirety of the Mythmaker's broadside. The leviathan will begin its assault, and with our crew's current state, there'll be no defense."

She nodded. "If we can get our tail end facing that thing, it's almost certain we'll escape."

Barloe returned a few minutes later, trailed by three people: Howell Ridel, the seashocker commander; Benji Gora, firefighter commander; and Evelyn Tesai, the lone Stillian on the ship. She wasn't a commander by title, but Agnos was happy Barloe had brought her anyway. The squallblaster commander, Troy Sulia, was still at his station in the crow's nest, which was exactly where Agnos wanted him.

"This isn't going to work!" Agnos shouted, gesturing toward the main deck. "So, welcome to a lesson in delegation! Each unit will have a role as we prepare to enter our most vulnerable position. The squallblasters will remain in the nests and fighting tops, helping steer and propel our path away from the leviathan. I need all firefighters and seashockers to position themselves on the port side of the ship. Most need to stay on the upper decks, but some can drop down a floor and work via windows."

An explosion of wood cut him short. He flinched and ducked, throwing an arm over his head. Most others did the same. The crew's roars grew louder. He quickly raised his head and looked toward the forecastle, where significant damage had been done to the deck. A boulder sat lodged in the crater of shattered wood.

He turned and gaped at the leviathan in the distance, where three massive figures stood just above the ship's bow. They were giants, and they had managed to clear a couple of leagues' distance by simply throwing a boulder. That should have been impossible.

More stones began to fly toward the Mythmaker, most coming up short or missing to the sides, smacking the sea with enough force to form waves that lightly rocked the ship.

"Sometime this century, Captain!" Barloe shouted.

"Mr. Gora, have your firefighters form a smokescreen by weaving a wall of fire to the port side of the ship! Mr. Ridel, I want the seashockers to focus on targeting any incoming—" he paused, flinching again as a boulder rammed into the longboat that hung at the center of the main deck, sending it crashing down into the lower deck. "Focus on any incoming stones! Do your best to disintegrate them with electrical attacks."

They stood still for a moment, as if waiting for more orders.

"Go, now!" Agnos barked. "You too, Barloe! Join the firefighters' efforts!"

"Yes, Captain!" they said, scattering across the deck.

He looked at Evelyn. "I'm not exactly sure what you have up your sleeve, but I'd appreciate any help."

She turned and grasped the deck's railing. The utility specialists were already getting into position along the ship's left side as a blazing wall of fire began sprouting over the sea just outside the ship's perimeter. A thick curtain of black smoke rose into the air just as the ship's port side faced the leviathan.

Stones and boulders continued to penetrate the smokescreen, but their trajectories were erratic and off target. His seashockers did well in disintegrating the stones headed for the Mythmaker, but their attacks were useless on the larger boulders, their electricity not strong enough.

"I think we should be fine," Evelyn said in a bafflingly calm manner. "You've set up an excellent illusory defense. And you seem to have the personnel to execute it."

"Your help would still be greatly appreciated," he said.

She shrugged. "Perhaps I could partake in the efforts now that there's a smokescreen. I hadn't planned on doing any weaving because I didn't want to show my hand. If that leviathan found out there's a Stillian on this ship, they'd relay that information to other vessels in their alliance. As of right now, we have the element of surprise in case we need it down the line." She shook her head and gazed at the wall of fire. "And it looks like we will. Once we flee this whirlpool, there will be no finding another one … not without Gray Whale."

Another slab of rock struck the ship, a perfect shot to the hull. He heard screams from below and dreaded the thought of how many of his crew had fell victim. Evelyn took that as her cue to join the firefighters and seashockers.

A young pirate—Tryties by name—climbed the stairs from the main deck to the quarterdeck. She stopped in front of Agnos, sweat dripping down her face. "Damage to the hull of the ship, but nothing catastrophic, Captain. Two dead, three critically injured."

He closed his eyes and exhaled slowly. "Is Ronnie already tending to the injured?"

"Yes, Captain. He's taken them to the infirmary quarters."

"Good. Thank you for the update, Tryties."

The woman scampered back down the stairs and disappeared within the ship, where most of the crew had fled to. If they weren't vital to the current objective of escaping, then they weren't needed above deck. They'd only get in the way, risking their lives for no reason whatsoever.

Being the physically inferior human that he was, all Agnos could do was watch while his crew went to work. He appreciated every single one of them. The recruitment process before his voyage to hunt the chronicle had been the most important part of his pirating career. While most people would have strived to acquire only the greatest talents, he had focused more on their personalities. What was their stance on loyalty and camaraderie? Cohesion was more important than having a bunch of skilled individuals who only wanted to compete with each other.

A boulder darted out of the smokescreen and crashed directly into the Mythmaker's port side, blasting into the guardrail and utility specialists. Many writhed in pain, while two pirates lay motionless, likely dead upon impact.

The main deck's latch opened, and several pirates who had heard the collision climbed up, each grabbing a specialist under their arms and dragging them to the specialty quarters below Agnos.

With the barrier of smoke obscuring the leviathan, it was difficult to judge how many degrees they had made it through their turn. He spun toward Gunther. "How much longer?"

"Almost there!" she screamed, leaning into the wheel. "Inform Master Stefania and Commander Sulia to prepare to shift directions."

He craned his neck, eyes raking the sails until he spotted Squallblaster Commander Troy Sulia in a lower nest of the mizzen mast. He climbed onto the stern deck and yelled, "Troy!"

The man peeked over the side of the nest.

"Get your team to shift weaving directions eastbound! We're almost out of the turn!"

"Yes, Captain!" Troy said, disappearing once again.

Agnos headed for the stern deck's lone door. He opened it, revealing the room that sat underneath the rear deck, the navigation room. An old woman sat in a chair, scribbling away across some parchment. She looked up with violet eyes encased in wrinkled skin. She was the same age as Gray Whale, but, unlike the Whale Lord's captain, her posture was evident of it.

"Captain?"

"Master Stefania, it's time we adjust the sails."

The Sailing Master nodded, carefully rising from her seat. He jogged across the room and put his arm around her back, guiding her toward the door. "You're such a sweet man," she said.

"You're a sweet young lady," he said.

After a small chuckle, she patted his chest. "I do love our banter. Can you grab my ancient for me, please?"

He stopped at the door and let go of her to grab an item that hung from the wall: a pair of wooden manacles connected by a rod. He handed them to Stefania, the sole person in charge of the rigging in case of emergency. She opened each bracelet and trapped her wrists in them, pinning her arms together. It was a strange ancient.

He stepped into the daylight and helped her to her station at the front of the stern deck. The helm could typically be found here, but the Mythmaker had been constructed in a way that allowed for a secondary steering device. The guardrail had a series of holes in four of its poles, each small enough for Stefania to press one of her fingers against. They acted as gateways, guiding her weaving ability to different sections of the ship, where other tiny holes and hooks were scattered throughout the architecture.

He lowered her to the floor. She sat with her legs crossed, reaching out her handcuffed arms and pressing a finger against each hole. Closing her eyes, she released a sigh. Strings shot from her fingertips, nearly invisible to the naked eye. The ship's rigging sprang into motion, ropes pulling and rotating, sails shifting. Not a single rigger was needed. She conducted the role of what normally required dozens of men. This ship was now her puppet.

Agnos gently placed his hand on her shoulder. "Make sure we stay on the right track. If you feel the squallblasters filling the wrong sails, adjust how you see fit."

"I shall give them a piece of my mind, Captain."

He left the stern deck and returned to the helm, where Zorra had finally appeared standing next to Gunther.

"You missed it," Zorra said.

"Missed what?" he asked. He scanned the decks, realizing the tranquility of the crew. Were they not in the midst of battle?

He noticed everyone was looking toward the back of the ship. He turned and spotted a young woman with frost-bitten blue hair standing on the rear deck, facing the opposite direction.

"Evelyn Tesai is a force to be reckoned with," Zorra said. "She may have singlehandedly gotten us out of harm's way."

"What'd she do?"

The biggest slab of marble he'd ever seen cut through the dense smoke that was now behind the ship. It spelled doom for the Mythmaker, the Powish likely slinging it as a last resort.

Evelyn thrust out her arm, palm open. A beam of ice blasted through the air, forming a colossal claw shape at the end, acting like an extension of her arm but a thousand times longer and more powerful.

The boulder walloped the frozen claw and came to an abrupt halt, frost crumbling into the ocean. Ice slowly crept across the slab, fully encasing it. The claw clenched, the boulder shattering into thousands of fragments that sunk into the sea.

Agnos tilted his head.

"She did *that*," Zorra said.

# 52

# A Job Well Done

Olivia, Vuilni, and Fane sat at one end of a long table in a royal dining hall. Silverware and empty plates were placed in front of them. At the table's opposite end was a lone, vacant chair, much larger than the rest. A royal guard stood around the hall's perimeter, holy wood warped around their bodies as armor. There were roughly twenty of them, all eyes glued to the three guests.

"She's late," Fane said.

Vuilni's posture was stiff. "I haven't ruled out the possibility of this being a trap."

Eyes trained on the guards' armor, Olivia asked, "Do you think we could punch through holy wood?"

"I'd like to see you try," one guard said. His face was masked by the supposedly indestructible material, holes cut out for the eyes and nostrils, a slit spread across the mouth.

Her lazy gaze landed on him. Perhaps she'd take him up on that offer if things were to turn south. She'd refused to attack any of the holy trees in Asalka out of respect for the Primmish religion, but that didn't mean there wasn't an urge to test her strength after hearing about their reputation.

"I see that look in your eyes," Vuilni said. "Don't get any ideas, Olivia."

Fane raised an eyebrow at the violet-haired woman. "I don't know how you could possibly read her face."

Olivia shrugged and closed her eyes. "I'm not Bryson. I don't fall victim to such petty bait."

"You're more like him than you think," Vuilni said.

The doors to the dining hall opened, and in walked Prim Queen Inedibus. She was a rounder lady, roughly the size of Passion King Damian. Her hair was a chestnut brown with graying roots wrapped around the top of her head in a single braid. An extravagant crown of holy wood nested in the center, strange lettering etched into its sides. She wore a matte gray dress that hung listlessly around her legs, its hems a clean ivory. There were no ruffles, frill, or lace—just a sleek satin fabric.

A guard had approached the head of the table upon her entry and was now waiting as she walked toward her seat. He pulled out the chair, gesturing toward it. She smiled and nodded as she took a seat. His face twitched with effort as he tried pushing it back in. He was lucky she didn't have eyes in the back of her head.

As guards closed the double doors, three smaller doors opened along the side wall. Waiters carrying plates of food filed out of them, practically gliding through the room as they balanced wonky silver trays next to their shoulders with little effort. They passed Olivia, Vuilni, and Fane, distributing plates of steamed vegetables, an abnormally large baked potato, and a bowl of noodles with onion and peppers mixed in.

Olivia frowned. As good as it all smelled, it seemed the trend of a no-meat diet extended into the royal palace also.

"Thank you," the queen said, smiling at her food as the waiters exited the hall. She grabbed a napkin from the table and placed it on her lap, then dove straight into her meal.

Olivia, Vuilni, and Fane watched, unsure of what was proper protocol in the presence of Prim royalty. The queen looked at them while carving into her potato. "You may eat."

Olivia grabbed her fork and stabbed at some broccoli, biting into it with little enthusiasm. Food had already been low on her list of desires at the moment, but without meat it might as well have been a plate of rocks. She was in this dining hall for one reason only: to find out what happened the night of the Prim Prince's assassination.

"Not that I care all that much, but Partus spoke rather highly of you three," the queen said. "And I suppose out of the Monsignors, she's the only one I'd actually trust in terms of judgment."

"If you trust her judgment, why did it take so long for you to accept a meeting with us?" Fane asked.

"Because she's still a Monsignor, a pathetic leader of a deceased religion." She twirled her fork in her noodles, lifted it, and let it sit in front of her mouth. "Not to mention, when your son is killed in one of the most secure locations in all of Kuki Sphaira, you tend to lose the ability to trust anyone." Her eyes skated to the sides, regarding her guards. "Including those who serve to protect you."

Olivia studied the masked men surrounding them.

"In my profession," Fane said, "one learns loyalty can be a whimsical concept for some."

The queen's eyes narrowed, studying him as she closed her mouth around her fork and began to chew. "Are you the one with black fire?" she asked.

"That's correct, and I deeply apologize for my ruse a few weeks back."

She shook her head. "To think I have an assassin in my midst. My son is likely rolling in his grave."

"We're not bad people," Vuilni said.

"But you spread lies," Inedibus said. "You have somehow convinced the Monsignors their god is alive. You've breathed life into their nonsensical preaching."

"Dimiourgos is alive," Vuilni said, making Olivia wince at the absurdity of the name. "I've seen him with my own two eyes."

"And according to the Monsignors, they've recently seen dimiours. Yet they can't provide me with any such proof, claiming they allowed these figments of their imagination to travel to the Power Kingdom." Inedibus sighed. "Really … humanistic animals from before our timeline walking the land? How stupid must I be?"

"I can't blame you, Queen," Fane said. "I would have never believed it had I not seen it."

Several minutes passed in silence before Olivia grew exhausted. They weren't achieving anything. It was time she cut to the point. "Do you know why we requested this meeting?"

"You want to investigate my son's assassination," Inedibus said. "You believe it will help True Light in the war against the Rogue Demon."

Olivia nodded.

"Well, that's not happening. We don't divulge information to anyone outside of the palace. I am a kind lady, but I do not respond well to meddling."

"Then why entertain this arrangement?" Vuilni asked, dropping her fork onto the plate with a clang.

"Because of what I was offered," Inedibus said. "I guess the Monsignors grew tired of my constant denials, so they did the unthinkable and offered me a greater share of their holy trees." She pursed her lips and glanced to the side in thought. "I was shocked to find out they'd go to such lengths, especially after centuries of their firm disposition on its rationing."

"That alone should tell you enough," Olivia said, growing impatient. The last thing she wanted to find out was that she had come all this way and wasted all this time for nothing. "They're willing to risk something so sacred to their beliefs because of what they witnessed. The dimiours told them to help us."

Inedibus scowled. "Stop with the dimiour nonsense. Dimiourgos died years before our timeline, as did his power over this kingdom. The royals took his place and have been ruling since then. We should have abolished religion long ago, just like the other kingdoms did during the first couple of centuries." The queen stood. "Instead, we nurtured those fanatics and zealots, turning them into something far stronger than they should have been."

"We just want—"

"I don't care what you want." Inedibus dabbed a napkin against her mouth and pudgy cheeks. "My son is dead. That's all you need to know. How that piece of information even managed to escape years ago befuddles me." She released a cathartic breath, face relaxing. "I've granted you an audience. Now, I demand your dismissal." She turned and headed for the doors. "General Pinillias will escort you out."

She walked out of the hall, and a man standing by the doors looked back at the table. Unlike the other guards, he didn't wear a mask. His hair was fully gray, slicked back with an oily substance. "Follow me," he said. "I will show you out."

Olivia shared glances with Vuilni and Fane before leaving the table and following the general out.

"That was a complete failure," Vuilni said. She looked at Fane. "I thought you would have provided a lot more help."

"I don't know why."

"Shouldn't you be good at coercing people into giving you information?"

"I'm an assassin, not a spy. And if you want me to even attempt at mind tricks and deception, I'd need my partner with me."

"And who's that?" Vuilni asked.

He smiled at some fond memory. "Horos Vevlu."

While Vuilni and Fane bickered, Olivia observed their surroundings. She didn't recognize this corridor as one they'd walked through on the way in. There were no windows and candles were sparse, providing little light. She came to a stop, Fane and Vuilni bumping into her.

"Give us a warning next time," Vuilni said, lifting her foot and rubbing her toes through her shoes.

"Where are we?" Olivia asked.

Pinillias turned, hands clasped behind his back. "Somewhere we can't be overheard." He looked past the three of them, then closed his eyes and lowered his head. "Everyone always speaks of the prince as if he'd been the only one assassinated that night. Everyone forgot the other death that day."

"The general," Olivia said.

"Yes, my predecessor. He'd been a victim of betrayal, stabbed in the back by a woman who abandoned us years prior."

The corridor fell silent for a moment. "How much can you tell us about that night?" Olivia asked.

"Everything, but it must be done away from the palace. I have my monthly prayer in the northernmost holy tree of Asalka in two weeks. That is where we can discuss it."

Vuilni tilted her head. "Prayer? I thought this palace separated itself from religion."

He shook his head. "The queen likes to feign blasphemy, but even she hasn't completely rid herself of her beliefs. I think that night took a lot of faith out of us all." He fell silent, eyes growing somber. "We never would have expected it from Kadlest."

*     *     *

Getting out of bed was one of the hardest things Bryson had ever done in his life. His chest and head were still wrapped in bandage, and small movements created searing burns in his sternum—a jarring change to his body's frigid temperatures.

He was supposed to be bed-ridden for another few days, but he couldn't lay idly by any longer. He had spent too much time in Brilliance. With his success in regaining his electricity and gaining entry into Mendac's old laboratory, he'd accomplished everything he wanted to in this city. There was nothing left for him here.

He exited the room and limped aimlessly down a hallway, possessing zero knowledge about Jugtah's estate. It didn't feel like a home as much as it did a large, empty building. The man had only moved in a few weeks ago and was still trying to settle in. Something told Bryson there was too much space for one man anyway.

After a hopeless hunt inside the house, he took his search outside to find success. He edged his way around the estate and spotted Jugtah seated at a patio table, sipping on what looked to be champagne. The man he sat across from gave Bryson pause: Benedict Ronal, the head steward of the Intel royal family.

After a momentary lapse, Bryson made his best attempt at a jog toward the patio. He flinched every few steps, reaching for his chest, but he'd never been so happy to see a fresh face. Benedict caught a glimpse of him, eyebrows climbing his forehead. He was likely just as stunned to see Bryson rushing in his direction. After muttering something to Jugtah, the surgeon turned Bryson's way with a grin.

"Benedict!" Bryson shouted, stepping onto the patio. "I've never been so happy to see you!"

The steward raised an eyebrow before chuckling awkwardly, placing his hand against the back of his head. "What exactly did you tinker with in his head, Nyemas?"

"Is that not the greeting you would have expected?" Jugtah asked.

"All is in the past," Bryson said, limping his way across the patio and coming to a stop next to their table. "Being stuck in this city has made me appreciate the people in Dunami."

"That bad, huh?" Benedict said.

"Bunch of Mendac worshippers."

"Well, it's good to see you, too, milord," Benedict said. He stood and extended a hand.

Bryson beamed, firmly grasping it. "How did you get in here?" he asked. "I thought there was a strict policy about people entering the city."

"If King Vitio puts his foot down on a matter, Wendel cannot refute it," said Benedict. "As much as that man wants to believe he's above our king, that has never been the case. However, I have agreed to stay away from any building that practices weavineering—not that I possess any desire to see them."

"Have you come to take me back?"

"I have," Benedict said, smirking at Bryson's weak excuse of a fist pump. The pain was still overwhelming. "The moment Lilu informed us of your surgery, Princess Shelly demanded I come up here to make sure everything went smoothly. She wants you back as soon as possible."

Bryson swooned at the name of his love. He missed her and his son dearly. "And they're just going to let us out of here?" he asked. "I thought Wendel would have a lot of questions for me."

"That man is irrelevant," Benedict said. As sure as the steward sounded of himself, Jugtah's eyes widened at those words. But, he didn't speak on it. "He can do nothing. If he wants Lilu to stay in Brilliance, he'll squelch those curiosities."

"That sounds great to me," Bryson said. "When do we leave?"

Benedict eyed Jugtah, who responded with a dismissive wave. "Whenever you want," the steward said, turning to Bryson again.

"Tonight?"

"So it will be, milord."

*     *     *

Bryson had finished packing his belongings and was now standing in the doorway of his townhouse room. He surveyed its bareness, smiling at the pile of memories he had accumulated in the short span of a few months: the late nights sitting on the balcony with Lilu and Frederick, admiring the two of them as they pretended to not be madly in love with each other; the frequent disappearances of Limone and Gracie, only to be followed by questionable noises from a floor above.

Lilu had built herself a wonderful team here in Brilliance, one that sorely reminded him of the Jestivan. Perhaps, that was where she had siphoned her inspiration from. The four weavineers were serious about their purpose while maintaining a fun workplace. They meshed well together and fed off each other's vibes. It did make Bryson miss his life at Phesaw, those brief two years as a Jestivan—even if most of that time had been spent in disarray.

He shut the door and left the townhouse. During his walk to Steel Field, he thought of Lilu. This trip had found success in unexpected places. He felt like he had mended his relationship with her. Not only that, but it was stronger than it had ever been. He supposed he had Gracie to thank, for she'd been the one to knock some sense into him.

Thousands of Intelights fluttered high above, swallowing the Bastion's cavernous ceiling. Light poured through a skylight, splashing the weavineer town in dusk's hue. As he neared Steel Field, he was confused by the silence. He should have heard the conversation of weavineers and hammering of metals in the distance. He'd grown anxious to see what kind of progress they'd made while he'd been out of commission.

He broke free of the Bastion's final block of buildings and was met with cacophonous cheers. A horde of weavineers in white lab coats expanded before him, with Lilu, Gracie, Frederick, and Limone standing in front. His friends smiled while their subordinates continued their frenzy, many placing their fingers in their mouths to expel high-pitched whistles. Dozens of scattered travolters towered over the crowd. Between their sheer size and the twenty-foot cannons extending ahead of them, they were menacing beasts—like ships on land.

He stepped onto the hard surface of Steel Field and limped his way toward Lilu, gawking at the beauty of her innovations. He'd hate to be the unfortunate enemy to step in front of a travolter.

Frederick embraced him in a hug, patting his back with one hand while Lilu laughed. He stepped away, and Gracie gave him a tighter squeeze. Limone elected to simply shake his hand, which Bryson didn't mind at all. He was euphoric to have met Lilu's friends, and he couldn't thank her enough for giving him the opportunity to take a step into her world for a short while—even if he was ready to rid himself of this place.

They split away, but Lilu remained standing in the same spot, arms crossed with a sly quirk to her lips, a pink begonia nestled into her hair. He walked forward and reached out for a hug, but she raised her hand and wagged a finger. "Your mission here isn't complete."

He scoffed. "Like hell it isn't."

"Let's go," she said, turning and walking toward the crowd. The weavineers split, clearing a path for Bryson, Lilu, and her friends.

People beamed at him as he passed. Some nodded, others clapped, a few reached out to try to shake his hand. Even those who resented him at first because of his comments about Mendac seemed to have forgotten all about their feelings. He should have been flattered, but he only felt discomfort. Why did they praise *him*, as if he was the one responsible for their recent success? If that's what they thought, then they were due for a reality check.

The path brought them to a travolter. He found himself in awe now that he stood directly next to it. Part of him couldn't believe he knew the woman responsible for inventing such a technological marvel. But, he wasn't surprised that it was Lilu of all people. She'd been the one to teach him how to properly weave in the first place. Even Agnos had viewed her as an equal, though their areas of expertise were on opposite ends of the scholarly spectrum.

The two Jestivan peeled off from Gracie, Frederick, and Limone and rounded the vehicle, where a set of stairs climbed up its backside. He followed her up, and suddenly the scope of the crowd really hit him. There were more weavineers here than what was seen on a typical shift. Had the whole town been invited to witness this?

They dropped into the cockpit, where there were six seats, two to a row. He didn't even bother trying to make sense of the levers, buttons, and wheels. All he knew was that he felt invincible up here, staring down at the people on the ground as if he was one of Pilot Ophala's hawks. The massive cannon loomed above him like the bowsprit of a galleon. What could possibly take this behemoth down?

"We're not going to drive this thing, right?" he whispered, leaning toward Lilu.

"Of course not, but you *will* place your stamp on this project. You played a part, and the team wanted a way to truly celebrate your visit."

He twisted his lips in thought. "I didn't really contribute to this," he said. "You made this happen, and they need to realize it. If you're not going to address them about that, can I?"

She paused, then laughed. "You want to defend me?"

"Only if you're comfortable with—"

"Go ahead," she said, cutting him off with a shrug. "At least you asked, which means you're learning. Besides, I'm interested in what you have to say."

After a smile, he hopped onto the cockpit's edge, balancing perfectly on the guardrail.

"I was brought here with many objectives in mind," he announced, raising his voice to make it heard as far as possible. "One of those objectives was to provide a source of inspiration for all of you. Because of my last name and direct relation to a certain man, the commissioner thought it wise to put me within eyesight of his weavineers, which implies he doubted the ability of many of you."

He scanned the crowd in efforts to spot Wendel, thinking the man wouldn't miss such an occasion. His gaze shifted to the distant balconies, but the commissioner's was empty. Would he not show his face?

"I believe that I had nothing to do with the successes I see around me today. This was accomplished because of your own skills, but more important, the woman who led you. She was the one who imagined the idea at the age of eleven, sketched the blueprints and diagrams, calculated the formulas, and ultimately constructed the prototype. That travolter that has sat next to the stage all these months—the very one you've all been trying to replicate—was a product of Lilu."

She tugged at his pant leg and whispered, "People helped me on that."

He smiled and nodded. "Of course, she had the help of Gracie, Frederick, and Limone, too. But even they achieved it under her guidance." He took a deep breath. "This city didn't need me. This day would have come with or without me. In fact, it seems there was more progress while I was on leave this past week than there had been over the course of the three months I watched from the stage."

Reaching back, he offered his hand to her. She grasped it, and he pulled her onto the rail. She stood gracefully and effortlessly—a credit to Debo.

"Lilu Intel's genius, hard work, and skill as a leader created all of this. I wasn't around during the beginning of this project, but one thing I do know is that all of these travolters are a sign of the level of respect you have for her. If you didn't care, this day wouldn't have come." He looked down, images of Shelly and L.K. flooding his mind. "Soon I will no longer be a LeAnce, and I'm proud to know I'll share the same last name as a woman like Lilu. And it pisses me off that I have to say this, but everyone should revere a mind of her caliber."

Steel Field exploded into a cacophony of cheers. The crowd roared. The travolter rumbled beneath his feet, sending vibrations up his legs. He felt the response in his bones, piercing his core. A euphoric spirit blanketed the atmosphere, and he almost felt as if Jilly was with them.

He turned toward Lilu, who was failing miserably at wiping away tears. She was clearly sniffling, but he couldn't hear it above the deafening blare of the crowd. He could barely hear his own thoughts. For a moment, he forgot about the pain in his chest and the frigidness of his body. Ever since meeting her when they had become Jestivan, he'd noticed she received very little recognition for everything she provided to the group—he was a guilty member of that party.

She stepped back, dropping into the cockpit. He followed, briefly cringing at the pain in his chest. She crouched and opened a latch in the floor, still wiping her face with her other hand.

"You idiot," she said. "This was supposed to be your day."

Gingerly, he lowered himself next to her. "I don't deserve a day," he said. "In a city where women like Gracie have to grow up thinking she's less than someone else because of her gender, you have continued to call bull crap on such a notion. I admire every ounce of your personality and how you carry yourself."

She released a weak laugh and grabbed his wrist, placing his hand above the latch. "I give you the honor of being the first person to fill the supply of a travolter's cannon—outside of the prototype, that is. If we ever enter battle, this travolter will lead the charge and fire the first few shots. It will serve as a wake-up call to the world, and I will steer it."

He stared at her and nodded, then looked down and released a blast of Intel Chains into the supply, weaving carefully to follow the ridges carved within. His clout felt different than it had his entire life, but he liked it. Whatever Jugtah had done inside his body had worked.

They were invisible to those on Steel Field, crouched within the cockpit, but the cheers continued to rattle the vehicle. He lifted his hand, and she slapped the latch shut. Then she wrapped him in a hug.

"Thank you for coming, Bryson. You're a welcome addition to my family."

# 53

# Sky-Skimmers

Himitsu would never grow tired of the Central Grasslands' sky. It was the bluest he'd ever seen, as he lay back on the sloped roof of Pluzina's cottage. Since arriving here, he'd spend at least an hour a day in this exact spot following a search of the surrounding prairie. What made it even more serene was the company of Kaylee. She lay next to him, shoulder to shoulder, knees folded and feet planted on the shingles. An occasional breeze blew her wispy silver hair into his face, which he didn't mind. It had a gentle floral scent—nothing too thick.

He turned his head to look at her. As always, her face was buried in an open book, her eyes narrowed as if she was questioning the truth behind every word written on the page—like she knew more than the author, which wasn't an absurd notion.

"I just don't see it," she said, the book looming above her face.

"See what?"

"The argument that inducing a coma in order to force life-saving surgery against the wishes of a terminally ill patient is, somehow, morally correct." She scoffed after reading a bit deeper. "The scenarios painted by Doctor Ricter are absurd."

"Tell me one," he said.

"Let's put the two of us in his first scenario," she said, rolling onto her side and nearly on top of him in the process. "If death was certain for me, but there was a surgery that could better my chances, would you want me to do it?"

"Duh."

"And if I didn't want to?" she asked, eyebrows rising.

"Why would you rather die?"

"Because the solution the apothecary uses to put me under during the surgery is a heavily toxic one. It'll put me to sleep and numb my pain receptors, but it's highly probable I awaken with permanent amnesia."

He shrugged. "I could win your affection back."

She shook her head with a grave look and returned to lying on her back. "I wouldn't want to wake up without my memory. Even though I wouldn't know what it was I had missed, I'm sure I'd realize its impact over time. I'd have to relearn motor functions or just the simple action of forming words."

"So this Doctor Ricter guy says a surgeon should be able to place a patient in a coma without their consent in order to perform the surgery?" he asked, trying to make sense of things.

She nodded. "And a scenario he uses is what if the patient has a loved one who threatens suicide if the surgery isn't done."

Mouth curling into a frown, he tilted his head and scratched his head. "That is an *extreme* hypothetical ... and it's kind of twisted."

"It is," she said. "As the apothecary in that situation, I would advise the loved one to seek professional help. I'm not doing something to someone if they don't want it, even if it's to save their life."

He sighed. "I wouldn't threaten to take my own life, but I'd hope you'd want to live."

"Doctor Ricter is a genius, but I don't like his practices," she muttered.

"Speaking of geniuses, have you made any progress on Pluzina about Neeko?" he asked.

"No, but I'm connecting the dots when she answers certain questions. I have a theory on the status of Neeko's whereabouts, but I can't jump to rash conclusions ..." She trailed off, setting her book down. "Or maybe I just don't want to accept the possibility."

"Of what?" he asked.

"I think he's dead."

He sat up, hands planted behind him for support. "I'd say it's a rash conclusion. What would have even caused it? He wasn't in danger."

"Old age is a thing, Himitsu."

He looked at her, trying to make out what she was feeling through those narrowed eyes as she stared at the sky. How handy it must have been to read auras.

"I entertained the possibility once I noticed her sorrow every time I mentioned the man's name," she said. "I thought it might have been that his name reminded her of their childhood, when Neeko and Mynute were good friends, but her pain seemed too intense for that. It felt like a fresh wound."

"So you assume he's dead based on that?"

"Obviously not, but I dug deeper by asking more direct questions. Even though she's very skilled at masking her aura, I sensed hints of guilt laced within her sorrow. This led me to believe Neeko had come here sometime after Mynute's death. Perhaps, that guilt stemmed for her turning him away." She paused. "Or maybe it came from something else. I asked if she thought Neeko was still alive."

"What'd she say?" he asked.

"She said he died decades ago in the Warpfinate, but it took a moment for her to answer. And when she did, not only did her sorrow thicken, but the guilt did as well." She looked at him, gaze softening. "She's lying, Himitsu. When I asked about any of Neeko's possible keepsakes, she continued her story about not having seen the man since she was young."

He sat up and placed his forearms across his knees, gaze falling to the roof. "What do we do then?"

She sighed. "I don't know how we're supposed to find a dead man."

He did, but it would require the keen eyes of Skyrise.

*       *       *

Yama couldn't remember the last time she'd felt gut-wrenching fear. It was a foreign sensation, and right now it was tearing at her insides as she stared over the Adren Kingdom's Edge. It was nothing but a blanket of blue stretching into the distance, the sky plunging beneath her with no ground in site. All that could be seen was the cragged wall of the floating island. It dipped inward and jutted out, shaped by countless millennia of natural erosion. In some places, spires thrust out from the wall, making it hard to find a clear spot to jump.

Across every kingdom of the Light Realm, typically the Edge was heavily guarded. But, Yinyon's Edge was one of the few unobstructed locations. Anyone could walk up to it and fall victim to the crumbling precipice. But Yama was no victim. She'd throw herself over.

She inched forward, allowing the toes of her leather running shoes to hang over nothing. The crust wanted to give way beneath her, and she liked that thought. If nature did the deed for her, there'd be no second-guessing. Glancing behind her, she longed for the life she was supposed to have in this village. A mile of grass separated her from the nearest pasture, not a tree or bush in between them. Nobody cared.

She exhaled slowly through circled lips, looking over the edge once again. Wallowing in self-pity had never been her forte, which was the main reason why she'd never gotten along with Agnos. In this moment, however, she felt she could connect with the fellow orphan. He'd owned that part of him while she hadn't—not until now.

Closing her eyes, she detached her sheathed sword from her hip and placed it in the grass. It didn't deserve this fate. In a way, she felt like she was betraying a loyal companion. That blade had been the only thing to stick by her side through thick and thin. Her family had abandoned her, just like Toono and Jilly.

But who was she to make such complaints? She had abandoned the Jestivan to join their enemy, only to follow that up with the ultimate betrayal … taking Jilly's life, robbing the world of her spirit.

She opened her eyes, determined to watch every bit of her demise. She'd absorb every detail of her plunge and wither in the terror. If karma knew any better, perhaps she'd make impact with a spire. Her chest swelled as she inhaled deeply, spreading her arms to the side. She fell forward, accepting that there wasn't anything left for her here.

"What do you think you're doing?"

Yama's eyes widened, the collar of her tunic choking the front of her neck as someone grabbed the back of her shirt. She leaned over nothingness at an unnatural angle, her feet barely on the precipice, hair dangling below her face. Who had stopped her? There had been nobody around for at least a mile just a second ago.

She turned her head, spotting the youthful innkeeper, Kolver. What was this man? How much ground had he just covered in the blink of an eye?

"Are you an idiot?" he asked. "No Fuuna I've ever known would commit to something as asinine as this." He yanked her back, stepping to the side and allowing her to tumble across the ground.

She reached for a handful of grass and heaved a forceful breath from her lungs. He stood over her, watching curiously.

*I just tried to kill myself,* she thought incredulously. All it had taken was that split second when she dove for her death to regret it. Luckily, Kolver had interfered.

Sobbing, she pounded her fist into the sod, lying hopelessly in the innkeeper's shadow. She looked up from the ground and gasped at the woman who lay in front of her.

Jilly's golden hair split at her shoulders, some spooling atop the grass, the rest lying on her back. An enormous sunhat sat on her head, shadows enveloping her entire face save her glowing blue eyes.

"Jilly …?" she croaked.

The dead girl's ghost sported a pronounced frown, her chin resting between both palms, elbows planted in the grass. Her legs were kicked up behind her, ankles entwined and bare feet tapping against each other. The bottoms of her feet were dirty, as was always the case with a girl who spent all of her time playing outside.

"You're judging me, aren't you?" Yama asked.

A pool of crimson soaked the grass beneath Jilly. She didn't seem to notice, her eyes trained on the swordswoman. Yama squeezed her eyes shut, shame consuming her once again. She hated every fiber of her existence.

"Did you just have an out-of-body experience or something?"

Kolver's question jolted her to her senses. She opened her eyes, but Jilly was no longer there. She pushed herself up to a knee. "How'd you know where to find me?"

"I went looking for you on the hill. When I didn't see you, I thought you had finally wised up and left." He paused, looking away from the distant hill to regard her. "But then I saw you walking toward the Edge and thought, well, that can't be good."

"I checked my surroundings before jumping. Nobody was near me."

He shrugged. "We have a saying here in Yinyon: *Distance is relative*. For me, anyone within a few miles is within reasonable proximity."

She wiped her cheek, ashamed of the emotions slapped across her face. "I don't understand how you've managed to achieve such a speed percentage. With such skill, you shouldn't be in a remote village this far away from civilization. You'd do great things elsewhere."

He offered his hand, which she accepted. "I'm exactly where I need to be," he said, pulling her up to her feet.

"Was this not where I needed to be?" she asked, looking back at the village. "Was that why I was cast out as a child?"

He sighed, following her gaze. Cows grazed in the pasture closest to them. Sheep raced into a pen in the lot next door, chased by a shepherd dog. A woman stood close by, keeping a watchful eye on the process.

"Look," Kolver said, "I'm not in the business of allowing someone to kill herself, nor do I fancy the idea of feeling responsible for it. I was told to introduce you to some people only in the case of emergency. Attempted suicide falls under that category in my eyes." He looked back at her. "I can't guarantee you answers, but I will show you a glimpse of what is behind

Yinyon's infrastructure. We are more than just a rural village … much more."

"I'm not surprised," she said, eyes rolling toward the two oaks atop the village's distant hill. "You bred the likes of Ataway Debonicus Kawi and Leon Suadade." She raised an eyebrow at him. "And you have proven to be quite the specimen yourself."

He turned for the village. "Come, and don't make me regret this."

They didn't head for the mayor's building at the heart of the village like she'd expected. Instead, they wandered through a corn maze for several minutes before arriving at the door of an unassuming barn house.

Kolver entered without knocking. She remained outside for a moment, hesitant of what came next. "Let's go," he said, glancing back outside. "We don't have all day."

She inhaled deeply and stepped inside. Straw covered the ground, providing a healthy crunch with each step. Sunlight streamed through glassless windows near the top of the walls, reflecting off the golden-brown haystacks of various heights scattered throughout the barn. Besides the blocks of hay, it was an empty structure. She saw no tools or livestock, and the air was fresh, not a scent of animal dung lingering through it.

"You can come out," Kolver said. "I've brought Yama. She tried to kill herself."

"And you didn't let her?" came a woman's voice.

He paused, mouth agape. Then his brows furrowed. "Should I have?"

"She doesn't exactly deserve to live, so who are we to stop her from casting judgment upon herself?"

"We're better than that," he said.

A long pause followed. "Better than allowing one less evil to walk the land?"

Yama didn't blame him for falling silent. The mysterious voice had a point, though she was curious of its source. Was the woman hiding behind one of the taller hay stacks?

"Do you request I take her away?" he asked.

"That would be wise."

He sighed, turning toward the exit. "I tried," he whispered to Yama.

She didn't move. "I deserve to know why I was abandoned as a child. I'm owed that answer."

He squeezed her arm. "Don't push your luck."

"Some would say that act alone was responsible for the path I took," Yama said, ignoring him.

A small laugh carried through the barn. "Is that what you claim? Are you so mentally weak to believe someone else made all your decisions throughout your life?"

"I made those decisions," Yama said, Kolver's grip weakening. "I was given one task when I was abandoned, and that was to train as hard as I could until I reached a certain speed percentage. Instead, I chased companionship, stemming from the absence of a mother, father, or siblings."

"You bend easily," the voice replied. "That's what I'm hearing. You've returned to Yinyon without completing your task. Worst of all, you've returned as a demonic thing, fighting for the Rogue Demon as one of his lackeys … taking the life of a dear friend."

"I can help you!" Yama exclaimed. "I have useful information about Toono and his side!" She didn't understand why citizens of such a remote village cared, but if that's where their interests lied, then she'd cater to them.

She blinked, stunned by the image before her. There were now three other people in the barn, appearing casually out of thin air. Two men—long, lean, and burned by the sun—sat atop smaller straw bales.

The third person was a woman, who sat on top of a rolled up hay bale between the two men. She wasn't as tall as them, but her heightened position demanded more of a presence. She sat with one leg folded, an arm resting across the knee, and the other leg hanging down the front of the bale. Strapped to her back were two long swords, a hilt protruding above each shoulder. Her hair was a faded violet.

The woman shook her head with sorrowful eyes. "To think I spawned such a wretched thing."

Yama dropped to her knees. "Mom?"

"You will address me as Master Soraku."

The barn fell silent, the tension thick enough to hold back Yama's tears. She couldn't believe her eyes. She stared at an older version of herself, making her wonder if she possessed *any* traits of her father—not that she even knew who the man was. She studied the two men, seated just as leisurely as her mom. Were either of them her dad?

They both looked the same age as Soraku, likely early on in their fifties. The man to the left had a head of gray hair, speckled with black. A spandex singlet squeezed his rugged frame. The other gentleman was lankier, and looked to wield a scimitar based on the shape of his scabbard across his back. Amber hair flirted between brown and red, his forehead stretching up his skull, paving the way for a bald spot in the shape of a crescent moon. He may have been younger than the other two.

Despite the age in their faces, their bodies were as fit as Yama's. And considering the fashion in which they arrived—seemingly teleporting into her vision—there was more to envy beyond their statures.

"I think what makes everything worse in my eyes," Soraku said, "is that you had the nerve to try to wriggle your way out of your nefarious deeds by means of suicide." Her eyebrows furrowed. "Such a cowardly act. Can you not face your demons?"

"I'd hit rock bottom when I returned here only to be met with Kolver's spurning hand. After a lifetime of believing my purpose lay in this village, one could imagine my dejection."

"Nobody pities you, Yama," her mother snapped. "We are good people here, and we respect good people. We've had someone in True Light's ranks for a couple years now. And even before that, he or she was close to people you were close to. That person has kept tabs on you and those you've surrounded yourself with, relaying information back to us when appropriate. We know not only of your deeds, but the present day status of the world. Soon, we'll come out of hiding and join the efforts of those whom we believe to be the good guys."

"I can help," Yama said.

"I don't care. Us three" —she extended a hand toward the two men flanking her— "are all we need. We're the only three of our kind." She paused, gazing down at the balding man with amber hair. "I suppose there's a fourth now, but we're waiting for their return."

"What is 'your kind'?" Yama asked.

"The world has thought us to be extinct," Soraku said, "which we were nearly so. All things considered, I suppose I can let you in on our secret. The world will find out anyway."

Yama fell backwards, hands landing in straw, her mother now standing directly in front of her. Yama's jaw dropped. She'd always considered herself to be a master swordsman with elite speed, yet she couldn't track this woman. It gave her flashbacks to the Generals' Battle, when she'd come face-to-face with a teleporting Devish man in the stands.

Soraku had covered roughly fifty feet in a flash, creating no smeared trail of colors, not even a blast of wind. She'd moved with the ferocity of a bolt shot from a crossbow and then stopped with the delicacy of a child's whisper.

Yama looked up at Soraku in shock. With her mother this close, Yama could see the woman's tight wrinkles, subtle age spots, and loose skin in her neck area.

"A long time ago," Soraku said, "our distant ancestors were known as Wall-Runners or Sky-Skimmers."

*No way*, Yama thought, immediately recognizing the terms.

Her mother's gaze hardened. "Now, you'd call us Adren Assassins."

# 54

# The Heir to House Gromel

Creep sat in a lavish carriage, complete with a drinking fountain in the back that must have been connected to a water store somewhere beneath the floor. He maintained a calm demeanor despite the roving eyes of his travel companion. Rose wore the wealthiest of Powish attire: black slacks that nipped at her ankles, held up by suspenders that looped over her shoulders. No matter how long he spent around Powish aristocrats, he couldn't get used to their sense of fashion.

"Let me do all the talking, and we'll be all right," she said with a sweet smile.

"Fine by me," he said, peeling back a curtain and watching as they neared a small manor. They were in Stratum Four, a few stratums below the likes of Rose. He didn't know much about her, but she was part of Rattius's group, so he'd trust her until given reason not to. Most members of SLO were mysteries to him. While they may have known each other quite well, they were guarded when around him.

According to Rose, her appearance at this ball would be of colossal significance. It was unheard of for a citizen of her stratum to attend such a lowly house's event. But, to the few lordlings in attendance privy to SLO, they'd understand what her presence implied.

"You're so mysterious, so *entrancing*," she said, whispering the last word.

"I'm a claimed man," he said, giving her stern eyes even he didn't believe.

"For how long?"

He shook his head and returned to his sightseeing, reaching a hand up his sleeve and running a finger across the edge of his favorite knife. It was such a grounding weapon, a reminder of why he no longer called the Light Realm his home. *Soraku, what has come of you now?*

The carriage rolled to a stop, and the side door opened. As he followed Rose outside, he sighed with relief at the manor ahead of him. He appreciated its more modest size. And unlike the buildings of the upper stratums, regular wood composed its bones.

He didn't have to sneak his way inside like with the Gromel Ball. He trotted up a few stone steps, strolled down a walkway, and then ascended some more stairs before entering the manor. He lengthened his strides to keep up with Rose.

The inside of the house matched its exterior—no gold, marble, or silver, just a lot of polished wood. Murals weren't quite the size as those seen hanging in Gromel's estate, nor were they as intricate. The smaller windows lent to a dingier atmosphere, too. It seemed Creep had become quite a harsh critic, which made him want to gag. It was still a manor, and a palace when compared to the things slaves called homes in Stratum Zero.

Even though he shouldn't run into anyone familiar here, he'd still taken precautions by changing his appearance. A bowler hat now joined his ensemble, a mustache was glued above his mouth, and a pair of thick-rimmed, black spectacles sat high on his nose. These were bothersome. How people felt comfortable with such weights pressing into their face was beyond him.

Rose led him through the foyer with a hooked elbow, wending between guests, all of whom turned and stared at the couple. Their eyes were first drawn to her, but they'd quickly skate to him, their expressions of awe twisting into confusion. He found it odd how people from Stratum Four could recognize someone from one of the higher stratums so easily. Stratums One through Four didn't mix with Stratums Five through Eight … *Unless Rose was an exception to that rule?*

Nobody greeted the two of them, nor did anyone even attempt at approaching them. Guests moved out of the way, parting like the sea before the bow of a ship, only to converge again behind them. He looked up toward an overlook, where one woman stood like a perched owl, her gaze following them. They had obviously caught the eye of someone important.

Rose, too, glanced up, but only for a moment. The two ladies knew each other, leading him to believe the one on the overlook was a SLO lordling working under Rattius.

"Is she one of us?" he muttered out of the corner of his mouth.

"Kind of."

He looked over his shoulder toward the overlook, but the woman had vanished.

Upon entering the grand hall, resembling one of Phelos's ancient cathedrals with its arching windows and stained glass, those already seated at tables slowly took notice of Rose and her mysterious companion. She sauntered straight down the center of the hall, practically pulling him along. It didn't help that the walkway was built like a pageant runway, elevating the pair above the other guests. They even beckoned the attention of those at the head table, the only other area of the hall matching their height.

The six people at the head table stood as Rose came to a halt. They looked to be a family—a mother, father, and four children whose ages likely fell somewhere between six to seventeen. He glanced back, observing the ball-goers. A good majority of them were preoccupied with food, conversation, or dance. Upbeat chatter and the music of a stringed quartet filled the hall, offering a more authentic ambience than what he'd experienced at the Gromel estate. He was also pleased with the severe drop-off in the slave count.

"We've been expecting you, Rose," the older man said. Oil caked his round bald head. He looked toward Creep. "And we're excited to get to know the new guy." He leaned over the table, which somehow braced itself against the weight of his belly. "It's kind of exotic, the thought of working with someone from your king—"

"I'm going to stop you right there, Pongrotto," Rose said, holding up a hand. "Show us our seats and get this thing over with. That way we can get to matters of importance."

He straightened up and nodded. "Of course, of course. And I promise it will only last a couple of hours." He extended a hand toward an empty table near the front of the floor. "I hope it's to your liking."

She nodded toward the others at the head table before departing for their own. Her elbow remained locked with Creep's until they arrived to their seats. He cringed as he rubbed his shoulder, thankful that ruse was over.

"You're not doing a great job at playing the part," she said with a wry grin. "You're supposed to be accustomed to these things, Mister Lattimore."

Creep paused, forgetting that was his alias for tonight. She lifted an eyebrow, and he said, "Yeah, well, I work best from the shadows, not in the thick of it all." He wasn't Praetor, whose maxim had always been: *Hide in plain sight; disguise with light.*

A slave visited their table and read out the specials for the event. While Rose requested a spiced carrot hummus, he focused on the slave's skin. The man seemed to be relatively unharmed—not a scar or bruise in sight.

"Snap out of it," Rose said.

Creep blinked, eyes rolling up to the slave's face. "I'm not hungry, thank you."

As the man walked away, she narrowed her eyes at a table behind Creep. "I've caught the attention of the family from Stratum Five that Rattius lured into attending this ball. And it seems the young heir has taken a fancy to you."

He brushed his napkin onto the floor, pretending to have dropped it. As he leaned over to pick it up, he snuck a peek behind him and immediately recognized the too-tall bun of hair standing atop a young girl's head. He snapped upward, body rigid as he stared at Rose. "What are they doing here?"

"I'm not sure, but Rattius insisted they be here." She leaned in and whispered, "He made sure rumors of my attendance here reached their house. House Itria is a rather pretentious one. They cling to anything or anyplace that hosts higher families." She chuckled softly. "It's why they keep sneaking glances at me. Yesenia, however, only cares about you apparently."

He recalled the night of House Gromel's ball, when events had gone south for him. During his desperate attempt to flee the mansion while being chased by a giant, Yesenia had helped him, pointing him in the direction of Rattius while sending the giant the other way. This raised a question.

"Is Yesenia part of SLO?"

Her brows furrowed. "A child, especially one from that family? Definitely not. What would make you ask that?"

He didn't respond. If that was her reaction, then either Rattius withheld that information from her or Yesenia's motives that night had genuinely been to help Creep escape via a misdirection ploy. That would have meant running into Rattius had been a matter of convenience, but that didn't seem right.

"Then why would Rattius go through the trouble of luring House Itria here?" he asked.

"He wants me to speak with Ernest and Lana, which will require a brief retreat to a private parlor. I'm to pry information out of them about their slave-handling practices." She shivered after those words. "Will you be able to handle yourself here alone?"

He leaned back and sighed. "Don't be shocked if you come back to an empty plate. I'm not one to watch food go cold."

She stood up and adjusted the cuffs of her button-up. "You didn't even order any food, but help yourself. I'll be back in a bit."

He didn't bother turning to watch Rose exit the hall with Ernest and Lana. He only hoped they hadn't seen through his disguise. But if Yesenia had been staring that hard, then that didn't bode well.

The hummus arrived, and he tried to resist stealing it. That only lasted about ten minutes. He reached across the table and dragged the plate to his side. He lifted a spoonful of the dish and closed his mouth around it, swooning from the complex blend of spices. Glancing up toward the head table, he met the eyes of Pongrotto. The man gave him a nod, and he tilted his head in response.

A small body cut in front of him and swooped into the chair Rose had occupied earlier. He froze, spoon trapped in his mouth, as he stared at the amber-green eyes of Yesenia Gromel.

"And what are you going by today, stranger?" she asked.

He lowered his spoon and studied her for a moment, lifting a napkin to his mouth. "You're quite astute for someone so young."

"You're bad at your job," she said.

His lips flattened. "This isn't the kind of spy work I'm used to."

She giggled, placing both arms on the table and thrumming her fingers. "So you're getting to know the lower families?"

"How much do you know?" he asked.

"I know my parents are stupid and are being fed a spoonful of crap in that parlor right now," she said, casually glancing toward the doors at the distant end of the hall. Her gaze slowly roved back to him. "I know a lot. I'm not an official member of SLO, but Lord Rattius makes use of me. None of the members know about my role. I'm a spy of sorts. Because I'm a child, it's very easy to access a lot of aristocratic homes via play dates. I learn about slave treatment in the various houses."

"So you're familiar with those at the head table?"

"The Nedda family?" she asked without turning to acknowledge them. "Of course, but they don't know that. I don't bother with them since they're already allies of Lord Rattius's efforts. They're likely questioning my conversation with you, viewing it as an odd arrangement."

He nodded, peering elsewhere in the hall and trying to ignore the girl's impressive vernacular. Like was the case with most wealthy families, someone had taught her well.

"Who are you looking for?" she asked.

"I saw a woman earlier on the foyer's overlook. Not quite a giant, but tall enough to not seem human."

"Was she wearing slave garb, but with wooden rings piercing the sides of her ears?"

"Yes," he said, turning back to her.

"She's called the Beacon, and she's one of the most important people in SLO."

"How so?" he asked, leaning in.

"When Lord Rattius initiated the organization, he needed both sides to participate. While he was the mouth of the aristocracy and nobles, someone needed to be the mouth of the slaves. He ended up choosing that woman you saw earlier, giving her the title of Beacon Uni. They collaborate from time to time, making sure both sides of SLO are moving at the same pace."

Scratching at his beard, Creep raised his eyebrows and frowned. "A complex system he has operating in the shadows."

"More complex than either you or I know," she said. "Luckily, we don't have to worry about the finer details … just focus on our parts. SLO has been in operation for fourteen years—longer than I've been part of it. During that span of time, there have been too many failures for it to keep going much longer. Your arrival has breathed new life into the members. Rose was supposedly known for her infectious charm a while back; I've never seen it … not until tonight, with you.

"They've become so desperate that they haven't even bothered trying to figure out if you actually have a group in Stratum Zero or not. They're blindly trusting you, and I find that troublesome …" She shook her head, gazing emptily into the distance. "Lord Rattius believes this is SLO's last chance to liberate the slaves." She shrugged. "It falls on the shoulders of a Primmish … if that's even what you are."

His gaze hardened, jaw stiffening. He almost wanted to remove his hat, glasses, and mustache as a gesture of greater sincerity. "I do have a group, and we will make this happen."

The girl pulled down the collar of her shirt, revealing the upper area of her chest. A mighty bruise lay across her skin. His eyes widened. "This was from my mother," she said. "I'm not a fighter; I have no skill in that regard. My intellect doesn't get me very far when faced with her club."

Rage bubbled inside him. "Why did she do that?"

"She's done it many times, which she can get away with because I'm Powish. My body, like most people in this kingdom, can take quite a beating. Every time she's caught me playing, talking, or even laughing with a slave, she swung her club at my chest. It got to the point where if I even granted them the simple respect of eye contact, she'd beat me without thought."

He closed his eyes, ears growing uncomfortably hot. He recalled all those times Rhyparia had referred to this mission as more than a simple rescue job, even when her comrades only viewed it as that. This was a journey of retribution and reckoning, and he'd wondered what made her feel such malice. Perhaps she'd heard a story like the one Yesenia told now. If so, then he understood that rage.

"That is inhumane," he finally muttered.

"But the beatings I could endure," she said, lips beginning to quiver as she gazed emptily at the table. "There was another half to the punishment. They'd torture and kill whichever slave it was who they claimed 'distracted' me. They'd make the slave lay on the floor as a giant walked across them. I'd have to watch, my mother's hands clasped down onto my shoulders."

Creep's mouth dried, suddenly wanting this city burned to the ground.

# 55

# Five Locks

"Lilu and Limone are suckers," Gracie said, snickering evilly to herself as she relaxed in an armchair in the living room of their Bastion townhouse. Blue stained her lips after finishing her third ice pop in thirty minutes.

Frederick sat on the floor, buried in Mendac's theory notes on the coffee table. He'd become a fixture of the room, his time spent in the same position evident in his cracking joints whenever he tried to stand and reprieve himself. "And why is that?" he asked absentmindedly.

"They're out there on Steel Field on a Sunday, working those poor weavineers like dogs," she said. "This is supposed to be everyone's day off."

"Urgency has been increased," he said, flipping over a sheet of parchment and placing the feather of his quill against his cheek in thought. "With Bryson returning to Dunami, she thinks the war will hit hyper speed."

"This war that nobody in this city even understands?" she asked, raising an eyebrow. "Brilliance isn't exactly on anyone's radar. We have a wall around us, and entry from outsiders is rare." She paused to give it some thought. "Heck, *information* is rare."

"This city has lulled its citizens into a false sense of comfort," he said. "Thankfully, we have Lilu here, so she understands the dangers of what is happening across the world. That's why she's working on a Sunday. If her name is called and the service of her travolters is needed, then she wants to make sure they're ready, including the weavineers who will be manning them. You can't forget now that they're being built successfully at a steady rate, instruction must shift to the operation of the vehicles."

"Push the switch, press the pedal, and turn the wheel accordingly," Gracie droned.

He barked out a laugh. "That's why you won't be driving the damned things. Stick to manning the cannon."

Her eyes narrowed in suspicion. "How much can you gather from continuing to read through those notes?"

"Well, I'm not just reading anymore," he said, leaning back slightly to get a broader view of the parchment strewn across the table. "A lot of this is my own notes, as I've been jotting things down and trying to comprehend some of Mendac's unfinished claims. His lab notes were very much incomplete, like there were missing pages or he had been interrupted during his recordings. I'm simply using context clues and prior knowledge to tie up loose ends."

"How boring," she said through a yawn.

"I've made some intriguing discoveries, and I believe I may know the answer to something Lilu brought to my attention a long time ago."

"And what's that?"

"Remember when she told us about Olivia's water ability?" he asked.

"Yeah."

He shrugged, as if his discovery wasn't all that impressive. "I figured it out."

*     *     *

The tunnel was becoming narrower and shorter in height the farther the dimiours traveled. Weeks of digging had depleted their stamina. The food and water being brought by Saikatto was becoming increasingly more meager. Even Moros, the spunky weasel, had resorted to spending more time attached to Biaza's back than actually digging. Biaza and Atarax were really the only two putting in any effort, clawing their way through the crust.

The fact that they were nearing Stratum Zero was the only silver lining. Therapif had burrowed down into the tunnel from the surface a day prior, informing Atarax and Biaza they needed to shift their tunneling more northeast. When a putrid scent had sunk into the tunnel through the hole, they knew the stratum's sewage-strewn streets were close.

Atarax's paw made contact with an embedded rock, forcing him to shift his position and dig elsewhere. Despite the distance between them and the rabbit hole from yesterday, they could still smell the sewage. It had penetrated into the ground, and he began to question whether this was only dirt he was digging through.

"We might have to redirect," Biaza said through heavy breaths. "I'm getting nothing but rock."

He nodded. "Hopefully, we can go around it. What do you think, right or left?"

"What's that?" Moros asked, pointing over Biaza's shoulder.

They followed his finger and spotted black sludge seeping out of the crack between two stones. Rayne, who stood behind them and watched their backs, approached and extended her torch.

Atarax leaned forward and sniffed it, only to recoil backwards. "There's the sewage," he said, hacking up his lungs.

"If that's the case," Biaza said, "then we have to be very close."

"You're right underneath it."

They whirled. Therapif, Saikatto, and Kakos stood several paces away, merely shadows in the waning light.

"And you've come across a particularly useful bed of rocks that extends above ground," Therapif said. "I was hoping the direction I had you going would result in your arrival here. They can serve as a hidden entry point for the slaves."

"And where's Prakriti?" Rayne asked.

"Since he has the outwardly appearance of one of the more deprived slaves," Kakos growled, "we thought it wise for him to infiltrate Stratum Zero and walk among them."

Therapif frowned, looking up at the wolf. "I wouldn't phrase it so tactlessly. However, he is making my job a lot easier. The slaves respond better to another human rather than what they see as a talking rabbit."

"And how'd you sneak him in without Rhyparia or Creep?" Atarax asked.

"Do you forget I'm Adrenian?" Saikatto said with a smirk. "And a very skilled one at that. I was once a Jestivan just like Rhyparia."

The fox nodded. "I see. Then, that makes sense."

"You've earned a break," Therapif said, hopping toward them. "Lie down and let me examine your bodies."

Atarax and Biaza both fell to the ground and slumped against the wall. They welcomed this time to recuperate and offered no objections.

"How much longer?" Atarax asked, eyes heavy. "I've lost track of time down here."

"The time table isn't fixed," Therapif said, lifting up Biaza's eyelids. He reached back toward Rayne, who had been holding onto his purse of medical supplies while he'd been in Stratum Zero. He dropped it on the floor and rummaged through it.

"But, if Rhyparia and Creep are doing their best at trying to meet the deadline," he said, "then we have only but a few days before these tunnels need to be accessible from above. Tomorrow, we start digging smaller tunnels and finding other access points."

Rayne smiled. "Remember when Musku spoke about rescuing the Powish and Primmish slaves all those years ago, Saikatto?"

"Like it was yesterday."

"It's bittersweet," she said. "To be a few days away from our goal, but to not have him with us."

"He played his part," Saikatto said. "And it was the most important one. Don't ever forget that."

*       *       *

"You've been on the move too much, milord."

Bryson opened his eyes, blinking away the haze. How was Benedict still seated with his bench swaying to one side?

"Milord, you're going to—"

Bryson fell sideways, head smacking the bench. He released a muddled groan and grasped his bandaged temple. So *he'd* been the one tilting, not the bench.

Instead of jumping to Bryson's rescue, Benedict sat calmly on the other side of the carriage. A grin slipped onto his face. "I'm glad to see you're still the same naïve and relentless man I brought to Brilliance. Your surgeries weren't that long ago, yet you try to function like there aren't fresh stitches keeping you together."

Easing himself into an upright position, Bryson winced. "I felt fine the day I was scheduled to leave Brilliance."

"Because you were riding a high, milord," Benedict said. "The excitement about knowing you'd be on your way back to the capital, where your fiancée and son wait for your arrival, outweighed your pain."

"Anything I must be warned about before stepping foot in that palace again?"

The steward shrugged. "You should fear the princess's wrath about the news of your surprise surgeries. She wasn't pleased. With that said, she's missed you dearly and will likely push that aggravation to the side once she sees you alive and well."

"Has there been any news from Himitsu, Olivia, or Toshik about their missions?"

"I wouldn't know," Benedict said. "I'm not privy to that information."

Bryson nodded and slumped against the wall at the bench's far end. "I think I'll sleep."

"I think that's wise, milord."

*       *       *

It was difficult for Bryson to explain his euphoria when stepping out of the carriage in front of Dunami Palace, his fiancée and future in-laws waiting for him on the steps. While the overcast sky was identical to that seen in Brilliance, there was something more freeing about it. Perhaps, it was the absence of the skyscraping towers that fought for space amongst the clouds.

He stood outside while Benedict carried his bags out of the carriage and toward the royal family. "You know either of you could move, right?" the steward said, setting Bryson's bags next to Shelly.

"I refuse to be that woman who runs toward you," she announced.

Bryson smiled at her before eventually releasing a laugh. Of course she wouldn't do that. He climbed up the stairs, stopping a few steps below her. He opened his arms, and she covered the tiny distance left between them, wrapping her arms around his neck. The impact sent pain through his chest, but he didn't show it.

"Good to see you, my boy," Vitio said.

Bryson winked at the king while still trapped in the embrace. He smiled at Queen Delilah, who returned the gesture with grinning eyes. It felt good to be home, and it no longer felt weird to call it that. He had moved on from his childhood house, though the memories shared with Debo would always remain.

Shelly stepped away with a resentful glare. "Don't ever do what you did without my knowledge again."

He rubbed the back of his head, guilt seeping from every pore of his body. "I'm alive, aren't I?"

"You might not be once I'm through with you," she said.

He felt the color drain from his face. "Don't hurt me."

Vitio gave a hearty chuckle. "What's the verdict? Did Nyemas perform another miracle?"

Bryson turned and pointed a finger behind him. A barrage of electricity passed over the carriage and hit the pond of water beneath the marble fountain. A dazzling display of blue and white lights forced him and the others to shield their eyes. Benedict, who had just stepped out of the carriage with another bag, cocked an eyebrow. "What the hell was that?"

Bryson's toothy smile was as bright as his voltaic theatrics. "I'm back and better than ever."

*       *       *

The walk through the palace was filled with lighthearted conversation between Bryson, Shelly, Vitio, and Delilah. He had a family here in Dunami, a strong, loving support system. Upon their arrival to the nursery, Vitio and Delilah split off from the young lovers, allowing them time alone with their child.

Bryson opened the door, and Yusif, the caretaker, looked up from his knitting on the sofa. He placed his supplies on the end table, rising to a stand. "Welcome back, Prince," he said, approaching him to bow.

Bryson raised a hand. "None of that."

After a pause, Yusif asked, "Why, Prince?"

"Do you want to hug or shake my hand?" Bryson leaned in and whispered, "For the man who does so much for my fiancée by granting her temporary relief, I hope for a hug."

The two men pulled each other into a powerful embrace. "I must admit," Yusif said, "the princess doesn't require my help that much. She is a fine woman."

Bryson stepped back with a nod. "I believe that. Now let me see my son."

Yusif exited the room. Bryson sauntered across the nursery while Shelly stepped slowly, watching from behind with keen interest.

Their time was spent in silence at the beginning, as he lifted L.K. from his crib and cradled him gently in both arms. The baby's thin blond hair was a mess, showing the unruly signs of his father's. When his eyes opened, Bryson gasped, two vivid pools of emerald looking up at him. They had changed over the months.

"He has your eyes," he said.

Shelly walked forward, stopping behind his shoulder with a smile. "Your hair, my eyes, your nose, my mouth … a miraculously balanced offspring."

"That's perfect," he said. "It means he's gotten the best of both worlds."

"Which means he doesn't have a brain," she said.

They both laughed, and L.K.'s eyes lit up, contributing to the jubilance with noises akin to laughter. Bryson's heart melted. "I didn't know babies were so cute."

She reached a hand past him and tapped L.K.'s nose with her finger, siphoning another infectious giggle.

He walked over to the couch and sat down, his son still in his arms. She chose an armchair. "What was it like up there?" she asked.

"Like a different world," he said. "Streets narrower and more congested, buildings of gray and white that stretched into the sky like giant rectangular blocks … Intelamps everywhere. It was like an evolved civilization."

"Sounds kind of unbelievable." She frowned. "I'm jealous."

"The culture was toxic," he said, making a funny face at L.K. "A lot of them still envy Mendac, and they're very much a culture that believes women cannot achieve what men can."

"I bet Lilu is changing that perception, though," she said.

"She is." He looked up at her with wide eyes. "Did you know about the Board of Directors in Brilliance?"

"I won't learn anything about that city until I become the royal head," she said.

"They're the city's leaders, and one of them is the Commissioner of the League of Weavineers. Want to take a guess at their last name?"

She shrugged.

"LeAnce," he said. "They were responsible for adopting my father when he was younger."

Her mouth wiggled, as if she was grinding her teeth from anger. "I hate my dad," she finally said. "He doesn't tell me anything. Were they as evil as you'd expect?"

"It was hard to get a read on them," he said. "They were a stern bunch capable of rubbing you the wrong way, but nothing they did seemed evil. That doesn't mean much, I suppose. I was only there for a few months."

She sighed and plopped back in her chair while he continued to play with L.K.'s face. "What have you been up to down here?" he asked.

She groaned and rolled her head. "Wedding planning. My mom has been all over me. Between color palettes, flowers, guest lists, locations, and music, it's been an endless process." She paused. "Which reminds me, thank you for your input on the flowers. I'm sure Lilu was a great help."

He blushed. Had it been that obvious?

She laughed. "If you want to pretend you were the brains behind the decision next time, don't give me an explanation as to why you made the choice you did. You're not an expert on flowers. That answer reeked of Lilu's insight. However, I suppose it was a good thing. She made an excellent choice." Her smile faded. "She better make it down here for the wedding. She no longer has an excuse based on what I've heard about her recent successes."

Talk of Lilu made him think about a few others. "Has Vitio heard anything from Himitsu, Olivia, Toshik, Agnos, or Tashami?"

"Olivia and Toshik's groups haven't been in contact with us. They're in the Dark Realm after all; communication isn't that simple. Agnos is in the midst of a voyage that should take him through a whirlpool into the Dark Sea. Himitsu's doing fine and making some progress, but ultimately hasn't achieved his objective. As for Tashami, he's guarding our kingdom's teleplatforms as the head officer."

"None of that sounds promising," Bryson said, eyes falling to L.K.

"Himitsu and Tashami should be able to make it," she said. "But I understand the importance of Olivia's attendance." She gazed toward a window on the far side of the room. "According to my father, her mission wasn't supposed to be as lengthy as Toshik's. I'd expect her arrival soon … or, at least, I hope."

After no response, she smiled. "Of course, we can always push the date back. No big deal."

"No," he said. "I want to marry you. The sooner, the better. You are the mother of my child, and it's about time I get to call you my wife."

*　　*　　*

Illipsia sat in bed, fidgeting with padlocks scattered around her. Twilight cast a dim blue tint through drawn curtains, providing just enough light. The room was almost empty save the presence of Beren.

She eyed him as he paced back and forth, biting his nails. He was waiting for her arrival, or so he believed. She'd told him earlier to wait in her room at dusk since it'd be the best time for privacy, her roommates using those hours to study in the Warpfinate. Guilt forced her to look away from him, shoulders drooping as she continued to press fingers against multiple keyholes.

The poor boy had no idea she was already in the room. She supposed this was a good sign. It meant she was successfully multi-weaving the manipulation of lock-picking while also maintaining a hallucinogenic wall between the two of them. She was also using clairvoyance to track the movements of anyone outside her door or window. She wasn't a fighter—her clout was average at best—but her skills as an intelligence officer would have made all of Prayoga jealous.

A collective series of clicks sounded at once, and she had to clamp her hand to her mouth to stop from gasping. Five locks lay disjointed. She'd finally passed the final barrier and could now focus on achieving her main objective.

She flinched as Beren swore to the ceiling. He looked up, seething, and then gazed toward her bed. The sun had set. He stomped across the room and swung open the door, slamming it shut behind him.

Just like that, she hated herself and the stupid locks.

# 56

# Erafeen: The Boundless Wonder

"Why do you know nothing?" Toono asked, sitting on his bed.

Meow Meow gasped, awkwardly slung on a bed post. "How dare you insult me? Do you not know who I am?"

"I know exactly who you are," Toono said. "But why do you seem to not know who you are?"

"I look at myself as the much-needed comic relief of this doom-and-gloom climate you've manifested over the past few years."

"But you're not funny."

Another gasp. "Only a villain would hurt me so."

He sighed and got out of bed, approaching the wardrobe to find a suitable outfit for the day.

"It's five in the morning," Meow Meow said, looking at the first-night sky outside the window. "Why such an early start?"

"There are a lot of things that require my attention, and I must evaluate the progress made by my peers." He reached into the wardrobe and

560

retrieved a blue robe, its collar embroidered in golden moons and stars. "I've put my trust in a lot of people in order find success."

As Toono pulled off his nightwear, Meow Meow closed his eyes and gagged. "Can you at least turn me around first?"

"For someone who was supposed to have been a mighty ruler a long time ago, you don't possess the disposition of one."

"Me, a mighty ruler?" Meow Meow asked, eyes still closed. "That's a bit farfetched when considering the condition I'm in. I can't even move of my own free will. I have no body."

"I wonder where it is," Toono said, thinking back to his first quest with Kadlest, obtaining his first sacrifice in the Prim Kingdom. It felt like a lifetime ago now.

"Are you finished yet?" Meow Meow asked.

"I am." Toono's eyes narrowed as he caught a glimpse of something strange in his peripheral vision. He sauntered across the room and took a gander out the window. A mass of pitch-black darkness consumed a distant city block, erasing the stars and moon from that area of the sky above. It had been a little over a week since the infiltration of the assassins, yet their progress seemed sluggish—not that it mattered much to him.

Still, he smirked. For assassins, subtlety didn't seem to rank too high on their list of importance.

*     *     *

Agnos had yet to inform Eet and Osh about the deaths of Gray Whale and her crew. The reality of the situation still hadn't completely dawned on him, as he struggled to come to grips with it. He'd viewed the acquisition of his own ship as a major stepping stone in his life's journey, and it was. However, even while captaining the Mythmaker, he'd never been at sea alone. When chasing the Thunder Queen's chronicle, the Whale Lord had trailed him. During this voyage, it led him. It wasn't until these past few days spent looking for the galleon's ghost around him that he realized the level of comfort its presence had given him.

He stood at the front of the navigation room, gazing out a small circular window. The room sat on the stern deck, which allowed him a view of most of the decks. His focus, however, was on the sea in front of them. Empty. Lacking. He'd grown so accustom to the Whale Lord sailing ahead of them.

Zorra and Barloe bickered behind him, leaning over opposite ends of a chart of the Sea of Light. The quartermaster had a tendency to oversee and micromanage the navigator's work. It was a bad habit of his, and Agnos once would have told Barloe to get out. Navigation was solely Zorra's job, and if she did need help, it would have come from Agnos, Stefania, or Gunther—not Barloe.

But, there was nothing he could do to separate the two of them, for this tension stemmed from something deeper than stubbornness. Despite Barloe's intention to marry Zorra before their arrival at the whirlpool, the plan had never come to fruition. She was to blame for that in his mind, for her focus had been on preparing for the whirlpool rather than a wedding. Then, once the fiasco with the leviathan happened, any thought of a wedding was tossed overboard. Nobody wanted to celebrate a marriage after watching their allies die.

"This is growing intolerable," Stefania said. The sailing master was the only other person in the room, seated at a desk and fidgeting with a compass on a map of her own. "Both of you should be thrown into the brig."

"He's the insufferable one," Zorra said, jabbing a finger into Barloe's brawny chest.

Stefania waved her free hand at them. "If the quarrelling doesn't stop, it's going to hurt the ship. The crew has begun to sense the dysfunction among leadership. If we're to be entering battle soon, the last thing we need is a crew in disarray."

Zorra straightened up and crossed her arms, sighing as she closed her eyes. "That's if we even make it before the battle starts. We're on the opposite side of the sea from the Intel River's connector. Queen Apsa was blunt in her message: time is of the essence."

The room fell silent. Agnos pressed his forehead against the glass. She was right. The Spirit Queen had made it sound like the dozens of ships that had been spotted exiting whirlpools over the past few weeks were now coming together to form a massive fleet, and they were already bearing down on the blockade at the Intel Connector. The worst part of that news? Four ships in that fleet were leviathans. Based off what he had just witnessed a few days ago, that spelled certain doom for True Light. His rational mind told him they couldn't make it there on time. And even if they did, how much help could one more galleon provide?

He spotted the smaller frames of Eet and Osh dash across the stern deck and leap over the rail to the quarterdeck. When he'd retrieved them from the hold after escaping the leviathan, he'd lied to them, telling them Gray had made it through the whirlpool and was now in the Dark Realm, but the Mythmaker had to retreat because of a tactical flaw in their approach that led to hull damage. This had caused them to miss their window of opportunity, and now the two cabin kids thought he was simply hunting down a new whirlpool to try to rejoin Gray in the other realm.

He'd have to tell them the truth eventually, but he was too much of a coward. He didn't want to watch their hearts break.

*     *     *

Eet bolted past Gunther and leapt over the rail, plunging down to the main deck. Osh landed next to him, and they both ran for the door to the specialty quarters. He swung it open, having to fight his way through. She rammed him into the wall and burst forward, but he thrust out his foot and caught her ankle. He ran past her flailing body, hearing a smack behind him as she hit the floor. He turned and laughed, placing his hands on his hips and thrusting out his chest. "Not this time!"

She scowled his way and tried to get up and run, but he was already rushing into the captain's cabin. Yanking open the bottom drawer of Agnos's desk, all he found was scrap paper and junk. He continued to pull open drawers with no luck. He was finally going to be able to read from the translated documents, and now he couldn't find them?

"Looking for something?"

He looked up. Osh was holding a stack of parchment in the middle of the cabin, a wry smile etched into her face. He rushed forward. "Where'd you get that?"

She pulled back the parchment as he reached for it, extending her other arm and holding him back with one hand. "No, no, no. Remember, I do the reading."

He growled into her palm, frustrated that he had yet to mature like her. Why was puberty such a hidden treasure for him? Her voice was already beginning to deepen.

"Have a seat," she said.

He stopped struggling and dropped to the floor, arms folded in front of him. She pranced toward the desk and hopped on top of it, standing above him like a queen addressing the masses from a stage. Clearing her throat, she began to read.

"The Boundless Wonder has many names …"

*　　*　　*

The Boundless Wonder has many names, and it usually depends on which kingdom you are from. In my kingdom, the Light Knowledge Kingdom, it is exactly that: the Boundless Wonder. Elsewhere that name has no meaning, yet Mialo knew exactly what I was referring to when I mentioned it during our second day together.

"You vaguely mentioned the Boundless Wonder last night," I said while we sat at a patio table outside.

"Is that what it's called here?" he asked.

"What do you call it?"

"The Warpfinate."

I pondered on the obscurity of the name, but it did make sense. "So, this prophecy you saw pertained to that?" I asked.

His golden eyes smiled softly. "I'm no prophet."

"What else do you call visions about something nobody has ever seen before? I'm sure it wasn't a dream; you wouldn't go to this extent to demand action."

He chuckled and took a sip of water. "What I saw wasn't by mere chance," he said. "It didn't just dawn upon my conscious from some inexplicable force. I sought it out. By weaving my energy with the Essence in a specific pattern, I grabbed truths from its consciousness that it had buried deep within. I wanted answers ..."

I nodded. "And you found them."

It's always important to note—and I know I've stated this countless times already—that Mialo is a fascinating man with a mind that surpasses even my own. Granted, it took me some weeks before accepting this, but it had been dumb pride that got in the way of that truth. He is an innovative thinker—a theorist, of sorts.

How many of the Originators would have conducted such a test? No, the real question should have been: how many would have had the will power to neglect harvesting for as long as he did, starving themselves of their Essence? Then, have the proper state of mind to return to their Essence not to harvest, but to try something different by expelling their energy into the belly of the beast?

And to this day, as I flee for my life and prepare to die just a few leagues outside of the Boundless Wonder, I question his ability to think in such a way. He had reversed the harvesting process. Instead of consuming the Essence, he had fed it his own energy. In doing so, he learned his energy was an extension of himself that granted the sense of touch. He became the man who discovered what the Originators fear today ... *weavists*.

We're not going to make it to the Boundless Wonder. Of course, if you're reading this chronicle, you know this. But even if we miraculously did, we aren't certain we'd find success. Does our intellect and wisdom meet the unknown, intangible quota that's needed to reach the forgotten gods, Tahara and Mulawith? Or would our limited perception spell doom inside of the otherworldly phenomenon?

Because inside the Boundless Wonder—or Warpfinate, as Mialo so often demands it be called—there are one of three troublesome outcomes for those who are intelligent enough to gain access to its greatest depths.

First, you either die from depravation caused by entrapment. The Warpfinate's shadowy depths are replaced by menacing black walls that mimic shadows, barring your progression deeper into the structure. This scenario tends to stem from a lack of knowledge on a topic of rational thinking—a question and answer based on facts. It's a miserable way to die, but there are ways to combat it. Mialo believes the information needed to break down those walls would be hidden somewhere you've already explored. Alas, that's hard to do when riddled by starvation and thirst.

Second is death by illness, caused by toxic areas of the Warpfinate that stem from unresolved personal issues of morality. If there is something from your past that stirs emotions of shame or guilt in your conscious, these toxic wastes will be something to fear. And it takes more than simply facing your demons and admitting that you were in the wrong. It requires a meticulous psychological self-examination. Unless you can truly comprehend the reason for your actions and prove that it was, at its core, done without malicious intent, your body will degrade from an excruciating disease.

The third outcome is, perhaps, most terrifying in terms of adrenaline-pumping fear: a death of violence, which is caused by ignorance. It seems the Warpfinate really hates those who aren't just wrong, but believe with conviction that they're right. This pertains to the matter of black, white, and the morally gray. The degree of violence is determined by where the issue your ignorance stems from falls on this scale. What makes it more mortifying is that matters of either ethics or intellect could create this outcome. The more the arbitrary needle leans to black or white, the more violent the foe if your belief is wrong. When the needle falls in the gray area, which is usually ethical dilemmas, the aforementioned death by illness can become a cause for concern.

I think Mialo explained this to me on the fourth day. I'll never forget what I said in response: "I've committed acts that I'm still shameful of to this day."

"As have I," he said. "Nobody makes it through the Warpfinate without facing at least one of those hurdles, if not all three. At least, that's what was implied when I saw what I did. We'd likely run into a threat of illness, violence, or both. If that's the case, it doesn't mean immediate doom. There are ways out of each fate, but we must be able to either understand our rationale behind our immoral actions or accept the fact that we're dead wrong with certain subjects."

"I am quite stubborn," I said.

"We are very similar."

"You seem to not be worried about the first possibility, death by depravation."

"Individually, each of ours scope of knowledge is unsurpassed," he said.

I raised an eyebrow at that. Even I wasn't that arrogant. "But there are definitely things we don't know," I said.

"That's why there will be two of us. Where my knowledge falls short and those walls begin to spring up, your intellect will make up for it. You'll teach me what you know and knock those walls right back down. If we come across something we're both unaware of, then we'll hunt down the answers elsewhere in the Warpfinate."

I smirked. "That's why you want two people."

"That's one desirable reason for it, but it also stems from a matter of necessity."

"How so?"

"One cannot reach the Warpfinate's end alone. The more, the merrier. Such a quest requires the participation of a being from each realm. Both must be highly intelligent in order to even reach such depths. And they must possess opposing energies, for that's the only way to manifest the final corridor."

Reaching the Boundless Wonder is already difficult enough while trying to traverse the Region of Raging Tides and fleeing from a fleet of ships captained by Originators. To think this is supposed to be the easy part, dwarfed by the scale of what is supposed to follow: the excavation of the Boundless Wonder and search for the forgotten gods.

I stared at him long and hard. With each passing day, his explanation of this massive mission had become exponentially more complex, but infinitely more wondrous. This was no ordinary quest, but an epic. A journey suited for gods.

# 57

# A Fair Warning

Kadlest was happy to be away from Adren's capital. She had been cooped up in the royal estate for far too long. Now she stood in an office on the third floor of the transit building that sat near the Adren teleplatforms. Just outside the building was a military encampment the size of a small town. She smiled. To have a militarized zone of this magnitude filled with Dark Realm soldiers in a Light Realm kingdom was credit to how far she and Toono had come. And now they were closing in on their goal.

This was years in the making.

A teleplatform connected to the Dev Kingdom began to spin, soldiers taking position around it. They had expected guests, for a messenger had been sent nearly a week ago warning them of visitors.

The platform reached an incredible speed when a group of people appeared out of thin air, holding onto the support beams. It slowed, and the frost-entwined hair of Still Warden Moroza became evident before anything else. Standing next to her was a man Kadlest had yet to meet. He was tall and dark, with an unsheathed sword of glistening ice strapped to his back. Steam rose from its blade, giving it the signature look of something out of the Still Kingdom. That was no ordinary ice.

Her eyes narrowed. He must have been the Still Diatia, Groto Yuln. It was a shame that this man was the only Diatia they could gather for their forces. The group was severely splintered, having become inoperable long ago. Chelekah, Bruut, Jina, and Halluci were dead, Vuilni and Evelyn had joined forces with True Light, and the other three—two Prim and a Cyn Diatia—wanted nothing to do with the war. Ipsas, like the realm it represented, was a sorry excuse for a school. Yet, somehow, it remained standing while Phesaw lived as a shell of its old self.

Kadlest descended to the bottom floor and exited the building, taking a short path between a few tents to reach their reinforcements. Moroza was now standing a few feet away from the platform, pushing away any soldiers who tried searching her. Groto stayed by her side, hand casually drawn above his shoulder as he grasped the hilt of his blade, looking more like a personal body guard than her student.

"Good day, Moroza."

The warden turned her head with a disdainful frown. "Call off your men, please. I needn't be frisked by such animals."

Kadlest's eyes slowly raked her guards, who were waiting for her instructions. Not all of them were men, but in the eyes of a proud Stillian woman, the men would have been the ones to stand out. Moroza's belief of male inferiority was strong. To have them patting her down and digging into her belongings was a nefarious crime.

Nodding, Kadlest said, "I can search you if you'd like. Either way, you're not taking any more steps into this kingdom until I feel safe with your presence."

"Need I remind you that the Rogue Demon sent me here?" Moroza said, now turning fully and inflating her chest.

Silence followed, tension palpable. Over a hundred pairs of eyes were trained on the two women.

"That would be unnecessary," Kadlest said. "And that's cute, referring to him as the Rogue Demon. That speaks of your reverence for him. Awfully embarrassing for a woman who despises the idea of male authority." Groto's brows crumpled, his grip tightening on his hilt. "I, however, am one of only two people who could call Toono their equal. We are partners in this mission. You are simply a subordinate."

"I don't care about the man's goal of resurrecting some hallucinating king," Moroza spat. "I'm in this war for one reason only: to avenge my kingdom and its queen."

"A queen who no longer possesses such an aspiration and has flipped her allegiance to the very side you're trying to defeat," Kadlest said. "Which explains my reasoning behind searching you and confiscating any weapons during your stay here in our camp. When the time comes to depart, we'll return those weapons."

Moroza hesitated, then muttered low enough to not be heard by the soldiers, "You can't do that."

Kadlest grinned. "I can. You are my subordinate."

The two women stood across from each other, both ready to pounce if provoked. Groto stepped forward. "You're a fool if you think you can speak to a warden of Ipsas in such a way."

"Is that so?" Kadlest asked, curious eyes darting toward the Diatia.

"You're not a Gefal, Bozani, royal, general, warden, or director," he said. "You have no titles and haven't established any sort of name for yourself in this world. Toono also isn't any of those things, but he has at least established a reputation. He's a demon." He paused. "So I ask again, what gives *you* authority?"

Her smile faded, no longer amused by their ignorance. She regarded his grip of his sword's hilt. "Try me," she finally said. "Let it be known to those around us that I am inviting your attack. I will give you one chance, and I promise you no repercussions even if you land a blow. I won't use a shield and I won't dodge. If you draw blood, I'll allow you to keep your weapons."

He looked back at Moroza, who nodded once in return. He turned to regard Kadlest. "This is an ever-ice sword from the second highest peak in the Still Mountains. You're a bigger fool than I thought."

"Swing, child," Kadlest said.

He pulled his sword free from its straps, lurched forward, and swung in a mighty arch toward the top of her shoulder. He was faster than she'd predicted, wielding a sword as large and heavy as herself. But—and as painful as it was to admit—he was no Yama.

She raised a hand, catching the sides of the blade with her fingers and thumb before the sharp edge struck her palm. He looked up, balking at the point of contact between his blade and her hand. A stunned silence blanketed the encampment.

She pushed the sword back, throwing it over his shoulder and causing him to stumble backward as the weight dragged him with it. Moroza's eyes narrowed as she watched the young man struggle to regain his balance.

Kadlest opened her hand, unscathed from the Diatia's failed attack, toward the warden as proof of no blood. She turned to walk away. "You will give your weapons to my officers, and then they will search you for more."

"Who are you?" Groto asked.

She stopped walking, but didn't turn to look at him. "Someone willing to do whatever it takes."

As she continued toward the transit building, the sound of a teleplatform caught her attention. There weren't any other scheduled arrivals. Her concern heightened as she turned and noticed it was the teleplatform that connected to the Intel Kingdom.

Soldiers raced into position more urgently than before. She remained calm as she watched the platform spin, waiting to see who'd be bold enough to enter a SCAPD-controlled kingdom so recklessly. As it hit its maximum speed, she caught a brief glimpse of a figure before it disappeared. Her eyebrows furrowed, having never witnessed such an aberration. Had a glitch in the platform been exposed? Had someone teleported in and out during the same rotation?

Soldiers fell to the ground, screams ringing through the air, gashes slashed across chests, thighs, and faces. Blood sprayed and heads rolled, yet there was no culprit.

It ended just as quickly as it had begun. Soldiers stopped falling, but the agonizing cries and writhing bodies of those who had been cut down made it not seem to matter. Kadlest looked around in horror as medics spilled out of the base's tents to tend to the wounded. In the span of three seconds, fifteen soldiers had fallen.

She crouched near one of her top officers, a Powish woman whose face was now unrecognizable because of the gash across it. She was still breathing, though it sounded more like a wheeze. It only took a glance for Kadlest to know it was a sword wound. She looked down to her right, where a decapitated head lay face-first in the grass.

The attack had happened right next to her, yet she hadn't seen the assailant during any of it. Possibilities raced through her mind. An Adrenian with an unprecedented speed percentage? If so, there had still been something odd about the style of movement.

She recalled the many times she'd witnessed Yama's speed. While she could never visually track the swordswoman, she could always *feel* her movement because of the wind it'd create. When Yama ran past someone, it felt like they were being sucked into a tornado.

This was different. She didn't feel the tug of a sudden gust. It was as if a ghost had attacked them. A Dev Assassin? But that didn't make sense for a number of reasons.

Looking toward the Intel platform, Kadlest questioned everything. It sat motionless with nobody on it. If their assailant had been that skilled, what stopped them from wiping everyone out? Where had they gone? Were they still here, disguised as a soldier with the intention of causing distrust within the ranks of her military?

Fearing the worst, she stood and began barking orders. True Light had made a fantastic and shocking move, and now her camp was in disarray.

*　　*　　*

Despite great progress toward Rhyparia and her friends' goal of freeing the slaves, something still bothered Creep. He didn't know what she was planning. She continued to hint at something "big," reiterating how vital it'd be to not only get the slaves out of the upper stratums, but far away from Stratum Zero. At first, he was keen on seeing where this path would take her, but after meeting Yesenia and the members of SLO, he realized something a younger him would have understood before he even took part on this mission.

This wasn't a scenario of good and evil. Not every free citizen was an enabler or spectator. There were activists here, people who despised the institution of slavery and had been trying to abolish it for decades. He had to do something about this. He either had to force those in SLO to flee with the slaves or convince Rhyparia to rethink her strategy. Otherwise, a lot of innocent people would die.

He stood at the window of his room in a quaint inn provided to him by Rose. He was presently stationed in Stratum Five after a few days of scouting Stratums One and Two, which were slums for the most part. While there weren't many slaves, he'd remained meticulous in his search. Even Stratum One required the attention of SLO, which said a lot about the character of such a group.

Stratum Five allotted him some height up the hillside, so he had a wide view of the lands surrounding the city below. He could see the blanket of black that hugged the base of the hill's perimeter, belonging to Stratum Zero. They had no Intelights, and torches weren't bright enough for him to see at this distance. Despite second-day approaching and the laborers of the upper stratums heading home for an evening of relaxation, he knew the slaves would continue to sweat over their duties.

Shaking his head, he looked straight ahead, where the Malanese Peaks stood erect in the distance, like the jagged bottom teeth of a hyena against the starlit sky. There were even slaves out there too, their job to mine the provod sources dry until they replenished again in two years. With the mission's climax so near, Saikatto and Rayne were likely already on their way to the mountains to free the miners.

Every time Creep thought about the goal this ragtag group was chasing, his doubt festered. This was a widespread mission, and they were few in numbers. The possibility of combat with daunting foes was high, and he'd never seen any of these dimiours fight. Would Rhyparia's group hold up against Powish giants? And what about the royals? If needed, could she take on the Power family? There was more to fear than just the queen.

He turned away from the window, rubbing his eyes in frustration. He needed to take a walk, try to rid his mind of apprehension. Maybe he'd swing past a certain house.

*　　*　　*

If any of SLO knew Creep walked the streets of Stratum Five alone, they'd have his head. Since his debacle at the House Gromel ball, he'd been advised to only enter public eye when instructed to do so by an elite member of the organization.

Today he wore a pewter bowler hat with a raven feather pinned to the side, a matching pewter button-up, black slacks, and suspenders securing them at the waist. It was just how the Powish did things. They dressed to impress, especially in the upper stratums. Time of day or matter of occasion didn't matter. One could have been doing something as simple as paying a visit to the butcher shop for meat, yet they still wouldn't be caught dead in something destitute.

He stuck to the busier sectors of the stratum, hugging against the crowds to better blend in. Occasionally, he'd pass a wide, dead-end alleyway. Some were empty, others were occupied by a Powish officer atop a barreler, waiting for some kind of excuse to storm the street and pulverize someone for any petty crime.

As he passed one, he made it a point to continue looking forward, though it was difficult to not see the engorged, reptilian gorilla. It was only a week ago when he witnessed a woman fall victim to the fists of a mounted barreler. Apparently, she'd looked at the officer the wrong way and for too long. The beast didn't hesitate, leaping from the alley and pouncing on top of her, raining scaled fists.

It had been a terrifying scene that Creep had learned wasn't uncommon here. Because of the Power Energy flowing through these people, they could withstand unimaginable forces. To them, the assault of a barreler was like someone from any other kingdom getting beat by a heavy club. Painful, yes, but not life-threatening for a healthy Powish adult. If one of those things pinned Creep, however, he'd die quickly.

After an hour of walking, he slowed, realizing the direction in which he'd headed. He thought he'd been wandering aimlessly, but it seemed as if his subconscious had a destination pinned all along. He stood on one side of a residential street, not a single person to be seen nearby. Across the street was a small estate with a humble front yard, fenced with black iron columns. Welded letters stood atop the main gate: ITRIA.

He had walked all the way to the property of House Itria, home of the deplorable lords, Lana and Ernest, and they're kindhearted daughter, Yesenia. Why? Had guilt brought him here? And what did he look like standing by his lonesome on an empty residential street, staring at their house from afar?

He turned, spotting some bushes on an unfenced property. He ran toward them and jumped in, making no noise thanks to his boots and gloves. Once situated, he peeled apart some of the leaves and watched the estate. Three slaves worked in the yard. Two hacked at an oak's errant branches while another scooped them off the ground and slung them into a wheelbarrow.

He watched them for a few minutes, unsure as to why. They were all about their business, heads down as they refrained from conversation. He knew this wasn't of choice, but because it was likely enforced. Lords Lana and Ernest Itria eventually left the premises and disappeared down the street. He was pleased by their disregard of the slaves. It meant they weren't punishing them—at least, for now.

His eyes narrowed as the front door opened again. Yesenia stepped outside in beige shorts and a sweater vest. She leapt down a few stone steps and bolted for the front gate. Grabbing onto the bars, she looked both ways down the street as if making sure the coast was clear. Once satisfied, she smiled and turned to sprint toward the slaves.

It was the first time he saw them look up, and the joy on their faces was a foreign expression. They laughed—a newfound euphoria to their essence. Reaching the tree, she leapt off the ground with her unmistakable Powish strength and grabbed hold of one of the oak's lower branches. She hung there for a moment, shaking off leaves as she impersonated a monkey. The three men guffawed as they looked up at her.

Creep wanted to escape the bush and join the fun, but he didn't know who was in these neighboring homes. And the last obstacle SLO needed was his capture.

All thoughts of "fun" fled his mind, however, as he spotted a few figures down the street, walking in the direction of the estate. It was difficult to tell who they were with the second-day sun beaming directly behind them. By the time he noticed who they were, it was too late. Ernest and Lana had already returned from wherever it was they had gone, and now they were accompanied by a giant.

The two lords saw Yesenia before she saw them, and the mixture of disgust and rage on their face said it all. The girl's eyes widened, dropping from the branch as her parents opened the gate, Lana leading the way. The woman marched across the grass with Ernest in tow. Yesenia ran in front of the slaves with her arms spread wide.

"It's my fault, mother!" she screamed. She must have thought her parents would be gone much longer than a few minutes. Otherwise, she would have stayed inside and not done something so irresponsible.

Creep looked around as the doors to other homes opened, their tenants stepping outside to watch what would unfold. He wondered if this was a common occurrence. Nobody seemed all that surprised.

"I knew this would happen!" Lana screamed. "Why do you think I bought the services of a giant for the day? I can't even pretend to go out for dinner without you taking advantage of that fact!"

"You tricked me?" Yesenia asked, seeming to whimper.

Lana reached for her daughter's arm and yanked it to her right, flinging the girl into the grass. The giant, not able to fit through the main gate, had stepped over the fence. It took only a few strides for him to reach the slaves.

Yesenia jumped back to her feet and ran toward him in hysterics, throwing out her hands as if that would do anything. The giant slapped her out of his way with a simple wave of his hand. He scooped up all three slaves, two to one hand and one to the other. His fists tightened around them, disfiguring their skeletons and causing them to release the most agonizing screams Creep had ever heard in his life. Their cries rang down the street, fazing none of the neighbors. Lana's grin was evident even from this distance, and Ernest appeared unmoved.

The giant dropped the slaves in a contorted heap, somehow still alive. Creep closed his eyes, realizing he could do nothing about what came next. His stealth abilities didn't work in this situation. They would have seen him coming no matter what.

The giant lifted his foot and stomped as hard as he could. Yesenia's scream was drowned out by the thundering of the ground upon impact, despair painted thick over her face. Her mouth hung open; snot leaked from her nose, the skeletons of her friends crushed in a split second by the sole of a giant's boots.

Before long, neighbors retreated into their homes, and the Itria lords dismissed the giant after thanking him for his service. It had been a routine execution, albeit quite a public one. The families on this street would carry on with their evening as if nothing out of the ordinary had occurred, meaning this was a problem too deeply rooted in their culture for there to be a quick fix.

Lord Lana kicked her daughter in the chest, pinning her to the ground with her foot. Yesenia fought, grasping both hands around her mother's ankle, but with no luck. Creep couldn't hear Lana, but he assumed she was threatening the girl. These parents had left the house, luring their daughter into a false sense of security just to catch her in the act of showing empathy toward the slaves. All of it had been a sham with a goal of making a firm statement.

Lana and Ernest went back inside, leaving their daughter in the grass. Yesenia pushed herself onto her elbows, rolled onto her hip, and then crawled toward the mangled bodies of the slaves. She sat on her knees and stared at them before bringing her hands to her face and crying.

Creep stepped out of the bushes and walked across the cobblestone street. He stood outside the fence, no longer caring about who might have spotted him from a window. "Yesenia."

The girl looked up, the right side of her face badly bruised and already beginning to swell. Grass stains ran down her left sleeve.

"Come with me," he said, extending his hand through the fence. He glanced at the slaves and regretted it. This little girl shouldn't have had to see horrors like this. For the hundredth time, his opinion on Rhyparia's motives had flipped. He wanted her to do whatever it took to make these people pay.

"Tomorrow night, this city will never be the same again," he said. "And I want you to meet the woman responsible."

*     *     *

"This was reckless, Creep," Lord Rattius said, closing a door behind them.

Creep shrugged. "We only have one more day of this charade anyway. I couldn't sit by after what I'd seen."

They were in a basement chamber of one of SLO's most trusted members. He didn't know whose home they were in exactly, but they were filthy rich. To have a mansion of this size in Stratum Eight meant one had to possess unprecedented wealth and status. He guessed Yosetti Equious. The chamber was to serve as their meeting spot for the night, a meeting originally intended for only three people: Rattius, Creep, and Rhyparia. Yesenia made it four.

Rattius sighed, lowering himself into a long-backed armchair of plush red. He looked at the girl, pressing his lips together as he shook his head. "The tortures you've endured."

She remained silent, seated on the floor at the base of a display table, legs folded against her body. She didn't acknowledge either man, but instead focused on the floor, likely replaying the day's events in her mind.

"I need to make sure she gets out with everyone else tomorrow, Rattius," he said, glancing back at the lord. "I don't want her in that house when everything goes down."

"I still don't know what you mean when you say that," Rattius said. "You make it sound like everyone—even SLO—must fear for their lives.

578

Why have we been advised to flee with the slaves? Isn't your partner going after the royals?"

Creep's gaze fell. "She is, and I'm part of that plan. However, I think she's keeping me in the dark about certain details."

Rattius remained quiet, studying Creep with an unreadable expression. "That doesn't sound promising," he said.

The door opened. Rhyparia NuForce sauntered inside, hands placed casually in her pockets and an umbrella strapped to her waist like a sword. The door shut behind her, seemingly by itself. Unaware of her ability, Rattius gaped at the woman before regarding the door in wonder. A simple blast of a lateral gravitational pull had caused the door to swing shut.

She looked absolutely dashing in her Powish attire. For a second, Creep found himself admiring the style now that he saw it on her. She resembled Rose with her matured frame and facial structure, minus the oversized muscles. It was hard to believe she had counterparts in their early twenties somewhere in the Light Realm. This wasn't a young lady tiptoeing the path to adulthood; this was a motivated, experienced woman—a very frightening one, at that.

Rattius stood and extended a closed fist, expecting the traditional handshake between a Powish and non-Powish in which the latter places their hand atop the former's fist. This was done in fear of crushing a foreigner's hand with a normal handshake.

"A proper handshake will do," Rhyparia said, hands remaining in her pockets as she eyed his fist.

He hesitated and then opened his hand. She smiled and grabbed hold. "It's an honor to finally meet the head of such a respectable organization. You've made mine and Creep's job here a lot easier."

They released their handshake. She turned and offered Creep a nod while Rattius returned to his seat, stunned. It took him a moment to recover before saying, "If I was really all that respectable, I wouldn't have allowed my wife to continue her tirade for the past few decades."

"That is partly true," she said, electing to remain on her feet. "But I understand the power of your wife and the rank she holds among aristocratic families. She is not someone you could easily deceive or dispose of. One, she'd fight back. And two, even if you did manage to overcome her, Queen Gantski wouldn't be pleased."

He raised an eyebrow at her. "And how do you know all of this?"

"What do you think I've been doing these past few weeks?" she asked, frowning as if he'd humiliated her with such a question.

"Exploring the sewers," he muttered.

She laughed. "That was my job during the first week, and I think it went well. Have you made use of my maps?" He nodded. "Good, then I expect every refugee's safe arrival to Stratum Zero tomorrow night. I went through a lot of effort to find the specific pipes that would lend well to human passage."

"It's all taken care of," Creep said. "We have SLO officials positioned in the safe houses, ready to funnel refugees through."

"Very well …" she trailed off, catching sight of the young girl sulking in the shadows. "Who is that?"

"Yesenia, the unfortunate heir to House Itria," Creep said, gazing back at the girl. She continued to regard only the floor.

Rhyparia sighed. "I understand. It's the families like Itria that galvanize me to execute the mission I came here to achieve."

"Forgive me, but I must ask how you know so much about the Powish aristocratic and political structure," Rattius said timidly. He sounded like anyone did when faced with Rhyparia, like if he asked the wrong question or said too much, she'd smite him where he stood. She did tend to carry an intimidating disposition.

"I've spent the past few weeks in Stratum Nine," she said.

"What? How?" he exclaimed. "The royal stratum is heavily guarded."

"Because of my ancient, it's easy for me to sneak around when it's dark. It's also why I was able to scout the sewers so efficiently. I can move freely, without the limitations of natural laws."

His eyes dropped to the umbrella at her hip. Somehow, he knew. "I see," he said, eyebrows raised. He turned toward Creep. "You were right; she's quite formidable."

Creep gave him a nod.

"It's settled, then," she said. "Now that it's confirmed everyone is in place and preparations have been made, it's official. When noon tomorrow strikes and second-night descends upon us, Creep and I will execute our plan in the palace. During that time, SLO will aid the refugees in their escape. My friends will be awaiting their arrival in Stratum Zero."

"What about SLO members?" Rattius asked. "Should they be worried about their own safety, too?"

She stared at the lord, firmness in her set jaw. "If anyone wants to escape alive tomorrow, I'd advise them to flee with the slaves. This city is as vile as the sewage it sits upon." She turned, the door swinging open on its own. Her single braid trailed behind her, a burgundy bandana tied around its tail end.

"For this," she said, moseying out the door, "clemency will not be tolerated."

# 58

# A Resilient Soul

Bryson fidgeted with the collar of the military uniform Vitio had forced him to wear. It was an insufferable thing, thick and heavy with material that's sole purpose was to trap in heat. He looked like an uptight, high-ranking officer. His coat and pants were a matching blue, while the trimmings, cufflinks, and buttons were real gold. It was the exact kind of thing no practical warrior would wear into battle.

He sighed. At least nobody had forced him to tidy his hair.

Shelly sat next to him in an ostentatious dress, looking equally as unhappy as him. Her mother had picked it out for her, claiming it was the only attire suitable for a royal lady when posing for a portrait. As uncomfortable as they were, they resisted the urge to argue. When the time came, they'd sit for another portrait more suited to their liking.

L.K. sat on Bryson's knee, held in place by both him and Shelly. He squirmed and fought their restraints, and it was only a matter of time before it led to a tantrum. No infant could sit still for three hours with a stranger—

in this case, the artist—staring at him so uncomfortably from behind his easel.

The wedding shower took place in one week in the second quadrant of the palace's western grounds. He wanted his friends to attend, but it didn't seem likely following his discussions with Vitio. With Olivia and Toshik's groups still in the Dark Realm, communication was impossible. Agnos was on an important mission given to him by the Spirit Queen. Even Himitsu, who was in the Archaic Kingdom and could have easily made it on time, didn't sound promising. He was too close to finding whatever he was looking for. Tashami was the only Jestivan who'd attend the shower since he was right outside Dunami at the teleplatforms.

Thusia's likely absence bothered Bryson the most. Not just because he wasn't allowed to have a Branian at such a public event, but because even if he wanted to break that rule, it would have been impossible anyway. Since the night she'd helped him infiltrate Mendac's lab, he hadn't been able to summon her, marking the second time this has been an issue. Suadade was also unresponsive.

Benedict snapped at Bryson, which meant he was moving too much for the artist. Vitio beamed just next to the steward, sending a tinge of guilt up Bryson's spine. Neither he nor Shelly had yet to inform the king about the absence of their Branian, fearing the alarm it'd cause. The war was in its most critical point, and all hell would break loose if people found out two of the most important people in True Light were without their celestial guardians.

L.K.'s screams suddenly pierced the peace and quiet of the showcase room—a mostly decorative chamber that received little to no attention throughout the year. Bryson sniffed at the air and frowned, noticing warmth on his knee. He picked his son up and held him away, arms outstretched. Benedict rushed forward, grabbed him, and carried him out of the room.

Delilah stepped behind the artist. "Very good. See why I had you paint L.K. first?"

"Very wise, milady," the artist said.

Vistas entered the room, taking full advantage of the now-open door. Bryson tried to get the servant's attention by straightening up, but he bypassed both Delilah and the painter without a single glance in Bryson's direction. Vistas stopped in front of Vitio, his back turned to most of the room. After a bout of whispers, both men swiftly exited the room.

Bryson tried to rise, but Shelly's arm pinned him. Though he could have easily overpowered her, he remained seated. Still, he was antsy. Whatever Vistas had just shared with Vitio hadn't been good news. The look on the king's face had been forlorn as he followed the servant out.

*     *     *

Bryson burst into the war corridor, where Delilah said Vitio could probably be found. Sure enough, the king stood behind a lectern while Vistas and General Peter sat in two foldable chairs.

"Bryson, how'd the portrait come out?" Vitio asked, trying to hide his fluster. The red in his face spoke volumes.

"Nobody cares about that," Bryson snapped. "What's happening?"

"Nothing. Routine meeting."

Bryson barked out a laugh and then looked at Vistas, hoping for a tell from one of his most reliable friends. The servant remained facing forward, likely knowing Bryson would try such a thing. His jaw clenched. "Tell me what's happening," he repeated.

"Nothing major enough for you to concern yourself with. Queen Apsa has it covered," Vitio said. "I'm about to speak with her right now and receive a status update."

Bryson marched deeper into the room. "Good, then I'll make myself comfortable."

"I must ask that you leave."

He stopped, brows furrowed as he regarded Vitio. "I'm part of this alliance."

"You are," Vitio said, closing his eyes with a nod. "But this isn't something you must concern yourself with. It's far below your place in this war. You're needed for bigger threats."

"At least give me an explanation. I need to be in the loop."

"You need to not be in this room."

Bryson's face soured, a pitiful curve to his eyebrows. "I'm your greatest fighter."

"And you're my daughter's greatest love," Vitio rebuked softly. "She needs your undivided attention for the next week, at least until the shower. Then I'll fill you in while she prepares for the wedding in a month. If matters concerning someone of your skillset surface, I'll descend upon you like Magnifica's meteorite. You'll be the first to know."

Silence. Vistas and Peter continued to ignore Bryson's presence. Vitio had a pleading look in his eyes. The man was lying, but Bryson did as instructed. He left the room and closed the door behind him.

*     *     *

Vitio released a long breath as the door shut.

"Are you sure it's wise to value their relationship more than the kingdom's safety, milord?" General Peter asked, seated with hands clasped on his lap.

"That's not what I'm doing," Vitio said, turning toward the two men serving as his audience. "There is simply nothing Bryson could do in this situation. What do I have to gain from telling him this? He can't provide help in such a location, so it's better his focus is here. Vistas, is everyone ready to connect?"

"Yes, milord."

"Go ahead then."

Three holographic displays lit up the corridor, each a product of the servant's right eye. His other eye turned burgundy, fixing itself on Vitio. Queen Apsa, Director Venustas, and King Sigmund were each pictured in their respective display.

"How many ships have collided with the blockade?" Vitio asked, skipping any hellos.

"Forty-three," Apsa said. "A battle is taking place right now. I've been watching some of it through a broadcast connection between Joy and a Dev servant on one of my vessels."

"How's it looking?" he asked.

"Quite evenly matched, but I don't know how much longer it'll stay like that."

"What do you mean?"

"I spoke with Pilot Ophala an hour ago," Sigmund said. "Her birds have spotted dozens more SCAPD ships pushing toward the Intel Connector. The blockade might be overwhelmed with such a massive scale of reinforcements for their opponents."

Vitio rubbed his eyes. "Number wise, what's it looking like? Who has the advantage if the SCAPD reinforcements make it to the blockade?"

"They'll have roughly a hundred ships to our hundred and twenty," Apsa said. "We must factor in our own ships near the outer edges of the blockade, which have yet to join the fray."

Vitio lifted his face. "Then why are we so worried? I was enjoying a pleasant time with my family only for it to be interrupted by this horrifying news. That's a twenty ship advantage."

"And aren't the Whale Lord and Mythmaker returning to the connector right now to help out?" Venustas asked. "With those two in the mix, our odds increase exponentially."

"The Whale Lord was defeated at a whirlpool," Apsa said dryly. "According to Captain Agnos, the ship was crushed by a leviathan. There were no survivors."

"Are you serious?" Vitio muttered to himself.

"Which is exactly why our number advantage doesn't tell the whole story," Apsa explained. "Of those thirty or so SCAPD reinforcements, *four* of them are leviathans. A single leviathan has the destructive capabilities of multiple ships. Reinforce it with a small unit of stoneslinger giants ... then it suddenly has the presence of fifteen ships. Toono likely planned this maneuver on purpose, delaying the leviathans to arrive when all of our forces were distracted by Dev, Cyn, and Adren galleons."

"So the Mythmaker won't make much of a difference," Venustas said.

Apsa sighed. "I'm not sure. Once those leviathans arrive, it could spell doom for our blockade. I've dispatched more galleons from other connectors, but they probably won't arrive until after the current battle's conclusion. If SCAPD forces penetrate into the Intel River, my reinforcements will have to chase them down from behind and hopefully catch them before they reach your kingdom's mainland river, Vitio."

Vitio placed his elbows atop the lectern and buried his face in both hands. This was bad. If one of those ships housed Toono, he'd have a way into the Intel Kingdom.

"As all of you know," Apsa said, "I provided Agnos and his crew with a formidable unit of sailors, led by a Still Diatia and Troy Sulia. If the Mythmaker can catch the SCAPD fleet, I like our chances. However, Vitio, I implore that you ready land forces down the mainland's river banks. I've already contacted your navy headquarters at Intel Bay. They're in the midst of preparations now."

Vitio straightened up and inhaled. "And I still have to worry about this being a misdirection ploy, trying to take my attention away from the teleplatforms."

"Even though we've locked Dark Realm teleplatforms, definitely don't take anybody away from there," Venustas said. "We know they have control of the Adren Kingdom and are likely looking to penetrate that way, too."

"At this point, I'm looking to just destroy the teleplatform to the Adren Kingdom," Vitio said. "That way they have no way in."

"Don't do that," Venustas said. "It'd only make our enemies teleport somewhere else as a midpoint. Besides, we want them to try that method of entry. It's a bottleneck. Your soldiers would slaughter them as they teleport in. Also, I'm currently near my kingdom's platforms, waiting to teleport there at a moment's notice."

"Do you need more military help?" Sigmund asked. "I can send more soldiers."

Vitio shook his head. "No, all of you have already rationed too many soldiers my way. I can't ask for more. Also, I have a plan should the SCAPD fleet penetrate the bay, too."

Sigmund leaned back in his throne. "I'll send whatever help you need when the time comes. I have reinforcements stationed at my teleplatforms waiting for my word. Good luck, Vitio."

The royal heads and Director Venustas said their goodbyes for the day. The displays disappeared, and Vitio looked at Vistas. "Have Radon fly a message to Wendel."

"What should it say, milord?"

Vitio squeezed his eyes shut to restrain tears. He was going to send his daughter into war. *"Deploy south."*

*     *     *

Agnos stood in the crew's quarters of the lower deck, watching as boatswains finished patching up parts of the hull damaged by the leviathan's stoneslingers. Several days had passed since the incident, and he was impressed by not only the speed at which his crew worked, but at the quality of the repairs. This wasn't simple patchwork, nailing boards across holes. They'd spent their days and nights carving and shaping wood to become perfect fits to fill in the gaps.

A boatswain hammered the final plank of wood into place, the crew's rumblings growing into a roar at the sight. Agnos's face brightened as different members approached the boatswains and congratulated them, praising them for their hard work. Rum made its way around the deck. Pirates raised their mugs before tilting them back, harsh liquor sloshing down their gullets.

Evelyn stood next to Agnos. "A crew that backs its boatswains and swabs with such enthusiasm is not something I've ever seen before."

"They're just as important as I am," he said.

"As the captain?" she muttered with a smirk. "I don't know about that."

He shook his head as Barloe grabbed a boatswain around the back of the neck with a massive arm. "I'm glad to see them so happy," he said.

She turned and eyed him, allowing a moment of silence to pass. "It's difficult for you," she finally said, lifting her mug toward the chaos ahead of them. "To act like them … when you're still mourning her."

"It wasn't just Gray," he said. "There were a lot of people on the Whale Lord who I had grown close to." He closed his eyes, envisioning a young man with a mullet. "Like Crole, one of my favorite people in the world."

"Be prepared to lose more."

He glanced at her with scornful eyes. "Quite rude," he said.

"You're about to enter a battle on the sea between two fleets. I'm expecting somewhere around two hundred ships, four of them being leviathans. I just want you to be prepared," she whispered.

"I'm not too worried."

Her eyebrows rose. "Oh? That's coming from you?"

"I still have personal dreams to achieve. Turns out, what I found in the seafloor cavern was only a stepping stone to the next journey. This means I still have purpose, and there is no way I'm going to die before achieving it. The Warpfinate beckons me."

"You make it sound like this is your last voyage as a pirate," she said.

"That's because it is. I'm not exactly sure what we're about to sail into, but I do know once we survive the ordeal, my career as a pirate will come to an end."

She shrugged, tilting her head with a frown. "It may have only lasted a few years, but you accomplished more in that timespan than any other pirate would during a lifetime. I understand the decision."

Rum splashed onto his shoulder. The woman responsible stared at him, but then guffawed drunkenly. "Sorry, Captain!"

He laughed along with her, clutching at his chest in the process. She dragged him into the crowd. As the festivities swallowed him, Evelyn observed from afar. He looked back at the Diatia, wondering what was on her mind. Did seeing this make her miss her friends, or did it make her yearn for something she never had? *Camaraderie.*

"Everyone!" It took a few moments for the cheering to die down. Gunther, the ship's helmsman, poked her head through the trapdoor from the main deck above. "Come see this! It's a miracle!"

She disappeared. The crew paused, but then they all scattered for different ladders that led to the decks above. Agnos was jostled in the crowd, lost in the fray. By some miracle, he made it to the decks above, sunlight pouring down on him. He headed for the back of the ship where pirates had congregated. They split as he pushed his way through with Evelyn, whispers shrouding the air.

"No way."

"That can't be possible!"

"She's invincible!"

He fought his way harder to the head of the crowd. Barloe, Zorra, Troy, Eet, and Osh stood against the rail, peering out across the sea. As he squeezed between two of them, his jaw dropped and eyes swelled.

A pod of massive whales neared the ship, the upper halves of their bodies exposed above water. Atop the head whale stood an indestructible woman, her grand staff Marigium in hand.

It seemed not even the sea could claim Gray Whale.

# 59

# The Heir to the Sky-Skimmers

Himitsu frowned as he stood in the pea plants of Pluzina's front yard. Hands placed behind his head, he surveyed the prairie grass that circled the house. Sal was crouched a couple rows over, picking pea pods and throwing them into a wooden pail. Pluzina had grown weak over the past few weeks, so the overgrown teddy bear had resorted to helping around the house. Himitsu usually did the same, but he was far too annoyed this morning.

His time wasted here was starting to get the best of him. He'd been keeping track of the days and knew Bryson and Shelly's wedding shower was no more than a week away. This mission should have been completed weeks ago. Twisting his lips, he wondered if Olivia and Toshik had already completed their objectives. If the two groups that ventured into the Dark Realm returned before him, it'd cast shame upon him, made even worse by the fact that his mission hadn't been assigned by a royal head. He'd given himself this assignment.

"She's got her crying again," Sal said, craning his neck to see above the plants. "That girl is putting her through torture. It's a damn shame."

Himitsu turned to look over his shoulder. Pluzina and Kaylee sat on the front porch. The widow rocked in her chair, fingers trembling in her lap. He'd thought that was a sign of old age, but Kaylee had explained it as her fingers being used to the motion of knitting. Arthritis no longer allowed the woman to do such an activity. According to Kaylee, death was nipping at Pluzina's heels.

The widow's tears had become a staple of their mornings in this house. Even when Kaylee decided to give her a break by not questioning her about Neeko, Senex, or Poicus, Pluzina found a way to cry. She was emotionally devastated, and the simple answer could have been the death of her husband. Kaylee, however, was convinced that sorrow stemmed from something deeper. But were they that desperate to find answers?

He turned forward again, wiping beads of sweat from his forehead. Time of year didn't matter; the Archaic Kingdom's Central Grasslands were almost as hot as the desert surrounding it. "If we have no answers within four days, we're leaving here," he said. "That should give me enough time to get to Dunami for my friend's wedding shower."

Sal nodded and bowed his head to return to his harvesting. "This has been quite an exhausting few months. Ever since we saw what we did in Accus Canyon, I've wanted to return to Phelos."

A screech ripped through the sky. Himitsu looked up, using his hand to shield his eyes from the sun. He spotted a falcon soaring toward them. "Skyrise?" It plunged out of the sky, spreading its wings as it slowed its descent and landed in the grass. He ran toward the beautiful bird. "Skyrise!"

He dropped to his knees and ran a finger over its beak, taking the folded parchment from its talons. He nearly ripped it in half as he unrolled it. His eyes darted side to side, reading the message.


*Hello, Son.*


*All is well here in Phelos. It seems moves are being made by SCAPD forces. While I wouldn't raise the alarms quite yet, I will say the war's climax is quickly approaching. I'm sorry I've kept Skyrise for so long, but I've needed his speed as a messenger.*

*I'll lend you his services for the next week. Anything you need from him in order to accomplish your mission, he'll do to the best of his ability. Alas, if you don't have anything by the week's end, I ask that you abandon your mission and head for the teleplatforms. The Intel Kingdom would benefit greatly from your presence.*

*With all the love the world has to offer,*
*Your favorite parent,*
*Mom.*

Himitsu looked up at the falcon with a glint in his eyes. "I've been missing you, buddy. I'm in need of a bird's-eye view. Can you do me a favor?"

Skyrise stepped forward and met his gaze.

"Kaylee believes Neeko is dead. I need you to find his grave."

*      *      *

Since the revelation of the identities of the Adren Assassins inside the mysterious barn house, Yama had been shunned from returning to the building's vicinity. She had tried a few times, but Kolver always managed to stop her. Clearly, he'd been assigned to keep a watchful eye on her from afar.

She sat on the hill of Debo and Suadade's graves, basking in the shade of the giant oaks. Ever since her suicide attempt, she stuck to this spot. She didn't know why, but something about her proximity to the grave of a man like Ataway Kawi grounded her. She wanted to get away from the Edge and this village, but that was impossible with Kolver, once again, watching her every move.

Yama had spent the past weeks speculating on the identity of the Adren Assassin who had infiltrated Phesaw years ago according to her mother. Had such a talent been around her without her knowledge? It could have been anyone. She thought she'd soon discover their identity based on her mother's comment about the person returning to the village, but that was weeks ago now. Had she lied?

The village below, a sprawling expanse of farmlands and pastures, gleamed of gold where fields of wheat and barley grew. It was difficult to believe that such a skilled group of individuals came from a place like this. They were the most elite order of assassins, yet they led simple lives. Agriculture dominated Yinyon, partly because they had to stay hidden from the rest of the world for so long. The history of Adren Assassins during the first couple of centuries wasn't the prettiest thing.

Yama's posture heightened as she noticed activity below. Farmers could always be seen tending to their crops or livestock, but this kind of movement was different. People left their homes, heading in the direction of Kolver's inn and the lone dirt road at the front of the village. She stood and narrowed her eyes as she tried to make sense of it all. Even with her elevation, it was difficult to see the main road, hidden behind the inn and the bevy of oaks lining it.

She looked into the distance, where the plains stretched between the village and the faraway Spunka Forest. Squinting, she tried spotting any oddities on the horizon. She had almost given up by the time she noticed a lone figure approaching the town. Finally, was that the assassin?

She sprinted across the hilltop and flew down its side, twisting between tombstones that dotted the ground. Despite the distance, she reached the main road in under a minute. She forced her way through the crowd until reaching the front. The three assassins stood well ahead of the pack, awaiting their guest's arrival.

Kolver stepped next to her. "There he is."

"The fourth assassin my mom spoke of?"

He nodded. "You'll recognize him, I'm sure."

"There's one thing I don't understand," she said. "I knew a Passion Assassin at school. How did he never sense this guy's presence if he was frequently around us? Can't assassins sense each other?"

"Only when using their technique. Assassins don't sense the presence of another assassin; they sense their ability. Master Fuuna gave him orders to never use his abilities around people. Of course, he still had to refine his skills, so he'd have to take his training elsewhere. I also believe he found another hobby while away from Yinyon, something quite foreign to Adrenian culture that doesn't involve a sword."

"An Adrenian who doesn't use a sword?" she muttered, still squinting at the approaching figure.

"Oh, don't get me wrong," he said, chuckling softly. "He can still use one quite proficiently. However, because he was trying to hide the fact that he was Adrenian to the public, he couldn't show that expertise."

Her eyebrows furrowed. This greatly expanded the possibilities of who it could have been. Up until now, she'd been recalling any Adrenian she had met in her life. Now it was a crapshoot.

As the traveler neared the village, his qualities became more distinctive. Her jaw dropped. She only knew him by association, for she had never talked to him. She couldn't even remember his name, though it was on the tip of her tongue. He was young ... sixteen, perhaps. His long hair was tied in a red bun atop his head, like a flame atop a torch. He wore ragged, holey clothes, his tunic a dirty tan but stained so badly it had yellowed. And he wore no shoes. A scabbard clung to his hip while a marvelous bow and quiver of arrows were crisscrossed on his back. As he neared, she could even distinguish the freckles on his cheeks.

She hadn't seen him in a few years. Since then, he'd matured from a child with missing teeth. Most had dismissed him as nothing more than a young fan, as he was typically seen drooling over the skills of one of her fellow Jestivan, Bryson LeAnce. Suddenly, it all made sense.

She remembered overhearing a conversation between Bryson and this boy a while back. Bryson had asked him about his summer working the fields with his father. She recalled the ragged, poverty-stricken image of his clothes at the time. She turned and noticed the same theme throughout the villagers, and it all began to click.

The boy stopped on the other side of the road. Now that she knew what he was, she no longer saw a weak child with delusions of splendor to become a Jestivan ... She saw a strong young man hidden beneath the frayed clothes. His arms and legs were toned, his jaw well defined for his age. His freckles seemed like an erroneous mistake of his genetics when plastered against such angled cheekbones. He had also sprouted several inches since she'd last seen him.

His gaze fell on her, and there was nothing pleasant about it. No longer did he possess that naïve disposition of an innocuous child. He didn't look at her as if she were a long-lost friend or acquaintance. He bore daggers into her soul, looking every bit like the fabled sky-skimmer he was.

"He really liked Jilly and what the Jestivan represented," Kolver whispered, leaning closer to Yama. She swallowed a wad of spit. "If there was anyone you shouldn't have made an enemy out of, it was Simon Skimentis … the only remaining heir to the race of Sky-Skimmers."

# 60

# Ulna Malen in Crisis

Creep sat on the roof of the Gromel estate, looking up at the Power Palace perched on the hilltop. It loomed over every side of the hill, serving as a fixture in the sky to the capital below. With the amount of Intelights that illuminated its walls, it feigned a constellation submerged in the sea of stars, serving as a constant reminder to the people of how small and insignificant they were. It seemed so far out of reach, yet Rhyparia had spent weeks scouting that stratum as if it were nothing.

Creep found himself on this roof to keep watch for a signal that would appear at any moment. And once it did, the mission to free the slaves— most of whom were already huddled in the basements of mansions—would commence. While they'd begin descending the sewage pipes into Stratum Zero, he would head in the opposite direction, climbing to the highest stratum where the royals lived.

A window opened behind him, positioned in a block of permanence jutting out from the sloped roof. It led to the estate's attic. He turned to find Yesenia Itria crawling onto the roof and carefully sliding down next to him.

"You should be in the basement with the others," he said, turning back toward the sky. "I want you out of here as soon as possible."

"I'll wait here until the signal," she said.

"Rose is going to be irate when she finds out you're missing."

"I'll say you kidnapped me," she said with a shrug.

He smirked. "Good tactic."

They sat in silence for a long time, soaking in the capital's visuals while they were still intact. Nobody knew what this city would look like once Rhyparia was done with it. The tiny voice in his head burrowed its way to the front of his mind again, telling him to stop her war path. But what could he have done, in all honesty? Verbal persuasion was a pipe dream, and he definitely couldn't overpower her.

"Are my parents going to die?"

He exhaled harder than intended at the girl's question. The swollen bruise on the side of her face may have been a product of her mother's hand, but she still pitied the woman. How dare that wench take advantage of a daughter's unconditional love?

His face hardened. "Probably. Does that upset you?"

"No. As long as my family's slaves make it out okay."

"Ruby should have that covered."

"Couldn't you have lent us any of your companions?" she asked.

"Mine are busy elsewhere," he muttered. "A couple of them are in Stratum Zero, two are in the Malanese Peaks to rescue the slave miners, one's handling things at the port, and some others will be joining my efforts in the palace to free the royal slaves."

"Lots of moving pieces around this kingdom today," she said. "Yet the only one that truly matters is that woman I saw last night. If she doesn't distract the royal family, Queen Gantski will unleash her wrath across the capital."

He regarded the palace once more. "Based off what Rhyparia has told me, it's not even the queen we must worry about. She has a son in his twenties."

"Why would he worry you more?"

"Royals try to keep this fact hidden to commoners—especially in the Dark Realm—but a royal firstborn possesses a genetic trait that grants him or her a celestial guardian known as a Bewahr or Branian from the empires. They awaken this bond usually in their late teens or early twenties, but then lose it as they approach age thirty. The prince looks to be in his twenties, and even though Rhyparia hasn't seen any evidence, she's approaching this as if he has one."

"You're not making me feel any better," she said. "To think the royals have such a trick up their sleeve."

"It's a nice perk they only have for a decade at a time. We were unlucky enough to strike during one of those decades. The Dev Kingdom recently had such a period, but it came to an end during a fight with a Jestivan. King Storshae's Bewahr was defeated in battle."

"And Rhyparia was once a Jestivan?" she asked.

He nodded silently.

"These Jestivan sound unbelievable. They make royals seem like peasants."

"Yes, well, the young man who defeated Storshae's Bewahr had a gimmick of his own that allowed him to win. If it had come down to raw talent between the two of them—at least, at that time—the Bewahr would have won without question." He sighed. "We can't rely on such a phenomenon occurring twice. Rhyparia can't hope for fate to swing her way."

She groaned and dropped her head. "We're doomed."

He looked at her and placed a hand on her shoulder. "We'll see. I've heard her infiltration strategy. She has a good plan in place that should position us well. She's no spy, and I don't know where she learned to think like one, but she's proven she has the ability to orchestrate an assassination as if she was one. Now it simply comes down to execution."

Something soared through the sky like a bird, but its silhouette was the shape of a woman. A single braid whipped behind her as she flew toward Stratum Nine from one of the stratums below. Yesenia stood, nearly losing her footing on the slick shingles as she stared in awe at the woman who mirrored an eagle taking flight.

"Is that her?" she asked.

Lazily, he stood himself up. "Yes, and that's our signal. Get to safety now."

She squeezed his waist, and he placed his hand on the back of her head. "Your gratitude is appreciated, but you were the one who helped me escape that giant the night of the ball; I'm simply returning the favor." He ran down the roof, leapt off the edge and exclaimed, "Let's free your friends!"

*     *     *

Wind buffeted Rhyparia's face as she soared high above the stratums in an elastic wetsuit similar to the ones Yama used to wear. Its drag resistance was perfect not only for the high speeds of an Adrenian, but for someone who could fly. With her umbrella strapped to her waist, she'd become so familiar with the ancient and skilled at weaving that she no longer needed to hold it in order to maximize its potential. She could achieve most feats as long as it was simply touching her body.

She glanced down toward Stratum Seven, the estate of House Gromel sprawled below. Creep was likely somewhere on one of the rooftops, reacting to her appearance in the sky. He'd be making his way up to the palace at this very moment, taking advantage of her diversion of the royal guard.

"Here they come!" Biaza screamed.

Rhyparia looked up at the palace. Stones and boulders were already being flung at them. She and Biaza dipped right and left in order to dodge the plunging projectiles, all while keeping control of her current weaving patterns. She rocketed higher into the sky, moving at a speed that would have bested an eagle. Biaza did the same just a few feet away—a flying honey badger … What an entrance.

After a steady barrage of stone, she looked down at the sound of destruction. The attacks were missing their intended target, but because she wasn't doing anything to deflect them, they were crashing into the streets of the lower stratums where the hill was wider at the base. How many of those buildings were safe havens for the slaves?

She looked up again, drawing her umbrella from its special scabbard. Pointing it upward and opening it, she expelled a blast of reversed gravity from its tip. Dozens of boulders exploded into tiny pieces above them, caused by the sudden impact of the opposing force. She then swept her umbrella to the right, pulling the rubble away from the hill and flinging it into the distance toward the desert.

An arrow skimmed past her cheek, making her happy she'd tied her hair back into a braid. A bevvy of more arrows rained upon them. She continued to twist in the air as she ascended, clearing Stratum Eight and entering the aerial zone of Stratum Nine, where she spotted the archers lined atop the wall to the palace grounds. The strings of their massive bows—thicker than her arm and taller than any normal-sized human—were drawn back as they took aim, adjusting their angles as she continued to rise.

They released. She turned to face them—they were now below her— and thrust out her open umbrella once more. Hundreds of arrows scattered midflight, deflected in every possible direction but her own.

Giants leapt from palace grounds, blasting small craters in the stone from the force of their takeoff. She'd witnessed the mighty jumps of a Powish before; Vuilni had displayed such a skill in the tournament at Phesaw, years ago. This, however, was far beyond that level.

Her eyes widened as two giants appeared just below her in an instant. Some two hundred feet from the ground, one grabbed hold of her. It took only one hand to ensnare her entire leg. Her body lurched, the giant's weight dragging her down. Biaza faced a similar predicament, the other giant having grabbed hold of her tail.

They plunged. Rhyparia didn't want to try to counter the combined force of normal gravity in addition to the giant's weight; otherwise she would have taken the giant with her to their destination. She also couldn't adjust the gravity around only herself, for that'd cause her to rip her leg from her body, and there was no surviving an injury involving such a major artery.

She'd try something she hadn't practiced since her decades training with Musku—a technique she had refined off to the side and without the old man's knowledge. He would have scolded her for attempting something so brutal. She called it a crossforce.

She closed her umbrella and pointed it down at the giant as he reached up with another hand to grab the rest of her body. His current grip was tightening, and she felt her leg muscles starting to give out. If she didn't finish this within the next five seconds, he'd break every bone in her leg.

She did a bit of complex multi-weaving, creating two colliding gravitational forces at once. Both forces hit the giant on opposing sides of his body, essentially sandwiching him between two invisible boulders. He roared, relinquishing the strength of his grip. This mammoth of a man, an edifice of muscle some fifteen feet in height, was crushed. She watched his face contort and narrow unnaturally, his entire skull flattening until his ears were a mere centimeters apart. Then the giant let go and plummeted to the ground.

A blast of dirt rushed into the sky upon impact, swallowing Rhyparia whole. She expelled it with an effortless gravitational adjustment and then quickly served the same fate to Biaza's captor.

She and the dimiour took to the sky again, this time at a more breathtaking speed, skimming up the side of the building. Three more giants tried leaping for them, but now she was prepared, smacking them back to the ground with a downward blast of gravity.

They cleared the banister of the balcony she'd been targeting this entire time, some twenty stories off the ground, landing softly on the stone. It was mostly quiet at this elevation, though they could still hear the frenzied shouts from the soldiers below.

Several hundred more Intelights began to illuminate the walls as the palace's alarms were raised. In just seconds, the royals would be disturbed from their slumber and put on high alert.

She stepped across the balcony with Biaza next to her. She had learned a lot about the man on the other side of this door, for this led to the quarters of the Power General, grandfather to a young Diatia she once knew.

The door burst open as she sauntered toward it. The general sat on his bed with a goblet the size of a serving bowl in his hand. Clearly, the alarms had yet to reach this section of the palace. He was a big man, bordering the line between human and giant. And the room's furnishing had obviously been built to accommodate someone of his size.

Another man stood at the center of the room, using an ottoman as a stage. His top half was exposed, brandishing the vivid scars of whips across his chest and abdomen, and he was in the midst of pulling off his trousers.

The slave startled upon Rhyparia's entry, but the general didn't even flinch. He simply looked toward the balcony as she stepped into the room with a honey badger at her side.

"General Rath Schaap, grandfather of Bruut?" Rhyparia asked.

He took a long swig from his goblet. "What's it to you?"

She glanced at the slave, rage boiling within her. "Get out. Follow Biaza. She'll lead the way."

Biaza sprinted across the room. The slave hesitated, but then followed her into the corridor outside. Rath didn't seem perturbed by Rhyparia's gall. He reached back and placed his goblet on the nightstand.

"I don't know who you think you are," he said, "but I don't appreciate this lack of respect." His body began to inflate as he stood, his veins bulging as they were compressed between muscle and skin. "You're a special kind of stupid, and I will—" He paused with a gape, watching as she strode toward the room's exit without sparing him a glance. "How dare you!"

She couldn't hear what he screamed next over the sound of the crumbling ceiling. While the palace's exterior walls may have been composed of layered Permanence and holy wood, the floors and walls within the structure were made of normal stone. The roof collapsed above him, burying him in heavy debris. The entire room caved in on itself as she ambled into the hallway, leaving the general in a grave of stone.

She met little resistance as she climbed within the palace. Many soldiers tried to impede her, their efforts in vain. They were either slapped to the sides or flattened into the floor with minimal effort on her part. Even a few elders chose to stand their ground before her; they, of course, were met with the same fate.

On one floor, she was able to clear an entire auditorium of human-giant hybrids with a simple gravitational increase. Nobody could lay a finger on her. She walked amidst the destruction and death as if this were nothing but a stroll of leisure through a meadow. Everyone in here deserved it, and those who didn't were currently being escorted by Biaza and Moros to the palace's dungeons. Creep would have already cleared their path by eliminating any threats in the lower floors. Biaza could handle any strays who managed to survive.

As Rhyparia set foot onto another floor, she found it mostly empty. This wasn't an area that typically housed any guards or soldiers—only advisors. Ten of them lay in pools of their own blood, slumped against the walls of the narrow corridor. Someone had already taken care of this floor, and the man responsible occupied the window at the corridor's far end.

Creep sat casually, a leg kicked onto the ledge, the back of his head resting against the side frame. His trench coat spilled to the floor, the other half dangling outside the window. He was using a bloodied glove to wipe off a small blade. With the Intelights and candles in the hallway extinguished, he appeared as no more than a silhouette against the night sky.

She stood frozen at her end of the hall, impressed by the man's timely arrival. Creep was exactly where she needed him to be. He turned his head to face her, and they exchanged a nod. He crouched atop the windowsill, then leapt upward and disappeared.

She turned and climbed the next set of stairs. The throne room was only a few floors away.

*    *    *

Biaza ran down a hallway with Moros skittering beside her. For once, the weasel wasn't attached to her back, which allowed for full range of motion. A long time had passed since her last combat scenario, so she couldn't allow any hindrances—especially with a stampede of slaves and sympathizers relying on her from behind.

The floor shook beneath a hundred trampling feet. People of all sizes had been waiting in different sections of the building for Biaza and Moros to run past. SLO had planned this flawlessly, placing refugees in perfect spots along their path to the dungeons. How difficult all of this would have been without the organization's connections on the inside.

Three soldiers stood in front of a stairwell just ahead. Most potential threats they had run into up to this point had already been slain by the hand of Creep. Rhyparia had warned her that there still might be some opposition, considering he didn't have enough time to dispose of everyone.

Biaza picked up speed as the soldiers set their stance, granite mauls in hand. "Go get 'em!" Moros screamed from behind.

She leaned forward and began sprinting on all fours, clearing several tiles of stone with each stride. A thrill ignited in her that most dimiours had been trained to suppress—a sensation that flourished in the Unboundants of the Archaic Mountains.

The soldiers drew back their mauls to attack. Two of them hacked downward with mighty blows, annihilating the stone floor, which she sidestepped with ease mid run. Her agility was beyond Kakos and Atarax, and nearly on par with Moros.

As the third soldier swung in a sweeping motion, she leapt forward, landing on the maul only briefly before lunging directly at the man wielding it. She clawed at his face, tearing off a chunk of skin with a single swipe. He grabbed his face and screamed, but it became a gurgle as she used her other hand to gash out his throat.

"Get this ugly one!" Moros shouted.

She looked back upon landing. The weasel had climbed atop another soldier and was now hanging from the back of his stone helmet, tiny arms wrapped around his head and hands, covering the man's eyes.

The soldier bellowed, trying to grab the pesky weasel, but Moros only skittered around the man's head, neck, and shoulder area, narrowly dodging his hands. She lunged just as the soldier finally grabbed his helmet while Moros was on it. He flung it across the hall, where it then smacked the wall with enough force to crack it. Moros dropped to the floor in a daze, having narrowly avoided being pancaked.

She clutched onto the soldier's chest, claws digging into his stone armor. She could always rely on the strength of her claws; they were her greatest asset in fighting.

He pounded at his chest. She leapt and rotated backward, tail curling out of the target area. His fist struck his armor, obliterating it upon impact. As her body arched, back parallel to the ceiling, head facing away from the soldier, she thrust out both of her clawed feet and dug them into his eyes. The man howled, warm blood seeping into her.

The third and final soldier readied her granite maul above her shoulder, preparing to swing down on a hapless Biaza like a blacksmith striking an anvil. The floor shook as she began to swing. Biaza tucked her chin to look back at the source of the vibrations. Slaves rushed forward, their collective war cry dominating the roar of the lone soldier.

While they weren't trained in combat, they had the advantage of massive numbers. They stormed past Biaza. Several caught the woman's maul while the rest piled on top of her, wrestling her to the ground. She sunk in a mass of flailing bodies like they were quicksand.

Biaza cringed, her back smacking the floor. Moros arrived and helped her to her feet. "No time to lie around, Biaza!"

She brushed rubble from her shoulders and then bolted forward. The slaves followed suit. With the dungeons just a floor below, freedom was within their grasp.

*　　*　　*

*You know, Creep, there are people who do evil things, thinking they're justified because they believe they're doing the world a favor ... Genocide, for example. It's hard to believe someone could think that wiping out an entire race of people is just, and all because they fear the actions of a few elites.*

Soraku's voice kept playing in Creep's head as he scaled the side of the palace, leaping effortlessly between balconies and windowsills, matching the speed at which Rhyparia was climbing within the building.

Soraku had been referring to her own race, of course. Sky-Skimmers had thrived near the beginning of Known History before being eradicated around the same time as religion. Only a handful of them still existed to this day, living secretly in a remote village.

He couldn't help but draw parallels between what happened to the Sky-Skimmers and what was currently unfolding around him. He still didn't know what Rhyparia had planned, but every time she spoke of it, it sounded catastrophic … no, *apocalyptic*. Was that justifiable?

His mind drifted from Lana and Ernest Itria to the slaves in Stratum Zero whipped by taskmasters, and to those working sixteen-hour shifts in the mines of the Malanese Peaks. Each image was a reason for him to climb higher. He hated those who preyed on others.

He reached a curtained window which, according to Rhyparia, was a floor below the throne room. He crouched against it and waited for the signal. A force pushed up against him from below—a gravitational fluctuation. She had woven a cluster of Archaic Chains through the glass, for if she had tried to do the same through a wall, it wouldn't have worked.

He floated upward, gripping the bottom of the next balcony's banister and pulling himself up so he could peek just above the floor. This balcony was unlike any other, as spacious as a dining hall and complete with outdoor decoration and furniture, some sized for the average human and others equipped for giants.

Through a glass doorway framed with painted Permanence, he spotted the back of a throne with a table in front of it. The balcony's extinguished Intelights allowed for clear vision inside, well lit by the Intelian inventions. He couldn't spot the queen from this angle, but he could see the two lines of officers bordering the sides of the throne room. A few of them were giants.

A young man standing next to the throne drew Creep's attention. He sported a buzz cut and wore long, flowing robes with the sleeves torn off at the shoulders. His height was that of a normal human, but the girth of his muscles weren't humane at all.

The towering double doors at the far end of the throne room burst open. Doors of such size would have required unimaginable strength to blow open like that. The throne obstructed Creep's view of the culprit, but he had a hunch.

A figure stood from the throne, a bald woman whose oily scalp shone beneath the chandeliers. She circumvented the table while the young man rounded the other end.

With all eyes inside trained on the intruder, Creep took this opportunity to pull himself over the banister and onto the balcony. He crept toward the glass door, hugging the balcony's rail along the perimeter. As he reached the door and gazed inside at an angle unobstructed by the throne, his eyes widened.

Power Queen Gantski and Prince Zorn stood in the middle of the throne room. Rhyparia stood just a few steps within. The double doors she had blown open—constructed of holy wood, some fifty feet in height—now hung from their hinges, the surrounding wall splintered as if punched by a giant.

Just when he thought nothing could interest him more than a fight between two royals and a Jestivan, a shadow engulfed not only the balcony, but the entire palace. The light of the stars and moons had vanished, replaced by pitch-black darkness.

His brows furrowed as he craned his neck to look up. His expression softened, and his arms fell limp as he had to stop himself from dropping to his knees.

Nobody told him Rhyparia was a god.

*    *    *

Rhyparia waited just inside the throne room doors, confronted by the Power Queen and Prince, both of whom stood several paces away. They didn't stand as tall as some of the giants lining the walkway, but their presence managed to dominate the room. They were taller than her, their bodies seemingly molded out of stone, their skin squeezing every single curve and ridge of their muscles.

"You've made an enemy out of the wrong kingdom," Gantski said.

Rhyparia looked away from the queen, completely unconcerned. She eyed the officers surrounding them, knowing she needed to dispose of them first. She required everyone's undivided attention, but with the way the officers were positioned, their eyes could easily wander and catch sight of the flank she'd prepared.

Because of their rank, these officers were well armored. A thick layer of Permanence coated nearly every part of their body. Even their joints were protected by a complex system of Permanence scales that could shift with their movements. While it may have limited their agility and dexterity, these two traits weren't a priority to Powish. Pure strength composed their repertoire.

Thus, she focused on the one weak spot, a small slit running laterally across the front of their helmets, too narrow for any blunt weapon to enter or average swordsman to strike. She didn't use normal weaponry, however; and her weaving skills were refined far beyond anything they could have imagined. If she couldn't kill them, she'd blind them.

In the blink of an eye, all twelve officers dropped to their knees. Some ripped off their helmets. Others grabbed at the slits as if trying to claw their way inside. They screamed as blood seeped down their faces from crushed eyeballs.

Gantski's face turned red as she watched her highest ranking soldiers writhe in agony. She threw off her robe and charged. She didn't wear armor, and Rhyparia was curious to find out why.

She ducked under the queen's left hook, knowing the last thing she desired was a blow dealt by a Powish fist—especially a royal head. Gantski followed it with an immediate hammer fist with her right hand. Rhyparia hopped back as the Powish fist demolished the stone floor.

She looked for Zorn, who was the real threat, remaining aware of his location. Gantski may have been powerful, but divinity didn't wait in her wings. For now, he only spectated, but Rhyparia needed him to enter the fray. She needed his life to feel endangered.

She hurled herself in the air, adjusting gravity so that she flew just below the cavernous ceiling. Gantski looked up at her with livid eyes and then noticed the direction she was headed.

Rhyparia increased gravity and dropped directly above Zorn. Gantski ran back in her son's direction and stuck out an open hand to catch Rhyparia's fall, but the queen apparently hadn't realized her ability.

Just before landing in Gantski's hand, Rhyparia increased the gravitational field around her. Gantski's arm snapped at the elbow upon impact, and Rhyparia continued her plummet with little resistance. Zorn dove to the side, narrowly avoiding the blast.

Rhyparia hit the floor with the force of a boulder hurled from the sky. Rubble burst to the sides. Broken stone collided into officers, one slab striking the prince square in his face.

The royal duo recovered quickly, sprinting at her with raised fists, the floor shaking from their footfalls. The queen seemed unbothered by her now-broken arm. As Rhyparia rose from the crater, she tried clearing her head. The impact of her fall may have done more damage to her than anyone else. By the time she looked up, their fists were only an arm's length or two away. A split-second decision followed.

She raised both hands with lightning speed, collecting energy from the ancient on her hip into her body, and expelled a negative gravitational force from her palms. As their punches struck an invisible cluster of Archaic Chains coating her hands, their bodies rebounded backward, hurtling into the steps that led to the throne's stage.

Stone shattered from the explosive collision. Clouds of dust spewed from the wreckage, illuminated by the blue Intelights bordering the room.

To nobody's surprise, the two royals slowly pried themselves out of the newly formed cavity. As veins bulged from their temples, their eyes looked on the verge of popping out of their skulls. And neither of them heard or noticed the assassin in their midst. The balcony doors behind them edged open as Creep slipped inside.

An inexplicable black mist began to swirl along the floor between Rhyparia and the royals. It spiraled upward, and for the first time in decades, fear prickled down her spine. It wasn't that she didn't have faith in her ability when faced with a Bewahr, but that she was operating at a quarter of her strength right now, with her weaving focused elsewhere. This had been the case ever since flying up to the palace earlier in the night. Without such a handicap, she would have disposed of these royals much quicker than this. But this was why she'd included Creep in the operation.

The black fog turned into an elderly man, his skin as wrinkled as the leather of a well-worn belt. His ivory hair circled a crescent-shaped bald spot atop his head. And his eyes ... he had none. He couldn't have been Powish.

And then he punched the air.

Everything in front of the old man dissembled itself, seemingly blown to pieces by the force of his strike—like a hurricane had descended upon only one half of the room. Rhyparia crouched and crossed her arms in front of her, clenching her jaw to muffle a scream as the bones in her forearms splintered.

He punched again, sending another wave toward her. She leapt straight up, unsheathed her ancient, and used its looped handle to hook onto a rafter. As she hung there, she attempted to crush him within a crossforce.

She sandwiched him between two gravitational forces, but he stood unfazed. How strong was this man's body? She saw no muscle.

She whirled, weaving a lateral force to yank her to a rafter farther away, her objective being to have all eyes follow her. With each lunge, she narrowly dodged the blast of a Bewahr punch. He punched holes through the ceiling into the quarters above without moving from his spot. Fighting this man required all of her strength and attention, which she didn't have at the moment.

Reaching the room's final rafter, above where the twin doors hung on their hinges, she turned and dangled from a weakened arm. The Bewahr no longer looked in her direction with those empty sockets. He was being consumed by the same black smoke that had brought him here.

And that's when she saw Creep with a lifeless Prince Zorn folded backward against him. A blade extended partially from the prince's throat, inserted through the back of the neck.

The Bewahr vanished as Creep yanked out the blade. Zorn collapsed, and Gantski lunged toward the assassin.

Rhyparia flung herself across the room with a mighty gravitational blast, tackling the queen and rolling across the floor toward the balcony. Gantski kicked her through the open doorway. Rhyparia surged across the balcony, crashed through the banister, and was sent flying into the open air thousands of feet above ground. Quickly, she wove a gravitational field that flung her back toward the balcony.

She hit the stone, keeping a tight grip on her parasol and using it as a crutch to rise to a knee. She opened her eyes, blackness swallowing her, the bright throne room ahead like daylight at the end of a tunnel.

Gantski's eyes narrowed as she stared outside, noticing the peculiarity of the scenario before her. A hundred possibilities likely ran through her mind to try to explain the darkness outside. Rhyparia, of course, knew the reason.

"Needed an accomplice to take us on?" the queen asked, referring to Creep.

"It was one against three," Rhyparia said. "And I was fighting at only a fraction of my full strength."

Gantski unleashed a hysterical laugh—odd, considering the state of her son just a few paces behind her. Had she passed a point of delusion, unable to cope with the crumbling state of her reign?

"Are you out of your mind, Rhyparia?"

Rhyparia glanced at Creep. The despair haunting his face was a strange complexion she had never before seen from the man. She looked up, spotting the reason for the sudden blanket of black smothering the city— the reason she'd fought with a handicap just moments ago.

"You know of Vuilni Gesluimant?" she asked, looking back down at Gantski.

The queen wiped a trickle of blood from her chin. "The vile Diatia who betrayed Bruut."

"This is for her, and all those you and your predecessors have oppressed over the centuries."

Rhyparia wove a lateral force. Creep seemingly fell sideways, passing through the room and out the doors until landing in her open arm. She cringed, pain shooting through her forearm.

"What do you mean?!" Gantski shouted, sprinting for the intruders. But she stopped as she stepped onto the balcony, gaping at her regime's approaching doom above.

There was no sky—only a falling moon.

# 61

# The Falling Sky

Rhyparia leapt from the banister, soaring high and far in order to clear Ulna Malen's hill in a single bound. She needed to move fast if she wanted to escape the moon's landing zone. By now, slaves should have been well on their way through the tunnels to the shipyard.

Holding Creep at her side, she could feel his horrified gaze fixed on her. She kept her attention downward.

"What are you?" he asked.

Briefly, she closed her eyes, the question having once been one of her own throughout her childhood. At the tender age of seven, she had annihilated an entire sector of a city, killing hundreds of innocents. It had led to years of viewing herself as a monster, her potential unreached because of it. At fifteen, she had squashed a restaurant, claiming the lives of dozens more. And at sixteen, she had murdered a general of an allied kingdom.

During her time spent training with Musku, she'd come to grips with these realities. And though she didn't inform the man of all the toxic thoughts plaguing her mind, that didn't mean she didn't make use of them. They fueled her.

She had decided that if she was going to be a weapon of mass destruction, it might as well have been with the purpose to eliminate evil. The direct culprits and those who benefitted while turning a blind eye in this city were exactly that. They didn't deserve the lives given to them.

"You will crush more than just the city," Creep said. "I don't know what you thought this would achieve, but by doing this, you're just as bad as the Powish culture you're trying to eliminate."

She broke her Archaic Chains around them, allowing natural gravity to pull them toward the ground again. She didn't respond to any of his comments. Nothing he said would convince her to turn back now.

They landed in the chaos of Stratum Zero, their feet sinking in a foot of sludge. It seemed certain slave rebels—the men and women who still had some sort of muscle mass—had remained back to fight off taskmasters. A barreler who had gotten separated from its owner rampaged through the streets, destroying shanties with massive scaled fists.

Rhyparia pointed the tip of her umbrella at the beast and two taskmasters in succession, lifting each of them off their feet and tossing them into the sky. Wide-eyed slaves spun around in confusion, searching for their savior.

"*GET OUT!*" she screamed. "*NOW!* Get to one of the tunnel entrances and escape!"

They hesitated in a stunned silence, but then bolted in the opposite direction. A vicious growl ripped through the streets from just around the bend—the unmistakable cry of pleasure that could have only been from a certain wolf. Kakos had found his calling in this fight.

One person didn't turn and flee like the rest; his bald head and feeble frame were unmistakable. He stood at the center of the sewage-flooded street, staring back at her with sorrowful eyes.

"You should leave, too, Prakriti," Rhyparia said. "Lead Creep to the closest tunnel." She squatted low and vaulted thousands of feet into the air, leaving those whom she had saved and those whom she was about to kill behind.

*     *     *

Prakriti watched Rhyparia's ascent. He could see her silhouette plastered against the gargantuan white canvas of the moon directly above. Tears spilled down his cheeks. He'd feared something catastrophic, but of this scale? This was divine in the ugliest way.

What would his father have said had he seen what this woman was doing? The man would have never advocated it. And had he known, he would have never trained her.

Someone grabbed his arm and pulled him backward. "Let's go," Creep said. "Get us out of here. There's nothing we can do but escape at this point."

"How did you let this happen?" Prakriti asked, continuing to look over his shoulder as he led the assassin.

Creep shook his head. "I didn't know what she had planned until it was too late—nor could I have imagined something of this scale."

"This was only supposed to be a rescue mission, yet you propelled her toward this outcome," Prakriti said. "The lives about to be lost are equally placed on your shoulders."

"This was her decision," Creep snapped. "No amount of persuasion— whether from you or me—would have made any difference. She's a grown woman." He closed his eyes. "You didn't see her tenacity—her resolve—as she took on the royals and a Gefal. If that's what one Jestivan is like, I don't want to meet the rest of them."

They rounded the corner of an intersection, where Kakos escorted the few remaining slaves into a shack. His eyes locked onto Creep and Prakriti. A slew of taskmaster corpses lay around him.

"I warned you, Prakriti," Kakos said as the two of them came to a stop before him, breathing heavily. He looked up at the approaching moon with a fang-bearing grin. "She's no martyr of peace."

615

Prakriti was hunched over, hands on his knees as he gasped for air. A simple sprint had been enough to exhaust him. "I never thought I'd see the day when I'd doubt my father's judgment."

"I must give Musku credit," Kakos said. "I didn't think he could create such a beast." He looked down at them. "Now let's get underground and as far away from this soon-to-be wasteland as possible."

They bolted inside and dropped into a hole, determined to avoid the fate of those still in the city.

*  *  *

Rayne ventured deep into the provod mines of the Malanese Peaks, rendering countless taskmasters unconscious while slave miners fled for the exits, where Saikatto dealt with guards stationed outside the cave entrances. She did her best not to kill the taskmasters, as deplorable as they might have been, but there were times when she had no choice. It pained her to kill, which was the complete opposite of who she had been during her teenage years as a Jestivan.

Musku's instructions before death had been clear. He made Saikatto and her promise him they would never revert to their old ways. She'd honor that oath to the best of her ability.

A taskmaster grasped her wrist and tugged back, trying to entrap her in a grappling technique. Rayne expelled energy at the point of contact, and a burst of flames ran up the man's arm. He howled and pulled back, waving his arm as if that would have any effect on putting out the fire. She kicked his chest, slamming him into the cavern's rugged wall.

As she sauntered toward him, she paused at the sound of an eruption of screams outside. She glanced down the tunnel lined with torches, noticing the apparent stillness of the crowd outside. What was happening?

She extinguished the taskmaster's arm and kicked him once more in the face before sprinting toward the exit. Did Saikatto need her help? Had he run into someone far beyond the talent level of the taskmasters?

She reached the back of the crowd and forced her way through. As she broke free, she spotted Saikatto crouched at the edge of the precipice, a look of longing on his face as he stared in the direction of the distant capital. Following his gaze, she raised a hand in front of her open mouth.

What they were seeing wasn't of this world.

*     *     *

Pushing seven feet, Atarax had always been considered a tall individual. And the fox's lean frame only added to his presence. But as he stood in front of two giants—his head level with their waists—he couldn't help but feel small.

He'd dealt with most of the port's staff by now, defeating dozens of navy sailors and random crewmen within a few minutes. None of them possessed the vision to keep track of his movements or the skill to force him to use his second or third sword. These giants would probably be a different story.

"I'm sorry," he said, unsheathing his second sword with his left hand and the third with his tail. "But I need these leviathans." He turned, hearing what sounded like a stampede behind him. A horde of slaves, led by Therapif, Biaza, and Moros, were spilling out of the shipyard and rushing the port. But they weren't what caught his eye. One of the moons was … different. Bigger, perhaps? Lower to the ground?

He sighed. "And it appears my timetable has been cut short."

He staggered his steps like a lumbering Powish giant, but moved with the speed and grace of an Adrenian officer. He leapt, slashing the chest of one giant with the swords of both hands and cutting the other's neck with a flick of his tail. They collapsed with a resounding crash. Slaves swarmed the port, following the dimiours as they boarded the leviathans.

He sheathed all three swords, turning once more to regard the distant capital. He slouched and leaned back against a wooden beam, eyes growing heavy. As he watched the descending moon, he muttered a prayer.

*　　　*　　　*

The light of second-day began to illuminate the outer reaches of the Power Kingdom. As two leviathans disembarked from the port, people bunched against the guardrails to watch what was unfolding at the kingdom's center.

Shadows swallowed most of the land, the moon now a breath away from crushing the palace that acted as a figurehead to the capital's hill. Atarax couldn't believe the sheer size of the thing. Nobody ever really knew how big the moons, sun, or stars were. They were impossible to measure when they hung at such grand distances. But now he understood the scope of what they were dealing with.

This behemoth in the sky would crush the capital and all of its surrounding terrain—the dense jungles and deserts. And if they didn't hurry up and sail out of this bay, they, too, would fall victim to its wrath.

He stood between Rayne and Saikatto. Their arrival from the peaks had been later than planned, but they'd just made it in time regardless. Like everyone on the leviathan, they were speechless. There were no whispers. Nobody wept. They just watched in awe.

This was beyond any fairy tales, legends, or myths. The *Of Five* couldn't compete with this, and he couldn't help but think the Originators would have been equally hopeless. The closest comparison, in terms of raw skill, he could think of was the tale of Gatal Accus, *First of Five*. He'd apparently summoned an unknown rank of Bozani by the name of Magnifica, who proceeded to redirect an incoming meteorite.

The moon obliterated the top of the palace, eliminating spires of varying heights one by one. Its plunge couldn't be countered, and it would only be a matter of time before the hill gave way beneath it. Atarax supposed its slow descent was a silver lining. The astral object wasn't in a free-fall. It seemed to sink as though falling through water, granting the leviathans time to escape before also being crushed.

"Anyone else curious as to where Rhyparia is?" Kakos asked, approaching their side. "According to her plan, she should have been on a ship by now."

As Atarax continued to watch the destruction, he said, "I don't think she was going to ever honor that part. She'll die with them."

619

# 62

# The Lost Boy, Found

Olivia walked with trepidation through the branches of Asalka's most holy space, the Glades. She didn't know what made it such sacred ground, but she knew to not take it lightly. She'd never forget the day she regained consciousness directly on the stage of her own execution. It had been a strange day, complete with appearances by animals that walked and talked like humans.

Prim General Pinillias sat cross-legged between two massive roots. He didn't acknowledge the arrival of his guests, but continued to stare at the trunk of the massive willow.

She stepped over roots, keeping an eye on the five birches that circled the perimeter of the Glades, wary of their hollows.

"Nobody is there," Pinillias said. "The Monsignors stopped calling this home ever since the arrival of the dimiours. In fact, this past month has been the first time anyone associated with the royal family has been allowed access here since the dawn of Known History."

As she took a seat on a root a few paces behind him, she asked, "Why were they so protective of this tree?"

"It is believed that Dimiourgos lived here."

"Because it's documented or because it's big?"

Pinillias looked back at her. "Please don't mock us."

"Sorry."

Vuilni punched her shoulder. "Way to go."

He faced the tree again. "Because inside its trunk, you can find his body."

Olivia nearly lunged from the root before Vuilni's grip held her down. "Interesting," Vuilni said, speaking to Pinillias but scowling at her friend. "Do you know that for a fact?"

"Not exactly," he said. "I don't dare set foot inside. But I believe the Monsignors. They say he was born here, too. But how much do we know about the birth of the Originators in the first place? Do beings such as them even experience a human's birth?"

"Agnos would die if he knew we were in a place this important," Vuilni said.

"What's more," Pinillias continued, "these roots are responsible for half of the world's ancient pieces. Dimiourgos supposedly molded them from these roots. Not only is this holy tree the only one of its kind, but it's indestructible, which is why ancients are impossible to break."

Fane raised an eyebrow. "But there are a lot of ancients not made of wood."

"Ancients from the Archaic Kingdom," Pinillias explained, "which are derived from the pious minerals of the Thousand Layer Loess. They, too, are indestructible."

"And they can be used interchangeably by both Archains and Primmish?" Olivia asked.

"It's why our kingdoms are unique from the rest. People of both kingdoms have nearly identical energies flowing through them. But they each have a unique additional ability granted to them by their energy. Ours allows us to morph holy wood." He paused. "This tree, however, is an exception. Only Dimiourgos could craft from it."

Fane leaned forward, his interest piqued. "You're saying that Archains have another ability that doesn't rely on ancients? Why have I never heard of this?"

"Because the practice was outlawed, along with the worldwide abolishment of religion, in the first century. Over the subsequent centuries, I suppose knowledge of morphing pious minerals became lost to the Archains." The general turned on his root to face his guests. "Since we're the only kingdom that didn't commit to such a blasphemous scheme, we still know how to make use of our extra ability." He sighed. "The Thousand Layer Loess is shrouded in mystery, and because of this, its secrets definitely don't reach this far. What I've said is the extent of what I know."

"It's not what we're here for anyway," Olivia said. "Can you tell us about Kadlest?"

His eyes grew somber. "Kadlest was our general a long time ago. Outside of that, there's not much I can say about her. I was too low in the military's ranks to be privy to anything involving officers, especially the highest ranking one. The royal family loved her, though. That much was certain. So it came as a shock the day she relinquished her position and abandoned the military."

"Did it seem voluntary?" Fane asked.

"Nobody knows. The royals kept a tight lid on the subject. She just sort of … disappeared. But that's not the part that bothers me. It was the night she returned after more than a decade of absence. The palace rejoiced, accepted her without question—even her young friend whose head was bandaged. That night, those two went on to murder the general and assassinate the prince."

Olivia frowned, recalling just how difficult it was to gain access into the palace. "They just let him in because he was accompanied by her?"

"Not just that; his story was convincing. Supposedly he was a practicing priest Kadlest had found in the kingdom's outer reaches. The bandage around his forehead symbolized the silver headbands the Primmish priests wear. Who knows? Perhaps that was truth. Some believe he'd been an assassin from this city's religious sector. The two factions had feuded for centuries."

"Then why aren't they at each other's throats right now?" Fane asked. "Surely, if the royals believed the zealots were responsible, this city would be in chaos."

"Because the Monsignors said they had nothing to do with it. They claimed they didn't even know who he was. If he had been part of their ranks, then he'd been a rogue priest led astray by Kadlest. Of course, their word alone didn't resolve much, but not even the royals wanted to start a war with the Monsignors."

"So, he's a priest of Primmish descent?" Vuilni said.

"That doesn't make sense," Olivia said. "Agnos was friends with Toono at a young age. They lived in an orphanage in the Archaic Kingdom when Kadlest entered the picture."

"It's likely Kadlest took him under her wing and converted him," Fane said. "One thing is certain. She lied about where she had met him."

"Does your culture know a good amount about Earth and its purpose?" Olivia asked.

"We once knew more than most—which still isn't much—but the world caught up when Dev King Rehn had his 'vision' or whatever it was."

Olivia glanced at Vuilni and Fane, each coming to the same disheartening conclusion. This mission had been a waste of time, amounting to no information of value to True Light's efforts.

"Are you not satisfied with what I've shared?" he asked. "I'd hope so, considering the sacrifice I've made to share it."

"Sacrifice?" Vuilni asked.

"They'll kill me for this," he said. "But this is the extent I'm willing to go in order to avenge my predecessor and kingdom. I'm not as arrogant as my queen. I know we cannot continue living like this during a war of this magnitude. If nobody else will serve as the catalyst for the Prim Kingdom's involvement, then I'll take that initiative."

Olivia stood. "If they try to kill you, you can flee with us. While the information was useless, the effort was there. And I respect you for that."

"You'll flee, will you?" asked a mysterious voice.

All eyes darted toward the wall of branches behind them. The plump queen stepped into the Glades. Fane and Vuilni stood at Olivia's flank, ready to protect themselves and the general.

Inedibus held up a hand and closed her eyes. "I brought no reinforcements with me for a reason; I do not wish to fight." This didn't make them relax. "Have a seat," she said. "I will tell you everything you need to know about Kadlest, and why it all unfolded how it did. Pinillias doesn't know the half of it."

"Why are you telling us?" Olivia asked.

She paused. "Guilt. I feel responsible for Kadlest becoming what she did. We were very different people, and I couldn't hide my annoyance with that fact. That ultimately led to our unraveling."

Fane took a seat first. Olivia and Vuilni followed.

Inedibus released a long breath. "Let me start by saying the True Light alliance has fallen victim to misdirection."

*　　*　　*

"How do you advise we do this?"

Toshik rolled over in grime, his face pressed against a cold brick wall. It marked the hundredth time he'd woken up through the night, but this wasn't any type of new development. Sleeping in dirty alleyways beneath the chilly night sky didn't allow for tranquil slumbers. And the two old men conversing nearby didn't help matters.

"The options are minimal," Kuiku muttered.

"More like nonexistent," Horos said. "Infiltrating Cogdan Castle is impossible under the current circumstances. The city is on high alert ever since Toshik's idiotic stunt to puncture its perimeter."

"You're an idiot," Toshik mumbled into the wall as his stomach growled.

They continued their conversation, ignoring him. "We better find something out fast," Kuiku said. "We have no idea what's happening in the war while we're creeping around the slums of this city."

"One thing's certain," Horos said. "We know Toono's still in the castle. We haven't seen any activity that would imply he's left the city."

"Who knows what that man's capable of doing?" Kuiku said. "He could have teleported for all we know."

Horos laughed. "That sounds plausible."

Toshik rolled over. "Can you idiots take this seriously?"

The two men looked at him sternly. "I operate best when relaxed," Horos said. "Allow me my comforts."

Toshik groaned, facing the wall again. "Whatever."

Silence fell over them. He almost told them to go back to talking. He hadn't realized how much their conversation blocked out the awful visions of Jilly. Balling up his fist, he squeezed his eyes shut and fought back the pain.

He heard shuffling behind him. "I suppose I'll begin my shift on the rooftops," Horos said. "If I see anybody trying to leave the castle, I'll let you know."

Toshik pushed himself off the ground. "I'll go."

"I don't need you passing out on the job," Horos said with an eyebrow raised.

"I'm awake. I need time to myself anyway." He hopped onto a dumpster and grabbed a windowsill, pulling himself up to a low roof. He glanced at the sky and paused, frowning.

"What's wrong?" Kuiku asked.

"Does something seem off to you about one of the moons? The small one is positioned strangely."

Both men joined him on the roof. "That *is* odd," Kuiku muttered. "Almost seems like it's falling."

"That's what the moons do," Horos said dismissively. "It's simply nearing the horizon."

Toshik's eyes roved toward the other moon, the bigger of the two. "I'm not sure of that."

"Their alignment is askew," Kuiku said. "Freak accident?"

Toshik lowered his head. "Whatever. It doesn't concern us," he said, sprinting across the roof toward another building.

*   *   *

Overcrowding had become a concern for the Mythmaker. It turned out Captain Gray hadn't been the only one who had managed to survive the collision with the leviathan, but a sizable portion of her crew, as well. Her whale pod had carried many of them in their mouths as they tried to find Agnos's ship. To his dismay, Crole wasn't one of them.

He sat in the captain's chair of his cabin. Gray and Evelyn sat across from him on the other side of his desk. It was a strange position to be in, for he'd grown accustomed to being on the other side—at least, when Gray was in the room. This was the first time she'd ever been in *his* cabin.

"How are we to fight those leviathans?" he asked.

"We hope there are enough capable seashockers in the blockade at the connector," Gray said. "Which I believe is the case. Queen Apsa would have prepared for such a disaster."

"I guess we'll find out soon enough," Evelyn said. "I spoke with Zorra earlier; it won't be long before we're nearing the connector."

"Should we send your whales to scout ahead?" Agnos asked.

"I think we'll refrain from showing our cards for now," Gray said. "In a battle at sea on that scale, there will be dozens of submerged sea scouts, whose only jobs are to watch the perimeter of their ship's hull. I don't want one spotting my whales."

Evelyn nodded. "The leviathan we met at the whirlpool likely informed the other SCAPD ships here in the Light Realm about what happened to the Whale Lord. They think Gray's dead. Let's keep it that way."

"Crews drop scouts into the sea during battle?" he asked. "I've never heard of that. Wouldn't that make them easy targets for seashockers?"

"Rubber suits," Gray said. "It'd take an inhumane voltage to penetrate them. As for why you've never heard of such a thing, that's because it's a strategy belonging to navy ships. Pirates don't conduct such practices because it's extremely rare for pirate ships to participate in multi-ship battles—which is when it's most useful. Not to mention the astronomical cost."

He leaned back and rubbed his chin. "Interesting. So we're heading into this blind."

"Pretty much," Gray said.

He sighed. "Since you'll be orchestrating your whales from within the ship, make sure you keep Eet and Osh by your side."

"Why not let them join the fight?" Gray asked with a maniacal laugh.

His eyebrows fell flat. "You're not funny."

After calming her hysterics, she shook her head and regarded him. "How long are we to continue the charade?"

He paused. She was speaking of the lie he'd told Eet and Osh, how the two ships had become separated at the whirlpool, the Whale Lord crossing into the Dark Realm while they had to stay behind. With Gray's surprise return from the dead without her ship, he'd been forced to complicate the lie, saying her ship was destroyed while trying to traverse a Dark Sea whirlpool to return here.

"For as long as time allows," he muttered.

She shook her head. "And you truly believe you have the ethical abandonment to commit to such an extended farce?"

He started to say something, but someone banged on the door. His eyes narrowed. "What is it?"

"Captain, come outside and look!" The person didn't wait for a response. The sound of footsteps quickly grew distant.

All three of them stood. "That sounded like Barloe," Gray said. "That oaf."

They exited the cabin and walked through the narrow hall of the specialty quarters with a lot less urgency than whoever had knocked. Stepping outside onto the main deck, they saw the crew crowding against the rails all around the ship. Some separated, clearing a path for Agnos and the two ladies.

His face paled as he approached the banister. Surrounding them was no battle at sea, but the remnants of one. The waters were nearly indistinguishable, blanketed by shattered wood, broken masts, torn sails, along with other flotsam and random knickknacks that bobbed in the water … everything, but survivors. There was no evidence of a standing blockade, and not a single vessel could be seen.

And the worst sign of it all? Most of these sails were marked with the insignia of a True Light kingdom.

"SCAPD won this battle," Evelyn said. "Safe to assume they're already approaching the Intel Kingdom's bay."

Agnos winced, spotting a body skewered by an errant piece of wood. He couldn't even imagine what this battle had been like. Soon, it'd no longer take imagination. He turned and bellowed for the empires to hear:

"*FULL SPEED AHEAD!* We'll catch them on the river!"

*　　*　　*

Himitsu lay on his side in bed, staring at the star-strewn sky through the window. His days here in the Central Grasslands were numbered, with Pluzina's mysterious illness consuming her entire body. The woman was now bedridden, and Kaylee had pinned the blame on grief. To think an emotion could grow heavy enough to cause physical ailments.

He'd leave this place with nothing to show for it, his mission resulting in no answers. Neeko had earned his title as the Lost Boy for a reason. Even now, in his old age, he was impossible to find.

The door creaked open behind him. He rolled over, expecting to see Sal attempting to creep out of the room. Instead, he spotted Kaylee, her ivory hair luminescent in the moonlight that splashed across the room. He stared at her for some time before rubbing his eyes, certain this was a dream. She would never enter his and Sal's room if it wasn't an emergency.

"What's wrong?" he whispered, bolting upright.

She shot a finger in front of her mouth. Sal stirred in his sleep. Himitsu's brows furrowed as he tried to get out of bed, but she was already halfway across the room.

"Is Pluzina okay?" he asked.

"Yes," she said, rounding the foot of his bed and approaching the other side.

"Then what's—" he paused, flabbergasted by what unfurled.

She kicked off her slippers and took a seat on the edge of his bed, her nightgown barely reaching the top of her thighs. Heat rushed to his face.

628

"Slide over," she said, kicking her feet onto the bed and making herself comfortable.

"It's only a twin," he whispered.

"We'll make do," she said, lying down on her side, back facing him. "I guess we'll have to squeeze together."

His eyes enlarged to twice their normal size. He opened and closed his mouth a dozen times, grabbing at his face and hair in exaggerated motions, pulling his head back in disbelief.

"I see you, moron," she said.

He froze. He gazed over her back at the nearby window, where he saw a nearly invisible reflection of her staring at him. He blushed, smacking his head back onto the pillow.

"You're going to fall off like that," she whispered.

He brought his hand to his face and pinched the bridge of his nose. What had come over her? It's not that he didn't like it; he just didn't know what to do. He had no experience. He glanced over to his other side and nearly yelped. Sal was wide awake, staring at Himitsu with a devilish grin. Sal mouthed something, but Himitsu couldn't decipher the movement of his lips.

Rolling his eyes, Sal extended a finger and began to draw letters in the air.

*Spoon her.*

Himitsu's mouth dropped open.

Sal nodded and silently gave him a thumbs-up.

Himitsu scoffed, but after a few seconds he rolled over and slowly raised his arm above her waist. She grabbed his wrist and pulled it the rest of the way, pressing it against the sheets in front of her. He lay stiff, unsure of what to do next. He no longer had Sal in his sightline to offer advice.

"Relax," she whispered. "You're tense."

"What do you expect me to do?" he asked. "I don't think I'm ready—"

"I know that. We'll go at your pace. Just hold me and try to sleep."

He brought his hand to her face and swept a few loose strands of hair behind her ear. It calmed him. His muscles relaxed and his breathing steadied.

"And how long have you been waiting to do that?" she asked.

He smiled. "Since the first time I saw you do it."

There was a long pause. He thought she might have drifted off. But then she laughed through her nose. "It's about time."

*    *    *

Himitsu's dreams that night were euphoric. He'd never slept so well, so deeply—

*Tap, Tap, Tap.*

He wriggled his nose at the noise, but fell back asleep effortlessly.

*Bang, Bang, Bang.*

His eyes jarred open. He stared at the ceiling, having rolled onto his back sometime during the night, his right arm pinned beneath Kaylee. He pushed himself up and glanced at the window, where Skyrise was perched between plant pots on the windowsill.

"Kaylee, get up," he said, shaking her shoulder.

Sluggishly she opened her eyes and turned her head. "Why?" she groaned, frowning.

"Over there," he said, using his free hand to point at the window.

She followed his directive. All it took was a single glance for her to spring out of bed and dash for the window. He rolled over and swung his freed arm to his other side, catching it with his left hand. It felt like a million spiders were crawling beneath his skin. As she opened the window, he approached.

"Did you find something, Skyrise?" he asked, leaning forward.

The falcon's head twitched up and down before taking to the sky.

"Was that a yes?" she asked.

He smirked and leapt through the window, landing on the sloped roof of the front porch. "He wants us to follow him. Let's go!"

She plunged to the roof behind him. He reached back, grabbed her hand, and they both jumped to the ground. They stomped through Pluzina's gardens and burst through the wall of the surrounding grasslands. They fought through the grass, breathing heavily, their bodies adjusting to the early-morning run. Skyrise remained high in the air, giving them a good view of his massive wingspan.

They ran for what felt like an hour, tripping over their feet several times in the process. The dark-blue sky faded into the gray of dawn. The crispness of the grasslands' morning dew bit at his nose.

"There!" Kaylee screamed.

Skyrise had taken a nosedive just ahead. Himitsu picked up his pace, sprinting full steam ahead, forgetting she couldn't match his speed percentage. He broke free of the grass and came to a halt in a tiny patch of open land. A tombstone stood at one end.

Kaylee stopped at his side only seconds later, her hands on her knees as she tried to collect oxygen. "Go back and get a couple of shovels," she said. "We have to dig."

They were about to become gravediggers and potential grave robbers depending on what they found. Himitsu read the inscription in the headstone once more:

*To the Lost Boy,*
*The reclusive child of Phesaw's troublesome three:*
*You have been found.*
*Neeko Lefolli.*

# 63

# The Catacombs

Toshik sat on a rooftop in Cogdan, a few blocks away from the castle's outer walls. His hand gripped the top of the scabbard at his waist, his thumb pressed upward against the crossguard as if he'd have to draw his sword at a moment's notice. He watched the walls to palace grounds, waiting for anyone to spot him. Wanting to be spotted, he'd forgone any attempt at remaining covert. Horos and Kuiku would have had his head if they knew, but this process had taken too long. He needed to speed it up.

A breeze whistled past his ears, kicking up strands of unkempt hair. If the Toshik of a couple of years ago had seen him in such condition, the verbal lashing would have had no end. But, he wasn't that naïve teenage anymore. He was well into his twenties, and he'd made a decision on that day in the mountains—when Jilly's body lay lifeless next to him—that he would never return to his old mindsets. He'd cut down anyone who opposed him, regardless of their reason for doing so.

He stood, annoyed by the lack of activity. Did he have to shout to get their attention? They should have seen him the moment he'd climbed up here.

The castle grounds' northeast gate began to open, gliding silently despite its iron rungs and hinges. Nobody pushed it open, and there were no mechanical contraptions to move it, just the telekinetic abilities of a slew of officers nearby.

Toshik leapt onto the roof's ledge, squatting low, perched like a bird. A line of carriages rolled through the gate, each one bordered by officers mounted on horses. He counted three wagons, their gaudy exteriors implying they carried something or someone of value. The number of well-equipped escorts made it more telling.

Was Toono in one of those wagons? Would he leave in such a manner, knowing there were intruders in the capital either trying to kill him or get to Rehn's body? Of course he would. Toshik felt he knew what kind of man Toono was. The demon didn't fear anything.

He traversed several roofs and dropped into the alley directly between Horos and Kuiku. "Three royal carriages escorted by a small cavalry just departed the castle grounds."

Both men stood. "It's time," Horos said. "Who goes for the carriages and who infiltrates the castle?"

"You definitely need to be the one infiltrating," Kuiku said. "Your abilities are most suited for it. But do you need one of us to accompany you?"

Toshik had crept to the front of the alley and was now peeking into the street. He glanced back and said, "I'm going for the carriages. Don't bother coming with me."

"Are you sure?" Kuiku asked. "If Toono is actually in one of them …"

"Who cares? If that's the case, then that means Rehn's body is too. I'll kill two birds with one stone."

Horos stuck his hands in his pockets and sighed. "Suit yourself, Toshik. Just approach with caution and make sure they're not luring you into a trap."

"I got it." Toshik leapt onto the building and began sprinting across rooftops, his eyes focused on the carriages a couple of streets over.

*　　　*　　　*

Another day of classes at Phesaw had come to a close. While most refugees filtered out of the main building, Illipsia lingered in the lobby that circled the central auditorium. Today she did so in an obvious way, not worried about masking her movements from the groundkeeper's shifty eyes.

She opened a door and entered the auditorium, already knowing who waited inside. Yvole turned to look up at her from one of the lower rows of seats, his customary pipe gripped between his lips. He turned forward again. "You've become brash, Illipsia."

She descended the steps into the lower part of the bowl-like seating area. He only said this because she'd been letting him believe it. In reality, her actions had been quite the opposite. She'd moved covertly over the past couple of weeks—he simply didn't know that. No matter how many times she'd crept through Phesaw after school hours, he always missed her. When he did catch a glimpse of her in the auditorium with a book in her lap, pretending to study, it was because that's what she wanted him to see.

"Brash?" she said, choosing a seat just behind him. "Such a word would imply my actions are done in fear of consequence. What consequence is there for choosing this place as an area of study? It provides the peace and quiet one cannot find elsewhere on campus."

"Is that your excuse for visiting here so often, hiding behind your scholarly façade?"

"I don't know what else I'd have to gain."

Smoke curled upward, ascending until it disappeared well beneath the ceiling. Had Mrs. Neaneuma lifted her smoking ban? He glanced at his wristwatch. "It's past five. All students should've exited the building by now." He paused. "That includes you."

She rose. "Very well. I simply wanted to speak with you, find out where your head is at. I find your watchful eye that seems to linger over only me to be disturbing. I thought this conversation could ease my nerves."

He chuckled. "Is that so?"

"Apparently not." As she shuffled her way out of her row and headed up the stairs, he didn't say another word.

Just before opening the door, she wove a wall of Dev Chains behind her, projecting a moving image she'd created in her mind. She stepped off to the side and remained inside the auditorium, but to the eyes of Yvole, turning to witness her exit, he saw the girl walk outside and the door close behind her.

He faced forward again, likely satisfied with her departure. Only she never left; she simply waited in the back row.

*      *      *

Evening progressed and the sky grew dark. The sunlight that streaked through the circular window in the ceiling eventually faded into a faint blue streak of the moon. Yvole finally ascended the steps and departed from the auditorium, on his way to make his rounds of the rest of the building. Not once did his eyes glance in Illipsia's direction.

Another man walked in to take his place, but he remained glued to the outer wall with an air of boredom. She stayed in the back row even after Yvole left, using her clairvoyance to track his movements in the lobby outside. He took his time scouring its space before continuing into the school's Knowledge Wing.

Once satisfied with the distance now between the two of them, she made her move down the steps. As she wove a Hallucinogenic wall between her and the new watchman, he didn't stir or seem fazed. Then again, his eyes were half-closed as he teetered on sleep's precipice.

She climbed onto the stage and headed for the ringed podium. She hopped over it, landing in the gap at the center. Squatting low, she found the five locks underneath. Using her clairvoyance once more to search for any unexpected presences approaching the stage, she leaned in, pressed a finger against each hole, and began fidgeting with the locks.

Their complexity didn't shock her. She'd predicted this, which was why she'd taken several months to practice. There were hundreds of spindles inside each lock. Considering the fact that they had to be picked simultaneously, this meant she had to manipulate over a thousand spindles into their precise location with five different fingers.

Sweat beaded on her forehead, the intricacy far more complex than anything on which she'd practiced. She wondered what kind of key even worked on a lock set like this. No normal one, of course.

Her clairvoyance fell by the wayside, this part of the process requiring too much of her attention. Besides, the hallucinogenic wall she'd woven above her was weakening, and she needed to put what little amount of spare focus she had into strengthening that.

She failed multiple times, fingers growing slick with sweat against the lock. The work was arduous and time-consuming. She wanted to finish before Yvole returned to the auditorium to find his the watchman asleep. He would then scold the man for his incompetency, expecting everyone else to possess the same resistance to exhaustion as he did.

*Seriously*, she thought, *when did that man ever sleep?*

The locks clicked. She fell back on her bum and nearly whimpered in relief. But there was no time. A small latch swung open, revealing a lever. She pulled it, and the platform below her sunk.

She returned her efforts to clairvoyance, immediately detecting a disturbance at the edge of the auditorium. The presence moved swiftly down the auditorium stairs and dashed across the stage. While she could mask imagery and fool someone's eyes, sound was a different beast she'd yet to explore. The watchman had definitely heard the platform's jarring screech as it disconnected from the stage and began its descent.

Looking up, she continued weaving the hallucinogenic wall at the top of the podium as she sunk into what felt like a well. A face peeked over the podium, looking down in her direction. The man's brows furrowed with confusion. If she had woven correctly, then he saw only the floor of the stage despite the reality of what was beneath him. He lingered for a moment before disappearing, hopefully blaming it on deliria from his sleep.

As the stage closed above Illipsia, she inhaled sharply, a weight lifted off her shoulders in the most gratifying way. So much preparation had gone into this moment.

She didn't mind the slow descent. It allowed her a moment of reflection and peace. She'd become proficient in the Secondary and Tertiary skills of Grandeur's Three: clairvoyance and hallucinogenics. Complement such skills with her telekinetic prowess and broadcasting and recording abilities, and she couldn't help but feel good about herself.

There was still more for her to learn, however. Telepathy and puppetry were two other elusive techniques rare enough to be considered impossible. Rumor had it Tazama was capable of the latter to a minor degree. Then there was the Primary of Grandeur's Three: teleportation. Despite its proof in Devish history, she still found it to be the most daunting skill of the three, so much so that failing to achieve it wouldn't have annoyed her.

Her descent through the tube brought her into pitch-black darkness, but she understood her location. Simon had told her every detail of the Jestivan's descent beneath the stage on the day of their inauguration, which he'd learned from Bryson LeAnce.

She sunk through the lake at this very moment, or that's what Bryson had believed apparently. That didn't make sense to her, seeing that Phesaw's two lakes were in Phesaw Park and nowhere near the school building. Also, they were tiny enough to be mistaken for ponds.

No, she believed this was the Sea of Light—the only thing that would have made any sense. She wished she could see it in its full glory during the day.

She closed her eyes, searching for the now-familiar connection of her mother's presence in the Dark Realm. Once found, she connected a transmission.

"Illipsia?" a voice said.

"Everything's good to go," Illipsia said.

"Really? I'll tell Toono right away. Where are you exactly? Give me a timetable."

"I'm descending into the catacombs. Another fifteen minutes or so, and then I should be ready."

After a long pause, Homina whispered, "I'm so proud of you."

Illipsia gritted her teeth and inhaled softly to remain calm. She'd never met the woman, so how was she supposed to respond to that? Kadlest was more of a mother to her than this woman.

Illipsia ignored her statement and asked, "Will Toono be ready?"

"Everyone will. They've been on standby for over a week, waiting for the official signal. The ships have penetrated Intel Bay, too. Your timing couldn't be better."

"That's good news," Illipsia said. "I look forward to seeing everyone." The connection split, and her mind freed itself.

Talking to Homina was bittersweet. Illipsia had never yearned for a mother in her life. Even before Toono and Kadlest had entered the picture, bringing her on journeys and treating her as family, she'd never craved dependence. She'd been raised in Cogdan Castle by a small team of intelligence officers who taught her a lot of the basics when it came to weaving. But they were teachers, nothing more. And that had never bothered her.

Her platform broke free of the tube, and she sunk into a large chamber. Despite the depth of this place, the walls were made of perfectly smooth stone, the floor constructed with hardwood. After a brief glance below, she noticed its emptiness first. There was no furniture or decorations, just the orange glow of dozens of torches lining the walls.

*Strange*, she thought. *Did they always keep the torches ablaze?*

The platform lowered to the balcony overlooking the rest of the lobby. At the far ends were two separate staircases leading to the main floor below. She hurried down the steps to the left, whirling at the bottom and spotting a doorway beneath the balcony.

She froze, realizing a person stood in front of the doors. The hunched frame of Shea-Ley Neaneuma stared back at her with indignant eyes. "Tell me," she said. "What do you wish to find down here?"

Illipsia's gaze flicked to the closed doors once more. She'd hoped to avoid confrontation, especially with a woman of this caliber.

"Planting a Dev Assassin in our midst is quite a tired tactic," Neaneuma said. "But I'm a bit shocked to find one of your age placed in such a dangerous position. The Rogue Demon has earned his title for a reason, I suspect."

Illipsia locked eyes with the woman. An assassin? She supposed that did make sense. While a skilled Dev Assassin of only fifteen was uncommon, it was nowhere near as incredulous as Illipsia's reality. Even Neaneuma's flourished mind couldn't fathom the possibility of hallucinogenics.

"I'll ask again … why the catacombs?" Neaneuma asked.

Illipsia had no reason to answer truthfully, and she didn't know if the director had any idea about what was hidden at the end of this maze of corridors. According to Toono, only two people did: Tazama and Mendac.

"A body?" the woman asked. "Whose body would you need and for what reason?"

Illipsia remained silent. She cared little about any of the cadavers buried down here, resting places reserved only for the most historic figures in the school's history.

Neaneuma sighed. "I don't want to strike a child."

Illipsia did a quick scan of the room just beyond the doors with her clairvoyance. Nobody else seemed to be down here, and why would they? Neaneuma didn't need reinforcements—at least not against one girl. If Illipsia could just get to her desired destination, then this woman could be dealt with.

But how? Illipsia wasn't a fighter. She was every bit the intelligence officer she'd been groomed to become. The art of puppetry would have been useful in situations such as this, but she couldn't do that. She'd have to resort to her usual parlor tricks.

She wove a cylindrical wall of Dev clusters around her, creating a hallucinogenic effect from every angle. Neaneuma's eyes narrowed, pupils skating across the room. To her, Illipsia had disappeared.

Illipsia charged, but then stopped, noticing Neaneuma's remedy to the unfavorable situation. She'd backed against the doors. If Illipsia wanted to get through, she'd have to make contact, which would be a death wish.

Illipsia paused to assess the situation while Neaneuma's eyes continued to scan the area. She released her hallucinogenic shield and became visible again. It was a real pain—this being the only doorway into the catacombs.

"I advise you leave here and return to the surface," Neaneuma said. "Otherwise, I'll have to apprehend you by force."

"A bit extreme when considering I've committed no crimes," Illipsia said.

"And that's why I'm offering you a chance to walk away." She closed her eyes and pursed her lips. "Though when we return to the surface, I'll see that you are sent straight back to the Dev Kingdom."

Illipsia tried telekinetically turning the handle, but Neaneuma had a tight grip of it behind her back. "That won't work."

Stepping back, Illipsia nodded. "I suppose you'll have to kill me then. I'm not leaving."

"Why are you throwing your life away, young one?"

Illipsia's eyes grew heavy as she glanced off to the side, a momentary lapse in thought. She wanted to wrap her hair around her wrists, but it was too short to do so. She wasn't throwing her life away. She wanted to do this for the man she wished was her father.

A gale burst from Neaneuma's stomach and struck Illipsia, ripping her off her feet and slinging her into the wall several feet behind her. Pain shot up her spine, a deafening ringing in her ears. Shadows pooled around the edges of her vision as she dropped to the floor in a heap. Blood trickled from her ears and mouth; she'd bit her tongue when she hit the floor. This woman was far too strong.

Neaneuma crept forward, a frail stature that shouldn't have been capable of such power. Illipsia knew she was well into her nineties, just like Poicus and Senex had been. Alas, age was no hurdle for such beings.

Another blast of wind slammed into Illipsia, smacking the back of her head against the wall. This was more than a gust. It didn't relent. It continued to buffet her like the winds of a hurricane, gales peppered in. Her face flattened, excess skin morphing with the storm. She couldn't even stand.

The wall behind her splintered like a spider web, and a gash formed in the stone, pushing her deeper into the wall. The pressure was unimaginable, her bones on the verge of snapping.

Neaneuma came to a stop a few paces away, the severity of her glare foreign on the normally pleasant face. Wrinkles of wisdom and peace were now rifts of disdain.

Illipsia struggled for breath within the torrential wind. If she didn't do something, she'd die. Hadn't she just threatened to struggle so hard Neaneuma would have to use lethal force? There was no struggle here. Besides, it seemed the director had no desire to let the girl live anyway.

Squirming, Illipsia tried moving her arm. There was a technique she'd yet to fully master, but in a situation as dire as this, she had no other choice but to put it to use. Daunting even under normal circumstances, achieving this technique in the midst of a cyclone was asking for a miracle.

She concentrated on a visual in her mind and then wove a hallucinogenic wall behind Neaneuma. It was one of her crueler ideas, but she needed to do something. Slowly, she lifted a shaky arm and pointed behind the director.

Neaneuma turned, and the wind relented—not because she wanted it to, but because of the shock of what lay before her eyes.

Two men hung from the banister of the overlook, strung up by their necks: Archaic Director Senex and Grand Director Poicus. Beaten and disfigured, blood ran down their legs and dripped from their bare feet to the floor below. The fact that Illipsia could even imagine such a morbid image said a lot about what she'd experienced in her young life.

Neaneuma struggled for words. "How can this be?" Did she realize the level of Devish she was dealing with now? If so, it was too late.

Illipsia got up and wove a cylindrical hallucinogenic wall around her, making her invisible to the director's eye. She sprinted for the doors, breaking through the projection that depicted the two hanging directors, causing it to shatter. Neaneuma remained rigid, a look of horror on her face.

Reaching for the handle, Illipsia adjusted the weaving pattern of the projection behind her, making the door appear as if it remained shut. She opened the door and closed it behind her, careful to not let it click. With no time to waste, she ran for a side wall once in the next empty corridor. Neaneuma would make sense of what was happening eventually.

Illipsia crossed through several rooms, following the directions Toono had given her, which he'd received from Tazama. She passed many caskets, some adorned more beautifully than others. Some rooms were exclusive to only a couple, while others housed several dozen. Each room seemed to sport a theme, too.

She reached the catacombs' final room. A single casket sat atop a polished mahogany bier, engraved with a series of insignias across its side: the Passionian burning heart, Spiritian windblown soul, Intelian electric brain, Adrenian blades, and Archain mindful eye. Strung together by a line, they represented the union of the five kingdoms of the Light Realm.

It was the magnificent crypt for the Founding Director of Phesaw: Sunir Ermonia. As mighty of a man he'd been during his lifetime, she had no interest in him. What she cared about was on the far end of the room.

She rounded the elevated stage on which the grand bier sat and approached the far wall. Besides the massive painting of Founding Director Ermonia, it was a relatively unadorned wall. A series of black tiled squares—each one almost as big as her—made up its design, appearing to hover against the wall. When she took a closer look, she saw that they were attached to the wall by a short rod ... a rather modern aesthetic for such an ancient crypt.

She backed away, counting tiles and recognizing the pattern Toono had told her to look for. It was a complex puzzle lock made specifically for a skilled Devish.

She telekinetically pulled squares from the wall, shifting them up and down or side to side before locking them into place. There were three dozen precise movements in order to solve the puzzle correctly, but there were over a million incorrect possible combinations. No mind would have been able to crack the code since none of the square pieces had any distinguishing traits.

Luckily, they had the woman who crafted this on their side: Tazama Bandia.

Illipsia placed the final piece, and the puzzle clicked. To any normal eye this would have simply been the design of an architect, which it had been originally. It took a scientist from Prayoga who had knowledge of Devish locking systems to make a functional use of the aesthetic.

She glanced back, anxious about Neaneuma's progress through the catacombs. There was no way the director thought she was still only an assassin.

One of the lower squares popped free. She yanked it open the rest of the way and lunged inside, maneuvering through a crawlspace after closing the square behind her.

She ended up in a crude, small cavern much different than the rest of the catacombs. It had been dug up by Tazama and Mendac long ago. The only bits of stone in the room sat at the center, the reason why Illipsia had tried so hard to get down here. A circular platform of Permanence sat on the floor, from which two support pillars vertically extended. A control panel stood off to the side.

She hurried to the panel and tried to yank the lever. It didn't budge at first, requiring a second and third attempt with more strength. It squealed once she finally managed to wedge it free. The teleplatform spun, taking entirely too long to build up speed. It rattled with each rotation as stone collided with the hard dirt floor.

She'd come all this way just for everything to fall apart because of this? How long had it been since this was last in operation? Mendac was likely the last one to use it, marking the passage of, at the *very* minimum, sixteen years. Were there enough Dev Chains still bouncing around inside the supply to support teleportation?

She looked back at the crawlspace, though she wasn't sure why. There was no way Neaneuma would have figured out where Illipsia had gone or even how to access it.

She covered her ears as the platform hit its maximum speed, banging violently against the floor. The cacophony likely pierced the wall of the Founding Director's crypt—a dead giveaway to anyone outside.

A pair of blurred figures appeared on the platform, gripping the support beams like their lives depended on it. If they let go, their fate would have been plastered against a wall of this cramped corridor.

It slowed, and the sharp bangs became dull thuds, Toono and Tazama appearing frazzled. It was a tiny teleplatform only big enough to support two people, but made with the purpose of only holding one: Mendac.

Toono was dressed in combat attire, which for him meant light clothing. A small tunic, a pair of skinny trousers that tucked into bandages circling his lower legs, and durable footwear that protected his ankles. He had a cane strapped to his waist, a deadly ancient he'd scavenged from Grand

Director Poicus. Resting atop the cane's looped handle was the decapitated head of a being considered half god, half ancient: the lynx known as Dimiourgos … To a select few, the kitten hat known as Meow Meow.

Like always, bandage wrapped Toono's temple. When anyone spoke of the Rogue Demon, the first descriptor used was always this. There were several theories, a wound being the most common. But others had started to speculate about a tattoo or some kind of insignia.

Illipsia's eyes widened as she regarded what he carried over his shoulder. "Is that him?"

"Hello to you, too," he said with a smile. "It's been a while." She rolled her wrists and looked down. "I still feel terrible about making you cut your hair. But it seems to be growing back fast."

"I'm happy to see you again," she said, looking up. She glanced at Tazama, intrigued by her blue hair and eyelashes. "Hi."

Tazama smiled and offered a courteous nod, stepping off the platform with the grace of a celestial queen. Suddenly, Illipsia understood how this woman could manipulate men so easily. Toth hadn't been her only victim.

"As for your question, yes this is the Oracle," Toono said.

She regarded the body slung over his shoulder, wrapped in bandages from head to toe. Despite the sheer size of the cadaver, he carried it with ease.

He looked toward the crawlspace. "That'll be a pain."

She turned. "That's not even the problem. You'll be met with resistance somewhere in the catacombs—possibly, right on the other side of this wall."

"Is that what took you longer than expected?"

"Yes, dealing with Director Neaneuma required some trickery. I wouldn't have been able to beat her in a fight."

He approached the crawlspace and climbed into it. "Shea-Ley, huh? I suppose that could be a good warm-up for the real thing."

"Or you could have one of us deal with her," Tazama said, now behind the control panel and pulling the lever. The platform spun, and two more people appeared: Dev Warden Gala and a woman with long raven hair in a loose ponytail, hanging just above the floor.

Illipsia stared at the woman in silence, unaware of Toono's smile as he observed from behind. By process of elimination, the raven-haired woman was her mother. Homina gazed at her daughter with teary eyes, but kept her distance after stepping off the platform.

"Hello, Illipsia."

Illipsia didn't know how to react. She'd never known her mother, so she had never longed for her presence. Was she supposed to have some sort of empathetic reaction?

Gala brushed past Homina and gagged. "Enough with the sentimental nonsense," she said, cutting through the silence. "This is about as awkward as it gets. She doesn't care about you, Homina."

"Gala …" Toono said sternly, eyes fierce and arms crossed as he blocked her way to the crawlspace. Rehn's body was now slumped against the wall.

She stopped and said, "You know better than anyone … we're here for business. The Dev King isn't going to bring himself back to life."

Tazama, whose gaze hadn't left Illipsia, nodded in agreement. "This is a time-sensitive mission. Kadlest, Moroza, and Groto will make their move very soon. And our forces stationed at the Dev Kingdom's teleplatforms are waiting for one of us to give them the cue."

"And the fleet crossing into the Intel Kingdom's mainland river," Gala said. "We have this synchronized beautifully. Let's not mess it up because of your strange infatuation with this hopeless family reunion."

The mother and daughter continued to stare at each other in silence throughout the discussion.

"Fine, let's go," Toono said. He turned and climbed into the crawlspace, dragging Rehn's body behind him. "Who wants to deal with Shea-Ley Neaneuma?"

"The Spirit Director is down here?" Gala asked. "A warden of Ipsas against a director of Phesaw? It'd be my honor."

"It's settled then," he said. "Let's go you two!"

Illipsia turned, ripping her eyes away from Homina and following Tazama and Gala into the crawlspace. She required time before simply jumping into her mother's arms. Hopefully this approaching battle for the final sacrifice didn't cut that time short.

Death sat on the horizon for many. She wasn't too young to understand this.

*     *     *

Faced with the crypt of Phesaw's Founding Director, Toono had to force himself to keep walking upon exiting the crawlspace. This was no time for scholarly wonder. This theme continued as they traveled through many rooms, each one occupied by a casket he wanted to admire. But there was one corridor that caught the attention of more than only him.

"Is this that rotten fiend King Rehn killed when the original Jestivan first tried invading our kingdom?" Gala asked, approaching a blue casket embroidered in gold at the room's center.

"If you mean Thusia, then yes," Toono said, coming to a stop a few paces away.

"Still odd that she's the only Jestivan who was buried here," Tazama said, looking around the space.

"Well, we don't even know if three of them are dead or alive," he said.

Gala pushed against the lid's lip, but it didn't budge. She grunted with effort. "Dammit. Someone help me." She straightened up and looked back at Toono. "Use your ancient to crack this thing open."

"No, thank you. And weren't you just the one preaching against wasting time?"

"This is different," she snapped. "This wench started it all!"

Tazama stepped forward and pressed a finger against a keyhole. After a few seconds, it clicked and the lid lifted. "I must agree with you, Gala," she said, looking down into the casket.

Toono sighed. "Not you, too, Tazama."

"Nothing's been the same since that fight," Tazama muttered. "It's difficult to act like she wasn't partly to blame."

"Your blame is misdirected," he said, keeping his distance with Illipsia and Homina.

The holograms that circled Gala left her body and wound around the casket like a tube, increasing their speed. Her fingers fidgeted at her side. The symbols slowed and began to vibrate, morphing from gold to blue. They hovered momentarily before converging upon the casket from every angle, shattering it into thousands of pieces, debris flying everywhere.

He ducked, shielding his face with his free arm, Rehn's body nearly toppling out of the other. Illipsia and Homina didn't flinch, the wreckage deflecting around them as it hit an invisible force field.

He opened his eyes, bone lying beneath him. Thusia's corpse lay in a dozen pieces scattered throughout the room. He straightened up, brushing dust out of his hair. "Satisfied?" he asked.

"Not really," Gala said, making her way to the next door. "Still have to bring my king back to life."

As the women entered the next room, Toono lingered in the wreckage. "My apologies," he whispered.

He joined the women in an empty cavernous corridor just as they were crossing into what should have been the catacombs' entry foyer, where the platforms sunk from the auditorium stage thousands of feet above.

"If we haven't found her yet, then she has to be in here," Illipsia said, standing in front of the door.

Gala grinned and pulled the double doors open. She sauntered into the foyer, looking hungry for a fight. The rest followed, but only to find it empty.

"Strange," Illipsia said.

"She might have returned to the surface to warn school officials and the rest of True Light," Homina said.

Toono walked out onto the open floor and turned, looking up at the overlook. No sign of Neaneuma. "Unfortunate," he said. "I hoped to achieve this without alarming anyone." He headed for a side staircase. "We must move now."

Once on the overlook, everyone got into position. With a platform missing, Illipsia and Toono were forced to share one. They each pressed a foot into a secret switch disguised in the floor next to their platform.

Nothing happened.

They tried again. Nothing.

"These things work, right?" Gala asked with frustration, glaring at Illipsia.

"How else would she have gotten down here?" Homina snapped, catching the warden by surprise. Even Toono raised an eyebrow.

"That's not good," Tazama said. She'd gotten off her platform and was now on all fours, inspecting something beneath the raised platform. "My supply's latch is open. It appears Shea-Ley emptied the Permanence vessels of their Intel Chains. She plans to trap us here."

"What a joke," Gala said. "There has to be a failsafe … a secret stairwell."

"No worries," Tazama said, stepping back onto her platform. "We're Devish, so we'll simply use our telekinesis to raise the platform."

"I don't have that ability," Gala muttered. "My specialty is holograms."

"Join Homina," Toono said. "She'll get you there."

Gala's nose wrinkled as she walked in the opposite direction of Homina. "I think I'll go with Tazama."

Toono inhaled to calm himself, Gala's defiance getting to him. "Let's begin the ascent," he said. "If this doesn't work, I have a fallback plan." He said the last part reluctantly. He didn't want to rely on *that*; it would expose too many of his secrets.

Illipsia, Homina, and Tazama lifted their respective platforms. Toono looked up as they entered a tube of shadows. There was still the matter of the closed stage above, but he had a trick up his sleeve to deal with it—even if it pained him to do so.

# 64

# The Wedding Shower

Spirit Queen Apsa stood on the balcony of one of her palace's highest floors. She looked down upon Saido, a city of multicolored buildings and rolling hills. Her eyes roved toward the gulf, where merchant ships docked at the port and smaller vessels stuck to the harbor. To the east, the mighty masts and sails of her navy's galleons loomed over headquarters.

The winds at this height were powerful, whipping her hair toward the navy base, tugging her in its direction. She almost felt like she should follow its heed and join the battle about to commence on the Knowledge River.

She closed her eyes, as if that would bring clarity to her muddled mind. Her efforts had been hopeless. The blockade at the Intel Connector had been decimated, and she'd just received news of the same fate at Intel Bay. Despite the clear blue sky of dawn and the crisp air blowing in from the gulf, this was a grim morning. The salt of the gulf only made her think of blood's sharp scent.

Most of the SCAPD fleet would soon turn south onto Dunami River, until deciding to drop anchor and head east to the capital. She supposed the one silver lining was that the leviathans wouldn't be able to traverse the Dunami River.

Still, the Intel Kingdom—a world power for several centuries—was in trouble. She only hoped Agnos and Gray had closed the gap. If they could reach the fleet before those galleons headed south, there was hope.

"Queen Apsa."

She glanced over her shoulder at Joy, her most trusted Dev servant, unsettled by the tremble in her voice. "Good morning, Joy. What can I do for you?"

"Reports are coming in from Reikon Gate. Over a hundred refugees have arrived through teleplatforms from Phesaw in a span of only a few minutes."

Apsa whirled. "Why? Is Shea-Ley with them?"

"No," Joy said. "But we found the person in charge of the operation and asked him—goes by the name of Yvole. He said Director Neaneuma instructed him to immediately evacuate as many refugees as possible. He wasn't sure why at first, but then he saw the reason right before departing the school." The servant bowed her head, as if she didn't want to mutter the next few words. "Tazama, Dev Warden Gala, two other women, and the Rogue Demon are, *somehow*, in Phesaw."

Apsa balked. "Have you relayed this information to Flen or Vistas?"

"Already contacted both of them, milady. But I fear the circumstances are unfavorable for the Intel family. The wedding shower for Princess Shelly and Prince Bryson was supposed to start this morning. A large amount of the societal elite is concentrated in the heart of the capital. The most skilled individual they have at their teleplatforms is Tashami, but that's only one Jestivan."

Apsa spun and gripped the banister, bowing her head with eyes squeezed shut. What could she do? She was a royal head who'd yet to produce an heir, so she couldn't risk her life. Besides that, Reikon Gate sat on the opposite side of the kingdom. It'd take her days to get there. At least Felli Venustas was stationed at the Passion Kingdom's teleplatforms for this very scenario.

"Connect me to Felli," Apsa finally said.

"I had a feeling you were going to demand that," Joy said. "I've had her on hold."

"Queen Apsa, what is it?" came the director's voice.

Apsa looked up at the sky, not even turning to acknowledge the holographic display. "Head to the Intel Kingdom right now. We can't let them fall."

"Got it."

A breeze blew past as she envisioned the collapse of the greatest world power. If the Intel Kingdom perished, the Spirit Kingdom was next.

*We need another miracle from you, Bryson.*

*     *     *

Bryson gagged, his necktie tightened to the point of suffocation by Benedict Ronal. "If you're trying to kill me before this wedding shower ..." he paused and gave a wry grin in the mirror ... "I appreciate it."

Benedict frowned, though a smirk eventually fought its way through. "Don't take today lightly, milord," he said, picking up a lint brush from the dresser and running it down the front of Bryson's suit. "I know it's customary for the bride to be the star of such an event, but this is a royal shower of the most upper echelon. You will receive your fair share of attention."

Bryson nodded, fidgeting with the knot of his tie. He looked himself over once more as Benedict took a step back. This outfit was nothing like what he'd wear at the wedding, but it was still a far cry from mundane. The silver cufflinks and tie pin sparkled against the room's Intelights.

"Have you ever found love, Benedict?"

The steward paused, his back turned to the mirror as he rummaged through an open wardrobe. "When you live to be forty-two, you'll find it in a few places over the years." He reached in and retrieved a belt, turning to approach Bryson again. "That, however, does not mean I've invited it in."

Bryson took the belt from Benedict before the man tried putting it on for him. He could dress himself—at least in that area. "And why is that?" he asked.

Benedict stepped back and seemed to ponder for a moment. "A few reasons," he said. "I come from Ipsa, a quaint town at the heart of the Lingens Rainforest. I left when I was sixteen, and since then I've never returned. I've found chances at love here in Dunami, but I've had to resist any temptation, for I can only love an Ipsanian."

"That's what they call someone from your town, I'm guessing?" Bryson said.

"It's what they call the people of a specific tribe from my town. We are experts in archery, and many archers of the Intelian military are sent to our village to refine their craft—only the most promising, though. My elders don't accept average talents."

Bryson's eyes widened. "That must have been where Simon had gone. He told me he went to the rainforest."

"Is this Simon fellow a world class archer?"

"Understatement," Bryson muttered, shaking his head. They both fell silent. "Are you a great archer?"

Benedict laughed. "I was an abomination to my family and the blight to the Ronal name. It's part of the reason why I ended up here in the first place." A knock thrummed through the door. "But that's a story for another time. It seems our guests are ready for their prince's arrival."

Bryson practiced patience during the long trek through the grounds. He wanted to continue pestering Benedict about his home life and how he wound up in the position of head steward, but he realized he only wanted to use the conversation as a distraction. Unprepared for the insufferable stares of aristocrats and wealthy business owners, anxiety crawled up the hairs of his arms. His one goal upon arriving at the shower was to find his bride-to-be as soon as possible.

Easier said than done.

The western grounds' second quadrant was packed full of people Bryson didn't know. General Peter—a very nice man, but one not really suited for such a title—had been standing at a private entryway between hedges, apparently awaiting the prince's arrival.

"Just follow me and nobody will bother you," Peter said, leaning in.

Bryson fell in line behind the man. Despite the title of general, Peter wasn't talented enough to have properly earned it. He was older, in his sixties perhaps, and had only been a corporal just a few years ago. But with the abrupt deaths of both General Landon and Major Lars—who had stepped up to take Landon's place—the Intel Kingdom didn't really have any other choice. Bryson would have been the most viable option, but he couldn't act as a general. He was a Jestivan and a prince.

Benedict fell in behind Bryson as they walked through the crowds. Stringed instruments were being played somewhere in the distance, but nobody danced. A steady murmur hummed across the quadrant, as guests mingled and drank. Security was suspiciously lax for an event of this status, officers few and far between, stationed around the hedge perimeter. He guessed the several security checkpoints between the palace grounds' main entrance and here made up for that.

As they reached the quadrant's western edge, they found the head table draped in gold cloth. The silver tableware seemed to gleam blue beneath Intelamps hanging above.

The painting of Bryson, Shelly, and L.K. stood in front of the table. It was a beautiful thing … Too beautiful. It didn't capture any of that day's truths: the crying baby, the discomfort in Bryson's face after sitting there for hours, or King Vitio's sudden departure from the chamber to deal with matters of war.

Something about it didn't sit well with him, but it wasn't the painting itself. Was it the positioning? The way it separated the royal table from the rows of guest seating … it reeked of a funeral, like when a portrait of the deceased was placed next to the open casket. It felt like an omen.

A chill coursed through his body. He turned, eyes skating across the many faces that dotted the field. The amount of people here made him uneasy, the security-to-guest ratio unfavorable to the royals. Had someone slipped through the cracks? Was he being paranoid?

He glanced toward the empty head table once more. Why was he the first one here? Where were Shelly, Vitio, and Delilah?

The murmurs of conversation from the crowd behind him began to morph into something more frenzied. He spun, seeking out the reason only to find officers ushering guests out of the quadrant. People started tripping over each other as they tried to squeeze through the hedge entrance.

As Bryson slowly approached the fleeing crowd, he heard some of the commands being shouted.

"Return to your homes and lock yourselves in!"

"Get underground if possible!"

"Public landmarks are open as safe havens!"

"Stay off the streets and out of view!"

His heart began to race. There was an imminent threat to the capital, and who knew how close it was. He ran for one of the officers, but General Peter grabbed his arm and turned him around.

"Prince, you're needed in the war corridor for an emergency meeting."

"What's happening? Are Shelly and L.K. all right?"

"Everyone is fine for now. They're not saying much. But the city is in grave danger!"

Bryson took off, cranking his speed percentage to its highest point for the first time in what felt like forever. Speed percentage had always been a tricky thing. Just because he may have been skilled enough to reach a high number, that didn't mean there weren't repercussions. Running at such speeds tore leg muscles like paper, especially for a non-Adrenian.

He was across the grounds and in the palace within seconds, blowing parchment out of the hands of shocked advisors in the halls. From their perspective, it would have felt like an inexplicable gust of wind, their eyes not trained well enough to track him at such a speed.

He made it to the war corridor within minutes, where King Vitio, Vistas, and a few officers huddled around a lectern at the far end. They each turned at his intrusion.

"Bryson, I wish there was time for small talk," the king said.

"Save it. Where's Shelly and L.K.?"

"In her room with Delilah," Vitio said. "It's the highest point of any manmade structure in the city. I figured they'd be safest up there."

"And she was cooperative with that?" Bryson asked.

Vitio sighed. "What do you think? She doesn't want to be up there."

"I'm glad you didn't cave. She's most needed near L.K., where she can protect him." He rushed toward the lectern. "Fill me in. What's happening?"

"What's *not* happening would be a better question." He pointed toward a map of the eastern half of the Intel Kingdom. "SCAPD ships are currently making their way west on Knowledge River. Some of the smaller ships—the galleons—are turning south down Dunami River."

"The galleons are *smaller* ships?" Bryson asked incredulously.

"Yes, they have four leviathans on the Knowledge River. We thought they would drop anchor near the bank, then head south on foot this way, but now we fear they're heading straight for the port city of Continon, where they'd likely wreak havoc without having to leave their ships since the city sits right against the river."

Bryson studied the rivers for a second, observing the locations of SCAPD ships on the map. He nodded. "Okay, so where do you want me to go first? West to confront the galleons or north to deal with the leviathans?"

"You need to stay here," Vitio said. "We fear this might be a diversion."

Bryson's gaze dragged up to the king's face. "And if it's not?"

"It is," Vistas said.

All faces turned to the Dev servant, whose eyes were closed momentarily before opening. "That was one of the intelligence officers at the teleplatforms."

"No ..." an officer whispered. Bryson clenched his fists.

"It seems the Phesaw, Dev, Cyn, and Adren teleplatforms have become highly active; SCAPD forces are now arriving in droves."

Vitio slammed his fist upon the lectern. "I need everyone to their stations! Secure the palace first. I want melee specialists and swordsmen on the ground around the wall's perimeter. Archers and specialists to the top of the wall. Stealth units report to their assigned emergency posts throughout the city, preparing to strike at any moment. And I want a special class of soldiers on the offensive, splitting into three groups: one heads west, one to the east, and one to the north. Be wary of civilians, as they are already in the process of trying to reach the safety of their homes or safe houses. We must defend the city at all costs! Show these animals why we are *the* world power! Now *MOVE!*"

"Yes, milord!" the officers shouted in unison, exiting the corridor without a bow or salute.

"Where's Flen?" Vitio asked, looking toward Vistas. "I need his aid. You can stay by me, and he can go with Bryson. This way the two of us have a constant line of communication."

"Honestly, milord, I don't know where he is," Vistas said. "He's been disappearing on his escapades ever since becoming a free man. And even if I knew his location, I doubt he'd help since he is no longer obligated to."

"I'm not waiting on him anyway," Bryson said, approaching a canvas map of Dunami hanging from the wall. He studied every district and street east of the palace. He knew the city very well, but it didn't hurt to know *exactly* where he was going. "I'm leaving," he finally said, satisfied with his refresher.

"I want you here, Bryson," Vitio said, face red and lathered in sweat. He looked … absolutely horrified.

*Some king*, Bryson thought. Queen Delilah's assessment of her husband had been correct. Vitio wasn't just a man scared of death, but one who allowed that fear to hold him back. She'd claimed to like that about him, but Bryson couldn't see the appeal.

"I'm not sitting in this palace," he said.

"I don't expect you to, but I need you in its proximity."

They both went quiet, noticing Vistas had closed his eyes again. He opened them and said, "A man with bandage on his head, believed to be Toono, just arrived at the teleplatforms. He's carrying a carcass over his shoulder."

Bryson shook his head and let out a yell of frustration and rage. "I'm leaving! I'm going to end this!"

"Hold on now, Bry—"

"*SHUT IT!*" Bryson bellowed, leaving the king speechless. "If you're not going to fight—if you're going to act like a scared child—then at least do this for me …" He paused, looking down at this clenched fists. "I'll try to lead the fight elsewhere, but I can't make any promises. If I'm not successful in doing so, and Toono and I clash in the streets, then a lot of people will be in danger."

Vitio nodded slowly. "What do you want me to do?"

"Evacuate the entire eastern half of Dunami."

# 65

# Assault on the World Power

Shelly stood in the lobby below her bedroom, the many portraits of past Intelian firstborns circling her. Nearly all of them sported golden locks, but she broke that trend with leafy green hair. Her mother had, somehow, managed to pass on that trait.

While she hadn't heard much of it in the past decade, as a child she knew of the gossip that consumed this city. The citizens feared her, as if she was an impure royal. An Intelian with green hair? It was why she'd begun styling her hair in a pixie cut at the age of twelve, as if shortening it would make it stand out less.

Now that same green-haired Intelian firstborn was set to marry a Stillian royal firstborn. And of course the city reeked of gossip regarding this fact, too. Would they blame these peculiarities for the regime's demise? The woman who looked nothing like her predecessors; the woman who betrayed her heritage by having a child with a foreign royal?

There were many reasons why she wanted to be out there fighting right now. This was one of them. She wanted to not only defend this city, but also defend her honor. She could fix this.

Her mother wasn't a fighter; her dad was too scared of death to even try to fight, fearing he'd miss out on the lives of his two daughters. She had neither of these issues. The only thing holding her back was responsibility. At barely a year old, L.K. couldn't defend himself, making it her duty to fight on his behalf.

She refrained from blinking, tears pooling in the bottom of her eye. She thought of the greatest man she'd ever met, though he made it difficult to consider him a man sometimes. She hadn't even been given the chance to speak to him before being ushered up here.

*Bryson, you better not die on me*, she thought. *If so, I will never forgive my father … I'll never forgive myself.*

*   *   *

It wasn't Tashami's normally scheduled shift atop the watchtower of the Intel Kingdom's teleplatforms, yet he found himself seated on its edge, heavy eyelids wanting to snap shut. Ever since receiving news of a SCAPD fleet penetrating Intel Bay, forces at the teleplatforms had been on high alert. If Tashami wasn't sleeping—which there was little time for—he was posted at the top of this tower.

He'd just finished a graveyard shift. The morning sun climbed above the horizon when the rooftop door opened behind him.

"My savior," he said, turning to find his relief: a man by the name of Ruth in Intelian military garb.

"I don't know how you do it," Ruth said, walking with his hands tucked in his pockets. "Especially when we all know it's pointless. Nobody is dumb enough to attack the Intel Kingdom—not even the Rogue Demon."

"Well, it's my duty," Tashami said, rising to his feet and finishing with a back-breaking stretch. "If my queen asked me to do it, then I refuse to ignore her request."

Ruth took a seat on the ledge where Tashami had been. "The fact that the Spirit Queen feels this obligated to help protect a kingdom that isn't her own tells me everything."

"And what's that?" Tashami asked with a frown, looking back at the watchman.

"We're the most important land in Kuki Sphaira, and even a nation as powerful as hers feels it must do everything it can to protect us."

Tashami turned away, shaking his head. "I think that says more about you than it does my queen." He headed for the door. "Anyway, have fun."

"Enjoy your four hours of sleep."

Reaching for the handle, Tashami stifled a sigh. He hated that Ruth was right. Six hours was allotted to him for relaxation, and he tried to spend all of it sleeping. Alas, he spent a third of that time worrying about Agnos and Gray. Today, he'd spend it feeling guilty about not attending Bryson's wedding shower.

He pulled the door open, but then he heard a commotion from below: the shouts of soldiers, loud bangs, and explosions. If he didn't know any better, he would have thought he was on the Whale Lord again, in the midst of battle with twenty Adrenian naval ships.

He looked back, panic on his face. Ruth now stood on the ledge, hands out of his pockets and instead gripping onto his pant legs. Tashami ran for the ledge and looked at the teleplatforms, where a battle had begun, appearing out of nowhere.

"So much for nobody being 'stupid' enough to attack your kingdom," Tashami said. He glanced at Ruth, whose face reflected terror. "Hurry up and get down there!"

After another pause, the watchman finally scurried toward the door and disappeared. Tashami remained on the rooftop of the tower, surveying the field from above. Where did it look like the enemy pushed through True Light forces with the most ease? That was where he'd put most of his focus. Fortunately, he saw no such areas. True Light seemed to have the edge in the skirmish, but how long would it last with the teleplatforms continuing to spin?

This bothered him. The platforms connecting to enemy kingdoms shouldn't have worked. The storage vessels had been emptied long ago, fearing an invasion such as this. The only way anyone should have been able to teleport into the Intel Kingdom should have been from Phesaw, the Passion, Archaic, or Spirit Kingdoms. Not even the Still Kingdom's platform was in operation.

And even if an enemy had entered through a friendly teleplatform and began fighting, the operator had orders to immediately halt its functionality. How had so many people made it through? Why were they still in operation?

Tashami spotted the operator's station, where traffic was conducted via a large panel of switches and levers. His brows furrowed. The operators lay face-down on the stage, and a new person—a woman with radiant blue hair and dark skin—flicked switches and filled vessels with what had to have been Dev Chains, handling the panel like an expert.

Another lady stepped onto the stage. She wore extravagant robes with blue holographic symbols that spiraled up her body. He'd never seen anything like it. Unlike the woman who had taken control of the platforms, this lady stood still, observing the battles around her with an air of authority.

What was her purpose? Was she the overseer? The general?

Tashami shook his head. What did that matter? He needed to take care of the woman controlling the panel. The sooner he rendered the platforms useless, the quicker this fight would end.

He stood on the ledge of the roof and flicked each finger of his right hand, shooting four wind bullets at the intruder. With her focus on the panel and the speed of his bullets, she wouldn't be able to evade.

*This seems too easy*, he thought.

A series of holographs peeled away from the cloak of the nearby lady, unwinding like a luminescent ribbon and darting in front of her partner. They absorbed the blows of the wind bullets, a holographic character shattering with each impact.

Tashami balked. He'd never seen or heard of such an ability from a Devish. That wasn't telekinesis or telepathy. The operator hadn't even flinched, likely trusting her partner's defensive prowess.

He wiggled his fingers, weaving a barrage of wind bullets. She couldn't stop all of them, right?

This time the holographic ribbon burned gold, morphing from its normal blue, and split into narrower strips. They whipped at the air in front of her partner like dozens of glowing tentacles, smacking every wind bullet out of their path and shattering in the process.

The woman's eyes roved upward, spotting Tashami on the watchtower. She smirked and gave a patronizing wave, fluttering her fingers as if to say: *I see you.*

He scowled, leaping into the air and weaving a gale behind him. As he soared, he spotted someone dangerous in his peripheral vision, someone who made these two women seem like grunts, a man whose identity the entire world had become familiar with over these last several years.

He carried a body over his shoulder and stood next to a raven-haired woman. A cane was strapped to his waist, and bandages wrapped the top of his head directly over his eyebrows. As he stepped off the teleplatform, it was like time froze around him, skirmishes coming to a stop as soldiers from both sides moved out of his way.

The Rogue Demon had arrived, the magnitude of his presence immeasurable.

*        *        *

Toono marched through the skirmish, a path opening before him. Lazily, he scanned the chaos in search of his most trusted companion. "Where is that woman?" he asked.

Homina, who walked at his side, shrugged. "I don't know."

Kadlest was a spontaneous soul at times, and when surrounded by this much bloodshed, he understood it could be difficult for her to not join the fray. Taking into account the nearness of their objective, it would have made even more sense. How could he expect anyone to hold back in this situation?

A fluttering cloak in the sky caught his attention. He spotted it just before the man wearing it landed. The ivory hair and way he rode the wind was telling. Tashami Patter, a Spirit Jestivan, was here. He disappeared in the crowd, but the direction of his descent looked to take him to the operator's stage.

*Smart*, Toono thought, expecting nothing less from a Jestivan. Prioritization was crucial in Tashami's position. Yes, he could have gone directly for Toono, but what good would that have achieved? Not only would he have lost, but it would have been in vain—a mistake someone like Toshik would have probably made. No, Tashami targeted Tazama and Gala, understanding he needed to close the gateways between kingdoms.

"I'm here, I'm here," a woman said through heavy breaths.

Toono glanced to his left. Kadlest, face already streaked with blood, had finally joined him. "You wasted no time," he said.

"What better way to get the adrenaline pumping than by winning a few duels? Though I had to be careful … not everyone here seems to be cannon fodder." She laughed. "Turns out Neaneuma just arrived right after us."

"I sense powerful fights in the crowd," Homina said. "It's difficult to distinguish in the commotion, but there are spots where power levels are clearly superior than average."

Toono nodded. "As expected. True Light wouldn't be unprepared for such an infiltration, however unlikely it might have been. But we're not to worry ourselves with this clash. Our targets are deeper in the city."

"Is Illipsia going to be okay by herself so deep in enemy quarters?" Homina asked.

"Don't worry, Homina. She's not by herself. Our inside source is waiting for her, and based on what he's told us over the past few weeks, none of the Jestivan are around to stop her." He glanced at Kadlest, face growing austere. "I know you're excited, but don't underestimate your foe."

Kadlest spit. "I will choke the life out of that cowardly king."

*    *    *

Tashami fell from the sky, landing on the stage in a squat, pausing as he looked up at the holograph-cloaked woman. A smile snaked its way onto her face, unfazed by the nature of his entrance. He swiped at her legs with a short blade.

She didn't jump, but why would he have expected that considering what he'd seen earlier? The holographs spun faster at the hem of her robes, glowing a brighter blue and parrying his attack. The blade flew out of his grasp as his arm recoiled. It felt like he'd struck steel.

She kicked. He hopped backward, a gust aiding his efforts. A holographic ribbon burned gold and snaked toward him, whipping at the air just as he planted his feet and leapt into a backflip.

The ribbon extended farther, slapping at him again. This time, after landing, he sprung even higher into the air, twisting his body to narrowly dodge the rapid crack of the holographic whip. He landed upside down on one hand and flipped himself back into an upright position, his shoes sliding through the sod as he bent low to keep his center of mass.

He lunged forward, a gale carrying him toward her. Another ribbon streaked toward him, but he dodged with a blast of wind into his side. She tried the same attack thrice more. Each time he dodged midair without sacrificing forward momentum, shooting wind bullets at her in the process.

None of his bullets missed, per say, but they didn't exactly hit either. They'd collide with a blue holograph, shattering it upon impact.

She casually stepped to the side, moving out of the way of his landing. He hit the ground and immediately pivoted, lunging at her with a punch.

"Have you not learned?" she asked.

Just as his fist was about to connect, her holographs froze at the area he was targeting. He paused. She stared at him in confusion, but then her eyes widened as a blast of wind erupted from his other hand hovering at his waist.

Another cluster of holographs raced toward the targeted area, but her late reaction proved disastrous. The strange lettering shattered, and she was shot backward into the operator's stage.

He ran at her; hesitation had no place in a fight like this. Whoever this woman was, she was powerful and skilled. He sprung into the air, his path dictated by the gale at his back.

The woman pushed herself onto her feet, the smirk no longer evident on her face. Wind bullets cut through the air, but her holographs absorbed the impact with ease.

The cloak's revolving holographic ribbon unraveled, loosening around her. It shifted from blue to gold, and this time he knew what it meant: an offensive technique.

It bolted toward him. He wove a crosswind to change his path, but the ribbon reacted accordingly, fraying in a dozen different directions. He dodged most of them with crosswinds, but one strip slapped his shin.

He yelled, a burning sensation tearing at his skin. Then his leg became strangely numb, and the pain vanished. He looked back, gawking at the point of contact. Three characters had been burned into his now-paralyzed leg.

The shock distracted him from what else loomed behind him as he fell toward the woman. The main ribbon he'd dodged earlier banked a turn and darted toward him from behind.

It caught his other ankle, wrapping around him with the strength of an iron chain. It tugged backward, stopping all momentum and nearly tearing his lower leg from his knee. It lifted him and flicked him toward the ground, keeping a firm grasp of his ankle throughout it all.

With the split-second speed in which it happened, there wasn't much time to think. He pointed a finger somewhere down the length of the ribbon while plummeting, leading his aim to account for distance and speed of motion.

He shot. The wind bullet hit the ribbon and shattered a holographic character, breaking the link. The tug at his ankle disappeared, but he couldn't stop his plunge. He'd only softened the inevitable impact.

A bolt of pain shot up his spine as his back struck ground. Air expelled from his lungs; vision cut to black. An unnatural, high pitch noise pierced his ears, drowning out the clashing of swords and grunts of soldiers in a way that made him feel as if he was miles away from the battlefield.

His vision returned just in time to see the blasted golden ribbon bearing down on him from above, ready to pierce him into the ground. He rolled to the side and evaded the attack, the ground shattering next to him.

He hopped to his feet and stumbled, the feeling in his left leg slowly returning. What had she done to him?

He regained his bearings and hunched over, gasping for air. The knot in his chest gradually loosened; the throbbing pain in his head softened; and the ringing in his ears dulled.

Looking up with one eye closed, he spotted the woman. She stood with a frustrating nonchalance, her grin evident once again. "You're as good as my Diatia were," she said. "If not better. But we wardens aren't like your directors; we're no pushovers."

Tashami straightened up and glanced past the warden. A fight had erupted on the operator's stage, distracting the blue-haired lady from her duties. Spirit Director Neaneuma had arrived.

*     *     *

Tazama spun, deflecting a gust with a wave of her hand. The hunched stature of the gray-haired woman stepping onto the stage could only be one person: Shea-Ley Neaneuma—or Tide's Winds, as she was called at a younger age.

Another gale, another wave of telekinesis to disperse it.

Despite the casual ambience of both ladies' approach, their attacks collided with ear-shattering violence. This wasn't a frenzied duel. These were two highly experienced women who would rely on their masterful weaving skills, like Dev Warden Gala was presently doing against the Jestivan—a young man who hadn't aged or seen enough in his lifetime to form the same kind of discipline.

Swords, knives, and all sorts of weapons were tugged out of the grasps of surrounding soldiers, Tazama's telekinetic mastery proving too powerful for their common strength. They hovered for a second, rotating so that they were aimed toward the director, then converged from all angles at an alarming speed.

A gale exploded from Neaneuma's body, blasting outward and rippling the air like a shockwave, her body its epicenter. A hundred weapons were

666

slapped out of the air with ease. Soldiers were sent flying with them, unable to hold up against such a mighty wind. Only Gala and the Jestivan remained on their feet.

Tazama scanned the area, eyes narrowed. *Well, that certainly helps limit unintended casualties*, she thought. She looked back at Neaneuma. *But I suppose I should be more concerned with my own life.*

"You can deflect someone else's abilities with your Dev Energy?" Neaneuma asked with a hint of intrigue. "Inanimate objects are one thing, but to manipulate my wind—even if for only a split second—is not a talent I expected to run into."

Tazama nodded curtly. "I appreciate the flattery, but I know a mere skill such as that only acts as a minor hindrance to a woman of your caliber."

"Such modesty for someone with your youth ..." Neaneuma trailed off, shaking her head with a smile. "Director Venustas could learn a thing or two from you."

"Mid-forties is hardly young."

"A matter of perspective, seeing that you're half my age."

Wind began to swirl at Tazama's ankles, drawing her attention downward.

"No burst attacks, then," Neaneuma said. "If you can fend them off so easily."

The winds stirred and then erupted like a geyser around Tazama. A twister wrapped around her, her hair whipping her face erratically. The stage's floorboards ripped from their bindings, sucked in by the torqueing winds.

Tazama covered her face with her arm, raising her other hand and curling her fingers. Dozens of shields from fallen soldiers darted toward her. She clutched her hand, and the shields froze in the twister's winds, acting as a wall to impede the gale's path. The twister strengthened in response, forcing her to place all of her focus on holding the shields in place.

Normally, she didn't have to use her hands when weaving, but when confronted with this much force, she had no other choice. Neaneuma was not an enemy to take lightly.

Tazama widened her base and lowered into a squat to prevent a loss of traction. One by one, shields were ripped out of their fixed positions, overtaken by the winds. She needed a quick solution. Better yet, she should have avoided this situation before it started.

Her feet were yanked from the ground, her body sucked into the howling winds. Round and round her path went, revolving at uncontrollable speeds. She couldn't stop it, and her vision spun too fast for her to target anything with her telekinesis. She knew she'd traveled a great distance upward in a short time; the soldiers below looked like bugs.

The twister lost its grasp of her, the winds weakening near the top. She flew through the sky, debris fluttering around her. She spotted a billowing wave of flame collide with a wall of ice below—another duel between two skilled adversaries.

A hammer-like blast of wind hit her from above. She plunged, land approaching faster than she would have hoped. And once again, she was at a loss for options.

Her body flailed, gaze toward the sky as her back turned toward the ground. As she closed her eyes and accepted death, she hit something soft, her free-fall quickly losing speed.

Glancing to her sides, she saw a glowing violet grid of foreign symbols. It stretched as it gave way beneath her weight, acting as a holographic net. This was Gala's doing. Had she defeated the Jestivan?

Tazama rolled onto her side as she sunk, glancing below. She located the warden just as the Jestivan broke through her defenses, connecting with a punch to her cheek. Tazama's eyes widened. Gala had averted her attention from her own fight in order to save a comrade?

The net shattered into pieces right after the warden received the blow, but by that time, Tazama was low enough to land safely in the grass. She leapt onto her feet and faced Neaneuma, this time stepping back into a ready stance as she was determined to not make the same mistake.

She wiped a bead of sweat from her brow, the heat becoming insufferable as the Passion Director clashed with Still Warden Moroza somewhere nearby—just another bout between mighty foes.

Despite the insanity, Gala had taken an interest in and saved Tazama's life. These women all fought with the same collective goal: bringing their rightful king back to life. It seemed even Gala's pride wouldn't interfere with that.

*     *     *

Director Venustas and Warden Moroza clashed in a symphony of fire and ice.

In normal elements, one should have had a clear advantage, but that wasn't the case when dealing with the frozen attacks of a Stillian.

Waves of heat and cold alternated in the atmosphere. Soldiers fell one by one around the dueling women, bodies succumbing to the shock of rapid temperature shifts.

Venustas screamed, a wide-sweeping inferno surging toward Moroza. A frozen wall shot upward, blocking the director's attack. Flames billowed outward and dispersed upon impact, only managing a dent in the barrier.

A pillar of ice burst through the flames, its pointed tip ready to impale its target. Venustas turned her shoulder, feet planted, as the pillar shot past. She grasped it with one hand, its frostbitten cold piercing through her skin. She released fire from her hand, coating the ice and melting it.

Moroza's assault relinquished. Ice and fire dwindled into nothing as the two women caught their breath, a comfortable distance between them.

Venustas lunged forward. Her shoulders dipped and rolled as she evaded ice stalagmites that protruded from the ground in a domino effect. She opened her mouth and shot a ball of fire through a stalagmite that had risen in front of her.

Leaping through the newly-formed hole, she flung two more balls of fire from each hand as she landed. They zoomed toward Moroza, twin trails of smoke behind them.

The warden crouched, holding out both arms as if she was scooping a body up from the ground. She then stood and roared, a glacier rising in front of her.

Venustas slid to a stop, planting her feet and squaring her base. She opened her mouth and blew a breath of fire at the wall, this time concentrating her Passion Chains into a narrow cluster. It provided an inferno's wrath, but packed into a single stream.

Flame collided with the wall and didn't relent. Slowly, her fire breath tunneled its way through, searching for the other side. Undoubtedly, Moroza would feel the fire's efforts against her Still Energy in the frozen wall. Venustas wanted her to. She was trying to redirect the woman's attention.

She extended both arms to her side, mouth still agape while breathing fire. Dozens of fireballs erupted from her arms and hands, soaring into the sky and arching over the top of the wall where they'd rain upon the warden.

Massive spikes extended from the wall, forcing Venustas to leap backward. The wall then vanished, Moroza now visible as she stood beneath an ice shell, flame raining around her like molten chunks of lava.

Venustas sighed, crossing her arms with a frown. "This is no good," she said. "A battle between Passionians and Stillians, in most instances, end in a stalemate."

The fire shower came to a stop, and Moroza exited the shell of ice. "This will come down to wits, and who can be the cleverest with their ability."

"Such a chore," Venustas said.

The warden nodded. "I agree, but this seems to be the luck that was dealt to us."

Venustas's eyes raked the field around her. She was participating in one of four critical duels scattered amongst the warring soldiers, the other three containing the pairs of Tashami and Warden Gala, Director Neaneuma and Tazama, and a newly formed bout between two men who wielded ice. This pair confused her.

"You get to see a Still Diatia in action," Moroza said, likely noticing the look on Venustas's face. "Against a traitorous—and frustratingly skilled— soldier in Titus. Unfortunately, he's not your average cannon fodder."

"Traitorous? Hasn't Still Queen Apoleia aligned with True Light? Wouldn't that make you the traitorous one, fighting on behalf of her enemy?"

The warden scowled. "My queen has clearly lost her backbone. I don't fight with Intelians—nor will I ever!"

Ice crept down her arms, starting from her elbows down past her fingertips. They took the shape of jousting lances, acting as extensions of her arms. Long and powerful, they expanded her reach by several feet.

She thrust, forcing Venustas to leap back. She swiped with the other lance, the director ducking beneath it. A kick followed, a frozen spike extending from the warden's boot. Venustas caught her ankle and coated it in flame.

Prepared for such a maneuver, Moroza jabbed with her frozen lance once more. Venustas lost her grip trying to dodge. The warden took that opportunity to look down and blow cold air in the direction of her torched leg.

Venustas raised an eyebrow, watching as the frigid air swirled around Moroza's ankle and doused the flame with ease. She'd have to watch out for the woman's breath, its temperatures likely capable of frostbite.

She sighed. "And we're back to square one, it seems."

"Not at all," Moroza said.

Ice accumulated at her boots, creeping downward into the grass. It spread across the battlefield with a cracking noise until it surrounded the two women.

Venustas shrugged, focusing her energy into her feet. She kicked off her shoes and rolled up her pant legs. Fire erupted at her feet, melting the ice below her. "This will come down to sparring, warden of Ipsas."

The two women set their jaws and charged.

# 66

# The Raven Wraith

Bryson stood in front of the eastern gate, a minor entrance to palace grounds. The defenses here were nothing like those at the southern or northern gates. With arms crossed and eyes as fierce as a hawk's, he stood eerily still. There wasn't any reason for him to enter the maze of city streets; that'd only make it easier to miss Toono, giving the man free access into the palace.

Half a dozen Dev servants—lent to the Intel family by allying kingdoms—were stationed at key areas throughout the eastern half of the city. Each was positioned in a way that wouldn't allow Toono to flank the palace unnoticed. If he did try such a strategy, Vistas would alert Bryson immediately. This entrance served as a choke point.

Bryson wasn't alone. Over a dozen archers lined the top of the wall behind him. He'd requested Simon's presence, but apparently Commander Magnolia hadn't seen the boy in several days. They feared desertion, but

Bryson couldn't believe that. In spirit, mind, and duty, Simon was of a rare breed.

This did worry him, however; the boy wouldn't leave of his own accord. Had someone hurt or stolen him?

Bryson closed his eyes in efforts to quiet the mental noise, but that only caused images of Thusia's face to materialize … another presence he wished he had right now. He'd tried many times in the past hour to summon her, but received no response. This had been a problem since the Blizzard of Blood, outside of the one night she'd helped him get into Mendac's lab. But even that only happened because she'd managed to 'escape,' according to her words.

He supposed that was better than Shelly's situation. Branian Suadade hadn't made a single appearance as of late.

Simon, Thusia, and Suadade weren't the only allies Bryson was missing. Himitsu, Olivia, Toshik, and Lilu would have tipped the scales in the Intel Kingdom's favor had they not been scattered around the world. He turned, gazing back through the gate, locating a spire of the palace that disappeared into the overcast sky. Shelly, too, would have been a reliable partner in battle. Alas, her duties were needed elsewhere.

Was Toono just a lucky man or had he somehow known about the scattered condition of True Light's most elite individuals? If the latter, it'd imply someone on the inside leaked information.

"*IT'S HIM!* And he has company!"

"Get ready, men!" Magnolia bellowed. "Nock your arrows!"

Bryson turned, allowing his vision to pan slowly. As he detected three figures at the end of the main road, his vision blurred then refocused. An inexplicable rage burned within him, causing heat to build in his chest.

What was this feeling? A loss of consciousness? Sanity? He knew he was heaving, but he couldn't feel it. His mind raced, but he couldn't think. Overwhelmed by everything happening within him, his sensory intake of the outside world seemed convoluted. He couldn't hear the world, but he could decipher the acute sound of this one man's footfalls as he sauntered toward the gate. And despite his hazy vision, the sharp features of the demon's face emerged with prominence.

Bryson reached up to touch his face. He couldn't feel it. He bit his lip and experienced the same numbness. His sense of taste, however, was at an absurd high. Blood seeped between his lips, soaking his tongue in a strong metallic taste. A mixture of angst and adrenaline swirled within him.

"I'll take the two women accompanying him."

The voice startled Bryson out of his trance. He glanced to his left, where King Vitio's tall and burly frame stood. When had he arrived?

"Are you sure?" Bryson asked. He'd never witnessed the man fight. The one time the opportunity had presented itself—against Archaic King Itta during the Generals' Battle—he only dodged.

"I may not be a Jestivan, but I am a royal head," Vitio said. "Since Shelly was born, I've lived my life fearful of death. There are no excuses now. My girls have blossomed into two successful young women, and one has made me a grandfather. I've done my job." He looked down at Bryson with somber yet peaceful eyes. "Now you do yours."

Bryson knew that look, but didn't address it. He walked forward, planning to meet the demon halfway. "I don't know how this will end, so I will say this now …

"You took me in when Debo died, and for that I thank you."

*　　*　　*

After departing Phesaw's Telejunction to the Dev Kingdom's teleplatforms and alerting the force of soldiers stationed there that Tazama would soon open the gateway into the Intel Kingdom, Illipsia headed for a platform designed specifically for her by the same woman.

She found it hidden in the grass roughly a mile northwest of the normal platforms. It was small and crudely built, meant to be unnoticed by any passersby. Even Illipsia's tiny frame had problems staying within its bounds, forcing her to hug the lone support beam at its center.

She telekinetically flipped a lever installed in a Permanence vessel on the ground. She hoped the person they had working for them in True Light's ranks was waiting for her on the other side.

The platform jarred into motion, drawing a sigh of relief from the girl. In moments, the device reached its maximum speed and all became black.

Her vision settled as the platform slowed. She was somewhere dark and cramped, lit only by a lone candle held in someone's hand nearby.

"Are you the girl the Rogue Demon referred to as the Raven Wraith?"

She looked above the candle in search of the man's face, but he held it too low for her to get a proper look. She supposed it wasn't necessary. If he knew her by that name—an alias recently constructed to prevent potential enemies from knowing her real identity—then he was definitely the spy Toono and Tazama had been in contact with.

"I am," she said. "And you are?"

He lifted the candle, exposing a pale face and sleek black hair. "Name's Flen. Welcome to Dunami Palace."

*     *     *

The room Illipsia had arrived in was a tiny thing, a single chamber nestled in the bowels of the palace. Mendac had built this teleplatform a long time ago, but only with the functionality of teleporting out. However, with the combined efforts of Flen here and Tazama building her own platform in the Dev Kingdom, they managed to rig it to accept incoming transports.

They climbed a narrow staircase ending with a closed door. Despite Illipsia's reassurance from her clairvoyance, Flen opened the door and peeked outside. He then stepped out fully, looking both ways for any bystanders. He waved her out.

The hall was a glorious spectacle, furnished with gold and lacquered maple, floor carpeted in lush blue. It was a befitting image for the centerpiece of the world's wealthiest city. Strange, though, considering the dark, dingy basement that branched off from it. She cringed at the amount of detail in the architecture,

675

"We must stick to the walls and keep the scope of the image I must recreate as focused as possible," she whispered. "My hallucinogenics can only do so much if I'm not familiar with my surroundings."

"I understand. The fact that you can do it at all is impressive."

Their climb through the palace was mostly unobstructed, save the occasional guard patrolling the more trafficked corridors. With Flen's guidance, they cut through lesser used passageways and shortcuts. They spent their journey in absolute silence, as they couldn't risk being caught by anyone. Despite Illipsia's weaving prowess, there was still a chance she could miss an approaching presence with her clairvoyance. She wasn't perfect.

Just like at Phesaw, she found herself conducting an infiltration mission—though this was different. Instead of trying to blend in with a crowd of refugees, she didn't want to be seen at all.

After several minutes, she no longer knew where she was. She'd even given up on tracking their turns, her trust falling solely on Flen—a reliance that could get her in trouble.

She stopped him just as they were about to turn down another hallway. "Strong presence down there," she whispered. "Is there another way?"

He raised an eyebrow. "Anyone noteworthy should be outside, and we aren't near Princess Shelly. I'm not sure who it could be."

He crept toward the wall's edge and peeked around the corner. He snapped his head back. "What is that fool doing here?"

"Who?" she asked.

"My brother, Vistas." He looked back down the corridor they currently occupied. "There's no use; this is the only way."

"Is he a skilled fighter?" she asked, biting her lip.

"Not at all. But he's not far behind me in weaving talent. He's also very observant." He sighed. "I fear he might see through a hallucinogenic front."

She frowned. "And this was going so smoothly."

"It's a nuisance, that's for sure," he said. "Since he is my identical brother, I've had to constantly bunker my thoughts the past few months. It'd be easy for him to get into my head—even on accident."

"So if my parlor tricks don't end up working, do we restrain him?" she asked, unsure of herself. "Could the two of us even do that?"

"Both my brother and I are physically weak, unlike our other brother, Tristen. I believe we could do it if we combined our efforts." He glanced around the wall again. "He's just standing at the far end, reading a book. Does he not realize what's happening outside?"

"I don't like this," she said. "Feels like a trap."

"Does sort of smell like one, doesn't it?" He pulled back, straightening his posture. "We're going to have to split up here. Your destination isn't far anyway." He looked down at her and must have noticed the doubt in her eyes. "You don't have to walk down the hallway he's in. You just have to cross this end of the corridor and continue down the other side of the hall we're already in. Trust me; you'll know which room you're looking for when you see it."

"I still have to cross through his sightline, so I'm faced with the same predicament," she said.

"Not if I divert his attention." He looked forward, eyes empty as he stared into nothing. "My brother is a fool. He's been lulled into a false sense of security for far too long in this kingdom. He's forgotten all that's been taken from him. If the Intel family has been able to trick him for this long, then I should be able to manage a few seconds." He swept around the corner and out of sight without another word.

She hurried toward the corner, pausing to hear Flen's distant words. Moments later, an incoherent conversation began. She wove a wall of Dev Chains across the width of the corridor, illustrating a still image into the cluster. She then ran across without hesitation.

Absent of thought, she sprinted the rest of the way. Adrenaline coursed through her as she looked for anything noteworthy in the corridor beyond. She spotted an opulent stairway leading upward.

*This is it*, she thought, recalling Toono's words of encouragement to her several weeks ago ...

"We've acquired an inside man on True Light's side," Toono said in a broadcast, sitting back and paying his lunchtime meal no mind. "As you know, Illipsia, we've been struggling with this dilemma of how you're supposed to get into the palace. This acquisition should stifle such qualms."

"You think I'm up for it?" she asked, using her mind to telepathically communicate through Homina's transmission.

"I understand it's a lot to put on your plate with you already trying to reach the catacombs over there in Phesaw. It's just one more thing to weigh down your thoughts." He smiled. "But I'm only asking this of you because I'm confident in your ability."

"Getting through Dunami Palace will be difficult," she said.

"Not with the plan the ladies and I have put into place. The Intel Kingdom will be attacked from so many different directions at once, the last place they'd expect an enemy to appear is inside the palace."

"I believe in you, Illipsia," said a woman's voice.

Illipsia paused, questioning the point of her mother's vote of confidence. It didn't mean anything to her.

Toono's face became grave. "I know I'm applying the pressure here, but you are the most important part of this whole operation."

"I get it," she said.

He nodded, and a smile spread on his face. "Do it for Kadlest."

# 67

# Battle on Knowledge River

A somber aura shrouded the Mythmaker. Hours ago, during the heart of twilight, they'd crossed through Intel Bay only to witness a scene identical to that of the Intel Connector. It seemed the SCAPD fleet had once again disposed of True Light forces, crossing past the Intelian naval base with little resistance, likely due to the leviathans.

Now Agnos's ship sailed down the Knowledge River, which was wide enough to make both shorelines seem invisible when at the center. It reached depths that could support even a leviathan, but the primary mainland river in nearly every kingdom was usually this big.

"I fear what waits on the horizon," Barloe said.

Agnos, Evelyn, Gray, and he stood on the forecastle, all eyes trained on the waters ahead.

"You know what awaits us," Gray said, her ancient Marigium in hand. "The odds are against us, but we can't back down."

Barloe nodded, and Agnos allowed her words to sink in. She'd sent ahead scouting dolphins after finding the destruction at Intel Bay. They had returned within an hour, offering only bad news. Four leviathans and several galleons from other SCAPD kingdoms were pushing down the river unobstructed.

"I don't know how we're supposed to stop them," Agnos said. "We'd need a hundred seashockers just to hurt *one* of those Powish ships."

"I have a plan," Evelyn said. "We may not be able to damage them, but I think I can impede their movement."

"Let's just make sure we first take care of the two Devish ships I saw at the rear," Gray said. "If they have talented enough wavewielders on board—and I'm sure they do—then it will require more than my whales' efforts to take them out." She looked at Agnos and narrowed her eyes. "Did you inform the seashockers to not electrocute the waters, no matter how many enemies may fall overboard?"

"Yes, they know better." He knew Gray was worried about her whales falling victim to friendly fire.

"There they are," Evelyn said with a squint. She shook her head in awe. "Those leviathans are terrifying."

Agnos's mouth hung open. He had seen one of them before, its hulking frame big enough to dwarf a galleon. But to see four of them lined up side-by-side in the distance … that was an entirely different matter. He could barely distinguish the galleons around them, sailing in their shadows.

"It's a miracle they haven't taken over the world with weapons like those," he muttered.

"The Prim Kingdom only exports a limited amount of holy wood for this very reason," Evelyn said. "Like I said, their glaring weakness is electricity. They can't sail in storms. All it takes is one strike of lightning, and they're finished."

"… or thousands of average Intelian weavers," Agnos said, sounding hopeless.

"Doesn't sound as simple when you put it that way," Barloe droned.

Agnos sighed. "What I wouldn't do to have Bryson right now."

"Bryson …" Evelyn muttered. "Isn't that the LeAnce boy? Mendac's son?"

"I think he prefers 'Still' to 'LeAnce,' but yes."

The four of them fell silent, watching the small fleet ahead of them grow nearer. They were each in their own heads, predicting the outcome of the impending battle. The most likely probability was utter annihilation, for they were only one ship against an ungodly force.

"Any commands, Captain?"

Agnos turned. Troy Sulia, commander of the squallblasters, stood in waiting. "I suppose we should start moving," Agnos said. "Get everyone into battle-ready positions."

"Yes, Captain." Troy turned and began shouting orders.

Agnos returned his focus to the ships ahead. "That man's expertise has been a real life-saver."

"I have plenty of that, too," Gray said. "But we need more than just experience in this fight."

"Like a lot of luck," Evelyn said.

Agnos drew a sword from its sheathe on his left hip, positioned for easy access by his only arm. All eyes turned toward him. He didn't have to look to know there were shocked faces all around.

"I thought you'd go into hiding with Eet, Osh, and that book of yours," Gray said with a slight tone of bewilderment.

"I will remain on these decks throughout it all. I won't seek a fight, but I refuse to back down if someone confronts me."

A deep chuckle thrummed out of Barloe. "Let's make sure our captain doesn't die for the sake of looking cool."

A breeze carried through Agnos's bangs. He closed his eyes and inhaled. Whether met with victory or defeat, this marked the Mythmaker's first and *final* battle.

*　　*　　*

A geyser erupted to the ship's left from a stoneslinger's boulder narrowly missing the hull. Water rained on the deck, an impressive feat considering the height of a galleon. A splash reaching that high said a lot about the size of the boulders and strength of the Powish sailors.

Agnos stood on the stern deck with Sailing Master Stefania and the helmsman, Gunther. "Whatever you do, don't let this ship turn sideways!" he screamed over the din of the crew prepping for battle.

Stefania smirked at the sword in his hand. "What are you going to do with that, Captain? Carve some knowledge into their minds?"

Gunther cackled, but Agnos's gaze fell flat. "Really, Stefania? Is this the time or place? There are lethal projectiles flying at us, and it's only a matter of time before we enter attacking range of their other utility specialists!"

"Don't worry about us," Stefania said. "Our job is done. The Mythmaker's course is set straight."

"Thank you, ladies," he said, turning toward the rail of the stern deck, which overlooked the quarterdeck, main deck, and forecastle.

Despite the unfavorable odds, Agnos felt a sense of comfort because of the pieces set around him. Besides his personally selected crew, he'd acquired several other talented individuals to fill vital roles in case of a battle such as this.

Squallblaster Commander Troy was stationed in the foremast's fighting top, already committed to deflecting the stoneslingers' attacks with mighty gales. He also served as the figurehead for his squad stationed across the ship's decks and throughout the masts. They'd look toward him for any direction.

Quartermaster Barloe stood at the center of a huddle of melee specialists on the main deck, most of which were Adrenian swordsmen and women. They went over tactics of boarding enemy ships if it came down to that, which for some reason Evelyn thought probable. Agnos just couldn't picture a scenario where he'd want part of his crew to jump into the waters, nor did he desire getting close enough to an enemy vessel in order to board it.

Gray Whale was behind Agnos, occupying the tail end of the ship on the rear deck. She held Marigium in her hand, the staff ancient that stood taller than her. From there, she'd fight through her whales, directing them into the enemy fleet ahead with the smaller galleons as their targets.

Then there was Evelyn, standing on the bowsprit at the very front of the ship with her arms crossed, her frost-entwined blue hair sparkling beneath the sun. Her posture displayed nothing but confidence. And though he couldn't see her face, he could guess at the nature of it: sagacious and austere, unwavering to any threat that lay before them. Her presence was like having another Jestivan onboard, which made sense since she was a Diatia, the very rank created to counter forces like Bryson, Yama, or Tashami.

She was the one who had warned him of the true dangers of the ship turning sideways. He'd feared becoming a bigger target to the stoneslingers, but she'd been more worried about the Devish wavewielders. With their ability to capsize a ship, her efforts to counter would only forge a massive wall between the Mythmaker and the fleet, allowing their escape.

Still, this made any aggression difficult. Without turning the ship, Agnos's crew was limited in space for assault positions. This allowed only the most skilled pirates to be positioned at the rail at the front of the ship, led by Firefighter Commander Benji and Seashocker Commander Howell.

Agnos's eyes narrowed, observing the fleet. *Where's the signal?* They had closed the gap, sailors aboard the two Devish galleons at the fleet's tail end were now discernible on their decks. Skilled Adrenians would have been able to board the vessels with a simple push-off from the Mythmaker's rail. The monstrous leviathans were just beyond them, and another group of galleons led the way near the front, which was where Agnos's attention was.

After a few agonizing minutes, three whales emerged from the river ahead of the leviathans and collided into the hull of a Cynnish ship sporting gray sails, converging in a way that obliterated the ship's tail end, damaging the stern in the process. Relief rushed through him as he spotted the now-splintered keel, the single most important foundational piece to a ship.

"*NOW!*" Gray shouted from the rear of the Mythmaker.

Agnos's crew erupted in howls, footsteps, and screaming metal as pirates drew their weapons. Troy deflected two stone boulders into nearby waters and then raised his arms in a cross above his head, a signal to his squallblasters in the nests behind him. Mighty gales formed, filling the sails and propelling the ship with alarming speed.

Flame erupted from the front of the ship as firefighters joined the action. The inferno took care of incoming arrows, but spears and blades flung telekinetically required the efforts of squallblasters who weren't busy filling the sails. Adrenians helped, too, fending off projectiles with their swords.

Thousands of arrows soared upward into the sky from both Devish galleons, rising in waves and arching at the height of their climb before falling in the direction of the Mythmaker. Some firefighters redirected their attention upward, but they couldn't do anything to stop the impeding shower. Their flames would only damage the sails.

They had prepared for this, though. A few squallblasters positioned near the top of the masts wove mighty gusts, deflecting most arrows out of the sky. Alas, many still made it through their defenses, ripping sails and striking the decks with sharp thuds, some felling pirates. One unfortunate soul next to Agnos took an arrow to the chest.

Why weren't the wavewielders striking yet? Did they plan to cause disarray aboard the ship first, to distract them from what was happening to the river around them? No, that wouldn't make sense.

"I don't think we planned for that."

Agnos turned, forgetting that Master Stefania sat on the deck next to him, fingers pressed against holes in the rail's wooden columns. "For what?"

"Look at the two leviathans at the center," she said. "Tell me if my eyes are deceiving me."

He glanced forward, eyes widening. So focused on the rear galleons, he hadn't even noticed the massive backdrop's shift. Two leviathans were turning very slowly, the Dev galleons looking to split the behemoths.

"Are they trying to wall off our path?" he asked.

"Seems so," she said. "And they'll also be positioned to strike us perfectly. If they turn successfully, we're dead."

"*FOCUS ON THE LEVIATHANS!*" Agnos screamed.

"That won't do you much good, Captain. What will focusing on them achieve if you don't have anyone capable of taking them out?"

He stammered, trying to form a strategy on the spot. "All squallblasters report to the back of the ship to fill sails! We need to shoot the gap!"

She smiled as pirates scrambled to send word to those who couldn't hear his orders. "That is better. We take advantage of a leviathan's weaknesses, their lack of speed and unresponsive steering, by out-sailing them to the spot."

Agnos shook his head. "I don't know about this. If we try to squeeze between them, it won't be smooth passage. Stoneslingers will drop boulders on us. We'll have to try to stay close to the hulls of both ships. That way we won't be visible from the decks ... and that seems impossible. We saw what happened to the Whale Lord when it got too close to one of those things."

"The Whale Lord didn't have Gunther and me," she said. "Nor did they have a squallblaster like Troy Sulia. It will be a risk, but I believe in ..." she trailed off as they both noticed an enormous shadow engulfing the Mythmaker.

They looked up, mouths agape as tidal waves converged on them from both sides. The wavewielders had finally made their move. Agnos had feared capsizing to one wave, not being sandwiched between two. The SCAPD fleet had orchestrated a flawless battle strategy. They were trying to wall off the Mythmaker on three sides, the only exit route being behind them. Could squallblasters make a ship sail in reverse?

A cacophony rang out across the decks. Nobody had planned for an attack of this scale and complexity. Agnos couldn't even tell if Gray's whales were still finding success at the front of the fleet through the chaos.

Boulders crashed into the ship while arrows struck screaming pirates. Agnos could do nothing but look up as the two waves curled toward them. If he had been more adept with Orbaculum—the ancient gifted to him from Toono—he could have protected his crew. Perhaps with a monstrous bubble capable of engulfing the Mythmaker. Unfortunately, he'd refrained from using it ever since his mission to find the Thunder Queen's chronicle.

But then his mouth closed, and the ruckus surrounding him slowly died out. His brows furrowed, absorbing what had just transpired. The tidal waves were no longer rising masses of water, but concave glaciers like jaws protruding from the river. A chill crept through his body as the temperature dropped to freezing in an instant.

He looked for the only person who could have been responsible for this. Evelyn still stood on the bowsprit, but with her arms stretched to her sides, pillars of ice connecting her hands to each glacier like branches.

And that wasn't all she had frozen solid. Most of the river around them had become a floor of ice, mimicking the Still Kingdom's Diamond Sea. The only unaffected area was a narrow strip of water that served as their pathway through the ice-capped river.

The surge of relief vanished as the leviathans continued to turn. Their holy wood-constructed hulls barreled through the ice, demolishing it like it was nothing. Evelyn had warned Agnos of this. She could only freeze the surface a few inches deep—not enough when faced with a leviathan.

"It seems like she only stalled our death," he muttered.

"Sometimes, all you need is a little bit of extra time for luck to swing your way," Stefania said. "That maneuver of hers could be the difference between defeat and victory."

Agnos squinted, spotting several whales in the distance as they broke free of the ice and attacked more ships. The ice was paper thin at that distance, so even galleons pushed forward. The ice only slowed them down.

Two more boulders hit the decks with an explosion of splintering wood and flailing bodies. Evelyn wove ice walls in front of the Mythmaker, but she couldn't stop every attack.

Agnos looked down at his sword, feeling stupid for believing he could contribute anything to this battle. His eyes roved toward his missing arm, as if having it would have made any difference. He only had himself to blame for his physical shortcomings. He'd never trained for combat or cared about strengthening his body. His mind had always taken precedence over everything else, but what good did that serve him right now?

A blinding flash of white light drowned his vision. He ducked and covered his ears, hearing a clap of thunder and an ear-shattering explosion coming from nowhere. Had that been the Mythmaker? A mere boulder couldn't have caused such a ruckus. And if that had been an attack on his ship, there was no way it'd still be upright.

He rose from his crouch, looking up with hesitance. The entire crew did the same. Even Stefania had to recover from being knocked backward.

He stepped forward, dropping his sword in awe. The two rotating leviathans were now smoldering in flame, their entire framework split in half as both sides tilted into the mostly frozen river.

"What the hell did that?!" Agnos bellowed, his crew roaring in approval. There had been no warning.

Another flash of white cut above the river, striking the other two leviathans that had gone ahead, a highly concentrated stream of electricity cutting them in half. It had come from the northern shore, a considerable distance away. Was it another ship?

He glanced that way only to find nothing of the sort once the ship sailed past the frozen wave. A line of strange vehicles rolled toward the shoreline from the prairie. From this distance, he couldn't decipher much, but they were hulking beasts. How were they moving? They had to have been heavy enough to render pushing, pulling, or pedaling out of the question.

Another voltaic stream shot from a pipe attached to one of the contraptions, darting across the river and colliding with a leviathan.

He glanced down at the quarterdeck, where Zorra had a spyglass raised to her eye. He hurried down to her. "What do you see?" he asked.

"Stone huts on wheels?" she said, sounding unsure. "Err … with pipes that shoot lightning on the top?"

His brows crumpled. It was rare for him to find something that baffled even his mind. These things seemed to defy logic, but he wasn't so foolish to believe that. If they approached the northern shore, that meant they had to have come from Brilliance, a city renowned for its weavineering studies. Those things were likely a secret weapon they'd been working on for quite some time.

"THE ENEMIES ARE ABANDONING SHIP!"

Agnos spun, spotting the wrecked leviathans. Powish sailors dropped from the decks and rained down upon the ice, several giants included. Though their landings blasted craters in the surface, they didn't stumble. They crouched and lurched forward, charging the Mythmaker with powerful strides.

A young pirate stopped at Agnos's side. "Evelyn requests a command on whether or not to melt the ice, Captain."

"No, we'll fight on it," he said after giving it some thought. "We've sustained too much damage to continue sailing anyway. And something tells me those Powish would still cause us problems in the water. Tell her to leave it, and if she can, strengthen it. I want those things on the shore to be able to travel across."

"Yes, Captain!"

As the pirate ran away, Agnos glanced back toward the shoreline.

"There are roughly fifty of them," Zorra said, an eye still glued to the spyglass. "And one seems to lead the charge. Unlike the others, which sport rustic gray exteriors, this one is draped in a sky-blue fabric engraved with the Intel Kingdom's insignia."

After receiving Agnos's relayed commands the crew threw shrouds down the sides of the ship. Pirates began to climb down while others slid down massive frozen slides crafted by Evelyn.

"A young lady with green hair is positioned in what I assume is the coach's seat," Zorra said, causing him to freeze. "She, too, has a spyglass and appears to be waving in our direction … with a beaming smile."

As more electric attacks were shot at the SCAPD forces, Agnos asked, "Is there a flower in her hair?"

Zorra lowered the instrument and turned toward him. "Yes, do you know her?"

"That's Lilu!"

*     *     *

Lilu was all smiles as she stared at Agnos through her spyglass. It had been quite some time since she'd last seen him, and damn had he changed. A patchy beard now consumed his baby face, but his charcoal hair was as unruly as ever. He waved at her and then beckoned her forward, as if telling her to charge onto the ice.

She lowered the instrument and gazed across the frozen river, contemplating the practicality of such a maneuver. Her travolters seemed to have no problem reaching the battlefield with their cannons at this distance, so she felt comfortable here. However, now that she noticed Agnos's crew charging across the ice toward SCAPD sailors, she feared accuracy would become more difficult to obtain. Once the two sides mixed, there'd be no avoiding friendly fire.

"Those first four shots were amazing," Frederick said, still staring in awe from the driver's seat. "I'm surprised the cannon didn't backfire with that much power being released at once."

"That's Bryson for you," she said emptily, distracted by tactical maneuvers being visualized in her mind. "But we don't have any more shots from him, so don't expect that level of destruction from this point forward."

He nodded, looking up at her as the blasts of travolter cannons thundered across the shore. She had to squint, the constant flashes of light sending her vision into a tizzy. "You see the ships trying to get away at the front?" she asked.

"Yeah, just barely," he said. The powdered ice from the electric blasts lay thick in the air.

"Take the travolters down the shoreline and aim for those ships. I see whales trying to obliterate their hulls, but the ice isn't doing them any favors." She turned and glared at him. "Don't hit them!"

"Got it," he said. "I'm glad. I thought you were going to have us ride these things out onto the ice for a second."

"Of course not. That ice could disappear at any second, and we don't have the tread for it. We'd be stuck."

Frederick stood and grabbed a pole from the backseat, a giant black flag attached to one end. He raised it into the air, facing the travolters behind him, and waved it to his left. The vehicles responded immediately, halting their fire to turn parallel with the river.

He dropped back into the coach's seat. "And what are you going to do?" he asked, cranking the travolter back into motion and turning the steering wheel.

She leapt onto the cockpit's ledge and stood there for a moment, surveying the ice-capped river. "I'm going to honor my title as a Jestivan and finally join this fight in all of its glory—headstrong and without thought, just like Bryson."

He grinned, shaking his head. "Good luck, Lilu."

She looked over her shoulder. "I've got something to say to you, Frederick," she said in a suspiciously proper tone. "But I must survive this battle first."

He frowned. "That's just mean."

With a mocking cackle, she leapt off the travolter and plunged to the ground. Landing with the grace and balance taught to her by Director Debo, she pushed off and broke for the ice, a miniature arsenal of blades strapped to her waist and forearms.

She felt alive. For once, she would finally fight in the war. She squeezed a folded note in the palm of her hands, sent to her through Radon a week back. She still couldn't believe the message inscribed within.

*You, Shelly, and Delilah are my world. Because of this, I've sacrificed your space to blossom by shackling your freedoms. If you want to fight, so be it. Round up your travolters and travel south to the Knowledge River. A SCAPD fleet might make it through the bay, and I want you there waiting for them as a final line of defense.*

*I love you, Lilu Sun-Lily Intel. Don't you ever forget that.*

*~ Father*

Lilu cranked up her speed percentage, traversing the uneven ice with ease. Receiving that note had been one of the best moments of her life.

*Thank you, Father.*

*     *     *

The Mythmaker was empty save for two presences at the front: Agnos and Gray Whale. Agnos oversaw the war ahead of them as waves of brown clashed on the white canvas below. The pirates were significantly outnumbered by the massive crews of the leviathans. They also had to deal with giants wielding blunt weapons big enough to smash a dozen people at once. The only reason the pirates were even able to hold their own was because of Troy and Evelyn, but mostly the latter.

The Still Diatia mowed through enemies like they were mere pests. She was worthy of her title, and likely an equal, talent-wise, to most of the Jestivan. When not skewering sailors on ice spires, she struck them down with frozen projectiles. If she got close enough to touch someone, she'd simply encase them in ice.

Gray Whale wasn't paying much attention to the battle. Her eyes were closed, all of her focus on the galleons trying to escape up ahead. Wavewielders had resorted to manipulating the currents and waves in a way that countered the whales' movements.

An electrical blast fired from the shoreline, but this time it happened more than a mile ahead. Gray's eyes jarred open, seemingly flustered by something.

"It seems that Lilu girl you mentioned has moved down the shoreline and is now firing at the galleons," she said, searching the distant shore. "That blast spooked the whales and made them scatter. Not even I can gain control of them now."

More beams of light struck the fleeing ships, damaging their framework with each collision. Something had changed about them, though. They didn't seem nearly as powerful as the shots that sunk the leviathans.

"The whales did well," he said. "Let's put the rest of the ships in Lilu's hands, that way we can focus on the battle directly in front of us."

She looked down at his sword. "I thought you were going to fight."

"Only if forced," he said. "As if I'm going to seek out a duel with a skilled combatant."

She guffawed, head tilting back. "There's the Agnos I remember." Taking a moment to regain her breath, she sighed and gazed to the right of the ship, where the ice was void of action. "I suppose you're not needed anyway."

Agnos raised an eyebrow as Gray stepped onto the rail. "You're joining the fray?"

"It'll be like old times," she said. "When I was in my youth, fighting on the decks." She lowered herself, grabbing hold of a rope that had been slung over the rail. "Also, it seems the royal is joining our efforts. I like our chances with her here."

Gray dropped below the rail and disappeared. He gazed at the empty bit of ice she'd regarded just seconds ago. Sure enough, a beautiful, green-haired Jestivan with two roses pinned in her hair ran straight for the battle.

Maybe they could win this.

*     *     *

Towering over the hundreds of scrums, the giants caught Lilu's eye before anything else. She counted twelve of them, and they were causing the most chaos across the battlefield. Three seemed to be focused on one person, though she couldn't see who it was through the throng of warring seamen. Frozen spires jutted up from the crowd in attempt to impale the giants, but they did well in dodging them.

How many Stillians were on Agnos's crew? Surely, one person was not responsible for all of this ice—even the spires seemed too rapid and numerous.

Lilu burst through the exterior wall of sailors, dipping beneath and sidestepping errant blows. The scrum was a cluster of flame, electricity, wind, thrown blades, rocks, and dueling swordsmen. At least eight of the ten kingdoms were represented in this fight.

She electrocuted SCAPD navy sailors as she ran, enemies easily distinguishable by their uniforms—the pirates wore commoner's garb. To think she was fighting alongside pirates, supposed criminals of the seas … To think that Agnos was a pirate. She'd have to talk to him about it afterward.

She cursed as a knife whizzed past her shoulder, cutting her sleeve and grazing the skin. The damned Devish were always the most bothersome.

A man's fist approached in her peripheral vision. She leaned back, caught his wrist and intercepted his lunge. Twisting her body, she used his momentum to flip him over her back and throw him onto the ice. He landed on his back and gasped desperately, the air knocked from his lungs.

She stood and screamed toward the empires, feeling a rush she'd searched for ever since becoming a Jestivan. A few men turned in the midst of combat to stare at her in shock.

Looking around, she saw giants in her proximity, but getting to them would be a pain. She wanted to skip the foot soldiers in order to reach the bigger threats. Then an opportunity presented itself just ahead.

She charged, a blade sliding into her grasp from her forearm. She dropped to her hip, slid across the ice at an unprecedented speed, and slashed the ankles of any poor saps who weren't wearing boots. Bodies dropped behind her like dominoes.

A sharp slope formed in the ice ahead of her. She hit it and was sent airborne, soaring over the battle with an unsuspecting male giant in her sights. She landed on the nape of his neck, thrusting her blade into the area directly below his skull. The giant roared, twisting to and fro as he tried to grab her off his back.

She released a surge of electricity from her entire body. It coursed up his neck and trapped his head in a voltaic sphere, slowly frying his brain. He dropped to his knees, shattering the ice.

She fell from his back and immediately focused elsewhere. Number-wise, it was a lopsided war. For every five SCAPD sailors, there was one pirate. But considering those odds, they seemed to fair well.

There was a method to dealing with the giants, and a rather easy one at that. Perhaps it had been all the training with Debo in her past, but she was too quick for them, their movements sluggish as they grasped at air. In roughly ten minutes, she'd taken care of three of them.

She found her way over to a large group of giants, all of whom were preoccupied with only one person. They struck with blunt weapons or threw their heavy fists at the same spot, but their enemy went unfazed.

She stopped, noticing the woman responsible for their frustration. Her hair sparkled within the billowing powdered ice as she executed a flawless combination of defensive and offensive maneuvers. She wove shields of ice when someone came at her blindside while attacking with spires from multiple angles.

Lilu joined the battle, placing her back against the Stillian's. "Who are you and why are you so awesome?" Lilu asked.

"I'm a Still Diatia," she said, continuing her onslaught. "Name's Evelyn. Pleasure to meet you."

Two giants aimed their fists at Lilu, but an ice wall sprouted before her, receiving the blow instead. She smiled. "That's handy. My name's—"

"You're Lilu, a royal daughter of the Intel family and a Jestivan," Evelyn said, rotating with Lilu as they continued to watch each other's back. "Agnos told me."

Ice shattered from a massive fist, the casual conversation between the two women doing nothing to calm the giants.

"Shall we team up and make quick work of these overgrown brutes?" Lilu asked.

Evelyn turned, facing the same way as Lilu. "It'd be an honor to fight alongside a Jestivan."

# 68

# Untimely Discoveries

They began digging before daybreak. Himitsu had never dug a hole in his life, but he was quickly learning just how deceptively difficult it was. With the pointed end of his shovel, he struck hard into the sod. It reminded him of trying to spear something with an enormous spoon. He pressed the flat edge of the spade with the sole of his foot to push it even deeper into the ground. Then he used a combination of bending, pulling, lifting, and twisting until he was able to hurl each scoop of dirt off to the side. After so many repeated efforts, the exhaustion had begun to set in.

Kaylee dug next to him, creating her own dirt pile on the other side of the grave. Grime coated her giant blue gloves. Sweat lathered her face, causing her hair to become too drenched to fall loosely as it normally did. They didn't speak nor even share a glance. With their goal directly beneath them, they refused to allow anything to distract them from reaching it.

It was a common practice in the Archaic Kingdom to bury the dead with their ancients—a reason why the kingdom suffered from so many grave robberies. Despite the practice's normality, burying an ancient was actually illegal according to Archain law. Those who robbed graves made a living off it. Elites in the black market—sometimes even the royal family—would pay a pretty coin to those who possessed formerly buried treasures. Depending on the ancient, the reward could vary from a measly amount to something grand enough to buy one a mansion.

If they did find Neeko's ancient here, Himitsu had no intention of claiming a reward. He only sought information, something that could aid True Light's efforts in this war against the Rogue Demon. The more they knew about that man's desires, the better prepared they would be.

An hour of digging had passed when the sun fully cleared the horizon, its light illuminating the entirety of the Central Grasslands. Besides the physical exhaustion, Himitsu fought through mental fatigue, which he mainly blamed on a lack of sleep. He should have grabbed Sal, a man with shoulders suited for this kind of work.

Himitsu stopped digging when he heard a bang. He regarded Kaylee, who had struck something hard with her shovel. She dropped to her knees and brushed dirt aside, revealing wood. She looked up at him, eyes wide with either shock or relief.

"We've reached it," she said, "but keep digging so we can open it cleanly."

A burst of energy returned to both of them. Their motions now became faster and more fluid. He hacked at the dirt wall to widen the size of the hole, clearing a way for the coffin's lid to open. They were minutes away.

"That's enough," Kaylee said through heavy breaths, bunching herself next to him. "Don't break the wood, if you can."

They'd only cleared off about sixty percent of the coffin, but with the way the lid had been crafted, they could open just the top half. Himitsu stepped forward and began to hack away at an iron lock with his shovel, the sound of clanging metals ringing into the sky.

After about a dozen strikes, the lock broke. He stood still for a moment, wiping sweat from his forehead. This would have been a lot easier with Sal.

Himitsu kicked the lock away and then backed up toward Kaylee. He reached over and pulled the lid open, exposing the decomposed remains of a man. Kaylee broke down in tears almost immediately, somehow recognizing the gnarled facial structure. He watched her for a moment, but then his eyes roved toward the corpse's chest.

Neeko's body was clutching a book within crossed arms. Pinned between the two longest fingers of his right hand was a quill. Himitsu didn't care about the quill, but he did struggle with the arms to get at the book. Out of respect for both Neeko and Kaylee, he tried to be delicate with the man's body.

He sat back after freeing it, holding it in front of his face. He turned to look at Kaylee, whose face was tucked between her knees. "Go ahead," she said shakily. "I'm not going to look."

He believed her, but he turned so the book's pages didn't face her when he opened it. He hadn't forgotten her warning. If people read their own dream, they died.

Flipping through the book, he spotted many names he didn't recognize, dreams written just below. Based off the changes in penmanship every few pages, it was clear this book had been passed down from different owners over the centuries.

Himitsu decided to skip straight to the back of the book and found Kaylee's name immediately. He glanced away and spotted the name on the next page over: Agnos. Again, he turned the page without reading any further down. The idea of reading someone's tethered dream seemed invasive to him. It also didn't help that these were written in their blood.

His eyes widened as he read the next name: Toono. This had been written during a time when the young demon was just a boy—twelve or thirteen, maybe. With what he had grown into, such innocence was impossible to imagine.

As Himitsu read Toono's dream, his face drained of color. He feared it and knew the entire world should, too.

*     *     *

Olivia, Vuilni, Fane, and Prim General Pinillias sat on separate roots of Asalka's most cherished holy tree, the supposed home of Dimiourgos, King of Ethos. Queen Inedibus continued to stand at the edge of the Glades, making no effort to walk any closer to the center. This made sense, considering the story she'd just shared.

If it wasn't for the sniffling of one woman with tears streaming down her cheeks, the silence would have been deafening. Olivia was crying, and Vuilni couldn't quite believe her eyes. Even Fane stared in wonder.

Vuilni recalled the rumors from years ago, when Dev King Storshae and Toono had invaded Phesaw. She'd been in a separate area of the campus, but word had gotten around afterward that Olivia had exploded in an emotional fit. It had been difficult to believe, especially back then, when the girl was known for being absolutely emotionless. Since that invasion, she had begun to express herself more often, but only sparingly. And when she did, it was subtle. She definitely didn't *cry*.

"That's our story," the queen muttered, staring down at the roots. "It's a stain on our kingdom's history for many reasons."

Olivia looked up, wet eyelashes stuck to her skin. "We need transport to the Light Realm immediately."

Vuilni found it difficult to move. There was something haunting about those tears, something that sucked her spirit dry.

Fane stood. "I agree. Our time here is done."

"I'll send for a Prowler to escort the three of you to the teleplatforms," General Pinillias said.

As the four of them exited the Glades, stepping past the queen, she said, "I do apologize for all of the trouble we've caused you here. And I do hope you can make it back in time."

*　　*　　*

Toshik didn't wait for the royal convoy to exit the capital before making his move, nor did he try to approach covertly. He struck just before first-day's dawn, glimpses of gray from the sun's approaching light appearing on the horizon. Civilians departed from their homes, dressed in their finest robes for an honest day's work.

Pedestrians slowed as they noticed the three royal carriages flanked by mounted officers, an uncommon occurrence in any kingdom. One royal carriage was enough to cause suspicion, but *three?* And with a small cavalry to boot?

Toshik watched from the roof of a holovision shop—whatever that was. The convoy had just turned down his street and was heading straight for him. He stooped low and waited patiently, ready to pounce.

As the carriages neared, he noticed the coachman's eyes were closed. *That's a red flag,* he thought. *And his robes are even more delicate and intricately designed than the mounted soldiers. What's that gold-embroidered eye on his chest? That's no normal coachman.*

Before Toshik could even connect the dots, the man had already opened his eyes to reveal nothing but white. He pointed in Toshik's direction. This coachman was an intelligence official, and a very skilled one at that. Toshik should have expected this. Toono would only entrust his safety with the most elite of his men. But this was good news, for it had to mean something or someone integral to SCAPD operations was part of this convoy.

Blades and daggers darted toward him, but he'd already moved from his spot. He hit the ground with one foot and pushed off, drawing his sword. One head rolled, then two. A dozen more joined them in the following twenty seconds. He didn't even break a sweat as horses bucked and spun, tossing the limp bodies of decapitated soldiers from their backs.

The carriages rolled to a halt, and Toshik stood still for a moment as headless bodies bled out around him. The screams of fleeing civilians pierced the morning air, and horses ran wildly down the busy streets.

He spotted a little girl gawking at him, tears bubbling in her eyes. What did Toshik look like in that moment? Something worse than Yama? An entity that didn't care about the lives of those who opposed him? He hoped so. Fighting that wretched woman would require that exact mindset.

He exhaled and swung his sword toward the rear carriage. The force of his slash rippled through the air, cracking the ground and splitting the carriage in half. He did the same with the other two. He searched the second and third carriage only to find them empty before stepping between the two halves of the head transit. A man sat in the back with his hands shackled to a bench.

Toshik gazed at him with little interest. Horos and Kuiku had been right. He'd been lured away from the castle. The shackled man squirmed, fearing Toshik's presence.

"Please don't kill me!" he screamed. "My name's Garlo, and I was once the general for the Still Queen. We're on your side!"

Toshik looked away, staring at the towers of the stone castle in the distance. There were many miles between him and it, but he'd sprint any distance to find the man partly responsible for Jilly's death.

Noticing Toshik's disinterest in him, Garlo's pleas became more insistent. "Can you free me from these chains? They have Permanence gloves around my hands and wrists, so I can't freeze them off."

Toshik flicked his sword, cutting the chains with the resulting wind. He then sheathed his sword and bolted back toward the heart of the city, leaving behind a street stained in red.

*     *     *

"Getting here was too easy," Horos said, descending a narrow, spiraling staircase holding a torch he had nabbed earlier from a guard he'd rendered unconscious.

Kuiku followed. "This is a trap, without a doubt."

"Or they just don't care if we come down this way. We could be doing them a favor by doing so." Horos paused and looked back. "You should stay at the top of the stairs, just in case."

Kuiku nodded, then turned and disappeared around the curving wall.

It was a crude stairwell, crafted entirely with uneven stone. It seemed more fitting for the entryway to a primordial crypt than that of a recent king. As he reached the bottom, however, the architecture shifted.

Gold decked the floors, walls, and ceiling, illuminated by large flames in the crypt's four corners. Even the golden coffin at the center of the crypt sat atop an equally dazzling bier. The amount of money that had been wasted on this one room could have fed a town for over a year.

He crept toward the coffin, testing each step by tossing a coin ahead of him. His eyes roved over every fine detail carved into the surfaces around him, looking for anything that might have resembled a trap. After a lifetime spent as an assassin, he was well-versed in this type of scenario. Booby traps were nothing new to him.

Once at the center, he placed his hand on the coffin. The surface was cold, trapped in the bowels of the castle for decades. As he ran his hand across it, he kept his eyes peeled and senses alert for threats. He listened for any clinks or other odd mechanical noises; he sniffed, searching for faint odors; and he felt for any anomalies in the coffin's surface.

Eventually, feeling as secure as he possibly could in a situation such as this, he began pushing the lid aside. Its weight squelched any doubts about the gold's authenticity.

He managed to push the lid askew atop the casket, exposing only the top half of its interior. He straightened up and gazed into the coffin, raising an eyebrow.

*This isn't good,* he thought.

# 69

# The Sacrifice

Vistas lowered his book as his identical brother walked down the hall. He'd seen little of Flen ever since returning from the Still Kingdom several months ago. The man had become as elusive as any assassin, oftentimes disappearing entirely from palace grounds. Vistas had chalked this up to typical behavior. The only reason his brother had become subservient to the Intel family was because the king had paid him to do so.

But with the king's blessing months ago, Flen could now roam the palace and city freely. He leeched off the royal family without having to grant any favors. He had taken full advantage of this fact, running amuck with different women depending on the night of the week … or so Vistas had thought.

It couldn't have been mere coincidence that Flen decided to show himself now, while SCAPD and the head of the operation, Toono, assaulted the kingdom. Flen had been the most hesitant of the triplets when joining the Intel family as servants. Because of this, he had developed a rebellious reputation. The amount of compassion, money, or goods King Vitio gave him didn't matter—it had never been enough to heal the wounds caused by Mendac.

It called to question: What had Flen been doing since becoming a free man?

"Hey, brother," Flen said, coming to a stop and leaning against a sidewall, hands stuffed in his pockets. Vistas eyed him curiously. "I figured I'd show my face during all of this, step in if needed." He smirked. "After all, an attack on this kingdom is an attack on my well-being."

Vistas gazed down the hallway. "Who was just with you?"

Flen paused, appearing dumbfounded until finally managing a smile. "That pesky clairvoyance." He shook his head and laughed. "A lady friend. You had to see the freckles on this one. A cute thing, she was." He gazed longingly down the hall. "Alas, considering the circumstances, we had to part ways for now."

"And why would she be interested in heading *that* way?" Vistas asked, placing the string of his bookmark between the pages and closing his book. "That's a peculiar direction."

"Well, I can't let her leave the palace at a time like this," Flen said without skipping a beat. "And with the lack of security I'm seeing inside the place, I felt she'd be safest deeper in the building."

Vistas pushed off from the wall and closed his eyes, tracking the mystery person's position.

"Can you give my future wife some privacy?" Flen asked. "What's gotten into you?"

Vistas opened his eyes. "I should be asking you that question. Since my return from the kingdom of ice, you've uttered only a few sentences to me. You've stood me up on several occasions."

"Come now, brother," Flen said, sighing as he titled his head and gazed at the ceiling. "You know it was earlier than that. Our communication has always been terrible, even back home in Tames. Tristen was the mediator, the glue. When Vitio sent him back to the Dev Kingdom as a spy, you and I drifted. Then when he died, our relationship nosedived."

"If you'd just accept—"

"Accept what?" Flen asked, straightening up and turning toward Vistas. "I know how much you like to stare at that holopic on the mantle in your room, thinking you're innocently reminiscing. But it's more than that. You're *longing* for that time, those days when you, Tristen, Marcus, and I were the greatest group of friends anyone could ever ask for." His jaw set. "But now Marcus and Tristen are gone, just like Brintlen."

Vistas blinked, hearing the name of his brother's girlfriend for the first time since being taken from their home.

Flen raised a hand, pointing upward. "And this family is to thank for all of it. They allowed that man to wreak havoc across the Dark Realm. And you bend to their will, doing whatever it is they ask of you. Why would I want to spend time with you?"

Silence followed. Vistas wasn't looking his brother in the eye … rather, gazing straight through him, recalling his teenage years that had been stripped away. The memories were nasty buggers, visuals he'd buried so far back in his mind they were impossible to dig up—until now, at least.

Fires, lightning, blood, corpses, and shouting soldiers.

Vistas shook his head. "Flen, Vitio didn't know the nature of Mendac's actions in our kingdom until after the fact. It wasn't his or this family's fault."

"Then he should have killed Mendac and returned all of the Devish people the moment he'd discovered what happened," Flen said. "Instead, he gave his general a slap on the wrist and told him to not bring soldiers with him the next time he tried traveling to a Dark Realm kingdom for 'research.'" His voice fell. "And look at what that led to: the rape of a princess."

Vistas closed his eyes and bowed his head, understanding his brother's perspective. Vistas couldn't counter; he couldn't find a reason to defend the Intel family … and this frustrated him. They'd enabled some abhorrent actions by simply playing ignorant.

"I don't know who was just with you, but I don't feel comfortable with what seems to be her destination," Vistas said. "You'll regret this decision, and the world will pay for it."

Flen crossed his arms in defiance. "If you want to stop her, you'll have to go through me. But while Tristen may have been far superior to both of us in terms of combat, you were definitely the weakest out of the three of us." He paused, eyeing Vistas with an icy glare. "Don't make me kill the only brother I have left."

*       *       *

A comfortable distance sat between Bryson and Toono, the entire city quiet enough to make a breeze seem startling. The army had done a good job with evacuating the eastern half of the city, as Bryson had requested.

Vitio stood next to him, and two women flanked Toono. Bryson instinctively clenched his fists, looking to leap forward at a moment's notice.

"How many innocents are in range?" Toono asked, speaking just loud enough for Bryson to hear.

"A few," the woman with long black hair said. "We should take this to the plaza we passed through earlier. I didn't sense a soul there."

He nodded, his eyes still glued to Bryson. "What do you think? I suspect you don't want to hurt any civilians, so let's fight where we can really let loose."

"You care about innocents?" Bryson asked.

"Of course."

Vitio scoffed, but Toono and the two ladies turned, heading back in the direction they came. "I assume you know of which plaza Homina spoke of, seeing that this is your city," Toono said. "Come."

"No."

Toono stopped, but remained facing the other way. "This isn't a trick."

"You're trying to lure me away from the palace," Bryson said, "which I refuse to let happen. Every gate is heavily manned. If you want a sacrifice, it will have to be me."

"Very well, then," Toono said. "Homina, Kadlest, you head to the plaza with the Intel King."

"I can take him myself," the brutish woman with brown hair said.

"Kadlest, he is a royal head—and a well-aged one at that. I want both of you around to fight him. We're not failing at this point because of pride."

After more hopeless insistence from Kadlest, both women eventually turned in the direction of the plaza. Bryson grabbed Vitio's arm before he pressed forward. "This isn't smart. He's trying to circumvent killing me by luring you away. He's used royal heads as sacrifices before, has he not?"

"Yes, but I—"

"Are you nothing but confident in your ability to not die in this scenario?" Bryson asked. "I can't fight this guy while also worrying about your state. If he tries to pull away from me mid-fight to land a finishing blow on you elsewhere, I can't guarantee I can stop him since I'm not familiar with his abilities or speed percentage."

"You have a point," Vitio said. "But I need to protect this kingdom."

"And I'll reiterate what Toono said to his buddy over there: this is no time or place for pride. You'll do best to protect this kingdom by staying alive and limiting the chances of the Oracle returning to life." Bryson's gaze fell onto the body slung over Toono's shoulder. "I just need you to stay behind me for now—better yet, behind the gate. The archers have already abandoned their posts under my orders. If you feel I'm losing this fight, step in and help." He lowered his voice. "I don't have Thusia."

A long pause followed, during which the two women stopped walking and faced Toono again. They stood still, noticing Vitio's hesitance to join them.

"Fine," the king said, following a long sigh. "If they try to interfere, though, I'm stepping in." He turned and headed for the gate, taking a seat on the pathway on the other side.

The two women each sat on a stone guardrail of a building's stoop down the road.

"Clever thinking," Toono said, reaching down the collar of his robes and rummaging for something around his abdomen. "Even if it wasn't my intention to attempt such a ploy, I respect your ability to sniff out the possibility. You have a general's mind, much like Mendac. I guess I'm not surprised."

He pulled out a familiar animal head, excess fur spilling beneath it. Bryson's heart raced. He hadn't seen Meow Meow since he'd been taken from Olivia, which was years ago now. Bryson leaned in, noticing something odd about the fur hanging from its head—five gems in the shape of a star. Four of them glowed with an unnatural light, overpowering the sullen atmosphere of the overcast sky. One seemed dim, bearing a soft glow that looked ready to burst.

"I believe you're familiar with the lynx, Dimiourgos," Toono said, placing Meow Meow on his head.

Something about it appeared more menacing than Bryson remembered. This wasn't the cat that used to sit on Olivia's head. It looked every bit like a lynx, just as the demon had said. Its fangs curved over Toono's bandaged temple, its ears tall and crooked along the sides, eyes fierce. Even the fur had darkened from the usual sandy brown.

"He's not quite the same as you remember him," Toono said. "Since acquiring him, I've learned that his appearance, personality, and scope of knowledge shift depending on the person whose head he sits on. And when he's taken off, he loses the memories specific to that person."

"*MEOW MEOW!*" Bryson shouted, uncaring of how silly it sounded. "It's me, Bryson!"

The lynx's fierce gaze focused on him, but there was no hint of recognition. "I've found myself in a strange predicament," it said, its voice deep enough to stun Bryson. "I don't want to fulfill this man's desire, but I don't have the means to stop him. He's a powerful weavist—that I sense. I can also feel the Gems of Anathallo raging within me, at the cusp of breaking the sacrificial threshold." Its eyes closed. "The intention of this rebirthing ability was never for this reason. My ninth and final life will be wasted on an undeserving soul."

"Ninth life?" Bryson muttered to himself, confused to the point of annoyance. None of that made sense.

"That's enough of that," Toono said, flinging the Oracle's body backward toward Kadlest, who caught it with ease. Her muscular frame was for more than just show apparently.

The demon raised his cane in the air and hacked at the ground with a mighty roar. The road split, a rift racing toward Bryson as fast as a top Adrenian officer. He dove to the side, rolled and sprung back to his feet. He knew that ancient; he knew that power. "That's Grand Director—"

Another swing. Another crack. Bryson simply sidestepped the crevice this time, prepared for the ability. It seemed Toono's patience had run thin, prepared to fight until one of them died. Words no longer served any purpose.

Bryson would commit every ounce of his being to this fight, unleashing his constraints on his clout and speed percentage. He lurched forward, closing a gap of thirty paces in less than a second. Even from his own perspective, it felt like he'd teleported.

He punched, but then Toono was gone. He whiffed, then spun, leaping as the cane hacked at his waist. He twisted in the air and kicked at Toono's face. The demon caught it with his other hand, flinging Bryson down the street.

Bryson flew in a straight line, the force behind Toono's throw proving just how strong he was. Bryson screamed as he crashed into the gate's iron bars.

Toono was upon him immediately, ready to slam his cane into Bryson's stomach. Electricity burst from Bryson's palm, forcing Toono off his path. The side of a distant building exploded from the dodged attack.

Bryson shot three more voltaic beams, yet the demon evaded each one, causing more buildings to erupt into rubble.

Toono struck the ground. A third crack ran down the street, widening at an alarming speed as it tried to swallow Bryson. As the ground crumbled beneath his feet, abandoned carriages and military tents fell into the void.

He cranked up his speed percentage, tearing his calves slightly in the process. He reached solid ground, but the quakes still thrummed through the soles of his feet.

He bent to the side, narrowly evading another downward strike by Toono. How had he gotten here so fast? He'd just been forty paces away! How could an Archain move like this?

Bryson tried grabbing Toono's arm, but he yanked it away. Obviously he wouldn't make it that easy. If Bryson could just make physical contact, he could release a direct and lethal surge of electricity into Toono's body. But the damned demon knew this.

Bryson started to believe a fight at close quarters would favor him. However, all Toono needed to do was connect with a swing from his cane. Both men's abilities were extremely deadly no matter the distance.

*I suppose I'll try my hand at sparring.*

Bryson pushed off, throwing a left jab at Toono's chest. Toono skipped back, dodging the fist. Bryson followed with a high right cross, missing as Toono's head twitched to the side. Stepping through the punch, Bryson planted and pivoted his right foot, twisting his body and swinging the heel of his left foot around for a reverse hook kick.

Toono stopped his backwards movements, seizing the perfect opportunity to close the gap between them, taking advantage of the two downsides to such a kick: its extension and the lack of vision it gave the assailant. He stepped forward, enveloping his body within the back of Bryson's hooked leg and thrusting the butt of his cane at the ankle of Bryson's planted foot.

Bryson had planned for this. Using the hook kick's momentum, he sprung off his planted foot just as the cane hit the ground, another rift cutting across the street. He barrel rolled over Toono's back, kicking downward like a pendulum. The top of his foot molded to Toono's ribs as it connected, slamming the demon into the cobblestone with enough force to blast a crater into the ground.

Bryson landed, skidding backward with a voltaic orb forming in his clasped hands. He thrust out his hands. Lightning bolted toward Toono, who tapped his cane against the ground, a hole forming beneath him. He dropped out of sight just before the attack landed.

Bryson narrowed his eyes, the scorched cobblestones showing no signs of a body. Buildings across the street continued to fall into the previously formed chasms. He stared at the black hole in the crater, hesitant to approach but also wary that standing still wasn't likely the best option.

Tremors suddenly shook the street as loud bangs rose from below the ground. Was Toono breaking the crust underground and burrowing through passages?

The road split beneath Bryson, forcing his legs to widen as a foot was planted on each precipice. As he began to fall, he lunged toward one of the chasm's edges with both hands, desperate to not drop into the void.

He hung from the edge, holding on with all of his strength as the chasm widened. Rock and dirt crumbled around him, pelting the top of his head and filling his nostrils with dust. He coughed, looking up just in time to see a three-story building leaning over the rift's mouth, its foundation groaning from the awkward angle. It'd collapse directly on top of him if he didn't move.

Panicking, he glanced down in search of a foothold or anything on which to grab. Then he located Toono watching from below, standing comfortably on a ledge that jutted out from a cave in the wall's side. That ledge formed switchbacks leading from the rift's shadowy depths all the way up to the surface.

Bryson swung to the right and dropped toward Toono just as the building plunged into the abyss.

The demon held his cane at his side, preparing to swing the moment Bryson landed. Bryson couldn't change his trajectory mid fall, and there was no such thing as blocking that ancient—not unless you wanted to sacrifice your bones.

He sent three blasts of electricity toward Toono, forcing the demon to move from his spot. Bryson landed as Toono dashed backward up the switchbacks … and right into Bryson's trap. A bolt of lightning dropped from the sky and struck the demon, causing a flash of white to illuminate the void.

The ledge gave way beneath both of them, and Bryson cursed at his own stupidity. They fell next to each other, their bodies smacking the cragged rocks of the wall. Toono reached up with his cane and slammed the hooked handle into the wall, slowing his descent while carving a gouge up the chasm wall.

Bryson reached out and grabbed hold of Toono's ankle at the last moment, his weight yanking the man deeper. Bryson swayed as he dangled over nothingness. Was there even a bottom?

Toono began to kick, but Bryson refused to let go. He wouldn't die like this. He looked up, gaping at how far they'd fallen. The surface seemed hundreds of feet away.

He reached up and grabbed around Toono's knees, pulling himself up farther. The cane's handle dug deeper into the wall. He pulled himself up to

Toono's waist, then his back. Before long, he placed his feet on the demon's shoulders and climbed onto the sloped bottom of a gouge. It looked like half a crater blasted into the chasm's side, sloping up to the surface.

Bryson turned and stomped at Toono's face, but Toono ripped his cane from the wall and dropped into the darkness. Standing at the precipice, Bryson stared into the black void. Collapsed buildings rolled down the chasm's sides, an avalanche of wood, stone, and metal.

He released an immense amount of clout, and three lightning bolts dropped in front of him, illuminating the abyss below. Toono was gone.

Bryson sprinted up the gouge with the surface in his sights. He didn't want to fight down here where Toono clearly had the advantage. Sidestepping to avoid fallen wreckage, he heard a crack to his right and saw Toono leaping out of another crevice in the crust.

Toono nearly matched Bryson's speed up the slope, smacking the ground with his cane every few feet. Countless clefts opened up and shot toward Bryson, but he outran them with ease.

Upon reaching the surface, he was met with a horrifying scene. The street was no longer recognizable, the surrounding buildings gone— including the eastern gate. Toono's attacks had stretched into palace grounds.

A network of intersecting fissures and chasms, dotted with craters, had replaced what once were several city blocks. It was as if the ground had been shattered, like a sheet of glass dropped on stone.

As Bryson heaved, he glanced at Toono, who stood some fifty paces away. His two female companions had repositioned themselves, now standing in front of faraway buildings.

He turned, pleased to find Vitio still heeding his warning, though the king had been forced to retreat a considerable distance. He now stood on a patio in a gardened area, watching with wide-eyed shock.

Still, that wasn't far enough away. The scope of this fight had become unpredictable. He needed Vitio nowhere near this mess. He bolted toward the king, hurling himself over a chasm in a single leap.

"Get out, now," Bryson said, sliding to a stop. "Get inside the palace and get to Shelly's room. Then round each of them up and head southwest, out of the city."

Vitio gawked. "I need to …" He trailed off, his gaze roving toward the destruction behind Bryson.

"I can't worry about you during this fight!" Bryson shouted. He glanced back to keep an eye on Toono. Surprisingly, the man stood patiently while observing from afar. Bryson turned to Vitio again. "This fight requires all of my focus and energy. They could easily attack you while I'm distracted. You cannot serve as their sacrifice!"

Slowly, Vitio nodded. Then he turned tail and ran for the palace.

"And that includes Shelly, Delilah, L.K., Vistas, and Flen! *GET THEM ALL OUT OF HERE!*"

Bryson continued to regain his breath as blood dripped down his face. He turned, immediately faced with Toono's cane.

Bryson ducked into a squat, butt directly above the ground. His knees recoiled, springing upward and blasting a crater into the ground. His shoulder collided into Toono's chest, carrying them both into the air.

They scuffled while airborne, the city growing smaller below them. Bryson tried reaching for Meow Meow, but Toono caught his wrist and twisted it. Bryson howled, the joints of his wrist, elbow, and shoulder trying to rip free from their sockets as Toono torqued midair.

Bryson expelled electricity, shocking Toono and forcing him to release his grip. They separated as they fell—Bryson crashing into the wooden roof of a split-in-half building, Toono hitting the ground with a resounding crash.

Bryson plunged through two more stories before landing on the ground floor. He groaned, pushing himself up out of the wreckage. Dusting off his shoulders and rising to stand, he found himself in a bakery. Judging by the aroma, it had been abandoned in the heart of a busy morning, fresh muffins lined in rows in a glass display case.

He cringed. His pinky and ring finger were broken, and he didn't have to look at them to know it. A searing pain stabbed at his whole body; bruises spotted his skin; and cuts ran across his face, warm blood seeping out of them.

He'd never experienced a fight like this, one with such brutality—not with Storshae, the Dev Assassins, Warden Feissam, or the Linsani at the Blizzard of Blood. The closest comparison would have been the beating he'd received at the hands of Olivia and Apoleia before learning they were his sister and mother.

He exited the bakery. He and Toono had flown a considerable distance. They were now farther away from the palace than even the two women. They continued to spectate with a calm intrigue, Kadlest still carrying the body of King Rehn over her shoulder. Neither woman had attempted to take advantage of his distracted state.

Why weren't they concerned with getting into the palace and targeting one of the royals? Did they have that much confidence in Toono?

At this distance, the street was unblemished by chasms. The buildings, however, sported heavy damage from Bryson's errant electrical blasts earlier. Toono heaved a slab of stone off his leg and slowly rose to his feet. He tore off a partly ripped chunk of sleeve that hung in the way of his hand.

Bryson surveyed the street once more, his eyes dragging between Toono, Meow Meow, and the Oracle's body. Perhaps, he'd fallen victim to tunnel vision. There was more than one option here. Defeating Toono wasn't the only method to stopping the rebirth. What would happen if he could get his hands on the Oracle's body and run ... or destroy it?

*Might as well give it a shot.*

He darted straight for the brunette, noticing the smirk slip from her face. Had they not planned for this? Before she could blink, he planted in front of her and kicked. Then Toono appeared, hooking Bryson's foot with the looped handle of his cane.

Toono gave his ancient an effortless flick, sending Bryson skipping across the ground like a pebble across a pond. Each impact was a burst of stone as he tumbled through the air. Eventually he rolled to a stop, pain swelling all over his body.

Rising to stand and regaining his wits, he spotted another chasm racing toward him. He ran to the side as it widened. Toono appeared in front of him and slammed his cane against one of the few still-standing buildings. A crack ran up the wall, splintering it as it climbed. The structure crumbled, entire sections collapsing within moments.

Bryson lunged through raining debris, arms crossed in front of his face as heavy stone pelted him. As he cleared the wreckage, he slung electric whips through the air. Toono dodged them effortlessly.

Bryson landed and lurched forward with a relentless barrage of punches, elbows, knees, and kicks. Toono leaned to and fro, stepping this way and that, evading each attempt with casual grace. Had training with Yama made this man able to track anyone's speed?

Bryson was sick of it.

He skipped back and kicked a voltaic orb at Toono. The demon skirted the blow, but a flash of white and a bolt of lightning cracked the ground right where he had moved to. He dove out of the way, but not fast enough to save his left arm, now scorched up to his shoulder.

A storm of lightning struck the street, claps of thunder splitting Bryson's ears as if divine giants were applauding them from the sky. Lightning either blasted craters into the ground or disappeared within the shadowy depths of fissures.

Bryson stood at the core of it all, a glowing orb of white enveloping his body, lightning branching off of him like he was the trunk of some kind of voltaic tree. He detected Toono in the chaos, sprinting around like a chicken with its head cut off as he tried to find a clear area.

This was no longer a city street, but a desolate warzone forged by the powers of two young men—a void of civilization and nature that stretched for miles. The palace itself was on the brink of being devoured.

Bryson dashed through the storm, twisting between blasted chunks of ground and bounding between rifts. The flashes of light, billowing clouds of dust, and showering stone made sight difficult, but he caught glimpses of the demon every now and then.

Bryson crouched and tried to sweep Toono's legs upon reaching him, the lightning storm rescinding. Toono leapt over the leg, but Bryson had prepared for this, refusing to be caught off guard by the demon's timely reflexes again. Still, reacting this well while getting hammered by bolts of lightning was beyond miraculous.

Already low to the ground and using the momentum gathered from the sweep, Bryson spun on his hands and kicked upward, connecting with the leaping Toono's gut and sending him higher into the air. Bryson pushed off with his hands and rocketed upward, hooking the top of his foot around Toono's waist and kicking downward.

Toono plunged. The land splintered. Bryson hurled voltaic orbs downward as he fell, not even sure if he was hitting his target.

A seismic explosion consumed most of the battlefield, shaking the city for leagues. Precipices crumbled as rifts caved in on themselves. Electricity randomly discharged in the atmosphere, crackling around a massive galvanic sphere that swelled where Toono had fallen.

Bryson landed outside the blast, arms up to shield his eyes from the light. His hoodie whipped behind him, the detonative force attempting to toss him away.

Eventually, the sphere subsided and disappeared, leaving behind a crater as wide as a palace in its wake. Bryson gasped for air, collapsing to all fours. He crawled toward the crater's rim and stared into it. All that was left was charred rock ... and a hole at its center.

*No way ... he couldn't have escaped that.* Bryson whirled in a daze. The world swayed around him, causing stars to swirl in his vision.

He looked for the two women, but only saw one—the lady with jet-black hair. Where was that Kadlest woman with the Oracle's corpse?

The ground cracked ahead of him, and the demon climbed out of the gap. Both Toono and Meow Meow were in terrible condition. The lynx's fur was burned, exposing pink patches of skin. Toono's limbs were charred black, while ash collected on his skin elsewhere. Blood ran thickly down his arms, legs, and chest. His robes had been ravaged to near-shreds. Even the bandage around his head looked ready to fall.

Toono pounced. Bryson collapsed, limbs flailing as a pathetic defense. At this point, they both flirted dangerously close to death. Neither of them would survive if this continued, and Toono had to have realized this.

The demon grasped Bryson's neck and pinned him to the ground, knees trapping his arms at his sides. Blood dripped from Toono's face onto his.

"I had a feeling it would come to this," Toono said, barely managing words between breaths. "I tried to envision every possible outcome, and this was, unfortunately, always one of them." His eyes fell to the *T2*-shaped scar on Bryson's chest, hovering there for a moment. He squeezed his eyes shut and shook his head. "But it's the scenario that makes the next most sense."

"Where did that woman go?!" Bryson said.

"She's bringing the Oracle's body where it needs to be," Toono said, tears now falling with the blood. A blade dropped into his hand. *"This is what needs to be done!"*

"You won't be able to speak to the Dev King," Bryson said, heart racing as Toono raised the knife. "You won't survive those injuries."

"I know this. Even if I sink this blade into your throat, I'm a dead man."

It was clear Toono was losing his mind, unable to contain his emotions. Bryson stared in shock, nearly forgetful of the situation before him. Where was the demon's composure he'd heard so much about?

He closed his mouth and recovered his wits. "If you know you're going to die, then why even do this? It's over."

Bryson's breaths came easier as Toono's grip weakened. Then, the demon ... *smiled?*

"You don't understand, Bryson. There was really only one of two options for the tenth sacrifice all along. It was either you ..." He paused, tears now spilling out of him as he reached up toward his head. "Or *me*." A cluster of sparks emitted from his fingers—the fingers of an *Archain man*— and burned the bandage.

Everything Bryson knew went out the window. Time seemed to slow down, the bandage sinking in tatters toward the ground, revealing an all-too-familiar scar on the man's forehead.

Leaning in, Toono whispered, "Avenge our mothers properly."

The demon cut his own throat, spewing blood on Bryson's face before falling limp. Bryson didn't even bother trying to push Toono off. He lay there, frozen with shock and grief from what had just been revealed.

The ability of electricity.

A scar on his forehead that read: T1.

# 70

# The Rebirth

King Vitio turned down a corridor, coming to a halt at the situation before him. Flen sat casually against the wall at the far end, one arm resting across a bent knee. His identical brother, Vistas, lay motionless on the floor beside him.

"*FLEN!*"

The former Dev servant looked up lazily. "Calm down. He's not dead."

"Who did it?"

"You're not going to like the answer."

The king's eyes narrowed, a fury painted red on his face. "Who is it? Where'd they go?"

"It was me, old man. But, like I said, he's not dead. I wouldn't kill my brother."

Vitio paused, taking entirely too long to find the right words. "Why?"

"Because he deserves it, as well as you, your family, and this kingdom. This has been a glorious morning."

Vitio marched down the corridor, his rage blinding him from the fact that his current mission was elsewhere.

"You better check on your daughter and wife first," Flen said. "They had a visitor just recently."

A fist connected with Flen's jaw, knocking the Devish across the floor until he rolled to a stop. Vitio bent down and lifted Vistas, tossing the scrawny man over his shoulder. He turned and walked back down the corridor.

"The one time I see you fight, and it's to strike a weak man such as myself," Flen croaked from behind. "You're a coward, Vitio."

The king continued walking, thankful to hear shallow breaths from Vistas.

"I know I've said this many times before, Vistas, but I apologize for what I put you through by sending Mendac into your kingdom. The graciousness you've shown this family over the years ... well, we haven't deserved it. You were a big part in raising my daughters, teaching them the ugliness of bigotry."

Vistas gripped the back of Vitio's shirt. "My brother was fooled," he wheezed. "They aren't targeting the princess or queen. And I believe it's too late to stop them."

"L.K.?" Vitio asked.

"Something far worse, milord."

"What could be worse than—*aargh!*" Vitio dropped to his knees, Vistas rolling off his shoulder and crumpling atop the floor. The king looked down at his stomach, where a sword extended outward, blood running the length of its blade.

He looked back, eyes wide with horror. Flen remained seated at the end of the corridor, but two more swords hovered in front of him, ripped from a plaque hanging from the wall.

Flen's cold gaze regarded the king. "This is for my town, livelihood, and parents. This is for Brintlen, Tristen, and Marcus."

The two swords darted down the hall, impaling the back of Vitio's neck and head. The last thing he heard before it all ended were the cries of Vistas as the servant caught Vitio in his arms.

*Shelly. Lilu. Delilah. I love all three of you. I suppose this coward couldn't run forever.*

*     *     *

Bryson remained still under the weight of the dying demon. Meow Meow's eyes glowed gold, Toono serving as the tenth sacrifice. Had Bryson seen it correctly? He kept replaying it in his head.

The electricity. The scar.

He screamed and pushed Toono to the side, losing any bit of sanity he might have had left. He was in the middle of a scorched and shattered chunk of land stretching for miles around him without a living enemy in sight, yet he felt no safer because of this.

Something was terribly wrong. He accomplished what he'd set out to do—defeating Toono—yet he could have never accounted for the man having Intel Energy. Despite victory, Bryson now felt responsible for offering the tenth sacrifice.

*Is this even a victory?* What did one classify a fight that ended with someone's suicide?

He wiped blood from his eyes, smearing it across his face. He grabbed Meow Meow and pulled him off the demon's head, fur unraveling below. The lynx's eyes continued to glow despite not being attached to its Archain wielder.

"It's too late," it said. "The process has begun; my life force has latched onto a nearby cadaver."

Bryson looked around, disoriented by the uneven terrain. He was in a sinkhole surrounded by cobblestone that sloped upward, forming dozens of tiny plateaus.

He glanced back at the lynx. "I just have to take the gems out," he said, rummaging through the excess fur. "That should work."

The lynx looked at Bryson. "I don't know why you continue to call me 'Meow Meow,' but I am the being who created half the world's ancients. And I was close friends with the woman who created the rest. I know how they work." He sighed. "The gems are irretrievable once the threshold of ten sacrifices has been reached."

Bryson found the gems and tried prying them free, but they flared white with celestial light, pulsating like a heartbeat. They grew unbearably hot, forcing him to rip his fingers away.

"*You* can stop this!" he yelled, desperation ringing through his voice.

"Toono activated it with *his* energy," Meow Meow said. "The process has begun."

"*FOR OLIVIA!*" Bryson screamed, knowing how ridiculous it sounded.

"I know no such name."

Bryson dropped the head in annoyance, and then struggled to stand. He guided himself up, placing one hand on the ground and the other on a knee.

Where had that woman gone with the body? Now he understood why she'd fled earlier. She'd wanted to reach somewhere Bryson couldn't find her and interrupt the process. She could have been tucked away in any one of these chasms, concealing herself within a cave Toono might have strategically placed.

He scurried up a sloped plateau, reaching the edge and staring down the cliff. Spread before him was a shattered wasteland, buildings barely noticeable in the distance. He turned left, spotting the unharmed palace. Its tallest spire stretched above the low-hanging clouds of the overcast morning sky.

Were Shelly, L.K., and Delilah still up there or had Vitio retrieved them and escaped?

He narrowed his eyes, detecting two figures on the palace grounds, just outside of the battlefield's reach. One was the raven-haired woman who had accompanied Toono and watched most of the fight. When had she gotten over there? She stood patiently, seemingly waiting for the other figure that had just exited the palace.

He didn't recognize that person—and he knew everyone in that building. Who was she and how had she infiltrated its walls? She was young, in her mid-teens perhaps. Her hair was also midnight black, but significantly shorter than the woman's.

Bryson tilted his head, curious of what hovered next to the girl … an open casket, and a very ornate one at that.

He leapt from the plateau, landing clumsily on jagged rock below. He ran toward the grounds, but his speed percentage had taken a mighty hit, his entire muscular system suffering from lacerations. Staying in front of Agnos would have been difficult at this pace.

The girl seemed to be telekinetically carrying the open casket by her side as she walked down the steps from the palace's side doors. Then it hit him, the short hair having thrown him off at first. Her name was Illipsia. She'd been Simon's lady friend a few years back, during Phesaw's final school year.

Illipsia came to a stop next to the mysterious woman, the casket lowering to the ground. Another woman stepped into view … Kadlest. Only now, she didn't hold the Oracle's body.

As the casket began to glow, Bryson panicked, tears spilling from his eyes. He tried to run faster, but he tripped over himself from atrophied strength. He stumbled forward, throwing out his hands to block his fall. Cragged rock cut into his palms, but he leapt back into a stand without thought.

While he'd never bothered visiting the room in which it was held, he still knew that casket. What else could it have been? The designs were too extravagant; its marble finish too lavish. What the hell had Toono done?

This entire time, he had led the world astray. He'd made everyone believe he wanted to resurrect an evil man, only to distract them from his true monstrous target.

A skeleton sat up in the casket, its upper torso exposed. Internal organs bubbled into existence within its ribs; sinuous muscles crept along the bones, blanketing them for protection and strength; thin layers of fat appeared in certain areas; and then skin slowly coated it all, trapping everything prior like a human bag. Lastly, hair stretched out of the scalp in messy golden locks, the roots a striking gray.

Bryson dropped to his knees, mouth agape. Repulsion and devastation swept over him at the image of the resurrected man. This wasn't the Oracle. This was a disgusting thing truly worthy of the label of beast, for there was nothing humane about him.

The man stood, a fiendish grin on his scarred face. He flipped over his hands and arms, observing them as if to make sure they were real. And during all of this, the two ladies with black hair seemed to shout at the brunette named Kadlest.

She appeared unresponsive, instead staring at the revived man in reverence. He returned her gaze with a discomforting leer, holding out his hand. As she placed her hand in his, he looked forward and locked eyes with Bryson.

Bryson wanted to scream and charge, but his body wouldn't budge. Everything was numb. Energy and physical exhaustion held him hostage. Even his mind was a mess as it tried to make sense of all that had unfolded in the past five minutes.

The man nodded at Bryson, wings of wispy black smoke extending from his back—similar to the shadowy body of the Linsani he'd fought in the Still Kingdom. The wings slapped downward, and the man's feet lifted off the ground, Kadlest pulled up with him.

As if enough already didn't make sense, now Bryson watched as his father took to the sky, making it apparent to the world …

Mendac LeAnce was alive again.

*　　*　　*

Horos didn't know exactly how to react as he stared into the casket of Dev King Rehn. Entering Cogdan Castle and reaching this crypt had been entirely too easy. He'd feared traps because of this, yet nothing had been triggered. And the reason why lay before him.

A man wrapped in bandages from head to toe rested comfortably inside the deathbed. It could have been the body of anyone, but the crown entwined with Chocolate Cosmos flowers perched atop his head made Horos think otherwise.

*No*, he thought, *this has to be a decoy.*

But if so, it was a stupidly obvious attempt at deception. Was the real body in the royal transit Toshik had chased, accompanied by Toono?

He sighed, staring at the mummified body. He didn't want to do it, but he had no other choice. He grabbed the crown and tossed it across the

722

crypt, placing his other hand on the abdomen of the corpse. It erupted in black flame.

This could have been an innocent person's body for all he knew, but he had to play it safe. He closed his eyes and whispered a prayer, something he'd spent a lot of his time doing while held captive by the Amendment Order. It was one of those things that people did in silence, for being caught doing so was cause for death.

He turned and ran back up the spiraling staircase, where Kuiku awaited his return.

"No issues up here" Kuiku said. "What'd you find?"

"A body with the Cosmos Crown, implying it was someone of royal descent. Its mummification made verification impossible however." He paused. "I burned it just to make sure."

Kuiku nodded, looking down the hollow stone corridor of the castle's dungeons. "Something's wrong," he said. "Toono has to be in those carriages Toshik chased after."

Hurried footsteps were heard in the distance, and a tall, lean swordsman appeared in the torchlight. Both men furrowed their brows. "What happened to the carriages?" Horos asked.

"False bait," Toshik said through heavy breaths. "Nobody of importance occupied them. In fact, two of them were empty. Checked for false bottoms and everything. I came rushing back as soon as possible." Horos and Kuiku exchanged skeptical looks. "Is the body still—"

"We need to scour the castle quickly," Horos said, cutting Toshik off. "If we don't find Toono or any noteworthy subordinates, I think it's fair to say the demon has left the capital."

"But how?" Toshik asked. "We've been watching the exits for weeks!"

"I don't know," Horos muttered. "He had that Tazama woman working with him. She could have built him another teleplatform … and if that's the case, he could have teleported directly out of the castle. He could be in hiding somewhere or …" He fell silent, an ominous cloud of dread hanging above them.

Kuiku finished the assassin's sentence. "He could have already attacked the Intel Kingdom."

*　　　*　　　*

Olivia, Fane, Vuilni, and the Prowler who led them were only halfway through a three-day journey. For Olivia, sleep had been elusive, making the already painful horse ride west through the Prim Kingdom even more arduous.

She'd sulked most of the way, sticking to the tail end of the group. She was thankful for the solitude. It allowed her time to absorb every bit of the Prim Queen's story. It also granted her time to regret not killing Kadlest when she'd had the chance years ago.

Kadlest was a mysterious woman, even more so than Toono. Some would say she was the biggest question mark of the entire SCAPD force. But because of her position, she'd never beckoned the same amount of attention. The world viewed her as a sidekick when, in reality, she'd been the catalyst to the entire operation. Without her, none of this would have happened.

Kadlest had served as the Prim General long ago, which explained her rugged build. And despite the trust Inedibus had in Kadlest's ability as a fighter, she despised the woman's nature.

Raised in a family of priests, Kadlest was an avid practitioner of religion in her youth until she parted ways with her family to join the royal sector, a permanent stain on her reputation with the religious zealots.

But no matter how deeply she lodged her way into the role of general, she could never fully pry herself free from her curiosities when it came to faith. She became enamored with her culture's deity, Dimiourgos, leading her to chase things she had no business chasing.

Olivia didn't care about any of this. It was the revelation of a man, a traveler by the name of Mendac LeAnce, entering the picture that took her by surprise. He'd wanted to negotiate a trade deal with the Primmish for their holy wood and ask for permission to build a cross-realm teleplatform on their land.

Olivia had heard a similar story before from the perspective of her mother, except Mendac had claimed he wanted to barter for the Still Kingdom's ever-ice. In both cases, these "negotiations" were simply tactical ruses in order to lodge himself into the kingdom's circle of elites with an ulterior motive.

Kadlest, however, didn't resist Mendac's charm like Apoleia had. She fell in love with the man and eventually fled her kingdom as an outlaw after committing a terrible crime: sharing secrets of the Primmish religion with an outsider.

After that, Queen Inedibus's story became vague. It was clear she hadn't wanted to say too much and risk committing the same atrocities as Kadlest. But she did say the woman returned nearly five years ago with a young man who she claimed to have been a practicing priest. And on that night, they killed the general and prince.

The final sentence of the queen's story sent a chill up Olivia's spine …

*I don't know why, but Kadlest loved that man and she wants him back.*

*　　*　　*

Sal couldn't keep pace with Himitsu and Kaylee, forcing the two lovebirds to stop and wait for the lumbering man to catch up. This grew tiresome and annoying, considering they were trekking through a desert with a destination to reach and little time to do so.

"Just tell me what it said," Sal pleaded, sweating profusely beneath the Archaic Kingdom's blazing sun. "I've come all this way with you guys. I think I deserve to know."

Kaylee glanced at Himitsu, whose eyes remained locked on Sal. "If you move a little faster, I will," Himitsu said, arms crossed in front of him.

"I'm not a runner," Sal said. "Not since my mother had me thieving in the markets."

Himitsu turned and decided to walk for a little bit. He felt Kaylee's frequent looks in his direction. He knew what she was thinking, that he should just tell the poor guy. It wasn't like doing so would have hurt them in any way.

He was frustrated with Toono's vague dream. He didn't know exactly what it meant, but he believed it could help in some way. Perhaps, if he combined his information with whatever Olivia might have discovered in the Prim Kingdom, the True Light alliance could finally become the aggressors in this war.

The one near-certain revelation of the dream was that the woman Toono's been working with this whole time was his mother. Something horrendous must have happened to her in order for them to go through all of this trouble to resurrect the Oracle.

"Come on, guys," Sal said.

"Enough's enough, Himitsu," Kaylee said, turning toward Sal and repeating the words written in blood:

*I will become my mother's avenger.*

# 71

# The Last of his Kind

Ophala had received word hours ago that the Intel Kingdom was under attack. It had come as no surprise to her; she'd given constant updates to King Vitio about the situation with the SCAPD ships. Despite these warnings, he'd shown no urgency when dealing with the matter. Spirit Queen Apsa had tried her best, but her blockade might as well have been a fleet of canoes when faced with four leviathans.

Skyrise had arrived just an hour ago with rather shocking news from Himitsu—news that would have changed True Light's approach with the Rogue Demon. The discovery was the very reason why the alliance had sent some of the most skilled Jestivan out on these faraway missions. Alas, the information had come too late.

Having just dismissed the Dev servant who was trying to achieve a connection with Vistas or Flen in the Intel Kingdom, Ophala could do nothing but sit at her desk and stare at a bottle of brandy, an empty glass in her hand as she pretended there was liquor in it. She dared not actually drink anything in case Phelos came under attack.

Nobody could get in touch with anyone in Dunami, which was unnerving. She couldn't even imagine what it was like at that very moment—fleeing civilians, warring armies, destruction, and perhaps a cataclysmic battle between Bryson and Toono.

She felt for the innocent Intelian populace, recalling her own experience with a similar situation. Phelos's uprising had been brutal and, in some ways, maybe more tragic. The Archains didn't have time to flee back then; the citizens of the capital were caught by surprise and sucked right into the violent operation led by Toth Brench and Wert Lamay. *What a terrible day that was*, she thought.

There'd been many days like that one in the past several years. The Generals' Battle, Rhyparia's execution, Phesaw's invasion, the Blizzard of Blood, and now Toono's attack on Dunami. The formation of the Jestivan couldn't have been timelier. Without them, the Light Realm would've succumbed to Storshae and Toono long ago.

A knock sounded from the door. "Come in."

Rathania, a young female courier, entered. She was a bright mind who Ophala had begun mentoring. "Pilot Ophala, urgent news from the Power Kingdom."

"Did you inform King Sigmund first?"

"Yes, Pilot. He then sent me to you."

"Excellent," Ophala said, satisfied with his decision to not come to her directly. He was improving on his ability to delegate. "Now, what is it?"

The messenger took another step inside and closed the door. "Details are minimal, but one thing is apparent ..." She trailed off, as if she didn't want to transmit the message.

"Surprise me," Ophala said, as if it were a challenge. She doubted anything could at this point.

The messenger pursed her lips, brows furrowed. "Well, Pilot ... as you're well aware, people have become confused by the disappearance of one of the moons over the past few days." She took a deep breath. "Apparently, it *fell* on the Power Kingdom, crushing Ulna Malen and most of the land surrounding it."

Ophala's empty glass shattered on the hardwood floor as her hand fell limp. She stared at the messenger, dumbfounded. Had she heard that correctly? "You said, 'fell'?"

"Yes, Pilot. And that's not even the half of it."

"What else could accompany such news?" Ophala asked in bewilderment.

"There were sightings of animals that acted like humans, standing tall on hind legs and even speaking." Hurriedly, Rathania added, "I promise I'm simply the messenger, Pilot Ophala. This all sounds ludicrous."

Ophala's face fell into her hands. *What had they done?* If the dimiours were there, that meant Rhyparia was, too. Her stomach fluttered as realization dawned upon her. The moon hadn't fallen; it had been dropped.

Swiping a hand across the desk, parchment fluttered into the air, the vase of fake flowers joining the glass in its shattered state on the floor. Ophala had freed that girl, knowing she'd been an innocent soul preyed on by her mother. This outcome couldn't have been foreseen—not even by the likes of a woman such as herself.

Musku and the dimiours were supposed to groom Rhyparia into a delicate soul in efforts to help heal the wounds of her past and the memories of all those she'd killed as a child. But it seemed they only worsened them. Or perhaps she'd been too far gone, and Ophala had been naïve to expect such a dramatic transition.

Either way, the guilt fell squarely on her shoulders.

*    *    *

The Intelian teleplatforms sat at the center of a field of death. Soldiers sporting colors of nine different kingdoms lay in bloody masses—some tangled together, others all alone. The battle had come to an end, but the misery would remain for some time for those who survived. War was an ugly thing, blanketed in long, empty stretches of anticipation and splotched with a battle's vivid red. This battle was the biggest splotch, the period at the end of a sentence, marking its end.

Among those dead were several notable names from both alliances: Dev Warden Gala, Still Warden Moroza, Diatia Groto, and Shea-Ley Neaneuma. There likely would have been a couple more added to True Light's tally if it hadn't been for their opponents suddenly dropping dead.

Tashami stepped around dead or dying bodies, many of which had fallen in the same inexplicable manner. He'd defeated Warden Gala and was in the process of lending aid to Titus in his fight against the Diatia when the phenomenon had begun.

"Did you see anything?" Titus asked, favoring his left leg.

"No," Tashami muttered, crouching next to the Still Warden's body. Director Venustas knelt nearby, a hand pinned to her bleeding shoulder. "What about you, Director?"

"Flip her over and check her chest," Venustas said. "I couldn't see her through the inferno I had weaved between us, but I heard a high-pitched whistling noise the moment before she collapsed."

Tashami flipped her over and sighed. "You're right. Arrow shafts directly into her chest where her heart is, likely broken in half when she fell." He picked up the fletched ends that lay in the grass—a single golden feather with a unique spiraling shape. "Someone has a very good shot."

He looked up and scanned the area, noticing the same injuries to those who had suffered a similar fate. "We had archers here," he said, "but I don't recall anyone this good."

"Let's not question our good fortune," Titus said, gazing back in the direction of the capital. "We need to get to the palace immediately."

Tashami nodded. "Go ahead of us. We'll be right behind you." He stood and limped his way over to the corpse of a woman very dear to his heart: Spirit Director Neaneuma.

He hadn't seen her in a long time—Jilly's funeral being the most recent memory—but she'd been largely responsible for the maturation of his character and weaving abilities. He and Jilly became her personal students when the Jestivan was formed. She'd taught him to stop holding back his power, an issue derived from the fear of repeating his father's journey. She'd led him and a few others into the Void, traveling with them as reassurance and guidance …

"She was the sweetest woman I ever knew," Venustas said, surprising Tashami as she stood next to him. "We butted heads often, but never out of contempt. She saw me as the young airheaded bimbo, and I saw her as a stubborn old hag. Still, we threw those insults at each other out of love."

He looked down at Neaneuma. "She was the only one left from the older generation," he said. "Now she joins Grand Director Poicus and Director Senex."

"A new wave has risen," Venustas said.

He surveyed the field around them, but saw no sight of Neaneuma's opponent. "Where did that blue-haired woman go?"

"Tazama might have escaped … like she always seems to do," Venustas said. She sighed. "Quite a pity. She's been one of the bigger nuisances in this war. Would have been nice had this mysterious archer taken care of her too."

Tashami stood and headed toward the capital. "Let's go find Bryson." He paused, gaze lured toward the sky in the distance. Something—no, *someone* was flying through the air, massive wings of wispy black extended from his or her back. Another figure trailed as if along for the ride.

Venustas ran past him after noticing the same thing. "We must hurry!"

*　　*　　*

Illipsia craned her neck, staring straight up at Mendac and Kadlest as they grew smaller in the sky. Tears rolled down her cheeks, an uncontrollable heat in her face. The last time she'd cried like this was during her stint in the Void, but those had been forced out of her by the Linsani's distant shrieks.

*This* sorrow came from within, rooted in betrayal. Years of hard work and life-threatening missions had just amounted to nothing. This hadn't been the plan. After Mendac's rebirth, Toono and Kadlest were supposed to capture, torture, and expose him.

The man's death had been sensationalized throughout the Light Realm, painted as a heroic sacrifice to protect the Intel Princess—which might have been the case. Nobody knew much about his death. However, Toono and Kadlest had planned to make the world see the man for what he really was. Kadlest wasn't supposed to take his hand and be swept away in his embrace.

Illipsia looked down, her vision swirling in tears as she scanned the remnants of what should have been the heart of the city. She'd heard and felt the destruction while in the palace, but nothing could have prepared her for the hard proof. Spires and plateaus jutted from the ground at random angles, fissures laced between them. Craters dotted the disaster, one much larger than the rest.

"I must admit," Homina said. "I'm confused."

Toono hadn't told anyone outside of Kadlest and Illipsia about the plan to restore Mendac's life rather than Rehn's. Even Illipsia had only recently found out, before splitting from the main group to start her journey as a refugee. She didn't care to explain any of it to her mother—at least, not now. There were more pressing matters to address.

Where was Toono? He definitely wasn't dead, for Mendac's rebirth made that evident. She noticed someone crawling across a slanted chunk of land. She tilted her head, realizing it was Bryson LeAnce.

*But how?*

She broke into a run, ignoring the pleas of her mother from behind. She wanted answers now. She approached to find Bryson's head bowed as he hacked blood into his hand. His body was bruised and bloodied to a point beyond recognition.

"Where is he?" she asked. "If you're still breathing, who did he sacrifice?"

He croaked out something that may have resembled a word, but she couldn't distinguish it. Before she could ask again, he collapsed.

She grew lightheaded as she stared at him, stomach doing flips as nausea set in. She followed Bryson's trail of blood up the slope until she reached the lip of an enormous crater. At its center lay an unrecognizable man, skin scorched black. The decapitated head of Dimiourgos sat off to the side, its fur burned off in most spots. The smell was putrid, reeking of charcoal and sulfur.

She dashed down the crater's side and nearly stumbled several times, her feet unable to keep up with gravity's aided push. Then she saw it without even getting close to Toono's body … his eyes a lucid white, just like those who were his first nine sacrifices.

*You jerk!*

There was no way he'd left her like this. Had he predicted this outcome? He'd said he wanted to avenge Kadlest, who had supposedly been a victim of Mendac just like Apoleia. But how did that explain the woman's sudden acceptance of the man's hand when he rose from the casket? Several lies had been spun here, and she didn't know who was responsible: Toono, Kadlest, or both of them. It was a convoluted mess filled with contradictive motives.

She broke down in tears as she sprinted for his body. Then a whistling sound cut through the air, and something pierced her thigh. She collapsed into rock, her leg giving way to the pain.

Another whistle. This time, something sharp struck her hamstring. She screamed with all her might, the physical agony only lumping onto the mental despair. One hand went for her blood-soaked trousers. The other tried to latch onto her hair and twist it around her wrists—hair she no longer had. Why'd she keep forgetting this? Instead she grasped a rock and squeezed.

She peered down at her wounds to find arrow shafts protruding from them, a golden feather fletched at their ends. *An archer?*

She pulled herself toward Toono's body, careful to twist her leg in a way that wouldn't disrupt the arrow shafts and shift them inside. Someone stepped in front of her, a pair of slim running shoes beneath lean legs.

"This is disappointing."

She knew that voice, and it only made her cry more uncontrollably. She refused to look up at him, so he purposefully crouched into her view. He wore an elastic bodysuit like Yama and donned a scabbard at his hip. There was no sword in his hand, however. He wielded an ivory short bow with intricate etchings that didn't make sense. A quiver of gold-feathered arrows was strapped to his back, complementing his fiery hair. His face had hardened into something more mature, freckles faded somewhat. And the baby fat was completely gone.

"You played me for a fool, Illipsia." He sighed, looking up at the sky. "But I'm guessing you now know how that feels."

# 72

# Toono's Past: Trailblazers

"I can't believe this. This is the last favor I ever do that woman."

A ten-year-old Toono looked up at Dynamo, the man who'd made the comment. He'd been assigned as Toono's escort by his mother. The boy looked forward and shrugged. "It's not like I want you here either."

Dynamo chuckled. "I don't know if that bold nature will get you very far at this orphanage. I've heard some brutal stories."

"I can stay out of trouble," Toono said.

"True, as long as that self-righteousness of yours doesn't affect your judgment."

They were in the city of Balle and had just crossed into the street that wrapped around the iron gates of Lost Wisdom, an orphanage notorious for its shady practices. The staff had supposedly grown bolder under the regimes of King Dolomarpos and now King Itta. Such men didn't care about rumors of abused commoner children.

"It's a nice place," Dynamo noted as they crossed the street. "At least from the outside."

They stepped through the gate's main entrance. Gardeners and yardmen nodded at them as they strolled up the path. The place seemed friendly enough, but of course Toono realized this was likely a ruse.

The main foyer bore the same beauty. He could nearly see his reflection in the hardwood floors, the polish having been coated on so thick. The secretary eyed them suspiciously as they approached the front desk, their outfits drawing attention from others too. They looked nothing like Archain citizens ... they were Primmish, after all.

Long robes of white draped down their bodies, trailing across the floor. Rope bound to their waists like belts, and their sleeves hung well past their hands. As they grew closer, however, the woman's eyes were drawn to their temples, both of which were wrapped in bandage.

Before taking the teleplatform into the Archaic Kingdom, Dynamo had taken this precaution in order to protect the secrets of the Primmish people. Typically, he wore a prestigious headband marking him as a high priest, but he couldn't wear such a thing here. Needing something to cover the five-pointed star tattooed onto his forehead, he decided to use medical bandage to make it appear as if he had a head wound.

Toono had mimicked this image, wrapping his head the same way. It did well in hiding the scar blemishing his temple, the reason why he could never become a priest. He wished he knew who'd given it to him. It'd probably be the one time he sought out a fight. The scar prevented him from his dream of priesthood, for his temple needed to be unsullied to fulfill such a role.

"What is it I can do you for, sir?" she asked.

"I'm here to drop off this boy," Dynamo said. "He's become too much of a pain."

She stood and looked the boy up and down. After a frown and shrug, she sat again. "I'm assuming you know how this place works. Are you willing to pay?"

Despite knowing of this beforehand, Toono was still perturbed by the question. Lost Wisdom didn't simply accept children—and they definitely didn't go around picking them up off the streets. They only took in those who miraculously had money to fork over—and a large sum of it at that.

This meant any orphan in this building was put here by a very wealthy individual. And the younger the child, the more expensive the price.

Dynamo dropped a sack of coins on the desk. "I'm well prepared, ma'am."

"And how old is the boy?" she asked without even sparing the money a second glance. She licked her finger and grabbed a blank sheet of parchment from a stack at the desk's edge.

"Ten."

Nodding, she dipped a quill in an inkwell and then began to write. She continued to ask for information about his physical measurements and traits: height, weight, eye color, and etcetera. Surprisingly, she showed an interest in his personality and hobbies, too.

"And how do you put this information to use?" Dynamo asked.

"Do you really care?" she countered, looking up from the parchment with a raised brow. "If you did, you wouldn't be here right now."

He started, but closed his mouth and nodded. "I suppose you're right."

She returned her attention to her writing and said, "This information is what determines who he mentors under. And from what I've heard so far, he'll be in rare company. Neeko doesn't accept just anyone." She paused and glanced at Toono again. "We'll see what the old man thinks."

"What's this Neeko guy like?" Dynamo said.

"No one knows," she said with disinterest. "He keeps to himself. I guess you'd expect it from the head librarian."

Dynamo fluttered his eyebrows at Toono, knowing how much the kid loved to read and study. Libraries were his playroom. He wasn't a normal child.

It took a couple of hours of sitting in the waiting room, filling out paper work, and interviewing with orphanage officials, but eventually Toono found himself teary-eyed as he said goodbye to a man who had practically raised him with his mother.

"How long do I have to wait?" Toono asked, wiping his eyes with the back of his hand.

Dynamo sighed. "I wish I knew the answer. I guess when your mother's done with whatever she's doing. I don't even know where she is."

"Is it something dangerous?"

Dynamo looked up in thought. "Well, it is Kadlest we're talking about. Odds are … yes." He glanced back down at Toono at the sounds of his sniffles. "This isn't like you."

"I miss her," the boy said.

"Just hold out a bit longer, bud. Now give me a hug."

Toono practically fell into the man's embrace. They remained like that for a whole minute, knowing it'd be a while before they saw each other again.

"Be good," Dynamo said as he released Toono. He turned and headed for the orphanage's front doors. "And don't burn the place down."

Toono watched as the man exited the building, unaware that he'd *never* see him again.

*　　*　　*

Toono's first experience in Lost Wisdom was lunch, kids and teens of all ages packed into a mess hall bathed in the dim light of oil lanterns lining the walls. There were dozens of rectangular tables scattered throughout, each seating eight. Larger groups connected tables. These orphans were noisy and hyper, often times shuffling seats for no apparent reason. He hadn't expected this atmosphere, given the reputation of such a place. He thought antics like this would be cause for severe disciplinary action.

Pleased with this twist, he smiled and found a table that sat a pair of smaller children. He sat in the middle seat, directly between the boy and girl seated at the ends. He kept to himself for a few minutes, twirling noodles around his fork and lifting them into his mouth, waiting for some kind of conversation.

Alas, words never came. The girl ate in silence, and the boy paid more attention to an open book propped against a stack of tomes just beyond his plate. He hadn't even acknowledged Toono's arrival. In fact, he seemed to *purposefully* avoid eye contact. He was a feeble thing, skinny and short. Toono leaned back and checked under the table to find the recluse's feet dangling high above the floor.

An older boy approached the table. He was well-built for an orphan, leading Toono to believe there was some kind of gymnasium around here. He came to a stop behind the frail child, a sneer on his face. Toono didn't like that look.

"Leave it to Agnos to pay more attention to a book than the pretty girl directly across from him!" the boy jeered.

Agnos's eyes remained glued to the page of the book in front of him, but they had stopped scanning back and forth. The bully's shadow swallowed him.

Toono couldn't help but focus on the fallacy of the bully's "insult." Agnos had to have been anywhere between five to seven years old. While books—especially those of that size—weren't something someone so young would typically find an interest in, *girls* were definitely the last thing on the boy's radar. Toono was only ten, and he *still* didn't understand the fascination of the female sex.

The other issue that struck him? This bully was older than Toono, maybe even in his teenage years. Why had he called this girl "pretty?" And if that wasn't disturbing enough, the lust in his eyes as he stared at her was bothersome. Still, Toono continued to eat his noodles, hoping the oaf simply walked away. Causing a scene would have been less than idea for Toono, but restraining himself when provoked was not quite a simple matter.

*No matter what injustices you see, don't get involved.* He practically scoffed at Dynamo's warning. The man understood Toono's character. He fought for injustice; he protected those who couldn't protect themselves.

A hand smacked the back of Agnos's head, sending his face into a plate of pasta. The plate clattered atop the wooden table, and the mess hall erupted in laughter. Toono's mouth fell agape as he regarded the assailant. What purpose had that served?

Agnos pried his face from his meal. Melted cheese plastered his face, strings of it connected to the splattered pasta. A trail of red ran down his chin from his lip. The hall continued to ring with laughter, many orphans in the distance standing on their chairs to get a better look.

Where were the adults? The authority figures?

"You're a weak little thing," the bully said, an evil curl to his lip. Then he frowned, laughter dispersing into silence, as Agnos did the unthinkable. Even Toono hadn't expected it.

The boy grabbed a napkin and wiped the cheese from his eyes, ignoring the rest of his face. He then reached out, flipped a page in his book, picked up his fork, and continued to read.

A grin spread across Toono's face. It was in that split second that he decided he was going to befriend and defend this young scholar. The bully had enforced his physical will upon Agnos, yet Agnos was the one who came out of it looking as ruthless as ever. That image would stick with Toono forever.

The bully's frown deepened, but it wasn't until the little girl across the table started giggling when a fury painted his face red. His nose curled up and eyebrows furrowed, lips trembling. Once again, this girl must have been half his age and unable to grasp the concept of a relationship, so the guy's reaction pissed Toono off.

Someone from across the hall screamed, "Hey, Ethan! The weakling just shrugged you off like a bug!"

The rage on Ethan's face vanished, masked with a calm smirk. "No, I just forgot what to target. The boy can take a beating, but if you really want to break him" —he reached over Agnos and slapped the propped book down into the pasta— "you hurt his precious books."

Now Toono could spot tears in Agnos's eyes, the hysteria returning to the hall. Toono couldn't blame him. Was there anything more important to the world than books? Air, maybe. But even that said a lot.

Ethan leaned in, curling his body around Agnos's shoulder. He grabbed the boy's head and twisted it to get a better look at his face. "Yep, there's the waterworks. What a weird—UNGHHH!"

The noise that belted from Ethan's mouth was drowned out by a vacant chair shattering beneath him. Toono stood over him, the heel of his clogs digging into the back of Ethan's head. The bully struggled to rise beneath him, writhing in agony from the splintered wood in his face. Toono didn't care.

The mess hall had fallen still and silent, stunned by Ethan's defeat at the hands of a stranger in white robes.

"From now on" —Toono pointed at Agnos— "no one will bother this boy. It's the young minds like his that grow to become leaders, and I will make sure he sees that day."

*     *     *

Toono didn't peruse the spines of books lining the many shelves of the library. He rummaged through the neglect bins, which were crates of books that were either nearly damaged beyond recognition or hadn't been touched in years, sometimes decades. Whether it was because of boring prose or damaged pages, these were the neglected texts of the world. Every library had such bins, but people usually avoided them like the plague.

He wasn't like most people, however. While useless and mundane books frequented the neglect bins, a few gems could always be found buried somewhere within. So he dug for hours, not bothered by how much time passed. He was supposed to have met with this Neeko gentleman much earlier in the night, but apparently the librarian wasn't one for punctuality.

He pulled his arms free of the sea of books and turned, hearing a door creak behind him. He stepped around the end of a row of bookcases and spotted Agnos exiting a room. The boy continued down a separate aisle with a book at his side. Toono nearly gave chase, but an old man poked around the door, eyes trained on him.

"Toono, is it?" he asked with a smile. "Come, let's talk."

After picking up a few books from the floor and returning them to the bins, Toono ran for the room. It was a humble office, not that big, but not too small that it felt cramped. There was just enough floor space between the desk and the door. A small spiraling staircase stood in the room's far corner, leading up to a loft. This was not just the man's place of work, but his bedroom too.

"Good evening, Toono," the man said, taking a seat and leaning back with hands folded on his lap. "My name is Neeko."

"How are you?" Toono said, sitting in the lone chair across from him.

"Very well, actually. It's always exciting when I hear word of a potential new recruit."

"Potential?"

Neeko nodded. "There have been many orphans who I've shown brief interest in at first, but I don't decide to mentor them until some preliminary discussions."

"So, an interview," Toono said.

"I don't like that word," Neeko said with a grin. "Sounds so staged … so artificial. I want this to flow freely. An exchange of meaningful thought involving two willingly participating parties."

"Well, I'm definitely here of my own accord," Toono said. "And I enjoy meaningful thought."

Neeko chuckled hoarsely. "You're strange, just like Agnos."

"What do you mean by that?"

"You're an adult trapped inside a boy's body. The way you speak and carry yourself is nothing like any other child."

"Where I'm from, this is fairly standard," Toono said.

Neeko's eyes fell to the boy's robes and then flicked up to his bandaged temple. He didn't address it, however. "You'll need to lower those standards now that you're here. Otherwise, you'll be faced with a lot of disappointment."

A frown curled onto Toono's face. "I've already witnessed the barbarity firsthand."

"I've heard. Agnos told me about lunch today. In that way, you're very different from him."

"I'm not in trouble, am I?" Toono asked, sinking in his seat.

"For dealing that boy exactly what he deserved? Of course not. But don't make a habit of it. If it becomes obvious to any of the people in charge here that you possess such strength …" Neeko trailed off, pursing his lips and shaking his head. "Well, they'll do whatever it takes to sell you for a great price."

A long silence followed. "S-sell me?"

"It's been a practice I've tried fighting for decades," Neeko said. "Alas, King Itta not only supports it, but participates in it. He's bought a few orphans in recent years. It's always the older ones, fifteen to seventeen, either for potential child-bearers or military might. In fact, General Inias was an acquisition of this orphanage."

"Why are you telling me this?" Toono asked, a hollow pit of disgust forming within him.

"So you know what kind of world you've stepped into. While the Dark Realm has a few kingdoms with renown morbid and suppressive cultures—the Cyn and Power Kingdoms, for example—the Light Realm also has one, and you're sitting in it."

Toono squirmed with discomfort as Neeko retrieved a sheet of parchment from a drawer. "Anyway, I've noticed a few things about you," the librarian said. "In your applications, it says your interest is reading. It also says your dream is to discover things long forgotten." He looked up with narrowed eyes. "Strangely ambiguous."

"And for good reason," Toono said.

"I believe that," Neeko said, glancing at the boy's temple again. "Give me a rough estimate on the number of books you've read in your life."

"Seven hundred and eighty two."

Neeko's laugh wheezed through the office. "You vomited up that answer as if you'd been waiting for the question."

Toono's face reddened with embarrassment. "I record a list of titles of the books I've read and segment them into genres or categories. In doing so, I also tally them up as I go."

"And I assume all of these books are from your place of residence before coming here?" Neeko asked.

Toono nodded, feeling as if words would betray him and reveal too much about his home.

"Then you have a lot more reading to go! I saw you rummaging through the neglect bins ..." Neeko's eyes twinkled with satisfaction. "That's a good sign. When Agnos and I saw you buried headfirst in the forgotten texts, we were pleased."

"You were spying on me?"

Neeko pointed across the room, where there were small rectangular panels in the wall. "Peepholes," the librarian said. "I don't like to be seen all that much, but I must make sure nobody's destroying my precious library."

Toono tilted his head, unsure of how he felt about the revelation. He turned, hearing Neeko's chair grind atop the hardwood. The man rose and walked toward a sidewall.

"I've made my decision," he said, pressing his fingers into a disguised handle and pulling at the wall. It slid open, revealing a hidden row of bookcases. He walked the width of the room and did the same on the other side. "I have a task for you. I feel I don't even need to ask to know your answer, but I suppose I still owe you that birth-given right of choice." He turned with soft eyes and the warmth of a grandparent's smile. "I want you to read every book in the main library twice over. Are you up for it?"

"Duh."

Neeko laughed. "And once you do—" he extended his hands toward the wall of bookcases— "I'll offer you the chance to read books of my own personal collection—or *try* to read them, I should say." He leaned forward, cupped his hands to the sides of mouth, and playfully whispered, "Most of them are in forgotten languages from a time *long* before ours."

"So you've chosen to mentor me?" Toono said.

"I have."

"Because I read?"

Neeko shook his head, holding up a single finger. "Because you seek the forgotten." He looked up. At what, Toono didn't know. "You and Agnos will blaze the trail to a new world."

*   *   *

After an extensive hunt later in the evening, Toono finally found Agnos in one of the group dorms. Eight bunk beds were spaced against the wall of the circular room, a window splitting them at the middle. Agnos sat on the wide set windowsill with a book in his hands, the moon casting his shadow across the floor.

"Hey," Toono whispered, careful to not wake those who had gone to sleep early. "What are you reading?"

Agnos regarded him apprehensively. "It's a study on the viability of relics in the hands of a commoner ... some light reading."

Toono smirked, understanding why Neeko had compared him to the boy. Hearing someone so young speak with such intelligence and fluidity was a bit jarring. "I'd have to say the viability is zero."

Agnos nodded, looking back at his book. "Risetto Yumen believes only a few people are born with the ability to wield relics. It's not something just anyone can learn to do—no matter how hard they try. They could practice every day of their life for twelve hours a day and would still never make it operable."

"And what do you think about that?" Toono asked.

"I find it depressing. What if I can't make a relic work?"

Toono pushed himself onto the windowsill. "The chances of you ever obtaining a relic are pretty close to zero anyway."

"Neeko has a few."

Toono fell silent, but didn't show a reaction. Agnos had said that so casually, as if relics were as common as trash in the streets of the slums. Neeko had a *few* relics? If so, he should have long been retired, living in the wealthy lakeside homes of Soulful in the Spirit Kingdom or Ara in the Passion Kingdom.

"You've seen them?" Toono asked.

"Yes, and so have you."

Toono raised an eyebrow. "Really?"

"Those glasses he wears."

Toono tried to recall the details of the old man's spectacles, but had trouble doing so. He wondered if their core was made of holy wood or pious minerals. "I guess I'll pay more attention next time."

Agnos looked up from his book. "How did you get so strong?"

"My mother," Toono said. "She's a warrior. She taught me how to fight. Apparently, there are other reasons for my physical abilities, but she never says much."

"Oh ..." Agnos looked out the window. "So you've known your parents before."

"Just my mom."

"And she decided to discard you after all this time?"

Toono's eyebrows crumpled, unprepared for the indelicate word choice. He decided to bite his tongue, however, considering the unknowns of the boy's family. "I guess," he said. "How old are you, Agnos?"

"Six, almost seven."

"And how long have you been here?"

Agnos shrugged. "Since I can remember. I have these vague memories of a lavish nursery, but I think it's my mind playing tricks on me."

"They have a nursery here?"

"Yes, but it's on the opposite end of the building and heavily guarded."

Toono gazed at the beds of the dorm. "That's interesting. The amount of money someone would have to pay in order for this place to accept an *infant* has to be an obscene amount."

"It's never made sense to me," Agnos muttered, gaze distant as he stared at the windowsill between his legs. "Why would someone pay an orphanage to take their infant child? Especially one as notoriously cruel as this one? If they don't have the patience to raise the child themselves, then what would make them throw money away for the sake of the child?"

"That's a good question," Toono said. "And why is the nursery so far removed and protected from the heart of the building?"

"Neeko says there's no way in without authoritative permission. Even he has tried on several occasions, but it's simply impossible."

Toono leaned back against the window and frowned. "Lost Wisdom's operations are befuddling." He glanced at Agnos. "Have you ever been curious about the identity of your parents?"

"Of course, but I don't dwell on it—nor does the uncertainty bother me. I don't need to know. If they were willing to stick me in a place like this, then why should I care?" He paused, smiling at his book. "Besides, they did me a favor. That decision led me to Neeko, who then nudged me in the direction of my dream. I'm just waiting for my tethering."

"Your tethering?"

Agnos's eyes widened, bringing a finger to his mouth. "Don't tell Neeko I said that."

"A secret, eh?"

"You'll find out when he wants you to," Agnos said. "But that's not for me to determine. You'll really like him—" He paused and snickered. "I don't even know your name."

"Toono."

"I like it."

"You better, if we're supposed to be best friends and all."

Agnos's cheeks flushed red. "Best friends and fellow trailblazers?"

"Sure … not that I know what Neeko meant by that … a 'new world.'"

Agnos placed the side of his head against the window and looked up at the sky. "We can't see it here, but supposedly those in the Dark Realm can."

Toono stared at Agnos in interest, understanding what it was he was referring to. Toono had seen it many times in the night sky. It was so commonplace that he'd never even paid it much attention, treating it like the moons, stars, and sun.

"One day I'll see it," Agnos muttered. "That place the Oracle called 'Earth.'"

# 73

# Toono's Past: The Avenger

"I've never seen someone read so fast," Neeko said, limping his way around his desk and past Toono. "I thought for sure that you'd cheated."

"I would never do such a thing," Toono said.

Pausing in the middle of the floor, he turned and smirked at the boy. "Now that you've passed my exam with only three incorrect answers, I see that. If you had skipped books or skimmed pages, you would have failed miserably." He carefully lowered himself to the floor, grunting in the process. "Still, reading nearly two thousand books in only a year—twice through? That's some kind of processing ability your mind has ... actually, it's inhuman. Even Agnos has been at it for two years and is still just finishing in the next couple of weeks."

Toono twisted his lips and shrugged. "To be fair, Agnos is only seven. It would have been challenging for me at that age, too."

Neeko lifted up a small section of the floorboards, revealing a stone safe. Toono rose from his chair and craned his neck as he watched Neeko insert a key and twist it. This guy was full of secrets. The space beneath the safe door revealed a small dark cavernous space.

Reaching into its shadowy depths, Neeko closed an eye with a look of pain on his face.

"Do you want me to do that for you?" Toono asked.

"No, thank you. You never know what might try to bite you." He cackled afterward, making Toono question the threat's authenticity.

"How vast is that thing?" Toono asked after several moments of rummaging.

"Vastness is a term I don't use lightly." Neeko released a sigh of satisfaction as he withdrew his arm from the hole. Toono's face twisted with shock as the man pulled out a book … and then a staff as tall as him. It had three holes at the top and a fourth one at the bottom. Neeko beamed as he rounded the desk and returned to his seat.

"Typically, I offer a gift to my students once they pass the exam. But since your birthday also falls on this day, you will receive two—a rare treat in a place like this, where most children have no clue when their birthday is."

Toono looked at the floor. "It's why I haven't told anyone."

"As expected from a considerate person such as yourself," Neeko said, leaning the staff against the desk. "Fair warning, however: I did tell Agnos. He was more than ecstatic about it."

Toono smiled. "I suppose he can know."

"Moving on to your gifts. I tried to revolve them around a curiosity you've expressed every chance you've gotten since beginning these lessons." The librarian chuckled. "You and Agnos are awfully persistent with this Earth business. But you fail to realize that I don't magically have the answers to that mysterious blue marble in the Dark Realm's sky."

He held up the book. "While this also fails to possess any answers of a concrete nature, it does vaguely hint at ways to find those answers."

"Another book is my gift?" Toono asked, his lips curling slyly upwards. "I think even I have had my fair share of those over the past year."

"No, this is your final assignment. It's a book written in an old Primmish language that died out in the early centuries of Known History."

The smile slipped off Toono's face, a dumbfounded expression taking its place. He'd had a feeling that Neeko had always known about his true identity as a child from the Prim Kingdom, but this was the first time the man had made such an obvious hint. Still, Toono tried to lie. "If it's anything like some of the books from your personal collection, I won't be able to read it."

"First of all, I think you can," Neeko said. "Secondly, this language is nothing like those you saw in my personal collection, which are written in dialects not just before *our* timeline, but long before that, too."

Toono's eyebrows climbed his forehead at that revelation. How long ago was he talking about?

A twinkle burst from Neeko's eyes. "Languages older than the Thunder Queen herself—a woman you'll come to learn a little bit about by reading this." He pushed the book across the desk. "But, just in case you can't actually read it, I present to you your first gift." He removed his circular glasses and placed them on the desk. "You have the weaving talent to use them properly."

Slowly, Toono's eyes roved from the book to the glasses. "You're giving me a relic? I find that slightly insane."

"It does me no use."

"Are they translators?" Toono asked, picking them up and inspecting them.

"Yes."

Putting them on, he glanced at the book's cover. He didn't need to weave, for he already knew how to read the language of Dimorian. However, to keep appearances, he made it seem like a struggle. "*What Lies Below the Sea*," he finally muttered after sounding out the words.

His next question gave everything away. Malice coated every word, as if he was accusing the librarian of something vile. "How did you obtain this?"

Neeko held his gaze for a long moment. "Why does that matter?"

"It seems like something the Primmish would go to great lengths to protect."

"I would never infringe upon the protected property of such a well-guarded culture. Like libraries have neglect bins, the world has one of its own. And that's where I found this."

Toono's eyes narrowed. "What?"

"It's a vast entity, an elaborate labyrinth too complex for someone of your age ..." Trailing off, he shook his head. "Too complex for someone of any age."

"I don't—"

"It's not something you must worry yourself with—not now, at least. For now, I want you to read that book ... and *really* absorb every detail. Agnos's exam is in two weeks. When he passes, both of you can analyze the text together. In five months' time, I'll have a discussion with both of you about it."

"You're being—"

"As for your second gift," Neeko continued, paying Toono's rebuttals no mind, "I give you this." He laid the strange staff on the desk. "An ancient of the artifact tier, Orbaculum. A great tool to aid any of your future aspirations."

"What does it do?"

"Practice with it and find out," Neeko said. "You're a human who enjoys discovery. I know a lot of things, Toono. But, I'm not here to answer everything, just nudge you in the direction you want to go."

As Toono continued to inspect the staff, his mentor waved him off. "Now go have an ethical birthday. In five months, we'll speak again."

"Five whole months?"

"Yes. Try being a kid for a bit."

*　　*　　*

"That's really cool, Toono!"

Agnos was looking around a janitorial closet with Toono's new relic on the bridge of his nose. Toono sat on the floor, using an overturned mop bucket as a table for his pastries. Agnos had snuck several of them out from the mess hall in celebration of Toono's birthday.

"I wish I had something to translate!"

"It doesn't work on any languages that are too old apparently," Toono said through a mouthful of doughnut. "No matter how good of a weaver you are."

"And the staff ... have you figured out what it does yet?"

"I find it hard to believe I'll ever have an opportunity in a place like this."

Agnos spun, scanning a sign that noted the rules and regulations for sanitation practices. It was written in perfect Sphairian, so Toono didn't know what the boy was trying to achieve. A bruise on the back of his neck caught Toono's eye.

"What's that on your neck?"

Agnos whirled, a guilty look on his face. "I slipped and fell."

If Toono hadn't been so angry, he would have laughed at the absurdity of the lie. "How must one slip to acquire such a peculiarly placed bruise?"

"Backwards ... a rock lodged into the back of my neck."

Shaking his head, Toono regarded his pastries and grabbed another piece. "Who was it?"

"No one, I promise."

"You're lying."

Silence.

"It couldn't have been Ethan," Toono said with a clipped, business-like coldness. "He's learned his lesson plenty of times by this point."

"Don't worry about it." Agnos took off the glasses and handed them back to Toono. A pout had formed. "You don't always have to avenge me."

"It's what I do. I make sure bad people get what they deserve."

"But does that make you a good person?" Agnos asked.

Toono froze, fixating his gaze on the grimy floorboards. He felt like he was back home. Those who knew him in the Prim Kingdom would call him the judge and jury. A few went as far as accusing him of playing god, as if he were the ultimate form of justice. It was just another reason why he scared the priests. They didn't like his violence, no matter the reason for it.

"I don't understand why you were assigned an Adrenian protector," Agnos said. "That Yama girl doesn't have to do anything because no one even looks at you the wrong way."

Toono shrugged, regaining his wits and continuing to chew. "She's good company and offers new perspectives on life."

Agnos gave the door shifty eyes. "It's a miracle we were able to lose her for these brief ten minutes."

The door's handle turned just after he'd said it. They both remained still, horrified by who might enter. Then one of the mentors peeked inside. "Of course," she said. "I knew I'd find you here. Toono, you have a visitor waiting for you at the front ... brutish looking woman."

Toono bolted upright, knocking the bucket and pastries onto the floor, exiting without saying a single word to Agnos. His mother had returned from her mission.

*     *     *

Toono ran down the path that cut through the front grounds of Lost Wisdom. He leapt into the arms of the woman he'd missed so dearly, but she didn't return the embrace with the same gusto. He stepped back, searching her face for any semblance of relief or joy. Alas, he saw only hollowness in her eyes as she feigned a smile.

"What's wrong, Mother?"

"You cannot call me that anymore."

Tears swelled in his eyes. "Huh?"

"Your father ... he ruined everything."

He didn't know what to say to that. He didn't know his father, nor had he ever heard her utter a word of the man's existence. "What happened?"

She broke down in tears. "He hurt me. He always has."

Then she told her story.

*     *     *

There was a deafening silence to Toono's world during the months following his mother's visit. Agnos and Yama had tried speaking to him every chance they got, but none of their words stuck. He only cared about his mother. He may have been only eleven years old, but that was old enough to have known the pain behind his mother's words. The piles of psychology books he'd consumed in his lifetime only made him more aware.

He sat across from Yama in the mess hall for dinner one night, poking at a flimsy hill of scrambled eggs, replaying the entire conversation he'd had with his mother that day in his head. She'd flooded him with information regarding her past, which included the identity of his father and the nature of their relationship.

He hadn't asked for any of this, and upon hearing it his immediate reaction had been a selfish one. *Why did you have to share this with me?*

But after some reflection, he realized why she'd decided to be so blunt with a child. It was because she knew her son. She knew his nature. She knew he'd want to inflict just as much pain on the man as she did.

Alas, how could they do this if Mendac was dead? The news was that he had fought and died valiantly in battle with a madman to protect Intel Princess Shelly. The realm was celebrating the man's life, parading his accolades around as if he were one of the greatest heroes to ever live. He had brought teleplatforms into the Light Realm, sparked trade between the Still, Power, and Prim Kingdoms, slain the "evil" that was Dev King Rehn, and defeated the Dev Kingdom with a bold invasion.

Nobody focused on his atrocities. How could they? None of them knew. The lengths he had gone to achieve his scientific breakthroughs was horrifying. He'd killed and manipulated people all for the sake of data. And for some reason, Toono was part of said data, used and tossed aside during his years as a toddler.

There was a silver lining, though. His mother had discovered highly classified documentation from a holy tree in Asalka with the help of Dynamo, who had apparently achieved a very high rank in the religious sector. It contained information on one of the most dangerous ancients to ever exist, one that required the head of the Primmish god, Dimiourgos. With it, they could bring the demon back to life, expose him for what he really was, and make him suffer pain the likes of which would make the flames of the Passion Kingdom's Volcanic Quadrant seem tame.

"You've grown so despondent," Agnos said, taking a seat at the table.

"Let him be," Yama said. "If he wants to talk, he'll talk."

Agnos glanced at Toono before digging into his food. "I suppose."

"I don't know how much longer I'll be here, guys," Toono muttered.

Agnos's fork clattered against his plate, and Yama's unfazed demeanor withered into worry. "Why do you say that?" she asked.

"It's just time for me to leave."

"Then I'm going with you," she said. "You were assigned my charge, so I'll stay by your side every step of the way until you're eighteen."

Toono looked up from his eggs, a bitter coldness laced in his eyes. "I don't need you."

Agnos pounded his fist on the table, eyebrows furrowed. "Why are you being such an—"

"Don't defend me!" she screamed, the rowdy mess hall drowning it out somewhat. "You're the *last* person I need speaking on my behalf."

Agnos sunk into his chair, remembering why he preferred to stay quiet. He'd spent so much time with Toono over the last year and a half that he'd forgotten about his tiny voice and weak will.

Toono's eyes shifted to Agnos. "You'll be fine without me. I've never met anyone with more drive than you." Blush flooded Agnos's cheeks. Toono sighed, trying to form a believable façade in his expression. He needed to lie. "I still have my same goals, but I'll achieve them another way."

"You still want to get to the Thunder Queen's chronicle?" Agnos asked.

"No, but I have a different path in mind to obtain the information. And I shall do it alone." He gazed around the mess hall. "I want you out of here, Agnos. I'll make sure it happens."

"But Neeko is here."

"Neeko is old. You don't know how much longer he'll be around to rely on." Toono grabbed his glasses that hung from the collar of his shirt and slid them across the table. "I want you to have these. You'll make better use of them."

Agnos stared at them, flabbergasted. Yama's solemn eyes had yet to unglue themselves from Toono. "You can't shake me," she said.

"Don't underestimate me, Yama," Toono said.

"How do you expect to do it?" Agnos asked. "What other avenues could there possibly be?"

Toono stood and turned to leave. "It's nothing to concern yourself with."

*     *     *

"Today's the day!"

Toono had never seen the old man display such fervor. While he'd always been a joyful spirit, he usually kept it blanketed in tranquility, showing it through witty remarks of elderly wisdom. Today he seemed like a child at a candy shop.

"You only made me wait five months," Toono said with a wry grin.

Neeko leaned forward, placing his forearms across the desk. "So, let's get to the good stuff. What'd you think of the book?"

Toono's smile faded. He'd hoped for some cushion before jumping straight to that. He wanted small talk ... he wanted to stall, hesitant to break the news to the old man.

"It was interesting."

Neeko raised an eyebrow. "You'll have to give me more than that."

"And a bit farfetched."

"I must agree, but a curious thing," Neeko said.

"There are too many hoops of logic that would have to be conveniently bypassed in order to believe a book wound up in a seafloor cavern ... then survive a millennium and a half without degradation from elements."

Neeko leaned back with pursed lips. "I see."

Toono opened the book and pointed at the front matter. "Not to mention, this was written by a notorious priest who even the Primmish believed to have been slightly mad. Rolto Aricrates? His name is one of the few things their kingdom couldn't contain in their secretive history. Most scholars throughout the world know of his antics."

Neeko studied the boy during a stretch of silence and then burst into laughter. That wasn't exactly what Toono had expected.

756

"You are full of surprises," Neeko said. "Here I was thinking we were going to tackle the topics of the supposed weapon in the sky and the Thunder Queen's interest in it."

"If anything, this book killed my desire to chase her chronicle," Toono said. "It reeks of folklore."

Neeko raised his hands and pressed his fingertips together. "You're being awfully blunt."

Toono extended his hand, palm up. "I know my dream, Neeko. Can we get this over with?"

The twinkle in Neeko's eyes vanished. Wrinkles became less pronounced as any sign of an expression slipped from his face. He stared straight through Toono. "What did that woman do to you?"

"What woman?"

"Agnos tells me things. I'm aware that you received a visit several months ago."

"Don't meddle in my personal business."

Neeko sighed, grabbing an ivory quill with a long silver-tipped feather from an inkwell nearby. He pulled out a sloppily bound book from a drawer under his desk and placed it on the table, opening it to a blank page marked with string. "I'm on the last page. Looks like I'll have to add another for Agnos."

"Can you get Agnos into Phesaw?" Toono asked.

Neeko looked up. "I could try, but I'd have to pull some strings. I suppose it'd be good for him, seeing that the most critical part of his journey lies on that campus."

"Thank you," Toono said, ignoring the vague remark at the end. "Now back to the matter at hand."

Neeko didn't hesitate, going straight for Toono's palm with the quill. The boy yanked his hand back, surprised by the immediate action. He'd expected a fight.

"There's the apprehension," Neeko said. There was no kindness in the thin line of his lips. He was as serious as Toono had ever seen. "Are you sure you know what you're doing here?"

Toono scared himself with his own hesitation. "Ye-yes," he stammered.

"There is no turning back."

Toono closed his eyes and took a deep breath. He was doing this for his mother … for justice. He stuck out his hand. "Do it!"

The quill cut his palm and drew blood, its warmth seeping down the side of his hand. Quickly, Neeko set the book on a raised podium and brought the quill's tip to the page. "Tell me your dream, Toono."

Tears rolled down the boy's cheeks. "I will become my mother's avenger."

# 74

# Recruits of Divinity

Dunami was in a state of stagnation as city officials began the road to recovery. Three days had passed since the Rogue Demon's invasion, yet it would still be weeks before any of its citizens could begin the daily routines of their lives again. The economy was frozen. Businesses were closed, and nearly sixty percent of the capital's eastern half had been demolished.

Elsewhere, families slowly trickled into their homes, but only after inspectors deemed them safe. Those whose houses had either been wiped out or on the verge of collapse were sent to temporary group homes set up in rec halls or other large establishments. Some families elected to permanently leave, taking one of many caravans that would travel to the kingdom's smaller cities and towns. They no longer felt safe in the capital.

The only people who had paying jobs were the architects, engineers, and manual laborers, those most responsible for repairing the city. Volunteers from the general populace were paid with hot meals—up to four portions—that could be taken back to their families for the night. Rebuilding would take a collective effort and *a lot* of money from the royals.

The young man partly responsible for the destruction lay in an infirmary bed inside Dunami Palace. This marked the third straight day of sleep, and those closest to him began to wonder if he'd ever wake. Princess Shelly, who sat at his bedside, seemed the most troubled.

Since being placed in the private medical room, Bryson had received dozens of visitors outside of his fiancée. They had trickled in, slowly arriving from missions or jobs elsewhere in the world. Now they all sat in the room, scattered throughout with grave faces. Despite a supposed victory for True Light, the auras of those who fought on its behalf were sorrowful. It didn't take Kaylee's eye to see it.

Lilu sat just behind her sister, staring over her shoulder at Bryson's heavily bandaged body. Olivia sat on the other side of the bed with an unreadable expression. Simon and a teary-eyed Himitsu sat at the foot of the bed, while Agnos, Tashami, and Vuilni kept their distance, each leaning against a section of wall.

They remained in these positions for hours, not bothering to utter a word. While they all had things they wanted to say and topics they needed to discuss, nothing felt as urgent as Bryson's health. In many ways, he felt like the core of everything. And that feeling only intensified with the recent rumor spreading throughout the palace: Mendac LeAnce was no longer dead.

The death of Intel King Vitio had also been a crippling blow. Nobody had seen Queen Delilah in days, as she spent all her time in her living chambers. Her wails pierced through the thick walls. They grew worse at night, haunting the surrounding corridors. Perhaps this was why Lilu and Shelly spent their days next to Bryson. With their father gone, their last hope was in this young man.

A lot had to be revealed. Olivia and Vuilni needed to tell Prim Queen Inedibus's story about Kadlest, Himitsu and Kaylee had to share what they read in Neeko's book, and Simon had to explain his desertion right before the invasion. Together, these revelations would fill the holes of Toono and Kadlest's stories, but leave them with a few contradictions in need of sorting out.

None of it mattered at that moment.

They simply waited for the eyes of one young man to open—a captain of the Jestivan, royal firstborn of the Still family, and the hero of True Light.

*          *          *

Pilot Ophala had arrived at Dunami Palace four days after the invasion. She'd taken a detour to Phesaw in order to discover how Toono had penetrated the school the way he did. It didn't take long, however, to quickly find the stage at the center of the main building's auditorium blown to pieces. A peculiar discovery, considering the stage had been constructed with holy wood ... meaning someone with obscene clout and Intel Energy must have been responsible. Had SCAPD possessed an Intelian in their ranks?

Ophala sat in an infirmary room at the bedside of Passion Director Venustas, who was recovering well from her injuries.

"Why aren't you with Bryson like everyone else?" the director asked.

"I'm waiting for it to empty out."

"*Pssh*, good luck with that."

Ophala nodded, understanding her implication.

"I know this might sound harsh," Venustas said, "but I'm curious as to why you've sat by my side for two hours now. Outside of a few broadcast meetings, we've spoken rarely—and we don't have a personal relationship." She smiled. "Though I must admit that I'm honored to keep such company."

"You were once the Passion Director at Phesaw," Ophala said quietly. "You personally trained my son when he became a Jestivan, taught him hand-to-hand combat and fighting without gimmicks. I thank you for that."

Venustas chuckled. "He was quite adept at sneaking around in the shadows, but shine a light on him and he became a cornered mouse."

"He has his father to thank for that."

Silence followed, and Venustas spotted the change of tone in Ophala's voice at the mention of her husband.

"Still no sign of them?" Venustas asked.

Ophala shook her head. "I'm so worried; I haven't touched alcohol in five days."

Horos, Toshik, and Kuiku were the only three who had yet to return from their missions abroad. She'd already lost her husband twice, each time to imprisonment at the hands of King Damian and Toth Brench. At least, during those occasions, she knew where exactly where he was.

"They'll show up," the director said. A long moment of silence passed, and Ophala nearly got up and left before Venustas asked, "Have you ever seen someone walk on air?"

The shock of that question quelled Ophala's anxiety. "I don't think anybody has witnessed such a spectacle in twelve hundred years."

"You're going to call me crazy, but I swear I saw it."

"Adren Assassins are long extinct," Ophala said. "Just like every other type save Dev, Passion, and Still."

Venustas's eyes narrowed at the ceiling, replaying the images in her mind. "It was mostly a smear of color, so my eyes could have been deceiving me. That still wouldn't explain the arrows that rained upon the battlefield."

"When's Jugtah getting here?" Ophala asked, gazing back toward the door. "I'm afraid we need a better doctor. Maybe he can fix delusion."

Venustas laughed, squeezing her ribs and finishing with a groan. Ophala regarded the director with a satisfied grin. "At least I know alcohol isn't the reason for my comical genius."

*　　*　　*

Mendac climbed out of a stone cube where a statue in his own image had once stood. He carried a bag over his shoulder. In it contained any and all of his remaining research, data, and essays from his first life that he could scavenge from his old lab. He noted a few missing lab notes and theoretical essays, but he chalked that up to the Branian who'd killed him: Ataway Kawi. He must have taken or destroyed them. Thankfully, Mendac had a flawless memory.

It was well into witching hours. The only people who had been awake to see him were those who patrolled Brilliance's main intersection. But they were now nothing but corpses, strewn around the block of stone in puddles of their own blood.

Wings of black mist lurched from his back, and he took to the sky. He cleared the city's towering wall and descended on the other side, where Kadlest waited patiently.

But she had company.

Three figures surrounded her, humanistic things cloaked in shadow. Mendac landed next to her, regarding them with a skeptical arch to his right brow. He'd never seen such creatures.

"Mendac LeAnce," one of the figures said. The voice was unnaturally grating, deep and powerful like thunder, yet strangely distant.

"Yes?" he answered.

"You have been recruited to fight in the Empirical War."

"I suppose you're not offering me a choice," Mendac said, eyeing the ambiguous figure of shifting black mist he believed to have spoken.

"When it involves the orders of Dark God Mialo, former King of Minds, there is no choice."

"And if I fight?" Mendac asked, feeling Kadlest's sweaty hand grasp onto his.

"There'd be no fight," another figure boomed. "There'd be no struggle. We may be missing two of our numbers, but three is overkill as it is."

Mendac turned slowly, studying each of the creatures. It didn't take a scholar to realize these were high-ranking Gefal, not the run-of-the-mill Bewahr of a royal firstborn. He sighed.

"You can take me, but Kadlest must come, too."

The figures converged on them in a rush of roiling shadows, swallowing them in a suffocating ball of anguish. Then they were gone, transported to a place they knew nothing of.

*     *     *

The tears that streamed from Rhyparia's eyes weren't a result of the scene in the distance: a perished kingdom crushed beneath the weight of a massive moon. She'd prepared herself for this moment for many years. This was inevitable.

What she couldn't have accounted for, however, was life still being breathed into her lungs. She was supposed to have died. If her destruction of Olethros and the collapse of the restaurant had both been enough to send her into a coma, then surely something of this scale should have killed her outright.

Yet life seemed a stubborn concept as she remained the only breathing soul in the Power Kingdom. The only person either not to have fled by ship or fallen victim to the moon's impact.

And what did she have to curse for her continued life? A pair of wings formed of black mist and tipped with flickering violet tendrils that had inexplicably sprouted from her back. Despite their outward beauty, she knew they represented the vilest parts of her soul.

"Rhyparia NuForce."

The powerful, stern voice of a woman thundered above her. She glanced up from her crumpled position on the ground. Two figures stood in front of her, their bodies nothing but coiling shadows.

"You have been recruited to fight in the Empirical War."

"I'm done fighting," Rhyparia muttered, not even trying to make sense of what she was seeing.

"We were told we'd be met with reluctance, but there is no denying the Dark God."

Rhyparia's brows furrowed. *What the hell is happening?*

"While you have those wings, you can't escape his grasp. If necessary, God Mialo can and *will* take control of your body."

Rhyparia grabbed a blade from her waistband and brought it to her neck, but her arm froze in place by some inexplicable force. No matter how hard she fought, she couldn't move it.

"You will play a major role in the war between empires," the entity said. "A war that won't end until one of two gods die: Mialo or Tonitrua."

Sphaira Publishing and David F. Farris hopes you enjoyed the final book of Erafeen's first act.

The series is not over. There is more to come.

To remain updated on the author's work:

www.erafeen.com
www.twitter.com/DavidFFarris
www.facebook.com/DavidFFarris

THE ERAFEEN SERIES:

THE JESTIVAN
THE UNTENABLE
THE UPRISING
THE CHRONICLE
THE SACRIFICE

BOOK 6 – COMING SOON